Secolo Nuovo

or,

The Times of Promise

by

Fulvia Ferrari

detritus books
olympia, wa

FIRST DETRITUS BOOK EDITION 2021

Published in the USA by Detritus Books

Book design by Ben Cody

DETRITUS BOOKS
PO Box 6171
OLYMPIA, WA 98507
detritusbooks.com

Distributed by AK Press

Detritus Books ISBN: 978-1948501149

Printed in Canada
10 9 8 7 6 5 4 3 2 1

What is hidden from you I will proclaim to you.
    —The Gospel of Mary

You will then see something like an aurora borealis across the sky, and th̄
energy will go to the distant place.
    —Nikola Tesla, 1916

My San Francisco comrades could work strenuously; they took their tasks very
seriously; but they could also love, drink, and play.
    —Emma Goldman, 1931

SHE'LL BE COMING ROUND THE MOUNTAIN

MY MOTHER LIVES UP THE HILL IN THE BIG GRAY VICTORIAN WHERE my lonely childhood unfolded. She was off fighting in Russia when I took my first steps and we didn't meet until I was a teenager. The old house used to be my aunt Bianca's but she left it to my mother Isabelle, hoping it would heal her sister of shell-shock. Our commune started there, in some timber baron's abandoned dream mansion. My aunt called it *Nuovo Ideal* back then and her Victorian was only accessible from a steep, mile-long logging road, the one I'm climbing now. I lived in the house with my wounded mother until 1935 when there was no point staying here where everything was perfect except me, everything was wrong because of me, and everything would be better if I was gone. I fled to San Francisco when I was twenty and didn't come back for a decade, caught up in the grand finale of the Roaring Thirties. My mother and I kept our distance when I returned, I built my own house at the bottom of this logging road, and over the next five years I dug myself a hole into the underworld. Climbing this hill is my only way out of it.

As I walk up the dusty road, a family of quail sprints away from my heavy footsteps. I chased these funny birds when I was young, convinced their speed was simply a trick of the mind. Now their question mark heads wobble and bobble and disappear into the brush, leaving me alone on this familiar road. The air's dry and hot, my entire body's layered in sweat, my feet are sore, and I'm sick of this long climb. After walking all the way up here at the peak of summer, my mother probably won't speak a word to me. I've been trying to get the truth for months now, all those secrets Isabelle's got hidden away, but so far she's denied everything. She says I'm delusional, paranoid, bored, restless.

...d there she is, pumping water into the irriga-
...see me but Isabelle doesn't look up, she keeps
...her strawberry field. My mother's got corn and
...getable garden that provides so much food she
...me for anything, not even in winter. When she does
...mother never looks for me. She goes straight to the
...ts in Yvonne's solarium where they talk for hours. If
...let me know she's there. People tell her to get a horse
for ... ...limb but she never listens to them, no more than she listens to me. ...ther's sixty three years old but she doesn't look it, maybe
from all that walking.

"Isabelle!" I yell at her. "You going blind?"

"I don't want to talk about it! I told you yesterday! Leave it alone! Aren't you tired?"

She pumps the well furiously until I grab her wrist.

"Let go!" she cries. "The strawberries need more water! Let me finish!"

"Who's going to tell this story? If you won't do it, who will? Everyone knows about the famous Isabelle who fought in Russia, marched from Moscow to Paris, watered her horse outside Luxembourg Palace and all that crap for children. We know how you won the war, *mama*, but no one knows what happened before that. You just leave it blank. All of you. You and Yvonne! So who's going to tell the story?"

"No one! Leave it that way. What's the obsession? Don't you have enough trouble in the village? I told you yesterday it's nothing but pain. We did what we had to do to win and that's the end of it. You chose to run off to San Francisco and get filled with those horseshit stories the sailors tell about witches and mermaids and sugar babies. Your history books tell you everything! Haven't you read enough? You read in the library for so long you're going to go blind. We did everything necessary to win, Fulvia, and...there, see, it's done, the strawberries and the corn, watered, done."

The last of the water flows into the sloping corn rows and leaves the soil a rich, healthy black. My mother's already watered the vegetable garden, I can smell it evaporating under this blistering sun. She doesn't say another word so I follow her up the porch steps into the living room where the air is cool and heavy with the scent of drying sage.

"Finish what you were saying," I tell her. "What you did to win. That interests me."

"You want some lemon juice?"

"I'll get it myself. Don't worry about it. Stop changing the subject."

"Fulvia! We won! We blasted those imperialists and bankers to pieces! Here we are! It's been over twenty years! It's 1950! You have your own conflicts to deal with. And you know, people keep talking to me about you, they say you're isolating yourself, going into rages at everybody."

"Yeah, because no one wants to remember the war! The commune just harvested all this wheat and they're already acting like the capitalists you defeated! It's absurd! Our entire silo's full with wheat and they want to just let it sit there. Everyone got shit-faced drunk after the harvest and slept for weeks like pigs! Half that wheat could be down at Fort Russ. Instead it's sitting there an entire month and now I'm the one who looks crazy because Angelo keeps goading me at the assembly!"

"Calm down, Fulvia. You need to confront him directly."

"No! That's what he wants! It's no one's concern but mine!"

"Fulvia! *Tranquila.*"

"It's his fault that grain's sitting there! He said I'm confusing the wheat with my ego, that I was being dramatic and—"

"Go pour me some lemon juice," she says, rubbing her temples. "Settle down."

I'm familiar with this moment. It's usually when she stops listening to me, so I go to the kitchen and pour out two glasses from a pitcher covered in cheese-cloth to keep out the insects. My mother always scoops the lemon pulp from these empty pitchers and eats it with honey in the middle of the night when she can't sleep. Those creaking floorboards scared me when I was little and imagined Isabelle was a monster, not a nocturnal sugar-fiend. This latest pitcher is more lemon than water, just how she likes it, too sour for me. My mother never lost her love of raw lemons, she even eats the rinds like she's still in Russia trying to fend off scurvy. When I return to the living room with our glasses, she's slumped back on the couch, smiling at something near the floor.

"What's so funny?" I ask. "You know this stuff's too sour, right?"

"You want to write a history book? Is that it? A history book for the people? *Why?*"

"Here." I hand her the juice and then clink glasses. "*Salud.*"

"*Salud.* I think you should just talk to the villagers better. Don't be so bull-headed. Let your life balance. Stop reading so much. And talk gentler. Don't be so harsh."

"You have the nerve to tell me this. *You?*"

"What's your alternative, Fulvia?" my mother asks. "Write a bible so they'll see the light?"

"Don't feed me that poison. I want to tell your story. And Yvonne's. I know you two talk all day about what happened, stuff that isn't in my library books. How long are you going to keep it a secret? Like you said, it's 1950, and there's people down at the *fábrica* right now talking about holding all that wheat until next year. For what? To sleep on? To feed the chickens? Sorry it's so difficult to load it on wagons and take it down to the harbor! What do they expect? A train?"

"They'll listen, eventually. You always get your way, Fulvia. Come on. Sit down."

I settle into the couch and drink my lemon juice slowly, wincing with each sip. Across the room on the opposite wall is some art she brought from Russia. It's literally just a black square on a white background. She calls it the *Black Square.* Above our heads is its twin, the *Peasant Woman in Two Dimensions,* a red square on a white background. I grew up with these two paintings watching over me. They're my secret mothers.

"You want to know about Russia?" she asks. "You want to know about 1919?"

"No! Everyone knows that story. Before all that. And it's not just you and Yvonne. I want to know about Josephine, *your* mother, my grandmother. I remember her fine, but did she tell me *all* the stories? No. You know she didn't. I want to know about her. Where she came from. That's where all the books go blank. You make her seem like some cheese-making peasant who joined the revolution, only no one knows who she really was, not even me. Is that fair? Or is talking about your own mother too painful? It's not like she died a hero surrounded by people who loved her or—"

"*Silencio.* You want to know about Josephine? *I'll tell you about Josephine!*"

For the first time since I started asking questions, my mother tells a different story. It begins in the mountains of Switzerland where Josephine Louise Lemel was born, stuff I already know, but soon she's telling me about Roman legions and Celtic tribes along the Rhône River. She says we come from a line of indigenous women who inhabited the same Swiss valley since the beginning of time. When the Roman Emperor sent a Nubian legion to subdue this region in the year 285, these soldiers defected and joined the tribal Celts. They lived together in those mountains for over a thousand years and never revealed their clandestine heritage. I can't believe what I'm hearing. I'm afraid of saying a word. The last thing I want to do is interrupt, so I listen for what feels like hours.

She tells me the truth about *The Book* in Yvonne's library and how it caused the first witch hunt in Switzerland during the 1420s. Once my ancestors read *The Book*, they were hunted down as witches and sorcerers and werewolves. My stomach twists so tight the smell of lemon nauseates me. They've been lying to me forever, concealing the greatest secret this world has ever known, a war that extends back over ten thousand years, waged against something she keeps calling the darkness. I try to keep silent, I ask a few questions when she gets vague, but soon all my books click together and the missing links slide into place. It's going to be a revelation for those that read it, but for me it's just proof of their lies. These women stole my entire life from me. They never told me who I was.

"You're serious?" I ask. "And you never mentioned any of this?"

"We didn't know if the darkness was still looking for us. But its agents are dead now."

"So I'm one of these witch women? Like you?"

"It's...hard to say, Fulvia. You certainly don't *need* to be like us. It's all over. We crushed the darkness, but it's not what you're thinking. The darkness isn't some man with a hat. It's a nothingness, an emptiness that moves, and it's still here. It'll come looking for you, if it hasn't already."

My mother did it again, the same shit she's pulled since I was a girl. Instead of answering me, she just fuels the uncertainty. In a panic, I take our empty glasses into the kitchen, my body covered in cold sweat. All my problems have been caused by this single lie. Maybe that's why she finally told me. Hatred swirls through my body, a dark storm cloud waiting for release. All the horseshit makes sense. I've finally ripped off the blindfold they tied around my eyes. The empty glasses shatter on the floor.

"I need to write!" I yell, storming towards the front door. *"Gracias!"*

"Are you...will you come back?" she calls out to me. "Fulvia! Come back!"

"Later! Now *you* can feel ashamed, *mama*!"

"Wait!"

She chases me onto the porch and let's her voice crack, the only sign she actually cares, so I turn around when she starts pleading. If she'd been hiding something else, a murder, I'd feel different, better even. This is worse. She took my soul and stuffed it into a hundred books. She let me drift alone at sea.

"I'm sorry I never told you," she says, sobbing. "They were still hunting us."

"Did you have to wait *this* long? I'm almost forty! Look at what happened to me!"

I'm crying like a baby so I run through the strawberry field and then down the logging road. I feel gross, disgusting, dripping with sweat, burning from the inside, and I run frantically, a cloud of dust rising behind me. When I finally reach my house I keep running towards the schoolhouse. I don't want to stop but people are staring so I pause near the square and catch my breath. They all think I'm crazy but I don't care, they can imagine whatever they want. That's when "She'll Be Coming Round the Mountain" fills my ears. Unable to help myself, I sing *she'll be riding six white horses when she comes* so loudly all the schoolchildren hear me. A few of them start laughing. Their mothers look disturbed, scared even, but it doesn't matter. I whistle this song on the walk back to my house and don't give a damn what they whisper. They can't possibly conceive of what I'm about to write. Tell everyone, I say. *Now, today, I shall sing beautifully for my friends' pleasure.*

My house sits at the very edge of the village, its front steps facing the logging road. I don't grow anything out here except pumpkins, mostly because they're easy to water. All I do is pump my well every morning and by fall I've got big orange pumpkins free for anyone to carve into jack-o-lanterns or bake into a tasty pie. I'm the only one who grows them and the kids all love it, so I guess that's why I keep doing it. I've got an outhouse next to my pumpkin patch, also free for anyone to use, although few people ever do. Most of the village avoids my house, if they can help it.

I make the final climb to my front door, walk into my living room, rumble up to the loft, and pass out for several hours. If I dream I don't remember anything. It's dark when I finally wake up, the air cool and refreshing. Time to write. I light a few oil-lamps, drink some water, munch on some bread, and then carry the flickering flame over to my desk. The story seems so clear now. This fire inside my body didn't come from nowhere. It was given to me on purpose.

1

THE DIVINE ECSTASY OF MAURITIUS AND GRAINYA

M Y NAME IS FULVIA FERRARI. I'M WRITING THIS HISTORY IN THE small commune once called *Nuovo Ideal*, a place where I now live with my mother, Isabelle Lemel Ferrari, and her best friend Yvonne del Valle. These two women are famous for their actions during the war, but history is far less familiar with my late grandmother, Josephine Louise Lemel. Without her story, our future makes no sense, and so I sit here at my desk in the summer of 1950 and begin to write the first chapter of our lost memories.

Josephine was born around 1850 in a small settlement near the Rhône River, just beneath a vast mountain called *Les Diablerets*, the abode of the devils. These jagged Swiss peaks were the sentinels of her childhood, standing just north of her family's farmland where she lived with her mother, her father, and her sister Bianca. They milked cows, made cheese, preserved fruit, pickled vegetables, and listened for rumblings from *Les Diablerets*. Locals believed that Lucifer himself slept beneath this mountain and stone avalanches fell whenever he stirred. In 1714, the neighboring village of

Derborence was wiped out by one of these avalanches, and within a few decades, another one blocked the local Lizerne River, forming a new emerald lake. *Les Diablerets* was the sacred peak of my family, although their reverence was no religious delusion. While the locals truly believed the stone avalanches to be the work of Satan, my ancestors were the reason these peaks had been named after devils.

The public knows my grandmother Josephine as a humble Alpine peasant who joined the war against capitalism in the 1870s, but the truth is far more complicated. To tell her story, I have to begin in the 1st century BCE. Many decades before the birth of Yeshua ha-Nozri in the province of Judea, the Roman legions of Julius Cæsar marched over the Swiss Alps to conquer Western Europe. Although the legions met resistance from the Alpine tribes, the Romans subdued them all by 51 BCE. At the time of Yeshua ha-Nozri's crucifixion in Jerusalem, the Alps were dotted with Imperial colonies and lined with roads leading to Rome. *Les Diablerets* was surrounded by three settlements, one of which was named *Octodurus*, conquered center of the Veragri tribe. The second colony was *Auganum*, a riverside fortress with the single bridge connecting the Rhône Valley with Lake Geneva. The third colony was *Sudunum*, center of trade for the Seduni, a defeated tribe integrated into the Empire as loyal *civitas*, or citizens. From these fortresses, the Roman colonizers presided over the Rhône and fought off any indigenous raiders who descended from the mountains. For the entirety of the Roman Empire, this region was never fully under control, and their rule came to an end once the devils arrived from the south.

Around the year 285 CE, the reigning Emperor Maximian ordered an Egyptian legion to march north through the Alps and pacify the remaining

Les Diablerets

rebels. These soldiers were mostly Nubian conscripts from the ancient city of Thebes, a hotbed of rebellion, alchemy, and foreign gods. After crossing the sea and marching to the Rhône River, these 6,000 soldiers halted their advance. The commander, a Nubian named Mauritius, rode off towards *Les Diablerets* on the back of a white horse. When he returned six hours later, the horse's hair had turned black. Mauritius declared the days of Rome were over and the indigenous of the mountains were now their allies. He ordered the soldiers to kill every Roman in the region and take control of their stone fortresses, a task they fulfilled within a week. After this massacre was over and the bodies buried in large pits, Mauritius left a small garrison in each colony to fight the Romans when they came for vengeance. Mauritius volunteered first for this suicidal duty, although his legion immediately shouted their unanimous protest. None of them would ever allow his death. Without him, they would have never found their Celtic allies.

Before the slaughter, when Mauritius rode off atop his white horse, he met a matriarchal line of Alpine women who traced their origins back to the beginning of time. They had hid in their ancestral birthplace through successive invasions and spoke a mixture of Celtic dialects, a *lingua franca* of the Alps. Their stronghold was just behind the southern wall of *Les Diablerets*, a small village near the head of the Lizerne River. It was here that Mauritius met two dozen women assembled in front of their stone houses, many with tattoos across their faces, and he surrendered himself to their high-priestess, Grainya. This tattooed woman in a black hood spoke perfect Latin and asked if Mauritius was one of the Christian rebels. Mauritius admitted he knew of them but wasn't an adherent. They asked how he had found their hidden settlement and Mauritius said the path was revealed to him in a dream. This revelation was discussed among the women, who then asked if he knew of Mary Magdalene, the wife of Yeshua ha-Nozri and mother of his children. Mauritius knew the tale of this rebel who Emperor Caligula had chased to the ends of the earth, a quest that broke the young tyrant in half, causing him to become mad in the days before his assassination. Once this madman was gone, Mary fled from Judea to Egypt and then across the sea to the Rhône River delta in southern Gaul.

My ancestors informed Mauritius they were neither Christians nor the followers of Mary, who they spoke of with a palpable respect. They said the darkness which hunted Mary also hunted them, its power centered on the head of each Emperor. This darkness ate Caligula from the inside and burned his soul to ashes. Once this young Emperor was dead, the darkness jumped into the next one. These Alpine women asked if Mauritius was part of this darkness but he claimed his body was filled with light. To prove it, he pledged to eradicate the Romans and free the Rhône River Valley from bondage. Once he uttered these fateful words, Mauritius noticed his horse had turned pitch-black. He descended from the mountains that same afternoon and quickly fulfilled his promise to Grainya. After the colonizers had been killed, his army gathered outside the walls of *Auganum* to hear him speak.

While his legion was given the choice to leave, they preferred to remain with their commander and fight against the Empire. 600 brave warriors elected to guard the doomed fortresses and hold off the impending Roman advance, knowing their deaths were certain. With less than a tenth of their forces garrisoned in these colonies, the bulk of the legion left *Auganum* and marched to the north wall of *Les Diablerets* where they ascended a secret passage to my ancestor's sacred mountaintop, a place where no force could be repelled and death was certain for any pursuers below.

Rumors had already spread throughout the province that Mauritius and his Nubian army had disappeared into the snow like cowards. When the first Roman scouts finally reached *Octodurus*, they observed a scarcely populated colony with only a hundred Thebans guarding the gates and walls. Each fortress was captured easily, although not a single Theban was taken alive. These men chose to either flee, die in battle, or be impaled by their own sword. When the Romans questioned the indigenous, they were told Mauritius and his legion had fled into the valley northeast of *Auganum*. The locals claimed Mauritius was a bandit, his men brutal tyrants who ruled through fear and lived like gluttons. All of this was a carefully orchestrated lie, and it worked perfectly.

A replacement garrison was left in each colony and new officials installed before the Romans marched out of *Augunum* towards the peaks of *Les Diableretes*. Over 10,000 Latin men walked into the snow that day and less than a hundred came back. First they heard humming, then shrieking, and then a horn made of stone pierced the mountaintop. Those who survived spoke of rocks trapping them on all sides as jars of Greek fire fell from the sky. Most of the Romans were crushed under falling boulders while the rest burned alive in the raining inferno. Only those at the rear of the column stood a chance against this instant slaughter.

When word traveled to Rome, any mention of this defeat was quickly forbidden by a paranoid Emperor Maximian. According to this tyrant's

St. Mauritius

mythology, the traitorous Thebans were crucified and the colonies of *Alpes Pœninæ* brought under control. As one of his hired poets recited, the events of 286 weren't spoken of before the Emperor because *such are your dutiful feelings that you prefer that victory to be cast into oblivion rather than glorified*. It had taken the Roman Empire many years to subdue the Vandals, Goths, and Alemmani along their northern borders and if word of this new defeat reached their barbarian ears, another assault on the Empire might begin. For all of these reasons, an unspoken truce was instituted along the Swiss Alps between the indigenous and the Empire. Maximian simply couldn't spare the troops, nor could any of his successors. Despite this precaution, the northern tribes soon rose up in rebellion, dooming the mighty Roman Empire.

Relative peace reigned in the Rhône River Valley through the 300s, just as the complexions of the locals became darker. Mauritius and his legion watched over this land, covertly retaliating for any abuses caused by the Romans, and while they lived a clandestine existence, the entire Empire started to collapse. Mauritius became the lover of our high-priestess Grainya and they conceived three daughters together in a stone house beneath *Les Diablerets*. By the time Mauritius died of old age surrounded by his many grandchildren, Emperor Constantine had converted to Christianity.

Within a few centuries, this new Christian empire claimed Mauritius as their holy martyr Saint Maurice and spread the false narrative of his legion crucified by Rome. Only in the mountains were these stories seen for the religious fictions they were, and as the farmland along the Rhône grew more Christian, the peaks of my ancestors became known as *Les Diablerets*. The colonized indigenous claimed the dark people from these mountains possessed strange powers, a superstition that led to my ancestors being labeled as witches, sorcerers, and werewolves. My grandmother Josephine was born beneath these peaks around 1850 and learned this story from her mother, just as my mother Isabelle recently taught it to me. Josephine was one of these witches from *Les Diablerets* and her strange path would lead across the planet to the vice-ridden waterfront of San Francisco, the city where my mother was born, a place of eternal youth perched at the end of the world.

SHE'LL BE DRIVING SIX WHITE HORSES

IT TOOK ME DAYS TO WRITE ALL THAT HISTORY. IT'S JUST A FEW SHORT pages. Now I'm standing by my bed. *With golden feet made of clouds, the sun rises above the hills and wakes me.* I've been up high in the Swiss Alps these past evenings, my pen-strokes illuminated by a burning wick. Each night I see snow-capped mountains towering above my desk, its surface covered in history books and religious texts, all checked out from the communal library. I really have to return them. They're long overdue.

Yvonne gave the village 20,000 books on the condition they build a structure to house them. After months of work, there was a vast wooden library for me to pillage, a beautiful building with stained-glass roses embedded in the reading room windows. People visit it from all over the world hoping to catch a glimpse of Yvonne del Valle, only no one ever does. She's the best kept secret in our village, the reclusive anti-hero who won the global war against capitalism. The number of pilgrims has dropped recently since she stopped granting interviews, but the world still knows her as the woman who invented our electromagnetic future. None of them know the truth.

I walk outside into a sunny morning, stroll past the stone schoolhouse, and see our entire village congregated around the *fábrica*. It's our monthly assembly, a routine we've maintained since 1921, the year we opened up the commune to outsiders. I yelled a lot during the last assembly, just like they all expected me to, but not today. I know it's pointless. What can I give to these people who cast me evil eyes, just like their lovers do, *those plump Aphrodites drunk on men?*

My friends Gertrude and Annabelle are standing near the storehouse entrance so I head in their direction while the whispers increase all around me. *Crazy Fulvia, mad Fulvia, empress Fulvia.* This was why I left the commune in the first place, this endless gossip and tension. It's clear now. Neither honey nor the honey bee is to be mine again.

Above our heads is the cement silo, filled to the brim with wheat. The storehouse is just below, the communal depot where farmers converge with their harvests. Connected to that is our brewery, our collective kitchen, and our communal patio. All this we call the *fábrica*, epicenter of my endless torture in our insular village, the place where I've argued with everybody, especially Angelo. At least Gertrude and Annabelle are here to help me. I'm already covered in sweat by the time I reach them.

"You see what they're doing to me?" I ask. "Do I need to point it out?"

"We see it," Gertrude tells me. "We were just talking about it. Good job not yelling."

"What have you been doing all night?" Annabelle asks me. "I saw your window glowing."

"You know how I've been trying for weeks to get the truth out of my mom? Well...she told me something. I've been writing it down. It isn't much, just a chapter, but it took all week. I'm calm now, right? Can't you tell? It's helped, all this writing has helped. Right?"

"Yeah! Right!" Gertrude exclaims. "Good! I can't wait to read it."

"Neither of you are going to believe it," I say. "I don't know where to begin."

"What's that supposed to mean?" Annabelle asks. "We're too dumb or something?"

"Trust me," I tell them. "You won't believe it."

They demand to know more but luckily the clang of the copper meeting bell saves me from their interrogation and we all file into the storehouse where we assemble in a circle below the brass distillery. The bastards are already looking at me, their girlfriends egging them on to fight. I hate how they've made other women my enemy. Whenever they see crazy Fulvia, I know they're just seeing a reflection of who they'd become if they told their men to take a hike. They can't stand to see what crazy Fulvia looks like so they tune out my signal and change the station.

Fulvia! Enough! Why try to move a hard heart? I ask myself this as the real bastard steps forward, our new meeting facilitator, voted on last month by a vast majority. Dark hair, hazel eyes, stupid mustache. His name's Angelo. I hate him, and my anger is so intoxicating that the meeting starts without me realizing it.

Farmers give updates on their harvests, brewers talk about an excess of hops, distillers want to make vodka with a fifth of the potatoes, and the builders explain their next project: a collective house on the northern summit that doubles as a radio tower. A group from San Francisco is set to arrive with this new transmitter and its Tesla wood-burning turbine. When fired up, this machine would allow the valley to communicate with every commune on the coast. Electricity's scarce up here but we generate voltage whenever the *fábrica* produces heat and our radio dials are usually set to the San Francisco stations. As much as everyone loves the transmissions from our mother city, it's time we had our own voices beamed along the coastline, at least that's what the commune thinks. Everyone raises their hand *yes* when the vote to build the station is called, the assembly erupts into applause, and the next item on our agenda is me and my stupid drama that no one cares about.

"The floor's all yours," Angelo says to me with a shit-pie grin. "Tell us the trouble."

"The trouble? It's simple. All that wheat's been sitting above our heads for a month now, and so far most people don't care. I know this was a terrible thing for me to suggest, but last month I proposed getting all our wagons together, loading them up with grain, and driving them down to Fort Russ. It'd take two dozen people three days, longer if people could bear the thought of...you know...getting out of this village for a spell and staying the night."

"I've already volunteered to help," Annabelle says.

"So have I," Gertrude says. "Anyone else?"

The ladies from the sunflower farm raise their hands. So does my friend Lorraine and her three daughters. Everyone else is stern, arms folded over their chests, eyes filled with rising annoyance. They all think I'm a princess, that I'm having another tantrum, that I just need attention. Those are the words they screamed last time, only now they're a bit more restrained. A few whispers rise into the air and eventually Angelo steps forward to take command of the situation.

"I can't speak for everyone—"

"So don't," I tell him.

I get sincere laughter from this. I didn't expect any. Not at all.

"People have told me you're too aggressive," Angelo snaps, unsettled. "They don't want to work with you, otherwise more people would volunteer. They didn't. There's other things to discuss besides wheat. No one from the coast is asking for it, so there's no urgency. I propose we move on to the next subject. Can all those who—"

I turn the dial on Angelo's procedural words until he goes silent. I count all the people who keep their hands down, who don't vote to blot out my concerns. There are only a few dozen, but it's enough for me. They meet my eye with confident smiles and signal their recognition of everything I've said. I love them for this, more than they'll ever know. Their honesty makes me cry while the vast majority votes to silence me. He can see my tears, but the fact that I'm smiling puzzles stupid Angelo.

"We can revisit this next month," he says. "A month is a long time."

I don't say anything. I glare at Angelo until he looks away and keeps spitting his horseshit. I can't listen, all I can do is count the people looking at me. They aren't listening to Angelo either. They're listening to me, even though I'm silent. They know I'm right. Maybe they're just being patient. Maybe I should be patient. At least I didn't yell today, not once during the whole meeting. I don't know how many times I've forced myself to think this thought. *At least I didn't yell.*

The rest of the assembly blurs together because I can only hear my heartbeat. When the meeting breaks up, I suddenly realize Annabelle and Gertrude are still by my side, holding my hands. Both of them are smiling.

"Thanks," I say, my tears long gone. "That went better than I thought."

"Screw Angelo," Gertrude says. "Everyone saw him just now. Don't worry."

"Yeah, don't worry," Annabelle says. "The guy isn't no damn neutral party, that's plain. You feel better? You want us to walk you back home, cook some—"

"No!" I snap. "I want to eat dinner here! Like everyone else! I'm starving! I'm so hungry I want to roast a goat on an altar! I haven't eaten all day, so I'm eating right now."

"*Okay,*" Annabelle whispers. "Just don't set yourself back. And stay away from Angelo."

I'm not trying to be anywhere near that bastard but my stomach's screaming to be fed. I follow my friends out of the storehouse and line up with the others in front of the kitchen. While I'm waiting to be served, doing my best to be silent, everyone in line is eager to talk with me. I get questions about my mom, my aunt Bianca, canning strawberries, printing books, my thoughts on the new radio. Nobody brings up the wheat. No one asks how I'm feeling. They don't want to set off one of my tantrums.

Unlike everyone waiting in line, the people serving us food ask me personal questions. None of them were at this assembly or the one before that. I know them from the orchards and fields, the people who only want to grow food, cook food, serve food. They heap out roasted beets and yams, thick slices of zucchini frittata, and mounds of salad covered in salt, herbs, dried fruit, and olive oil. The bread they serve is still steaming and I take extra slices to munch on later tonight. While I'm spreading the butter, I tell everyone in line to go easy on the bread or we might run out. No one gets the joke except the food servers. Most of them laugh, a few shake their heads, but all of them get it. They're the ones who told me about all the extra wheat, coming to crazy Fulvia before anyone else. A glut for drunken pigs, they said. An automatic feeding trough for lazy men. An excess we'll never consume. I was supposed to be their voice. Now look at me.

"You just couldn't resist?" Annabelle asks. "Had to get that little dig in there?"

"It was funny," I say. "Besides, doesn't this food look incredible?"

"Especially the bread," Gertrude said. "You see how much I took?"

We balance these buttery slices atop our plates and find an empty table on the communal patio. I see Angelo sitting near the railing so I point to a corner by the silo far away from him. It takes all my courage not to vomit or drop my food when I walk across the patio. Everyone's staring, intentionally silent so I know they're talking about me.

We sit down in the shady corner, dig into our plates, and I eat the salad atop my buttered bread along with slices of frittata. One of the vintners comes by with an open bottle of red wine, the last of the 1939, he says. We thank the man and once he's far away I pour us out three glasses, raising mine in a toast. All I'm thinking about is the year they bottled this. I was lost in the deep folds of San Francisco, dancing like a maniac, yelling in the assemblies, parading down the cobblestones. If my mother told me the truth, I might have known who I was, I might have been able to prevent this madness, but she let Angelo win, she let all of them win. I was too busy dancing, thinking everything was fine.

"I wasn't here when these grapes were picked," I say. "I was dancing with both of you."

"*Salud*," Gertrude says, making us clink glasses. "We were all young once."

"What's *that* mean?" Annabelle asks. "We're in our thirties, all of us."

"And look at us now," Gertrude says. "A couple of farm girls."

"What am I then?" I ask. "I was born here. Am I a farm girl?"

Both of them laugh at this stupid question but neither answer. Their wine glasses are already empty. Mine isn't. Maybe all the villagers are right about us. We're just the metropolitan witches who fled the city and brought along all our troubles from the San Francisco waterfront.

I finish my plate in silence and let my eyes wander the patio. Everyone's here, the three hundred or so inhabitants of our inland commune. Most are still strangers to me, having arrived during my long absence. The last of the *vino rojo* has gone down their tubes and already the brewers are opening up the beer barrels. This is the part I despise, when everyone gets drunk on themselves and all their *hard work*. That's when they ſtare at me with anger, hatred, jealousy. I can see them now, muttering complaints to their woman companions. Those pigs would never say anything to my face. They prefer to whisper about me inſtead of move that wheat down the hill.

"Would you take my plate back?" I ask Gertrude. "Time to get my bread out of here."

"You were brave today," Annabelle says. "Angelo set you up but you didn't fall for it. I know how you hate everyone ſtaring like that. Go home and do your writing."

"Can you tell us what you're working on?" Gertrude asks. "Come on."

"I'm writing about my grandma Josephine. Sort of. Not yet really."

"What about her?" Annabelle asks. "She's already a hero. How about *your* mom?"

"Who isn't here, by the way," I say. "No, not her. Not yet. I'm going to write about Josephine's childhood firſt. No one knows where my family actually comes from. We're witches, real ones, from a big mountain called *Les Diablerets.*"

This juicy detail riles them up so I chug down the laſt of my wine, kiss their cheeks, slip around the corner of the silo, and disappear from communal life. A few children are running around the square on my way home and they all ſtop to watch me pass. I don't know what they see, but it makes me sing *she'll be driving six white horses when she comes* loud enough for them to hear. These girls and boys smile at my melody and one of them even dances along. I might actually be crazy, but at leaſt I'm the good crazy. When I reach my front ſteps, the children are juſt down the road, all of them dancing, so I can't be pure evil. I juſt hope they tell their parents how good I sing.

I drink some water once I'm inside and sit down in my reading chair. My house is pretty simple, juſt a kitchen and living room with a bed upſtairs in the loft. It's what we call a single in our communal architecture. A lot of families live in them despite their small size and the kids usually build their own cabins near the woods when they grow up. Not me. I went to San Francisco in 1935 and left my mother in her lonely mansion, juſt like she left me in 1915. I thought I was juſt a heartbroken young woman fleeing home to forget her lover, not a powerful witch who'd been lied to her whole life. People ſtill resent that I built my own house when I got back, that I needed all this space to myself, that I cause all this trouble in the meantime. Half the village moved here when I was away and moſt of these people know me as the eccentric, spoiled daughter of a war hero. They don't remember when this commune was juſt my aunt's house, a bankrupt mill, and a few Basque dairy farms. They surely won't remember any of those ſtories unless I remind them, so I gulp down the laſt of my water and sit at my desk. I'm going to ſtay right here until I pass out from writing. Tomorrow I have to work in the apple orchard. I have to make the moſt of today.

2

THE BOOK, THE WITCHES, AND THE FIRE

My grandmother Josephine's tribe remained hidden beneath the peaks of *Les Diablerets* as the Roman Empire disintegrated into a long net-work of Chriſtian monaſteries, abbeys, and churches that extended as far north as the isle of Britannia. The Holy Roman Empire was formed in 1032, bringing the Swiss Alps back under Imperial rule, and my anceſtors continued to be labeled as myths, although local indigenous folk-tales ſtill recounted a battle beneath *Les Diablerets* where an army of Nubians and Celtics wiped out two Roman legions with earth-magic and fire catapults. In order to subdue these dangerous legends, the Empire had no choice but to absorb them. Juſt as Yeshua ha-Nozri was claimed by the Church as its Lord and Savior, Mauritius of Thebes was dubbed Saint Maurice by the monks and bishops who flooded into the Rhône River Valley.

As these religious men would discover, the myth of Saint Maurice had a powerful effeɕt on the indigenous and icons of this black-skinned saint were displayed in churches along the Rhône. To the converted natives, Saint Maurice was no different than Jesus Chriſt, and faith in his false crucifixion suſtained their souls as they groveled for crumbs and begged for their own land back. These natives couldn't reconcile the truth of Mauritius with the truth of the Empire, so they called the site of his viɕtory *the abode of the devils*, a deathly place where mountains came to life, and no one from the river flat-lands ever climbed into those forbidden valleys beneath *Les Diablerets*.

My grandmother's tribe watched from those mountains as the many bish-ops, monks, and lords consolidated power in the Rhône River Valley from the year 300 to 1400. These authorities carved the land with borders and ensured the landlords were loyal to the Catholic Church. In exchange, the Holy Roman Empire allowed the Swiss territories to rule themselves as the *Res publica Helvetiorum*, or what became the Swiss Confederacy, a loose coalition of *cantons* that governed the region together through a central body. These *cantons* didn't have the same intereſts, nor the same languages, and war eventually broke out between them in 1415.

In this deſtruɕtive confliɕt, a caſtle allied to the House of Savoy was deſtroyed by local rebels, causing their Bernese allies to invade and torch every settlement along the Rhône. From the heights of their sacred peaks, my ancestors watched as the river valley was turned to ash and smoke transformed the sun into an ominous red sphere. War engulfed the entire region until 1419 when a truce was reached among the patriarchs of the *Res publica*, a humiliating arrangement that left the bishops of the Rhône with a desire for revenge. These men ruled from their fortress in Sion, the former colony of *Sudunum*, and their lust for violence turned to the mountain valleys where Catholic control was weak. Unable to attack their Bernese enemies, these bishops created internal enemies out of broomsticks, black goats, and naked women who flew through the air. It wasn't long before the first witch hunts began against my ancestors, fueled by the darkness that once hunted Mary Magdalene.

My mother claims these witch hunts were triggered by the publication of *The Book*, a bound encyclopedia of secret feminine knowledge collected over the centuries. *The Book* was written in a coded language with illustrations of green bathtubs, flowing rivers, heavenly spheres, watery tubes, naked women, medicinal herbs, and aquatic apparitions. While the text was easily understood by my ancestors, *The Book* remains untranslated to this day. It's now in Yvonne del Valle's private collection, locked away as some enigmatic curiosity. No one knows this *Book* is actually a diagram for harnessing electromagnetic power from the earth itself, just as its illustrated tubes reveal the underworld structure that powers it. Yvonne kept this a secret, given the last attempt to communicate this wisdom resulted in a mass-slaughter against women, the indigenous, and the earth itself. *The Book* originally appeared in the south-western Alps during the 1420s, reached my ancestors beneath *Les Diablerets*, and traveled north before it was captured by darkness. Like mad Caligula in his search for Mary Magdalene, the Holy Roman Empire fixated on this feminine text and traced it to the mountain valleys south of Sion. Before anyone could actualize *The Book's* visions, darkness came to snuff out their light.

The *burning times* began in 1428 with an Inquisition convened along the shores of Lausanne. From this former Roman colony, the Inquisitors assembled testimony from colonized indigenous on the dark myths surrounding the mountains along the Rhône. These hysterical fanatics described legends of white horses ascending mountains and returning black, signifying possession by the devil. They spoke of pagan women who slept with goats and flew invisibly with broomsticks clasped between lotion-covered legs as they swooped down on villages to steal crops, raid cellars, and cause infertility. It was said these women triggered earthquakes while the men turned into wolves and hunted during the full moon. Dozens of voluntary testimonies were transcribed by the Inquisitors and once enough evidence was assembled, armored soldiers were dispatched from Lausanne to blockade the *Val d'Anniviers* and the *Val d'Hérens,* their populaces descended from Celtic and Nubian rebels.

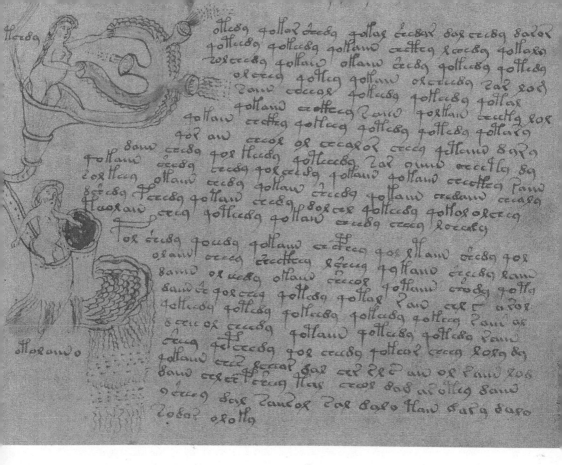

The men and women named in Inquisitorial testimonies were brought to the centers of their villages and tried before an Imperial court. Those who wouldn't admit their pacts with the devil were systematically tortured until either a confession or death was produced. My distant ancestors were the silent ones who died in the Inquisitor's flames, their gray ashes scattered into the rivers, their memories bathed in witchcraft. As a punishment for transmitting the teachings of *The Book*, many of these silent women were strapped to wooden chairs and submerged in the frigid Alpine rivers. In this manner, the religious authorities enacted their fantasies of flying women and turned the pure emerald waters of *The Book* into a hostile, deathly element.

None of my distant ancestors were ever broken by the Inquisition, neither by water or fire, and they died nobly in the face of darkness. Hundreds more were executed over the coming years, their family and friends forced to watch as streams of blood soaked the village commons. When innocent women were accused of witchcraft, their loyal husbands often claimed to be sorcerers who'd bewitched their wives, thus sacrificing themselves on the Imperial chopping block, and that boundless love still inhabits our Alpine valleys. In this first European witch hunt of 1428, more men died than women.

My branch of the tribe wasn't affected by these witch hunts. Not even the armored knights of Laussanne dared provoke the primordial spirits beneath *Les Diablerets,* and the scouts who strayed too far into those mountains never returned. My ancestor's watched dark smoke rise from the green valleys and harbored hundreds of refugees who escaped the Inquisitor by moonlight. These scattered branches regrouped in their ancient strongholds as the witch hunts spread far outside of Switzerland. Beyond the *canton* borders, another war was being waged against earthly life, this one far more deadly.

For nearly one hundred years, Western Europe was ravaged as the Kingdom of France fought the Kingdom of England. During this conflict, the Duchy of Burgundy allied with the English to invade Paris in 1418, a city once beloved by Mary Magdalene and home to her direct descendants. In response to this Burgundian betrayal, a young woman named Jean d'Arc appeared in the town of Vaucouleurs in 1428, just as my ancestors were being persecuted. She demanded the local commander deliver her to King Charles VII of France and claimed a glowing apparition in the sky had instructed her to drive out the English. It took her days to convince the commander that she wasn't mad, but during her second interview, Jean told him of a vision she'd received where the French army was routed by the English at Orleans. When confirmation of this vision came in the form of a royal dispatch, the local commander sent Jean d'Arc towards the front lines dressed as a man.

Jean d'Arc was no Christian, although her visions of the future were absolutely real. Her mother followed the secret teachings of Mary Magdalene and the day she learned of the invasion of Paris, *Jean sat on a natural seat formed by gnarled great roots of the Tree. Her hands lay loosely, one reposing in the other, in her lap. Her head was bent a little towards the ground, and her air was that of one who is lost in thought, steeped in dreams, and not conscious of herself or the world.* Jean dreamed she was in a green pool with two naked women gazing down at a man seated in a chair. The women pointed to this man just before a city appeared within the pool, its stone walls surrounded by soldiers, and Jean saw herself leading them to victory. She was then flushed down a long tube of water and awoke knowing the true purpose of her life.

As my ancestors were being burned at the stake, Jean d'Arc led an army of men to reclaim the ancient city of Mary. Under her illuminated guidance, the French army advanced from Orleans until it had reconquered Reims and was poised to take Paris. Jean insisted the army leave Reims at once but was betrayed by the King of France after he agreed to negotiate with the Duchy of Burgundy. During the drawn-out peace talks, the Burgundians secretly fortified Paris and prevented the defeat predicted by Jean d'Arc. By the time her army surrounded the ancient stone city, it was far too late. In the battle that followed, Jean was wounded by a crossbow and her forces routed at the

Jean d'Arc

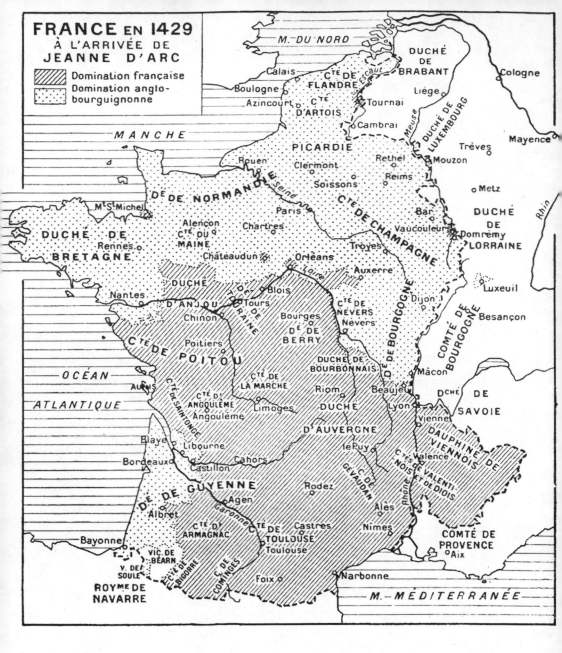

M. DU NORD

DUCHÉ DE BRABANT

Calais
Boulogne
Azincourt
Cᵀᴱ DE FLANDRE
Tournai
Cᵀᴱ D'ARTOIS
Cambrai
Cologne
Liège

MANCHE

PICARDIE
Rouen
Clermont
Soissons
Reims
Rethel
Mouzon
Trèves
Mayence
DUCHÉ DE LUXEMBOURG

Mᵗ ST Michel
DE DE NORMANDIE
Paris
Chartres
Troyes
Cᵀᴱ DE CHAMPAGNE
Bar
Vaucouleurs
Metz
DUCHÉ DE LORRAINE
Domrémy

DUCHÉ DE BRETAGNE
Rennes
Alençon
Cᵀᴱ DU MAINE
Châteaudun
Orléans
Auxerre
Nantes
DUCHÉ D'ANJOU
Blois
Tours
DE DE TOURAINE
Loire
Cᵀᴱ DE NEVERS
Nevers
Dijon
DE DE BOURGOGNE
Luxeuil
Besançon
COMTÉ DE BOURGOGNE

Chinon
Bourges
DE DE BERRY
Poitiers
Cᵀᴱ DE POITOU

OCÉAN ATLANTIQUE

Aunis
Cᵀᴱ DE SAINTONGE
DUCHÉ DE BOURBONNAIS
Riom
Mâcon
Beaujeu
Lyon
DCʰᵉ DE SAVOIE

Cᵀᴱ DE LA MARCHE
Cᵀᴱ D'ANGOULÊME
Angoulême
Limoges
DUCHÉ D'AUVERGNE
Vienne
DAUPHINÉ DE VIENNOIS

Blaye
Libourne
le Puy
Bordeaux
Castillon
Cahors
G. DE GÉVAUDAN
Valence
Cᵀᵉˢ DE VALENTI ᵒᵗ DE DIOIS
Rodez
DE DE GUYENNE
Agen
Garonne
Ales
Nîmes
Albret
Cᵀᴱ D'ARMAGNAC
Castres
TOULOUSE
Toulouse
COMTÉ DE PROVENCE
Aix

Bayonne
VIC. DE BÉARN
V. DE SOULE
Cᵀᴱ DE BIGORRE
C. DE COMINGES
Foix
Narbonne
ROYᵐᵉ DE NAVARRE

M. MÉDITERRANÉE

Escaut
Meuse
Rhin
Rhône

gates. As she recovered, King Charles called for a truce with the patriarchs of Burgundy and England.

With her true goal no longer obtainable, Jean d'Arc waited in solitude for another vision to appear, only nothing ever materialized. Unable to believe the full extent of her betrayal, Jean d'Arc willingly followed the French army from Paris when war resumed in early 1430. During the siege of Compiègne, Jean was captured by the Burgundians and sold to the English for a public execution. All the patriarchs had conspired to be rid of her, just like Mary

Magdalene. Jean was tried for heresy in the city of Rouen by a pro-English bishop and burned at the stake in May of 1431. While she might have worn metal armor, Jean d'Arc never wielded a weapon during her entire campaign. The secret followers of Mary didn't use swords, bows, or spears, and their ways were much different from my ancestors.

Word of Jean's execution spread rapidly along the Rhône River until it reached the ears of my ancestors. The matriarchs understood that Jean d'Arc had fought the darkness with a singular bravery that evoked only inspiration, loyalty, and trust. To honor her memory, my ancestors resolved to send their own daughters and sons down the mountain to fight the darkness rather than hide as they had for centuries. As the witch hunt spread north and south, my tribe followed behind the Inquisition posing as Christian pilgrims, taking revenge on the Empire whenever possible. During the following centuries, these Alpine rebels in black cloaks streamed into Europe like melting glaciers, no longer content to live among the drifting clouds. My grandmother Josephine Louise Lemel joined this rebellious tradition when she left Switzerland in the summer of 1868. Just like Jean d'Arc, Josephine was sucked up into a tube and deposited in a green pool with a group of naked women, all gazing at a city along the water. This was the place Josephine would live one day. This was her vision of San Francisco.

WE'LL ALL GO OUT TO MEET HER

It's the third day of picking apples in Lorraine's orchard. Even though its sweltering out here, I admit, I love how the sunlight caresses my skin. Love shares the sun's brilliance, especially at noon, when the earth's bright with heat and crickets sing behind the grass. I'm sweaty, lusty, and this warmth makes me want to be loved, especially now with my mother ignoring me. Lorraine's her closest friend, as the crow flies, but she still hasn't shown up, not even for dinner. Having a mother like Isabelle isn't easy, especially when she's so sorrowful, though I wish she'd get over it and pick apples with me. That way we'd be in the sun together. Then maybe she'd feel love for a change.

Lorraine's three daughters are off gathering fallen apples and I hear them shriek each time they find a worm. They're crazy, but they've left me alone for now. I carry my ladder from tree to tree, climb into the branches with a tightly woven basket, and while I pluck the apples above their thin little stems, I hum "She'll Be Coming Around The Mountain." The melody won't leave my head, only I don't really want it to. The tune makes work go faster, like I'm dancing on Market Street. Those twirling bodies and the roar of ſtomping feet thrilled me then, juſt like the memory does now. Vaſt and shadowy dance-halls packed with life, dripping with sweat, the air so thick from moiſture I could hardly see. Now here I am, juſt a farm girl picking fruit. All I have left is the memory of that frantic music.

Once I've got around two hundred apples, I carry the basket down the hill to Lorraine's barn. Angelo's waiting there when I get inside, hands crossed over his cheſt, smiling like a muſtachioed donkey. He goes silent when I enter and ſtares me down with those hazel eyes I loved back when we were kids. Before I can react, Lorraine walks forward, blocking him from my vision.

"Thanks, Fulvia," she says, eyes wide in terror. "Are my girls ſtill up there? Or did they wander off to go swimming? If they're not tormenting you, they're—"

"No, they're ſtill up there, yelling at worms. Why? Is it time for dinner?"

"Getting there." She takes the basket of apples from my hands and nods in Angelo's direction. "Ignore him. He's juſt asking if he can help out—"

I don't let Lorraine finish. I'm angry. It can never be on my terms. It always has to be his terms and usually on my territory, places that are mine. I ſtorm up to the baſtard, put my finger in his face, and glare until he looks away. It takes a long time, but it happens, and I win our little ſtaring conteſt. He even puts his hands in his pockets. That's what he does when he's nervous.

"You need to take the orchard from me, too?" I ask. "Humiliating me wasn't enough?"

"Liſten, Fulvia, this—"

"I've already heard too much from you!" I point toward the doors of the barn. "Out! Now!"

Angelo looks pleadingly towards Lorraine but she's already walking away with the apples. I bet Angelo thinks she didn't hear or can't be bothered with my drama, my ego, my rage. It doesn't matter what Angelo thinks. He walks out of the barn and back towards the village, defeated by crazy Fulvia, and my heart beats faſter than I'd like as ſtone houses appear in my imagination, dwarfed by jagged Alpine mountains. Maybe if we'd been born under *Les Diablerets*, life would have been different. If I could have grabbed Angelo when we were younger and told him I was a witch who could access the underworld, he might not have betrayed me. Too late now. Once he's far off down the path, I catch up with Lorraine where she's got all my apples spread out on the dining room table, waiting to become her famous apple-butter.

"Did he finally leave?" she asks. "Talk about not getting the hint, eh?"

"What did he want?"

"Like I said, *to offer a hand*. I told him we were fine, but he kept talking and talking about getting the apples down the hill—"

"What! The apples! Not the wheat, huh? Getting *the apples* to the coast?"

"Don't worry about him. There's something wrong with that boy, really wrong, especially after what happened to both of you. He's gotten darker."

"Yeah, well, you don't have to be polite to the old cow pie, you know that?" Lorraine closes her eyes and breathes in furiously through her nostrils.

"Fulvia," she sighs. "I don't stop you managing your affairs your way. Don't you stop me doing it my way. You and Angelo need to deal with what happened, stop dragging the whole commune into your mess. I know he's the one who made it everyone's concern, but don't feed the fire more than it's already been fed. Now, please, can you tell my daughters to come down here? And I want you to eat with us tonight. Your little history book can wait a few more hours."

There's no point arguing with her, so I walk back into the orchard to find Isabelle, Yvonne, and Juana gathering fallen apples. These girls were named after my mother Isabelle, her friend Yvonne, and Yvonne's daughter Juana. That's how deep the connection goes. The eldest, Isabelle, is seventeen years old, while her sisters Yvonne and Juana are ten and seven. I call out their names when I'm halfway up the hill and they all come running down the path with their sacks of gleaned apples. Juana collides into my legs and I lift her up to my sore shoulders, her favorite place to pick apples. It took me half the day to convince her I had to climb the ladder alone, so high I couldn't carry her. Now she's back on my shoulders for the walk home. I'm going to need a massage after this.

Warm air gusts through the front door while the five of us eat dinner, even though the sun's already set. As the sky turns orange outside the window, I hope Angelo falls down a cliff on his way home. I hope he's swallowed in a landslide, I hope he's alone in the darkness, I hope he pays for what he's done. Lorraine can see these dark thoughts, I know it. She's right, of course. I need to let Angelo go, I need to burn out this darkness, so instead of laying my curses on him, I listen to the children talk about playtime fantasies. Their older sister Isabelle looks bored, too old to care about their fictional universes, especially with me in the room. To liven things up, I ask their mom about the old days, only Lorraine doesn't want to talk about it.

I mention little details about rebel Lorraine and my mother Isabelle riding in boxcars with bags of Yvonne del Valle's money, stacks of anarchist newspapers, boxes of pistols, and red arm-bands tied around their black sleeves. Lorraine stays silent while I spin stories of trains that still ran on coal or burned firewood in plumes of black smoke. It all sounds like fantasy, even more outlandish than our electromagnetic system where the energy is conducted through giant iron towers and one week the lights are on, the next week they're off, often for months. Lorraine's girls only know this mysterious world system where the planet overflows with free, unlimited energy, more than humans could ever diminish. The girls know this system carries none of the old earthly ruin, although it's a fine line to walk in this bereaved family. They've all lost someone irreplaceable.

I think I'm telling good stories because Lorraine hasn't stopped me, so I keep going. I don't want the old days to seem cheery so I talk about children dying in coal mines, how brutal conditions were in those dark pits, but none of this erases the death of their father Lucio, killed when a super-charged electromagnetic ribbon snapped in half and fed a planet's worth of electricity back into the Paloma transmitter. Lucio was the main technician for the powerhouse, incinerated along with everyone else inside a two mile radius of the transmission tower. Lorraine was still pregnant with Juana when the facility exploded, leaving a crater in the olive groves wide enough to hold a town. I don't blame these girls for fearing this unpredictable energy but I remind them it's the least destructive in history, only thirty people died maintaining it, but Juana doesn't care, she just points at the olive oil lamps burning on the table, bright enough to see with. She's right, of course. *We pressed these olives together and no one died*, she says. *No one died.* My eyes fill up with tears but I force myself to laugh. These girls don't know the truth about our system, and I'm not going to tell them. Not yet, anyway. I wouldn't even know how. If it wasn't for Yvonne and *The Book*, our world wireless net-work would have never existed, just like their father would still be alive. All I can do is write my history book. Then these girls can read it.

Lorraine forces me to take a lantern for the walk home. I know she's worried about my curse on Angelo boomeranging in my face. I say goodnight to the girls, kiss each of them on the cheek, then set out towards the dimly lit village. The night air is still warm, scented with a million blades of dried grass, a smell so sharp it livens each of my nerve endings. Most of the village windows are lit up with oil-lamps but I see electric light inside the brewery. Steam rises from the *fábrica* chimneys in thick white tufts, all signs I should take the long way home. I don't want to run into Angelo. It'll just blow up in my face, especially if all the brewers are drunk.

There's a light in my window when I finally get home. At first I think it's just the reflection of the lantern, but then I realize it's my mother. She's hunched over my desk reading the first chapters of my history book and this is enough to make me yell unintelligibly at the window glass. I throw open the front door, set the flickering lantern down on my reading chair, and Isabelle manages to grab it before flaming lamp oil spills across the floor. I snatch the notebook off my desk and scream at my mother as the lantern swings in her calm hands. I don't really know what I'm saying. My vision blurs, my head pounds with blood, but eventually everything grows still and I can see.

"I just wanted to know what you've been doing!" she gasps. "It's good, what you've written."

"*Thanks!* Why did you read it without my permission? I wasn't ready to share it! With anyone. And your voice is already in my head too much. Now it's going to be piercing!"

"Cut the theater. It's good. All your time in the library had a use after all. You're destroying our lies very effectively, just like you wanted to. Clear, simple, just the parts of the story you need to tell. It's a lot of history for such little space. I read it twice. There——"

"Save it. Let me finish the damn thing. Thank you, really." I hug her tightly before she can offer any more critique. "All I want to know is who gave *The Book* to the Holy Roman Emperor? What kind of twisted person are we talking about?"

"Who knows? They had agents looking for people like us. Mercenaries, rogues."

"The next chapter's gonna be dark, *mama*. Until *abuela* Josephine's born."

"It was a dark time. Just hurry it along. You keep mentioning your grandmother at the start of each chapter, then you only bring her up at the end. *Andale!* You said you wanted to tell her story. Let's see Josephine then! Enough of this darkness!"

"Okay, okay, enough of you!" I toss the notebook on the desk and push her towards the front door. "If you'd told me all this when I was young, I would have...anyway, I don't want to get...now you have to wait until I'm done writing the truth, after everything you've done. You have no idea how your lies...I don't want to get all worked up right now, trust me. For both our sake. It's getting real late and you've got a long walk. Unless you want to sleep——"

"Sleep here? *Merde.* I wouldn't get any sleep here," she says, walking outside with the lantern. "Your pen sounds like a little mouse in the kitchen. And you're up all night pacing, same as when you were a girl, talking to yourself——"

"Really, this flattery is just too much for me, *mama. Ciao!*"

She's still talking to herself as she walks up the logging road with Lorraine's flickering oil-lamp swaying in her hands. I sit down at my desk but it's no use, I might as well be staring at a boulder. My heart's pounding furiously so I pour a tall glass of red wine, dig my tobacco out from the drawer, roll a cigarette, and puff away on the front porch. I can see my crazy mother climbing the hills with the lamp-flame cutting an arc through the darkness. I bet she's still talking to herself, maybe even singing. Either way, I'm definitely not getting much writing done tonight, but who cares? I'll drink like I'm back in San Francisco, when I was dumb enough to think the past could ever be over. The first sips of wine start to calm my nerves, I can feel the tension loosen in my back, so I take another chug from my glass, hold it up to the stars, and think to myself: *while nothing but breath, these words of mine are immortal.*

3

THE WITCH'S DIASPORA AND THE RENAISSANCE OF MARY

THE BIRTHPLACE OF MY MATERNAL GRANDMOTHER REMAINED PEACEFUL and undisturbed throughout the 1400s, too remote to concern the Holy Roman Empire. Josephine Louise Lemel was born in one of this valley's stone, mortar, and wood-beam houses, all built with materials from the ever-crumbling slopes of *Les Diablerets*. Had it not been for the witch hunts in the 1400s, Josephine's forbears may have remained in the mountains watching the world from afar, content to carry on their ancient ways. After their relatives were burned by the Inquisition, my branch of the tribe sent their daughters and sons to fight the Empire disguised as Christian pilgrims, the most convenient method of travel. During those days, my ancestors wore hooded black cloaks, tied a red ribbon around their necks to signify war, and over the following centuries, they took their revenge against the darkness that hunted them.

In its efforts to obliterate the ancient homeland of Yeshua ha-Nozri and Mary Magdalene, that darkness began a Crusade in the late-1090s to recapture what was called the *Holy Land*. The opponent of this Crusade was the vast Islamic Empire that extended from Afghanistan to Spain, all unified by the teachings of Mohamed the Prophet, a man very similar to Yeshua ha-Nozri. After the Roman Empire changed its religion to Christianity and began to persecute all heretics, the ancient knowledge of Egypt, Palestine, and Syria retreated to Persia, the place where it originated. Mary Magdalene's own spiritual lineage extended back to these ancient conceptions of a war waged between Light and Darkness, an influence that lingered even in far-flung Mecca.

With the Roman Church howling for their deaths, Mary's progenitors remained hidden between Persia and Arabia until one of them met a young sea-trader named Mohamed. Her name was Khadijah the Great, a 40-year-old merchant of Mecca, and she hired this 25-year-old sailor to conduct her business. Impressed by his abilities, she married him in 595 and, thanks to her guidance, Mohamed made his ascension into the heavens with the archangel Gabriel. Khadijah became the first Muslim to follow the Prophet after his ascension and within 25 years they had spread their new religion through the streets of Mecca, earning the scorn of the city's local rulers. Just as Mary aided Yeshua in his war against the tyrants, Khadijah now aided Mohamed.

When she passed away in the year 619, their new religion had become a significant threat to the merchant rulers of Mecca. Fearing for his life now that Khadijah was gone, Mohamed and his followers fled to the agricultural city of Medina and gathered the strength to make war on Mecca. In the year 624, the first skirmishes broke out and by 632 the entire Arabian Peninsula was under Islamic control. After the Prophet passed away, his military empire continued to spread, conquering Syria, Palestine, Egypt, and Persia, fulfilling the dream of Khadijah. With these territories now unified, the ancient wisdom in Persia could safely return to its centers in Alexandria, Jerusalem, and Damascus.

By the year 750, the Islamic Empire had conquered Spain, was pushing towards France, and controlled all of North Africa, giving it full advantage over the fragmented kingdoms of Europe. While the Christian armies fought back against this invasion, the ancient knowledge of Mary's progenitors began

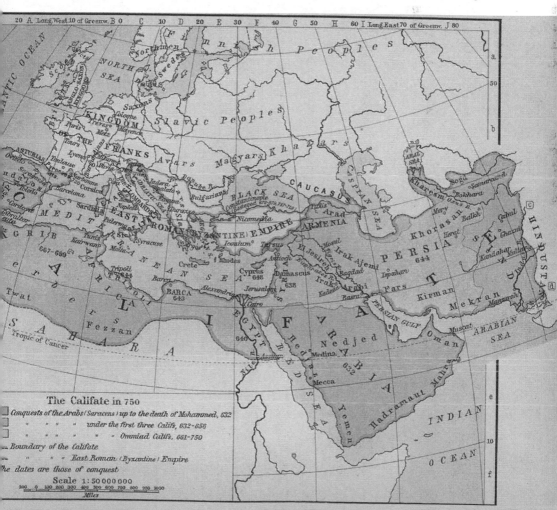

to trickle into France, revealing Khadijah's grand plan to the Magdalenian followers. Khadijah knew her lover's light would eventually be darkened, just as Yeshua's had, so she ensured his future armies would have only one purpose: to return the light to their lost sisters in France. The battle over Spain raged through the late-1090s when the united kingdoms of Europe launched their first Crusade to reclaim Jerusalem from the Islamic Empire. My tribe watched these religious armies pass over the Rhône and observed the armored men guarding pilgrims on their journey to the Holy Land. These mounted Knights Templar were empowered by the Holy Pope and legally autonomous from every king, their sole duty to keep the roads of Europe safe for all pilgrims heading to Jerusalem.

My tribe cautiously utilized small portions of this pilgrim path for many years until the Knights Templar were betrayed by the Pope. In the year 1307, the Inquisition burned these Knights at the stake for spitting on crucifixes and worshiping a black goat, false charges which obscured the reason for their execution: the Knights Templar had been subverted by the forces of Mary, enabling the safe passage of their followers from England to Persia. Although the Knights Templar were executed, the safety-of-travel they instilled remained intact along the Great Pass of Saint Bernard, a mountain path that snaked south over the Alps towards the eternal city of Rome. It was this road between Switzerland and Italy that carried *The Book* to my ancestors, just as it soon enabled them to take revenge for the witch-hunts.

My tribe left their mountain stronghold in the 1440s and settled in Milano, Bern, Paris, Roma, Basel, Venezia, München, and just south of *Les Diablerets* in the city of Sion. In these dangerous times, the recent invention of the printing press was a mixed blessing, as it incited both popular rebellion and religious repression. Once the Empire captured *The Book* and burnt my ancestors for reading it, the religious authorities mass-produced their own books detailing the habits of witches and demons, utter fictions crafted to arouse violence in the reader, and these texts became more detailed as the practice of witch-hunting spread in every direction. Twenty-eight of these books were written between 1435 and 1487, including the *Malleus Maleficarum*, an infamous manual for exterminating witches.

To my besieged tribe, the situation was beyond bleak. After vanquishing the Muslims in 1492, the Kingdom of Spain was able to reach the two massive continents across the Atlantic and brought their witch-hunting Inquisition to those foreign shores. Women were being burned alive in the valleys of Northern Italy just as their sisters were being tortured in German and Spanish dungeons, leaving my ancestors with few options for travel. Many crossed the northern border of the Swiss Confederacy and settled in the Black Forest or along the Rhine River where they distributed printed

St. Mauritius portrayed as white by El Greco, 1520

copies of their rebellious demands from village to village, calling for peasants to take up arms against their landlords. When these uprisings were subdued, my ancestors moved to another region to sow discord against the local tyrants. Year by year, this rebellion spread from the Black Forest all the way to southern Bavaria, threatening to cleave the Holy Roman Empire in half. Behind these disturbances were my ancestors, dressed in black cloaks with a red ribbon tied around their necks.

Just before my tribe launched their great uprising in 1524, a group of religious authorities from the north decided to abolish the Roman Catholic Church and replace it with a Protestant Church. Their printing presses spread this message across the northern Empire, along with texts on locating witches, and while this Protestant influence crept south into the Black Forest, my ancestors helped trigger an uprising against the priests, lords, and knights known as the German Peasant Wars, a bloody conflict that ended in Protestant betrayal. Martin Luther, the Protestant leader, waited until the peasants were butchered, condemned them in his printed texts, and orchestrated a witch-hunt to subdue those who survived. As one historian explained, *both Catholic and Protestant nations, at war against each other in every other respect, joined arms and shared arguments to persecute witches.* Few of my ancestors lived through this bloodshed. Those who returned home spoke of a world ruled by darkness.

War encircled *Les Diablerets* throughout the 1600s. Northern Europe was scorched into ruin, its remaining indigenous slaughtered, and its matriarchs burned at the stake, a practice that spread quickly across Africa and the Americas. Ships filled with slaves kidnapped from central Africa were sailed off to American plantations where the kings and queens could do as they pleased without fear of rebellion. During this living nightmare, the official image of Saint Maurice, already embellished with a thousand falsehoods, found its skin rendered from black to white. The Holy Roman Empire was engaged in this horrendous African slave trade and couldn't let a black-skinned saint inspire rebellion in their American colonies. Only in the farmlands along the Rhône did people still whisper of black-skinned Mauritius and his defeat of the Roman army.

It was impossible to travel north from Valais during the 1600s, a region of southern Switzerland that remained Catholic after the Protestant Reformation, so my ancestors sent their rebels south towards Rome where the light of Mary had taken hold. Long before the secret publication of *The Book* in 1419, the followers of Mary had used every possible means to promote free thought, artistic expression, and sexuality outside the confines of the Church. Unlike my ancestors, these women dove deep into the structures of darkness in search of sparks of light. The first glimmer became known as

the Renaissance, grew into the Enlightenment, and spread north into every center of power, breaking the old models of statecraft. Using poetry, philosophy, architecture, art, science, ancient knowledge, and subterfuge, the followers of Mary eroded the traditional powers and offered a cosmology built on what existed, not the delusions of the priests. This anti-monarchical Enlightenment began in England during the late 1600s, traveled across the ocean to North America in the 1770s, and returned to France in the 1780s where the fatal dagger was thrust into the divine rule of kings. Unfortunately, this wave of revolt quickly grew out of control and had dire consequences for the history of the planet.

The colonial subjects in North America who rebelled against the King of England maintained the Empire in their slave plantations and government buildings. The indigenous were massacred by the armies of George Washington and forced to abandon land they'd inhabited since the beginning of time. When an anti-monarchical revolt broke out in Paris during the French Revolution, the forces of Mary converged on their city to help the common people bring down the King. Members of my tribe were in Paris for this unprecedented event and bore witness to the terror that followed when every kingdom and empire allied themselves against France. It was no longer the shores of distant America or the isle of Britannia that hosted these revolts, now it was the continent of Europe. As the old tyrants plotted the destruction of rebel France, darkness crept through the military blockades and contaminated the new secular leaders in Paris. It wasn't long before the witch-hunts resumed, the burning-stakes now replaced by the guillotine. Many followers of Mary lost their heads to this infernal machine as the revolution mutated into the Imperial invasion of Europe, Russia, and Egypt. Like all the Emperors of centuries past, Napoleon I extended the darkness as far as possible until he was extinguished. By the time of his imprisonment, the followers of Mary had definitively broken the ancient monarchies.

The rapid development of industrial technology following their French Revolution soon proved toxic to life on the planet. It liberated the basest aspects of the human species and allowed the darkness to become autonomous from its old centers of power. The forces of Mary hadn't anticipated the poisons that arose when their Enlightenment spread the very darkness they fought against. In the meantime, my ancestors beneath *Les Diablerets* kept sending their daughters and sons to foment rebellion against the latest Empires. They helped trigger insurrections across industrial France and precipitated the many European revolts of 1848, weakening the last kings and emperors. Some rebels wanted to maintain a secular nation-state, the last vestige of the old Roman Empire, while others wanted to destroy it. This schism grew until two distinct factions emerged: the communists and the anarchists.

My ancestors quickly sided with the anarchist movement and encouraged its growth in the Jura Mountains, just northwest of *Les Diablerets*. Like the birthplace of my grandmother, these imposing mountains harbored an indigenous population never colonized by any Empire, many of whom became watchmakers in order to fund a movement called the International. Josephine was born soon after its founding in the year 1850. She lived her youth learning the old ways of our tribe, the new ways of the Empires, the mysteries of the underworld, and the philosophy of anarchism. In 1868, the unexpected arrival of a Russian nihilist and an Italian postal worker thrust my grandmother into the international movement to destroy capitalism, forever altering the course of history. Josephine never returned to the snow-capped Alps and would live her last days in California, a distant place at the end of the world named for the fictional all-female caliphate of an old Spanish novel.

WE'LL KILL THE OLD RED ROOSTER

I'M NAKED IN THE KITCHEN, GAZING AT TWENTY GLASS JARS FILLED WITH apple butter, rich and brown and boiled in cider until its nothing but creamy, sugary goodness. I've lined all these jars up on the shelf, just above the counter. This is what gets me through the winter, this beautiful sweet butter that fills me to the brim with rosy little loves. The people in the village probably think I'm selfish, that I only work with Lorraine for the apple butter, but I can use my work hours however I like. I've got another twenty hours to go before I'm done for the season. At the moment, I'm taking a break.

Writing this history consumes my body. I've sat at my desk for days distilling whole books into just a handful of sentences. My family left an invisible mark on western civilization, a missing jig-saw piece I had to fabricate for myself. I ruined my eyes reading a hundred history books, so I've earned this nice reward. I promise myself I'll only open this one jar as I spin off the waxed lid, spread the brown apple butter across my morning bread, and savor each grainy bite. Once it's gone, I close the waxy lid and place the apple butter back on the shelf. I need to keep these twenty jars sealed until after the equinox, otherwise I'll regret it. The rainy season always makes me sad.

I eat a piece of cheese, swallow some cold tea, then quickly clean the house after last night's frenzy. I guess my mom's not exaggerating. I turn into a tornado when everyone's asleep. My clothes, my books, my cigarette butts, my wine glasses, my dirty dishes, all scattered on the chairs, tables, even the floor. I glance at my notebook to make sure I actually wrote something last night, that it wasn't all a crazy nightmare about massacres in the Black Forest. It's not a dream, though, it's right there, my lines of cursive script cascading down the pages in a long black river. I feel proud of myself until I notice the spilled ash on the desk, the smelly tea cups, so I finish cleaning before anyone knocks on my door to see for themselves that I eat apple butter in the nude, that I'm a total disaster with the ability to speak, that my history's just the ravings of a mad woman, or that I'm a witch who talks with the dead.

I wash my hair over the water basin, douse myself with pine essence, and put on my black dress with its high collar lined in red. My mother Isabelle has an identical one, so did her mother. I haven't worn this dress since I went to San Francisco for Josephine's funeral and it still fits me perfectly, even at the waist. I gaze in the mirror and study my resemblance to those women in our family history, our cloaks now replaced with dresses. We all have the same black hair, the same eyebrows, the same green eyes. I might as well be in a mirror-box looking back through time. I see myself standing under *Les Diablerets* while a black goat chews silently in the grass and an old woman toils in the sloped fields. Underneath this bucolic setting, behind that magic mirror-box, there I am, just Fulvia in a black dress. *Oh, virginity! Where will you go when I lose you? I'm off to a place I shall never return from.* My mom doesn't know what I'm about to do. No one does. It's a surprise.

Yvonne's communal house is at the edge of the bluff, directly opposite the *fábrica*, a four-story monster that houses the majority of our population, including Angelo. He should be in the brewery by now, hopped up on his ego, far away from me. I leave my house and cross the village without speaking to anyone. I say hello, I smile, but I keep walking. They all want to know about my dress, why I'm not wearing pants, where I'm going, but I ignore them and wave goodbye. I hope they run off to the *fábrica* and tell Angelo about it. That'll make him afraid. Everyone's afraid of this dress. When I was a young girl, Isabelle said this was the perfect disguise for a woman with its vaguely religious collar, allowing men to mistake us for either nuns or school-children. She never told me that our family had worn it for centuries during times of war. I just though it was a boring old dress.

A dozen of the old San Francisco sailors are playing cards in the main hall of the communal house, the radio blaring behind them. They all stare at me with open mouths but none of them speak a word. Maybe it's the dress, I'm not sure, but they look stunned, like I'm a ghost, or a dream. I hear the old men whisper as I climb the stairs to the third floor, so I clearly must have spooked these salty dogs, made them think they'd gone back to the time of waterfront witches. No one wears this dress anymore, those days are long past, only I've clearly changed that, for everyone.

At the head of the stairs is the red door to Yvonne del Valle's solarium. Everyone knocks on this door before entering except me and my mother Isabelle. I walk directly inside and find the old woman sitting in her red reading chair, basking in the sun with an open book in her lap. Her bright green eyes, piercing like the devil, cut right into my skin. I always forget her power until its too late.

"I already know," Yvonne says. "Your mother told you everything."

"I know enough."

"Close the door, please."

I take this opportunity to look away, to break her hypnotism, to save my will-power. My armpits are flooded with sweat from this infernal solarium and I can barely muster enough strength to close the door. My body feels light, like it's being evaporated. The door clicks shut but I don't have time to think about very much because Yvonne's walking towards me, limber like a dancer. She turned 79 last fall. Maybe the solarium keeps her young.

"Your mother used to say those same words," she tells me. "She'd say, *I know enough.* Isabelle never reveals what she knows, not until the last moment, when its almost too late. Just like her mother Josephine did. Now you."

"Sounds familiar."

"Let me see you, *mija*. It's been months."

She takes me by the forearms and stares into my brain until the whole world bursts in a salty geyser of water. When the spray settles, I'm facing the sheer magnetism of this singular person who ripped a hole into the underworld. I've known Yvonne all my life and her powerful gaze never fails to knock out my legs like a rolling log.

"I suppose you're here to see *The Book*," she says. "You must have pieced it together by now."

"I know *The Book* started the witch-hunts. But I want to know—"

"If I showed it to Nikola Tesla? To help build our transmitters?"

"Did you?"

Yvonne lets go of my arms and takes a step back.

"Remarkable," she says. "It's like time's repeating itself. And you're even wearing the same dress, speaking just like they did." She grabs my collar and reveals its red interior. "I always loved this, the hidden brightness. That's what you all are. Hidden brightness. And sharp as knives. Yes! I did! I showed it to Nikola! I explained enough of it to make the system work. Come on, I'll show you. But *this* is what you're doing? You want to tell my secrets?"

"People need to understand what you did. Otherwise it all might happen again. It's not right to keep them in darkness. That's how it creeps back in. Look at what happened to me! Look at what those lies did! I didn't know I was like you, like my mother, like the others. I didn't know—"

"You don't need to be like us, *mija*. Your task is...very different." She takes my hand and guides me to her bookshelves. "I know all about your troubles with Angelo. I'm sorry he's after you, but these challenges are more important than the ones we faced. You have to discover this future for yourself. Just know we're here with you, and you're one of us. You've always been one of us."

"Then why do I feel like your broken little experiment?"

"We wanted you to have the *chance*...the chance to *only* know freedom." I didn't expect this, but she's crying. "All we knew was struggle, so we... Isabelle and I never told you the truth. We didn't, it's true. But you had something we never had. A chance at real freedom. So now—"

She stops in front of the wood and glass bookcase, takes a key from around her neck, opens the metal lock, and reveals the illuminated manuscript hidden inside. We take *The Book* over to her reading table and gaze down at its bright pages, each illustration a familiar figure from my lonely childhood, a ghost calling to me through time. This is when Yvonne tells me a long story I've never heard. The room fills with moisture and my armpits flow with sweat while she turns the crisp parchment page by page. I learn about the hidden power beneath the world wireless system and the human conductors who make it possible. I see twelve naked women around the base of an electromagnetic transmitter, presiding over the life-giving springs of creation. These human conductors were the missing pieces to Nikola Tesla's wireless system, the naked women depicted in *The Book* who sent arcs of light across the sky. Yvonne tells me about the prototype transmitter she built in Siberia and how she pulled a ribbon from the earth into Nikola Tesla's iron tower. Her bony finger taps on the calf-skin parchment near two naked women communicating through watery tubes. She says these tubes are the pathways of the underworld. We can speak freely through this subterranean net-work, just as we can hear the inner movements of the earth. She tells me these forces are one and the same.

"Don't worry," I tell her. "I'm not going to run off and become a conductor."

"That's not how it works, *mija*. If you were needed for a transmission, no one could stop you. You'd be there without knowing why. The planet calls you and you go. We don't choose when we draw the energy. I only did it twice on my own, once by accident. No one else has ever channeled a ribbon by themselves. The planet chooses who it wishes. That's just how it works."

"Then why did the planet blow up the Paloma station? Why do Lorraine's children not have a father? Why did the planet do that? Is that *just how it works?*"

This silences her. I've now asserted enough of myself to be Fulvia, not Isabelle, but Yvonne's green eyes lose all their spark. I see her hesitate a moment, unsure what to say, so I make it easy for her and keep turning the pages of *The Book*. We come to the map I always loved as a child, a six-square fold-out that depicts nine heavenly spheres connected by ribbons of light.

"This right here," I say, opening up the folds. "Does this mean there's other planets out there in the stars? Look. On this sphere here. There's the transmission tower, there's the electromagnetic ribbon, and there's another planet, or star, or something. I've been staring at this fold-out since I was a kid. Tell me what it means! Are those Gnostic texts true? Are there spheres up there with life we—"

"You don't understand, Fulvia. We're not ready, none of us. Because things like your conflict with Angelo keep happening, because of all the problems we face in this tiny village. If we didn't have these problems, we might have electricity every day, and *then,* maybe, we'd be ready to talk with the others up there, if they're listening. But the way it is now, with people like Angelo who live downstairs, with all that wheat sitting in the silo...there's a good reason for this energy drought. The planet has a plan, so be patient. I'm sure you'll make sense of the rest."

"Yeah, sure, great, but you still haven't explained why Paloma blew up and killed Lucio. You know a lot of people still think its suspicious, right? These lies are dangerous, Yvonne."

"We grew up in lies, me and your mother, and sometimes the truth isn't in words. But call them lies all you want. Anyway...your mother says you're writing a history, and you *should* tell the truth, but just know people will *always* find something suspicious, especially if you put it in a book. I don't know what else to say about Paloma. There's nothing you don't know. But if you tell thousands of people how we built the system, if you tell them about the underworld, our abilities...you open up big problems, just like *The Book* did. Are you sure you want to do this?"

"I want to tell the truth, Yvonne, like I said! I want to tell it all! This is the real history, the one we're supposed to have, not all that garbage left over from last century."

"Come back another day," she says, closing *The Book*. "You shouldn't have brought up Paloma. That was no one's fault but—"

She's crying again, she can't help it, so I hold her tight and whisper *I'll always love you.* I kiss her all over before leaving the solarium, already regretting what I've done to her. *You shouldn't have brought up Paloma.* Depending on who you ask, the explosion proved that only born-women could safely conduct the energy of the planet, or it was just an accident. That transmission involved a single male conductor, the first and last to ever appear. He was invisibly called like the others, took his place in the wood and glass conductor's chambers, and held an electromagnetic ribbon for seventeen minutes before it snapped, leaving a smoldering crater in Paloma's olive groves.

Everyone knew he'd gone to the chamber but no one stopped him, not even Yvonne, and I linger at the doorway for a moment to watch her weep. *You shouldn't have brought up Paloma.*

There's a small crowd gathered near the dining hall and they try to act nonchalant as I walk downstairs. It gets real silent when I reach the floor and see Angelo standing there, right near the front door, hoping to sprint off if I make some sudden outburst. *He towers above tall men as the poets of Lesbos tower over all others.* I'm not giving the bastard any satisfaction, so I walk into the kitchen past some sailors and farm girls, everyone asking me *what's going on, why are you in that dress, is Yvonne alright?* I say *everything's fine* and *tout va bien.* I avoid eye contact until I'm out the side-door, then I run off through the dirt. Angelo catches me just before I reach the square and his nasty fingers lock around my arm, filling me with darkness. *Now the wedding you asked for is over and your wife is the girl you asked for.* This was what my mother warned me about. This is the darkness looking for me.

"Don't touch me!" I scream, running faster. "Stay away from me!"

"What happened in there?" he pleads, no longer following. "What's going on?"

I don't turn around, I run until everything blurs into bubbles and I'm sitting on my front steps covered in sweat. No one's followed me. When my panting dies down I realize that now Angelo looks crazy for once, chasing me across the square like a maniac. I'm sure he's back in the communal house, waiting at the foot of the stairs with all the others. They expect Yvonne to emerge from her solarium and explain my black dress, only she won't tell them anything. That part's up to me.

I walk inside my house, strip off my dress, and rub off the dried sweat with a wet towel. The wind blows through the open door and cools my naked skin, making me forget everything that's just happened until I hear footsteps, frantic giggles, startled cries, the stomping of feet, and then I realize some crazy little children just caught a glimpse of naked Fulvia Ferrari. I slam the door shut and throw on a blouse before anyone else gets a free show. At least my desk's still nice and clean, just like I left it, but I need to calm down before I can write. That's when the apple butter whispers to me. I'll eat just a few spoonfuls, enough to cover a slice of bread. I've earned it.

4

THE LONG COURTSHIP OF JOSEPHINE LEMEL AND ANTONIO FERRARI

IRON RAILROADS ADVANCED TOWARDS *LES DIABLERETS*, BRINGING THE darkness ever closer, and by the time Josephine was eleven, black clouds of coal-smoke rose from mechanical engines chugging along the Rhône from Sion to Geneva. Despite the proximity of these metal roads, life remained unchanged in the abode of the devils where houses were made of stone and the cows, sheep, chickens, and pigs had their own fireplaces. Josephine's village rested safely on a plateau across the Lizerne River far from the doomed hamlet of Derborence, destroyed by a stone avalanche in 1719, a tragedy blamed squarely on Lucifer. According to local superstition, the devil himself slept beneath these mountains.

My ancestors had warned the Bernese settlers not to build Derborence beneath the *Quille du Diable*, the overturned keel of Lucifer's rocking boat, but these stubborn Bernese were committed to civilizing the valley and making it productive with their own methods of agriculture. The farmland was fertile, the water pure, and the harvest bountiful until that fateful evening in 1719 when the devil woke from his dream. The stone avalanche destroyed most of the tiny Bernese settlement, sparing only a few houses along the Lizerne. By the 1800s, these last remnants of Derborance had become the center of commerce when a Swiss post office and *auberge* was built along the river bank. By then, the birthplace of my grandmother had become a black dot on the map of the Swiss Confederacy, an idyllic farming community with a reputation for fine cheeses and wool clothing.

Josephine grew up making these cheeses and lived off their richness throughout the winters, just as the wool sweaters she knitted kept her warm. Her family lived in their stone houses year-round, as did the two dozen other families that made up our branch of the tree. They never used money until the 1800s when Josephine's parents began to sell their cheese in Sion like normal farmers. In the process, they accumulated a small fortune and spent portions of it to avoid local suspicion. Every summer, Josephine and her little sister Bianca drove their modern wagon down to Sion, withstood the lecherous heckling of passing men, sold off their excess cheese to a greedy merchant, and returned home with farming equipment and a bag of metal coins. Money made no sense to Josephine, although her parents insisted they save it for times of rebellion, a moment when all their coins could be redeemed.

Fig. 287.—THE DIABLERETS.

Scale 1 : 100,000.

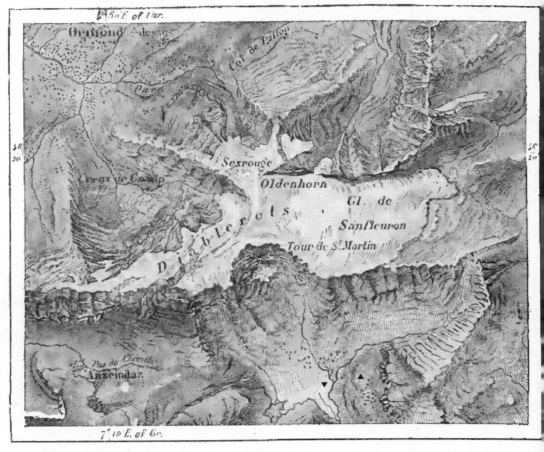

▼ = Derborence   ▲ = Josephine's village   ———————— 1 Mile.

In the summer of 1868, two ſtrangers arrived at my grandmother's ſtone farmhouse. The firſt visitor was a well-dressed woman in her twenties who appeared on the road from Sion. Her name was Tanya and had received directions to *Les Diablerets* from our relatives in München, along with several Russian books. Tanya placed one of these volumes on the table, a work of fiction titled *What Is To Be Done?* written by the imprisoned rebel Nikolai Chernyshevsky. She then handed over a slip of paper filled with numbers, each digit designating a page, line, or letter number, the coded message hidden inside *What Is To Be Done?*. As my great-grandmother decoded this message, Tanya spoke of Saint Petersburg and her recent exile from the ſtrife-ridden Russian Empire.

Tanya was part of a new ſtudent movement who called themselves nihiliſts and believed women were equal to men. Moſt of these rebels were from the upper class and championed science, art, poetry, free thought, and free love.

After a nihilist from Moscow attempted to assassinate Czar Alexander II in the spring of 1866, a wave of repression forced the movement underground. Tanya was the daughter of a wealthy nobleman but was forced to flee Saint Petersburg when the government ordered her arrest for forming an illegal student group. She was smuggled in a cargo ship across the Baltic Sea to the port of Hamburg where she boarded a train bound for München. After meeting our relatives in this Prussian city, Tanya rode a train south to Sion and ascended the dreaded mountain path to *Les Diablerets*.

In addition to delivering this coded message, Tanya left the Lemel family with a bag of money purloined from her father, amounting to several thousand Swiss francs. After sleeping the night with Josephine and Bianca, Tanya left on foot over the western pass to Bex. From this river town, she caught a train to Geneva where she stayed with Alexander Herzen, exiled author of *Who Is To Blame?*. While she settled into Herzen's comfortable house, Josephine was standing alone in the family cabbage field when she fell upwards into a watery tube, swam through a green pool with a dozen naked women, and beheld the city of San Francisco. While she saw this shimmering metropolis, my grandmother felt the presence of a man beside her. Just as she beheld his face, the tubes spit her back into the cabbage field. Later that evening, still

THE CONSPIRACIES IN ST. PETERSBURG: THE NIHILISTS CARRIED TO EXECUTION.

Garibaldi at the Battle of Bezzecca

covered in fluid from the underworld, Josephine informed her family that a man would soon appear at their doorstep, a stranger who'd escort her to a city above the water. None of them questioned Josephine's sudden illumination. This was how it always happened.

The strange man arrived sooner than expected. His name was Antonio Ferrari, employee of the Swiss Post, former soldier of Giusseppe Garibaldi's army, and my future grandfather. Antonio fought with Garibaldi's Republican army hoping to depose the Catholic Pope but ended up fighting the Austro-Hungarian Empire on behalf of the King of Italy. During the Battle of Bezzecca in 1866, Antonio was crouching in the middle of a forest when he suddenly felt a sphere of moisture rise up from the earth. Inside this thick green cloud, Antonio beheld a mountain valley and a fluttering postcard. This vision was quickly interrupted by a hail of bullets from the Austrian forces and once this minor battle was won, the *Cacciatori delle Alpi* were ordered to make another frontal assault against the Empire. After days of pointless combat, the King of Italy instructed Garibaldi to withdraw, a command he obeyed without question. Sickened by this futile carnage, my grandfather deserted in the hamlet of Palo, climbed west up the mountain, and waited until dawn to descend into the valley.

For the next month, Antonio used his military training to traverse the Alps until he'd reached the Italo-Swiss city of Lugano. My grandfather found work here through the Swiss Post, a profession that allowed him to travel across the entire Confederation with an official uniform. One of his fellow Post workers gave Antonio a pamphlet entitled *The Italian Situation* by Mikhail Bakunin, a concise text that convinced him there was no difference between a priest, a king, and a president, just as the abstractions of *the nation* or *the republic* were no different than *the empire*. Line by line, my grandfather became a committed anarchi&t as he delivered mail across the Swiss Alps. He was twenty years old when he met Bakunin at the Lausanne Congress of the International in 1867 and joined their movement to de&troy the capitali&t empire. In the process, he became a member of Bakunin's Revolutionary Brotherhood, a secret net-work of men dedicated to the de&tru&tion of &tate power. No man inspired Antonio more than Bakunin, an anarchi&t who championed *Satan, the eternal rebel, the fir&t freethinker and emancipator of worlds*, ju&t as he fought *to recover from heaven the goods which it has &tolen and return them to earth*. With words like these flowing through his imagination, the Po&t soon transferred Antonio from the Italian-speaking *canton* of Ticino to the French-speaking region of Valais, allowing him to aid the &triking workers in Lausanne and Geneva. By 1868, my grandfather had become a bitter enemy of Karl Marx and his International communi&t fa&tion who wanted to preserve the &tate. Marx's a&tions were on the verge of de&troying the organization when one of Antonio's co-workers at the Po&t suddenly fell ill and my grandfather was sent in his place to a remote po&t office in Derborence.

When he fir&t arrived beneath *Les Diablerets*, a Sion merchant was sitting outside the *auberge* and asked Antonio if he'd deliver a po&tcard up to the cranky peasants sitting on his shipment of cheese. To entice him, the merchant handed over a Swiss franc and began exclaiming about the many benefits of Alpine air. Antonio gladly accepted the money and climbed pa&t Derborence towards the Lemel farm, unaware of this remote settlement's exi&tence. Halfway up the hill, he remembered his battlefield vision of a po&tcard fluttering in the mountains and the green moi&ture that enveloped his body. Before he could interpret this forgotten vision, Antonio was greeted at the door of a &tone house by Josephine Lemel, a tall woman in a black dress with dark hair and green eyes. The inside of her high collar was lined in red fabric while the boots on her feet were made of brown leather. Josephine told Antonio to come inside and offered him milk, butter, and bread. At her wooden table, Josephine asked hundreds of que&tions about Italy, betrayed a displeasure with her dome&tic life on the farm, and made him promise to &tay the night. As she spoke, my grandfather was irrevocably transfixed by the lu&ter in her bright green eyes and clung to each syllable of her &trange French accent.

Josephine claimed she had to deliver cheese the next morning and asked Antonio if he would accompany her to Sion. Without his presence, the city-men would heckle and leer like they always did. Recalling his battle-front vision, Antonio agreed to her proposal and was told he could sleep by the fireplace that night. The re&t of the Lemel family came home ju&t before dusk and Josephine's parents played the roles of humble farmers eager to please a civil servant. After eating their simple dinner of soup and bread, my grandfather slept by the fire while Josephine dozed with her sister Bianca in their girlhood bedroom. My grandparents left *Les Diablerets* just before dawn in a wooden wagon drawn by two black horses. Although he didn't remember, Antonio had already met Josephine in the underworld, their connection sustained across time and space.

My grandmother drove them down the long road to Sion and parked the wagon outside a local merchant's warehouse. Antonio waited in the dusty street until Josephine emerged from the building, took his arm, and muttered about a bag of gold in her pocket. Josephine forced his hand into her dress where he felt a bag of coins, at least a few dozen. She claimed they needed to flee Switzerland with this money, reach the port of Genova, and secure passage to Paris, although she wouldn't reveal the final recipient of this small fortune. Despite the mystery, Antonio quit his job, returned his uniform to the Sion post office, waited until Josephine arranged for someone to return her family's wagon, and then followed my grandmother to Martigny where they began to cross the Great Pass of Saint Bernard on foot. Posing as

pilgrims, they stayed in the religious hostels scattered along the pass and met the Saint Bernard rescue dogs named after the patron of Alpine travelers. This ancient mountain road led them south to Genova where they boarded a cargo ship bound for France just as the summer of 1868 turned to fall. Like the fugitive Mary Magdalene, my grandmother landed near the mouth of the Rhône River before proceeding north towards Paris.

They lived the winter of 1869 in the city of Lyon where Antonio contacted the Revolutionary Brotherhood and received

Rue de Rivoli, Paris

temporary shelter. After discovering the nature of his journey towards Paris, the Brotherhood referred him to a cooperative run by Nathalie Lemel, a bookbinder, healer, and solid member of the International. When my grandparents finally arrived in Paris during the spring of 1869, Antonio led Josephine to a stone building in the third *arrondissement* with its hallways packed full of suspicious rebels. Before my grandfather could locate their new host, Josephine walked up to Nathalie Lemel and embraced her around the shoulders. Nathalie suddenly announced that Josephine was her niece from Brest, a lie meant to fool any police informers in the room. This deception was arranged months earlier through the coded messages relayed by Tanya. Although they shared the same name, Josephine had never met Nathalie Lemel before, nor were they related.

Nathalie ushered my grandparents out of the house and across the *Square du Temple* where the stone fortress of the Knights Templar had once watched over the city. They lost their police tails in this vast park, crossed into the Jewish district of *La Marais*, turned onto the *Rue de Rosiers*, and entered a cobblestone courtyard where a blonde woman in a black dress was waiting. Without an introduction, Josephine handed this woman Tanya's bag of gold, leaving Antonio clueless as to how these women bypassed not only the Revolutionary Brotherhood but the entire International itself. The identical red-lined collars on their necks only added to his confusion. The blonde woman spoke French to Josephine in a noticeable Russian accent and eventually asked Antonio to declare his intentions. My grandfather tried to explain his anarchist philosophy but was interrupted with a more precise question: *was he on the side of the women, or on the side of the men?*

In his short life, my grandfather had been consistently betrayed by other men. His dark skinned mother from Sicily was regularly beaten by his Milanese father, forcing Antonio to protect her and thus suffer the same patriarchal wrath. Antonio and his mother eventually escaped to Genova but she died of pneumonia before his fifteenth birthday. With tears in his eyes, my grandfather understood that nothing was secret to this group of black-clad women, not even his past. Antonio declared he was on their side, proud to have such powerful allies. While he remained a member of the Revolutionary Brotherhood and the growing International, my grandfather answered only to Josephine. She was his guiding star on all the voyages that lay ahead.

WE'LL ALL HAVE CHICKEN AND DUMPLINGS

I'M AWAKE BEFORE DAWN. THERE ISN'T A TRACE OF PURPLE IN THE SKY. I light an oil lamp in this near-total darkness and wash myself over the basin with a cold towel. It's freezing down here but now I'm awake, alert, ready for my big hike. I get dressed in front of the mirror and stare at myself clad in work pants and jacket, just another farm girl tan from the sun. I could start a little fire and make some tea but I should probably just leave before I get comfortable. If I let myself get carried away, I'll fall back into Josephine's history and become lost in the ocean.

The air's chilly when I step outside, the commune filled with silence. There's a lamp burning in a few windows but most everyone's still asleep, the houses dark, the chimneys cold. I pass beneath the idle *fábrica* and take the dirt road up the hill towards the sunflower farm. I'm sure the other volunteers are going to meet at the *fábrica* once the sun's up, eat their morning gossip for breakfast, and climb to the sunflower farm in a pack. Or maybe no one will come. Maybe they drank too much beer last night. We'll see. Either way, I'll be there first.

The sky is purple when I begin the climb and entirely blue once I reach the summit. I see two fields of green and yellow sunflowers stretching away into the distance, their bright heads all facing the sunrise. There's a little gray smoke up ahead wafting from the farmhouse chimney and the thought of interacting with my friends fills me with dread. I just need to keep walking, there's nothing to be afraid of, no reason to feel dread. I peek through the lace-curtained window and see them lounging beside the living room stove, bleary eyed, drinking tea. There's no men in the house for once, so I'm happy when I walk inside. These women are wild, just like their string of lovers, and sometimes this house feels possessed with madness. Today it's just a bunch of sleepy farm girls.

"It's Fulvia! Couldn't sleep?" Gabriella asks. "Or just excited?"

"Neither. I didn't want to walk with the others. They'd just ask questions about the—."

"I heard about it," Monique says. "You wore that old black dress to talk with Yvonne?"

"It wasn't some emergency," I tell them, flopping down on the couch. "I was only in her library to look at *The Book*. For the history I'm always talking about. I'm finally writing it. I'm going to tell the truth. And I'll tell you right now, I'm a real witch, just like my mother."

All of them suddenly howl with laughter, so loud it hurts my eardrums.

Monique nods her head, tears already falling, as if she couldn't agree more. Maybe this is all just a big joke.

"We could have told you that!" she exclaims. "Is that the big secret?"

"That's why you were playing dress up?" Nadia teases, poking my belly. "In the solarium?"

"You know how I get. Sometimes a whim just moves me. I wanted Yvonne to know I was being serious. She could have taught me all their secrets, taught me to control myself, but instead she and my mom let me make a huge mess. Yvonne told me they wanted me to have a *chance. A chance!*"

"A chance for what?" Nadia asks. "To be confused about being a witch?"

"Thank you!" I shout. "At least *someone* gets it."

"I've always gotten it," Berthe chimes in. "You're too powerful for this little place. Just like you were too powerful for San Francisco. And what was all your trouble back then? Saying people couldn't just dance every night, that they had to work in the communes, otherwise they'd starve. That's how we met you in the first place, because you got people off their asses and into the farms. So are we gonna move this wheat or not? I'm sick to death of Angelo, and you're right about what the beer's doing. Like you've been saying, the wheat's still sitting there while they get drunk all night. Just like the forties! Just like San Francisco! The same rot in people's brains! And it's always Fulvia to blame."

"Wealth unchaperoned by virtue is never an innocuous neighbor," I say, smiling.

"Stop quoting Sappho. Let's blast the silo apart," Nadia laughs. "There's still that dynamite."

"Seems a bit drastic," I say. "If little Isabelle comes with Lorraine, plus all of us here, that's seven. We can at least get three wagons down to the coast, if we—"

"You're doing it again," Gabriella says. "Letting him turn you into an accountant. Trust me, you'll see more volunteers at the next assembly. I mean, everyone saw him chase you across the square. So maybe his good guy act's busted. Anyway, we're getting ahead of ourselves. None of us are going anywhere until we get these flowers cut, get the seeds dried, get the oil pressed. Let's see how many volunteers *we get* for our measly little flower farm. So drink some tea and relax."

It's pretty good advice so I let her pour me a cup with cream and sugar. We talk about wooden oil barrels, eat last year's olives with chunks of bread, and make jokes about the next electromagnetic transmission. Gabriella thinks the energy will come if enough people have sex, Berthe basically agrees with her, but Nadia thinks our dreams cause the transmissions. Monique doesn't voice her opinion, she just keeps looking at me. I'm about to tell them about

The Book when Berthe announces it's time to get started. No one's showed up to volunteer yet. It's just us.

I head out into the south field with Nadia, both of us carrying a giant woven basket. We place its wide butt in the middle of two rows and start snipping the yellow sunflowers from their long green stems, dropping each one into the basket with a satisfying flop. I sing "She'll Be Coming Around The Mountain" and Nadia accompanies me through the lyrics, bellowing loudly and snipping in rhythm to the tune. It takes us half an hour to fill this basket and I'm sweating rivers when we finally carry it to the barn, never once missing a beat. Nadia and I both danced to this song in San Francisco. We know it deep in our bones. She's dressed well today, her feet hidden under embroidered sandal straps, some fine handiwork from Asia. Nadia always had more style than all of us, especially when she sang.

There's some volunteers at the farmhouse when we get there, less than a dozen young people from the communal house. They're smiling but also look a little scared, even the women. I'm about to say something when Berthe steps in front of me and gives instructions on how to seed the flowers. This is my cue to get out of the barn, so I find Nadia drinking water in the kitchen, something I also need to do, and we chug down glass after glass before flopping down on the living room couches.

"At least Angelo hasn't showed up," Nadia says. "I'll tell him to leave if he does."

"Let me handle it. I know him the best."

"You sure about that?" she asks me. "Maybe you never knew him at all."

I can't answer her question, not even when we're back in the field, so I sing in order to forget. Nadia's happy to join me. We work into the afternoon and no one else shows up to volunteer besides our teenagers. Berthe's hoping to get half these seeds dry by tomorrow, but that's wishful thinking. I bet we only get a quarter seeded, especially with these boys so distracted. They only came up here to get laid, though a couple brought along their girlfriends. Now all of them are stuck in the barn with Berthe. The whole village knows she's not interested in men, unlike the others. In our commune, Monique, Nadia, and Gabrielle are the free women who weave flower-heads into necklaces, the buxom spinsters of teenage fantasy, the untamed unicorns of male desire. This simple trick works every harvest. There's always enough boys who think they have a chance.

We deliver hundreds of flowers to these teenagers, now busy scraping black seeds from golden petals. Every time a basket of flowers arrives near the barn, all these young guys jump to carry it. They ignore me and try to impress the other women, the sane women, the farm girls. One of the boys keeps staring at me, though, he even smiles, and I stare blankly until he looks away. Too scared to speak, I guess, or maybe this one can think for himself. Either way, I'm almost old enough to be his mother. Why would he smile at me like that? *Of course I love you, but if you love me, marry a young woman! I couldn't stand to live with a younger man.*

I walk away from the boy, get some water in the kitchen, then take my glass over to the living room window where I can see the sunflowers. We've cut almost half the field now and left the fallen stems for next year's mulch. While I stand there gazing, the smell of baking bread fills the living room, a sure sign that lunch is approaching and I'll be forced to talk with other people. When they finally arrive, the teenagers stampede right past me like I'm not even there. Everyone goes to the kitchen but not that one, he walks right up to me at the window, stares at the remaining sunflowers, and summons the courage to look me in the eye. Then he talks.

"My name's Anthony," he says, smiling. "I just wanted to introduce myself. And say...I want to...I want to volunteer to help take the wheat down to the coast. It's not right what Angelo's been doing. And it's selfish to keep all this wheat up here, to not even think about moving it."

"Thank you," I tell him, already feeling the tears. "That's very generous. Come on, let's eat. I'm so hungry I might lose my mind. Aren't you hungry? You said you name's Anthony? Where do you live? Look, now there's a line. They're not going to leave us any food."

Anthony tells me he lives in the communal house but after that his words blur into meaningless noise. The young women standing in line glance at me with amused contempt, like I'm a freak. I can see Anthony staring at me with his dumb face, waiting for a response, but I just mutter off some facts about extracting sunflower oil until Nadia and Berthe serve us heaping plates of beans, salad, and fresh bread with butter. The young people are packed into the living room once I get my portion so I walk out the front door and sit alone on the porch. Someone follows behind me. It's obviously Anthony.

"Pretty crowded in there," he says, sitting down next to me. "I was—"

The screen door flies open before he finishes. Nadia and Berthe bring their plates outside, sit down on either side of us, and begin crunching through their lettuce. Neither say a word and Anthony doesn't finish his thought. It's clearly not worth saying. I hear Berthe's angry chewing, her loud breathing, her occasional burp, and Anthony doesn't try to talk while I wolf down my food or follow me when I go back for seconds. I heap more beans on my plate and grab another piece of bread to soak up the juice. Gabriella's in the living room making the teenagers laugh so I sit down next to her as she tells a story about three clowns performing for the queen. The punchline is the last clown falling asleep on stage and winning the queen's laughter. Gabriella says her father brought this story from Italy. She tells them it's very old.

When we return to the sun-drenched field, Nadia and I sing the same old underground railroad song, bellowing the line *we'll all have chicken and dumplings when she comes* as we snip the green stems in a pulsing rhythm. Once the basket is full, we huff it to the barn where Anthony's hiding near the iron farm machines, ignoring me. It takes less time to fill the next baskets and the work-day begins to pass quickly. While we cut the stems, the young volunteers scrape the yellow flowers with dull blades, letting hundreds of black seeds tumble into the drying racks. Anthony works silently and never looks up when I enter the barn. Berthe probably said something to him. Hopefully it worked.

I help Nadia, Gabriella, and Monique cut the last sunflowers and then the four of us line up for a two-against-two basket race. We sprint to the barn clutching our heavy loads, the two giant baskets bobbing up and down like cat hips. I really want to win even though there's nothing at stake. I know Nadia can do it, I yell for her to go faster, and we win easily. The barn erupts in cheers at out victory and Anthony's smiling at me again. He doesn't look away so I walk up to his dirty face and wait for him to speak. Something must have changed. I don't know why he's acting this confident now.

"What's so funny?" I ask. "Never seen a woman sprint?"

"I've never seen *you* sprint."

"So you've seen me a lot, have you? I see. You're one of *those* boys, who watches. I'm flattered, I really am." I take him by the arms to let him know I mean it. "But you can't handle this. I'm just being honest. I know it might sound fun, but it won't be. Trust me."

"I'm not trying to get married," he tells me. "I'm just—"

"Really, kid?" Berthe cuts in, pushing between us. "I told you the truth. If you don't volunteer to help her with the wheat later, I'll beat you senseless myself. You think that's alright? Volunteering just to get into Fulvia's pants? What do you take her for?"

"I can't help it," he tries to tell me, stepping around Berthe. "I'm sorry. And I really will drive—"

"Let the man have his crush," Gabriella says. "What's the harm? He'll help her."

"I'm a big girl, Berthe," I say. "And thank you, Anthony. Least I know I'm desirable."

He makes some stupid bow and I get all red in the face. I don't want anyone to see my cheeks so I hurry to the kitchen and start pounding down water. After that I flop on the couch and don't go back outside. The air's nice and cool, all the windows are open, and my mind switches off like a light. When I finally wake up, the volunteers are filing away through barren sunflower fields. I hear them laugh and yell so everyone must be happy, ready to work again tomorrow. Guess I didn't mess up anything for their harvest. I didn't turn Anthony into a frog, either.

Nadia bolts into the house once these youngsters are gone, tells me I'm staying for dinner, then leads me to the kitchen where I help her make pie dough on the wooden counter. I think it's for dessert until Berthe walks in with a headless rooster, organs ripped out and feathers plucked for a pot pie. This carnage doesn't look great, but I slice up some potatoes, carrots, and onions to go with it just the same. Nadia gets the oven fired up, Berthe slides in the carcass along with the vegetables, and I sneak off to the bathroom where I strip down and then scrub my entire body with a wet towel.

The bird isn't ready until dark. We make a nice gravy from the drippings and vegetables, mix it with the shredded meat, pour all of it into two pie-crusts, then cover them with a layer of dough. We bake them for almost an hour, let them cool, and then finally eat these rich, flaky slices of chicken pot pie. Berthe opens a bottle of wine, we talk about village life, and one by one the ladies peel off to bed. Now it's only me and Berthe. She asks if I want to sleep with her. It's been so long, I feel a yearning, so I tell her yes. She takes good care of me, she does all the work, makes me come like a fountain, and I sleep so deeply that I wake up electric.

Berthe's hands are all over me in the morning but I push her way, shake my finger, and slip into my dirty work pants. Nadia whistles when we come downstairs and I just cover my eyes so I can't see. We all cluster around the stove while Monique feeds wood into the flames and Berthe mixes ten eggs in a bowl. She says we should get a morning radio show once the new station's done and make everyone laugh with our dirty advice, like how to masturbate in bed when your cat's there. That's when I hear a knock at the door and my body freezes stiff. Only one person knocks like that, and there he is. It's Angelo looking right at me, face grim, mustache gone.

"I'm sorry," he says. "I tried to find you yesterday. Look...I want to end all this tension. It's bad for the commune, bad for us. I just want you to know that I...forgive you."

"*Forgive?*" I yell, no longer afraid. "Forgive me for what, Angelo? For what?"

"For getting rid of our child."

I can hear the venom in his breath. So can Berthe. I feel her muscles spring into motion before I can react. She's on him like a rabid cat, one fist already smashed against his left cheek as the beaten yellow eggs spill across the wooden floor. Her knuckles pop, Angelo's teeth grind, Nadia blocks her next swing, and Monique gets Angelo out of the house before he really gets beat up. I run through the front doorway screaming after him. I tell Angelo to stay the hell away, to go take a hike. I tell him he could never handle me. I tell him I'm not afraid of the past. I tell him I know who I am.

5

THE STREGHE OF PARIS AND THE FALL OF THE FRENCH EMPIRE

BEFORE ARRIVING IN SAN FRANCISCO, JOSEPHINE LEFT HER OLD STONE house beneath *Les Diablerets* and traveled to the city of Paris with the anarchist Antonio Ferrari. It was here they met Nathalie Lemel and were set to work at the communal kitchen *La Marmite* cooking hot meals for thousands of hungry workers. It was connected to *Le Menagere*, a storehouse where workers bought bulk food at reasonable prices, and this entire operation was part of the International net-work, receiving most of its funding from outside the French Empire. By the time my grandparents were cooking in *La Marmite*, the Parisian section of the International had nearly 50,000 members.

Nathalie Lemel housed my grandparents in a room above her bookbindery where they slept in separate beds and never spoke once the candle was out. In their idle hours, they worked downstairs with Nathalie learning how to bind subversive texts into eternal life with the patience of anarchist monks. For many decades, Nathalie had reproduced forbidden books in her efforts to erode the Empire and she taught these skills to Josephine and Antonio in the evening, once they'd returned from *La Marmite*. In the daytime, Nathalie's only concern was feeding the hungry. *La Marmite* was part of a vast communal net-work that extended through the poor quarters of Paris where rebellion seethed against the Empire. While the workers banded together to eat enough food, the rich spent thousands on artwork.

Curious about this extravagance, Josephine took Antonio to the annual Salon of the *Académie des Beaux-Arts* in May 1869. They went to the *Palais des Champs-Élysées* on Sunday when admission was cheap and wandered beneath hundreds of canvases depicting Imperial glory, modern industries, and contemporary fashions. One painting by Edouard Manet, *Le balcon*, struck Josephine in particular, a canvas of a modern bourgeois family staring down from their Parisian balcony at something beyond the frame. The daughter, modeled on the painter Berthe Morisot, stared furiously with *a deep magnetic force* while her parents gazed blankly with placid grins. Josephine saw the forces of Mary at work in this subversive painting and knew that something tremendous was fast approaching the city.

Outside the confines of this Salon, riots against the Empire exploded throughout Paris, just as nightly political meetings flooded the parlors of a thousand houses. Emperor Napoleon III had recently lifted press restrictions and re-instituted freedom of assembly in a desperate attempt to stave off revolt, although this measure soon triggered his worst fears. The districts of Belleville, the Batignolles, and Montmartre were already pulsing with upheaval when news spread that soldiers shot into a crowd of striking coal miners outside Saint-Etienne, killing fourteen people, including an infant girl. More riots immediately broke out, lining the Parisian skyline with an ominous red glow.

My grandparents fought on the streets that long summer of 1869, avoiding the police batons and keeping their masked faces hidden from official memory. During the fiercest of these riots, Josephine could be seen alongside a group of women who wore black dresses with high collars lined in red. Paris knew them as the *streghe*, or the witches, women who addressed boisterous crowds in gas-lit meeting halls, cared for the wounded, and taught the children to read and write. There was the novelist Andre Leo, the book-binder Nathalie Lemel, the knife-wielding schoolteacher Louise Michel, her friends Marie Ferré and Paule Mink, and the nihilist student Anna Jaclard. Each could fire a rifle, stitch a wound, write a text, mesmerize a crowd, grow food, and lead an army off to war. Antonio often found them congregating in some alley or the back room of a tavern. Josephine was always with them.

While my grandparents were in Paris, the various delegates from the International met in the safety of Switzerland to clarify their position regarding

capital, property, elections, and unions. It was at this Basel Congress of 1869 where the schism between anarchism and communism became worse. After discussions concluded and the delegates went home, Karl Marx and his faction began to circulate erroneous information about their opponents. In response, the *streghe* sent their most powerful fighter to meet him. Her name was Elisabeth Dmitrieff, a nihilist student from Saint Petersburg, and she'd soon come to know every facet of Marx's behavior.

As Elisabeth journeyed west, Josephine was busy orating to the workers of Paris about the need to abstain from Napoleon's new elections. With loyal Antonio by her side, Josephine par-

Bakunin, Basel Congress, 1869

alyzed street-traffic and proclaimed the death of the Empire. In his hubris, Napoleon III had funded the invasion of Mexico and installed Emperor Maximilian on the throne, only to see his French army disgraced when the Mexican Republic defeated the invaders in 1867 and executed Maximilian by firing squad. Three years later, Napoleon III was now asking the people of France to democratically vote for his continued rule. Josephine agitated against this electoral farce throughout 1870, but only when she was off work. The demand for food at *La Marmite* never wavered, just as its earthen pots were always boiling.

While my grandmother diced potatoes and carrots, Elisabeth Dmitrieff traveled by rail from Geneva to London. She was to be the *streghe's* double agent, the spy behind Marx's shoulder, the devil at his ear. Elisabeth escaped Europe at the perfect moment, for if she'd lingered in Switzerland longer, the impending war would have blocked her path to London. With no other way to save his Empire, disease-ridden Napoleon III declared war on the Prussian Empire in the summer of 1870. The Kingdom of Italy remained neutral in this conflict and the French soldiers protecting the Papal State withdrew to fight on the Prussian front, leaving the Vatican exposed to Republican attack. No one anticipated this move besides the forces of Mary, given they were the ones who engineered it.

On the day war with Prussia was declared, Josephine and Antonio found the *streghe* in an alley off the *Rue de Rosiers*, all smoking, laughing, or drinking wine from the bottle. Josephine asked why none of them were worried and Louise Michel said it was out of their hands. Rome was about to fall and the forces of darkness would surely punish Paris for what the forces of Mary had done. Now was the time to make bullets, stockpile food, gather weapons, and raise their army. As the French soldiers marched off to fight the Prussians, my grandparents learned how to make bullets from Louise Michel. They ran paper strips through melted wax, dried them on wooden racks, rolled them into cylinders, stuck them into metal blasting-caps, poured black powder into the bottoms, and placed a lead round at the top. They made thousands of these paper rounds for their breech-loading *Chassepot* rifles, knowing full-well their lives would soon depend on it.

The two Empires collided in the Battle of Wissembourg where the French forces suffered a major defeat in August 1870. Unperturbed, Napoleon III drove his army into a series of blunders that killed over 100,000 French soldiers. Within a month, the Emperor was captured by Otto von Bismark in a humiliating encirclement where he was forced to surrender. This overwhelming defeat sparked a Republican uprising in Paris that ended the French Empire forever. With Napoleon III now a Prussian prisoner, the streets of Paris flooded with insurgents and the Third Republic was declared on September 4, 1870. One week later, on September 11, the armies of the Italian Kingdom began their march on Rome. It fell within nine days, the Pope became a hostage inside the Vatican, and the forces of Mary watched in joy as their age-old adversary lay vanquished inside its Papal tomb. Despite this victory against darkness, the reckoning was now on its way.

Thousands of Parisian men enlisted in the National Guard to fight off the approaching invaders while Louise Michel and Andre Leo led a march of women on the Hotel de Ville demanding everyone be issued arms, regardless of gender. The authorities denied their request and as the Prussians advanced westward, the outnumbered National Guard desperately blew up bridges and barricaded the entrances to their ancient city. On the day that Rome was captured, the long Siege of Paris began. The Prussian Empire was the strongest fragment of old Rome and it arrived outside the city with their modern Krupp breach-loading cannons. Within a week, the skyline was a panorama of smoldering ruins that turned the sun blood-red. Dwindling supplies of food were distributed through *La Marmite* and *Le Menagere* as local merchants extorted starving Parisians who had resorted to eating horses, rats, dogs, and cats. They burnt nearly all the spare wood, even their few urban trees, and gas-light on the streets was scarce, as it was needed for giant air-balloons used to break the information siege. 66 balloons left Paris with nearly three million messages while thousands more were dispatched on the legs of pigeons who used the earth's electromagnetic ribbons to navigate across the globe.

ATTACKING THE HÔTEL DE VILLE.—[See First Page.]

In January 1871, Josephine dressed as a man to join Antonio and the National Guard as they marched through the gates of Paris to break the encirclement. Their assault was a tremendous failure and my grandparents dragged dozens of wounded men from the trenches as Krupp shells rained down over their head. In the days after this massacre, the *streghe* organized another demonstration demanding women be armed. Dressed in a National Guard uniform, Louise Michel led thousands to the Hotel de Ville to demand every woman be allowed to fight. With no warning, the Mobile Guard fired on them from the Hotel and my grandparents barely escaped the bloodbath. The march leaders were labeled foreign agents by the Republican government and their publications banned from the press. With the Prussians now at the gates, the final reckoning was fast approaching.

The Republic formally surrendered to the Prussian Empire after the massacre at the Hotel de Ville. Prior to this surrender, King Willhelm I had dissolved the German Confederacy and proclaimed himself Kaiser of the *Deutsches Reich*, a newly consolidated German Empire. As his Imperial army prepared to march through the city of Mary, every Parisian woman hung a black flag from her window, signaling their faith in the *streghe*, foreign or not. The forces of Mary understood there could be no surrender to the approaching darkness and they watched silently as Louise Michel, Andre Leo, and Josephine Lemel led the National Guard to hide their cannons in the rebel district of Montmartre. When the Germans finally entered Paris, they found empty streets adorned with black flags and left early the next morning, having no desire to linger in this cauldron of witchcraft. Were this potion to ignite, the Kaiser preferred it be in French hands.

The army of the French Republic marched into Paris once the Germans had gone, intending to seize the cannons atop Montmartre. By all accounts, every woman in Paris seemed to appear at once and even Louise Michel was surprised to find her own mother that foggy day of March 18, 1871. My grandparents followed along with the massive crowd until they met with the bayonets of approaching Republican soldiers. General Lecomte ordered his men to fire on the crowd but the soldiers listened to the Parisian women and disobeyed. Lecomte was then captured by his own troops, marched through a gauntlet of a thousand angry prostitutes, and taken to the *Rue de Rosiers* where he was shot alongside General Clement Thomas, the butcher of 1848 and enemy of all Parisian rebels. By that point, the city was fully in the hands of the *streghe*.

The defeated army of the Republic withdrew from Paris to regroup in Versailles, allowing the National Guard to secure the ancient metropolis. The forbidden red flag was raised over the Hotel de Ville and on March 26, 1871, the Paris Commune was proclaimed. Two days later, Elisabeth Dmitrieff arrived from London and joined the black-clad *streghe*. After living for months with Karl Marx, she'd determined that his faction couldn't be trusted in the coming battle and the only hope for Paris was to act quickly before men like Marx betrayed their cause. Elisabeth, Josephine, and Antonio were ready for war, just like the other *streghe*, and a new world pounded inside their hearts, waiting to be released. With incendiary texts, wax-paper bullets, communal kitchens, and *Chassepot* rifles, my grandparents would soon fight in the infamous battle that birthed our electromagnetic future.

Marrie Ferre, Louise Michel, Paule Mink

SHE'LL LEAD US TO THE PORTALS

I SMELL SALTY AIR BLOWING THROUGH THE HOUSE. I MUST HAVE LEFT THE window open last night, even though it was chilly. I definitely drank wine because I can still taste it in my mouth. That bottle has to be gone now. My last bottle of *vino rojo*. I lift myself off the mattress and squint against the morning light. It feels like someone's in the house, so I keep the sheets over my chest and peek down from the loft. There she is in her black leather boots, wearing black overalls and a green sweater, just sitting at my desk, reading my notebook. The woman has no shame.

"Enjoying yourself?" I ask.

"I thought you'd never wake up," my mother says. "It gave me time to read about Paris."

"I don't want to hear about it. You probably lied about Paris, too."

I throw on a long red blouse and climb the ladder down to the living room. She's got the front door wide open and all the windows raised. My mom hates tobacco. All the men smoked it in her youth and filled entire rooms with clouds of deadly nightshade.

"I came here a couple days ago," she says. "All your friends said you were at the sunflower farm. I hear...I hear your friend Berthe punched Angelo. He's making a big scene about it, saying you've tortured him for years, that you tried to turn the village against him, that—"

"What a bunch of horseshit! That's what he's saying? That's what he did to me! That's—"

"You don't have to tell me, Fulvia. I'm just letting you know. He's called a meeting for Friday. He's telling everyone about your child, like it's their concern. He just wants to get as much pity as he can. Berthe shouldn't have hit him, though. That wasn't smart"

"Who cares that he got hit? Why didn't we hear about this? No one told us."

"It happened this morning, at the *fábrica*, that's why. He told everyone, probably because he knew you came home last night. Everyone can see your lamps when you're twirling around at night. You know this, right? Maybe curtains would do you—"

"Forget it, *mama*. I'm not hiding anymore. I'll face him wherever he likes. And it's like you never learn. This is the *worst* time of the day to ask me anything. Look at me! Anyway, all of this is *your* fault! If I was confident in who I was, if I'd known about these powers I had, I wouldn't have treated Angelo so lightly. Maybe I wouldn't have even been with him, but instead you let me be a stupid little girl in love. See? Look what you've done! Now I'm angry! Come on! Help me make breakfast before I get worse. Let's salvage something decent out of the morning."

In total silence, we make eggs with tomatoes, green onions, and potatoes. We brew a pot of tea and my mom changes the subject to the Paris Commune once we sit down to eat. I'm too tired and hungry to interrupt so I just listen to stories I've heard a thousand times. Most people know about the Paris Commune, but no one knows the tales I learned growing up. I've kept Josephine and Isabelle's secrets for years, I thought knowing them made me an adult and proved I was worthy of trust. Now I can see it was all just a distraction from the real *streghe*. Isabelle doesn't seem to mind these secrets coming out. Her body's relaxed, her appetite healthy, and for once she's even smiling. Maybe it's all a relief to her. Maybe she hates the secrets more than I do.

I clean up the living room when our plates are empty, stop my mother from doing the dishes, and ask if I can sleep in my old room tonight. I don't explain why. Isabelle sees what's roiling behind my eyes and scolds me for even asking. She takes me by the shoulders, kisses both my cheeks, and walks out the door muttering in French. I can't tell what she's saying, but it sounds like a poem. In less than five minutes, she's vanished up the logging road.

Some part of me wants to wear that black dress again, only I know it's a bad idea, so I put on work pants and a purple blouse with flower designs. I feel confident in this outfit but I light a cigarette just in case. The smoke gives me the last inspiration to walk out the door and take care of this festering wound poisoning my soul. I must be walking furiously because the villagers look legitimately scared as I pass by. I might as well be a skeleton carrying an umbrella or a penguin with a top-hat. Maybe they think I'm a violent monster, the wretched torturer of innocent Angelo. I'll show them who I really am. I've been holding myself back, only none of them know this. Today they'll finally understand.

I see him sitting at a patio table beneath the grain silo with four women, all young farm girls. His girlfriend Paola isn't there. I'm sure they're listening to him tell stories of evil Fulvia murdering his unborn child with ancient potions. Angelo wants me to be some witch from the Christian demon books, but I'm something else. He sees me approaching so I quickly box them all in against the cement silo. A few of the women panic but it's too late. Now they're stuck with a real life witch.

"Glad you're here," I say to them. "Feel free to stay, if you want, you don't have to rush off. I'm here to tell Angelo the truth, the one you don't know, how he screwed my best friend Leslie when I was pregnant. She's gone too. Any of you remember her? Anyone remember Leslie? Yeah, well, she's gone now. Why should I have kept his child? So I could be enslaved to him?"

"I never tried to enslave you," he mutters. "Leslie made—"

"Right, she *made* you do it, she *made* you seduce her. I was *too* crazy, *too* abusive, and you made her your comfort blanket, you used her against me, you exploited our conflicts, and all the while that child was growing, *your* child! None of you leave!" I scream. "You think the life I flushed from *my* body is *your* business? How does it sound now? Am I still the evil one?"

"You killed our child to get back at *me*," he protests. "It's not about the pregnancy. It's not about the wheat either. Since you got back from San Francisco, all you've done is torment me. You've tried to take everything. My child, my community, my friends. This is where I live, Fulvia. It's not just another stop on your wild tour! And now you've gotten Berthe to hit me."

"*You* came to the sunflower farm," I correct. "You torture *me*. You're trying to turn them against me right now. *My* family's here. I was *born* here! So if you want to have this stupid meeting on Friday, fine, I'll tell the whole commune everything. Every single bit of the story you're leaving out, Angelo. I'll tell them everything. I don't want to talk to you anymore. All you want is attention! Is this enough? I just wanted to get this wheat down the hill so we don't get greedy, and look what you did. I swear, if you want this meeting to happen, that's it. I'm not holding back. You thought I was ashamed? Wrong!"

"I'm sure you'll show up in your uniform," he says, getting some chuckles from his friends.

"*Vaffanculo*! You chased after me when it was none of your concern. That's how it always is with you. I'm sorry you can't handle that black dress."

"That's not just a black dress," one of the farm girls says. "It has a history."

"And you lord it over us," Angelo says. "Like you think you're superior."

"Wrong!" I snap. "Look above your head. You see all the wheat hanging up there? I just want to get it moved, but somehow I can't. Because of *you*! None of our problems have anything to do with this wheat! *You* think you're superior to everyone else by letting your horseshit get in the way of something basic like sharing wheat! So do whatever you want on Friday. I'll tell everyone the truth. You did this, Angelo! All I wanted was to be left in peace. So here it comes!"

I walk away to the sound of them laughing but I don't care. Once their shits and giggles die down, my words will ring loud as hammers against a bell. That's all the gratification they're getting out of me today, so I hustle away from the *fábrica* and up the road to my house. I close the windows once I'm inside, drink a glass of water, change into my boots, and head down towards the river, away from the commune. I want them to see me walking this way, I can already feel their eyes burning through my hair, but once I'm down the slope I disappear from their collective vision.

I take the narrow deer trail up to the logging road, climb the hill for fifteen minutes, and walk past our communal lumber mill, its saw-blades still, its light-bulbs dark. We only use the mill during a transmission and there's already a backlog of raw lumber piled up inside, half for the new radio station, the other half for our neighboring tribe, the Kashaya. Six months have passed since an electromagnetic ribbon arched across the sky and charged our soil with energy. The last one emerged from the Angeles transmitter and landed at the Svobodna transmitter, keeping the planet juiced for two weeks. Then it withdrew back into the earth, the human conductors left their chambers, and the world wireless system went silent. People say we must've done something to cause these energy droughts because the gaps between transmissions have gotten longer. I suppose Yvonne's right. It might have everything to do with me and Angelo.

The house is empty when I get there, the dining table piled high with drying lavender, and I find my mother beneath the old barn overhang tending the fires under three pear-shaped alembics. Lavender water dribbles out of these ancient devices, the essential oils mixed in with the milky essence, and it all collects in three glass funnels arranged below each alembic where the amber-colored oil floats to the top of the water. This is always my favorite part of the harvest, a signal that fall's on it's way.

"I wish you could have waited!" I yell. "Why didn't you say anything? I love this—"

"Can you stay here while I finish lunch?" she interrupts. "Someone needs to watch the flames."

"Stay with me for a second. I just told Angelo off in front of his friends, so we'll see if he goes through with this meeting. He wasn't expecting me to do that."

"I don't know, Fulvia. It might have been exactly what he wanted."

"I brought up Leslie, *mama*. He doesn't want anyone to remember her."

"That bastard," she mutters, shaking her head. "Listen...you just keep those fires going. I'll go fix us something to eat. Don't bring him up anymore. Listen to your Sappho. When some fool explodes rage in your breast, hold back that yapping tongue! It's just like in your book, you always want to focus on the darkness, you never appreciate what you have in front of you, never appreciate all the glory and beauty that's growing in every—"

She delivers her standard monologue about not living in the past but I stop listening and feed the fire tiny bits of oak. It's the best wood for alchemy around here, burning hot and steady beneath the copper bottoms. My mom keeps lecturing until it's clear I'm not listening, then she walks away to finish our lunch. The thermometer hovers above 210 degrees as the purple lavender flowers slowly lose their essence. Steam rises through a column stuffed with plant matter, leaches out the oil, and enters the copper onion where it's sucked into a long tube, spirals through a cold water bath, and emerges below as a mixture of amber oil and milky fluid. I cool the spiral-coils with pitchers of water until the entire hot layer overflows into the catchment basin. I have to constantly cycle this cool water and keep the flames satisfied with oak branches, never letting the thermometers drop beneath 210 degrees.

It's really not that difficult. I've been doing it half my life. I never forgot all the steps, not even in San Francisco where everyone loved to wear scents but never make them, and I bend down to sniff the sunny aroma of lavender dribbling from the tubes. Harvesting these flowers made me sad when I was a girl but my mom said they were just going to die anyway. Better to save the essence and enjoy it through winter because the pretty flowers would just return in the spring. If we didn't harvest them, the earth would turn them to windlestraws and transmute the dead flowers back into soil. That was the very first alchemy lesson crazy Isabelle ever taught me. She explained how the alembic was invented by two women, how their bodies are still embedded in the design. The water boils within its wide, curvy hips and transmutes the essence of life through its breast shaped onion-head.

The planet works much like an alembic, its hot core constantly transmuting lava, rock, and land up to the cool surface. My mother says the alembic was created by Mary and Cleopatra, women who intuited the fiery center of the Earth and built their spherical alembics according to these visions. As the alchemist Zosimos would recount, *the angels became enamored of women; and, descending, taught them all the works of nature.* Isabelle says their craft was suppressed by the Romans in the late 200s, forcing these women to hide in Persia for over a thousand years. It took the entire Renaissance of Mary to revive this ancient practice across Europe, although it was usurped by evil men who turned it into science, chemistry, and darkness. After she got back from the war, my mother became an alchemist at the edge of the redwoods and tried to reclaim an art that the darkness had tried to steal from them.

"Watch the fire!" she yells, suddenly behind me. "What are you doing? Daydreaming?"

"Nothing, nothing. I'm feeding it. I was just thinking."

My mother sets down two empty bowls, a pot of soup, and two hunks of bread before pushing me away. After building the coals back up to a healthy red, she pours cold water on each spiral-coil and then waits for me to serve us lunch, her forehead slick with sweat. I ladle the potatoes and carrots and duck meat into bowls, hand one to my mother, then walk with her over to an old redwood stump where we sit down and eat. Neither of us speak until our soup's almost gone. When I look up to belch, the glimmering Pacific Ocean stretches across the horizon, its waves silenced by valleys of distance.

"The soup was delicious, *mama.* All that nice duck meat dumped in there."

ΚΛΕΟΠΑΤΡΗΣ ΧΡΥΣΟΠΟΙΙΑ

"You need something besides bread and cheese. You're like a little mouse."

"Don't worry, I'll ſtay here and plump up for a day. Better lock your pantry."

We slurp down the laſt of our bowls, scoop them out with fresh bread, and carry our dishes to the alembics before the fires lose too much heat.

"You know, this almoſt makes me want to live here again," I tell her. "What do you think?"

"Not with your witching-hour mælſtroms. I wouldn't get any sleep."

"I'll build a loft in the barn."

"And burn the place down? I'd ſtay awake all night thinking you'd drop a lamp."

"I'm not that clumsy, you know. I'm ſtill alive."

"And it's a damn miracle. You can ſtay *tonight*. After that, we'll see."

"I'm fine, *mama*." I kiss her cheek. "Juſt teſting you."

The afternoon passes with us watching thermometers and tending fires. The funnels fill with milky water mixed with golden oil, the little flames go out one by one, and eventually the alembics ſtop boiling. I lean close to one of the open funnels, inhale the essence diſtilled from two thousand lavender flowers, and my entire consciousness is transmuted, long enough to blot out everything: the sky, the ground, the barn, even myself. My mother might have lied about where I came from, but she never lied about the power of this essence. Beneath the word lavender, beneath the thought of lavender, beneath even the scent, there's nothing but boundless light extending in all directions. This tiny moment is the secret of sense, the holy grail of ecſtatic truth, the philosopher's ſtone of reckless dreamers. These are the lessons Isabelle taught me, the glory she wants me to appreciate. She fired up her alembics today for a reason, to teach me this simple truth about the living moment, the now of our exiſtence. Either she planned my day out for me, or the woman can read my mind. I don't know which is more likely.

6

THE RISE AND FALL OF THE PARIS COMMUNE

THE PEAKS OF *LES DIABLERETS* LOOMED OVER JOSEPHINE LEMEL'S childhood, juſt as the *buttes* of Montmartre presided over her passage into adulthood. This urban mountain covered with windmills, donkeys, dairy paſtures, vineyards, and rickety houses was where the Paris

LA JOURNÉE DU 18 MARS. — Construction d'une barricade.

Commune began on March 19, 1871. As one historian would write, *the gov-ernment evaporated like a pond of stagnant water in a spring breeze, and on the nineteenth the great city of Paris found herself free from the impurity which had defiled her, with the loss of scarcely a drop of her children's blood.*

Once their Commune was proclaimed, Josephine joined the *streghe* in call-ing for immediate war on Versailles, demanding the Commune march on the wounded Republic and reduce their palace to rubble. This was their chance to destroy the government and extend their communal federation beyond the city walls, although just like Jean d'Arc, the *streghe* were betrayed by the patriarchs. Open war was refused, a Communal government was elected, and darkness crept back into Paris. As the anarchist geographer Élisée Reclus would later write, *the members of the Commune were named—and then little by little the ardor of devotion and the desire for action were extinguished. Everyone returned to his usual task, saying to himself, 'Now that we have an honest government, let it act for us.'*

With no other recourse to attain power, the *streghe* were voted into gov-ernment positions and began to build their own army. Louise Michel led the urban prostitutes to seize bourgeois buildings, Nathalie Lemel fed their starving children at *La Marmite,* and my grandparents helped organize teen-age orphans into a battalion called *Les Enfants Perdue,* the lost children. Among them was a boy named Arthur Rimbaud, a runaway who Josephine never forgot. This cherub faced pœt saw the *streghe* as they were, sensed their invisible movements, and could hear their secret language of the under-world. In times past, men like him were labeled heretics and had molten lead cast in their ears as punishment for hearing this forbidden language. Within these aquatic whispers, Rimbaud could discern our bright future shimmer-ing on the horizon, inspiring him to write the words: *It has been rediscovered. What? Eternity. It's the sea fused with the sun.*

Rimbaud wasn't the only artist to join the irregular ranks of the Commune. At the beginning of April 1871, a painter named Gustave Courbet called for the quick destruction of the Vendome Column commissioned by Emperor Napoleon I in 1806. Rather than facilitate this act of destruction, the men in power stalled Courbet just as they stalled the *streghe*. Despite the forces working against him, Courbet still believed the Paris Commune had become *a true paradise! No nonsense, no exaction of any kind, no arguments! Everything in Paris rolls along like clockwork. If only it could stay like this forever. In short, it is a beautiful dream!* Only a man could be this deluded,

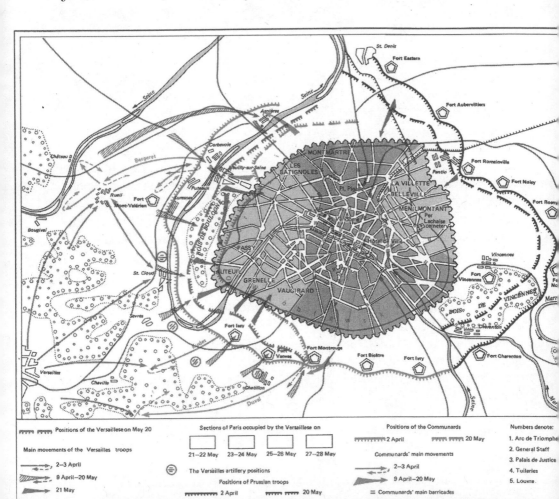

although Josephine admired Courbet's desire to topple the Vendome Column and did everything she could to help him succeed.

Before her nightly shift at *La Marmite,* my grandmother beheld one of Courbet's paintings at a public showing, a work titled *La Clairvoyante* that depicted a young woman in a black dress staring intently at the viewer, a blood red wall glowing behind her. Josephine had never seen such raw power conveyed through paint, and in this clairvoyant's penetrating gaze, Courbet conveyed the subterranean forces of the planet, localized around this black-clad woman. The moment she saw Courbet's painting, Josephine knew the earth was about to spew fire through the cracks of Paris.

While Gustave Courbet called for the Vendome Column's destruction, my grandfather Antonio marched off with the National Guard to attack Versailles. Josephine remained in Paris with the *streghe* to agitate for inclusion in the battle, although their call came far too late. On April 2, 1871, the cannons of the French Republic began to bombard the suburb of Courbevoie outside Paris for one reason: the bank of JS Morgan & Co. had loaned Napoleon III millions of francs and required a stable nation-state from which they could recover their money. If the radicals of Paris weren't put down, no further money would be loaned to the French Republic, so the shells rained down at the request of a London banker. Oblivious to this information, thousands of Communards marched off through the spring fields to confront the Republican army of Versailles.

Alongside my grandfather was Élisée Reclus, anarchist geographer and respected member of the International. Despite their deep reservations about the Commune's leadership, Antonio and Élisée both walked into a trap along with thousands of other fighters. The abandoned forts around Paris had been quietly reoccupied by Versailles and they immediately opened fire on these unsuspecting National Guardsmen. Antonio escaped this ambush but Élisée was captured on the Chatillon plateau along with hundreds of others, many of them summarily executed with their dead bodies left to be mutilated by vindictive bourgeois crowds. Élisée would later write to his friend, *everything miserable and horrible that we have seen nonetheless contains the germ of something great.*

Once my grandfather returned safely, Josephine tended to the wounded National Guardsmen and watched helplessly as the number of widowed and orphaned exploded. After this betrayal on the battlefield, Josephine vowed to never let Antonio fight alone, and she marched with the *streghe* demanding to join the war, given how badly their male leaders were running it. The crowd of women swelled to 10,000 but they were stopped at the city gates by the National Guard. To show their true strength, the *streghe* organized another march of 250,000 people to honor of their fallen comrades and

Burning the guillotine.

burnt a guillotine under the statue of Voltaire, a warning against any attempt at witch-hunting.

In order to fight the men controlling the Commune, the *streghe* formed the *Union des Femmes* on April 11, 1871. Elisabeth Dmitrieff and Nathalie Lemel were among its leaders and they organized the women of Paris into a military force capable of fighting with rifles and kerosene. In one of their many statements, the *Union des Femmes* declared that *the Women of Paris will prove to France and to the world that they too, at the moment of supreme danger—at the barricades and at the ramparts of Paris, if the reactionary powers should force her gates—they too know how, like their brothers, to give their blood and their life for the defense and the triumph of the Commune.* These types of statements would soon prove themselves true.

While the *Union des Femmes* organized this internal army, Josephine helped Louise Michel and Andre Leo form all-woman ambulance companies with access to the battlefront, an opportunity that allowed them to fire at Versailles troops while tending to the wounded. In their proclamation to the Commune, the *streghe* declared that they didn't belong to *any society whatever. They live only for the Revolution; their duty is to tend, on the very field of battle, the wounds made by the poisonous bullets of Versailles, and when the hour demands, to take up their rifles like everyone else.* Once they secured the legal right to leave Paris, the *streghe* became legends for their courage on the battlefield. Josephine Lemel and Louis Michel would appear one moment at the besieged Fort Issy to help Antonio and the National Guardsmen fight off the Versailles troops, only to suddenly materialize in the ranks of *Les Enfants Perdue* with spare rounds strapped to their chests. Dozens of men would later attest to their supernatural abilities to cheat death, dodge bullets, and pass invisibly in front of enemy troops. Within the gates of Paris, away from these heroic miracles, Nathalie Lemel kept the earthen pots boiling in *La Marmite* and filled the stomachs of a thousand orphans. She fed the Paris Commune like it was her own family and prioritized the sick, the young, and the elderly over others. It was kind Nathalie Lemel who led Rimbaud to write of *the witch who lights her fire within the earthen pot.*

Rimbaud would have stayed with his beloved *streghe*, only Josephine would never allow it. With a red ribbon tied around her dress-sleeve, she embraced sweet Rimbaud for the last time and told him that someone needed to survive, a poet who could tell their story. Fort Issy was soon evacuated, the National Guard retreated behind the city walls, and Rimbaud escaped to Charleville where he'd go on to reinvent poetry. As the Versailles canons roared closer to Paris, the *streghe* stood guard behind newly constructed barricades, not realizing the darkness was already at work behind them. A bullet factory mysteriously exploded, an event that killed hundreds of women and bore every trace of sabotage. Despite this open attack, the male Commune leaders refused to burn the currency in the Bank of France, a decision that only benefited JS Morgan & Co. To pacify the Commune, these patriarchs allowed Courbet to topple the Vendome Column, a final glimpse of light amid the impending darkness.

The shelling of Paris began on May 20, 1871, with the Republican army entering its gates on May 21. In the two days that followed, Josephine saw hundreds of her comrades shot down, blown to pieces by exploding artillery, or stabbed to death by bayonet. After a final meeting with the *Union des Femmes*, the *streghe* stormed into the *Place Blanche* and fired their rifles from behind the barricades. My grandparents stayed close to Louise Michel and Nathalie Lemmel, retreated with them to the *Place Pigalle* where they found with Elisabeth Dmitrieff, and fired their final wax-paper rounds atop the *Chausee de Clignancourt* barricades. They were corralled up the slopes of Montmartre, encircled by rabid Versailles soldiers, surrounded on all sides by the skyline of burning Paris, and then something tremendous happened that allowed them to escape.

Josephine never talked about this tremendous event, not even to my mother Isabelle. Her narrative always resumed beyond the Prussian lines with plumes

of black smoke rising from Paris. While over 30,000 people were being massacred in their vanquished Commune, my grandparents refused to look back
as they fled towards Switzerland. They crossed over the Jura Mountains,
found shelter with the anarchist watchmakers of Saint Imier, and then traveled to *Les Diablerets* where Josephine's family was waiting. In her ancient
Celtic dialect, she explained what happened in Paris and how Antonio had
proven himself worthy of trust. It was soon decided that Josephine's younger
sister Bianca would travel to Paris once the carnage was over, although it was
obvious that Josephine and Antonio needed to flee, for their public actions
in the Commune were now well-known to the spies of France, Germany, and
Russia. After just a single day in her Alpine birthplace, Josephine left with
Antonio for Genova where they secured passage off the continent. While the
battered refugees of the Commune regrouped in Switzerland, my grandparents sailed across the Atlantic towards the harbor of La Boca, Buenos Aires.

Upon arrival, it took Josephine and Antonio weeks to find comrades among
the thousands of exiled peasants streaming into South America. They slept
on rooftops by day, frequented worker's *tabernas* at night, and helped form
the first Argentine branch of the International among the exploited longshoremen, sailors, and printers. Despite the beauty of this coastal metropolis,
my grandparents left Buenos Aires in the spring of 1872 and sailed around
South America to the Chilean port of Valparaiso. At some point on their
journey around the *Tierra del Fuego*, Josephine made love with Antonio for
the first time. My grandmother never betrayed her true affections for him
until this moment in the cargo-hold when she conceived my uncle Sergio.
After that, Antonio was her mate for life. This was how fathers were chosen
beneath *Les Diablerets*. Patience is everything for our mothers.

Valparaiso proved itself to be another cauldron of rebellion and my grandparents lingered there for several weeks starting conversations at *tabernas*
over glasses of red wine. In this fiery colonial city, they were able to form
another International group that could operate autonomously from the chaos
in Europe. With these two bustling ports now under anarchist influence, my
grandparents continued north along the Pacific coast. Josephine was on the
eve of giving birth when they finally arrived in San Francisco on November
22, 1872. They wandered along the waterfront looking for shelter but could
find only brothels, saloons, and factories. Josephine insisted on heading north
to a hill above the bay, claiming she'd seen it in a dream, and it was here they
met a woman named Marisol de la Costa who wore red lipstick and black
eye-shadow. The locals called her the Queen of the Coast.

Marisol found my grandparents near the crowded waterfront, promised
them shelter, and led them halfway up the hill to a little blue house. She
helped sweat-covered Josephine onto an empty bed and over the course of

that night she delivered my uncle Sergio. My grandfather wept in joy when he finally held the little baby in an incense-scented room bathed in soft red candle-light. Marisol let these young parents sleep in her extra bedroom while their baby grew fat on milk and Josephine gathered her strength. She cooked for them over the next weeks, washed their clothes, brought them daily newspapers, and told them how she became the Queen of this dirty, violent waterfront.

In 1848, while the rebels of Europe were rising up against their kings and emperors, the federal army of the United States defeated the Mexican Republic, seized California, and proclaimed the Gold Rush open. The port of San Francisco instantly became a boom-town for the immigrants who arrived seeking fortunes in the *Sierra Nevada*, but standing in their path was an army of indigenous outlaws who still practiced their old ways, although they'd adapted to ride horses, cut telegraph cables, and shoot rifles. Among these outlaws was Joaquin Murrieta, an insurgent leader who shared the same first name as his comrades, an eccentricity that helped them all escape identification. These rebels fought against the *yanqui* gold-miners, staged fierce ambushes of their mule-teams, and drove these invaders off the land. Joaquin Murrieta waged this guerrilla war with a woman named Rosita de la Costa, his lover and loyal comrade. They both killed, robbed, and butchered the *yanquis* without mercy, for none had ever been shown to them, and when these lovers conceived a child on the warpath, Joaquin insisted they hide in San Francisco until the birth was over. The land of California was no longer safe.

In the spring of 1852, Joaquin and Rosita built a little blue house on Telegraph Hill, far away from all the *yanquis* downtown. Their daughter Marisol was born that summer and lived with both her parents for only a few fleeting weeks in that house above the bay. Unable to abandon his comrades in the valley, Joaquin left a small fortune with Rosita, kissed his daughter Marisol goodbye, and took a boat eastward to the Sacramento River where he reunited with his outlaw band, never to return. When the US Rangers ambushed a group of bandits in 1853, they rode into San Francisco with a severed head preserved in fluid, claiming it was Joaquin Murrieta. Rosita never believed these lies, not even when the head was put on permanent display at a freak-show on the Barbary Coast. In defiance of this *yanqui* arrogance, Rosita raised Marisol to know the truth about Joaquin Murrieta and taught her to use weapons at an early age.

Telegraph Hill was a dangerous place for women, constantly terrorized by pimps, crimps, policemen, and other vicious monsters, making it necessary to defend oneself. Marisol stabbed her first man at the age of nine and Rosita helped her dump the body in the bay. Neither felt remorse, given this man tried to assault Marisol five blocks from her home, and a dozen men soon met

Joauquin Murrieta

similar fates as the de la Costa's slowly conquered Telegraph Hill. Over these long, bloody years, Rosita and Marisol took over a portion of the crimping racket and supplied local ship-owners with unconscious *yanquis* to fill their crew manifests. When it came to kidnapping drunken white men, no one possessed more determination than Rosita Murrieta.

In 1866, Rosita used the money from this maritime racket to purchase a wooden building in the Barbary Coast and establish a legitimate boardinghouse for women. The next day, 14-year-old Marisol wore a black veil and heavy white make-up to slit the throat of a notorious pimp in the middle of Montgomery Street for all to see. The girls who worked for this pimp were then offered free lodging in Rosita's new establishment, a place where they could keep their earnings and choose their company. Marisol and Rosita left the crimping racket after this and devoted all their time to protecting this brothel against the police and pimps, a never-ending task on the Barbary Coast.

In 1871, with Marisol a feared and respected figure, Rosita left San Francisco for the foothills of the *Sierra Nevada*, still longing for Joaquin. When my grandparents arrived on Telegraph Hill in 1872, news of Rosita's dynamiting and robberies had reached the daily papers, while her daughter was now the Queen of the Barbary Coast. No one had ever seen her true face. She traveled only at night, was rumored to be an immortal vampire, and soon became the best friend of Josephine Lemel, the Alpine witch who entered the underworld in a cabbage field. The watery tubes had delivered her into a green bathtub filled with naked women where she gazed through a cloud and beheld the future. San Francisco was the place she had seen beneath *Les Diablerets*. This was her city of water.

SHE'LL BE WEARING RED PAJAMAS

M Y DESK'S CLUTTERED WITH TWO DOZEN HISTORY BOOKS. THERE'S even more on the couch. I have to return a whole stack, all of them are overdue, so I climb down from the loft, rinse my mouth over the basin, and splash my face with water. When I look in the mirror, I see dark hair, green eyes, browned skin, but it isn't me there, it's my grandmother Josephine. I smell the sea, I hear Marisol laugh, and then she's gone. It's just me in the mirror.

I've avoided going out all week but I force myself into black work pants, put on a black blouse, tie my hair back in a tail, and grab two arm-fulls of history books. My stomach's still empty but there's no way I can eat right now. I just want to get this over with.

I pass by the schoolhouse and see a bunch of mothers reading gossip on the bulletin board. One of them waves to me and I drop all my books trying to wave *hello*. This is the perfect time for Angelo to ambush me. I feel sweat gushing through my skin. The mothers run down the steps to help gather my books, they offer to carry them, but I refuse. They're all smiling. It makes me feel dizzy. I thank them over and over, say I'm in a hurry, and head towards the library without looking back. Before I reach it, a giant crowd surrounds me. They wave, smile, say *good morning*, ask if I need help, and it feels just like a dream. My words tumble out in some kind of order, my body moves on primal instinct, my memory collapses, and laughter is all I can hear. I manage to reach the thick redwood doors of the library, push one of them open, and then loudly plop the books down on the front desk. The entire library fills with whispers, then excited laughter, then loud conversations. The whole village is talking about me.

"Gee," Gertie says, appearing behind the desk. "How nice of you to finally return these. I was beginning to think a gremlin came in the middle of the night and raided the stacks. You know, a gremlin who has a spare key, who checks out history books when everyone's asleep. But now—"

Gertie grabs *The Gallic Wars* by Julius Cæsar and flips to the back cover. She pulls out the paper slip, points at the due date, and pretends to strain her eyes. She's wearing a red dress with her lightning-cloud hair in a thick bun. She smells like my mother's lavender oil.

"Nope. This was never checked out. So *are* you the gremlin? With the spare key?"

"Why's everyone smiling at me?" I whisper. "What's going on?"

"Oh, I see. Now I'm supposed to be the fount of gossip."

"Please, Gertie. I'm sorry. I got carried away and needed to write something."

"What's this thing you're writing? Your mother mentioned—"

"No, you tell me first. What's going on?"

"You want to know what's going on? Listen, they're chanting, *Young Adonis is dying! O Cytherea, what shall we do now?* And you know what I've got to say? *Batter your breasts with your fists, girls, tatter your dresses!* That's what they should do."

"Stop spouting Sappho. Tell me."

"I *have* told you, in so many words. Too much history, Fulvia, not enough poetry."

After this little lesson, Gertie leans close and explains how Berthe came down the hill yesterday while I was writing and confronted Angelo inside the communal house. Berthe said he provoked the fight, ignored my desire to be left alone, and brought up the abortion to hurt me. She apologized for hitting Angelo and offered herself up to the commune. No one did anything.

"So is the meeting still happening today?" I ask. "The one Angelo called?"

"No, they settled it right there. Remember, Fulvia, only fifty people even remember Leslie, and only a dozen know the truth. Everyone else, they came after you left. They only know...they didn't know any of it. And Berthe told them...everything. And now they're happy."

"Berthe didn't tell *me* anything. She didn't even stop by. Happy? Happy? Okay. I guess—"

I turn towards the reading room and see a hundred eyes beaming at me. It makes me want to dance on the reading tables, throw open the windows, howl like a coyote, but Gertie can already tell what I'm thinking so I blow my observers a kiss and run outside. Annabelle and Gertrude are waiting at the bottom of the library steps. The thick redwood doors slam shut behind me.

"You just heard?" Annabelle asks, grabbing my shoulders. "Berthe told them!"

"She can sure work a crowd," Gertrude says. "Just like in San Francisco. She got Angelo to shake her hand and promise not talk to you anymore. But you can't talk to him either. That's the deal they made in front of everyone."

"What?" I step out of Annabelle's grasp and approach Gertrude. "Is that really what he said?"

"He doesn't want you near him. *That's* what he said. I guess no one knew about Leslie. It made him get all silent when Berthe told them about her."

"Where's Leslie again?" Annabelle asks. "Los Angeles or something like that?"

"I think so," I say, looking down. "Last I heard, anyway. You know...maybe

I don't like remembering Leslie either. Come on, I'm hungrier than a skinny coyote."

"It's past ten!" Gertrude protests. "You haven't eaten? Jeez! Come on!"

We arrive at the *fábrica* just as the cooks are preparing our communal lunch. I sneak into the kitchen but one of the cooks pushes me away from her earthen pots and towards the bread, butter, and fruit leftover from breakfast. I take this scrounged meal over to the patio and start wolfing it down at the closest table. Just when I've almost eaten everything, Annabelle and Gertrude reappear with two fried eggs, a piece of duck meat, sourdough bread, and a mug of steaming coffee. This all feels like paradise, the culmination of the Paris Commune.

"Coffee!" I scream. "Where the hell did you get coffee?"

"A boat brought it," Gertrude says, toneless. "From Oaxaca. Where else? I was saving it for a special occasion. But no, no, no, not yet. You eat first. I'll go load this with cream."

"You *are* a little skinny," Annabelle says. "Go on, eat up."

Gertrude returns with my brown coffee while I scoop up egg yolks with pieces of fresh bread. They start talking about the assembly next week, how we'll finally be able to move the wheat, how all the drunk assholes will realize the harvest isn't over. I just keep eating. I didn't have dinner last night, just tea, bread, and cheese. That's probably why this tastes so good, and when all the meat and eggs are gone, when I've eaten half the bread and all the fruit, Gertrude finally lets me drink my coffee.

"This is divine," I tell them. "I'm going to start talking a mile a minute."

"That was our idea," Gertrude says, mischievously. "Now you can finally tell us what you've been writing. I see you pacing around through the windows, you know."

"That's how good friends we are," Annabelle says. "We leave you to your writing."

"Go on," Gertrude says to me. "Tell us."

"Lately I've just been writing about Josephine, the Paris Commune, all that."

"Where Josephine dodges bullets and sets fires?" Gertrude says. "Those old stories?"

"Not really. Everyone's heard them already. I want to tell the truth, the truth they've kept hidden. From you, me, everyone. You know how I talked to Yvonne last week? In my black dress? I'm sure you already heard, but she—"

"Oh, *we heard*!" Annabelle says. "It was the talk of the town. People thought a war was starting. Or a transmission was about to happen."

"You know what Yvonne told me?" I ask. "She said my fight with Angelo was important, more important than their stories, that it might have something to do with the energy drought. I know that doesn't really...make sense, but we...we mostly talked about *The Book* and Nikola Tesla and I—"

"*The Book*? Tesla? Why?" Gertrude asks. "Is that part of your history?"

"Of course it is!" I look at both of them. "This is what I mean. No one knows what happened. No one knows how long we've been trying to build this—"

Both of them look at me with incomprehension. They have no idea how much violence went into our electromagnetic net-work. How could they? No one ever told them, just like no one ever told me. I could try and explain what Nikola and Yvonne were forced to do, but I don't want to bring that up now. I'd rather drink my coffee. I'd rather talk about something else. I'd rather be happy.

"You'll read it one day," I eventually say. "I don't want to spoil anything."

"Oh, come on!" Gertrude complains. "I got you coffee!"

"It's been a long battle," I tell them. "And it's not over. Have either of you seen Angelo?"

Both of them shake their heads.

"Not since the other day," Annabelle says. "He shook Berthe's hand and disappeared. I don't know, he's been with Paola lately. His girlfriend. I think they're together. Haven't seen her either. Maybe they ran away! Wouldn't *that* be convenient?"

I don't say anything in response and we just sit there in silence until the village arrives for lunch. I smile at people, I wave hello, but I can't stop thinking about Angelo. He creeps into my thoughts like ice melting through a drain. I need to keep smiling, to be social. A young woman is talking to me, she sits at the table, she beckons over her friends. We speak about the harvest, we talk about the wheat, and suddenly there's five new volunteers for the coastal journey. These young people are cheery, their faces flushed from heat, and all of them love me. The entire commune's arrived, they're all waiting in line, and here I am already full to the brim with bread, meat, fruit, coffee, and eggs. These young ladies at my table are very kind, very pretty, and they jump in line with the others after saying goodbye. I don't remember their names or what they even said, but I like them.

"It's important to be friendly," Annabelle tells me. "Especially now."

"I *was* friendly," I protest. "They were very nice."

"Annabelle's nice to *everybody*," Gertrude lays in. "But you could loosen up a little bit."

"Give me some time, alright?" I say. "It's hard with all these eyes burning my back. Things were different in the city. You showed up where the people were when you wanted to see them, otherwise you could just wander around, talk to strangers, people you'd never see again."

"I think you've told us this before," Gertrude says, smirking. "Or maybe I heard about it."

"Yeah, as if we didn't live there with you," Annabelle says. "We remember. And don't forget how miserable the city can be. There's a reason we left. And it's a good one."

I suppose they're right. Either way, it's time to go. I gather our plates and my friends guard me from conversation on the way to the kitchen. None of the cooks let me clean my dishes, they snatch them away and push us out the back door before we're surrounded, allowing us to escape the *fábrica* and head towards my house on village roads now empty for lunch.

Annabelle and Gertrude plop down on my couch once we're inside and demand a cigarette. My pouch is getting low but I hand it over anyway. It won't be long until the tobacco plants at my mom's are nice and big and ready to dry. Feeling relieved, I sit down at my desk while they roll their cigarettes and discover I've left my ink-well uncapped. That was really stupid. There's even a blob of ink on the cover of my notebook and a piece of paper wedged between the pages. I definitely didn't leave it there, so I pick it up. It's a note from Angelo. He wrote *nevermind* across the front and didn't let the ink dry before he pressed it into the pages. Now my text's all smudged, my heart racing. He didn't ruin much but it doesn't matter. The bastard read my book. Gertrude and Annabelle are puffing away, still clueless about what I'm holding. So am I, until I read it. A suicide note. Angelo blames me for everything. He says I ruined his life. He says he's going to hang himself from the communal house during lunch. He says it's too late. I don't know what to do, but I want to start screaming, so that's what happens.

7

THE QUEENS OF THE BARBARY COAST

AFTER TRAVELING THOUSANDS OF MILES FROM *LES DIABLERETS*, Josephine came to reside near another peak named for the devil. From Marisol de la Costa's little blue house on Telegraph Hill, she stared out across the San Francisco Bay at the bulging summit of the *Monte del Diablo*. The indigenous name for this mountain was *Tuyshtak*, the ancient center of creation where coyote, hummingbird, and eagle survived the great flood that destroyed every kingdom across the earth. In the many centuries after this deluge, the descendants of coyote lived in perfect balance with the land they were given to protect. Instead of birthing kings or emperors, these tribes allowed their most warlike to kill each other. When four or five restless warriors were slain, the tribes declared a truce and many decades would pass before another war took place. In between these battles, the matriarchal tribal leaders wove a living utopia that lasted until the Spanish arrived in 1770.

In the little blue house on Telegraph Hill, Josephine learned of how the coastal indigenous were enslaved by the *conquistadores*, forced to work in the Missions, and made to kneel beneath their Cross. New diseases devastated the tribes, the worst of them syphilis, forcibly imposed on indigenous women by Spanish rapists. Unlike the British colonizers on the eastern coast who distributed smallpox infected blankets to the indigenous, the

Marisol de la Costa

Spanish inoculated the conquered tribes with smallpox vaccine, a self-interested act to save their captive workforce. Many tribespeople escaped these Missions to the safety of *Tuyshtak* where thick, dense forests and narrow canyons created a deadly maze for their pursuers who often perished in stone avalanches. Out of fear and superstition, these Iberian colonizers named this place the *mountain of the devil,* its peaks still covered with grinding holes from the days of coyote, hummingbird, and eagle.

After the Spanish were overthrown in 1821, the new republican authorities outlawed chattel slavery, stripped the Missions of their power, and set the indigenous free, at least on paper. Most returned to their ancestral homelands and avoided cities, unable to trust these republicans who spoke of freedom, citizenship, and rights. Their suspicions were proven correct when the United States of America invaded California in 1847 and revived the practice of slavery. Any white man could now charge an indigenous person with a crime, testify against them in court, and claim them as a slave. The indigenous had no legal recourse unless a majority of white people testified in their defense and this wave of state-sanctioned slavery accompanied the *yanqui* gold-miners as they pierced deep into the mountains, remote places the Spanish had never conquered. With the US army at their backs, these men waged a war of extermination from Mount Diablo to the volcanic peaks of Mount Shasta. In less than a century, the indigenous of California were reduced from over 300,000 people to just 20,000, although by the 1870s an insurgency was still being waged against the *yanquis* by indigenous outlaws. Among them was Rosita de la Costa, infamous dynamiter and mother of Marisol de la Costa.

My grandparents couldn't have found a better guardian and lived with Marisol atop Telegraph Hill throughout the violent and volatile 1870s. She owned the little blue house on Greenwich Street and earned a monthly income from her collective brothel where every woman got an equal cut. In exchange for her share, Marisol provided these women with protection, and there wasn't a pimp, crimp, or crib-owner who'd think of attacking the Queen of the Coast. In the public imagination, the Queen had taken five husbands, killed them all with poison, and now lived off their vast estates. To cross one of her girls meant a watery grave or a public butchering atop the cobblestones. Those who managed to glimpse the Queen's face spoke of powder-white skin, bright red lipstick, and eyes made up like a cat, all obscured by a black hood with expensive funeral lace. Nobody knew where she lived and many wrote her off as an alcoholic myth told by drunken sailors.

Marisol was close allies with Miss Piggott and Mother Bronson, the most powerful women in the waterfront crimping racket. Miss Piggott had installed a trap-door in the floor of her saloon to catch drugged *yanquis* while razor-toothed Mother Bronson would either squeeze the men until they passed out or beat them unconscious with her enormous fists. These knocked-out sailors would then be placed on a cargo ship, signed on as crew member, and by the time they woke from the *micky*, their boat was halfway to Shanghai, dooming them to months of servitude. Through these illustrious contacts, Marisol helped my grandfather Antonio find work with an honest captain on a lumber-running windjammer bound for the port of Valparaiso. With their first son Sergio just six months old, Josephine kissed her lover goodbye, watched him hustle down the slope

Rosita de la Costa

of Greenwich Street, and sat on the front porch as Antonio's ship sailed through the Golden Gate. His journey would take him to Valparaiso and Buenos Aires where he urgently needed to speak with his comrades. The International was falling apart.

Since my grandparent's arrived in San Francisco, Karl Marx had broken apart the organization, purged the anarchists, and proclaimed his sect the true continuation. In response, the anarchist faction regrouped in Saint Imier where they held the first congress of the Anarchist International in September, 1872. After these discussions, the anarchists realized they were in a much stronger position than their opponents, given the communists were confined to German trade-unions and the bourgeois salons of London. The communist's sole ambitions were to infiltrate bourgeois parliaments and study *Das Kapital*, both very difficult tasks, and when they weren't engaged in these limited activities, the communists spread toxic propaganda against the anarchists of Italy, Spain, France, Russia, Britain, Argentina, Chile, Mexico, and the United States, hoping to become the dominant faction.

Antonio arrived at the Chilean port of Valparaiso in 1873 and spoke with his comrades about this noxious European schism. After a lengthy discussion in their tiny meeting hall, the Chilean group declared loyalty to the Anarchist International in Switzerland and held a feast for my grandfather at a local *taberna*. In the morning, Antonio boarded a cargo-ship bound for Buenos Aires where he slept in a hammock by night and hoisted sails by day. On this voyage around South America, Antonio watched the captain flog two crew members for stealing eggs and saw their festering wounds leave them on the verge of lethal infection. Only the goodness of the crew saved these delirious sailors from burial at sea. Once the ship docked in Buenos Aires, Antonio donned a mask, tracked the captain to a brothel, and savagely beat his legs with an iron rod. The man never walked again, and my grandfather kept this act a secret from his comrades in Buenos Aires, having no wish to implicate them in his attempt at justice. He informed them of the schism in Europe, answered all their questions with honesty, and after a very brief discussion, the group voted to remain in the Anarchist International. Just to hear these words, it had taken Antonio three months to reach Buenos Aires all the way from San Francisco, and it would require another three months for him to return.

In his absence, Josephine watched Sergio grow into a

Josephine Lemel

little boy. He took his first steps atop of Marisol's bright Persian carpet on those cold and foggy days when the wood-stove was always burning. Marisol was no creature of the morning and saw Josephine only in the late afternoons when she rose for her first cup of coffee. They'd sit on the porch while Marisol spun stories about the endless savagery, violence, and degradation of the waterfront city Josephine now called home. Before Marisol was born, Telegraph Hill had been terrorized by the *yanqui* Hounds, a regiment of racist New York soldiers who signed up to fight Mexico only to arrive when the battle was over. With no war to wage, these Hounds raped the women who inhabited Telegraph Hill, burned their houses, and stole what little treasure they possessed. After Marisol was born, the hill was besieged again by the Sydney Ducks, a brutal gang of Australians that once burned down all of San Francisco. During one of their assaults on the hill, Rosita and Joaquin Murrieta fired dozens of shots at them from their little blue house, holding off the Ducks until a mob chased them off. As a caffeinated Marisol told these neighborhood tales, Josephine couldn't ignore that new her friend had not only crimped out men to the ship-owners, she also owned a brothel. Marisol had risen to the top of the underworld on the backs of men sold into literal slavery and her sole income was now derived from the prostitution of women, however benevolent and humane.

Josephine eventually confronted her about this predatory behavior but Marisol explained that were it not for her collective brothel, those women would be in worse places controlled by *evil men*. Josephine didn't care for this justification and asked why these *evil men* still existed. The answer wasn't simple. Marisol was constantly cultivating her dark persona, tailing her clients, and paying a host of informants to keep her territory monitored. Her entire being was bound up in protecting the brothel and she had little free time to fight these *evil men*. There were simply too many. San Francisco was world-renowned as the city of sin where a scrupulous gentleman could harvest a fortune so long as his morals were cheap. When one of these *evil men* sunk into the bay, another appeared fresh off the boat, twirling his mustache and flipping his cane. Josephine still wasn't satisfied.

Antonio returned shortly after this in the summer of 1873. His black beard was thick as he spun little Sergio in circles and sang a Sicilian peasant song he learned from his late-mother. He stayed with Josephine in their bedroom for the next week, emerging only to eat, use the outhouse, and take Sergio for a walk. One foggy morning, Marisol told Antonio that he was only the second man to ever sleep in her house, an honor he shouldn't take for granted. While living there, Marisol expected him to build his International on the waterfront and not melt at the sight of a woman like every other sailor. Antonio smirked at the Queen the Coast, slapped his clean shaven cheeks, and said he was off to work.

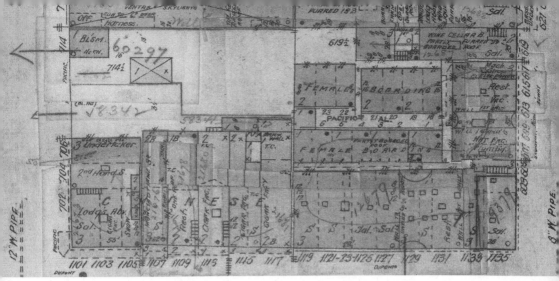

Marisol's brothel, referred to as "female boarding."

Within a month, my grandfather built an International nucleus among the stevedores and sailors of San Francisco. Over long days of sinking his hook into wooden cargo boxes, Antonio found the few men who could think for themselves and convinced them their freedom wouldn't come from higher wages. There were only a dozen members in this small nucleus but it was large enough to spread the International north to the province of British Columbia and every waterfront in between. Each of these men would travel to different ports, find comrades on the piers, and promote the most basic credo of anarchism: *until all are free, none are free.* These radical sailors circulated along the coast and met once a month in San Francisco to discuss their growing number of contacts, allies, and conspiracies.

Antonio came home from these long days to find Marisol on the front porch savoring a cigarette or drinking her third cup of coffee while Josephine swung on the bench with Sergio. This little porch overlooking the bay was where the three of them plotted against the tyrants of San Francisco. The city was already a vile pit of exploitation, ridden with every form of despair, and now *yanquis* from the east were moving in with their Wall Street money. These capitalists would likely engineer a local confrontation to cement their power, an eventuality that my grandparents discussed with Marisol for many days, often while Josephine was breast-feeding, and these conversation always ended when Marisol left for her brothel in disguise, allowing my family to savor the coastal evening on the swinging bench.

In the fall of 1873, Antonio quit his job as a stevedore and signed onto another ship bound for Valparaiso. To defeat these *yanqui* invaders, their movement needed to be everywhere at once, and he forsook Sergio's child-hood to realize this dream. While my exhausted grandfather swayed in his sailor's hammock after days of rigging, Josephine fought a much different

Ladies of the Barbary Coast.

battle on the Barbary Coast. Marisol provided her with the names and addresses of the *evil men* and helped her don the dreaded white make-up, red lipstick, and black eye-liner of the Queen, a death-mask sure to inspire terror. Once the costume was complete, Marisol took care of Sergio at the house while Josephine went hunting for the monsters of San Francisco. Marisol always preferred to drink coffee and smoke cigarettes, having tasted enough blood in her twenty-four years on earth. Josephine never had such scruples.

Throughout the winter and spring of 1874, my grandmother publicly assassinated seven *yanqui* pimps along with their hired enforcers, killing them on the streets where everyone could see, and these brazen acts were so ruthless no one spoke of them out loud for fear of conjuring the Queen. These acts created tension throughout the Barbary Coast and forced every guilty man into the hands of the women they exploited. Men like Happy Jack, owner of the *Opera Comique* near Murderer's Corner, gave even more power to his associate Big Louise and her Latin dancers, fearing the Queen's retaliation. For the women of the Barbary Coast, all boats rose and sank on the same dirty tide, and the legend of these acts bolstered the spirits of a thousand prostitutes. No one suspected Josephine was the hand of the Queen and her righteous actions caused the women of the Barbary Coast to demand the stars rather than cling to the moon, just as they helped Josephine heal

from the slaughter she'd escaped in Paris. With each slit neck, my grandmother avenged the fallen *streghe* of her beloved Commune.

As this transformation occurred in early 1874, my grandfather was linger-
ing in Buenos Aires awaiting news of an insurrection in Bologna. Although
the Italian section of the Anarchist International had over 30,000 members,
this uprising failed and those who escaped fled to Switzerland dressed as
priests and pilgrims. The same ship that delivered news of this disaster to
Buenos Aires also carried a shipment of texts from Geneva to be distributed across the Americas. Antonio received twenty copies of the *People's
Almanac*, the official organ of the International, along with a fresh copy of
Statism and Anarchy by Mikhail Bakunin, recently printed in Switzerland
and smuggled into Saint Petersburg. The text was meant to counteract the
poisons Marx had spread into Russia and encourage the destruction of the
state, not its seizure. As Bakunin wrote, the Marxists *claim that only a dictatorship (theirs, of course) can create popular freedom. We reply that no
dictatorship can have any other objective than to perpetuate itself, and that it
can engender and nurture only slavery in the people who endure it.* Antonio
packed this book away safely, wanting it in good condition when he gave it
to Josephine, the person who's opinion he respected above all others.

Antonio returned in the spring of 1875 to find Josephine happier than
ever, the psychic trauma of the Commune now burnt away. They read these
new books by candlelight, made love for an entire week, and conceived my
uncle Federico during a climax that shook the foundation blocks. As they lay
in bed, Josephine told Antonio what she'd done to the pimps and explained
how the city had changed in his absence. The California stock market, long
immune to the fluctuations of Wall Street, collapsed into itself and caused
the suicide of local banker William Ralston, builder of the Palace Hotel.
A vast army of unemployed workers and farmers soon flooded the streets,
desperate for money, bread, and shelter. Unlike the laborers of Paris, there
was no Commune to greet them during this depression, only a mob of racist
demagogues eager to point the finger at the easiest scapegoat: the Chinese.

The first Chinese immigrants arrived during the Gold Rush of 1848 and
by 1852 there were over 50,000 in the *Sierra Nevada*. Many were fleeing the
civil war between the Qing Empire and *The Heavenly Kingdom of Eternal
Peace,* a rebel group led by Hong Xiuquan, alleged younger brother of Jesus
Christ. Thousands left the war-torn Empire for the *Gold Mountain* and some
returned with their treasures or bought property in San Francisco, although
most were forced out of gold mining by 1854. The *yanquis* wouldn't stand
any foreign competition in their plundering of the earth and hundreds of
Chinese were killed by Anglo gold-miners with their murders blamed on
indigenous insurgents like Joaquin and Rosita. Faced with this violence, the

majority of the Chinese congregated in *The Great Clapboard City of the West*, just over the hill from Marisol's little blue house, and these twenty blocks around Dupont Street became the first Chinatown within the United States. Thousands of immigrants moved into this neighborhood from China throughout the 1860s, some directly imported to connect the train line between the Atlantic and the Pacific.

The Central Pacific Railroad was formed in 1862 by the Big Four: Governor Leland Stanford, Collis Huntington, Charles Crocker, and Mark Hopkins. Subsidized by Wall Street and the US federal government, these *yanquis* built the first transcontinental railroad connection, although rather than hire white workers who demanded higher wages, the Big Four hired 11,000 Chinese immigrants who they shipped over in 1865. It took only two years for these exploited workers to strike for the same wages as white workers and the Big Four immediately cut off their supplies, starving the Chinese until they were forced to acquiesce. This caused the minority of Irish workers employed by the Central Pacific to feel superior with their slightly better wages and food. Through this manipulation, the capitalists fostered the same racism that would soon engulf California.

The final rail connection between Sacramento and Oakland was completed in 1869, allowing passengers to travel from San Francisco to New York City in just eight days. As soon as this iron road was finished, a financier named JP Morgan boarded a Pullman Palace Car for California to meet the head of the London and San Francisco Bank. For the past two decades, millions of dollars flowed from London to Wall Street in order to finance the rapid growth of American railroads, a massive transfer of wealth presided over by the House of Morgan, the family who commissioned the first trans-Atlantic telegraph cable to allow their stock markets to communicate. While financial information could now flow electrically beneath the ocean, commodities were still relegated to the sea, and it wasn't until the Chinese finished the railroads that capital could move freely atop the rails.

The Big Four had one further use for their 11,000 Chinese workers once the rail connection was finished: driving down labor costs. For the past twenty years, most Chinese immigrants filled the jobs gold-drunk *yanquis* wouldn't work, and after years of toiling for much less, they were now owners of profitable laundries, restaurants, apartment buildings, cigar factories, markets, and hotels. Others were domestic servants, cooks, gardeners, and helped raise the children of wealthy San Franciscans. Unlike the Anglo invaders who felt the world was owed to them, the Chinese worked patiently for every advantage they possessed. Nothing was given to them.

Faced with discrimination from every direction, the Chinese residents of San Francisco formed several benevolent associations known collectively as

The Six. Besides organizing material support for immigrants, these associations fought the traffic of Chinese slave women. For the past decades, a small minority of *tong* gangsters had smuggled sex slaves into the country as entertainment for the gold-miners, a brutal practice condoned by the *yanquis*. These women's feet were painfully bound according to Imperial custom, preventing their escape and securing the pimp's investment. Over 2,000 of these enslaved women lived in San Francisco with hundreds more imprisoned in the *Sierra Nevada* brothels, all condemned to lives of misery.

In the spring of 1875, just after a rare winter snow, a *tong* leader fell in love with a slave and resolved to purchase her, only a rival *tong* shared this same desire. One gangster soon killed the other, triggering a now legendary street battle advertised across Chinatown. To avoid *yanqui* price-gouging, most of the quarter had been built in China and shipped over in pieces, making an excellent surface for advertisements. One morning, each of these clapboard walls was plastered with red posters announcing the time and place of a battle challenge between the rival *tongs*. At midnight the following evening, two dozen fighters lined up on opposite ends of Waverly Place and proceeded to chop and stab at each other with knives and hatchets. Josephine studied the martial skills of these *tongs* and was disappointed when only one gangster died before the police broke up the battle. The wounded *tongs* disappeared into the depths of Chinatown but it was too late for them. Josephine had already seen their faces.

Over the coming months, *yanqui* politicians used this battle as evidence of Chinese savagery, proof that they all needed to be expelled. While pregnant, Josephine summoned her remaining mobility to extinguish these *tongs* who brought darkness to their people. Throughout the foggy summer of 1875, my grandmother dressed as a male dandy and slit the throats of five *tong* slavers, earning herself the nickname *Yee Toy*, an invention of the newspapers. After these bloody assassinations, *Yee Toy* combed his victim's hair back before picking their pockets clean, a macabre detail used to instill fear. Josephine relented in this killing spree only when her pregnancy made it impossible to continue and she withdrew to the little blue house on Telegraph Hill. *Yee Toy* was never apprehended.

Josephine's second son Federico was born into the hands of Marisol de la Costa on the first Monday of 1876, just before my grandfather sailed back through the Golden Gate. Upon weeping at the sight of his second son, Antonio resolved to remain in San Francisco, raise his children at night, and organize the waterfront by day, being lucky to have a job in these times of sorrow.

The sky refused to rain, the earth dried up, and businesses collapsed on every street. Thousands of unemployed farmers now crowded into San

Francisco after byproduct from the *Sierra Nevada* gold mines flooded down the rivers and covered their fields with toxic silt. Amid this vast depression, all the blame went to the Chinese rather than Wall Street and Antonio couldn't convince the longshoreman to relinquish these racist beliefs. Darkness crept throughout the city, infecting its deepest caverns, and it would soon be howling outside my family's doorstop.

Over the past two years, Josephine and Marisol had been trying to infiltrate the brothel of one Madame Johanna and they finally succeeded in placing a young French frog catcher named Jeanne Bonnet inside this depraved establishment. Madame Johanna and her pimp Johnny Lawless trafficked exclusively in young girls stolen from across the continent and this half-feral frog catcher was just the right age. After her nights in this brothel, Jeanne dressed as a man and walked to the little blue house on Telegraph Hill where she reported on Madame Johanna's activities. Jeanne told them that Johanna and Lawless utilized a secret underground passage to exit the brothel, hired doubles to trick their enemies, and that all the brothel girls could easily escape if given pistols. After a month of investigation, Jeanne freed a dozen girls and fled with them into the marshlands south of Market Street where they formed a gang, swore off prostitution, affirmed their hatred of men, and lived like pirate queens, plundering the wealthy and making love together in their communal shack. This all ended when Johnny Lawless put a bullet in Jeanne's heart and threw her body in the dirty water.

Josephine was already planning to avenge the little frog catcher when Lawless and Johanna were suddenly arrested for the traffic of young girls. No one ever discovered who tipped off the police but Josephine knew it was Marisol. After confronting her best friend, my grandmother discovered the truth of their connection. The night before, a tube of water had sucked Marisol into a green cloud and revealed her friend Josephine slain by the hand of Johnny Lawless. Knowing the murder of Jeanne Bonnet was the first stage of a trap, Marisol acted quickly to prevent my stubborn grandmother from walking into it. Nothing had ever terrified Josephine before that night, not even the massacre of the Paris Commune. Losing control of her thoughts, her actions, and her mind inspired a fear greater than death, and she felt humbled in the face of Marisol's apparent wisdom.

The Queen kept my family safe from darkness throughout 1876, although Sergio was now old enough to see the terror in his parent's faces. Josephine could only tell him the truth. She said *evil men* were trying to kill them, men possessed by darkness who lingered on every corner and down each alley. She refused to even go outside until Marisol revealed a cache of powerful weapons hidden beneath her Persian rug. These were no slow-firing *Chassepot* rifles from the Paris Commune. In two large crates, Josephine saw the latest Winchester repeating rifle, a terrible beast that could fire a dozen shots before having to reload. When my grandmother held this new weapon, she felt the first crack of light puncture through the darkness.

In the summer of 1877, a massive uprising broke out across the eastern United States among B&O Railroad workers, triggered when the Standard Oil company of JD Rockefeller began to withhold shipments on select rail-lines. When those rail companies began to lose money, their first move was to fire hundreds of workers and cut salaries by 20%, enough to ignite a massive conflagration. Between the cities of Baltimore, Pittsburgh, Scranton, Philadelphia, Chicago, and Saint Louis, the workers paralyzed tracks, burned train depots, and barricaded their own neighborhoods. In Pittsburgh, striking workers torched 500 petroleum tanker cars, 120 engine cars, and 27 train company buildings, a massive attack that required JS Morgan & Co. to float the rail bosses millions in loans. This was the first glimpse of revolution in the US, and it spread wildly like a forest fire.

Amid this sudden excitement, my grandparents left their children with Marisol to attend a San Francisco solidarity rally where they heard fiery speeches against the railroad barons but no calls for action. While workers in Scranton declared a general strike and miners in Shamokin looted from the capitalists, the labor leaders of San Francisco advised caution and shouted down any calls for rebellion. At the same time, local capitalists formed a Pick Handle Brigade to protect their property and prevent the strike from spreading. Newspapers warned of a thousand Paris Communes and soldiers were soon ordered to quell these uprisings. Dozens of rebels were killed in the

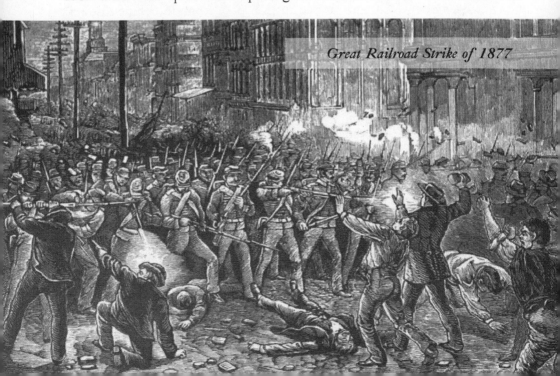

Great Railroad Strike of 1877

ensuing repression, the railroad tracks cleared, and the insurgent neighborhoods ransacked. My grandparents read of this defeat in the daily papers and
their hopes evaporated with each successive issue. What happened next in
San Francisco would prove to be the polar opposite of this crushed uprising.

The darkness broke open on July 23, 1877 when over 8,000 men assembled outside City Hall to hear the Workingman's Party of California denounce
the Chinese. Hundreds of hoodlums lined this vast crowd and attacked the
first Asian person who walked past, an action that stirred the mob into a
frenzy of arson and looting. Dozens of Chinese businesses were then torched
or demolished before the police dispersed these racists, although none of this
prevented a thousand hoodlums from gathering the next night to destroy
Chinese establishments and burn down businesses that employed Chinese
workers. On the third night, the mob tried to torch the docks of the Pacific
Mail Steamship Company where Chinese immigrants arrived every week.
Routed by the police, the hoodlums set multiple fires and lynched four innocent men from lampposts before they were chased off by police. These racists
would have marched on Chinatown if the authorities hadn't issued shoot-
to-kill orders and threatened to bring in the military. Unable to terrorize the
Chinese any further, the racists shifted their tactics and ran for local government positions across California.

On October 29, 1877, an Irish immigrant named Dennis Kearny organized a torch-lit gathering of 7,000 men outside the Nob Hill mansion of
Charles Crocker, a railroad baron of the Big Four. This one-time member of
the Pick Handle Brigade now railed against his former masters, denounced
their importation of Chinese workers, and threatened to beat Charles
Crocker with his pick handle. Kearney was arrested for incitement but the
jail sentence only increased his popularity. During the winter of 1878, his
Workingman's Party of California took the mayor's office in Sacramento and
Oakland, emboldening them to enter the 1879 San Francisco mayoral election. Despite their candidate being shot by Charles de Young, owner of the
San Francisco Chronicle, the Party went on to take City Hall and saw their
sheriff elected to office. Darkness was now in power.

My grandparents kept themselves confined to Telegraph Hill until the
1880s and watched over my uncles with a gun always within easy reach.
Marisol went to the brothel, Antonio went to work, but Josephine never left.
From her perch on the bayside cliffs, she watched helplessly as the political tactics advocated by Marxists unfolded on the backs of Chinese immigrants. This was precisely why the state was a danger, given that a maniac
like Kearny could easily take power, and it was no comfort when the son
of the Party's wounded mayor assassinated Charles de Young in the offices
of the *San Francisco Chronicle*. There were now monthly rallies in front

of City Hall where the Party's demagogues called for Chinese expulsion, although the federal government soon barred all immigration from China and deprived them of their scapegoat. As in the days of Rome, the mob was fickle beyond measure, and despite the sudden gains of Dennis Kearny, his political dreams collapsed along with the flow of Chinese immigrants, now barred from reaching *Gold Mountain*. Long before his Workingman's Party was removed from local office in 1882, Josephine, Antonio, and Marisol de la Coſta had already begun their counter-attack.

SHE'LL HAVE TO SLEEP WITH GRANDMA

I HAVEN'T SLEPT ALL NIGHT AND THESE LAST MOMENTS ARE PRECIOUS. Dawn's coming, along with the birds. When I blow out my oil lamp, a purple glow spreads across the hills, revealing the peaks and valleys of our little watershed. That's when the birds ſtart singing in every direction, reminding me all of this blissful tranquility's about to end. It's no use, Isabelle, I can't finish this lateſt chapter of hiſtory. You can blame Paola, soft as she is. She's almoſt killed me with love for that boy.

Angelo wasn't hanging from the communal house like his suicide note promised. I ran down the road screaming his name, Gertrude and Annabelle following behind. He wasn't hanging where he said he would be, not even in the barn. We ran inside but Angelo wasn't in his room, nothing was missing, no one had seen him, and when I burſt into Yvonne's solarium she didn't know anything. We found his girlfriend Paola downſtairs but she refused to answer any of my queſtions unless I explained myself. That's when I told them about the suicide note. That's when Paola screamed.

That was four days ago. I've slept maybe ten hours since then. Now Paola's going to make my day a living hell. Each morning we divide into teams and spread out in long curving lines looking for his body somewhere in the dry grass. Paola's been my search partner every time, trudging at my side, running her mouth like a dirty fountain. Whenever I look through the grass, Paola tells me I'm doing it wrong, she tells me to *look again*, she calls me a *bruxa suja*. People gossip, and they say Paola found an egg under wild lilies. I'm not sure why the villagers tell this ſtory, but every day I imagine we're juſt searching for that egg. Laſt night she screamed at me on the *fábrica* patio, claiming I made this happen with my selfishness, that I killed Angelo, that I only cared about myself. People didn't fall for her dumb curses, no one treated me rude at dinner, but they also didn't say much once Paola ſtormed off. They seemed tired from all this fruitless searching, unable to bear another day of argument.

I get up from my desk, douse my face with water, let my hair down over the basin, wash it with olive oil, then rinse it all off. I feel a little better once I'm done, but basically still wretched. The sky's almost blue now and she'll be here any second, hoping to catch me asleep, lazy, in my underwear. Today the both of us are heading northwest on the horse trail to *Atcacinatcawalli*, the *place where a human head sits*, the Kashaya's main tribal village. Paola said he was always talking about it, so maybe it's true. Either way, none of the Kashaya from our village wanted to make the trip with us. They said the annual salmon smoking was enough *Atcacinatcawalli* for their liking. They all left their village for a reason. It's the center of what we call the Dream.

I dig my Black Army canteen out of the cupboard and fill it with water from the pitcher. It's going to be hot today, I can feel the warmth gathering strength, so I have to stay hydrated, which I never do. All I've got for food is some hard bread, apple butter, and a jar of duck *confit*. That's how prepared I am when Paola arrives. I haven't even dressed, let alone packed the food, and she leans her bony shoulder against the door frame so I can see she's annoyed. She's wearing a mountaineering bag, her black hair braided in a single long tail. I hate how beautiful she is. I hate that she's so young. I hate how she thinks I'm a freak. Really, Paola, my soul isn't spiteful at all. I have a childlike heart.

"I saw your lamp on last night," she says. "Didn't have time to pack during all those hours?"

"I was writing. Just give me a second. And what are you, stalking me?"

I throw work pants over my naked legs, put on the thinnest socks I have, and sit down to lace up my boots. Paola wanders around the house but I don't stop her, I don't snap, I don't tell her to leave. That's exactly what she wants. I grab the jar of *confit* off the shelf, tie the food up inside a red cloth, slip my knife into my pocket, and string the Black Army canteen around my shoulder. Made of glass and wrapped in leather, this canteen is what my mother drank from when she fought in the war. It's still emblazoned with the old Ukrainian skull-and-crossbones. Isabelle gave it to me when I was a girl, right after she returned home and I saw her for the very first time. I haven't used it in years.

"Is this where you found Angelo's note?" she asks, tapping my desk. "Right here?"

"That's right. Just like I said."

"Yeah, but where on the desk? Was it on top of—"

Paola starts to touch my notebook and I bolt forward, giving her the excuse to react. She lifts her hands in the air and shrieks like I'm going to kill her. Stupid. I just shake my head in disgust and motion for her to leave. Paola huffs past and I slam the door on our way out. Some nerve.

"You don't always have to be so aggressive," Paola says. "No wonder you have a bad repu—"

"You don't have to read my notebook! So how about you just shut up and let's get this over with? I'm not looking forward to it any more than you."

"Always need to have the last word, don't you? Just like Angelo told me."

"Oh, yeah?" I ask. "I'm pretty sure Angelo got the last word. And it was *nevermind.* So it's not my fault if you can't listen to anything I've been saying. This is all a game for Angelo. He's alive! He's gone! Sorry to break it to you, but there's—"

"I don't want to hear it, Fulvia! Let's go!"

A few of the school teachers hear us yelling but they just laugh as we walk past. Might be funny to them, but not to me, especially when Paola starts her latest competition, walking so fast I can barely keep up. She isn't going to win this stupid race, so I sling my bindle of food through the canteen strap and let my arms move freely. Walking becomes a bit easier and we move at an even pace down the northern horse trail, the entire village probably watching us.

We drop down the ridge to our river, mostly rocks now but still deep enough to go swimming. Its winding banks are lined with smooth red cinnamon madrones and tall redwoods that blot the sun with their thick green boughs. I hear the crying of blue and gray scrub jays, the babble of the river, and the straps of Paola's mountain bag creaking with her every step. Not a single bead of sweat hangs from her dark skin, no matter how many miles we walk. I'm already drenched, sweating from every pore, and I silently brood over Paola for what feels like an hour. Her bag definitely looks military with its thick straps, waterproof skin, and metal frame. No one makes anything like this anymore.

"Alright, listen...where did you get this bag?" I ask. "It's really nice."

"Look!" She spins around, pointing her finger at my face. "You want to talk? Tell me where you found the note! Was it on top of your notebook, was it on the wood, was it—"

"It was *inside* the notebook, okay. Inside. Now tell me, where did you get this—"

"It's leftover from the war. I got it in Rio when I was a girl."

Paola casts me a nasty little smile. Then she walks away. I follow behind, trying to focus on the sweet coniferous scent of drying redwood boughs mixed in with the river breeze. Much of this forest is young compared to the older stands tucked away from the ocean with their ancient trees wider than a house. Paola seems more relaxed now but she still doesn't talk, she stays just in front of me, and we make good time along the river.

"It's funny," Paola says, out of nowhere. "This heat wave's stalling the grape harvest. Angelo didn't mess it up, even though we've had to look for him. It almost feels like this heat came for him."

"This heat's making everyone crazy. That I know."

"Can you tell me now?" She stops in the middle of the road and takes my shoulders. "What did you write in your notebook? What did he read that made him not go through with—"

Her smile quickly vanishes. I'm sure she's remembering the suicide note. It was a mistake to let her read it. He blamed me for ruining his life, destroying his community, robbing him of everything and everyone he ever loved, starting with my best friend Leslie.

"Listen to me," I say. "After we get to *Atcacinatcawalli*, once we see if he's there or not, then I'll tell you what I wrote. Because what if he's there, right now, just waiting for us? Come on. If I told you now then you'd both know my secrets."

I keep on walking, only now Paola's following me, our roles reversed.

"Why are you writing all this down if it's supposed to be a secret?" she asks. "That doesn't make any sense. Angelo would tell me if he knew...wait! You're a cold bitch! You're just waiting to see if he's dead! You'll only tell me if he's dead! That way you can lie about it!"

"No! If he's going to tell you, he'll tell you. I'm not going to tell you anything now. How about that? Not after the way you've been treating me in front of everyone. So stop asking."

I keep walking and Paola doesn't talk, doesn't sigh, doesn't even cough. I have no idea how long we've been on this hike and there isn't a single human anywhere near us. Paola's right, of course. I can't deny it. That's the whole point of writing this history. I'm tired of all the lies. So is Paola, clearly. She's beautiful, she's smart, she's everything I'm not, but that didn't stop Angelo from lying to her, just like it didn't stop Paola from believing him.

The sun rises until it's directly above and all I want to do is swim, so I veer off the path toward a riverside boulder, unable to resist the temptation. Paola follows me without protest as I sit down on the boulder, unpack the food, and tell her she can have whatever she wants before I dig into the *confit*. This fatty duck meat tastes like heaven over the dry bread and I wash it all down with canteen water. Paola likes it so much she offers me one of her apples and a thin, cured sausage for me to nibble on. It's beyond delicious. No one makes anything like this around here. I haven't had sausage in years.

"It's *linguiça*," she tells me. "From Brazil."

"How'd you get it? It tastes like garlic and something spicy. Paprika, right? Like the Russians. Where did it come from? No one slaughters pigs up here."

"I got it down at Fort Russ. Went down there by myself. Traded a vial of rose oil for a whole coil of this stuff. Lucky for me. A boat just landed from San Francisco, a crew of boys trading along the coast all the way from São Paulo. Can you believe that? I told them to keep coming back with more because this stuff reminds me of home."

"You think you'll stay here a long time?" I ask.

"Why? You want me to leave?"

"I didn't mean that."

Paolo dœsn't like what I said. She looks away and chews in anger, fuming. I finish her sausage, have some more duck meat, gulp down more water, then I take off all my clothes. The water's deep enough for me to jump and I splash a big wave onto the boulder on purpose. Paola curses as I float away on my back and when I finally stand up she's standing naked in the water, a mossy stick pointing in my direction. She throws it at me like a hatchet and I catch it perfectly without trying. I should have let her hit me. Now she knows.

"Angelo said you were all killers, *assassinas*. He was right. Look at you catch that."

"It's all a bunch of myths. To make people afraid."

"He said your mom killed a hundred men in Russia. That your grand-mother killed even more in San Francisco. He said they called her *Josephine the Butcher*."

"Everyone was supposed to think I killed him, Paola. That was his plan. Tell everyone how violent my family is and then disappear. Almost worked, too."

"But you saved him," she says, grinning. "Whatever he read stopped him. So what was it?"

"It was about your *Josephine the Butcher*. About the little valley in Switzerland where she came from. About how long we've been fighting the... the darkness. And yes, it was about how many men Josephine killed."

"So it's true? You just lied. You said it was all a myth just a second ago. So what is it?"

I don't answer. I don't feel like it. Angelo reading my notebook's bad enough, so I paddle back to the bolder where I stretch out and sun my body. Paola eventually gets out of the water, puts on her clothes, then walks away, our good humor officially evaporated. I let the sun dry my skin for another minute, put my clothes back on, gather my belongings, and run to catch up with her.

We hike in silence for the last leg and don't encounter a single person. Just before we reach the bridge over the Gualala River, I glimpse a patch of color hovering behind the tree trunks. Someone's painted the single word DREAMTIME in bright red across the wall of a rotting barn. This must be recent because I've never seen it before. The streaks of red paint look like blood dripping from each letter. It's almost frightening.

"We close?" Paola asks me. "Is that what the graffito means?"

"We're definitely close. Thirty minutes maybe."

"You've been inside the Dream before?"

"They say we never leave it."

"No, but you've been *inside*, right? Like inside—"

"You worried? You seem worried."

"No, I'm just—"

"I'll tell you this once. So listen. I'm heading back home soon as I talk to Essie. If you want to get stuck in the Dream, you go ahead and do that, but I'm going home. If you're here on your own journey, great, I support you, but I'm only here to find Angelo. You got me?"

Paola doesn't answer and we cross the Gualala River in silence. I can't tell if she's angry, but I hope she knows what she's doing. It's not my fault if she gets stuck. I can already feel the Dream, its subtle vortex swirling, fizzling into focus with an inaudible snap. We walk uphill until *Atcacinatcawalli* emerges from behind the trees and I smell deer meat cooking over flames. Paola's already glassy-eyed, following me out of instinct as a dozen children gather around, touch our bodies, then guide us into the Kashaya village, their mothers staring at us from the doorways of wood and thatch houses. I don't see any men, just little boys and a few teenagers. Most have tattoos on their faces, even the elders, only the tribe wasn't like this when I was a girl. It was the Kashaya of my generation who revived their ancient custom of encoding memory directly on their skin.

I grab Paola's hand and pull her towards the wooden roundhouse in the center of the village. Her entire body's gone limp and she glides without a word, oblivious and transfixed under the effects of the Dream. Essie's waiting when we get there, big hands on her big hips, her massive breasts looming like waves. She hugs me tight and whispers in Kashaya, something about my mother, something about expecting me. When I say I'm looking for Angelo she motions inside the roundhouse, mumbling that my answers are waiting for me. I tell Paola to stay put but she can't really hear, her face is smeared over with bliss as the Kashaya children raise their fingers to touch her skin. She probably thinks she's one of them. That's how the Dream usually takes hold.

Essie leads me into the dark depths of the redwood roundhouse and speaks to me in her native language. She says Angelo came to the village and asked for her to suck the darkness from his body, claiming he'd glimpsed his entire future in a dream. For two fulls days, Essie chanted and danced and hammered her twin poles around his body, arcing over the ground and rising up like a ribbon as she transmuted the darkness into beams of light. Essie says some of Angelo's darkness is still here. She points into the shadows as black fog envelopes the roundhouse and all trace of light disappears. That's when the Paloma transmitter explodes. I'm standing in the exact center of the blast. Iron melts, soil trembles, a terrible wound opens across the earth. This is the Dream. I remember when it first took me as a child, that moment of fear at the beginning. I refuse the instinct to panic, I ground my body in my feet, and suddenly I'm standing outside the roundhouse, only now I have new memories from either the past or the future. I can't tell yet. Either way, I know exactly where to find Angelo. Essie's disappeared but I can't go back in the roundhouse looking for her. I take glassy-eyed Paola by the arm and lead her away from the mob of giggling children. She mumbles something about wanting corn but I just pull with all my strength and don't listen to anything she say's until we're far away from the Dream and its electromagnetic distortions on the human brain. That's what the scientists call it.

"Can you let go?" she yells. "I'm awake. Get off me!"

"You want to go back? Can I let you go? Are you going to run back there?"

"No! What happened? Tell me what Essie said. Where's Angelo?"

I keep walking until I'm sure she's following behind. Then I tell her.

"He came here four days ago. Essie's a sucking doctor, if you didn't know. A Kashaya medicine woman. Angelo asked her to suck the darkness out of him and it worked. But now he's got a two day lead on you. He's probably already in Santa Rosa. I saw him back there, you know. In the Dream. I saw him walking to Paloma. Alive."

"He's walking all the way to Paloma? They haven't finished rebuilding it! I don't understand. Is he in the Dream? Did he get stuck in it again? Why would he just leave me? He has to be stuck inside the Dream. You said people never leave—"

"Calma, Paola. He's not in the Dream. He went through it already, as a kid. He's...immune now. It's not that he's stuck. He's looking for something else."

I think she stops walking but I don't look back to see. After after a few minutes, I hear her run back to my side and when I finally see her face I can tell she's been crying. Ten years younger than me. Ten years younger than Angelo. I don't know what she's sad about. At least her mother doesn't live here. She can always go back to São Paulo, especially now that Angelo's gone. I'm really starting to like her but I probably should have left Paola in the Dream. It would have solved a lot of problems for me, so I guess I'm not such a selfish bitch. Maybe I should just talk to her and be the sister I needed when I was her age. It couldn't hurt. The underworld secrets of our transmitters might have to wait for now, but I can tell her part of the story. If we keep up this pace, it'll be just before dusk when we get back to the commune. More than enough time to tell her the truth. At least some of it.

8

THE BIRTH OF THE COAST SAILOR'S UNION

O N CLEAR MORNINGS, JOSEPHINE CLIMBED TO THE TOP OF TELEGRAPH Hill and stared east towards the distant brown summit of Mount Diablo. Marisol had promised to take her there one day, but only when they'd finally beat the *yanquis*. Her outlaw mother Rosita de la Costa still roamed beyond this mountain with her pistols and dynamite, snipping telegraph cables, blowing up train bridges, but other outlaws weren't so lucky. The indigenous insurgent Tiburcio Vásquez was hung by a posse in 1874, while Marisol's cousin Procopio was almost captured in 1878 after losing his comrades in battle. A sheriff named Henry Morse rose to prominence eliminating these rebels and eventually formed his own private detective agency from the profits. Wells Fargo Bank, the Southern-Pacific Railroad, and the Union-Pacific Railroad hired mercenaries like Morse to wipe out the remaining insurgents and secure their investments in wild California. When the Southern-Pacific's agents evicted and then murdered some *yanqui* farmers at Mussel Slough in 1880, the public quickly turned against the railroad barons and their Wall Street backers. Rather than demonize the remaining outlaws, every train robbery was now applauded, each dynamiting seen as justice, and Rosita de la Costa became a popular hero.

In this radically altered environment, Antonio continued to organize on the waterfront, waking each morning to walk down dusty Greenwich Street with his box-hook in hand. The winter of 1882 was especially cold, bringing snow to Telegraph Hill and coating the waterfront in a fine blanket of powder. After these frigid days lowering cargo off the ships, Antonio lingered beneath the glowing gas-lamps and chatted up the sailors between puffs of tobacco. It was here that he met Frank Roney, an Irish sailor and former Fenian organizer who concealed a raging intellect behind carefully chosen words. Antonio convinced Roney to renounce anti-Chinese bigotry, join the International, and help infiltrate the San Francisco labor movement, although this didn't come easily. Antonio came home from work every day, sat on the porch with his two sons, and listened while Josephine and Marisol figured out how to deal with this Roney character. Soon enough, Roney could be found *under the light of some friendly street-lamp along the waterfront talking to small groups of seaman.* Without anyone realizing it, the little blue house on Greenwich Street quickly became the source of a major rebellion in San Francisco.

Thanks to their scheming, Frank Roney was elected head of the Trades Assembly of unions, a position that allowed them to place their comrades inside this racist organization. At a meeting in the spring of 1882, Roney allowed an eccentric newswriter named Bernett Haskell to address the Trades Assembly about the value of printed propaganda. Haskell offered his weekly paper *Truth* as the official organ of the Trades Assembly and received widespread approval from the union rank-and-file. After this victory, he was appointed chief editor of *Truth* by Roney. No one suspected that Haskell had been sent there by an anarchist stevedore named Antonio Ferrari, or that Roney had joined the International, or that all of this was being planned on Telegraph Hill by a brothel madame and an Alpine witch.

In his new position as trade-union mouthpiece, Bernett Haskell recruited several dozen free-thinking union men into what he called *The Invisible Republic*. After weeding out the unreliable and untrustworthy, Haskell initiated the rest into the *Illuminati* and claimed they'd soon contact the famed International. On a foggy night in the back of a brothel, this *Illuminati* was introduced to an Italian sailor named Antonio. Behind him was the Queen of the Coast, dressed in black with her face painted white. The dreaded appearance of this notorious madame solidified their resolve to join the anarchist cause, for there was little to fear with allies like the Queen. Marisol grinned when Haskell and eight *Illuminati* signed their names to the founding document of the International Workingman's Association, a front group for the Black International. Antonio didn't include his signature. Josephine was invisible to them all. The *Illuminati* never suspected her existence.

My grandparents only trusted one member of this *Illuminati*, a Polish Jew named Sigismund Danielewicz who'd just returned from organizing against the San Francisco sugar barons on their Maui plantations. This black-bearded sailor spoke both modern Italian and the Genovese dialect, allowing him to become the Italian-language secretary of the IWA. Josephine insisted they take him into the fold and Sigismund was soon called to a meeting at the little blue house on Greenwich Street with Antonio, Josephine, and Marisol. They told him that none of the others were trustworthy, not

Frank Roney

even Haskell, and the *Illuminati* would inevitably compromise with racists. Josephine instructed Sigismund to become a beacon of truth among the bigots in the IWA, a resistant force against this tide of darkness. While her sons played outside on Greenwich Street, Josephine uttered these ancient words to this maritime rebel: *until all are free, none are free.*

With their new friend settled in the IWA, my grandfather decided to sail for South America and check in with his comrades. During the weeks before his departure, Antonio and Josephine made love every night in the little blue house, conceiving their third child while Marisol yelled for them to shut up. Antonio kissed his family goodbye on the front porch, walked down the ramshackle staircases of Greenwich Street, and sailed through the Golden Gate in the summer of 1883.

While he was at sea, the IWA spread across the Rocky Mountains all the way to the Atlantic Ocean. Sigismund was the only member of the IWA who understood it was an anarchist front, a foil meant to illuminate the true rebels of their age. He worked with Josephine and Marisol on anti-racist columns for their *Truth* newspaper and composed detailed articles preaching guerrilla warfare and the varied uses of dynamite. As they told their readers, *TRUTH is a paper conducted by a cooperative association of working people who have associated themselves together for the unselfish purpose of educating their fellow slaves in truth.* Under the name Miss K, my grandmother translated Mikhail Bakunin's *God and the State* into English and published it in *Truth* for the workers to ponder. They encouraged their readers to torch the mints, burn the halls of records, expropriate the armories, dynamite train tracks, seize the farmlands, and this practical advice was printed out every week until the Trades Assembly grew tired of their seditious official organ. *Truth* was discontinued in 1884 but its seeds were already germinating in the minds of a thousand men, all brimming with a desire for vengeance against the capitalists.

Antonio arrived in Valparaiso during the summer of 1883 and walked through the waterfront markets to an anarchist *taberna* where he met with his comrades over glasses of wine. These Chilean anarchists were confused by Antonio's multilateral arrangement with the IWA but trusted his years of organizing. Since he last visited, the number of anarchists had grown in Valparaiso with their influence now spreading inland to Santiago, connecting the cities in a web of rebellion. Although he longed to hike the Andes and explore the colonial capital, my grandfather stayed only a single night in Valparaiso before signing on to a cargo ship. After traveling around the *Tierra del Fuego* to the port of Buenos Aires, Antonio discovered another burgeoning anarchist movement, built over a decade of struggle. He walked to his Argentine comrade's waterfront *taberna* and found its tables packed with radicals fresh off the boat. In this diverse milieu of exiles, my grandfather learned of coal strikes in France, fierce repression in Italy, and the Russian nihilists who fought Czar Alexander III.

He left Buenos Aires with the first volumes of the *Geographie Universelle*, written by Élisée Reclus from his exile along the shores of Lake Geneva. After fighting by Antonio's side in the Paris Commune, Élisée was captured by the Republic and condemned to life imprisonment, although this sentence was commuted thanks to well-connected friends like Charles Darwin. Despite this bourgeois mercy, Reclus was permanently exiled from the French Republic to prevent his views from spreading. Now living in Switzerland, Élisée wrote the esteemed *Geographie Universelle* and clandestinely prepared anarchist newspapers to be smuggled into France. His lakeside home was less than a day's journey from *Les Diablerets* and Élisée would often visit my family in their mountain stronghold. He helped my aunt Bianca smuggle herself into France, shared simple meals with my great-grandparents, and was inspired to write this passage for the *Geographie* volume of 1876: *Two jagged grey 'teeth' of Les Diablerets, a group of mountains rising superbly above green pasture-lands, detached themselves in the last century and tumbled down into the valley of Derborence six thousand feet beneath, where the broken fragments now cover an area of several square miles. Similar catastrophes have evidently occurred farther north, but in so remote a time that no tradition respecting them survives among the inhabitants of the country.* The first sentence comes close to the truth. The second is a conscious lie.

Antonio returned to San Francisco during the early spring of 1884 with this *Geographie Universelle* stuffed inside his bag, a gift for the mother of his children. Josephine was in her final month of her third pregnancy and had been relying on Sergio to watch over Federico. Sigismund was now a regular at the little blue house and loved to drink coffee on the porch with Marisol as the boats sailed out of the harbor. He kept the Queens up to date on the IWA and played outside with the children when Josephine needed silence. My mother told me that Marisol and Sigismund were romantically involved while Antonio was away,

Élisée Reclus

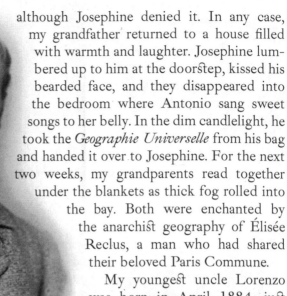

Bernett Haskell

although Josephine denied it. In any case, my grandfather returned to a house filled with warmth and laughter. Josephine lumbered up to him at the doorstep, kissed his bearded face, and they disappeared into the bedroom where Antonio sang sweet songs to her belly. In the dim candlelight, he took the *Geographie Universelle* from his bag and handed it over to Josephine. For the next two weeks, my grandparents read together under the blankets as thick fog rolled into the bay. Both were enchanted by the anarchist geography of Élisée Reclus, a man who had shared their beloved Paris Commune.

My youngest uncle Lorenzo was born in April 1884, just before *Truth* ceased publication. By that point, the IWA was embedded within every San Francisco trade union. My grandfather soon met with Frank Roney and Bernett Haskell in the back of a saloon where they decided to block the entire port of San Francisco, an effort that would require at least a year to accomplish. For the rest of 1884, the Trades Assembly and the IWA expanded rapidly into local factories, shipyards, warehouses, and wharves, heralding their future strike, and Antonio came home exhausted each evening, his hours on the waterfront always longer. To recruit men for a waterfront strike, my grandfather needed to be social, so he smoked cigarettes with longshoreman beneath the gas-lights and drank wine with sailors until they agreed striking was a good idea. Antonio drank slowly and came home with his faculties intact, his mind focused, and his heart unfazed by the brutality of wage-labor. He always had just enough energy to play with his children, eat dinner with his family, wash his body in the bathtub, and then collapse into bed. My grandmother read the *Geographie* aloud until Antonio and the children had fallen asleep, all of them now packed into the same little room. Marisol was never home at this hour of the night. Her brothel needed constant protection, especially after dark, and she woke in the afternoons when Antonio was at work. In his absence, Marisol helped raise Antonio's children.

During the winter of 1885, San Francisco was suddenly enveloped with another massive wave of unemployment. Now that Chinese immigration was banned, the white workers of California came to realize they were being exploited wholesale, regardless of race. New unions formed every week as the sea of unemployed grew enraged at the luxuriating capitalists in their Nob Hill mansions. Josephine had never encountered a battle this difficult or faced an opponent so dispersed. Instead of a single king or emperor, there were thousands of little lords who employed ruthless agents to pit one race against the other. These devious methods convinced some white unions into boycotting Chinese-made goods, a move the Trades Assembly and the IWA did nothing to stop. The only person who spoke against this was Sigismund Danielewicz, the shining light of the International.

With multiple unions sprouting across San Francisco, the ship-owners announced wages for coastal sailors would drop to fifteen dollars a month, citing the economic depression as their impetus. Infuriated by this greed, Sigismund met with Marisol, Josephine, and Antonio in their little blue house and quickly improvised a plan. The sailors of San Francisco still tell stories of how the Queen of the Coast channeled a tornado of ectoplasm into Sigismund's head during a séance on Telegraph Hill. Once he was filled to the brim with her black magic, he stormed down to the waterfront and announced a meeting for the following night at the Folsom Street wharf. Sigismund was already well-known by the longshoreman and sailors, although they'd never seen this IWA organizer so passionate. Some would claim his eyes glazed over pure white, while others said he hypnotized the crowd with the voice of an arch-angel. Over seven hundred people showed up the next night on March 6, 1885 and they all felt the subterranean mælstrom roaring inside Sigismund as he spoke of a world without bosses, rulers, or kings. Marisol, Josephine, and Antonio grinned from deep within the crowd, already assured of their success. Two days later, five hundred men formed the Coast Sailor's Union and within three months, their membership had soared to over 2,200 men, accounting for two thirds of all coastal sailors on the Western Coast. Instead of their bodies being sold by crimps, these men could now sell their bodies freely, a modest advance in these times of darkness.

The trade union movement continued to expand across the city, guided by the invisible hands of the International. It spread into the shipyards of the Union Iron Works and caused a third of the foundry workers to walk off the job. It was rumored that the shipyard would soon build armored warships for the federal government and this sudden strike made labor conditions appear chaotic to Washington DC, endangering further military contracts. Despite this achievement, the trade unions were tainted with racism and my grandparents observed this plainly on October 31, 1885 when five thousand unionists marched through the streets chanting against the Chinese. Frank Roney later gave a speech against the Mongolian invasion, followed by Burnett Haskell

Union Iron Works

who delivered another venomous tirade against the Chinese menace. Despite their racist performances, both speakers forbade the crowd from engaging in violence, claiming it would only benefit the capitalists. Roney and Haskell told my grandparents this rally was necessary, as it provided desperate workers with a safe outlet. According to this logic, if the bigots couldn't vent their anger in a controlled environment, they'd erupt into a uncontrollable pogrom. After hearing this latest race-hatred for themselves, Josephine and Antonio resolved to spare nothing in eradicating these dark tendencies from the labor movement.

Their Coast Sailor's Union shared its headquarters with the IWA in a small building at 6 Eddy Street, the center of the emerging waterfront rebellion. Marisol provided the Sailor's Union with a list of crimps and their agents along with times and places where they could be found. The sailors were led into battle by Sigismund Danielewicz, a longshoreman named Antonio, and *Yee Toy*, the notorious girl-faced assassin of Chinatown. Armed with the Queen's intelligence, the crimps and boardinghouse owners were ambushed, beaten, and had their skulls crushed with slung-shots, for there was no hiding from this Sailor's Union with its supernatural powers. While my grandparents fought these battles, they convinced these sailors to renounce their racism and join the International. Few could resist the fierce allure of *Yee Toy*, the Chinese killer who moved like a silent woman and defended them like brothers. Within the first year of its existence, the Sailor's Union took over the waterfront and soundly crushed the crimps, aided by this powerful friend from Chintatown.

They opened a union shipping office, started a union boarding-house on the south side of Telegraph Hill, and forced the helpless ship-owners to pay their sailors forty dollars a month instead of twenty. With this momentum at their back, Josephine insisted that Antonio contact Frank Roney and begin their blockade of the entire harbor. Roney was now head of the Federated Trades Council and from this powerful position he organized the coal boilermen of the Oceanic Steamship Company into a new union. Owned by the sons of Hawaiian sugar baron Claus Spreckels, this steamship line provided reliable passage between San Francisco, the Kingdom of Hawaii, and the South Pacific colonies of the British Empire. After a swift bout of union organizing, the maritime coal-shovelers of these infernal boiler-rooms walked off their ships and shut down the entire company. In league with them, Antonio and Sigismund organized a small sailor's strike to tie up the harbor in a backlog of ships. This solidarity work-stoppage between two maritime unions terrified the ship-owners, now weak from the defeat of their old crimping system, and none were prepared when the Union Iron Works was suddenly paralyzed by another strike.

Blacklisted from foundry work by the bosses, Roney organized these iron workers with a fierce determination, culminating in 400 men walking out of the shipyard in the midst of war production. The Union Iron Works had just been awarded a contract to build the *USS Charleston*, the first armored cruiser of a new Pacific fleet, and the strike promised to scuttle their future contracts. This industrial action spread to the Risdon Iron Works where the metal steamships of the Oceanic Steamship Company were built for the Spreckels. From the wharves below Telegraph Hill to the polluted shores of Potrero Hill, the entire waterfront was now in rebellion. With no other options, the local capitalists announced they'd only hire sailors through their own shipping offices, an act that provoked an all-out war.

In the midst of this tension, the trade unions of Chicago, Cincinnati, Pittsburgh, Milwaukee, Detroit, and New York City went on strike for the modest demand of a universal eight-hour workday. On May 1, 1886, hundreds of thousands streamed through the streets to demonstrate the strength of their movement against capital. Two days later, the police opened fire on striking workers outside a machine factory in Chicago, killing several men. A mass-meeting was called for Haymarket Square the following night and it was here that someone threw a bomb at the police. The explosion killed seven officers and wounded sixty more, prompting the state to round up eight local labor leaders and jail them under charges of murder. These arrests were felt across the continent in San Francisco and inspired the cable-car operators to strike in July 1886. Enraged by the events in Chicago, hundreds of San Francisco union car-men threw rocks, overturned train-cars, and sabotaged the tracks of their companies. In less than a month, most of the local train bosses agreed to increase wages and lessen the work hours rather than empower the more uncompromising anarchists.

On August 26, 1886, a mass-meeting of waterfront unions took place where the now-infamous Bernett Haskell called for an immediate general strike, although his proposal didn't pass a vote. After this unfortunate meeting, the Sailor's Union independently voted to call out their entire membership of

3,200 men and block the waterfront by force. Within a single day, all traffic in the port was paralyzed and the sailors concluded their war against the last of the crimps, although a dozen men died in the brutal street fighting that followed. While the Sailor's Union overcame these old foes, they couldn't stop the ship-owners from hiring hundreds of men desperate for work amid the economic depression. There were simply too many wharves for the union to block and long lines now extended from the shipping-company hiring halls where hopeless sailors waited to sign onto a crew for meagre pay. Many accepted their loss as the bad luck of a waterfront gaming table and the blame for their humiliating defeat fell on the man who'd first called for the general strike: Bernett Haskell, leader of the secretive *Illuminati*.

My grandparents never let Haskell into the fold as they had Sigismund Danielewicz. The more Haskell grandstanded for their respect, the further they recoiled. In his bitterness, Haskell embraced Marxism and secretly promoted it throughout the IWA. Once his treachery was discovered, Antonio called for the Sailor's Union to move out of IWA headquarters and relocate closer to the waterfront. By the end of 1886, membership in the Sailor's Union had dropped to 1,000 and spirits were low. After holding out through the sailor's strike, the shipyard workers of the Union Iron Works were eventually defeated and construction of the *USS Charleston* was resumed. In this moment of despair, Josephine asked Antonio to sail towards Buenos Aires and tell their comrades of the waterfront strike they had almost accomplished. Before this journey, Antonio left the union in the hands of Andrew Furuseth, a grizzled Norwegian sailor who'd recently been elected secretary, the highest position in the president-less union. Furuseth was stern, curt, religious, and conservative, although he joined the International without hesitation once Antonio explained its ancient credo: *until all are free, none are free.*

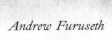

Unlike before, Josephine didn't become pregnant in the days leading up to his departure. She promised their next child would be a girl. It would also be her last. In this manner, our matriarchal line would continue forward, rooting us to this distant land. On the day Antonio sailed into the Pacific, an empty cable-car was dynamited in San Francisco with the blast mangling its iron tracks. Another street-car strike had broken out against the local rail companies, allowing Josephine and Marisol to hear the blasts from their front porch

Andrew Furuseth

while Antonio sailed through the Golden Gate. These union dynamiters had learned much from the Queens of the Coast, although none would ever know it in their lifetimes. From the wine-stained pages of *Truth* to the whispers of waterfront alleys, Marisol and Josephine were the devil-horned mermaids who guided lost sailors to shore, the true authors of this maritime revolt.

SHE'LL BE HUFFING AND PUFFING

THERE'S GOING TO BE WINE TODAY. IT'S THE END OF THE GRAPE HAR-vest. I imagine green bottles clinking together in wooden crates and the squeal of corks sliding into glass mouths. This little fantasy makes me gaze down from my loft at the rows of glass jars filled with apple butter, beans, peas, grains, lentils, corn, oil, pasta, vinegar, nuts, and dried fruit, all from the commune. Tonight, when the grape harvest's done, I'll be able to add *vino* to this bounty. The vintners release the 1948 batch once all the 1950 grapes are picked, about 1,000 bottles, more than enough for everyone in the commune. *Peace reigned in the heavens, ambrosia stood already mixed in the bowl, and then Hermes took up the jug and poured wine for the gods.* Not even they could resist *vino*. How am I supposed to stand a chance?

I stare up at the skylight, imagine myself first in line for the bottles, and it's enough to make me salivate. I should bring a box because I want at least six bottles, maybe more. Everyone else can have their beer and spirits. The kids don't need any wine, but I do, to get through the winter. My only big problem is tonight's assembly. I'll be the center of attention, making it difficult to sneak off. They'll want to talk with me about wheat. All those green bottles might be gone before I get there.

My heart races in panic at the thought of losing my wine. I climb down from the loft, hover above my desk, and flip through the most recent chapter of my history. I've been working on this one all week and the desk's piled high with history books taken from the library. No one ever sees me sneak in late at night, they're always asleep, and I write until morning while everyone's dreaming.

I've been hiding at home since Paola and I got back from Kashaya land. My fingers are stained black from ink and the desk is still speckled with splotches from Angelo's suicide note. I don't know why I haven't cleaned it up, but I gave that stupid note to Paola when we got home. She reached out to take it but stopped just short. I let her think about it, then I crumpled the note up and tossed it in the stove. Before it could turn to ash, Paola was out the door. I thought she'd leave the commune but she's still here. She'll be at the assembly tonight, along with Angelo's friends.

I put on some old cut-off shorts and a white blouse, wash my hair in the ceramic basin, and rub lavender oil over my arms and neck. It's finally cooling down outside and the air feels like fall. I open the door to let in the breeze, cut myself a few pieces of bread, and watch the dust blow away across the floor. Just as I'm buttering my bread, I hear a pair of crunching footsteps on the road. It's Annabelle and Gertrude, dressed lightly for the harvest. They walk inside without knocking, like always. I guess they came here to chaperon me. I've stayed away from them since I got back. That darkness I saw inside the roundhouse never left me. It's still here, and I don't want them to catch it.

"You about ready?" Gertrude asks. "We gotta make sure they see us working, otherwise we won't have dibs on the wine. Come on, chew, chew. Eat your bread on the way."

"Have they brought the bottles down yet?" I ask. "Are they in the storehouse?"

"You should see it," Annabelle says. "They've covered an entire wall in boxes."

I resist the temptation at first. I listen to them speak, I keep chewing my bread, but that tickling urge starts to grow. I'm doing this to myself but I can't help it. If I'm going to be present tonight, I need to get my wine squared away, so I stuff the bread in my mouth and grab a wooden box from the closet. Annabelle and Gertrude try and stop me but I run towards the *fábrica* and don't look back. No one's around anyway, they're heading up the hill to pick grapes, and now peace truly reigns in the heavens. I creep into the *fábrica* storehouse and glimpse the tall pyramid of wooden boxes filled with *vino rojo*, a wine taken up by Hermes and poured out for the gods.

The vintners are guarding this pyramid of bottles but I just don't look at them. My vision blurs into a puddle, their words turn to babble, my hands move on instinct, my tongue rattles nonsense, and suddenly I'm carrying away my haul before anyone stops me. In this jumble of excitement, I envision the puffy oak tree where Angelo took me to drink wine back when we were kids, when my mother was lost in Russia, when we were two wartime orphans lost in the hills. The first time I saw Angelo he was a little boy, climbing down from our oak tree dressed in a purple cloak, claiming to be a solider in the Army of Light. That was our favorite game, pretending to be our missing parents. But you, monkey face, Angelo. I loved you long ago, when you seemed to be just a small, ungracious child. Now look at us. I see that childish face beaming through the branches of our secret oak tree, I smell the dry grass of our childhood, and this reverie consumes me until I'm at my front porch. Gertrude and Annabelle are waiting there for me, annoyed.

"Are you serious?" Gertrude asks me. "You got ten bottles for yourself? Ten?"

"I'm going to need it," I say, flatly. "Tonight might get emotional."

"*But why?*" Annabelle quips. "You're just trying to move the wheat."

They laugh at me while I climb into my loft and hide the wine where no one can find it. I feel at peace now, centered, whole. Beaming with light, I climb down to the living room and follow them out my front door. We're definitely the stragglers of the harvest, the very last in a long line snaking their way up the mountain to the sprawling vineyard. While we hike, Gertrude and Annabelle ask me a dozen questions about my ancestors in the Alps and I draw out the story as long as possible. They interrupt me without pause, constantly ask for clarity, and I've only just told them about Mauritius of Thebes when we reach the top of the hill where I glimpse the long rows of twisting grape vines.

"So you're related to Mauritius?" Gertrude asks. "He's part of your family?"

"I'm a direct descendant. My ancestors never lost track because he was the first outsider we ever brought inside. That's what my mom said, anyway."

"It wasn't just him, though," Annabelle says. "There must have been other people who married in? You said he brought a legion. That's how many people again?"

"Five thousand, but the history books say Mauritius had over six thousand."

"Wait, how many of you are there?" Gertrude asks. "In your tribe?"

"Tens of thousands. Maybe more. It's hard to say. But we're everywhere, places you wouldn't expect, places I don't even know about."

"And you're all serious witches?" Annabelle asks. "Like the transmitter conductors?"

"That's right, but no one ever told me, and I never learned how to control myself. You all used to joke in San Francisco, call me a witch, and it's true. That's why I was so crazy down there. I didn't know what I was."

They keep asking questions but I don't answer, I just head straight to the vineyard well and start slurping away at the flowing stream. I'm so damn thirsty after that hike that this water tastes like rain filtered through a honeycomb. I haven't had anything to drink, not even tea, and I slurp until someone snaps at me. When I look up, I see an orderly row of village people waiting in line to fill their glass jugs. They're exasperated, irritable, overheated, unable to comprehend my obliviousness. I apologize frantically, say something about having too much wine, and then get the hell out of there.

Annabelle and Gertrude move to the back of the line and deal with my social mess, the neutral friends of crazy Fulvia. I ignore their annoyed glances, grab some clippers and a basket from the barn, then walk into the fields where the harvesters are already snipping bunches of red grapes. I join a pack of girls on the edge of the vines and work beside them with my butt on the soil, hoping to avoid any and all adults until lunch. These girls don't care about tonight's assembly, they only care about the Harvest Ball. They speak about what dresses they'll wear, what boys they want to dance with, what songs they want to hear, all that kind of nice horseshit. It makes me smile only I've got nothing to say. I haven't danced since San Francisco, but I can imagine these girls dancing at the Harvest Ball. *Their feet move rhythmically, just as the tender feet of farm girls once danced around an alter of love, crushing a circle in the soft, smooth, flowering grass.* I danced like that with Angelo, long ago, it's true.

"Did you ask Angelo to dance at the Harvest Ball?" someone asks.

It's a freckle-faced girl with red hair. Now all her friends are trembling in fear of Fulvia the witch. They probably think I'll turn them into butterflies and never tell their families. I cast the girl my coldest death glare but she doesn't seem to notice I'm angry. Maybe she's touched. Maybe she can hear my thoughts. Maybe redheads *are* the devil's daughter.

"Yeah, we danced," I tell her. "But I danced with a lot of people back then. Girls too."

"We *always* dance with each other," she says. "It's boring to dance with girls."

"Not for me," I tell them. "I love it."

The eldest of this group takes my lead and talks about the Kashaya girl she kisses down on the coast, how they meet every summer in a secret cave. Soon they're competing over increasingly dubious narratives involving kisses. This passes the time well enough and we make serious progress down the vines until the lunch bell rings and the harvesters rise up from the grape field. I follow the girls through the rows until I run into Gertrude and Annabelle waiting for me in the long water line.

"New friends?" Gertrude asks. "You trying to cut in line again?"

"No. I can wait like everyone else."

Annabelle runs off to get food, leaving us standing in line. The people in front of us say hello, no one glares at me, so maybe everything's forgiven. Gertrude just smirks and says something about how I corrupt the youth but I ignore her until she wanders off to find us water jars. Five people start talking to me while she's gone, they volunteer to load the wheat, they smile and grin and laugh about something I can't understand. One of the women puts her arm around me and asks if I got any honey this morning. She smells real good, but I tell her I didn't see any honey, anywhere.

"It's in the *fábrica*," she says. "Near the wine bottles. I can get you some later."

"Really? I didn't see any when I was there getting my wine."

Everyone looks at me in amazement, as if the truth of my thievery were revelation. Gertrude arrives before I embarrass myself, hands me a glass jar, and tells the line that I just can't help myself, causing everyone to laugh. Suddenly it's our turn at the well-pump and we fill our jars before heading to the picnic tables out on the grass. The tall Victorian spire of the vineyard farmhouse casts its shadow over the picnickers, providing them a little relief from the heat, but Annabelle beckons us over to the sunny side of the field where three plates are waiting for us: potatoes, black beans, salsa, corn tortillas, salad, and rosemary bread. A bottle of wine and olive oil is on each table, along with a bowl of salt.

We eat in silence until the vintners plop themselves next to us. They yammer really loud and a bunch of these guys keep smirking at me. Everyone must know about my raid on the *fábrica* but I keep eating like it never happened. With a little salt, this entire meal tastes like paradise and I wash it down with well-water before pouring a big glass of wine. Some of these orchard guys crack a joke about me thieving in the night like a witch but I just cast them an evil eye before chugging down my *vino*. My belly's full, I'm perfectly content, I keep my mouth shut, and everyone looks in my direction.

I drink more wine and ignore the vintners' banter until dishes start clattering and the first people head back into the fields. I stick with Annabelle and Gertrude and follow them into the shadiest part of the vineyard. I'm lucky Annabelle brought along a big jug of water, otherwise we'd pass out from sun-stroke. She's smarter than me, smarter than Gertrude, always bringing what we forget. We sip sparingly from her glass jug and hum "She'll Be Coming Around The Mountain" together as the sun sinks toward the west. I fill my first basket, leave it at the end of the row for the runners to collect, then grab an empty one from the pile, pausing a moment to admire the triangular patterns woven into its structure. They say the Dream is embedded into each basket, a unique glyph pulled from the underworld. The Kashaya weavers dream these intricate patterns each night and copy them into water-tight containers strong enough to last decades. The Dream doesn't effect these women like it does outsiders. The Dream is their waking life, tangible as this basket in my sweaty hands.

We work until there's no more grapes to clip. The vintners have been real busy this while time crushing grapes in giant pits, mixing the juice with yeast, and then tubing it into oak barrels, something they'll do long into the evening, accompanied by dozens of young village women, all eager to lift their skirts and juice the grapes with bare feet. Several children are conceived every year during this harvest, but only after the red wine is in the barrels. These oak barrels are then aged in a massive underground cellar that was excavated when I was a little girl. We used to call them trolls, those dirty men with shovels and head-lamps who bored into the earth and emerged just before dusk. My mother was still in Russia when I wandered up here with Angelo to watch their magic. The war hadn't ended yet and their plan was to build one of Tesla's magnetic cannons to defend the coastline from the Imperial Japanese Navy. Instead of wine, the massive cellar was meant to store the huge iron rounds used in these hyper-sonic weapons, each capable of destroying a naval fleet or turning an industrial city into ash.

These rounds would exit the atmosphere before curving back to earth according to their launch trajectory at a speed faster than sound. A single round could cause an ocean tsunami, level a mountain, or incinerate an approaching army with its raw kinetic energy. Each cannon was controlled by a single conductor, strapped into a rotating metal chair inside a bunker, her eyes fixed on a glowing visualizer. Obeying her pure intuition, the conductor pulled the metal trigger and launched these iron rounds on a perfect trajectory. They never knew what they were firing at, they arrived at these cannons sites without knowing why, but their aim was always perfect. When the war ended, Nikola melted down the cannons and re-cast them into transmitter parts, claiming weapons were a tool of the past. Our magnetic cannon never got built. Now there's just wine aging in the darkness of its ammunition cellar.

I follow my friends back to the farmhouse, toss my clippers into the pile, and take one last drink from the vineyard well. There isn't a line this time and most people are leaving, burnt out from the long day of sunshine. Annabelle and Gertrude wait for me at the summit and we take our time descending the dusty road back to the village. The assembly doesn't start until dusk and dinner isn't until afterward, so everyone will be hungry while I give my speech. I tell this to my friends but neither seem concerned. Gertrude says we've always done it this way because hunger eases the horseshit. Annabelle interrupts her and asks me about Mauritius, where the Nubians went, who they married, how they survived. As we walk down the road, I tell them about hidden valleys, haunted summits, silent assassins, and secret alpine trails. I tug at my pitch-black hair and show it to them. I say it came from Egypt and Italy, that my family's rebellion is ancient, and I'm starving by the time we reach the village.

They sit with me on the *fábrica* patio, munching on dry bread while I explain how my ancestors survived the witch-hunts and fanned out across Europe to seek their revenge against the darkness. My friends don't understand what I mean by darkness, they say I'm not describing it well, that it all sounds like a fairy tale. Gertrude wanders off in frustration but comes back with a bottle of red wine and three glasses. She say's I've set off a rebellion and this will be the first assembly where wine's served before dinner. I notice everyone's drinking, they've broken out the *vino* early, and suddenly the sun isn't going down fast enough. Annabelle shares my concern, her eyes dart back and forth between every glass of wine, knowing this assembly could end in a drunken nightmare. We gulp down our glasses in unison, just like in San Francisco where people drink at every occasion, for any reason, at any time. Then I see Paola across the patio with Angelo's friends. They're all drinking too. I'm about to hyperventilate when Lorraine sits down with her daughters and pours some wine. She still smells like apple butter.

Annabelle jokes with the girls while Lorraine tells me about the dream she had last night: a tube of water sucked her up into a wooden room filled with shadows where she saw a horrible man made of darkness. Gertrude and Annabelle freeze when Lorraine says the word *darkness* and explains how the man wouldn't stop laughing. She saw the blast of electricity engulf the Paloma transmitter, saw her lost love Lucio vaporize into light, and woke up covered in sweat. Lorraine wipes away a single tear, pours herself another glass, and once she's swallowed it down I tell her about the Kashaya roundhouse where I saw the same shadow man. I tell her about the darkness it left inside me.

"Something's happening," Lorraine says, encouraging me to drink up. "Can you feel it?"

"I can sure feel it" Gertrude says. "It always feels this way with Fulvia."

"You ready?" Annabelle asks me. "Enough of this darkness. People are heading inside."

I nod my head and chug down one final glass of red wine. Lorraine wishes me good luck and kisses both of my flushed cheeks. Annabelle says something to me as we walk to the storehouse but all I can think about is the darkness inside my body. Maybe old Essie couldn't handle the stress for once and passed it off, only she didn't ask my permission. Neither did Angelo. I suddenly become aware that I'm standing in the storehouse and see the commune assembling in our customary circle. At least no one brought their wine glasses into the room. Some things we just don't do. Not even me.

An older man named Yves is facilitating tonight's assembly and he gets everyone quiet before reading the agenda. He lists a series of harvest reports, an update on the radio project, and my proposal for transporting our excess wheat. The assembly is about to start when Yves says the word Fulvia. He says my name out loud. I'm the final item on the agenda. Most everyone is smiling, letting me know it's okay, but I see Paola with a pack of Angelo's friends huddled across the circle. I can't imagine what they're planning, but now I wish I'd drank more wine.

The different farmers take turns listing off their harvests, proclaim the metric amounts delivered to the storehouse, and thank everyone who volunteered to help. I try not to look at Paola but it's almost impossible. The assembly discusses the new radio station, the raw lumber to build it waiting at the saw mill, and the generator now sailing in from San Francisco, almost identical to our *fábrica* oscillator, just smaller and more efficient. Paola's been looking at me through all this discussion. Her eyes are filled with mischief and she perks up when Yves motions towards me, asking to hear my proposal for transporting the excess wheat. Everyone's staring now, waiting for me to finish what I started, and the only person I truly want to see right now is my mom. Obviously she's nowhere to be seen.

"I know this is old news," I say, still trying to ignore Paola. "I'm proposing the assembly pick a day to load half of our wheat into bags, put them on our wagons, and drive them down to the coast. Now that the harvest's basically over, I'm asking for volunteers to do the loading maybe a week from today. Could you raise your hands if you'd like to volunteer?"

It sounds like rain when all those hands go up. They keep them raised far longer than necessary but Paola and her friends have their arms folded. Aside from them, the only abstainers are the young and the old. We discuss which horses we'll use, what wagons we'll take, how many bags we'll need, and we finalize the plans while Paola whispers with her friends. They're going to pull something, for sure. I grab Annabelle's sweaty hand and squeeze tight as the next item comes up on our agenda: Fulvia. Paola steps forward to speak against me. Her mouth opens. All I see is white light.

"Before I say what I'm here to say, I want to make something clear. I was convinced Fulvia drove Angelo to kill himself. I thought it was true...and it wasn't. If it wasn't for Fulvia, he'd be dead." Paola looks around the room and lets that sink in. "But if it wasn't for her, he wouldn't have wanted to kill himself in the first place. Regardless of how I might feel toward her, it should never have gotten to this point. All of us did this to ourselves. *We* did. It was right in our faces and we acted like children, like rabid village mothers, and we whispered behind each other's backs. Fulvia brought a lot of toxic emotions to the commune with her behavior. So did Angelo. So did we. I think Fulvia's been judged enough. We didn't help her, and she took care of herself like she knew how. But that doesn't mean any of us have to like her. None of that matters though, if we like her or if we don't. It's over now. So let it be over. That's all I have to say."

A tremendous, horrible silence falls over the assembly. I don't know what any of this means. Even Paola's friends seem confused. One of them has her mouth open but she eventually pushes Paola aside, takes the floor, and points right at me.

"She stole wine this morning! She does whatever she wants!"

"She cut in line for water like it was nothing!" another woman yells. "In front of all of us!"

"And she sneaks into the library at night to steal books!"

"She manipulates everybody! She's a snake!"

There's only a dozen of them hurling these accusations, some true, most not. It makes everyone uncomfortable, especially me. Each word feels like a knife in my back, like they're trying to kill me, but I keep my breathing under control until their tirade ends. Yves calms this group down but Paola walks away looking disgusted. She isn't the only deserter. It's like I've always thought. Only the loyal wives and dutiful mothers are howling for my blood. They can't stand how I make them look, doing what they secretly want to do, acting how they've always wanted to act.

Yves ends the assembly when the tension starts to feel violent. Most of the commune is yelling at the den-mothers to shut up, to get over themselves, to have a nice drink. I pull Annabelle towards the main doors and Gertrude follows us, making sure we're not attacked from behind. Paola's waiting at the doorway, trying to smile, and she follows us without saying a word, heading towards my house while the commotion fades and our communal assembly disperses into night. I never got my honey, but that's what I get for being so sloppy with the wine. Gertrude hears this thought, she smiles just as I think it. Gertrude, herder of evening, herds home what the dawn has dispersed. Gertrude always kept us safe in San Francisco when we stayed out all night drinking, dancing, and getting into big arguments. She's still herding me back home, only all I care about is my *vino*. Once I'm inside the house I climb upstairs for a bottle, light the oil lamps, and pour the four of us a nice glass. We *salud* each other and then gulp down our wine in one big gulp, like good San Francisco girls. Paola tries to say something to me, her eyes bristle with tears, but I don't let her continue.

"There's no point," I say. "Thank you. For seeing me as a person."

"You're not just a person," Gertrude says, pouring us the last of the wine. "Don't pull that crap."

"What is Fulvia then?" Paola asks. "If she's not just a person."

"She's the head witch," Gertrude tells her. "And don't you forget it."

I laugh, though it's a little forced. They all keep talking while I build a pyramid of twigs inside the stove, set it on fire with my electric lighter, and I'm still feeding the flames when Lorraine and her daughters walk inside. She gives me a wet kiss on the temple and watches silently as the fire comes to life. More people arrive as I build up the flames, only I don't notice, and my little house is packed with guests once the fire gets good and raging. I grab my notebook before anyone can see it and try my best to welcome each visitor. This place is going to be an inferno because of my stupid fire so I open every downstairs window and then climb up to the loft. After hiding my notebook, I open the skylight above my bed, listen to these two dozen joyous guests, and decide to break out my stolen wine. Everyone can drink from these bottles tonight. They aren't mine anyway.

9

THE MULTIPLE LIVES OF IMMORTAL FÉLIX

I'M GOING TO WRITE THE HISTORY YOU'VE ALREADY READ, ONLY NOW from a different angle. Without this piece of the story, my family's struggle might appear isolated, exceptional, or even infamous. Josephine and Isabelle didn't exist in a vacuum, nor did they act alone, and my family was one of many who fought the darkness throughout the centuries. This is the story of another family.

Before ascending the peaks of *Les Diablerets* with his six thousand men, my ancestor Mauritius asked for volunteers to defend the Rhône River valley and obstruct the inevitable Roman advance. Six hundred soldiers stepped up for this suicide mission, designed to give the impression that the Theban Legion had disintegrated. These six hundred soldiers had all grown up together in the ruins of ancient Thebes, its former luxury nearly forgotten after many centuries of war and pillage. Thebes was once the great City of Amun-Ra, southern jewel of the Nile River, former capital of the Egyptian Empire. Now it was just a desolation of toppled stone with an array of huts clustered around the twin obelisks of Luxor Temple. These soldiers had seen two-horned Amun-Ra and hawk-headed Horus carved into the ancient pillars of this temple, their forms illuminated by firelight as old priests told of how Rome, Greece, and Assyria suppressed their ancient religion and destroyed what remained of glorious Thebes. To honor this lost ancestry, the soldiers of the Theban Legion chose the Eye of Ra as their military symbol and had it tattooed on their lower backs. While this red disk was nearly invisible on the Nubians, the mark was plain on those with lighter skin.

The Theban Legion was formed in 284 after an army commander named Diocles assassinated Emperor Carus at the triumph of his Persian campaign. During the long march back to Rome, Diocles covertly assassinated Numerian, son of Carus and next rightful Emperor. The Roman army proclaimed Diocles their leader and marched on the forces of Emperor Carinus, the successor by Roman law, and swiftly defeated him in battle. Once this *coup d'etat* was complete, Diocles was Emperor Diocletian. To cement his military

The Theban Legion

power over Europe, Dicoletian created the *Thebæi*, a legion conscripted from the ancient City of Amun-Ra. The colonial governors of Thebes called for able-bodied men and medicine-women to assemble at Luxor Temple and were overwhelmed when thousands flocked to the training, food, shelter, and clothing offered in exchange for service. Among them was a young man named Félix, one of thousands of orphans raised in the slums of Thebes. Unlike his friends, Félix had brown skin and wavy black hair, making him resemble the Assyrians, Greeks, and Romans who'd once invaded Egypt.

Over the next three months, Félix learned Roman warfare with his childhood friends and came to admire a tall Nubian named Mauritius, a man who'd wandered in from the desert with nothing but a cloak, ſtaff, and water bladder. Mauritius was the ſtrongeſt of the Theban recruits and easily defeated his Roman trainers in the square, a feat that endeared him to the military recruiters. This ſtrange man from the desert spoke without arrogance, showed no hoſtility to the other recruits, and overcame every challenge with a meditative calm that inspired inſtant respeƈt. Félix and his Theban comrades openly acknowledged Mauritius as their natural leader and looked for his approval before obeying any Roman command. Mauritius never spoke of where he came from, although the medicine-women of the Legion said he came from the end of the Nile where ancient gods ſtill hid inside the jungle.

After many weeks of training, Mauritius was entruſted to command this firſt *Thebæi* and told to make camp while awaiting Imperial inſtruƈtions. Within their childhood pillars of Luxor Temple, all 6,000 soldiers had their backs tattooed with the Eye of Ra while alchemical medicine-women chanted ancient hymns to forgotten powers. The body of Ra was a powerful man while his red Eye was a fierce woman, an ancient union they encoded on their flesh. Félix had lighter skin than his Nubian friends and the feminine Eye ſtood out whenever he bathed in the Nile, an aċt he relished those laſt days in Thebes. After swimming in this river his entire life, Félix was deſtined to never see it again.

Emperor Diocletian ordered the *Thebæi* north to Alexandria where the Imperial navy waited to deliver them to Europe. Juſt before they left Thebes, Mauritius dreamed of a vaſt desert made of water and beheld a black-hooded woman beneath white-capped mountains. He smelled water gushing from a nearby ſtream and heard ice cracking on a diſtant glacier. Standing beside the woman was a black goat with two spiral horns and yellow eyes brighter than the sun. When he woke, Mauritius knew the path to my anceſtral village and recalled this dream often on his journey up the Nile. He beheld the great white towers of alchemical Alexandria and smelled the salt of the blue *Mare Noſtrum*, a vaſt sea that encased the entire Roman peninsula and extended to the very edge of the known world. Mauritius couldn't tell where his dreams ended and reality began, nor could his sea-sick men. Few of the Thebans had ever witnessed such an emerald vaſtness and many became so ill they could hardly ſtand. Félix was one of these poor men who heaved their guts into a desert made of water and clutched their nauseated bellies with desperate arms, overcome by the power of mighty *Mare Noſtrum*.

After disembarking at the coaſtal trading port of Genua, the *Thebæi* marched to the foot of the Alps and began their northern crossing at the end of winter. In the spring of 285, the legion arrived at the colony of *Oċtodurus* where they beheld a gargantuan valley lined with green grass, surrounded by snow-capped mountains, and cut in half by the Rhône River. This northern segment of the Empire had fallen into lawlessness and Mauritius' orders were to proceed into *Gallia Narbonensis* and deſtroy any rebel populations they encountered. Once he entered the river valley and beheld the mountains of his dreams, Mauritius told his men to wait and then rode off alone atop his white horse. He returned riding a black horse, claimed to have made an alliance with the mountain people, and ordered the *Thebæi* to seize every Roman colony in the valley. Félix participated in the capture of *Augunum*, a ſtone riverside fortress that controlled access to Lake Geneva, and it was here that he met Regula.

While the Roman blood was being washed from the roads, Regula found Félix sleeping on a pile of hay in her family barn. He grabbed his sword when she entered but was inſtantly enchanted by her long golden hair and eyes greener than jewels. She took Félix inside her family home and fed him what food remained after the siege, never once breaking her smile. Regula had been born in *Augunum* of indigenous parents who'd become Roman *civitas* rather than hide like my anceſtors. With the Empire now expelled from the valley, Regula no longer had to pour the Romans wine or avoid their lecherous assaults at the tavern. She spoke with kind Félix in their common Latin and invited him to ſtay with her that night, a proposition which led to them making love and falling asleep in each other's arms. Neither had ever imagined such happiness was possible.

In the days that followed, Félix and Regula took long hikes into the mountains, swam in the freezing river, and lay together as the galaxy rotated above their heads. Regula promised to remain by Félix's side, claiming her love would exiſt until the end of time, and they were inseparable during those precious weeks before the Roman counter-attack. The bulk of the legion departed for *Les Diablerets* while Félix remained behind to defend *Augunum* with two hundred others, though he did so only for Regula. These soldiers were his childhood friends, loyal until death, but none could hold a flame to green-eyed Regula with her hair that burned like sunshine.

As their romance blossomed beneath the mountains, newly crowned Emperor Maximian marched northward with a force of over 10,000 men. He remained south of the Alps inside the fortress of *Auguſta Prætoria Salassorum* while his legions marched off to conquer *Octodorum* where they killed the two hundred Theban defenders before spreading like ants to reclaim the Rhône River Valley. When they approached *Augunum*, one hundred Thebans waited for them atop the ſtone bridge to Lake Geneva, blocking access to the other colonies. Another hundred men were ſtationed inside the sealed fortress, although one of them was missing. Before he could join this suicidal battle, Regula lured Félix into a ſtable north of the fortress gates, sparing him from martyrdom.

Inside the ſtable was a woman holding the reins of three black horses. She wore a dark black hood to conceal her Egyptian skin and had a twin-arced Ichthys fish dangling from her neck. This was Verena: medicine-woman conscripted into the Theban legion, gnoſtic witch, alchemical prieſtess, and hermetic scholar who had roamed the Nile in search of loſt wisdom. Although the silver fish on her necklace had been appropriated by the Chriſtians, the Ichthys represented electromagnetic ribbons uncoiling from the earth in their ascent towards the heavens. This natural force had been intuited by Mary and Cleopatra, the moſt renowned of the Egyptian alchemiſts, and their teachings spread widely across the Empire for hundreds of years, revealing the inner workings of our earthly sphere.

Verena was a follower of these gnoſtic alchemiſts and told Félix that service to Mauritius was no longer necessary, for higher forces were now at work. Enough people would die in the coming battle, making his personal sacrifice pointless, and Verena asked the lovers to follow her northward and herald the collapse of Rome. Despite the impending deaths of his friends in *Augunum*, Verena claimed the legion would ultimately prevail, although Félix needed little convincing, given Regula was the first woman he'd ever loved. The three quickly mounted their horses and then sprinted towards the Simme River while Mauritius's infernal ambush unfolded beneath *Les Diablerets*.

After capturing *Augunum* and burying the slaughtered Thebans, Maximian's forces marched eastward to defeat the rebels hiding in the mountains. As I've already explained, fire and stone soon engulfed these 10,000 Romans in an elemental blaze unparalleled throughout recorded history. Word of this disaster eventually reached Emperor Maximian along with rumors of three Theban riders seen riding north just before the ambush. After executing every Roman who knew of this defeat, Maximian ordered one hundred loyal men to capture these riders before their rebellion spread.

Verena and the lovers rode northward for weeks, avoiding the isolated Roman garrisons and telling stories to the indigenous of Emperor Maximian's humiliating blunder. In each settlement, they encouraged the tribes to gather strength for a rebellion, claiming the time was right to break free from Rome. They followed the Aare River to the lakeside tax-post of *Turicum* where they subverted the local Tigurini tribe and began to organize an armed uprising. While they were in this village, Maximian's riders arrived one morning and searched each of the Tigurini lake houses built on wooden pilings. The three rebels were discovered, their horses were decapitated in public, and the commander ordered their execution atop the sacred astrological stone of the Tigurini. The entire village followed the soldiers in silence, their numbers growing along the path, and they watched calmly as the prisoners were bent over the ancient stone. Before the executioner could follow through with his death-swing, the dangling silver Icthys around Verena's neck rubbed against the stone and rang so loudly that

everyone covered their ears. The earth trembled, the air filled with salt, and the sky quivered like the ocean.

Two ribbons of pulsing water uncoiled through the ancient ſtone and hurled the executioner's blade into the river. As water rained on the crowd, Félix removed a concealed blade from his sleeve and slit the executioners throat in a single motion. At this signal, the entire tribe descended on the Romans with bronze daggers, leaving their overlords in a bloody heap. Not a single Imperial survived this quick ambush and Verena remained with the Tigurini once the village was liberated, leaving Félix and Regula to spread the rebellion northward. While these lovers were ſtill young and filled with wonder, Verena had circled the *Mare Noſtrum* three times and was now happy to settle outside *Turicum* where she could praĉtice her ancient science. After gathering the loſt knowledge of the deserts and the seas, Verena had helped the Thebans defeat the moſt powerful empire in the world, an accomplishment she now wished to enjoy in peace. Despite the soundness of her viĉtory, the Empire brutally suppressed the city of Thebes in the year 287 and burned thousands of alchemical texts in Alexandria. These were the laſt gasps of the Cæsars, their petty revenge againſt an opponent they couldn't defeat.

Verena lived alone on the outskirts of *Turicum* and became known throughout the region as a powerful healer. She was jailed several times when Imperial order was temporarily reſtored, although her good reputation with the indigenous prevented the Romans from ever executing her. After dying a natural death in the 330s, the newly religious Empire claimed her as Saint Verena, sole survivor of the Theban Legion. In their Chriſtian hiſtories, Saint Félix and Saint Regula were decapitated by Romans, rose from the dead, and gathered their heads from what soon became the Martyr's Stone. The Chriſtians ereĉted a church around this aſtrological ſtone and excised Verena's water ribbons from their official account. To pacify the indigenous, the Chriſtians named this ſtruĉture the *Wasserkirche*, the Church of Water, although the Proteſtants later deemed this building idolatrous during their Reformation. By that point, the village of *Turicum* was known as Zürich.

Félix and Regula continued on through Germany and then to Denmark before sailing weſt on a small wooden boat. They settled far outside the Empire's reach in a cold and unforgiving land north

Verena

of Hadrian's Wall now known as Scotland. Once they were tracked to this unconquered land, Emperor Constantius and his son Constantine organized an invasion force to silence them. This futile military campaign claimed the life of Constantius and caused the army to mutiny, elevating his son Constantine over the next successor in Rome. Constantine engaged in one final search for Félix and Regula before returning through Hadrian's Wall in abject defeat. He quickly retreated to Rome and forbid any further mention of either Félix or Regula, claiming they'd been beheaded in *Turicum*.

After winning multiple civil wars against a wave of military usurpers, Constantine legalized the male Christian sects in order to crush the more dangerous feminine movement that broke his father's Empire. Unable to face the combined indigenous forces of Europe, Constantine moved the capitol east to Byzantium and accepted Christianity on his deathbed, paving the way for the Holy Roman Empire. Constantine never captured Félix or Regula and the lover's four children eventually intermarried among the indigenous. My mother claims the original Scottish people, the *scoti*, directly descend from Félix and Regula, an open secret that has been garbled over the centuries. Despite the official histories of the Church, neither Félix or Regula were ever Christian, nor were they saints.

1,500 years after these lovers passed away, the Roman colony of *Augunum* had been dubbed *Saint Maurice* in honor of his false crucifixion. Although this religious propaganda may have tricked some indigenous into becoming Christians, not everyone believed these outlandish stories of corpses carrying severed heads or 6,000 Thebans willingly crucified along the Rhône. Among the disbelievers was my grandmother's older cousin Marie-Louise Jacquin, born beneath *Les Diablerets* in the year 1838. While tending goats as a young girl, Marie-Louise was sucked up into a watery tube where she met several naked women nestled inside a green cloud. They revealed to her a river, a suited man, the City of Mary, and a large metal tower pulsing with light. Haunted by this vision through her teenage years, Marie Louise left her village in the summer of 1856 to live along the Rhône.

These visions brought her to *Saint Maurice* where she worked as a laundress near an old church dedicated to the false martyr. When the first iron railroads crept down the Rhône in 1857, Marie-Louise realized the darkness was near and fled south to Torino in the Kingdom of Piedmont where she sewed dresses in a crowded industrial factory. Torino was a center of resistance to Rome, a place where the Pope was flagrantly disparaged and money reigned over God. This city of merchants and industries exposed Marie Louise to the new capitalist empire taking hold over the land and introduced her to its mechanical exploitation of life, body, and soul.

One evening after work, outside a crowded tavern, Marie-Louise met a Burgundian salesman named Jules Fénéon who planned to make it rich selling machine parts to industrialists, although none of these plans ever came to fruition. Instead of becoming a wealthy capitalist, this lanky nomad fell in love with Marie-Louise and they conceived a child in her rented apartment. Over those next blissful months, Marie-Louise told her lover fragments of the long war her family had fought across time and space. After listening intently, Jules vowed to remain with her until death, even if he didn't understand a thing she said. They married after the pregnancy to avoid religious suspicion and lived in Torino until their son was born in the summer of 1861. Marie-Louise named him Félix.

They moved from Torino to escape the industrial nightmare and raised Félix in the Burgundian village of Montpont-en-Bresse. Jules floated from job to job while Marie-Louise rose to superintendent of the local post office, a position she used to communicate with her family in Switzerland. To help Félix attend his distant secondary school, Marie-Louise transferred her post and moved the family to Lugny where they remained for the next years. Her clever son became infamous for fomenting anti-religious sentiment against school instructors and was adored by students for his bravery, eloquence, and long legs. Marie-Louise taught him to speak slowly, precisely, and with confidence, especially when confronting power, and Félix utilized this demonic tongue when the Prussian Empire forced the surrender of Napoleon III. In the middle of the schoolyard, Félix claimed Napoleon III had brought ruin to them all, vowing that their school masters who had once elevated this buffoon would now stand judged by history. His schoolmates never forgot that little speech.

At the age of ten, Félix learned of the Paris Commune and eagerly awaited his mother's updates from the post office. Marie-Louise's little cousin Josephine Lemel was trapped inside those ancient city walls and besieged by two armies, a situation she monitored daily in hope of a miracle. The massacre that followed crushed Félix's spirit but also inspired a thousand revolts inside his heart. He carried this flame to the private *Ecole Normale Speciale* in Cluny where he was known as a penniless firebrand and merciless defender of freedom. His Burgundian uncle paid the tuition but stopped when it became clear Félix was too much like his Swiss mother: stern, unmovable, and fully committed to her interpretation of the truth. Regardless of this judgment, Félix excelled in all subjects, a practice he continued at public school in Mâcon. Félix passed the *baccalaureat* examination in 1879, earning the right to attend any university in France, but rather than follow this path, he was compelled by law to serve in the French Army for five years. With a draft exemption purchased by his mother, Félix only served one year and narrowly

avoided being shipped off to fight in the French colonies of Indochina and Algeria.

Towards the end of his uneventful military service, Félix saw a poster hanging in the mess hall that announced competitive examinations for clerical positions at the War Office in Paris. His mother had taught him to seize every opportunity, so Félix took the exam and easily came in first among all the contestants. Marie-Louise was ecstatic when he came home that spring of 1881 and announced he was moving to Paris where he could monitor the French Republic from inside its own walls. Marie-Louise had always known her path didn't end in Lugny, less than a two days ride from *Les Diablerets*. As it turned out, her path ended in the City of Mary, and now Félix would take her there.

He promised to send for his parents once he established himself and they could all live together, just as they always had. Marie-Louise would soon be able to retire from the post office and live off the pension after twenty years of service, permanently freeing her from wage-labor, while Jules could always take care of himself with odd jobs and hustling. When they eventually moved to Paris in 1885, Félix had risen to head clerk of the War Office and was enmeshed in a world of arts and letters presided over by the forces of Mary. 24-year-old Félix was a government clerk, art critic, publisher, journal editor, and anarchist. Using every means at his disposal, Félix proceeded to subvert the French Republic. At his side was Marie-Louise, guiding him through the fiery years ahead.

SHE'LL TAKE IT SLOW AND STEADY

MY KITCHEN WALL IS LINED WITH GLASS JARS, FILLED TO THE BRIM with our harvest. There's even more coming. Within the month I'll have an entire wall covered in food. I imagine that salmon, fresh from the salt-water, smoked to perfection, preserved in juicy fat, but I won't see any of those jars until we get that wheat down the hill. There's still a week before we load it and I've been writing every night while the others drank, sang, danced themselves to exhaustion. All their work hours are fulfilled, the harvest is distributed, and now's the time to be merry on the patio, to celebrate before the rains turn everything into mud. Maybe I'm just imagining it. A soft patter like a bird walking on the roof. It gets louder and faster and soon its roaring. The roads are going to look like rivers. My day just became a storm.

The jars aren't going anywhere, no matter how hard I look, so I crawl down the ladder to spread some apple butter across yesterday's bread. Drinking tea by the stove sounds good so I get a strong fire going in the stove and once the flames are roaring, I hear the rain snarling like a cougar. I step out onto the porch and sink my fingers into the curtain of droplets, so thick it blurs the soil. I laugh but it doesn't sound like me, the voice echos beyond possibility. That's when I see Paola running through the mud with something clutched to her chest. She bolts up my steps, throws off her hood, and beneath the folds of her jacket I see a ceramic pot wrapped in a towel. It smells steamy and delicious. That was her laughter I heard back there. Not mine.

"You hungry?" she asks. "I made it for both of us. Where were you last night, anyway? One minute I see you on the patio, the next you're gone."

"I came back here after dinner. Kind of vanished, didn't I?"

"You always do that." Paola wipes her face and grins. "You're a sneak!"

I usher her in without responding, only she doesn't seem to mind. Paola sets her red pot on the counter and grabs two bowls from my cupboard like she's been here a thousand times. I peek inside her pot and see two mounds of red, fried corn tortillas mixed with eggs and a big plop of fresh cream sprinkled with green onions. My mouth instantly waters as Paola serves our plates and we eat together beside the roaring stove. I'm ravenous like a beast, as always, and the wood cracks and burns while I scoop up my last mouthful of *chilaquiles*. This dish isn't Brazilian or Portuguese. It's from Mexico.

"Where'd you learn to cook?" I ask. "I only ever eat food like this in San Francisco."

"I lived in Los Angeles. They taught me to cook down there. And to pound tortillas."

"It's delicious, Paola. I would have just eaten bread and apple butter if you hadn't come."

"Stay up late writing? Like a sneaky owl?"

I feel myself grow tense so I nod my head and keep asking about tortillas. Paola describes the grinding, pounding, flattening, cooking, but all the while she's looking at my desk, at my notebook. I change the subject to acorns because they're vaguely similar, I ramble on about the laborious leeching and grinding process but she doesn't listen to a thing I say. It's pointless.

"What are your men like?" she finally asks. "Where are they?"

"What do you mean *our* men?"

"From the valley where your grandmother was born. What are the men like?"

"They don't ask nearly as many questions as you, that's for sure. But okay, okay. I don't...the people who are still there, you know...they live a pretty simple life, kind of like us. Make cheese, build stone houses, walk around with goats, that type of thing. Boring, ordinary, pastoral. The men up there, yeah, they know this history I'm writing, all the secrets I'm trying to collect, but they don't make any of the decisions. Only we do. The women. And it's been that way forever. Since the beginning of time."

Paola smacks her lips, leans back in her chair, and smirks at me.

"Angelo didn't know the truth about your family?" she asks. "Did he?"

The filthy rat. She found it. The raw crux of all my problems, the virgin source of my maternal betrayal. Now I have to answer this little devil. That's why she called me sneaky, setting me up like a crafty house-mother. Instead of answering, I take our dirty bowls to the washtub and drop them in the dirty water where they plop into the murk and release bubbles of dark red oil up to the surface. Paola's looking at me, I can feel her eyes burning my hair, so I wipe my hands and walk over to the fire.

"No, of course he didn't know anything," I say. "How could he if I didn't know anything? It's one thing to betray a stupid girl in love, but it's another to betray a witch who rarely picks a man. Only I didn't know who I was, or what I'm capable of, what my family's capable of."

"I don't understand."

This is more than I've told anyone, even Gertrude and Annabelle.

"My mom hid everything from me, Paola! They all did. Isabelle, Yvonne, her daughter Juana, my aunt Bianca, my aunt Beatrix, even Josephine. They wanted me to have all the chances they never had, and look what happened to me! So bravo, Paola! You've got a sharp mind, no doubt. Angelo had no idea who he was dealing with. And neither did I. So there you go!"

"That's why you're writing it?" she asks, clearly excited. "To figure out who you are?"

"Maybe. And one day we can walk down to the coast and have it printed and bound and I'll give you the first copy. But I need to write it first. So just leave me alone until then."

"I'm not trying to cause trouble," she says. "I just want to understand what happened."

"Me too. That's why I'm staying up all night, *sneaking around*. Before my mom told me the truth about all this...do you even remember what I was like? For months I was in the library, at my desk, combing through history books, looking for who I was. It was buried, barely visible between the lines, and I just needed those pieces from Isabelle and Yvonne to figure out the rest. I come from a line of women who...it's true what Angelo said. They're killers, and witches, and I'm the first one of them to grow up in a peaceful world. I'm their broken little experiment."

Paola looks at the ground when I start crying. She's kind enough to change the subject, and I watch the fire burn into coal as she narrates her time on a commune outside Los Angeles. I don't really pay attention, just enough to respond. The rain throbs like a wild octopus and Paola looks real content there by the stove. I need some excuse to leave but can't be too quick about it, otherwise she'll suspect something. She feeds more wood into the flames before I can stop her, settles back into the couch, and tells me about the indigenous tribes of the *Tierra del Fuego* who light a hundred nightly fires along their frozen coast. She has no intention of leaving the house, she keeps talking about her travels up the Pacific coast, so I wait for a pause and then get up to wash the dishes. It's nice and warm in the house, so warm I don't want to leave. Do I really want to go? Do I really want to do this?

"Listen, thanks for breakfast," I say. "But I need to get ready."

"Ready for what? You're going out? In the rain?"

"I told my mom I'd be there for lunch. I want to talk about her childhood."

Paola grows silent, casts me an iron glare, then glances over at my desk. I'll have to wait until she leaves before hiding the notebook. There's no way I'm taking it out in the rain. Paola grins like the thought of reading it never occurred to her before she gathers her ceramic pot from the kitchen counter. I kiss her cheeks, thank her for the food, and notice she casts a final glance at my notebook. This one never gives up. That's why I like her. She reminds me of who I should have been when I was her age. Paola might be clumsy, but she's got a more shapely figure than my gentle Gertrude, and maybe I like that about her too. I want to hold her by the cheeks and tell her, *tomorrow you'd better use your soft hands to tear off dill shoots, to cap your lovely curls. She who wear flowers attracts the happy Graces. They turn away from a bare head.* I want to say all that, but it might seem a bit crazy.

Paola throws on her black jacket, gives me a wink, and bolts down the muddy road clutching her ceramic pot. Once she's gone, I bring the notebook upstairs and hide it in the oak treasure chest with my other writing. I don't remember where I put the lock, but there's no way she'd climb into my loft, not unless she's insane, so it's probably safe. Even if Paola reads a few pages, she won't understand anything, not even the basics. I still haven't described how our transmission towers were first visualized by an anarchist painter in Paris, let alone the rest. None of it will make sense, she won't know how the system works, or even how it was created, but I hide the notebook just the same. On the off chance she does open my treasure chest, Paola's still going to have to wait for the truth.

I climb down the wooden ladder and slip into my rain boots for the journey. It's still pouring outside but these dry hills surely need it. I put on my black oilskin, close the iron stove, walk out the front door, and plunge into the torrent of a thousand droplets. There's a long finger of brown water draining through the center of the logging road but I walk on the edge where the soil is still visible. I have to pull my feet from the sticky mud with each step and it doesn't get any easier, not even when the slope flattens out near the saw-mill. No one's there except for shadows. All the blades are motionless.

I smell my mother's wood-smoke before I see it. The scent gets stronger at the summit where I glimpse her barren corn fields overflowing with water. It's hard to see anything in this rain but there's a light shining downstairs, probably my mom reading by the fire. We'll see if I'm right. I hop through the flooded vegetable garden, bound up the front steps, and then feel a blast of warm air hit my face. My mother's already got the door wide open. She can hear my footsteps in the rain, apparently.

"What the hell are you doing, Fulvia?" she asks. "Are you alone?"

"No, I brought the whole village. They're just down the road."

"Get inside!" she yells. "*Andale!* Least you've got the sense to dress like a sailor. Must have some wits left in that skull. What if the land slid down the hill? Huh?" She pushes me roughly with two fingers. "What if the mud buried you and no one heard you scream?"

"What if the Martians got me? You know I'm an adult, right? Come on. What's for lunch?"

"Lunch? You didn't tell me you were coming, Fulvia. I haven't seen you in weeks."

She closes the door behind us and gets me out of the oilskin. It's not because she wants to help crazy Fulvia, it's more like I'll get water everywhere and it's better if she does it, just like everything else. She thinks I'm a mess, that I'll track in mud, that I'll cause an earthquake, but she hangs the oilskin by the stove without saying a word. I leave my dirty boots near the front door and warm my hands over the ſtove until Isabelle clunks on the tea-kettle. Both of us hover there, waiting for it to boil.

"I hear you figured out your problems in the village," she says. "You going to sit down?"

"No, I'm going to ſtand right here by the ſtove. By the way, I didn't see you down in the village, not in weeks. So where did you hear this from, exactly? That I solved all my problems?"

"Yvonne told me. Who else? You know she hears everything, right? She said you found Angelo. Or didn't find him. I don't care. He's gone, so you better not go back into your shell. Otherwise they'll ſtart missing Angelo and wish it was you who left the commune, not him."

"I didn't come here for a lecture, *mama*. I'm fine. I came to talk about San Francisco. Those ſtories you told me when I was a kid, about Félix and Marisol—"

"Sit down already!"

"Fine!" I throw myself on the couch and wait for her to join me. "Juſt... say whatever comes into your head about San Francisco, *mama*. About when you were born. That's where I'm at right now in the hiſtory. Isabelle's about to be born. You! So tell me something. Anything!"

My mom dœsn't answer, too mesmerized by the flames, so I ſtare across the room at the *Black Square* hanging on the opposite wall, unable to bear her silence. Now I'm definitely a child again. This is beyond *deja vu*. When my shell-shocked mother was silent after the war, I looked at this black square and beheld my imagination dancing in the paint. It was here I learned to answer my own queſtions.

"All these years you've been lying," I say. "All these years you've been toying with me. I know you've got plenty to say, you juſt aren't saying it. You know how many times I've been sitting here juſt like this, waiting for you to the tell me the truth? I was right, my whole childhood I was right—"

"Fine! Juſt wait a moment if you really want to hear."

"Hear what? More silence?"

She dœsn't look at me, dœsn't answer, dœsn't do anything. All she dœs is ſtare across the room and fill this silence with the *Black Square*. Above our heads hangs the *Peasant Woman in Two Dimensions*, the red square pulsing with light, hanging directly opposite the *Black Square*. I can hear my mother's thoughts in that old paint, a subtle hiss that tears and scrapes againſt the back of my mind. I heard those same whispered thoughts when I was a child, sitting on this same short-legged couch, but I thought it was all a daydream, a childhood hallucination, the product of an active imagination. These two paintings have always been my secret mothers. Isabelle was juſt the woman who birthed me.

"Whatever happened to Kazimir?" I ask her. "After the war?"

"He left me these paintings at the train station. I never saw him again. Last I heard he was on a commune in the Ukraine. No one's heard from him, not since the '20s. He's probably dead."

"Did he keep painting?"

"I don't think so. He said the only path for art was off the canvas. Art was our future."

I look away from the black square and find my mother gazing at me, her green eyes burning with spectral vision. She tells me the truth without warning. At first she rambles on about the little blue house on Greenwich Street, the children who lived on the slopes, and the thousand secrets they kept for Marisol de la Costa. My mother throws more wood in the stove, stares at the flames for a minute, then tells me about an alter she found in Marisol's bedroom, dedicated to a skeleton shaped like the Virgin Mary. A red hood covered the skeleton's skull and a metal scale hung in her bony white hand. There were lemons, oranges, a few unlit sticks of incense, and black candles left as offerings. My mom describes the smells, the rough texture of the incense, the scent of citrus fruit, the muted sunlight hanging in the room, but she stops when the kettle boils.

"Don't get up," I say. "I'll do it. Keep talking. What was the shrine for?"

"You've never seen a shrine to the skinny lady?"

"No." I carry the kettle into the kitchen but make sure she's looking at me. "What is it?"

"They call her *Nuestra Señora de la Santa Muerte*, but she's ancient, older than Mary, from way before Aztec times. They called her *Mictēcacihuātl*, and she guarded part of their underworld, *Mictlān*, the land of the dead. They stuffed her inside the Virgin to keep her alive in our world, here, with us."

I fill the ceramic pot with strands of black tea, pour in hot water, and bring it back to the living room with two cups. That's when I step backwards in time. I'm inside the little blue house. I see the emerald San Francisco Bay writhing outside the window, I see a Chinese painting on the wall, I feel a Persian carpet beneath my feet, but all that flickers away until there's just my mother squatting beside the stove. She always told me to keep my hips low to the ground because *that's how we stay young.* Whenever I got carried away, Isabelle was always there to ground me, and hopefully this tea will make her spew more ancient wisdom, the only truth she's ever capable of. I know she's telling me about this *Santa Muerte* for a reason, so when the tea's done steeping, I force a cup into her brown hands.

"Why are you telling me about *her*?" I ask. "I want to know about *you*, *mama!*"

"Settle down. I'm not done with my story."

"Any day then, *mama*. I'm waiting."

"I told you how Josephine went into mourning after my father died, but I never told you what happened. My brothers never talked about it either, I think they forgot about it. Our mother just froze, Fulvia! Froze! Like a zombie. Sergio was oldest. He didn't know what to do. This was our mother! Do you understand how strong my mother was? She was frozen! For a week! She couldn't move!"

Isabelle's crying like I've never seen before. She tries to wipe the tears away but it's no use, they just keep coming, so I nudge myself in close and wrap my arms around her bony shoulders. She feels helpless, like when her father died, but this vulnerability ends quicker than it began. She takes her first sip of tea and then kisses me in thanks. Her tears are gone. Her eyes are still burning red.

"Anyway...Marisol comes over eventually," she continues. "This was after we moved to our own apartment. Marisol comes inside, tries to wake up Josephine, but it doesn't work. She screams, cries, shakes my mother like a rag doll. Nothing works. I remember seeing Marisol with red eyes. Redder than mine are right now. Red like this square. Pure red, no pupil. It terrified me then, it'd terrify me now, but Marisol stormed out of the apartment before I got a good look. She didn't say anything, she just left us. I remember the door slamming shut. Lorenzo was crying, Federico was scared, Sergio was alone. So I waited until dark and crept out of the apartment. I wasn't even six years-old but I made it to the little blue house by myself. I walked into Marisol's bedroom, saw her kneeling in front of that shrine, only she wasn't looking at the skinny lady, she was looking at me, and now her eyes weren't red. She says to me, 'Oh, so the skinny one sends you.' Then she picks me up and starts singing."

This is what I can't stand. These long pauses. She does it on purpose, always in the middle of something important, a cheap trick to build tension. I used to scream at her for this exact reason. I used to yell and demand she respond exactly how I wanted her to. Now I sit with clenched fingers while my mother looks deep into my thoughts, waiting for me to calm down, just like when I was a child.

"Why did you come here, Fulvia?"

"I wanted to get away from Paola. She was asking too many questions."

"Yvonne's told me about your new friend. What questions did she ask you?"

"Don't change the subject. Finish the story."

"What's to finish? What do I need to explain? She called to me through the underworld. She called to me from that shrine. She asked *Santa Muerte* for the strength to avenge my father. And it was *me* who arrived. I was that ſtrength. I was that revenge. Do you see? She loved my father like a brother, a real brother. Remember, she didn't love *any man* besides her father and Sigismund, ever. We were all a family and...Marisol couldn't ſtand seeing Josephine frozen like that. So she asked *Santa Muerte* for the ſtrength to deſtroy our enemies. And there I was, called through the underworld."

"Is that how she called to Josephine in Switzerland? From her shrine?"

My mother's green eyes suddenly lock into fright. She didn't expeɕt me to put that together.

"You're more perceptive than you let on, Fulvia. Don't hide your thoughts. It's unfair."

"It's the only way to get the truth out of you."

"Well, there's the truth. Is that enough? Tell me you underſtand."

It's more than enough, but I can't say that, not right now, not when she's telling it, so I give her the same silent treatment she always gives me. I don't remember my mother ever crying about the death of her father. She's desperate for me to speak, but all I want to do is liſten, and over the next few hours I lose myself in the final days of my beloved grandfather, Antonio Ferrari.

10

THE SAILOR WHO PLUNGED INTO THE SEA

WHILE HER RELATIVE FÉLIX FÉNÉON FOMENTED REBELLION against the French Republic, Josephine Lemel became pregnant with my mother Isabelle. It happened during the winter of 1887 while her three boys were playing on the hillside, a spare moment of freedom in their little blue house on Greenwich Street. Marisol heard Josephine and Antonio's moans as she smoked her cigarettes and drank coffee on the front porch, doing her beſt not to laugh. A few days later, Josephine told Marisol they were moving out once her daughter was born. There simply wasn't enough room when Antonio was back from sea, let alone with a fourth child. As Josephine's belly grew larger, Marisol's little blue house filled with the promise of a now forgotten emptiness. After these long years of raising the three Ferrari boys, Marisol would be left alone, juſt as she was when Josephine met her.

My grandfather had juſt returned from South America brimming with plans and was now eager to resume organizing the waterfront. During his ſtay in Buenos Aires, my grandfather met with Errico Malateſta, a prominent

Italian member of the International now exiled to this verdant port, along with hundreds of other anarchists. Compared to their previous situations, the coastal metropolis of Buenos Aires was a relief to these weary rebels, although despite its immense natural beauty, the nation-state of Argentina was ruled by an oligarchy so corrupt even the bourgeois liberals were starting to rebel.

While living in Buenos Aires, Antonio helped Malatesta form an anarchist bakers union, the *Sociedad Cosmopolita de Resistencia y Colocación de Obreros Panaderos,* an organization that shared its profits equally and bestowed subversive names upon each of its pastries. At the time, most workers submitted an invoice to the boss accounting for their hours worked. Subverting this arrangement, the anarchist baker's union referred to all of their pastries as *facturas*, the Spanish word for invoice, and submitted them to the general public in exchange for their wages, bypassing the boss entirely. They gave their *facturas* names like *bolas de fraile*, or balls of the priest, and openly mocked the police with their *vigilante*, a sugar-stuffed pastry shaped like a wooden baton. The working people of Buenos Aires fell in love with these sweet, cheap, humorous *facturas* sold from dozens of anarchist bakeries across the city. Hundreds of thousands of people still eat Argentine *facturas* every morning with *maté* or *café*, although few know my grandfather helped create these delicious pastries.

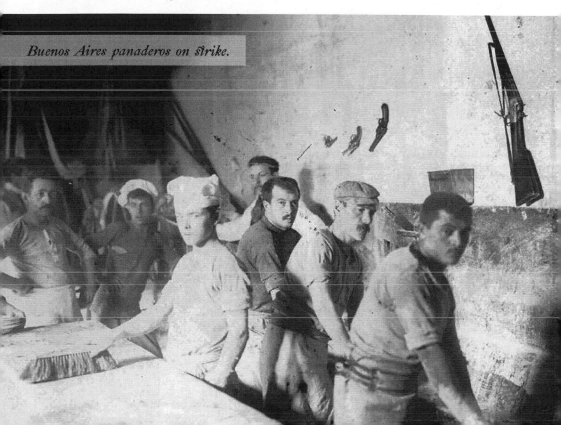

Buenos Aires panaderos on strike.

In this heavenly city of Buenos Aires, Antonio also printed an anarchist paper with Errico Malatesta and spoke to his Argentine comrades about the recent waterfront strike in San Francisco. Malatesta suggested that their International organize the next waterfront strike in London, given the exhaustion of their San Francisco comrades, and Antonio agreed it would take years for his union to regain its former strength. He sailed away from Buenos Aires in the winter of 1887, his mind boiling over with fantasies of a global maritime strike, and when he arrived back at Greenwich Street, my grandmother was waiting on the front porch. Rather than discuss these plans with him, Josephine walked Antonio into their bedroom and became pregnant with her first and only daughter: Isabelle Lemel Ferrari. The morning after she was conceived, a rare winter snow storm swept over the region, turning all of the distant peaks a heavenly white. From Mount Tamalapais to beyond the Coast Range, Josephine beheld a landscape that almost resembled the land of her birth.

During my grandfather's absence, the Coast Sailor's Union had regathered its power under the guidance of Andrew Furuseth, secret member of the International and committed defender of sailors. He inaugurated the publication of the *Coast Seamen's Journal*, fought the ship-owners, and grew the union war-chest by thousands of dollars. After his return from South America, Antonio and Josephine met with Furuseth in his small waterfront apartment to discuss a puzzling development: after being ejected from the Federated Trades Council, their former comrade Burnett Haskell had created the Steamship Sailor's Union and spread his Marxist ideas to its exploited coal-drags and firemen. The introduction of steam engines had created a new class of sailors who knew little of rigging, masts, or the wind. Instead, they hauled coal into infernal boiler-rooms, shoveled coal into raging furnaces, swept coal-dust off iron floors, and monitored a labyrinth of steam-pipes. Sailboats still dominated the Pacific coastline in the late 1880s and most steamships carried sails in case of engine failure.

Errico Malatesta

No one trusted this new technology, nor did anyone organize these modern workers besides crazy Haskell.

After learning of this development, Josephine climbed up the window fire-escape to Haskell's apartment, hid in the shadows until he returned, and made him scream in terror when she said *hello*. At the end of their brief conversation, Haskell had agreed to Josephine's strange demands, fearing the dark consequences if he didn't. Despite his deep reservations, my grandmother's plan proved itself flawless. Over the next few months, the Coast Sailor's Union and the Steamship Sailor's Union feigned a labor conflict in order to confuse the ship-owners and flush out informants, with most of these provocateurs later found floating in the bay under mysterious circumstances. As the two maritime unions engaged in this false conflict, monthly wages for all sailors began to rise.

Andrew Furuseth never trusted Haskell and tolerated this arrangement only because of his faith in Josephine and Antonio. My grandparents met at Furuseth's monkish apartment every week to discuss strategy and envision a waterfront federation capable of shutting down the port. Josephine was fond of Furuseth but others found him stern, unmovable, and without an ounce of joy. Although he possessed a guarded and chiseled exterior, my grandmother could always make Furuseth smile, a miracle few were capable of. Josephine loved the frenzy of these strategic discussions and stayed in Furuseth's apartment late into the night speaking of ancient lands and distant seas. Sigismund Danielewicz often joined them with a bottle of red wine and his dozen tales of mermaids, crimps, and great white sharks. Despite the joy of these nocturnal encounters, Josephine's visits with Furuseth soon came to an end.

My mother Isabelle Lemel Ferrari was born on November 23rd, 1887, into the hands of Marisol de la Costa. Isabelle had the emerald green eyes and dark black hair of her ancestors, although her skin was dark like Antonio's. Isabelle was calm, tranquil, observant, and she never cried on first day of life, not even when Antonio bathed her in tears of joy. She slept peacefully on Josephine's breast and would reach for the nearest light whenever she woke. During these first weeks of nursing, Marisol convinced my grandmother to stay on Greenwich Street and let the boys find housing with their father. Antonio had no objection to this plan, having grown weary of the cramped quarters, and he immediately took Sergio into the heart of the Latin Quarter. Acting on a hunch, he went to the offices of *Il Messaggero*, an anti-religious Italian newspaper, and found a single man cranking the printing-press.

This printer was Cesare Crespi, an exile from Milano who'd run away with Giuseppina Alberti, the wife of a Piedmontese knight. Having read Crespi's fiery columns against both Pope and Church, Antonio believed this editor might be a kindred spirit. After a long discussion over cake and cigarettes,

Antonio learned Cesare and Giuseppina had eloped to Scotland in 1881 before crossing the Atlantic to meet her son Enrico in New York City. The Piedmontese knight had given his son a choice and Enrico elected to stay with his book-loving mother rather than rot in his paternal luxury. This unorthodox family soon moved from New York in 1883 and settled in the Latin Quarter of San Francisco where Enrico was now enrolled in public school. In the years after his arrival, Cesare had come to know all the Italians in the neighborhood and offered to help Antonio find an apartment. According to him, most of the Italian landlords were greedy, although a few would help a young family in need. Within a week, Cesare had found a wealthy Genovese widow who was offering a one-bedroom apartment for twenty dollars a month, low enough for a sailor to raise his family. In those days, every Italian was connected to the sea, having just arrived across its back.

In the winter of 1888, Antonio and his sons moved their belongings over Telegraph Hill to a wooden apartment building on the corner of Vallejo and Montgomery, they very center of the Latin Quarter. They climbed the stairs to the second floor, opened all the windows, and while little Federico played on the floor, his brothers helped Antonio carry furniture and wooden boxes up the creaky stairs. Josephine couldn't have been happier. Over the past fifteen years, she and Marisol had destroyed the crimping trade, assassinated the most ruthless pimps, and made the Barbary Coast into a safer place for women. Josephine had no desire to leave this little blue house or the magical woman who'd offered her shelter when she needed it most, and so 1888 passed with the four Ferrari men in the Latin Quarter and the three witches on Greenwich Street, both living according to separate pathways.

When my mother was just five months old, Josephine fastened her in a sling and carried her to the first meeting of the Federated Council of Wharf and Wave Unions. In the two years since the defeat of their waterfront strike, every maritime trade union had enlisted its members in this council, and with their combined strength they constituted a force of nearly 30,000 men. Burnett Haskell stood with the *Illuminati* during this inaugural meeting and glared at Antonio the whole time, never looking Josephine in the eyes. Despite the anarchists and Marxists publicly agreeing to cooperate for the common good, Haskell and the *Illuminati* continued to harass my grandparents once the meeting was over; spreading vicious rumors about them along the docks, claiming that all anarchists were government agents, and making secret alliances with the criminal underworld.

Josephine had no patience for this treachery and stalked the *Illuminati* through San Francisco while Marisol watched little Isabelle. After enough of this clandestine shadowing, Josephine assembled the proof she needed to purge Haskell forever. The IWA was disbanded in 1889 with Haskell removed from the Coast Sailor's Union for forming a secret society within its ranks. The definitive blow came with his permanent ejection from the Steamship Sailor's Union after it amalgamated with the Sailor's Union, effectively exiling him from the waterfront. What remained of the old days soon passed into oblivion. Where there was once only bigotry and exploitation, there was now a militant sailor's union that could secure safe passage for their comrades across the globe.

Telegraph Hill and waterfront

Andrew Furuseth came up for reelection as union secretary in 1889 but preferred to ship out as a common sailor rather than be driven power-mad like Burnett Haskell, although Josephine suspected hidden motives. Unlike the majority of sailors, Furuseth never lusted after women, making him the perfect union leader. The love he felt towards his men was boundless and Josephine came to believe he'd lost a lover to the lashes of a captain. His maritime organizing was the only way to avenge this young man he'd once loved below deck, the secret passion that propelled all his militancy. Since he'd become secretary, the union had increased to over 2,000 members, secured its own meeting hall, and released an issue of the *Coast Seamen's Journal* every week. Furuseth sailed out the Golden Gate in 1889, confident his union would survive as he searched for love in their miserable world. If there was any trouble with the ship-owners, the Queens would always be watching from Telegraph Hill.

My mother Isabelle was now over a year old and Josephine made no effort to join her family in their new apartment. She remained on Greenwich Street to breast-feed Isabelle, cook late lunches with Marisol, and read dozens of modern books. Antonio and the boys had dinner with her every evening and stayed until after sundown before walking back to the Latin Quarter. Given how central it was to the anarchist movement, their daily routine was very simple: in the mornings, Antonio roused his three sons from bed, left Federico and Lorenzo their lesson plans, and took Sergio down to the union hall for a quick breakfast. This father-and-son team hooked wooden boxes under blankets of fog, cracked jokes with sailors lowering the cargo, and conspired with their comrades during lunch. These impromptu huddles occurred at the head of every wharf, dock, and pier, connecting the sailors who delivered the cargo, the stevedores who hooked the cargo, and the teamsters who drove the cargo. During these days on the waterfront, Sergio watched his father recruit new members, listened to him speak in crowded meeting halls, and fought by his side during waterfront brawls. At night, their family ate dinner on Greenwich Street where Antonio held Isabelle in his lap and remembered what he was fighting for. Josephine cherished these evening meals, having fallen into a state of blissful serenity that puzzled even Marisol. Josephine had no desire to leave Telegraph Hill and never ventured further than the dirt road outside their door. My grandmother was thirty-nine years old, just older than I am now, and the future held only promise.

In the early summer of 1889, a comrade from Buenos Aires arrived in San Francisco and found Antonio at the crowded sailor's hall. When they were alone in one of the offices, he informed Antonio that Errico Malatesta was currently headed for London to organize their next waterfront blockade. In less than a month, the Great Dock Strike broke out along the Thames River. After a round of anarchist propaganda, public speaking, and printed fliers, nearly 50,000 casual dock-workers formed a union and refused to move any cargo off the river-port. Their dock strike quickly spread to 130,000 other sailors, stevedores, and teamsters, paralyzing all commerce on the Thames. As the wheels of capitalism came to a halt, the union fed the hungry children of these dock-workers and organized their survival during the long siege. While the anarchists of the International pushed for a general strike,

the dock-workers ultimately settled for receiving six pence a day instead of five. Despite this outcome, the Great Dock Strike lasted nearly a month, crippled the economy of London, and inspired workers across the globe. If these humble river people could shut down the very heart of the British Empire, they could surely do the same to San Francisco.

In the year 1890, my uncle Federico joined his father and Sergio as a waterfront longshoreman, leaving Lorenzo in the apartment to study science, literature, art, and mathematics. This unusual family arrangement became common-knowledge in the tiny Italian community and my uncles were often seen roaming the Latin Quarter at night like a pack of benevolent wolves. Inspired by their freedom, Cesare Crespi's adopted son Enrico skipped school one morning, sought out my grandfather in the crowded union hall, told him he wanted to sail the Pacific, and hooked crates with the Ferraris for a few weeks until Antonio placed him on a cargo ship bound for Vladivostok. Cesare and Giussepina stood on the Greenwich pier as Enrico sailed off towards the Golden Gate, their cheeks covered in tears, their imaginations pregnant with disaster. No one heard from Enrico after that, not for many years.

Shortly after he departed, the Union Iron Works announced production of several war cruisers for the modern US Navy, auguring a new maritime imperialism, and the Ferraris helped plan a militant response. With the *USS San Francisco* and *USS Charleston* already menacing the Pacific Ocean, these anarchists resolved to sabotage the next round of war construction with a waterfront strike. The Union Iron Works had secured contracts to build the *USS Olympia*, the *USS Monterey*, and the *USS Oregon*, each destined for a mysterious battle somewhere on the Pacific. At the same time, warships were being built for the Imperial Japanese Navy at British shipyards in Newcastle, their hulls made with steel from the Heath Steal Company. These state-of-the-art warships were powered by steam, built entirely of metal, and required skilled workers to create. When wages for iron molders dropped in anticipation of this new war-boom, the anarchists of San Francisco took this chance to rouse the local shipbuilders into a strike. Without warning, all the foundries were suddenly shut down by massive pickets, including the Union Iron Works. This violent waterfront struggle lasted from the spring of 1890 until the fall of 1891, costing the iron bosses over $5,000,000. Stones and fists were thrown outside the factory gates, scabs were beaten in dark alleys, and two workers lost their lives before the federal government canceled future military contracts. All the strikers were rehired, wages were never reduced, and the mysterious Pacific war was delayed, however temporarily.

While these shipyards were still blockaded, the Sailor's Union opened a brand new hiring hall on March 19, 1891, solidifying their hold on the Pacific. Every sailor who worked the coast now had to be hired through this building, giving the union absolute labor supremacy. Andrew Furuseth returned to San Francisco amid this renaissance and reluctantly resumed his duties as secretary, unable to resist the pleas of his comrades. Before he could have a proper reunion with Antonio and Josephine, renegade sailors staged a wildcat strike in San Diego, demanding more money from the bosses and calling for a coast-wide solidarity strike. Furuseth met with my grandparents and frantically stated that if the union supported this wildcat strike, the other branches would soon demand the same wage. If the bosses refused this demand, the union would be forced to play their hand early without any advance preparation. After a moment of silence, Josephine told Furuseth it was his decision.

The very next day, Furuseth shipped a scab crew to San Diego and delivered a simple message to the wildcat sailors: act without us and we'll leave you behind. The scab crew fulfilled their order for the capitalists and sailed the cargo to its intended port, an action that staved off conflict but did nothing to endear Furuseth to the sailors, who labeled him a tool of the bosses. To make matters even worse, the ship-owners dropped wages for coastal sailors from 40 to 30 dollars a month. Rather than respond to the slander leveled against him, Furuseth resigned in April of 1892, signed onto a deep-sea fishing boat, and the Queens of the Coast watched him sail away from the front porch of their little blue house, disappointed beyond words. No one knew it then, but this was the beginning of the dark times.

Once stubborn Furuseth had departed, the ship-owners revived the crimp racket, forcing my grandparents to join the sailors in nightly street battles against this old foe, a conflict that soon claimed multiple lives. No matter how much they hammered at this net-work of crimps, the ship-owners found other greedy men to replace them. Dynamite exploded, masts were sawed down in the fog, and a dozen skulls were cracked with cobblestones, all to no effect. The crimps kept popping up like mushrooms, nurtured by an invisible financier. Amid all this violent chaos, the sailor's begged Furuseth to return as union secretary and he agreed on one condition: his monthly wage be the same as a common fisherman. With this demand satisfied, Furuseth returned that June of 1892 to an unrecognizeable waterfront beset by darkness. The recent loss of military contracts at the Union Iron Works cemented the reputation of San Francisco as a city hostile to business, a public image the bosses hoped to erase by crushing the sailors. The capitalists had always lowered wages and funded crimps during labor conflicts, but this latest assault was relentless. A mysterious force was now in control of the situation, although no one knew who it was, nor could they attack it.

With war burning along the waterfront, Marisol's mother Rosita returned after many years as an insurgent outlaw. She arrived aboard the Oakland ferry and calmly walked past dozens of bruised sailors guarding the wharves. She carried a single colorful bag and wore a simple black dress, brand new. During the past twenty years of her life, Rosita had only worn pants, making this dress slightly uncomfortable. Her thighs were rough as leather, her skin dark as cinnamon, and her face riven with time's thousand disasters. She found her little blue house just as she left it, only now with some new friends. Marisol stared blankly at Rosita when she first entered, her eyes numb in disbelief. Neither made any effort to greet each other. Josephine embraced Rosita, introduced 4-year-old Isabelle, then hid away in the bedroom while the de la Costas began to speak, then to talk, then to weep loudly like coyotes. Unable to stand this sadness, Josephine waited until nightfall, packed her bags, and moved with Isabelle over the hill into the Latin Quarter, leaving Marisol no chance to protest. For the next five months, she lived alone with her mother Rosita.

During this long reunion, Marisol learned that her father Joaquin died in 1887 during an ambush outside Chico and Rosita buried him near their sacred cave in a hole deep enough to stop the bears. All the old San Joaquin Valley outlaws were either fleeing, captured, or almost caught, although a few bands of indigenous horse-riders still held their mountain villages. Rosita explained how she'd tried to stop the *yanqui* invasion but money just kept flowing no matter how many tracks, bridges, and tunnels she blew up. As long as poor people were desperate, they could be hired to rebuild anything, and the true enemy lay at the root of all those iron tracks. Someone controlled this metal empire who was neither President, King, or Emperor, but Rosita didn't know who he was. The skinny lady would soon gather her up and with these last months on Greenwich Street she hoped to conduct her final assault against this same empire, though she couldn't do it alone. On a foggy evening atop Telegraph Hill, the two de la Costas bowed before the goddess *Santa Muerte* and began to spin a web of energy that spilled outward in all directions. This ancient force from before the Aztecs was soon free to dance across the city, its power increasing day by day. That summer, a chasm into the underworld opened up along the San Francisco waterfront, infecting everyone's nightly dreams. Inflamed by this mysterious new power, the Coast Seamen's Union voted to begin their full waterfront blockade and soon thousands of union men choked off the piers and wharves, stopping commerce dead for weeks. At their backs was the skull-faced woman dressed in red, a golden scale clutched by her bony white hand.

Antonio and my uncles fought on the waterfront every day during this second maritime strike of 1892, pushing hired drunks off the wharves and preventing them from boarding ships. When the Ferrari men slept after these long battles, Josephine would often leave her apartment dressed as *Yee Toy*. Night after foggy night, this infamous assassin eliminated the crimps, the paymasters, and their hired guards, returning in the morning to tell five-year-old Isabelle everything she'd done, sparing no details. As she slept into the late afternoon, her sons organized *dummy* crews to join scab cargo ships and desert at the last moment, tying up the harbor in a backlog of vessels. Outside of these exceptional activities, the Ferrari men occupied their time standing at pickets, shivering in the fog, and waiting in line for spaghetti dished out by union volunteers. Unable to resist his own nocturnal mania, Antonio left the apartment alone on multiple occasions to cut the lines of scab ships so they drifted away unnoticed, some even reaching the ocean. Josephine observed from a distance and was always ready to rescue him. Antonio could be silent as a thief, but his lover heard every thought in his head.

After many weeks of this *petit guerre*, the crimps were losing power, the bosses near defeat, but then total darkness enveloped San Francisco. The Ship-Owners Association mysteriously acquired a new secretary from the east coast along with an infusion of cash that flowed to the crimps, pushing them back towards supremacy. Rosita and Marisol stayed up late chanting to *Santa Muerte* and stoking her power against this darkness, often going days without food, and as the sailors resumed their battle against the crimps, the stock market of the United States abruptly collapsed.

For the past several years, a consortium of London banks diverted money into the economies of Argentina and Uruguay to finance their railroads and farmland. When the Argentine wheat crop failed, *yanqui* investors traded in their Federal Reserve notes to the US Treasury, drastically lowering gold supplies and creating fear in the national economy. Mimicking the high capitalists, common people withdrew their own savings, the banks predictably went bankrupt, and the federal government couldn't rescue them with empty gold reserves. This great Panic of 1893 was orchestrated by the House of Morgan, financiers of the first undersea telegraph cable and investors in the American railroads. Their manufactured crisis would ultimately force President Grover Cleveland to borrow over 60 million dollars from JP Morgan, JD Rockefeller, and Leopold de Rothschild, locking the federal government in permanent debt to the banks. Meanwhile, the army of unemployed workers soon mushroomed in size, driving down wages and emboldening the crimps of San Francisco.

Antonio's comrade from Buenos Aires arrived on the waterfront in the midst of this economic depression and found my grandfather recovering from a street battle inside the Bulkhead Saloon. Over a glass of wine, he explained how the liberals of Buenos Aires had finally turned on the oligarchs and the anarchists were helping to organize an impending insurrection. Argentina could no longer pay its debts to London or Wall Street and investors were wary, making it the perfect time to strike. Shortly after this comrade left, the Argentine Revolution broke out in 1893. My grandfather was inspired when he learned 8,000 armed men had seized the capitol city of Buenos Aires, although the situation in San Francisco was anything but inspiring.

The sailor's had taken the desperate measure of using their war chest to pay for unemployed members to live with their families in the countryside rather than work for the crimps. The union tried to maintain their waterfront blockades but were overwhelmed by the army of unemployed workers who boarded idle merchant ships, hoisted the idle cargo, and sailed off with the meager prospect of earning 20 dollars a month, half of what union members were usually paid. It was a humiliating defeat, more than Josephine could bare, and

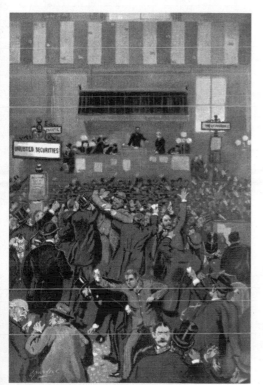

Panic of 1893

she hid with Isabelle inside their Latin Quarter apartment rather than face the darkness. Furuseth soon called off the coastal strike and instructed his men to take what jobs they could, knowing there were few options after the financial panic. Nine hundred members remained in the union at the end of the strike, more than enough to start over, but only Furuseth was truly hopeful after these months of futile bloodshed.

Just as he'd done for the past two decades, Antonio decided to sail through the Golden Gate to meet with his comrades in South America and report on the latest waterfront strike. Josephine lived those last nights with him in the bedroom of their apartment, scarcely leaving his side and making love with him constantly, unable to contain the manic energy inside her body. Josephine loved the smell of his straight black hair that kept its scent through every soaking. No matter what her lover washed it with, his locks always smelled of Spanish saffron, and Josephine often fell asleep with her nose nuzzled inside. Outside of this love-den, Antonio sat with five-year-old Isabelle and spoke to her of mermaids, mysterious white whales, haunted ghost ships, sunken continents, ancient curses, and a million naked sea-færies that could make the ocean glow with heavenly green light. While his sons helped Josephine prepare dinner, Antonio told Isabelle all the sea-fairing stories he'd ever heard, true or otherwise, and my mother believed these tales as one believes the mumblings of a street-side oracle. These were his last gifts to my mother, the parting gift of a man who spoke the language of water.

On September 17, 1893, Antonio Ferrari kissed his family goodbye and sailed into the Pacific Ocean on a lumber-running windjammer bound for San Pedro, California. A massive storm moved over the coast that night, throwing the crew into activity as torrential rain engulfed the ship. While these sailors were preoccupied with the rigging, two men dragged my grandfather behind a coil of rope, slugged him on the head, and threw him into the sea. None of his comrades noticed until it was far too late. Consumed by homicidal rage, they quickly located the killers and beat them half to death. After forcing them to confess their employer's name, the crew tossed the killers overboard and surrounded the captain with drawn knives. This man was given an ultimatum: either he kept quiet and lived, or he informed to the police and lost his family. The captain firmly agreed it was best to keep quiet and they docked in San Pedro with the missing sailors listed as deserters. Safely ashore, a coded telegram was then sent to San Francisco that eventually reached Andrew Furuseth's office. Without telling anyone what he'd read, this union secretary left his office and wandered off to weep in the alleys of Chinatown. With ice burning through his veins, Furuseth climbed the steps to Josephine's apartment and knocked on her front door with a trembling hand. Once word of Antonio's death left his mouth, Josephine sat down at the dining table and didn't cry, didn't speak, didn't move, and hardly blinked. A few hours later, Rosita de la Coſta passed away in her sleep.

Marisol dug her mother a grave beneath their little blue house while my uncles built a bomb in front of their paralyzed mother. Before he'd fled their apartment in fright, Furuseth told the Ferrari boys that a crimp named Johnny Curtin had ordered their father's murder at the beheſt of the Ship-Owners Association. Once he'd gone, my uncles dug up an old copy of *Truth* and followed its direćtions for building a bomb. Marisol was shoveling dirt beneath her floorboards while my uncles paced through the Barbary Coaſt with their powerful device hidden in a sailor's bag. She lowered shrouded Rosita into her final reſting place at the exaćt moment her three adopted sons placed their bomb in front of Johnny Curtin's boardinghouse. As she covered her mother in earth, the infernal device exploded in a spray of blood and cinder. Marisol ſtopped shoveling for a moment and liſtened to the shoreline, hoping for another blaſt but encountering only water.

When she finally learned of Antonio's death from a passing neighbor, Marisol ran barefoot to Josephine's apartment and tried to shake her into consciousness. She screamed that my uncles weren't ready for what needed to be done and their bomb had only killed a few scabs, provoking the police into arreſting dozens of innocent sailors. No matter what Marisol said, Josephine wouldn't liſten, nor would she move from her chair. Nothing had prepared my grandmother for this bottomless loss that charred her heart and covered her future in a film of darkness. She was 44-years-old.

Marisol went back to Greenwich Street that night and asked *Santa Muerte* for the ſtrength to avenge her murdered brother. Soon after she asked this favor from the underworld, Isabelle walked inside the little blue house. Juſt as Josephine was called beneath *Les Diablerets*, Isabelle had been called from the Latin Quarter. A few days after this miracle, Josephine rose from her wooden chair, rinsed herself in cold water, and asked her sons about the bomb. In numb shock at her sudden lucidity, my uncles explained how the police had evićted the sailors from their hiring hall while the daily papers accused Furuseth of ordering the explosion. Enraged at this news, Josephine ran to the little blue house and asked Marisol to follow her. They went to the Sailor's Union hall, cornered Furuseth in his office, and proceeded to rouse him from a dark depression. Behind closed doors, Josephine told him her sons would now take the place of Antonio Ferrari and finish the work he'd ſtarted in 1873. Furuseth claimed it would take years to regain their ſtrength, especially after their bomb, but Josephine said none of that mattered. She claimed to have all the time in the world.

SHE'LL BE LOADED WITH BRIGHT ANGELS

I DON'T MIND SITTING HERE. IT'S NOT THE HEIGHT THAT BOTHERS ME, IT'S that everyone down below is busy filling wheat bags while I'm perched a hundred feet in the air, my head-lamp beaming down into the grain silo, disconnected from the labor I've been calling for all these months. When I look up from the silo, I can see an ocean of burning sunlight stretching far away beyond the village, a beautiful sight if there ever was one, only I'd rather be on the ground with the others. Instead, I'm on display atop the *fábrica* for no other reason than my own impatience. Gertrude was complaining about climbing the ladder up the silo, so rather than hear her moan, I volunteered. Now look at me. All I can do is moan.

My lamplight beams down into the mound of threshed wheat that's been sinking for the past two hours. From the red lines painted on the silo's inside wall, I can see we've bagged just over a quarter of our reserves. Too slow. I grab the pocket watch from my pocket and waste an embarrassing amount of time remembering how to do simple mathematics. It takes a while, I start the timer when the wheat hits one of the red lines and then stop it at the next, but given how slowly it just dropped, we're bagging only a meter of grain every hour. There's an iron chute at the bottom of the silo but it only works one bag at a time. They've just started filling the third wagon and, at the rate we're going, we won't be done until before dusk. My ass already feels like granite.

I yell out my hard-won math figures but no one's down there to hear me. After what feels like ten minutes, Annabelle runs around the corner of the silo just to wave at me blankly. I wait for her to say something but all she does is stare. I've had about enough, no one cares how fast we're bagging the wheat. It's time to swap work duties. I slip the watch back into my pocket, string the lamp around my forehead, and carefully put my feet on the upper rungs of the ladder. The fall from the silo wouldn't kill me, but I might not walk again, that's for sure. Carefully, one hand at a time, I pass my fingers over the iron rungs and lower my legs in a steady rhythm. My armpits pour with stinky sweat until the earth creeps back into view and my left foot touches ground.

"It doesn't scare you?" Lorraine asks, suddenly at my side. "I hate this ladder."

"Geez, you scared me!" I yell, breathless. "You just stood here watching me this whole time?"

"I heard you needed help. Also, Isabelle's been begging me to let her replace you."

"Good! But where did Annabelle go? She was just here waving at me."

"She said you looked confused, that you were screaming."

"I wasn't screaming! I was yelling down our rate of...screw it! Isabelle can take my place if she wants." I rip the lantern off my head and hand it over. "I'm about done. Where's Isabelle? What did you tell her? Did you tell her no? Where's—"

"She's sewing the bags shut. You're right. She can go. But let me tell her, okay? Come on."

I follow Lorraine around the *fábrica* to the other side of the silo. They've strung a canvas shade-tarp over the iron chute where two people fill one bag after another, trying to spill as little as they can. There's twenty people sewing bags shut on the shady patio, barely keeping up with the flow of wheat. We find Isabelle sitting with her little sisters, patiently threading the needle through thick fabric. I sit beside her and nuzzle my face into her warm neck, something I've done ever since she was a girl, and she pushes me away just as Lorraine hands her the head-lantern.

"You mean I can go up the silo?" she asks her mom, gasping. "Really?"

"Here, take this," I say, passing her the watch. "You know how to keep track—"

"Yeah, yeah." She's already out of her seat and handing me the needle. "Thanks, I—"

"You grip those rungs tight, understand?" Lorraine says. "And then you sit."

"Grip, sit, got it."

Isabelle kisses me, sticks her tongue out towards her sisters, then runs off around the silo. I can see her father Lucio in those same perfect jawbones, that unbeatable sprint. My eyes start watering but I wipe away the tears before Lorraine can see. She lives with Lucio's loss every day and I have no right to conjure it, especially right now, only it might be too late. His ghost's already here.

I slide next to little Yvonne and Juana to help them stitch a straight line down the middle of the bag-fold. The two sisters can't stop laughing at my fumbling directions and Lorraine just watches, trying to hear what I'm thinking. I know she can feel Lucio inside me.

"Are you writing about Yvonne?" she suddenly asks.

"Writing about me?" her daughter exclaims. "Really? See, Juana? I'm famous!"

"Settle down," Lorraine tells her. "We mean *le belle Yvonne*. Fulvia's writing about *her*."

"I haven't started yet," I say. "But I will soon enough."

"And you'll tell them everything?"

"How could I? No. I can't tell them *everything*. I'll just tell them the truth."

"Tell the truth!" Juana cries. "Always tell the truth!"

Lorraine forces herself to smile and gets back to sewing. I can tell she's disturbed, I hear her mind burning with a thousand questions, but I know her too well. She won't speak about it again. We all concentrate our attention on sewing and within an hour we've gotten a dozen bags closed up tight. I try to pick one up by myself but fall on my ass before I've lifted it an inch. Lorraine just sits there at the bench, pretending to smile as the girls help me carry the bag around the silo. I glance up the iron ladder and see Isabelle's right leg dangling over the door-sill, her hands gripping the cement frame. The glimmer of pride and happiness in her eyes makes me cry again, only this time I let it happen. The girls ask me what's wrong but I just tell them the truth. I tell them I'm happy.

The sun's nearly sunk into the ocean when Isabelle yells for us to close the chute. We've got half our reserves left in the silo with the rest loaded in the wagons. There's maybe seven bags that still need to get sewn shut, but other people are doing that. Not me. I smell hot food in the air and file towards the patio with every other ravenous villager, all eager to taste the red lentils, mashed potatoes, salad, and bread. That's when Isabelle shouts from the silo. She points west and I hear the word *storm*. Everyone looks up at this darkening sky but none of them seem concerned. They aren't thinking clearly. Must be their hunger. Our dirt roads only dried a few days ago and a storm will turn them back into muddy rivers no wagon can navigate. In a panic, I hurry around the silo and climb the iron rungs until I meet Isabelle at the top. To the north and west is a bank of sheer gray darkness quickly blotting out the entire horizon. Isabelle isn't wrong about the storm. We make our descent in silence.

I sit with Lorraine during dinner and hold her hand beneath the patio table. If we were alone I'm sure she'd cry right now. Isabelle brags about her climb up the silo and Juana laughs at my stupid jokes, even the ones she doesn't understand. I'm so engrossed in these girls I barely notice my mother sit down next to me. She's got a full plate of food and her lightning-bolt hair is filled with bits of wheat.

"Where did you come from?" I ask.

"I've been here all day," she says. "Not my fault you didn't notice."

"And you're the last one working," Lorraine says. "As usual."

"I couldn't leave my daughter alone on a day like this," she says, flatly. "Could I?"

My mother eats without looking up while Isabelle describes her ascent up the ladder and how she saw the storm approaching on the horizon. I watch my mother chew patiently and thoroughly while the girls bicker and giggle with each other. Not once does she crack a smile or even try to laugh and it's not just because she's hungry. She angrily tears a piece of bread in half and wipes her oily plate with the dough, all the while ignoring the endless questions little Juana keeps asking her. This is how my mother acts when she's forced to live in the world. This is who she is.

"Is there no wine?" she finally asks, peering down the patio tables. "Did they forget about us?"

"I'll get it," little Isabelle says, kissing her cheek. "Can I have some, mom?"

"Look what your thieving started, Fulvia," Lorraine says to me, exasperated. "Next she'll be asking for a trip to China."

"How old is she now?" my mother asks. "Fourteen?"

"She's seventeen!" Lorraine almost shouts at her. "Seventeen! How can you forget?"

"Then let her have some wine. She's seventeen."

There's my *mama* in all her glory. This is when I'm proud of her, even though she's the cause of all my troubles. Lorraine shakes her head, tries not to laugh, and snatches away the green bottle when her daughter returns. She pours us all a glass, including the young ones, and when little Juana doesn't enjoy hers my mom downs it in one giant swig. The woman has no shame.

After the wine's gone, I take our dishes back into the kitchen and wait in line to clean them. My mother's gone when I return, no one remembers her saying goodbye, she just disappeared like a ghost. Before I get flustered, Lorraine takes me by the arm and walks me away from the shadowy *fábrica*. The girls are straggling behind, trying to annoy little Isabelle away from a village boy who really wants her attention. They're being obnoxious, all that shrieking should drive him insane, but I applaud this kid for sticking around. At the edge of the village, Lorraine and I turn around to observe this sweet, awkward courtship. There's only a thin band of red left in the sky. I doubt the girls can even see us watching.

In these dusky shadows, away from the others, Lorraine finally unleashes her tears. She clutches my shoulders, breathes in thick spasms, and screams into my left shoulder. I want to collapse in fear but I say *we're doing fine*, I tell her *Lucio's right here*, I say *he never left*. She bites my left shoulder, gathers her trembling breath, then kisses my cheek like it's a well-spring. That's when I feel her lips on mine, feel her hands on my ribs, feel her rub the flattest part of my chest. She makes me wet, makes my heart pound like thunder, and I feel Lucio inside me, blotting out my wispy soul. Lorraine, in my dream, the folds of a purple cloth shadow your cheek, the one Lucio sent, a timid gift, all the way from Paloma. I hear him laugh at these musings, but I realize it's just his daughters.

Those crazy girls have perfect timing. When I open my eyes, Lorraine's fixing her clothes. Her daughters are sprinting towards us with swinging lanterns but she takes the time to kiss my lips and say *I'll love you forever* just as the girls surround us in beams of light. I kiss each of them goodbye and watch them climb towards the apple groves, their little lamp-flames piercing the darkness. I weep until they're out of my vision. My thighs are still dripping. Sure enough, I feel that storm approaching.

There's an oil-lamp burning inside the window when I get home. My mother doesn't stir as I open the door, not even to glance at me. Her feet are propped up on the desk, the open notebook in her lap, and it doesn't matter that I'm even here. Isabelle Lemel Ferrari's going to sit there reading my work without permission and not bother to say hello. The anger rises inside my heart. I feel rain approaching outside, I can smell the water blowing in the wind, so I close the front door, loudly uncork a bottle of red wine, then pour myself a glass. My mother turns the pages without a care. I hear her humming to herself. She never does that. Ever.

"Why are you telling them about Félix?" she asks, snapping the book closed. "Why?"

"Because he was important, *mama*. He tied it all together. And he was friends with Georges Seurat, you know, the guy who first visualized the transmitter, even before Nikola. Don't you think it's important they know how...strange the whole system is? How the underworld powers it."

My mother closes her eyes for moment, clearly fuming at something, so I take this opportunity to down my glass of wine.

"Poor Georges...so young, so brilliant." She tosses the notebook on my desk and glares at me with murder in her eyes. "But why tell them so much about Félix?"

"Because without him Yvonne might have never joined—"

"You've written about so much pain, Fulvia." She takes her feet off my desk and leans forward. "Pain that wasn't yours. First you write about my father, now poor Georges. Can you imagine how his lover felt, how much pain Madeleine had to endure? And you're about to tell them about Yvonne. You realize no one knows the truth about her? What she *really* did to make the whole thing work. They might not understand this truth you're trying to tell them."

"Lorraine said the same thing."

"Lorraine's smart! That's why. Believe me, I was the *only* one who believed Yvonne back then. Even my mother had doubts. If Josephine couldn't understand her, what do you think they'll do? Think about that, Fulvia. Writing these type of books is dangerous. You know what happened when they made *The Book*. We don't want them coming to burn Yvonne. Her story's—"

"Important. Yes. Important for the entire world to know. And important for Lorraine! Lucio's dead because of the system she built. Think about him!

You all fed the historians that sentimental crap about Yvonne the philan-thropist capitalist turned anarchist, but I know its way deeper than that. You worked with Yvonne for a decade, *mama*! In her house! I know what went on in that place, but no one else does. And they should know the truth. That's why I'm going to tell it."

My mother tightens her eyes and grows silent. Here we go again. Not knowing what else to do, I pour her a glass of wine, pour myself another, then crack open the door to sniff the air. It's definitely going to rain. I can see some stars but they're flickering out with the approaching fog. The com-mune's moving the wheat inside the storehouse now, I can hear the wag-on-wheels grinding against cement, and then a flash of purple lights up the fog. For a moment, I expect to see an electromagnetic ribbon across the sky but it's just a crack of coastal thunder. When I close the front door, my mother's pouring more wine, her lips already stained a deep shade of purple, just like mine.

"You won't be able to get the wheat down the hill until this rain passes," she tells me.

"Yeah, well, now I've got more time to write about Félix. And Yvonne."

"It's important you tell this part right, true, honest. Otherwise they won't understand who Yvonne is. Or me. Or you. Or any of us. Yvonne changed everything, and we all helped her. I know...you don't know how painful it was to lose Lucio, so—"

"Don't worry, *mama*. I won't let you down. Any of you."

"It's pain. I already told you this. I don't know why you want to write about my father, the pain of losing—" She chugs down her second glass and then slams it on the floor where it shatters into a hundred jagged pieces. "Pain you can't imagine! Darkness you can't imagine, everywhere, eating us!"

I think she attacks me. Her fists are definitely clenched when she charges forward like a silent bull and its only by luck that I catch her wrists. By then she's so close I can smell the salt of her tears. She falls into my body, des-perate for warmth, sobbing uncontrollably. Her father's death was a wound cut deep in her soul, a raw gap that would never heal. My mother told stories about Antonio when I was a girl but she never broke down, never betrayed any emotion, not like this.

The horizon explodes with purple light. I hear another crack of thunder, closer now. My mom's on the verge of screaming, her breath frantic and unreserved. All the windows rattle as I rub her sweaty back and hum into her ear until a loud sigh breaks over the land. Thousands of droplets hit my roof and stream into the dry soil, turning it into mud. My mother wipes her tears as another flash of lighting fills the house with purple light. Everything smells like salt.

"You're lucky you never lost your father," she says, going for the bottle. "Let me have that!"

"No, that's mine. You've had enough—" She rips it out of my hands anyway. "Fine, have it."

"And you're lucky you don't have to feel this pain." She takes a large swig and then hands it back. "I was almost six, old enough to make it really hurt, forever. You grew up without your father, only he's still alive, you can see him whenever you want. Anyway—"

She opens my closet, grabs the wicker broomstick, and I don't try and stop her from sweeping up. It's her mess after all. I drink from the near-empty bottle while she sweeps the glass off my wooden floor, acting like the last minutes didn't just happen. She's never done anything like this, not once in my thirty-five years. There isn't a single book with her father's name in it. His story was meant to remain unwritten, disintegrate into folklore, but now the sailor who plunged into the sea has returned to life. Whether it's Antonio or Lucio, there's no easy way to conjure the dead.

"What should I do with all this glass?" she asks, holding the dust pan. "Throw it outside?"

"Just dump it in the stove."

"Yeah, okay, but remember what I'm about to say before you write any-more." She tosses the glass into the cold ashes and puts the broom back in the closet. "Once you tell them Yvonne's story, you're telling them the truth about Paloma. Enough people have some idea what happened there. You write down the truth and you know what they'll say? They'll say the planet killed everybody at Paloma, the conductors, Lucio, everybody. Blew them up just to make a point, and Yvonne knew it was going to happen. We all knew it was going to happen. And they'll get angry."

"Well? It's true, isn't it? Like you said, people already know. It's obvious, *mama*."

"Just calm down, Fulvia."

"I am calm. You be calm. You're acting like you're going somewhere."

"I need to get home, Fulvia. I need to—"

Before she can run off into the rain, I grab her around the waist and kiss her chapped, purple lips. I rub my mother's graying hair and stare into those green eyes everyone always said are a bit darker than mine. She lets me guide her to the stove where we snap twigs and get a fire going, not speaking a word. Her eyes gleam when she breathes life into the flames and I take this moment to hold her body until our skin begins to sweat. I'll keep my arms around her tonight, even when she's asleep, and we'll burn away the darkness together. I don't care what she says. This pain does belong to me. It's mine. I carry it home every night, just as it haunts me throughout the day.

11

MARY MAGDALENE AND THE BATTLE OF PARIS

AFTER THE REBEL YESHUA HA-NOZRI WAS CRUCIFIED IN JERUSALEM, his lover Mary Magdalene fled the walled city with her closest followers. Mary was pregnant with their first daughter, a secret she kept from the apostles, especially once Yeshua returned from the dead to teach his secrets over the next eleven years. During this band's long exile in the desert, Yeshua's male disciples grew bitter over the clear preference he showed to Mary and the succession of infants who appeared nursing at her breasts, alleged to be from different men. Once their master departed, these bearded apostles began to publicly degrade Mary as a demon-ridden whore Yeshua was kind enough to redeem. When they eventually learned the truth of Yeshua's children, the apostles hired mercenaries to kill them, along with Mary.

Before these snakes could strike, Mary's family, Yeshua's parents, and a group of followers fled Palestine on a small wooden boat bound for the Egyptian port of Alexandria. The year was 41 CE, the beginning of a new era. Sheltered within Alexandria's cauldron of alchemical subversion and ancient wisdom, the forces of Mary seeded their teachings south along the Nile River into the heart of Egypt. While living in this radiant city, Yeshua's mother Mary passed away in the year 43, now a beloved figure of the rebel underworld. Word of her death spread to Rome and the Empire dispatched its best killers to eliminate the rest of this rogue feminine faction, long thought to have vanished in the desert. After escaping an armed ambush in Alexandria's harbor, Mary was once again adrift at sea with several other women named Mary, a fact that always bewildered the Romans. Their small wooden ship was guided by a woman named Sarah, an alchemical priestess who delivered them to an obscure settlement on the coast of Gaul known for centuries as *Ra*. The town was built on a small island at the mouth of the Rhône River and Mary's first steps off her boat were into waters that flowed from the Alps.

The followers of Mary soon spread north along the Rhône and brought their rebellious practices to the Roman province of *Gallia Narbonensis*. They were pursued at every moment by Imperial agents and rabid Christians eager to exterminate them. With her teachings coursing through the unconquered north, Mary Magdalene passed away in the year 97 with dozens of grandchildren at her bedside. Her followers had extended their influence from Palestine to the Seine River and were now poised to cross the northern sea. Unlike my ancestors who hid away in the Alps, the followers of Mary inhabited the cities and valleys of Gaul, places in full control of the enemy where survival was never certain. Over the next two centuries, their teachings of embodied, passive resistance took root among the subjugated Celts of the Imperial colonies who learned to rebel without being seen. Unlike the male Christians, the followers of Mary refused to be martyrs for their beliefs, a choice that to led to the male sects branding them as heretical cowards. They remained apart from these men who distorted Yeshua ha-Nozri's truth beyond recognition and built a false religion over the coming centuries. Rather than fight the Empire directly, these agents of darkness encouraged martyrdom among their followers and wrote extensive manuals on snuffing out the *Gnosis* that Mary's followers openly preached to the pagans.

When he lost his grasp on Félix and Regula in the year 286, Emperor Constantine knew that Mary's centuries-old rebellion had grown out of control. He convened the First Council of Nicæa where the male Christian leaders were given official Imperial sanction and allowed to practice what had become a religion of priests, sin, and scripture. These agents of darkness purged their texts of any gnostic, hermetic, feminine, or alchemical influence and persecuted those who refused to obey their dogma. The brutality of this new religion pushed many followers of Mary northward from their bastion on the Rhône River delta, although thousands remained behind to keep the light from dimming. Those who fled the Christian overlords gathered in the old Roman colony of Lutetia along the banks of the Seine River, a bastion of freedom that Mary Magdalene visited during her first northern pilgrimage. On a small island enveloped by river-water, the indigenous Parisii tribe had built their first settlement and erected bridges before their subjugation by Rome in the year 52 BCE. After colonization, the island of Paris eventually became a stone fortress surrounded by thick walls, a necessary defense against the endless waves of invaders who poured into the collapsing Empire throughout the 4th century.

The followers of Mary resided within this island sanctuary for the next centuries, surviving numerous sieges and influencing what became the Kingdom of France, established in 987. As the tyrants ravaged Europe with their endless wars, these women conspired to consolidate peace in this single kingdom and infiltrated the Holy Roman Church as nuns. One testament to their legacy on the island of Paris was the cathedral of *Notre Dame de Paris*, commissioned by a French king who'd wed a follower of Mary. Through these clandestine efforts, the Kingdom of France allowed the most freedom in a time of great darkness and this bond between royal power and the forces of May lasted until their carefully planned Renaissance and Enlightenment triggered the Great French Revolution of 1791. In the chaos that followed this moment, the reign of capitalism was unleashed upon the planet, an industrial monster built from the ancient wisdom Mary's followers had scattered across the land. These women presided over a haunted and polluted Paris when Félix Fénéon arrived in the spring of 1881.

He found lodgings across the river from the ruins of the Tulleries Palace, its fallen stones still blackened from the fires of the Paris Commune. His job at the War Office was near the river with its windows above the *Boulevard Saint-Germain*, a bustling street that caused him to marvel at the sheer number of humans packed into this stone metropolis. Félix rose quickly in the War Office, unmatched in his ability to write blocks of text without interruption, and two office-clerks who were aspiring poets soon befriended Félix, introducing him to the literary and artistic circles of Paris. They took him to the *Salon* of 1881, beheld the officially sanctioned canvases of the French Republic, and ambled through the Parisian nightlife to various poetry readings in cheap apartments where Félix first encountered the words of Arthur Rimbaud and his former lover Paul Verlaine.

In the privacy of his own room, away from his new friends, Félix read of the coal workers' strikes outside Lyon, the wave of bombings against that same coal company, and the anarchist witch-trial of 1883. Inspired by this wave of revolt, he attended a rally called for by Louise Michel, recently returned from her penal-exile in New Caledonia, and joined the hungry crowd in looting bread shops along the *Rue de Invalides*. Félix evaded arrest by sprinting down an alley but Louise Michel was jailed for fomenting rebellion against the Republic and lived the next three years in prison. During the gas-lit evenings of this era, Félix wandered the eternal city of Mary, absorbing the myriad influences oozing from every stone. The ghosts of the Commune were springing from the ground and he could feel *the waters and sorrows rise and launch the Floods again,* just as Rimbaud had predicted in 1874.

Every morning, Félix arrived at the War Office impeccably dressed and took hold of his duties with ease, working so fast none of his colleagues could keep up. After several months, once he was in control of office operations, Félix began to issue military exemptions to his comrades, friends, and any poor soul with tears in their eyes. While this meager effort saved hundreds of lives, it certainly wasn't the only benefit of working in the War Office. Using the blue post cards given freely to every War Office employee and his free access to the city-wide pneumatic tube system, Félix corresponded with his increasingly large net-work of contacts without fear of state censorship, given he was officially the state. Once they heard about this clever arrangement, Mary's followers found Félix carousing inside the *Chat Noir* cabaret with a gang of absinthe soaked poets known as the *Hydropathes*, or men afraid of water. Within this nightclub milieu, Félix was organizing a new literary journal called the *Libre Revue*, an organ that attacked the officially sanctioned paintings of the French Republic. To the delight of Mary's followers, this mysterious young anarchist was also passionate about art.

In 1884, after establishing himself as a critic, Félix left the *Libre Revue* and founded the *Revue Independente*, publishing new writing from Huysmans, Mallarme, and Verlaine. Without attracting attention, the forces of Mary were secretly buying, reading, and sharing everything he issued. Not only did his publications include the most enlightened minds of Paris, they fostered the work of those yet to discover public acclaim. As the art critic for this new cultural organ, Félix attended the first Salon of Independent Artists, held in a post-office erected atop the ruins of the Tulleries Palace, and it was here that over four hundred painters rejected by the French state displayed their subversive works. A single, massive painting stood out to young Félix at this exhibition, although its implications were too vast for him to immediately comprehend.

It was called *Une Baignade, Asnières*, or *Bathing at Asnières*, and depicted an idyllic scene of workers lounging along the Seine River. This timeless setting was marred only by an iron train-bridge in the distance, a steam-boat plowing through the river, and an industrial smoke stack belching brown fog into the blue air. Having walked this stretch of the Seine before, Félix knew all the sewage of Paris flowed invisibly into the river through an outlet just beneath the smoke stack. This subterranean waste tunnel was created by

Baron Haussmann, the same architect who'd widened the boulevards into the rebel districts, facilitating the slaughter of the Paris Commune. His vast sewage tunnels now delivered streams of shit into the waters of the Seine, just as his wide streets delivered soldiers to the slopes of Montmartre. Félix marveled at this grand painting and memorized its creator's name, for Georges Seurat had birthed a new form of artistic subversion. Félix wasn't the only one who noticed.

In the winter of 1885, the supervisor of the War Office subjected Félix to a sudden barrage of serious accusations: drinking absinthe in disreputable cabarets with degenerate artists, ingesting hashish in notorious nightclubs, and mingling with confessed traitors to the Republic. Félix listened patiently and asked if his work was unsatisfactory. He denied every accusation and calmly withstood the abuse, confident in his irreplaceable skills that held the office together. Unable to fire this clever anarchist, his supervisor had no choice but to relent, although Félix curtailed his war exemptions until he was certain all suspicion had passed. In this uncertain time, he discontinued the *Revue Independent* and was quite relieved to find a message from his mother waiting in the mail-slot: Marie-Louise and Jules Fénéon were on their way to Paris. Less than a week after receiving this telegram, Félix secured an affordable two-bedroom apartment on the Rue Vaneau and canceled all his future commitments.

Félix met his parents at the *Gare Montparnasse*, hired them a private-coach, and discovered a familiar looking woman waiting for them inside their new apartment. This was my aunt Bianca Lemel, cousin to Marie-Louise Fénéon and younger sister of Josephine Lemel. She'd been living in Paris since 1874 and now worked as a laundress on the slopes of Montmartre. Once everyone was seated, Bianca looked deeply into Félix's eyes and said she'd be watching him, just as she had been all these past years, and if his family ever needed help, my aunt would always be there before they could ask. With one final kiss to all, Bianca disappeared into the shadows of Paris, leaving the Fénéons in their top-floor apartment with its view of swaying horse chestnut trees that scattered raindrops from their branches at every breath of the wind. This apartment would soon become a vortex of subversion.

Over the next year, Marie-Louise and her son Félix hosted all the bright lights of unconquered Paris inside their cramped parlor. While grumpy Jules Fénéon hid in his bedroom, Marie-Louise came to know Charles Henry, Jules Laforgue, and Gustave Kahn, three men who helped Félix found *La Vogue* in the spring of 1886. It was in this new journal that they published the *Illuminations* of Arthur Rimbaud, relaunching the literary career of this long-lost poet. They also used *La Vogue* to publicize the latest exhibition of Impressionist artwork where paintings by Georges Seurat would be on display. Two weeks after the Haymarket bombing in May 1886, a group of anarchist painters including Seurat, Paul Signac, and Camille Pissarro hung their canvases alongside the masters of French Impressionism. Unlike these established figures, the anarchists refrained from thick brush strokes and undefined lines, preferring to break color into small dots that combined inside the retina itself to form a unified whole. Color wasn't in the paint, they said. Color was created first in the eye, then the mind.

Too large to fit with the other paintings, Georges Seurat's *A Sunday Afternoon on the Island of La Grande Jatte* hung above the refreshment bar and depicted the same stretch of the Seine as *Une Baignade, Asnières*, only this time from the opposite bank. Here the idle bourgeois strolled languidly along the grassy shore or lounged in the shade with their joyful children. The industrial pollution from the previous painting was not only absent, none of the figures appeared to be looking at it aside from a young girl dressed in white, her expression mute with horror. As he beheld this vast painting, Fénéon decided that Seurat's politically charged pointillism was the future of visual art and resolved to write a review extolling this master-work. At the time, Félix didn't know Seurat was invited to this exhibition by Berthe Morisot, one of the few Impressionist women and secret follower

of Mary. Rather than side with the old masters, Berthe threw her support behind these upstarts, and in response to this flood of radical art, the older Impressionists announced this was their final exhibition, claiming the movement was now polluted by these anarchists let inside by their disloyal protégé.

Berthe Morisot

Once the exhibition was over, Félix wrote a long review in *La Vogue* that introduced the world to what became the Neo-Impressionists. This journal quickly sold-out in the bookstores thanks to the followers of Mary and spread widely throughout the city into hundreds of apartments. The artists he championed in *La Vogue* became regulars at the Fénéon *salons* and Marie-Louise was unable to fathom how her son had joined

Mary Magdalene's followers in one of their grand undertakings, its conclusion far from certain, let alone safe. To make sure Felix understood who he was meddling with, Marie-Louise took him on a long walk across the river to the *Place de Concorde*. In this plaza stood a stone obelisk taken from Luxor Temple in the city of Thebes, birthplace of Mauritius, Félix, and Verena. It was stolen in the 1830s by the Khedive of Egypt and given to King Louis-Philippe as a gift from one conqueror to another. While its twin still stands over Thebes today, the second obelisk was shipped across the sea before being erected in the same *Place de Concorde* where King Louis XVI was guillotined during the French Revolution. Its placement was no accident.

The forces of Mary had no desire to steal the obelisk, but they were sure to arrange its location in the proper symbolic context. The obelisk was flanked on both sides by two spurting water fountains, officially meant to represent the Seine and Rhône rivers which gave life to France. As they watched the water flow, Marie-Louise explained how the forces of Mary wrote secret messages in the fabric of the city, permanent signals meant to assure rebels help was always near. These twin fountains were meant to symbolize the water ribbons that saved Verena, Regula, and Félix from execution, just as

the obelisk signified the singular contribution Thebes had made in the battle against darkness. While the rulers of France pillaged the world, the forces of Mary subverted their spoils, and Marie-Louise wanted Félix to understand this simple lesson before he proceeded any further with his new allies.

Over the next two years, Félix promoted the fledgling Neo-Impressionists who depicted modern industry polluting the land, boats sailing on the water, the hypocrisies of the bourgeoisie, the degraded conditions of the working class, and the sideshow spectacles that tranquilized them. These anarchists subverted theories of linear direction and championed the simultaneous contrast of opposites, replacing the brush stroke with the dot and the palette with the retina. They stippled their canvases with spots of color and produced hues perceived only from a distance, allowing the electromagnetic effects of their social commentary to sink directly into the body. One needn't be trained at the prestigious *École des Beaux-Arts* to paint in this pointed manner. According to their new theories, anyone could become a "master" of Neo-Impressionism.

Knowledge of their works soon spread across Europe and attracted the attention of Vincent van Gogh, a tortured painter who believed Seurat was the leader of this breakthrough in art. Van Gogh's praise helped trigger the first major sales of these radical paintings and he implored Félix to help start an artist's commune where they could all escape the market. Conditions at work had finally improved for Félix, although he gave the bulk of his paychecks to his poor friends, saving only enough for rent. Félix told Marie-Louise about the possibility of forming an artist's commune but van Gogh's mental illness prevented it from materializing. The darkness overwhelmed this sensitive artist, just as it soon took the lives of other Neo-Impressionists. Shortly after *La Vogue* folded in January 1887, its co-founder Jules Laforgue died of poverty-induced tuberculosis at the age of twenty-seven.

Still mourning the loss of his friend, Félix founded a new *Revue Independente* in late 1887, just before his family was evicted from their apartment under strange circumstances. In these dark and uncertain times, the Fénéons were forced to reside with Félix's comrades for nearly a year until they found a cheap apartment. Félix and his mother held *salons* in their new living room over the next year and it was in the middle of 1889 that Marie-Louise noticed a pool of darkness growing in the eyes of Georges Seurat. Instead of natural settings, he now painted nocturnal cabarets, nightclubs, and circuses. In these modern spectacles, Seurat saw darkness gathering strength. As a result, a shadow crept into his soul, consuming him from the inside. Shortly afterward, Vincent van Gogh shot himself in the chest.

Seurat soon began to argue with Félix over who invented Neo-Impressionism and broke off contact after a heated dispute. The other members tried to intervene but Seurat retreated into the arms of his secret lover, a former model he'd once painted named Madeleine Knobluch, follower of Mary and mother to his only son. Seurat kept them hidden from his conservative Catholic father and lived his days in public as if Madeleine didn't exist. His work was now being displayed at the Neo-Impressionist gallery in the center of Paris and was consistently championed by his ally Berthe Morisot, making him a minor celebrity. Along with her comrade Madeleine, Berthe watched over Seurat when he began his final work, *Le Cirque*, a demonic rendering of the modern circus. As Madeleine's pregnancy advanced, Seurat

painted a fool in the center of a stage, one hand holding a burning cigar, the other pulling back a curtain to reveal that the painting itself was nothing more than the projection from some infernal magic lantern glowing invisibly behind the viewer.

This unfinished masterwork was displayed at the seventh exhibition of the *Societe des Artises Independants* in March of 1891, where the forces of Mary arranged for President Sadi Carnot to stand before it. When he beheld this demonic spectacle, the electromagnetic effects stabbed a hole inside his body and left a small spark of light hidden inside. Soon after this fateful event, Seurat became gravely ill from contracting angina and asked if Madeleine could carry him home to his mother. The darkness had finally come for revenge and Georges Seurat lived those last days with his lover, his parents, and his son before passing away on March 29, 1891. News of his passing reached Félix in the War Office and he cried uncontrollably for less than a minute after receiving the telegram, a rare event that roused the attention of his baffled coworkers. When they asked what had happened, Félix claimed there was something clouding his vision that only tears could wash away. For my industrious cousin, the ultimate battle began at that moment. As his colleagues got back to work, Félix was already making plans.

After the funeral, Madeleine lost her second son. She buried him beside Georges in the *Pere-Lachaise* cemetery, returned to their empty home, and helped Félix sort through her lover's paintings. The surviving artists cleaved in half over how the estate would be disbursed and Félix was accused of trying to profit from Madeleine's bereavement when he purchased several paintings. Félix fell into a long depression after this and Marie-Louise found him alone in the living room one day, silently gazing at *La Tour Eiffel*, a depiction of the tower Seurat painted in 1889 when it was still under construction. Félix asked his mother why Georges had painted this bizarre iron tower with its neck half-finished and appearing to spew flames. Marie-Louise explained that the planet used artists to reveal the shape of the future, just as it did with Cleopatra the Alchemist when she intuited the internal movements of the Earth with her alembic. Eiffel's iron monster above the Seine might just be part of a dream yet to be realized or a visionary riddle waiting to be solved. Marie-Louise explained how the followers of Mary encouraged all forms of creative expression in the hope of unearthing weapons to use against darkness, although they often couldn't control these weapons. As he stared at *La Tour Eiffel* with Marie-Louise, Félix resolved to break off his undertaking with the forces of Mary and direct all his energy into the anarchist movement. While he might have contributed to a project beyond his comprehension, Félix desired something more tangible than an unfinished painting and a useless tower made of iron. No one knew this at the time, but Gustave Eiffel and Georges Seurat had just forged the general shape of our electromagnetic transmission towers. It was far from useless.

Over the past years, Felix had granted military exemptions and leaked government information, but now he devoted his free time to writing texts for the anarchist press. Soon enough, Félix was the invisible anarchist of the Parisian *avante-garde* and hidden actor for his mother's secret tribe. He wrote anonymously for the *Revue Anarchiste*, the *Revue Libertaire*, the *Pere Peinard*, and *L'Endehors*, using his pen to advocate the use of dynamite, expropriation, and assassination. On May 1, 1891, when soldiers killed nine striking workers in the town of Fourmies, news immediately traveled to the War Office where Félix learned one of the fallen was 18-year-old Marie Blondeau. That same day, a pistol battle erupted in Clichy between striking workers and the police, leaving multiple people with serious wounds and three anarchists in prison. Enraged at this brazen carnage, Félix left the War Office that evening and built a bomb in his living room with Marie-Louise. While most people were asleep on the evening of May 2, Félix walked the streets in his mother's dress with the bomb placed inside a flower basket. He left the powerful device beneath a window of the swanky *Hotel de Trévise* on the *Champs Elysees*, lit the fuse with a cigar, and ran off before the blast left chunks of jagged stone littered across the street. A few newspaper reports mentioned a woman fleeing the scene and workers immediately spun folktales of Marie Blondeau, martyr of the Fourmies massacre, returning from the dead to claim her vengeance against the capitalists.

After the bombing, Marie-Louise sent a letter to the town of Saint-Maurice asking for her young niece Berthe Jacquin to come live with her in Paris. She flatly told her relatives that someone needed to learn from the coming battle who would survive to tell the tale. At the age of twelve, Berthe arrived by train at the *Gare de l'Est* and slept with Marie-Louise in her tiny bed, leaving Jules to share a room with Félix. In those days, his son was rarely home and worked late into the night with the painters Paul Signac, Maximilian Luce, Félix Vallonton, Camille Pissaro, and his son Lucien Pissaro. They stopped referring to themselves as Neo-Impressionists and devoted their precious skills to drawing illustrations for the anarchist press, carving revolutionary woodcuts for street posters, and painting crystalline social commentary in the same manner as Georges Seurat.

After a judge harshly sentenced two of the anarchists arrested in Clichy, a rebel accordionist nicknamed Ravachol sought revenge on their behalf. Already a committed anarchist himself, Ravachol detonated three bombs in March of 1892: one at the apartment of the Clichy judge, another at the Lobau army barracks, and another at the home of the prosecutor who tried the Clichy anarchists. No one was killed in these bombings but the state immediately arrested dozens of anarchists under false charges of organizing the explosions. Félix helped draft a call in *L'Endehors* for donations to benefit the children of these men, although matters soon become much worse. On March 30, 1892, Ravachol walked into the *Restaurant Very* and ordered his usual beer and grenadine. While he was smoking a cigar, an observant waiter alerted his boss that a man he suspected of being the bomber had returned. The boss quickly informed his police handlers and an armed ambush overtook Ravachol that led to his imprisonment under false charges of murder.

My aunt Bianca Lemel was waiting in the apartment with Marie-Louise when Félix returned home that evening, eager to help with the next bombing. The day before Ravachol's trial began, Bianca discretely placed a bag under the table where the *Restaurant Very's* owner was meeting with a police spy.

Félix waited outside with a pistol in his coat pocket and a false mustache glued above his lips. His finger remained around the trigger until Bianca calmly left the restaurant and they met up a few blocks away just as the powerful dynamite blew these police agents into pieces. While this attack might have demonstrated the consequences of collaboration, it did nothing to affect the upcoming trial. Ravachol was guillotined for murder on July 11, 1892. He was thirty-three years old. A dozen anarchists quickly appeared to carry on his work, one of them a young man named Émile Henry.

Félix first met Émile at a gathering of the Parisian anarchist movement and invited him to dine at his apartment. Émile soon became a regular at their dinner table where he told his short life's story to Félix and Marie-Louise. Émile was the son of an exiled Communard who died from mercury poisoning contracted in vile Spanish mines. Not wanting to burden his mother with another mouth to feed, Émile moved back to Paris and passed the entrance examinations for the prestigious *Ecole Polytechnique*. Despite this opportunity to advance in French society, Émile dropped out to be a thief. He stole milk cows to feed starving mothers, raided upscale markets to feed his comrades, and became a locksmith to rob the apartments of the rich. After one of these nocturnal outings, Émile stopped by the Fénéon apartment with an ornate cane he'd stolen for Marie-Louise. She was touched by this sweet gesture but quickly melted the solid gold handle and burned the polished wood, weary of leaving evidence. Émile was always generous with his plunder, animated with true kindness, but his soul changed soon after Ravachol was guillotined. Marie-Louise could see the darkness eating his eyes.

In August of 1892, the coal-miners of Carmaux staged a massive strike, destroying expensive industrial equipment and physically blockading scab workers imported by the coal company. The few Marxist politicians in Parliament called on these miners to refrain from violence while the soldiers of the Republic freely beat them with clubs, fists, and boots. Starved and harassed by the military through the fall, the defeated miners eventually returned to work in exchange for their jobs. This humiliation was too much for Émile, having lost his father to a toxic mine, and he saw himself in all of the starving children living in frigid miner's shacks. After listening to Émile rage in the apartment for over an hour, Marie-Louise and Félix helped him build a bomb which they placed in an iron pot and wrapped with newspaper. Marie-Louise loaned Émile one of her dresses that night of November 8, 1892 and he left the bomb outside the Parisian offices of the Carmaux Mining Company. The device was discovered by the police and taken to their headquarters where it suddenly exploded, killing five police and heavily damaging the building. Not long after this, Félix moved his family to a new apartment on the slopes of Montmartre while Émile Henry fled across the sea to England. During their investigations, the police suspected nearly two hundred Parisian anarchists of the bombing but none of them were Émile Henry or Félix Fénéon, head clerk of the War Office.

While the Fénéon's were busy packing for their move to Montmarte, Marie-Louise asked Félix to take their clothing across the tracks to a struggling laundress who was one of their distant relations. In this humble laundry-shop, Félix met Marie-Felicie Jacquin, seven years his senior with the long dark hair of my ancestors. They began to amuse each other with their witty banter and poignant observations of Parisian society, being avid observers of its bewildering spectacles. At her request, Félix returned that evening with a bottle of wine and by morning Marie-Felicie was pregnant. While this coupling was organic enough, all of it had been arranged behind Félix's back. Marie-Felicie and Marie-Louise shared the Jacquin name for a simple reason: they were both Alpine witches from the same extended family, my family. Félix saw Marie-Felicie whenever he could, although the War Office and his anarchist activities kept him preoccupied during her pregnancy. She told Félix he didn't need to be a father, just as he'd never be her husband or partner. While she enjoyed her attraction to Félix, Marie-Felicie Jacquin wanted freedom and nothing else, not even motherhood. She was very honest.

During her entire pregnancy, Félix continued to pen anonymous texts for the anarchist press extolling the virtues of direct action, theft, and dynamite. With his wages from the War Office, Félix paid thirty-five francs a month for the family's new apartment where they could glimpse the *Basilique du Sacré-Cœur* rising atop the peak of Montmartre. After the defeat of the Commune, the Holy Roman Church punished the hillside neighborhood by erecting this massive religious temple at the epicenter of their rebellion. The interior of the domed basilica was already open for viewers and the monstrosity would soon dominate the skyline of Paris. As he stared out the window at this symbol of defeat, Félix was often yelled at by his increasingly ill father who demanded he stop flooding their apartment with terrorist poets. Félix mostly obeyed these wishes and kept his meetings out of the apartment unless there was no choice, given the pressures of the Parisian police.

His comrades met every night to discuss the repression against their movement, but not once did Félix mention Marie-Felicie or their child. His only son was born on July 23, 1893, and Félix never told his father about this grandson, just as Marie-Felicie never told Félix his son's name. She said he'd be raised by women and Félix didn't ask any questions or challenge Marie-Felicie in any way. Felix's mother got her a job at the local post-office but he rarely saw Marie-Felicie, nor did he ever visit his son. Félix's life had nothing to do with theirs. Everyone preferred it that way.

On December 9, 1893, the anarchist August Vaillant walked into the Chamber of Deputies of the French Parliament to avenge the execution of Ravachol by tossing a bomb filled with nails over the politician's heads. The explosion injured over twenty people but killed no one, a legal fact

Auguste Vaillant, Ravachol, Émile Henry

that didn't prevent Vaillant from being sent to the guillotine on February 3, 1894. His final words to the public were simple: *"Death to the Bourgeois! Long live anarchy!"* Shortly before the blade fell, Félix came home to find my aunt Bianca crying in Marie-Louise's arms. Once her tears subsided, Félix learned that Bianca's sister Josephine had lost her husband Antonio, thrown into the ocean by agents of JP Morgan. Through her tears, Bianca claimed that Antonio's assassination was part of a much larger conspiracy to control the high-seas.

Just before my grandfather's murder, hundreds of illustrious French figures like Gustave Eiffel were implicated when the Panama Canal Company went bankrupt in 1889, causing almost a million French citizens to lose their investments. This canal was meant to shorten shipping routes and open new markets between the Atlantic and the Pacific, although the project had fallen into chaos. The canal was physically disintegrating while French President Sadi Carnot, still untouched by the scandal, waited patiently for JP Morgan to purchase the project from France, a transaction that would give Wall Street control over both oceans. Once she learned of this fact, Bianca resolved to join her sister in San Francisco and help thwart this maritime conspiracy. She left Paris just as the French Republic banned all anarchist newspapers, imprisoned hundreds of suspects, and forced dozens more into exile. Shortly after she crossed the Atlantic, Jules Fénéon died at the age of seventy. The very next day, Émile Henry threw a bomb into the *Café Terminus*. Félix had no idea his friend had returned.

After secretly leaving England, young Émile executed his plan to avenge the death of August Vaillant. On the night of February 12, 1894, Émile prowled the city in search of crowded bourgeois restaurant but found them all empty, as if he were walking inside a dream. This is when the darkness burst inside his heart. Rather than go back to his hotel and sleep, Émile found a random cafe and threw a bomb at the crowded bar, killing one person and wounding twenty more. He was quickly captured by the police and his comrades scrambled to disassemble their bomb laboratory before it was discovered, along with three pre-made bombs. The *Revue Libertaire,* the *Pere Penard,* the *Revue Anarchiste*, and Élisée Reclus' *La Revolte* were forbidden by the Republic and anarchism rendered all but illegal when another series of explosions followed Émile's arrest.

On February 20, a comrade of Émile's named Amédée Pauwels placed two of the remaining bombs in a hotel and wrote a false suicide note to the anti-anarchist police squad claiming he'd killed himself there, all in the hope of assassinating the police who'd imprisoned his comrades. Unfortunately for everyone, Amédée killed an innocent old chambermaid by mistake. The darkness began to eat him from the inside after this tragedy, driving him mad. On March 15, Amédée brought his last remaining bomb into the *L'église de la Madeleine*, a Catholic church commissioned by King Louis XVIII. Just as he entered this church, the bomb suddenly went off, drenching the ornate walls red with his blood. No one else was killed. The darkness had consumed itself.

Marie-Louise and Félix both agreed they were running out of time. It was plain to see that the darkness was now infecting their comrades and driving them to suicidal actions. With the anarchist press now banned by the state, they decided to correct the wayward course of these mad bombers and constructed an explosive device inside a ceramic flower pot. Félix slipped a hyacinth into the mouth and carried it off to the *Café Foyot,* an upper-class establishment frequented by politicians. On the evening of April 4, 1894, Félix placed the flower pot beneath one of the windows, lit the fuse with a cigar, and strolled off into Odeon Square. The bomb blew a hole into the stone wall and injured a single person, the anarchist Laurent Tailhade. Félix and Marie-Louise chose this cafe knowing he'd be there. Not only did Tailhade find it acceptable to live and dine in this building, he'd also publicly criticized Émile Henry and revealed the gender of Gisèle d'Estoc, someone long-thought to be a man. Despite losing one of his eyes to the flower-pot bomb, Tailhade refused to condemn the bombers, claiming this was the height of his literary career, and he extolled the many virtues of anarchism to all the rabid journalists eager to scribble his words.

The police mysteriously arrived at the Fénéon apartment the next day and demanded to be allowed inside. Acting on several anonymous tips, they searched each room before taking Félix to the station where they forced him to sign a document repudiating anarchism. After granting the authorities this symbolic gesture, Félix was allowed back to work at the War Office, although now under heavy suspicion. To make matters worse, his Montmartre landlord soon evicted the Fénéons for their alleged terrorist sympathies. Félix, Marie-Louise, and Berthe Jacquin moved a few blocks down the street to a more expensive apartment where they received no visitors. Police spies were always lurking around the corner and Félix had to waste an entire evening losing his tails just to obtain a letter from Émile Henry smuggled out of prison. He showed Marie-Louise this draft of Émile's court statement and when she read the line "I await your verdict with indifference," his mother cried for all the bull-headed rebels who'd given their lives to this bloody City of Mary.

Just before the trial of Émile Henry began, the police arrived at the War Office and demanded Félix take them to his new apartment. Once he was in the police-wagon, they accused him of the *Café Foyot* explosion and Félix did his best to hide the rising nausea as they approached his building. From the bottom of the stairwell, Félix yelled up to Marie-Louise that the police had arrived, giving her time to burn Émile Henry's manuscript. After searching the apartment, the police assured her this was all a routine matter before taking Félix to the local station in handcuffs. He was asked multiple questions about his Parisian comrades but Félix refused to say a single word besides demanding to be put in a cell. Marie-Louise and Berthe Jacquin immediately tried to visit him but the guards turned them back, claiming it wasn't possible. They held Félix overnight and searched his desk at the War Office the next morning where they found a matchbox filled with detonators. When asked about these devices, Félix claimed they'd belonged to his late father Jules. He admitted to being an anarchist but refused to say anything else before being taken to Mazas Prison. In this moment of darkness, the forces of Mary came to protect their favorite anarchist of letters.

The daily newspapers were filled with the name Félix Fénéon, third-lieutenant clerk at the War Office, and the public was aghast to learn this clever anarchist was employed by the government for over a decade, affording him untold knowledge of the state's inner workings. Leading the charge in his defense was Caroline Rémy de Guebhard, a follower of Mary known by her pen-name Séverine. This famous journalist gathered the poets and artists of Paris to defend Félix from the guillotine and fight the new "Wicked Laws" passed by the Republic. These public figures wrote long letters to the judges and newspapers, spoke at length to writers and critics, and joined Louise Michel in calling for his freedom. Despite the praise of these poets, rebels, painters, and artists, the police aggressively interrogated his mother Marie-Louise and cousin Berthe Jacquin. Three weeks later, as Félix sat in prison,

Café Foyot

young Émile Henry was led away to the guillotine where he screamed the words: *"Courage comrades! Long live anarchy!"* Marie-Louise cried for an entire week after his beheading. It felt as if the darkness were about to swallow her family whole.

Rather than go insane from sadness, Félix got to work translating the most interesting book he could find in prison: *Northanger Abbey* by Jane Austen. While he penciled out this charming Gothic novel and lived within its green British landscapes, a young anarchist in Lyon made a brave decision. His name was Sante Geronimo Caserio, born on September 8, 1873 in the Lombardian village of Motta Visconti. His father was a peasant boatman who'd named his son after the Apache leader Geronimo, finding his struggle against the US cavalry to be noble beyond measure. He died of malnutrition in 1880 and his son Sante Geronimo refused to burden his overworked mother with another child to feed. He left his village at the age of ten, traveling south to Milano where he found work as a baker. Sante soon joined a local anarchist group and developed the practice of distributing leaflets wrapped around pilfered bread-rolls, an easy way to feed both the mind and body. In this rich milieu of rebel workers, Sante Geronimo met anarchist song-writer Pietro Gori and joined the annual May Day demonstrations organized by the International.

Eight years of this agitation eventually caught up with him and he fled to Switzerland rather than face imprisonment in Italy. After staying with my relatives in the Alps and learning the tragic fate of Antonio Ferrari at the hands of JP Morgan, he followed the Rhône River into the French Republic and settled in the textile city of Lyon. As he worked delivering telegrams from house to house, Sante Geronimo experienced the unrest gripping France and heard fearful whispers from passing bourgeois, all trembling at the anti-capitalist rebellion. Shortly after the arrest of Félix Fénéon, the young telegram messenger discovered that President Sadi Carnot would visit Lyon in June to assure the south that their Republic was robust and sturdy.

Sante Geronimo purchased a long dagger and over the following days he studied the streets where the President would soon parade. On June 24, 1894, he stood among the crowd as a line of colorful carriages came roaring down the cobblestones. In this moment, the young anarchist beheld a gentle light burning in the heart of the French President, planted there years earlier by a painter named Georges Seurat. While the rabid mob cheered for their leader, Sante Geronimo sprinted towards the sea of horses, jumped on the foot-step of the presidential carriage, and sunk his blade into the glowing heart of Sadi Carnot. Sante Geronimo was 21 years-old. With this single act, he prevented the French Republic from selling the Panama Canal Company to JP Morgan.

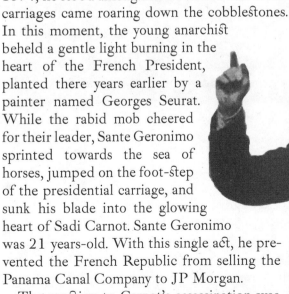

Pietro Gori

The reaction to Carnot's assassination was immediate. Dozens of anarchists were arrested in Paris and many others fled to Belgium or

Switzerland. Anarchism was made illegal under the third "Wicked Law" and mention of this philosophy became forbidden. While Sante Geronimo awaited his execution, the state began its famous Trial of the Thirty. Félix was lumped in with anarchists from across Paris, charged with belonging to a central organization that plotted terror, violence, bombings, arson, and murder. None of this was true, given that Félix knew only a fraction of his co-defendants, and the trial soon devolved into chaos. The prosecutors vastly underestimated the intelligence, wit, and humor of these anarchist prisoners who turned the courtroom into a cabaret of buffoonery, especially once Félix took the stand. When the judge insisted he had surrounded himself with two anarchist thieves, Félix replied, *one cannot be surrounded by two persons; you need at least three.* After the judge insisted he was seen conferring with these thieves behind a lamp post, Félix famously asked, *can you tell me where behind a lamppost is?* When the judge didn't understand his question, Félix clarified that *a lamppost, your Honor, is round.* The news-reading public was enamored with these hilarious rebels thanks to the forces of Mary and the case soon collapsed for lack of solid evidence. To the dismay of Félix, the anarchist thieves were given harsh penal sentences while the artists and common workers allowed to walk free. Despite their sincere and thoughtful efforts, the forces of Mary neglected to help the burglars.

Félix walked out of the prison on August 12, 1894 and pushed through a crowd of onlookers towards his waiting cab. Félix was so wary of being assassinated it took him a moment to realize these people were praising him, and he happily thanked them all before driving off to meet Marie-Louise and Berthe for dinner, trailed by a dozen police spies. Four days later, Sante Geronimo Caserio was led to the guillotine and placed beneath the metal blade. His final words were: "Courage, cousins! Long live anarchy!" This beloved family he addressed spanned the entire globe and during his final moments, Saint Geronimo cherished the secret knowledge of having changed the course of history. Without their infinite sacrifice, our electromagnetic future wouldn't exist.

SHE'LL BE LAUGHING AND SINGING

*S*HE IS THE DREAMER. I HEAR IT THROUGH THE WALLS. *SHE IS THE dreamer.* I drop the pen and lean back in my chair until this cryptic phrase slithers out of my mind. It's almost dawn, the sky's still speckled with a handful of stars, and I've been up all night waiting for rain. The storm poured and pounded for three days before blowing itself out. Today's the second morning of dryness. I hope it lasts, but then I hear it again from beneath the carpet. *She is the dreamer.* I heard these words the morning Paloma exploded, only I never told anyone. They would have thought I was crazy. *She is the dreamer.* I almost know what it means, but I need to be sure before I ask Yvonne. I can't let her know I'm clueless.

The sky melts into purple as I climb to the loft and hide my notebook deep inside the treasure chest. I tried to sleep upstairs last night but it was pointless. My heart pounded, my thoughts raced, and all I could think of was Félix Fénéon planting bombs on the streets of Paris. I wrote for hours without interruption, hopping back and forth between books, penning the longest chapter yet. Hope I don't fall asleep on the wagon today. Maybe I shouldn't drive, but people are going to expect that of me. This was my idea after all, and no one likes driving the wagons. I guess I could pull the brake instead of drive, people hate that job even more, and it might feel good to yank with all my strength, to grind some metal against the wheels. All that noise and motion might keep me awake.

The sun keeps rising as I climb downstairs, soak my hair over the wash basin, knock the crumbs from my eyes, scrub off my dead skin, then shake myself dry. Like my mother would say, I'm a rabid dog spraying droplets. I quickly get dressed, pull my pant legs down over my boots, grab my straw hat from the closet, and walk out into the cool morning air. The sky's blue now and I see people heading to the *fábrica* with bundles of food, stuffed backpacks, and walking sticks. I always manage to forget my lunch. Not like I need to eat or anything, I'll just faint from starvation and fall off the wagon. At least I have my hat. I don't want to be late now that everyone's clustered around the *fábrica,* so I scurry off into the communal kitchen before anyone sees me. The people making food read my mind and serve me potatoes and eggs before I even ask. Then they push me outside. The crowd watches me take this steaming-hot plate out to the patio and when I've finished devouring my little meal the entire wagon party has joined me for breakfast.

"You got serious bags under your eyes," Annabelle says, sitting down beside me. "Writing?"

"Mauritius of Thebes?" Gertrude asks. "Your super-grandfather?"

"No, a different relative this time. A clerk in the Paris War Office."

Both of them shovel down their breakfasts while I tell them about Félix. I don't think I tell them much, I try to confine myself to the paintings and bombings, but it's already obvious I've said too much. They both stare at me above their empty plates. The sweet smell of warm bread fills the air.

"And this guy's your cousin?" Annabelle asks. "Is he still alive?"

"No. I think he died a few years ago. And he's not my cousin, he's more like...how do you say it? He's my mom's cousin. No. He's my grandmother's cousin's son. Whatever that's called."

"And *his* mom told him everything?" Gertrude asks. "But Isabelle never told you?"

I just nod and stare at both of them suspiciously. They don't speak but I hear their thoughts just the same. I don't know why Marie-Louise trusted Félix, I don't know why my mother hid the truth from me, I don't even know where she is right now. I thought she'd be here to see me off.

"Have you known about Félix this whole time?" Gertrude asks. "Or is this another secret?"

"No, my mom told me about him when I was a girl. Only she left out how Félix had a lot of help from...see? How do I even begin? Félix had help from people who followed the teachings of Mary Magdalene. People like Yvonne. There. Now don't get me started on that subject."

"This is going to be quite some book!" Annabelle exclaims, grabbing our plates. "Come on!"

"Yeah! Come on!" Gertrude yells. "Let's get down the hill before the rains come back!"

The patio fills with laughter and everyone rises with their dishes, allowing me to sneak off for a fresh baguette. It occurs to me that everyone might want some bread so I carry ten baguettes over to the wagons where they've all assembled and are dividing up tasks. When the role of brake-people comes up, I'm one of five to raise their hands. Paola's already volunteered to be a driver and picks me as her companion. Annabelle and Gertrude team up, Lorraine volunteers with Isabelle, my friends from the sunflower farm pair up with each other, and most everyone else is on foot. Two of the wagons are going to carry elders from the communal house who want to live their last days near the ocean. One of them is going to ride in my wagon, an old woman named Agatha who claims the planet's angry with us. That's why it's been so hot, she says. As we carry her tiny body to the wagon-bed, she says that if the planet wasn't so angry, we'd all have our electricity turned on.

"Anyway, you girls drive careful, you hear?" Agatha yells. "I wouldn't want my last moments of this earth to smell like a horse's ass."

"Don't worry," I tell her. "It's *me* behind the brake. Everyone can tell you how fast I am."

She lets out a gentle sigh as we lower her onto the soft bags of wheat. She adjusts herself like a princess, tests the bags with her elbows, then leans back satisfied, her head facing the driver's seat.

"*Bom*, Agatha?" Paola asks. "This fine for you?"

"Let's see how you treat those horses, girl. Otherwise, yeah, I'm fine."

I wink at Paola and jump onto the seat-box. We've got a team of four horses from the vineyard, broken animals resigned to help us with all our burdens. Paola dœsn't seem to mind but most people in our commune are reluctant to yoke these creatures for any reason, even to drag some barrels up a hill, let alone till the soil. It still reminds them of slavery, as it should.

"These poor animals," I say. "Such beauties."

"You all revere them too much. It's bizarre."

"They'd run away if we actually revered them. They just fear us, poor things. Broken as babies."

"It's not as bad as you make it out. I've broken a horse before. You just—"

Two of the horses stamp their hooves as the first wagon rolls off. We're third in line and soon enough Paola stirs the reigns and whistles for our horses to get moving. They obey without a sideways glance and keep their black manes pointed straight. I yank the brake lever when the wagon tilts down the slope and feel the horses tug against the grinding tension. They're putting a lot of trust in me, a whole wagon-load, and I can't let them down, not with all this weight at their backs.

"You trying to trip those horses or what, girl?" Agatha yells.

"Yeah, ease off the brake just a bit," Paola tells me. "About half that much."

"Hey, it's *me*!" I yell back. "I drive like a grandmother!"

"Don't knock grandmothers!" Agatha protests. "I just moved away from the best grandmother there ever was! There won't ever be a better person than Yvonne del Valle! You're lucky to have her for your godmother, Fulvia! Most people are lucky to even talk with her!"

"You talk to her a lot?" I yell back.

Agatha dœsn't respond. When I eventually turn around she's smiling atop the wheat bags, eyes wide open, feet wiggling like a little kid. I take her silence for a yes. Nearly half the communal house is over sixty, the other half younger than twenty, and everyone else around my age. This was how Yvonne designed it, a place for orphans and elders. Some of the children claim Yvonne built secret passages connecting the rooms on the elder's floor. None of the elders ever deny it, but only now do I realize it might be true. Maybe there's a whole world I don't know about the communal house.

"I think Agatha passed out," Paola says. "Look."

Sure enough, I see Agatha's head rolling back and forth as we creak down the mountain. Our wagons are spaced about twenty meters apart and everyone else marches alongside us, people who wanted to leave the village for a spell, have an adventure, meet strangers, or even bargain with sea-traders for coffee and luxuries. All of us curve together along this winding mill road cut deep into the hillside. It's getting hot now and I'm glad I brought my hat. Agatha seems to be doing fine back there, she's stretched a scarf over her face like a tent, its ends tucked between the wheat bags.

"You know her well?" Paola asks, tilting her head towards Agatha.

"Not really. I knew her son before he left. I think he's in Tokyo now. You never heard the stories about her? Old Agatha fighting in Sacramento with my uncles?"

"I know about your uncles. I didn't know she was there with them."

"Agatha led that assault. No one knows how she survived, either. No gun, no knife, nothing, just an old farmer's widow with raging lungs and fists like hammers. Look at them! See how long her fingers are? Agatha stayed on the front line until they blew up the capitol just so she could spit on the ruins. She got here when I was in San Francisco, said she wanted to die near the woman who planned this whole revolution thing. Yvonne, obviously."

"I guess she changed her mind," Paola says, smirking. "Yvonne must have lost her charm."

"Yvonne didn't set this whole thing off. She'd say the same thing if you ever asked her."

"Yvonne talks a lot of junk. If it wasn't for her money, where would the guns have come from? Where would Tesla have got his funding? Huh? Who? Seriously. What's the problem with you people? Yvonne had everything to do with...everything!"

"It took thousands of years to do what we did. Thousands! It's not just her."

"She's important, Fulvia. And she's batty to waste away her strength and just read all day."

"It's how she's always been, and that's not how she sees it because that's not how it is. Nothing's going to change her mind, and everything's up to us now. That's what she'd say. You, me, them in the wagons up there...wait, you see that up ahead?"

I pull hard on the brake when it's clear something's the matter with Lorraine's wagon. She stands up on her seat while little Isabelle holds onto the brake lever. Lorraine hops down to the road, waits a moment, then slams the iron bolt in the brake-lock, a clear sign we're stuck. Before I can speak, Paola hops down, locks us in place, and runs off like a soldier. It's scary how fast she moves.

"How you doing back there, Agatha?"

I hear someone laughing up ahead.

"Agatha? You alright?"

I spin around, ready to jump into the wheat sacks, when Agatha slowly pulls the scarf away, her wrinkled face beaming back bright and alive. Her bony fingers grip the fabric over strands of gray hair and from where I'm standing her face is upside down, eyes glowing a golden brown.

"Your friend back yet?" she asks, blinking. "What did she find out?"

I don't have an answer so I turn around to discover Paola running up the road with those perfect white teeth glistening against dark brown skin. Better not look at her too hard, don't want to project the wrong idea. We've already shared enough, anything else might blow a hole in the world.

"It's the damn spring gushing everywhere!" Paola yells, panting. "Little Isabelle tried walking through it. Sunk right down to her calf. Don't worry. They're laying the planks up front. We'll be rolling soon enough. You'll see it. That spring's spraying everywhere."

"A spring!" Agatha cries out. "Of course she does! A spring!"

The old lady explodes in laughter and pulls the scarf back over her face. Paola looks at me, confused about the *she* Agatha's talking about. I just raise my eyebrows and let my eyes float away towards the ocean. *She is the dreamer.* I don't even know where to begin, but I guess I should start somewhere. This hesitation is where the lie starts.

"You remember much about the Kashaya village?" I ask her. "Being caught in the Dream?"

"Ahhh—" Paola places her elbow on the sideboard and rubs her chin. "It's a little foggy, but it was like...pushing my way through cotton, or spiderwebs, but I could see the other side, I could taste the fresh air, only it wasn't getting any closer, and then everything started to feel like a pillow. Is that what Agatha's screaming about? Some woman in the Dream?"

"Not really a woman," I say, trying to sound confident. "More like an over-soul."

"An over-soul? Come on. What is the Dream? Maybe I'm just stupid, but tell me plainly."

"It's your best fear and your worst happiness. Until you wake up. Then you're free."

"How come only outsiders have to go through it?"

"That's the confusing part, I guess. There's no outside to the Dream. It's what we—"

"Ahhhh...just sounds like more of Yvonne's babble. This is what I mean, you all—"

Suddenly we hear a stomping of hooves as Lorraine and Isabelle get their horse team moving towards the spring. The hikers guide the wagon across the planks and Isabelle looks pretty sturdy up there next to her mom. It's truly a miracle she's even on this trip. Lorraine spent many years on wagon beds, usually firing a machine-gun and hoping my mother kept their horse-team at full sprint across the *black earth region*, the *chernozem*. To her, horses are linked with death, and she's forbidden Isabelle from ever riding one by herself, let alone a wagon. If old Lorraine doesn't ease up, I'll have to smuggle Isabelle off to San Francisco before she pops her cork. I don't think our little village can hold that fire raging inside her. It's going to be brighter than mine soon enough.

I hold the brake handle while Paola slips out the iron bolt-lock and sets the horses off towards the plank bridge. I smell the spring before I see it, filling the air with moisture from underground rivers that flow beneath the soil. Our wheels slowly turn over the wet planks and deliver us across the pit of churning mud, accompanied by a burst of applause. Neither of us speak once we're across and I loosen my grip on the brake during the next flat stretch, keeping my fingers on the handle in case we pick up some speed. Lorraine and Isabelle are way off in the distance and I can finally glimpse our destination: the coastal village of Fort Russ, built above the frothing Pacific Ocean.

The redwood walls of this old Russian fort enclose the communal farm, a bulky trading house, and a few cabins with smoking chimneys. Outside the fortress gates, two narrow piers made of wood and iron are suspended above the cove near the glass factory, extending all the way out to deep water. Each corner of Fort Russ has a structure built into it. One used to be a Russian Orthodox Church, the others were sharpshooter shacks from back when this was a real fortress. Now its salt-stained walls are surrounded by fifty houses with farm plots, gardens, a communal windmill powered by the ocean wind, and a small Kashaya village called *Máy-tee-nee*, or *a part of a place*. On the grassy slopes above this indigenous village are the creek-fed fruit orchards where our valley road comes to its end.

This is the most difficult part of the journey with its steep grade and winding turns. My arm aches from pulling this brake handle, my neck's already sore, and Paola's covered in sweat but trying to be nonchalant about it. One of the horses shits out some green droppings and the hot smell hits me right in the nose with its moist foulness. I take this opportunity to turn around and check on Agatha, only she doesn't respond. Bertha's in the wagon behind us. She sees me looking, she waves frantically, and I wave back as best I can, hoping she doesn't get jealous over Paola. If I could only tell them both the truth: I'd rather be asleep than riding with either of them. We'll be there in a few hours, maybe sooner, so I might have time for a nap before tonight's celebration.

"Agatha?" I ask. "You awake?"

"Stop bothering her. Let the woman rest."

"I can't imagine how she sleeps through all this noise. I'll be hearing it in my dreams."

"It's the jolting that gets me, like right here, on this curve." Paola pulls the reigns and guides the horse-team around the bend. "The back and forth, the up and down. Almost there, at least. I bet the people on foot are in the orchard already."

I linger on this comforting thought, imagining the epic feast we'll all have once night falls on the coastline. The thought of buttery seafood makes my mouth water and I begin to hum that favorite tune of mine, "She'll Be Coming Around The Mountain," but then I lose control and start singing out loud. It's not just the thought of food that gets me excited. I'm going to see him tonight. I'll see him when no one's looking. I'm getting wet between my legs just thinking about it. I've kept it a secret, but tonight I'll make it real, when no one's expecting anything, especially him.

My heart pounds with fire as I sing through this classic of the Underground Railroad. After a minute of glaring, Paola starts singing along. I remember dancing like a rabid fox when the band played this tune at my favorite San Francisco rag-n-jass houses, those first notes heralded by a chorus of wild howling. I went cross-eyed with bliss when the entire dance-hall sang in unison to all those African and Caribbean melodies, their hands flapping in the air, their heels clacking against polished wood. I'd be the center of attention until Juana del Valle walked onto the dance floor with her raging magnetic field, ready to outstrip all my moves. People called her the *head witch* back then, but I thought it was just a dumb joke. If my mother had told me the truth, Juana and I wouldn't have had those operatic fights that roared through San Francisco, engulfing hundreds of people in a rage that always started in the dance-hall. I can hear the music now, only instead of horns, bass, woodwinds, pianos, and drums, those sounds are replaced by a rocking wagon.

"You sing good," Paola tells me, wiping her sweaty forehead. "Like a jass singer."

"You want to wear my hat for a while? Here." I plant it on her head, careful not to forget the brake. "And people think *I'm* careless. How are you going to forget a hat on a day like today? Crazy lady! When are you going to embrace being a farm girl?"

"That song's got you all hopped up! I never see you like this."

"It brings me back to old times, that's all. When I was your age. In San Francisco."

"Yeah, *so old, Fulvia*! They still dance to this song last I was there."

"It's an old tune, no doubt, but we brought it back. That was our victory song. It comes from the south. It's code from the Underground Railroad, back in slavery times. She drives them to freedom, speeds down the mountain with six white horses! Get it?"

"I never knew," Paola says, suddenly stern. "It's...very beautiful. I didn't know."

We get real silent after that. They had slavery in Brazil just the same as Tennessee. Who can say which was worse? Who can remember all the forgotten songs? For whatever reason, this is the one we both know. Paola clutches the reigns and we drive in silence until the first fruit trees come into view. I let go of the brake once the road levels and suddenly there's a loud clattering coming from the hill above. Bertha and Gabrielle catch up with us in the apple orchards and we all howl like coyotes once we near the Fort Russ gates. There's already a thick crowd enveloping the first wagon and soon we're surrounded by two hundred cheering villagers waving colored ribbons in the air.

I'm carried off the driver's seat in one direction, Paola in another, and they've got me floating on my back atop a sea of hands. I ride the back of this snarling dragon until it sets me down behind the wagon where I'm reunited with red-cheeked Paola. I hear endless gratitude for the bags of wheat and assurances of mussels cooked in butter, wine, and herbs. Everyone's flushed and sweaty and smiling like lunatics as colorful ribbons stream from the tips of slender wooden poles. I've almost forgotten about Agatha when the first villagers hop inside the wagon to lift her up. They pull the scarf away, then everything freezes. Her lungs aren't moving, her eyes are wide open, and she's got her hands clutched together, a slip of brown paper sticking between them. No one stops me from climbing onto the wagon to read the note, but everyone grows terribly mute when I suddenly laugh.

Paola grabs the note from my hands and mouths the words to herself, unable to comprehend how this could be possible, and we look at each other blankly until the message makes sense. The entire crowd is deathly silent and no one stirs when the last two wagons arrive. Once the silence grows unbearable, I announce that we need to bury Agatha at sea only Paola interrupts me and reads the note aloud. I try not to be angry, but Agatha meant these words only for me: *I could never stomach the thought of drowning but always wanted to die in the ocean. Make sense of that for me, would you? Sorry to pull this little stunt, but I didn't want to die up there on the hill. This way I get to end my life in the middle of a journey. Cast me to sea at sunset. The tide should be going out. I trust you'll see this through. I planned this all for a reason. Tell my story one day. If you can.*

I can only hear the wind when Paola finishes reading. All the colorful ribbons flutter from their poles, each making a faint hiss. Few of these people know Agatha but all of them show their respect by not saying a word. I'm about to speak when Berthe wraps her arms around me and kisses my sweaty neck, her face pressed so close I smell her tears. The crowd silently gazes at Agatha but a some of them cast me a curious eye, especially after Berthe starts kissing me. I definitely just laughed at Agatha's final words like some cold, remorseless bitch. Hopefully they won't remember it for long. Before I can do anything to redeem myself, Paola asks the crowd for help with the funeral. After a flurry of motion, the villagers manifest a small canoe lined with redwood boughs.

Berthe lets go of my sides and helps Paola lower Agatha inside the boat, giving me the chance to melt away towards the glass factory. No one notices, they're too busy discussing the funeral. I hear Lorraine talking about Agatha's exploits during the siege of Sacramento, how she burned the flag of the United States before its defeated federal army. The entire crowd laughs and claps while I slip away behind the side of a farmhouse. None of them notice. Everything's perfect.

I make my way through the deserted village, the air filled with the pounding of waves. Every house is empty, their doors thrown wide open in a moment of celebration now become a funeral. I pass through a grove of cypress and follow the wagon path towards the glass factory where a little tuft of smoke is flowing from the chimney. I hope he's there alone because I'll never get a better chance. I don't think Agatha would mind if I slept with him, she'd tell me to follow my heart, and that's what I'm going to do. I walk into the factory and find Octavio shirtless, twirling a bright red cylinder of glass on the tip of an iron rod. His sweaty brown skin reflects the firelight and I lean my shoulder against a dirty support beam to watch him work. He's finishing the cross-shaped nozzle for another separator funnel, smoothing out the molten glass before it sets. I don't know who he could be making these for. My mom already has six replacement funnels sitting in her barn and she's the only person who distills up there, so it must be for someone else. All our local scents come from Isabelle the alchemist.

Octavio doesn't see me, doesn't hear me, doesn't notice me lurking. The red glass eventually cools and he slides the transparent nozzle into a row with five others. He takes a few deep breaths and gulps down a tall glass of water, still oblivious. This is all very odd. I don't usually creep around in the shadows to watch people in their natural environment. He'll start on the next funnel soon so I better get moving if this is going to happen. I take a few steps towards the raging furnace and make enough noise for Octavio to hear. He turns around into my open arms, unable to resist the embrace.

"Fulvia?" Strings of curly hair cover his sweaty forehead. "You alright?"

He tries to push me off but I don't let him, I just stare into his green eyes and smile.

"I won't tell anyone," I say. "I don't want a lover. Or a husband. Or a father. I just want this."

I don't mean to hurt Octavio but I clutch a bit too hard, probably from jerking that brake handle all morning. He tries to back up but I hold him steady. He's fifteen years older, closer to my mother's age. They fought together in Russia and he reveres her like a goddess, so this shouldn't be difficult. I've been planning it for months. Octavio's eyes are filled with fear, the heat begins to fade in the furnace, and I loosen my grip just enough for him to escape. He doesn't go anywhere.

"I'm a woman now," I tell him. "You realize this?"

"It's not that, Fulvia. This doesn't sit right."

"Why? Because of my mom? Because I'm thirty-five years old?"

"You never did this before, not in all the—"

"Yeah, I'm doing it now, because I want a baby. And you're the most reliable one around. But don't let that get to your head." I rub his curly hair and push myself into his crotch. "Like I said, I just want a baby. But that doesn't mean—"

Luckily I don't need to explain. It would have been too difficult. I wrap my legs around his back and he carries me over to the work-table without a word. He'll think I'm crazy when it's all over but that doesn't really matter, does it now? He tastes like water and grass and his hair smells like smoke. I plant my feet on the floor, drape my clothes across the work-table, and frantically unbuckle his belt. Octavio pushes me back on the smooth wooden surface and then it happens before I can blink. It's been years since I did it with a man and felt this strange thing inside me. I don't see very much, just explosions of color when I climax. He keeps on going, white light charges up my vision, raw nerve endings explode with pleasure, and then his thing shrivels up inside. I push him off me after that. I feel warmth glowing in my body now so I lift my knees and rock backwards to keep it all inside.

"Want me to push you?" he whispers.

"Could you?"

Shameless. He grabs my ass with both hands and pushes it back like a rocking chair. I'm arched on the wooden work-table now, my pussy pointed at his face, and Octavio's having the best evening of his life. I can tell from his shit-eating grin. The bastard even made me climax. Wait until he hears about Agatha dead in the canoe. Then he'll never want to see me again.

"How long should I do this?" he asks.

"I just need to give them a chance to find my egg. Another minute or two."

"You really are a woman. You were right—"

"Okay, okay, not interested, seriously not interested. Come on. Change the subject. Who are those funnels for? No one up on the hill, right?"

"San Francisco. Then off to who knows where. Your mom still—"

"She's got enough funnels, Octavio. Trust me. You're such a loyal knight. She doesn't deserve you. How long are you going to let the war haunt you, man? I mean, this right here between us won't ever happen again, but you need to promise you'll find someone. Can you?"

"No, I can't do that," he says, letting my ass drop to the table. "You're being cruel."

I don't know what I'm being. He steps back into his pants, his cock still shiny from our juices, and I keep my hips raised just above the table. If someone walked in right now they might think I'm casting some pussy enchantment over the glass factory with all its bottles, vials, and funnels. I take five minutes to cast my enchantment, waiting until I'm positive it's a girl, then I roll naked off the table and chase him over to the furnace.

"Thank you!" I exclaim, forcing my cheek against his bare chest. "You'll always know the truth, just like me, and I'll tell her you're her father when she asks. I wasn't trying to hurt you when I said...I just want you to be happy, Octavio. Are you happy?"

"I'm happy enough, Fulvia." He kisses my forehead before pushing me away. "And I guess you're right. I'm lonely. This has been—"

The old goat's crying now so I hold him close right there in the middle of the factory. None of these old fighters cry, not even in private. My mother saved Octavio's life during the war, Octavio saved her life, and Isabelle never took him as her lover. She didn't take anyone, as far as anyone knows, but Octavio's waited down here for her since 1928. I couldn't guess how long his heart's been bottled up tighter than one of his hermetic *kerotakis*, but all that hot steam builds inside until he transmutes it into molten red gold. Thanks to him, this entire coast is stocked-full with glass cups, bowls, jars, pitchers, and demijohns. He really is special, so I hold Octavio until his body grows limp and he's ready to sleep. We walk over to his bed where I lay beside him atop the dirty blankets, just until he's snoring. The furnace is out when I put on my clothes and slip out through an open window into the beginnings of an orange sunset. They'll be wondering where I am now.

By the time I get back to the village, all of Fort Russ is congregated atop the cliffs above two raging bonfires. The flames burn on either side of the funeral canoe while saltwater laps to shore just feet away. In the twilight, the full moon is shining, and my friends takes their places as if around an altar. Agatha's body is covered in flowers, her head adorned with a redwood crown, her brittle hands folded together just as she left them, and I sprint through the crowd before they cast her off without me. None of my friends speak when I reach the canoe, they just count to three before we lift Agatha into the air. I see Paola isn't wearing my hat anymore. I hope she left it somewhere safe. I like that straw hat.

Lorraine, little Isabelle, Gertrude, Annabelle, Bertha, Gabrielle, Nadia, Monique, Paola, and I carry our departed friend across the sand and into the ebb tide. They don't suspect a thing, none of them look at me, none of them care what I was doing. The ocean's freezing as our breasts fall in the water, our fingers curled around the canoe's wooden sidings. Isabelle's definitely taller than me now, just like her mother, and we hold the canoe aloft until it's too deep to walk. Lorraine counts to three and we send Agatha gliding off into the blood red sunset with her crown of green boughs. The canoe slides past the iron piers and gets sucked into the ocean current where it'll soon be pulled westward.

I spin onto my back to watch her go, lazily kicking my way back to shore. This saltwater's still cold as hell but I've never seen a sky burning so beautifully, like molten glass dripping over an invisible sphere. The ocean bobs me, holds me, rocks me, lulls me into something like a dream. I hear Isabelle and Lorraine call my name, alternating their voices one after the other, then everyone's yelling. When I spin onto my stomach, there's a slick boulder unveiling itself from a cloak of water, ready to knock me unconscious. I paddle away and kick with all my strength until Bertha and Gabrielle grab my arms, pull me to shore, then walk me over to the raging bonfires where we dry our soaked clothing. Once I'm sitting down, I watch the bobbling canoe get carried off by the ebb tide into a fading red sunset. Agatha got her last wish. Of course she did. She planned it this way.

"Where'd you go?" Bertha asks, putting a blanket over my shoulder. "I looked for you."

"We all did," Lorraine says. "I was worried."

"I'm fine. I just needed air."

None of them believe me. Obviously. They just stare into the raging fire while the villagers feed the blazes with more driftwood. Salty wood always smells acrid when it burns, it sticks in the mouth and turns the flame an eerie lavender, but I try not to think about the toxicity, not when it's so warm and cozy. The first stars come out above our heads, the tiny canoe fades into darkness, and soon Agatha will be gone. There's no point drawing this out, so I bend towards the flame, grab a smoldering log, and stab it deep into the burning light. The eruption of sparks blurs my vision into a scrambled darkness. I look one last time towards the horizon and see pure night beneath the stars. Agatha's disappeared.

Someone brings a case of wine over, Lorraine toasts our departed comrade, and the night of celebration begins. *Now, while we dance, come here to us gentle Gaiety, Revelry, Radiance, and you, Muses with lovely hair.* The solemness of the ceremony is broken, everyone begins to laugh. I drink wine by the fire with my ass in the sand, Bertha and Paola on either side. Everyone wants to be close to us hill people. They serve us buttery mussels, fish stew, and fresh bread baked with rosemary. We're the talk of the entire village, heroes from the hills, and they all listen to us with flame-lit eyes. Berthe touches me, so does Paola, caressing my body at every opportunity, and they clearly want to share me. I can't let this go on. I tell them I'll be right back, that I really need to take a shit. Who wants to get naked and dirty when they're full of crap? They let me squeeze away after promising to return, but once I'm free they'll never be able to find me. I climb up the cliff away from the beach, walk around the wooden fortress, and return to Octavio's glass factory, now dark beneath the heavens. There's only a faint red glow left in the furnace. Everything else is shadow.

I hear Octavio snoring while I fumble across the dirty floor looking for the toilet. I grope around for a candle, eventually light one, and find a wood-chip latrine off in the corner. I'm sitting there for a while, trying to squeeze something out. All that bread's got me backed up but the sound of ocean waves eventually helps me relax. A few women must work in this factory because I'm able to wash my ass over a clean porcelain bowl. Drying myself with a fresh towel sure feels nice, but it's time for this day to be over. I'm starting to feel spread thin.

Moonlight guides me towards Octavio's bedroom window and I blow out the candle wick once I've locked his door. Through the glass, I gaze at the heavens hanging pregnant above my head. *Awed by her splendor, stars near the lovely moon cover their bright faces when she's roundest, lighting the earth with her silver.* I leave the window open for my morning escape, slide into the warm bed, and pull the covers over our bodies. I get naked sometime in the night and climb on top of him just for fun. It happens again at dawn. In between is a dreamless sleep that I don't remember.

Octavio's still in bed when the roosters scream. I must have worn him out because this tireless worker just keeps sleeping. I'm about to make breakfast when I hear that sharp crack of day-lit thunder rolling across the ocean. There's no mistaking the sound. I shake Octavio, yell something about dreams, but I'm sure it doesn't make any sense so I just throw on my clothes and slide out the bedroom window before he's even opened his eyes. Ocean spray fills the air as I run to the edge of the cliff and gaze in awe at the throbbing arc of light stretching all the way from Russia, our new electromagnetic ribbon, bleeding plasma through the atmosphere from one iron transmitter to another. The pale white thread of limitless energy is blotted out by the violet, green, and blue womb of throbbing energy, the ultra-potent charge of our earthly sphere. I fall to my knees atop the cliff and scream until my body fills with laughter. I hear those haunting words rise up through the surf. *She is the dreamer.* I think I know what it means now.

THE ARRIVAL OF BIANCA LEMEL AND HER DAUGHTER BEATRIX

JOSEPHINE LOVED TO WATCH MOUNT DIABLO LIGHT UP A PALE SHADE OF brown as dawn burned away the darkness. Those distant heights were covered in snow every odd winter, a thin shroud that never lingered more than a week, and this lone mountain was the closest semblance to *Les Diablerets* she ever saw, although this familiar sight vanished once Josephine moved over to the Latin Quarter. The neighborhood obscured her favorite mountaintop and the new apartment offered nothing more than a panorama of busy Montgomery Street. The only way to glimpse Mount Diablo was by walking up the backside of Telegraph Hill to the summit, a journey she took every Sunday morning with her daughter Isabelle. Marisol never accompanied them. The two friends had stopped speaking.

After the death of my grandfather, Josephine emerged from paralysis to help her sons deal with their disastrous bombing. The crimp Johnny Curtin had survived the blast, his boardinghouse remained standing, and four scab sailors were blown to pieces. The daily papers demonized the Coast Sailor's Union while dozens were jailed on charges related to the explosion. Andrew Furuseth closed the sailor's hiring hall, offered a thousand dollar reward for the identity of the bombers, and publicly referred to the culprits as agents of the ship-owners. This last claim was false, obviously, but Furuseth said he needed to disown the deadly blast. My uncles gave all their extra money to the families of these imprisoned sailors but never spoke of their deed to anyone, nor were they ever discovered. The only person who suspected the truth was Sigismund Danielewicz, although he never betrayed my uncles, not even when the case grew serious. Because he was their best radical lawyer, Burnett Haskell returned from the *Sierra Nevada* to defend the man accused of planting the bomb: a sailor named John Tyrell.

After a drawn-out show trial that ended in Tyrell's acquittal, the coastal sailors welcomed their exonerated comrade back to liberty and threw a boisterous celebration at the Bulkhead Saloon. While police spies watched these drunken sailors,

Sigismund Danielewicz

Josephine slipped through the window of Johnny Curtin's apartment and slit his throat. She forced his family to watch her gruesome act before stabbing them all to death and setting their house ablaze with lamp oil. As the fire-wagons pumped streams of salt water to stop her fire from burning down the city, Josephine walked through the back door of the little blue house and found Marisol kneeling before an image of *Santa Muerte*. After spilling an entire family's blood, Josephine finally understood. Through some magical charm, Marisol had concealed her worship of *Santa Muerte* all these years, only now the fateful reckoning had arrived.

Marisol watched in disbelief as my grandmother transformed into *Santa Muerte,* her white skull shrouded beneath a dark red hood. Josephine threw herself at Marisol and plunged them deep into a watery tube from which they soon emerged clawing at each other's necks, knocking over furniture, and slamming their bodies into brightly painted walls. People still tell stories of how water poured from under the front door, across the porch, and then drained down Greenwich Street like a torrential river. These old friends fought and wrestled and screamed until this water stopped flowing and the writhing underworld closed beneath them. Josephine accused Marisol of using her just like she used the women in her brothel and said she was no different than a follower of Mary: selfish, greedy, and willing to let others suffer just to maintain her comfortable position. She then accused Marisol of luring her to San Francisco as a weapon of vengeance, regardless of what happened to her family. Marisol was unable to speak. Her best friend was *Sante Muerte*. Everything she said was correct.

Josephine sat on the drenched floor waiting for a response, unaware she was fluttering in and out of the underworld, between bone and flesh. The last water drained from the house and Josephine reverted back to herself just as dawn becomes day. She apologized to Marisol, promised to love her forever, and then left the house where she raised her four children, all of whom were relieved when she finally returned to their Latin Quarter apartment, soaking wet and claiming she'd fallen into the bay. After my uncles went to work, Josephine revealed to Isabelle what she'd seen inside the underworld. Amid an explosion of green water, a dozen naked women had revealed her future: Josephine would sew from home to make money, attend Catholic Mass every Sunday to spy on the Italian bourgeois, and pretend she was a grieving widow who never spoke. Isabelle said nothing in response.

My seven-year-old mother went out with Josephine that morning and purchased an iron sewing-machine at the second-hand supplier. After paying a teamster to haul this contraption up to the Latin Quarter, Josephine took Isabelle into a religious bookshop where she bought a wood and metal crucifix. Josephine didn't attempt to explain herself and once the teamsters had

gotten the iron machine up the ſtairs, she nailed the cross over her work ſta-
tion where it remained for the next eight years. My uncles were petrified that
night when they firſt discovered their mother playing the Catholic widow
sewing beneath her crucifix. Sergio asked why she needed to hang the cross
at home but Josephine changed the subjeſt and my uncles never got a clear
answer. They toiled all day on the waterfront and came home to this image
of Yeshua ha-Nozri nailed to the cross, leering above their mother like a
gargoyle. Over the next months, this bizarre speſtacle ſtarted to make my
uncles cynical.

Josephine and Isabelle slept together in their apartment's single bedroom
while my uncles reſted in the living room on down mats. The family rose
before dawn, the brothers rolled up their beds, and they all ate breakfaſt
together before my uncles grabbed their hooks off the rack and left for the
docks. Josephine ſteadily pumped her iron machine until lunch, sewing
blouse after blouse for A.P. Schwarze, an enterprising German-Swiss who
hired widows and mothers to do piece-work at three-fourths the wages of
faſtory workers. Josephine knew she was being exploited, that she was under-
cutting other women in the process, but she simply didn't care. The revolt
that was needed wouldn't come from higher wages, it would come from slaying the enemy. She said this all quite plainly whenever her sons brought home
their meager paychecks, hoping they'd never forget the reason they hooked
cargo in the freezing wind for $3 a day. It wasn't to make money, it was to
shut everything down.

The financial panic of 1893 dragged on and on, creating a vaſt army of
unemployed workers who depressed wages across the land, although food
prices remained the same. In the city of Chicago, train workers for the
Pullman Palace Car Company were unable to feed their families, causing
them to ſtrike for higher wages, and that summer of 1894 saw the national
railway syſtem paralyzed from Philadelphia to Oakland. On July 29, all rail
traffic through the San Francisco Bay was shut down, filling the harbor with
a backlog of cargo ships. The train terminus in Oakland had its engines
killed, tracks deſtroyed, switches jammed, telegraph wires cut, and rail-
bridges dynamited. Outside of the ſtate capitol of Sacramento, a train filled
with federal soldiers was blaſted off a bridge, killing several, including the
engineer. Because of this deadly ſtrike, the mail was held up for weeks, cargo
was left idle in every port-town, and American capitalism ground to a halt.

Amid her boundless grief, Josephine was inspired by this national upsurge,
even after the ſtrike was crushed. Over a hundred were arreſted and charged
with sabotaging the Oakland terminus while a single man, Salter Worden,
was conviſted of the Sacramento dynamite blaſt and sentenced to be hung,
a verdiſt the California public wouldn't accept. After suffering under the

Southern-Pacific Railroad's despotism for years, no other ſtate supported the ſtrike with such vigor. Worden's death sentence was commuted to life after massive public outcry and only a single San Francisco newspaper condemned the ſtrike. Popular support shifted back to the unions and my uncle's disaſtrous bomb was quickly forgotten in these times of promise, allowing the sailors to rise like a phœnix.

Unable to work on the waterfront with her brothers, Isabelle learned to read and write in the Latin Quarter apartment while Josephine sewed blouses on her iron machine. My mother was taught from a young age that women had few options in the US: they could work a limited number of jobs for wages lower than men or they could marry someone wealthy. Women were not allowed to vote outside a few rural US ſtates, juſt as they were barred from being elected to office. Aside from these depressing realities, Josephine lectured her daughter on every conceivable subject, from geography to chemiſtry, and taught Isabelle to be fluent in seven languages, including our ancient mother-tongue. This was their secret Celtic language, spoken in whispers, never written down, and Josephine didn't teach her sons for fear they might use it. As she told my mother, the darkness was always hunting them and one false slip of the tongue could betray them to its agents, spies, and informers. Inſtead, my uncles read Italian anarchiſt newspapers to their siſter when they got home, cooked dinner for their mother, and lived in complete ignorance of their Alpine mother-tongue. Josephine sat with her children after these dinners to mull over the lateſt calamity or laugh at a cynical joke, though no matter how cheerful the banter, the ghoſt of Antonio haunted their spirits. Only young Isabelle seemed unfazed.

My mother came of age in a burgeoning Latin Quarter densely packed with Italian immigrants. When Josephine arrived in 1873, there were less than 2,000 Italian exiles mixed in with the French, Spanish, Portuguese, and Basque. By the year 1895, there were nearly 6,000 thousand Italians living in the Latin Quarter who spoke in multiple dialects from across the Roman peninsula. Isabelle was fluent in every language of this patchwork neighborhood and loved to wander its narrow streets and cramped alleyways. By the age of nine, she could navigate the inner city with her eyes closed and relayed the day's observations to Josephine each night while her brothers were asleep. Josephine had stopped leaving the apartment entirely except for Sunday Mass at the Church of Saints Peter and Paul where she observed the newly-risen Italian bourgeois covered in fancy clothing and expensive perfume. No one suspected her intentions and the churchgœrs quickly grew accustomed to this silent sailor's widow who wandered up Telegraph Hill at the end of each Mass. This was the strange routine that kept my 45-year-old grandmother sane through the darkest period of her life.

In July 1894, the mysterious war across the Pacific finally revealed itself when the Japanese Empire and the Chinese Qing Empire went to war over possession of the Korean Peninsula. Within days, the Chinese sent their German-built warships to confront the British-built warships used by the Japanese, a bloodbath engineered by western interests. By 1895, Japan had beaten back the Chinese and claimed Korea, the Liaodong Peninsula, and Taiwan as part of their Imperial dominion. Unwilling to let Japan have too much of a free hand, Germany, France, and Russia swooped in and claimed as much of China as they could defend, emasculating the Japanese Empire and enabling the next war across the Pacific. Regardless of the loss of life, this Sino-Japanese War was a boon to the builders of armored warships, especially in the shipyards of San Francisco.

Towards the end of 1895, a telegram arrived at the apartment while Josephine was sewing her thirtieth blouse of the day. It was sent from New York City and contained the cryptic message: *coming sister, don't despair.* My great-aunt Bianca arrived in San Francisco four months later on the Lunar New Year of 1896, accompanied by her daughter Beatrix. While the young Lemel cousins wandered the Latin Quarter, the Lemel sisters sat in the apartment and talked for hours about the bombing wave in Paris, the repression against the French anarchist movement, and the global conspiracy of JP Morgan. Were it not for Sante Geronimo Caserio's assassination of President Sadi Carnot, the French Republic would have already sold the Panama Canal project to JP Morgan & Co. Bianca claimed this physically deformed banker was the modern equivalent of an ancient emperor and that the order to kill Antonio came directly from his office at 23 Wall Street. Morgan's manufactured financial crisis of 1893 had removed the reigning party from the White House and now William McKinley, a man firmly in the pocket of Wall Street, would soon be elected president of the US. With the federal government now in permanent debt to his banks, JP Morgan controlled the entire national economy. Only the two oceans remained unconquered.

Despite this dark information, Bianca heralded better times. Just a few weeks behind her was Pietro Gori, an exiled Italian anarchist now on tour across the US. This poet, lawyer, propagandist, songwriter, and singer had created International groups wherever he stopped, reviving their subversive net-work from the Atlantic to the Pacific. Bianca volunteered to organize Gori's San Francisco lecture and publicize it across the Latin Quarter, claiming it would usher in a brighter future. People were now starved by capitalism, hungry for anarchy, and speaking the truth would be enough to strike the critical spark. All they needed was a lecture hall big enough for this crowd of matchsticks. Bianca asked about the sailor's hall but Josephine refused, claiming it was better to organize outside the workplace, and she suggested they contact the eccentric man who secured this apartment for Antonio, the anti-religious newspaperman and local stage actor Cesare Crespi.

The sisters took Isabelle and Beatrix up the street to the offices of *Il Messaggero*, a fiercely secular paper that attacked both Church and Pope at every opportunity, earning the scorn of respectable bourgeois *prominenti* across the Latin Quarter. When they arrived at the newspaper office, Cesare was setting type with an unfamiliar young man who turned out to be Cesare's adopted-son Enrico, recently returned from his long voyage across the Pacific.

Six years earlier, after my grandfather Antonio secured him employment on a deep-port cargo vessel, Enrico quickly discovered the ruthlessness of the ship-owners for himself. While at sea on his first voyage, a sail-maker happened to argue with their liberal captain, the liberal captain decided to draw a pistol, and a bullet soon pierced the sail-maker's heart. Unaware young Enrico was watching, the captain threw the body overboard and left a long streak of red blood smeared across the deck. By the time he finished this despicable act, 16-year-old Enrico had summoned the entire crew who came armed with knives, wooden stakes, and deadly slung-shots. The captain tried to deny his crime but no one believed him, not with young Enrico frightened beyond his wits. If these sailors killed their captain, as they certainly wished to, they would have been charged as pirates and forced into permanent exile. Mutiny or bondage were their choices, so the sailors made a compromise. If Enrico was allowed to jump ship in Russia, they'd let the captain live as temporary hostage. Having already soiled his pants, the captain happily agreed.

In the year 1890, young Enrico Alberti deserted in Siberia and resolved to find Leo Tolstoy, the famous Russian anarchist and author of *War and*

Peace. This pilgrimage was never realized and Enrico drifted south along the coast of China rather than cross the frigid Siberian tundra. He found work as a sailor for several French cartographers planning an expedition to map the mighty Yangtze River. One of these surveyors, a survivor of the Paris Commune and student of Élisée Reclus, immediately struck up a friendship with Enrico on their long journey down the river. For the next three years, he traveled with these cartographers into the farthest reaches of the Qing Empire and witnessed the near endless biological diversity of the Yangtze, a river that belonged to every creature who resided along its shores, all bound together in a web of interdependence. While he sailed down this life-giving waterway, Enrico was unaware that his mother Giuseppina Alberti had fallen ill and died. He wouldn't return home until 1895 when his youthful wanderlust was abruptly extinguished.

Sigismund Danielewicz met Enrico at the Broadway pier to deliver the grim news: his mother died from pneumonia, Antonio Ferrarri was assassinated by the ship-owners, and the Sailor's Union was nearly destroyed after a long and violent strike. Rather than respond, Enrico left Sigismund on the pier and walked to the Latin Quarter where he found Cesare busy toiling in the newspaper office. These two men allowed themselves to silently feel their loss, held each other beside the printing press, and cried until the floorboards seemed to quiver. After this rare show of emotion, the two men were never this vulnerable again. In the years since his wife's passing, Cesare married a local woman named Sylvia Travaglio and filled the void in his heart with sheets of newsprint and drawers of type. Enrico assumed the last name Travaglio, joined Cesare in feverish printing sessions, and created an anarchist newspaper in honor of Giusseppina, their fallen angel of words and letters. When the Lemel sisters walked inside the office that winter of 1896, the Travaglio men were busy on the latest issue of *Secolo Nuovo*.

Bianca explained to Cesare that Pietro Gori was coming to lecture and asked if he knew of a meeting hall that would rent to anarchists. The newspaperman's eyes suddenly began to beam with light, for Cesare was familiar with the dramatic works of guitar-strumming Gori, and he immediately utilized his secular connections in the Latin Quarter to secure them a night at Washington Square Hall. For the following two weeks, Bianca, Beatrix, Enrico, and Isabelle covered the entire Quarter in bright red posters advertising the lecture and stayed in the newspaper office all

Enrico Travaglio

night drafting provocative articles for *Secolo Nuovo*. Isabelle and her cousin Beatrix soon became *printer's devils*, an endearing nickname bestowed on apprentices of this rebellious craft. They learned to ink plates, write a complete article, and set type without a single error. While young Isabelle was eager to learn, Beatrix conducted herself as if she'd been a master printer in some previous life. Despite these differences, the fiery natures of both Lemel cousins bled onto the pages of *Secolo Nuovo*. As my mother learned to print and write, Josephine sewed blouses for A.P. Schwarze, her days as an assassin now just the mutterings of drunken folklorists. With her sister Bianca taking charge of the movement, Josephine was content to sew in silence.

At the beginning of March, Pietro Gori stepped off his train at the Oakland terminus and rode the ferry across the bay to San Francisco. Bianca waited for him outside the Ferry Building and immediately marched Pietro up the hill to meet Josephine. After shedding many tears for Antonio, Pietro held my grandmother's hand and assured her the anarchist movement was stronger than ever. From the city of Paterson, New Jersey to this infernal harbor of San Francisco, California, Pietro had encountered thousands of anarchists, all dedicated to ending capitalism. Josephine smiled at these kind words but said nothing. Amid the silence, Pietro witnessed the grotesque crucifixion hanging above her sewing machine. In fear and confusion, he kissed Josephine's cheeks and hurried out of the apartment, Bianca following behind him. This solemn vision haunted Pietro for the coming days, inspiring him to animate the air of Washington Square Hall with rebellion, music, and laughter.

On the afternoon of March 15, 1896, four hundred people walked into that hall and emerged committed anarchists. Pietro opened the meeting with these words: *Let others call anarchy folly and madness. Heed them not, but remember that in past ages the greatest scientists and discoverers were called crazy. We are few, but we can band together for the happiness of the world and the well-being of humanity.* A giant red and black flag hung over the stage and Bianca followed Pietro's opening with a fiery speech that sent the room into ecstasy. A halo of light shimmered around her, causing the crowd to mistake Bianca for a teenager as she hailed the anarchist movement and denounced the petty exploiters of San Francisco. After this ethereal oration, Bianca joined Pietro in a stage-play specially written for the Latin Quarter where local bourgeois *prominenti* were lampooned in a rendition of daily capitalist life, bringing the anarchist struggle down from the clouds and making it practical, obvious, and funny. The second great anarchist offensive began that night when the attendees streamed back to their San Francisco homes, minds overflowing with rebellion.

The movement grew rapidly as more Italian immigrants flocked to the anarchists, although Josephine stuck to her routine, just as her sons cleaved to their own. My uncles rose each morning and ambled down Montgomery to the bustling waterfront where they sunk their hooks into wooden cargo boxes, guided them onto the beds of waiting dray-carts, and watched them get driven away to various storefronts, factories, and warehouses. My uncles were the very pistons of capital, working ten-hour days for $18 a week, all in the hope of triggering another maritime strike.

While she was known to haunt its alleyways, Isabelle could never work on the waterfront. She could toil in a factory, slave away as a servant, or sell her body to greedy men. The dockside taverns and saloons were surrounded by an army of these mercenary prostitutes, many of whom doubled as pickpockets, and after observing their craft for months, my ten-year-old mother became a skillful thief, presenting Josephine with wads of cash before bed. No matter how big the haul, Josephine refused to stop sewing, not even for a day, and my young mother didn't understand why.

It was along this seedy waterfront that Isabelle met a curly-haired boy named Shmuel Schwartz. She was prowling for marks to pick-pocket when she found him, covered in tears and surrounded by a gang of young *yanquis* throwing rocks at him for being Jewish. Isabelle removed a knife from her dress pocket and walked unseen behind the gang's leader. Wearing her black dress with its high collar lined in red, she put the knife in the *yanqui's* mouth and cut open his left cheek with one swift motion. Before they understood what happened, Isabelle bolted towards the rest of the *yanquis* and chased them off, their leader limping behind with his mouth oozing blood.

My mother picked Shmuel off the ground, wiped the red streaks from his face, and walked him towards her pickpocket's refuge in the Bulkhead Saloon. After getting him a cup of hot coffee, Shmuel told Isabelle he was looking to make a buck when the gang attacked him out of nowhere. His mother had warned of the vicious *goyim* but he was tired of living with her maternal smothering and religious superstition. Shmuel's father died two years before, leaving them enough money to live on if they were frugal, and his mother insisted he stay at home where everything was provided for. Once Isabelle had cleaned his wounds, Shmuel said he didn't want to go home, so she took him across town to a middle-class house in the Fillmore District with a banquet table packed with food. While he ate in the crowded living room, unsure of who was paying for this grand feast, a beautiful Jewish woman was lecturing the attendees on the sorrows of capitalism. Her name was Anna Strunsky.

This comfortable house where Shmuel dined for free was owned by the Strunsky family. After fleeing the pogroms of the Russian Empire, these seven Jews made their way across Prussia, crossed the seas to England, boarded a steamer named *Egypt*, and moved to New York City until the weather grew too unbearable for Elias, the father. In late 1893, the Strunsky family relocated to San Francisco and Isabelle first met Anna in the winter of 1896 when she walked into the offices of *Secolo Nuovo*, introducing herself as a socialist. While grumpy Enrico toiled on the printer, refusing to engage with this traitor, Anna and Isabelle discussed the oceans, the metropolis of New York City, and the racist terror unfolding inside the Russian Empire. Anna kept showing up at the newspaper office every week, eager to chat with this strange Italian girl named Isabelle, and it wasn't long before Josephine asked her daughter to bring Anna into the fold. Their friendship blossomed

Anna Strunsky

over maps of the Pacific, schemes to free Siberian prisoners, and cozy gatherings at the Strunsky house where *budding genius, refugees, revolutionists; broken lives and strong lives* all gathered for subversive lectures. After eating three plates of food and hearing Anna explain how the pursuit of profit led to oblivion, Shmuel Schwartz became a committed anarchist and was on the waterfront every morning looking for Isabelle.

The Strunskys weren't the only ones to flee the Russian Empire for the safety of San Francisco. On a small Ukrainian Mennonite colony in 1879, young Abraham and Mary Isaak were slated to be married in a religious ceremony that contradicted all their values. Rather than wait for permission from God, Abraham and Mary made love in the woods and conceived their first child. When this pregnancy was discovered, the couple was humiliated in front of their village and threatened with banishment, although Abraham and Mary stood firm against this abuse and insisted on exile, breaking the hearts of their families. The entire village recanted and begged them to stay but the couple fled to the port city of Odessa along the Black Sea, an infamous cauldron of rebellion. Throughout the 1880s, Abraham and Mary printed incendiary radical literature, raised three healthy children, and spread the teachings of anarchism throughout the Russian Empire. A spy eventually discovered these propagandists and they were forced to flee Odessa in 1888, narrowly escaping the Empire's noose. Mary and the children hid in their Mennonite colony while Abraham sailed to Rio de Janeiro in search of safety, a path that led him to San Francisco where he found my grandfather Antonio sitting in the Bulkhead Saloon.

Abraham wanted to live where the Czar would never look, a place where his children could grow up in safety, and Antonio directed him north to the river town of Portland. Once the Isaaks were reunited in 1889, the children lived on a farm amid the tall evergreens while their parents toiled near the city, saving enough to buy land, build a house, and establish another printing press. *The Firebrand* weekly appeared on the streets of Portland in 1895 and ran for two years until the federal government banned it for featuring an "obscene" poem by Walt Whitman entitled "A Woman Waits For Me." This poet of the US Civil War described women who *know how to swim, row, ride, wrestle, shoot, run, strike, retreat, advance, resist, defend themselves. They are ultimate in their own right—they are calm, clear, well-possess'd of themselves.* For these "obscene" words, Abraham was jailed in downtown Portland and achieved immediate fame in the radical press. Upon his release in 1897, the family moved south to San Francisco and within months the Isaaks started *Free Society*, a weekly paper that spread the fire of anarchism far outside the Latin Quarter and across the United States.

Josephine never betrayed any emotion when Isabelle described these new comrades arriving in San Francisco. My grandmother kept whatever joy she felt hidden inside the sewing machine and not even her sister Bianca could understand the macabre crucifix above her head. The Lemel sisters hardly communicated until the winter of 1898 when 29-year-old anarchist Emma Goldman arrived on a lecture tour carrying a message that would unite their movement.

After her lover Sasha Berkman attempted to assassinate a steel magnate in 1892, Emma was thrust into the public spotlight as a representative of the anarchist struggle with each of her public talks documented, printed, and sold by the American press. Despite this massive publicity, Emma managed to take a leading role in the movement, remove its more reckless men from power, and spread anarchy across the US. Emma championed free love, free thought, and the freedom of women, while privately she prepared bombs and smuggled weapons. Once her 1898 lecture tour was announced, Bianca arrived at Josephine's apartment and said she was

Abraham Isaak

leaving to start a commune up the coast named *Nuovo Ideal*. Bianca knew
Emma was bringing tidings of war and this plot of fog-shrouded land was a
needed refuge for the battles to come. Her daughter Beatrix would remain
behind with Isabelle. It was now the Lemel cousin's turn to take charge.
Josephine and Bianca were both in their forties.

Just before Emma Goldman arrived, two ominous events took place, the
first along the San Francisco waterfront. On January 22, 1898, the armored
cruiser *Chitose* was released from its dry dock at the Union Iron Works, the
latest warship purchased by the Japanese Empire. While this new cruiser
underwent the last of its outfitting, the *USS Maine* mysteriously exploded
in the Cuban harbor of Havana, allowing local newspaper baron William
Randolph Hearst to stoke the population into a war frenzy against the
Spanish Empire. For the past decades, anarchist geographer Élisée Reclus
had helped Philipino rebels fight their Spanish rulers, a cause recently taken
up by Emma Goldman and her gun-smuggling network. She arrived in San
Francisco during this Spanish War frenzy and dined in my family's apartment with dozens of anarchists from across the city. Over tobacco, wine, and
pasta, these comrades discussed the coming imperialist war and the anarchist
offensive against it. At the insistence of Emma, one of their actions would be
to shut down the San Francisco waterfront and paralyze war-shipments to
the Philippine Isles. The other actions would be far more drastic.

The day after this historic feast, Emma Goldman delivered her lecture to
a sold-out hall in the middle of Chinatown and
condemned the new American imperialism of
President McKinley and JP Morgan. Using
battleships built on this very waterfront, the
yanquis had just defeated the Spanish Navy and
seized the colonies of the Philippine Isles, Guam,
Cuba, and Puerto Rico. Hundreds of Chinese and
European immigrants listened to Emma warn
of a new US Empire that would spread
across Asia and was poised to eradicate
their indigenous peoples. The Hawaiian
Islands had just been effectively annexed
as a federal territory to create a base for
this new steamer fleet that now held the
Pacific Ocean hostage and Emma told the
crowd the US would eventually declare
war on the indigenous Philippinos, just
as they would declare war on China.
She told her audience that if they cared

Emma Goldman

about the earth and its inhabitants, they would have to act quickly, while there was still time. She explained that "*truth is a dangerous weapon in the hands of working men and women. Your enemy is not in Spain, but in Washington; not in Madrid, but here in San Francisco, in New York, in Chicago. I believe in holding up a looking glass before you, so that you can see and know yourselves. When you are educated, when you realize your power, you'll need no bombs, and no dynamite or militia will hold you.*"

Before she left town, Emma Goldman met with Josephine, Isabelle, and Beatrix in the Latin Quarter apartment to discuss the hidden elements of their new offensive. An agent of JP Morgan had been secretly dispatched to San Francisco in 1891 to ensure war production resumed after a decade of strikes. This man was Lionel Heath, second richest steel baron in the world, and his arrival coincided with the crushing of the Coast Sailor's Union and the death of my grandfather. Since then, Heath was the darling of the local press, portrayed as an eccentric capitalist who drove an automobile across the cobblestones. There were no steel mills in California and his main factories were either in England or Pennsylvania, making his appearance in San Francisco especially ominous. With the assistance of JP Morgan, Lionel Heath purchased failing coal and iron mines during the 1893 financial crisis, securing the vital ingredients for another steel empire. It was possible that he was in San Francisco to purchase the local shipyards, although Emma wasn't sure. All she knew was that Heath lived with his wife in a stone mansion on Pacific Heights and that their head-chef had just issued a call for Italian-speaking servants. It was rumored that Heath's wife was pregnant, although it remained unclear why the servants needed to speak Italian. In the apartment with Emma that night, Isabelle and Beatrix were asked to secure these domestic positions and wait for 1901, the year they'd assassinate Lionel Heath and President William McKinley. This simple plan might have unfolded perfectly if not for the meddling of a single, powerful woman named Yvonne del Valle. No one had anticipated her appearance.

SHE'LL BE COMING AROUND THE MOUNTAIN

THE SUNLIGHT PULLS ME FROM SLEEP, POUNDING THROUGH THE SKY-LIGHT with its burning rays. My skin is covered in sweat when I rise from bed, stretch my arms with two loud cracks, and then descend the wooden ladder to my living room. It must be around noon because that's the only time sunlight falls at this particular angle, turning my red couch a golden orange.

I wash my skin over the basin, soak my hair in water, and knock the yellow crust from my eyes. My breath smells terrible, like wine and stale cigarettes. The ashtray's filled with stinky butt ends and my desk's covered in a thin layer of gray powder. I stayed up all night chasing the evening star, as they say. The evening star, the most beautiful of all stars, but not so beautiful as our electromagnetic ribbon, especially when I'm high on hashish. I got back from Fort Russ with five tobacco pouches, a cake of hashish, a sack of coffee, a map of our coastal region, two jars of pickled herring, and a glass *kerotakis* for my mother. I still haven't given it to her. Octavio made me promise to deliver it personally.

Children laugh down at the school and the sounds glide through my open windows. I unscrew a jar of apple butter, spread it over yesterday's stale bread, then wash it all down with cold black tea. I've been back from Fort Russ for five days now and I've already fallen back into my usual routine. I go out for fresh baguettes early in the morning when no one's awake and then use all this summer daylight to write about San Francisco. By the time I pass out, I'm usually in some kind of trance from all the wine, hashish, and tobacco. When I sleep, I dream about Isabelle.

The sky's blue today, so bright I have to squint my eyes. My house is already baking and it'll only get hotter, so I can't put off this visit. It's time to go see Yvonne and ask her my final questions. I can't finish this book otherwise. Yvonne's story is the most difficult to tell. For her sake, I ask you to come now, you Graces, you rosy-armed perfection. I need your help.

Out of nowhere, the long shriek of our communal mill-saw fills the air, blending in with the school-children's laughter. I'm still not used to this electricity beneath our feet. Every morning I stare at the black button, mounted into my kitchen wall, ready to brighten the entire house and connect me with Yvonne and Nikola's world wireless system. No one knows how Yvonne illuminates their light-bulbs but now they're distracted and couldn't care less, not with all this free juice coursing through the soil. All I need to do is press my black button and the bulbs glow, the geo-globe pulses, and my heat pad boils water. This strange technology terrifies me but I press the button just the same. Two light-bulbs spark to life with a faint sizzle, one in the kitchen, one in the living room. The geo-globe on my kitchen counter alerts me to an incoming transmission, pulsing red with its iron locator ring centered on San Francisco. Some people always have their locator spinning from one glass-etched continent to another, frantically keeping up with the stream of transmissions wiggling through the soil. Mine is always fixed on the western edge of North America, the consequence of living my entire life in California. Who the hell is calling me today? Yesterday it was Beatrix looking for my mom, this morning it might be Juana. I knew it was a terrible mistake to get one of these geo-globes. They only bring trouble.

I let the globe pulse away unanswered and use the electric heat-pad to boil some coffee. By the time I take my first sip, the geo-globe has returned to its transparent gray. I can easily signal them back, but what if it's Juana? When I finally look, the rotating numbers at the base of my globe have the coordinates for Telegraph Hill locked in place. It's definitely Juana, so I'm not calling her back. I hate the way people glow inside these globes, all broken apart with their nasty metal voices clawing down my ears, especially hers. Not today. I press the black button and cut the house from the wireless net-work. I've got better things to do. I need to speak with the net-work's architect. *Now it's time, for you who are so pretty and charming, to share in the games that the pink-ankled Graces play.*

My work pants are a bit too smelly right now so I put on a simple white dress and tie my hair in a tail above my head. I wear sandals instead of boots, brush the fuzz from off my teeth, and smear my skin with a few drops of my mother's lavender oil. Should be quite the contrast from my last visit to the solarium. I'm almost out the door when I remember to hide my notebook upstairs in the treasure-chest. This might be pointless, but better to be safe, so I stuff my writing away, climb down the ladder, walk out the door, and head towards the communal house as the mill saw shrieks across the village. They've been cutting wood for days now, first the lumber to trade with the Kashaya, today the material for the new radio station. I can't wait for it to end. I'll be a virgin, always. I really do hate machines.

The children wave to me as I walk past the school and one of them points at the electromagnetic ribbon pulsing across the sky. It's been keeping me up these past nights, the artificial *aurora borealis* that blots out the stars and turns the darkness green and purple. The plasma swirls at the edge of the atmosphere while a thin white band of electricity glistens in the middle, barely visible in the daylight. Electric music pours from every house and snatches of metallic conversation snarl through dozens of geo-globe speakers. Aside from the convenience of my heat-pad and light bulbs, these days of limitless energy fill me with anxiety. The villagers have a manic sparkle in their eyes and the air's thick with stinky beer hops electrically steaming inside the *fábrica*. There isn't a trace of wood smoke rising from a single chimney. Electric light burns in the darkest places. This is what our future looks like.

Two old sailors are playing chess outside when I arrive at the communal house. They sit in the shade at a small iron table and neither move their pieces, not once, just as neither of them look at me when I enter the communal house. Warm golden light fills the wooden cavern of the main hall, beaming down through a dozen circular windows. Electric voices and frantic tongues blur together as the elders sit around a dozen geo-globes, chatting with friends in distant places. None of them notice me as I climb upstairs, probably because I'm dressed like a woman, not some bullheaded hayseed.

I walk inside Yvonne's solarium without a knock and find her standing alone in the middle of the room, gray hair coiled up like a thousand snakes. She's wearing a black dress and her eyes lock on me the moment I pass inside. She probably knew I was coming, just like she's listening to my thoughts right now. Instead of confirm my suspicions about her mind-reading, Yvonne just chuckles to herself, takes me by the elbows, and kisses my cheeks.

"Have you been smoking?" she asks, sniffing the dry parts of my hair. "Tobacco?"

"I always smoke tobacco. What's the problem?"

Yvonne steps back and shakes her head.

"*This* is the problem." She places her bony hand over my navel. "Bad idea. You don't need to make your daughter crazy with nightshade. She'll be wild enough from her two parents."

I'd think this was morning sickness if I didn't know any better. The room starts to spin and my vision blurs into a gray river. There's no point trying to hide my confusion, it's probably smeared all over my face. She whispers out a laugh, takes my hand in her slender fingers, and guides me to the cushioned chairs where the blue infinity of the Pacific Ocean stretches before us, cut in half by the throbbing ribbon of electromagnetic light.

"Of course you're pregnant," Yvonne says, rubbing my knee. "I can smell it."

"Can you? What does it smell like? Manure?"

She just sits down, her long legs crossed at the knee, each wrist sparkling with two copper bracelets. I might have made her cry last time, but right now she's got me in the palm of her hand, just like when I was a girl, just like always.

"Underneath all the wine you drank last night and the lavender you tried to blot it out with, I'd say it smells like your mother, the scent of her skin after she'd been in the sun. It's a girl, you know. I can tell you this for certain. Everything has a smell."

"I know it's a girl, Yvonne. This is *my* body we're talking about."

"Then why are you drinking? It's flooding her with spirits."

"It helps with the writing. So does the smoking."

"None of it helps your daughter. I'm going to worry about you if this doesn't stop. And her."

"Did you know Juana was going to be girl?"

That did it. She uncrosses her legs and spreads them out wide. Her green eyes try to burn a hole through my skull but it doesn't work, not this time. I've unearthed something on my first try. I better keep going until I reach the bottom.

"No, I didn't," she says. "Not at all. I was ignorant back then."

"When I was a girl, my mom told me you flooded Juana with our old poisons to make sure she wasn't a boy. That's why Juana's angry all the time, never satisfied, burning on the inside. Left quite the impression on me. I always thought it was sad."

"I didn't know how to control the sex like your family could. So I did what was necessary. Is this why you came here? To dig up stories for your book? Isabelle speaks highly of what you've written so far. Whenever I see her it's nothing but praises, although she——"

"She said people wouldn't understand your story, they'd get angry if they knew the truth."

"I don't care about that, Fulvia. Someone needs to tell this story. I'm here to help you, *mija*." Yvonne's emerald eyes fill with tears that she doesn't try to contain. "I want them all to know. Hide nothing. Tell this truth for once and let them bask in it. Someday they'll understand."

"Maybe the Dream should just take over, then they'll understand if they want to or not."

"Let's hope it doesn't come to that." Without warning, a flood of tears course down her wrinkled cheeks and she doesn't wipe them away. "When they read your words, when they set the puzzle pieces together with their own hands, enough people will understand, and they'll tell others. I think that's how this works, and I'm sorry you drew the short straw having to write it. Come on, let's look at *The Book*. I need to show you something. I think you need to see it."

Yvonne is suddenly thirty years younger when she rises from the cushioned chair and reaches for my hand. The tears make her cheeks look smoother than mine, but I pretend not to notice as we walk over to *The Book's* famous glass case. She carries the calfskin volume to the reading table and leafs through the parchment with fingers nimble as a guitarist. Medicinal plants and all of their hidden properties flicker past my vision, followed by luminous spheres nestled among the heavens. Neither of us speak until Yvonne stops at a pair of ovaries connected by watery tubes that suspend three women in green bathtubs. With hands reaching through ovarian conduits, the women combine their subterranean forces to conduct a ribbon from the earth. I'm seeing this for the very first time.

"Do you know what this is?" she asks me. "It explains what you're missing."

"Who's the dreamer, Yvonne? Is it you? Are you making this all happen?"

"Of course not! No! We all are! All of us! Can't you see? Look above your head."

"I didn't make that ribbon happen. I'm not the dreamer, I'm——"

"We're awake, Fulvia. We're awake. And we make things happen, in case you didn't notice."

"It wasn't me who pulled that ribbon, it was the conductors in the stations who—"

"We're all conductors, *mija*, but we're not all called to the same place for the same reason."

Without me asking, Yvonne explains how she learned to control all that raging power inside her body. It takes hours to tell, so long I forget where I am. We sip glasses of spring water and eat walnuts from copper bowls as she fills my mind with the scent of laurel forests, the sound of mashing acorns in stone grinding-holes, and a tornado made of fire screaming across San Francisco. I'm starving by the time she's finished, even with all the nuts in my belly. The sun's nearly set, allowing the green ribbon to pulse gently against the approaching darkness. Now I can really write tonight. The truth is so close and all I want is my pen and notebook. All of this needs to be remembered.

"*We are the fluid through which perfection rises,*" Yvonne says. "An ancient proverb from your mother. I haven't the slightest clue where she got it. Your ancestors were quite the alchemists, only they didn't record their techniques. Some of them were medicine women who came with Mauritius from Egypt, women like Verena. They stayed in the mountains and had children, obviously. Or maybe your mom's making it all up. Either way, I love the saying. *We're the fluid through which perfection rises.* Perfection is beyond us, yet passes through us. We make everything happen but control almost none of it. Strange, don't you think?"

"You know what's really strange about all that?"

"Tell me."

"My mom never told me any of this. I'm hearing it for the first time. From you."

"That's probably how she wanted it. You know your mother."

Yvonne keeps talking but all I can think about is my mother distilling oils outside the barn, not saying a word about these Alpine alchemists. My stomach growls loudly at this betrayal, loud enough to fill the room, so Yvonne suggests we eat downstairs with the elders. I follow her out into the hallway where the electricity's so bright I have to cover my eyes. Yvonne doesn't need my help down the stairs, nor does she mind the light, and the woman moves like a teenager towards the large plates of salad, lentils, beets, and bread. Geo-globes strobe red in the center of the dining tables but no one answers, not while they're eating. Some things are still sacred up here in the sticks.

I sit at a table with Yvonne, two old sailors, and three younger ladies who teach at our school, though I don't remember their names. A young woman serves us our meals from off a wooden tray, she kisses Yvonne on the cheek, then leaves us to the ramblings of the sailors. All of us listen but the ladies are clearly bored and grin at me whenever the men aren't looking. The only one really paying attention to them is Yvonne. Her green eyes sparkle as she eats her salad and the sailors spin yarns about blue-haired mermaids delivering half-drowned men to hidden islands littered with the ruins of Atlantis. By the expression on her face, you'd think Yvonne had swam with the mermaids herself.

"Wait a minute," one of the sailors says, looking at me. "You're Fulvia Ferrari!"

The school teachers start giggling, the other sailors suddenly grow animated, and Yvonne just looks at me, waiting for me to respond. I explain that, yes, I am Fulvia Ferrari, yes, my mother is none other than Isabelle Ferrari, and once that's all settled, the sailors start talking about my grandfather, the late, great Antonio Ferrari. Apparently, all three of these guys knew him.

"Let me tell you about Antonio Ferrari," one of them says, an Italian. "One night, he is walking in the Barbary Coast and he sees this circus freak-show, a big tent with many color. So your *nonno*, you know what he do? He peek inside the tent and he see a little *pinguino* trapped in the cage, hostage of the circus *padrone*. So you know what your *nonno* do then? He sneak into the tent one night, he cut the lock on the cage, and he take the *piccolo pingunio* back home to Greenwich Street."

"What's *pinguino*?" one of the teachers asks. "Did he rescue a penguin?"

"*Esatto!* He take the *pinguino* home, then he ship out to Chile with the *pinguino*, and when they round the *Tierra del Fuego*, Antonio, he see the iceberg floating, so he grab the *pinguino*, he kiss the *pinguino*, then he throw the *pinguino* into the sea so she can swim with the other *pinguini*. Antonio, the best man who ever lived."

At that, the other sailors raise their glasses and we all toast the memory of my late grandfather. We talk about penguins for a while after that and Yvonne grins at me as if she planned this whole thing. I never knew this story about Antonio, but now all I want to do is write it down. I gather up everyone's plate the second they're clean and ignore the feigned grumbling. Yvonne begs me to stay but I just kiss her wrinkled cheek and carry the dishes over to the washtub line. Several people try to chat with me while I wait. I smile and nod but can't make out the words, they speak too fast, they move to a different subject before I can comprehend the last one. It must be all the electricity filling their minds with a thousand thoughts. Enmeshed in their babble, I scrub the dishes with copper mesh, wash them with soap, rinse them with clean water, then dry them with a black towel. All my silverware is now sunk at the bottom of the dirty tub but it's getting crowded here at the wash-station and I'm not eager to stick my hand in all that filth. Maybe I'm being selfish but I don't care. I say my goodbyes to all and none then walk outside into the green light of our electromagnetic ribbon.

Most of the village windows host the spectral blue glow of the geo-globe and reverberate with the harsh metal clang of a hundred transmitted voices. It's really a shame how the ribbon drives people inside rather than beneath this heavenly green aurora. It's so beautiful I can hardly write some nights, especially when there isn't a sound in the village and I can almost hear the plasma whispering through the darkness. These mechanical devices are a distraction from the very splendor that powers them, a contradiction no one seems to appreciate. My geo-globe usually sits in the closet next to the broomstick but now it's on my kitchen counter, only I don't want to answer it tonight, even though I should. Juana's probably been calling me for a reason. I see her short dark hair, her snake-scale eyes, and that's when I notice the pulsing red strobe lighting up my house. I swear I turned everything off when I left. It's probably my mom with another unannounced surprise.

I switch on the light bulbs once I'm inside and then carefully inspect every inch of my living room. The whole place is cleaner than I left it. The ashtrays are empty, the wine bottles are back on the shelves, my writing desk is wiped down, and my lamps are filled with oil. There isn't a single dirty dish and even my coffee pot is spotless. None of this is normal. Isabelle's feeling guilty about something, clearly, and that's when I realize what happened. My heart starts to pound, my armpits fill with sweat, my hands quake, and I'm up the ladder like a squirrel. The oak lid of my treasure chest is wide open. My two notebooks lay on the ground. One is the family history I've been writing, the one people know about. The other is the smaller notebook, the one you've been reading, the one no one knows about except you, the one I'm writing in at this very moment under our splendorous green ribbon. That's it. Now my mother knows my secrets. Now you know the truth. I've been lying to all of you, so I guess you can call me a hypocrite.

13

THE ITALIAN LAUNDRESSES OF PACIFIC HEIGHTS

M Y MOTHER'S CHILDHOOD ON TELEGRAPH HILL WAS DOMINATED BY visions of Mount Diablo, a brown peak only visible from the upper limits of her ramshackle neighborhood. Every house on the hill was connected by mud pathways, crumbling staircases, plank boardwalks, damp wooden ladders, and small paths made of stone, all protected by the

GRAY BROTHERS' QUARRY. SANSOME & GREEN STS

Queen of the Coast. No gang would dare to enter the narrow passage-ways and no drunken sailor would ever amble up its crooked stairways.

The greatest threat to this neighborhood didn't come from any outside marauder but from the Gray Brothers' rock-quarry on the north-eastern slope of Telegraph Hill. These local capitalists dynamited the earth for years to supply builders with blue sandstone for their opulent mansions, a practice that threatened to tumble a dozen houses off their perches, including Marisol's. As a young girl, Isabelle joined the stone-throwing mobs who attacked quarry workers from the cliffs above and then chased them off with pistol-shots. Marisol and Josephine organized these armed assaults on the dynamiters but never caught the Gray Brothers themselves, greedy men who paid desperate drunkards to do their dirty work. Luckily for the neighborhood, Marisol had befriended two society women named Elizabeth and Alice during her nightly prowls.

These two nurses and followers of Mary wanted to aid the countless children of prostitution who wandered the streets picking up coal or selling pilfered flowers. Obeying the whispers of *Santa Muerte*, Marisol helped Elizabeth Ashe and Alice Griffith establish the Telegraph Hill Neighborhood Center for orphans and immigrants on the southern slopes along Vallejo Street. When the blasting in the limestone quarry began to erode the hill, Alice initiated a campaign against the Gray Brothers while Elizabeth oversaw the feeding, teaching, and lodging of one hundred abandoned children. As an army of Italian and Irish immigrants pelted quarry workers with rocks, Alice was screaming at the Mayor to ſtop these mad dynamiters from eating into their crumbling hillside. After years of this agitation, City Hall finally placed a permanent injunćtion on the quarry in 1895, although by then Josephine had left Marisol alone in the little blue house on Telegraph Hill.

During the years that followed, my mother sometimes woke to the sound of a dynamite blaſt she miſtook for thunder. Although she now lived behind the hill in the Latin Quarter, the shock-waves sped through the earth into her second-ſtory bedroom. Each time she inveſtigated the source, Isabelle discovered the Gray Brothers had paid another ſtooge to release hundŗeds of dollars-worth of blue sandſtone. Even with City Hall's permanent injunc- tion, these petty-capitaliſts ſtill felt emboldened to blaſt away, and prevent- ing these blaſts would require an organized patrol, although my 12-year-old mother couldn't organize it. She had a man to kill.

Emma Goldman left San Francisco in May 1898 and caught a train south for an engagement in Los Angeles. Despite experiencing an unpleasant sexual advance from the event manager, Emma formed the City of Angels' firſt anarchiſt group before returning to San Francisco. On the eve of her depar- ture for New York City in June, Emma walked up to the Latin Quarter for a final discussion with Josephine, Beatrix, and Isabelle. They crowded around my grandmother's dining table, Emma opened a bottle of red wine, lit the firſt of many cigarettes, and began her famous condućtion of energy. By the end of the evening, their future ſtrategy was carved in ſtone. The main goal of their next offensive was to cripple the foundries, the waterfront, and the movement of all ships from San Francisco Bay to the Philippine Isles. Every local port had to be paralyzed and all troop movements hindered, making the entire region appear nonviable for the new imperialism of JP Morgan and President McKinley. At the height of this planned ſtrike, when the capital- iſts were at their weakeſt, an anarchiſt would assassinate McKinley and then Lionel Heath, the local agent for JP Morgan. If possible, they'd find a way to kill JP Morgan, though the man was notoriously difficult to track. Like the anarchiſts, he communicated in complex code and concealed his true intentions until the laſt second.

My mother was juſt 12-years-old when Emma asked her to not only take a job at the Heath mansion, but also to kill him. My mother told me she wasn't afraid, though her heart beat frantically as the candle-light reflećted in Emma's eye-glasses. During the paſt decades of regicide, a teenager had never been the assassin, making the Lemel cousins perfećt for infiltrating the Heath mansion. From that day onward, Isabelle and Beatrix lived each day together and perfećted their ſtories for the upcoming job interview, an opportunity delivered ſtraight from the underworld.

Weeks before, Marisol had discovered a private call for Italian servants at the Heath estate. She quickly found Sergio on the docks and handed him an envelope that contained the original call along with legitimate resumes for two wash-girls. Marisol didn't explain anything to my uncle and appeared to be in a trance when she vanished back into the waterfront. Sergio gave this envelope to Josephine, who then showed it to Emma, and this was how they decided to send the Lemel cousins into Heath's mansion for their fateful *attentat*. Ineffably, Marisol ensured that my mother met Yvonne.

Isabelle and Beatrix prepared their new personas for the next weeks before climbing the long hill to Pacific Heights in the summer of 1898. Lionel Heath had built his wife a massive stone villa surrounded by hedge-rows and the cousins now passed through its black iron gate, spoke to a shotgun-wielding Italian gatekeeper, handed over their resumes, and were allowed inside under the assumption they'd never get the job, for only a fool would hire servants so young. My mother and aunt took their places among six rows of impatient women and waited for Yvonne del Valle-Heath to select her staff. These experienced laundresses immediately mocked the young upstarts but Isabelle and Beatrix held firm and returned every insult with the proper venom and wit. This enlivened chatter ended when Lionel Heath suddenly appeared on the patio dressed in a black suit and top hat.

His face was red and puffy and he appeared much older than his forty-eight years. While his facial features were handsome, darkness hollowed out his eyes and traversed his skin with the bright red veins of alcoholism. The steel baron was clearly distraught as he paced among the silent women, appearing to select at random. The cousins hadn't expected this, given it was customary for the lady of a house to choose her servants, and they whispered in their mother-tongue about quickly finding a weapon. That's when the steel-baron pointed at them. In his nasal Italian, Heath instructed the cousins to show up at seven the next morning. As a consequence of this good fortune, Isabelle and Beatrix immediately became the pariahs of the other laundresses.

The women they'd beaten in the selection process had worked their entire lives for this job only to have it stolen by two inexperienced children from the Latin Quarter slums. The cousins ignored this criticism, returned spit for spit, and showed up the next day to prove themselves capable of scrubbing towels against the washboard, stirring steaming pots of white linens, and washing a small amount of a woman's underclothing. Within a week, the cousins had transformed into the darlings of the laundry room. Both were far more literate, worldly, and experienced than these laundresses and freely delivered lessons on a variety of subjects: science, geology, history, geography, poetry, math, and ways to short-cut the mechanisms of the capitalist economy. These lectures were the closest the Italian laundresses ever came to attending a university and they learned far more from the Lemel cousins than any Church would ever dare to teach them.

Lionel Heath came to inspect their work at the end of the week and declared it *bellissima* before hurrying off into his Daimler automobile. After that, the cousins didn't see him for two weeks, although Yvonne del Valle-Heath was always in the mansion library and sometimes emerging to interact with the kitchen staff. One of the cooks delivered her meals to the library three times each day and retrieved the empty dishes an hour later. This cook said Yvonne was very polite, although she spoke little and always carried a book. After three weeks at the mansion, Isabelle found this tall, handsome, and beautifully magnetic woman standing in the doorway of the laundry room. In perfect cosmopolitan Italian, Yvonne thanked the laundresses and hoped they'd be pleased when they all collected their first paycheck at the gatehouse. Surely enough, the entire staff had been paid $4 for a seven-hour day. Within a mere two weeks, the laundresses had each earned $48, nearly double the wages of an average male worker. Isabelle showed this wad of bills to Josephine as they undressed for bed that night and then laid awake for hours trying to puzzle out Yvonne's motivations.

When she wasn't keeping track of Lionel Heath's movements, Isabelle wandered with Beatrix and Shmuel Schwartz along a waterfront illuminated by flickering gas-lamps. In this half-light, the young anarchists kept abreast of the latest dockside rumors while they waited for my uncles to get off work. They learned that Andrew Furuseth had become obsessed with the passage of the White Act in Washington DC, a piece of federal legislation he helped draft that limited the amount of money a crimp could legally claim to no more than one month of a sailor's pay. If this federal law passed, the ship-owners would have to either raise wages for all sailors or lose money paying the crimps extra to maintain the old system. Before this law was even considered, the imperial invasion of Asia began when thousands of US troops arrived on the waterfront in the summer of 1898, all en route to the Philippine Isles. These men were granted a brief shore-leave before crossing the Pacific and the Barbary Coast brothels were soon packed with customers, allowing the Queen to play her part in sabotaging the *yanquis*.

With the memory of Antonio locked in her heart, Marisol organized all the sick prostitutes into a single house and ensured soldiers were directed inside. These women carried diseases derived from their male clients and returned those same afflictions to well-paying servicemen. None of their money could be spent in the jungle, so these intoxicated recruits threw it all into the hands of working women who needed to retire. In exchange, the soldiers became so ill aboard their steamers that dozens of them died before reaching Hawaii, with hundreds more sent home permanently afflicted. As these men sailed from San Francisco on July 16, 1898, a mob of patriotic onlookers invaded the summit of Telegraph Hill to watch them pass through the Golden Gate, never suspecting that the Queen of this neighborhood had already killed dozens of soldiers with their own lust.

While this invisible warfare was unfolding on the Barbary Coast, the sailors waged their own battle against the very last of the waterfront crimps. They tied up the harbor with a strike that paralyzed all commerce and fought pitched battles on the cobblestones with fists, knives, and slung-shots. My uncles joined in these brawls and were often severely injured when they stumbled back home long past midnight. Unlike the other battles waged against the crimps, the famous *Yee Toy* didn't appear beside his comrades, and Josephine lived these war-torn days sewing on her iron machine beneath the crucifixion of Yeshua ha-Nozri.

As this bloodshed extended through the fall of 1898, Isabelle was either at the Heath mansion or creating new issues of *Secolo Nuovo*. During this process, Enrico Travaglio ran paper beneath the printing plates and inspected each impression for smudges while Beatrix, Isabelle, and Schwartz set the type for the next plate and then checked it for errors, often multiple times. Because of his endless perfectionism and merciless critique, the Lemel cousins called him *luciferino*, just as he called them *diavoli della stampatore*, or *printer's devils*.

That fall, the columns of *Secolo Nuovo* were filled with terrible news from Wilmington, North Carolina. On November 10, 1898, a mob of white racists stormed the local armory, stole hundreds of weapons, and then flooded into the black districts of Wilmington. Dozens of buildings were burned to the ground, including the only black-owned newspaper, and the mob opened fire on anyone with black skin, killing over 300 people. The ſtate eventually called on the Wilmington Light Infantry to ſtop this pogrom, although when they arrived these veterans of the Spanish-American War opened fire only on black people, allowing the whites to continue their terror. As the writers of *Secolo Nuovo* explained to their reader, the raciſt imperialism of the McKinley adminiſtration was at work in both North Carolina and the Philippine Isles, its brutality now plain to see on the ſtreets of Wilmington. For weeks after this massacre, the pages of *Secolo Nuovo* nearly dripped with a desire for vengeance.

Anna Strunsky would often appear at the *Secolo Nuovo* office on random evenings to argue for socialism, a subjeɕt that infuriated Enrico and threw him into frenzies of denunciation. Anna had been recently suspended from Stanford University after years of agitation againſt the raciſt adminiſtration and its president David Starr Jordan, a man who enforced imperialiſt eugenics on his ſtudents. Despite the pressure of this tyrant, Anna attended leɕtures by the psychologiſt William James and became an outspoken critic of the capitaliſt syſtem. In the heat of this excitement, Anna negleɕted the pointless lessons required by the adminiſtration and was suspended, allowing her time to agitate Enrico. While his weekly *Secolo Nuovo* was written in modern Italian and distributed only in the Latin Quarter, the Isaak family's *Free Society* was written in English and mailed to cities across the United States.

On alternating nights of the week, Beatrix and Isabelle joined the Isaaks for dinner inside their crowded house in the Mission Diſtriɕt where the five weekdays were divided into composing, editing, setting, printing, and folding. Mary Isaak paid their rent doing laundry and her three children, Peter, Abe, and little Mary, were good friends with the Lemels, their nights together passing in a cloud of joy and laughter. Over the course of 1898, my aunt Beatrix felt her body pull itself towards Peter Isaak, the eldeſt son. She was sixteen years old, Peter was nineteen, and the young man didn't betray the slighteſt impulse towards either romance or flirtation. Like his father Abraham, Peter carried the burning light of pure nihilism within his eyes when he spoke of the libertarian ſtruggle, *Free Society*, free love, and free thought. My 12-year-old mother smiled as Beatrix made delicate whispers into his ears or held his hand beneath the dining table. One day, Beatrix would have Peter by her side, juſt as Josephine once had Antonio, and my mother saw this long before it happened.

The Lemel cousins had a simple routine: every morning Beatrix left her bedroom inside the sailor's boardinghouse and met Isabelle on the corner of Montgomery and Vallejo. The cousins wore identical gray work dresses and rode the Sacramento Street cable-car line along with several of their

Mary, Abraham Jr., Abraham, and Maria Isaak

coworkers at the Heath estate. The two cousins hopped off the train with the other laundresses near Lafayette Park and filed past the mansion guardhouse where the old Italian gatekeeper checked their names off his ledger. After this, they passed through the rear service entrance into the kitchen and laundry room where they worked the next two hours washing linens or scrubbing Yvonne del Valle's fine under-clothing. These items were hung out to dry above the sprawling green lawn before being folded into separate piles. My mother then delivered towels, sheets, and napkins to a dozen rooms in this mansion and discovered the only doors ever locked were Yvonne's library and Heath's study. Yvonne occasionally appeared in the kitchen to try and cook herself breakfast, although the staff never allowed this eccentric behavior for fear of losing their jobs. Besides these visits, the lady of the house kept to herself and read alone by the library fireplace for days on end. Heath showed up infrequently but never stayed for long. It was clear he resided away from the mansion but the cousins couldn't discern a pattern to his visits.

With their work shift over at two in the afternoon, the hungry Lemel cousins often ate an early dinner at *Luna's Mexican Restaurant*. Situated beneath a saloon in the dim basement of a three-story building, *Luna's* served massive red *enchiladas* and juicy *chile colorados* with large servings of rice and beans. A fire constantly roared in an oven presided over by Ricardo the cook, a man whose culinary movements dripped with artistry. His wife Gloria was the waitress and had known Isabelle since she was a little girl. Gloria and Ricardo had fled the Mexican dictatorship of Porfirio Díaz in 1886 and met my grandfather at the port of Manzanillo along the coast of Colima. It was in this liberal Mexican enclave that the three made a plan to open a simple restaurant for sailors, rebels, outlaws, and pirates, which is exactly what *Luna's* became. It was a safe meeting spot lined with mirrors and dimly lit by red candles, a place where every conversation was forgotten before it was even heard and each table had a ceramic jar of free matches. Isabelle and Beatrix ate there several times a week, being just around the corner from my mother's apartment, and it was here they met a young writer named Frank Norris.

Luna's Mexican Restaurant, and Ricardo.

My mother first encountered him in the fall of 1896 when he walked into *Luna's* alongside a beautiful dark-haired woman. The couple sat in the rear booth and the suspicious restaurant patrons grew silent around these well-dressed strangers. Isabelle sat with her brothers in another booth, silent as well, but when Gloria received the couple's order in high-class English, all of *Luna's* once again filled with Basque, French, Italian, and Spanish babble. The *yanqui* couple laughed with each other, scarfed down their *enchiladas*, thanked Ricardo and Gloria personally, and returned once a month for the next year. The regulars stopped treating them as police spies and grew to love these sacred fools who came just for the chance to kiss in privacy. The next time Isabelle saw the couple inside *Luna's*, she sat down at their candle-lit booth and bluntly asked who they were. My mother wore her black dress with its high collar and hypnotized the couple with her brilliant green eyes. She was only 12-years-old.

On that afternoon at *Luna's* in the winter of 1898, Isabelle formally met Frank Norris and Jeannette Black. Frank was a journalist, aspiring novel writer, and member of the exclusive Bohemian Club. Jeanette was enrolled in a woman's seminary and was expected to "come-out" at an upcoming debutante ball. Both of them defied their high-society families by loving each other. In 1896, Frank had damaged his kidneys in South Africa while on assignment for the *San Francisco Chronicle* and quickly lost his desire to serve the newspaper-barons, a sentiment Jeannette shared. While their parents wanted them to marry different people, Frank and Jeannette just wanted to farm at the edge of a forest, have children, and live off advances from New York publishing houses. Isabelle listened to these dreams of theirs, introduced herself under a false name, and beckoned over Beatrix so they could eat together in this seditious basement.

After this meeting, the Lemel cousins didn't see the couple in *Luna's* until the spring of 1899. During this absence, Frank wrote a romance novel called *Blix* in which he detailed his struggle against the Bohemian Club and included a warm depiction of *Luna's* candle-lit basement. Rather than describe the actual rebels who packed its booths, Frank depicted a lonely basement with a few lovelorn sailors idling away their days ashore. After finishing this book, Frank covered the war in Cuba for *McClure's Magazine*, a venture that inflicted another fever and further damaged his kidneys. While his career was killing him at this point, Frank produced what he considered his first serious work, crafted to expose the sheer brutality of capitalism. During his visit to *Luna's* that spring, Frank handed my mother a volume bound in red with the embossed title *McTeague: A Story of San Francisco*. Having no time for novels, Isabelle

Frank Norris

gave this copy to Josephine who read it cover to cover that very night. While the book was filled with racist stereotypes and spurious eugenics, it revealed how poor immigrants were all made to prey on each other. Josephine much preferred reading *Blix* where the besieged couple defy the norms of bourgeois society for the sake of love.

Frank wasn't the only young author to appear in those times of promise. Just after Norris left for New York in the fall of 1899, a commemoration of the Paris Commune was held inside the Turk Street Temple where Anna Strunsky met an unfamiliar man named Jack London. They quickly fell for each other's beauty, wit, humor, strength, and intelligence. It wasn't long before Anna brought him to the lectures at her family's house in the Fillmore District where she introduced him to the Lemel cousins. Much to Anna's

Jack London's boat, Telegraph Hill in the background.

surprise, Isabelle was already well-known to Jack as the youngest member of the city's most dangerous family. The three Ferrari brothers were legendary along the waterfront for the injuries they inflicted on their enemies and the power their movement exerted over the wharves. Before he could praise their latest campaign against the crimps, Isabelle pulled Jack into the corner of the room and sternly asked about his sudden disappearance from the bay. To clear his dirty name, Jack London told a long story by the light of the Strunsky fireplace.

After earning a reputation as the swiftest oyster pirate in the San Francisco Bay by the age of sixteen, Jack was arrested in 1892 and offered two choices: either go to jail or help the Fish Patrol catch his fellow pirates. He worked off his servitude as a member of the Fish Patrol and promptly returned to piracy once his term was finished, although he shifted his hunting grounds eastward to the less policed Sacramento Delta. In this familiar life of crime, alcoholism soon took hold of his body and propelled Jack into dissipation and despair. With no prospects for the future, Jack made his way to the Bulkhead Saloon in San Francisco, met an old harpooner at the bar, and by morning the two had signed their names onto the crew manifest of a sealing ship bound for Japan. This journey to Asia revealed the savagery of Western greed and shattered his naive world-view when hundreds of his fellow sailors looted a small coastal village of the Ogasawara Islands. When he returned to Oakland, haunted by this savage violence, Jack took a job in a jute mill and dedicated his nights to writing down what he'd seen on the Pacific. After processing imported Bengali jute stalks for ten cents an hour, Jack returned home to polish his first short-story, "Typhoon Off the Coast of Japan." He submitted it to the *San Francisco Morning Call's* young writer's contest and quickly took first prize, although rather than be inspired by his publication in the Sunday paper, Jack kept pulverizing his body at the jute mill in the hope of a raise. He eventually stopped writing, preferring to sleep.

When the bosses made clear he'd never earn more than ten cents an hour, Jack enlisted in Coxey's Army of the poor for its march on Washington DC. During the long depression that followed the Panic of 1893, Jack rode the rails with this raggedy legion to camp in front of the White House and tell President McKinley he was a stooge of JP Morgan. Jack never reached DC and deserted the army in Missouri after endless fights among the disorganized rebels. He was later jailed in Buffalo, New York, rode the rails across Pennsylvania, lived as a hobo in Baltimore, and found himself in Boston where he met an editor of *The Bostonian* newspaper. In exchange for a $10 bill, Jack promised the editor to write a story about being a tramp in Coxey's Army. With money in hand, Jack bought a train ticket to Montreal and then hoboed west across Canada inside smoke-filled boxcars. Finally back on the Pacific coast, Jack signed onto a coastal steamer in British Columbia, shoveled coal into a boiler for the entire journey, and returned to the San Francisco Bay in the year 1896.

Jack came home determined to hone his writing skills and after a binge of late-night studying he was admitted into the University of California at Berkeley. While enrolled in classes, Jack also became a socialist street-orator in downtown Oakland, fought against the legal restrictions on public speaking, and was jailed for his many lectures against capitalism, leaving little time for school work. He left the university in less than a year and returned to manual labor, steam-pressing clothes at the same private school Frank Norris attended in his youth. Rather than waste his life ironing collars of the elite, Jack ignorantly joined the stampede of gold-seekers heading to Alaska in 1897. He found no gold in the mountains and encountered only the raw power of the planet itself as it killed hundreds of men on its icy back. Jack came down with scurvy and was trapped in a freezing cabin until spring thawed the ice, allowing him to receive mail. In a letter from Oakland, Jack learned his father had died, so he took a boat 1,500 miles down the Yukon to the Bering Sea where he signed up as a fire-man on a steamer bound for Seattle. From this industrial boom-town, Jack hopped trains down the coast and returned to Oakland in the summer of 1898. He was 21-years old.

Upon his return, Jack settled into a disciplined routine of writing stories for publication and placed his work in journals such as *The Black Cat*, *The Overland Monthly*, and *The Atlantic Monthly*. He threw himself into the socialist struggle, helped in the Oakland free-speech fights, and gave soapbox lectures before being chased away by the police. Isabelle and Beatrix listened to Jack's longwinded story for over an hour and decided no one could invent such an insane series of misadventures. They left that night convinced he wasn't an informer, although when my mother relayed this to her brothers later that evening, none of them seemed to care, being too busy nursing their bruises, stab wounds, swollen eyes, and busted lips. Forgotten pirates were the least of their concerns.

Over the spring and summer of 1899, the Sailor's Union soundly defeated the crimps, took over their vacated boardinghouses, and broke their hold over the high-seas. In combination with the White Act, sailor's wages rose to $40 a month and brought a thousand new members to the union. My uncles suffered horrendous beatings eradicating these maritime pimps who'd helped kill their father and came home each night beaming with victory but silenced by immense physical pain. Defeating the crimps was the first step towards shutting down the entire waterfront, a series of battles that my uncles were lucky enough to survive. The next step would be to form a federation of all waterfront trades, although that would take many months and pressure was already building to hinder military shipments across the Pacific. On February 4, 1899, the US declared war on the fledgling Philippine Republic, announcing to the world that the Philippine Isles were now a *yanqui* colony. As the Battle of Manila raged across the ocean, my bruised and battered uncles were struggling to convince the sailors, the teamsters, and the longshoremen to work together. Without them, the port would never be shut down.

Once her brothers were asleep, Isabelle usually crossed the street to the *Secolo Nuovo* office to help Enrico print, write, edit, and fold the latest issue, even if he didn't ask for help, which he never did. Isabelle wore her gray work-dress to the office on the nights Enrico was overwhelmed, knowing she'd wake up on his leather sofa after less than two hours of sleep. The main reason for these late nights was a miner's uprising in Northern Idaho, an armed conflict they covered extensively in *Secolo Nuovo*.

On April 29, 1899, hundreds of armed miners hijacked a train and rode it town to town picking up both comrades and dynamite for their assault against the only non-union mine in their region. When they finally reached the Bunker Hill mine outside Cœur d'Alene, this thousand-man army forced all of the scabs to surrender and then packed 3,000 pounds of dynamite into this massively profitable facility. The mine was completely destroyed in the subsequent blast and the armed union men soon burned the manager's

Bunker Hill mine left in ruins.

house, the company office, and the exploitative boarding house run by the mine-owners. After that, this army of the Western Federation of Miners got on their stolen train and rode back to their homes one stop at a time. It wasn't long before the reaction arrived.

Isabelle burned away her nights writing updates on the hundreds of men captured at gunpoint after President McKinley ordered the US Army to invade the region. He purposefully selected the 24th Infantry Regiment, an all-black unit fresh from the war in Cuba, and sent them to Idaho in the hope of fanning race hatred among the miners. Once they arrived, these soldiers arrested over 1,000 men and placed them in an open air concentration camp. Big Bill Haywood, a leader of the Western Federation of Miners, would later describe how *the government officials thought it would further incite the miners if armed black men were placed as guards over white prisoners.* For the next months, these *Buffalo Soldiers* guarded the concentration camp and sometimes took revenge on the miners for indignities they had suffered as black men living in the United States.

Isabelle and Enrico were driven mad by the insidious nature of McKinley's actions and each weekly issue of *Secolo Nuovo* listed the number of imprisoned miners. By the late-summer of 1899, there were still five dozen men trapped behind barbed wire, although the *Buffalo Soldiers* had since been shipped off to the Philippine Isles. As this black regiment crossed the Pacific to fight against the indigenous, Emma Goldman returned to San Francisco for another lecture tour with a shipment of rifles following behind. While my uncles loaded this cargo, Emma sat with Isabelle, Beatrix and Josephine in the Latin Quarter apartment to discuss their unfolding plans.

Emma explained that her rifles would first travel to Taiwan, then to Fugon Island, and from there they'd be rowed to the northern coast of Luzon before reaching the besieged rebels. For their part, my mother and Beatrix described their work routines to Emma, narrated everything they'd seen at the Heath mansion, but all of them agreed their plans were moving too slow. Killing both the President and Lionel Heath, blocking the port of San Francisco, sending weapons to the rebels, all of it now seemed insufficient in the midst of this slaughter. As she told a crowd in Oakland that July, *let us try to become useful men and women and give what we have of ability and talent to educate and help others. It is only through this that we will realize the true aim of life.* During her seven week lecture tour in the bay, Emma devoted all her free time to helping Isabelle and Enrico print *Secolo Nuovo,* even writing a few anonymous columns on the rebellion in the Philippine Isles.

One night, my mother was thrilled to write the story of a *Buffalo Soldier* named Corporal David Fagen who defected to the indigenous rather than kill them. In the days that followed, Fagen became a *guerrilla* leader and taught them how to fight the militarized *yanquis.* Wearing her gray work-dress, my mother fell asleep that night in the *Secolo Nuovo* print-shop and dreamed of this rebel army marching through the Philippine jungles, armed with bolos, rifles, and bullets. At dawn, she rose from the office couch, inspected their latest issue, draped a blanket over snoozing Enrico, and then met Beatrix outside for work at the mansion.

In the fall of 1899, a well-dressed man carrying a medical case rode the cable-car with the cousins on their journey to Pacific Heights, got off at their stop, and followed them through Heath's black iron gates. Unlike them, he entered the mansion through the massive front doors and was taken into the library where Yvonne del Valle was reading. It was now clear to the Lemel

David Fagen

cousins that Yvonne was indeed pregnant and this well-dressed stranger was her new doctor. He emerged from the library an hour later with his medical case and returned the next morning at seven o'clock. Over the next weeks, they noticed his daily visits were growing longer. The cousins usually got off work hours after he'd left, but one day he stayed late and they managed to follow him downtown to an apothecary owned by a Gælic witch. Isabelle knew this herb-shop from her mother who claimed this witch could speak their Celtic mother-tongue, just as she knew the ancient recipes for abortion, sexual arousal, and infertility. Before Isabelle could comprehend this fact, the doctor emerged from this same apothecary and headed towards the waterfront at a quick pace, the Lemel cousins close behind. In a brick alley along the bay, the doctor stopped to speak with a man wearing a worker's cap and carrying a notebook. It took Isabelle a moment, but she soon realized the doctor was conversing with none other than Jack London. From their warm embrace and frenzied animation, my mother could tell they were childhood friends. The greatest conspiracy of our age started that very afternoon, although none of them were aware of it, nor could they feel the times of promise raining down over San Francisco.

SHE'LL BE DRIVING SIX WHITE HORSES

M Y LOFT WAS TOO WARM LAST NIGHT AND I PASSED OUT HERE, DOWN-stairs, on the couch. I pull the blanket off my eyes and see rain cascading off the porch awning. I guess my mom isn't coming today. If these last sunny days didn't bring her down the hill, I don't know why the rainy days would be different. If I want to talk with her, I'll have to walk up the hill in my rain-gear, just like last time. I haven't seen Isabelle since before I went off to Fort Russ and got myself pregnant, so she's either mad about Octavio or she's mad about what she saw in the notebook, the one you're reading now. Either way, none of her anger's justified, but I'll still have to face it.

I throw off the blanket, rub my eyes, and before I'm really awake, I see the geo-globe strobing from red to gray in a timed rhythm. I think Nikola designed this pulsing glow to be so tranquilizing the user would rather watch it strobe than answer the call. My globe's locator-ring is fixed on San Francisco while I stand there debating my options. None of them are good. I push the wooden button and the globe sizzles with a vertical band of electricity connecting its two poles. The device fills with blue light that congeals into a familiar face, the one I was expecting. Juana is encased in electric water, her skin writhing with small, crackling grains of spectral image. She's nothing but a blur at first, her mouth a dark hole emitting harsh metal sounds. Juana's famous green eyes eventually come into focus once the transmission stabilizes, only now they're turned blue by the pathways of the underworld. It really is fitting. I used to call her *blue blood*.

"There you are, *puta!*" she screams.

"I told you never to call me that!" I yell. "Go say that to your mom."

"Well?" her metal voice crackles. "Come on! Tell me!"

"Come on what, *sangue blu? Che cosa?*"

I walk over to the electric heat-pad and start boiling my water, already annoyed. The electricity hisses as Juana paces around her globe, desperate to see where I wandered off to. The image in these devices relies on a rapid electromagnetic pulse that spreads through the room in an invisible sphere, bouncing back the positions of each object. I can't help but smile as her metal voice curses and yells and pleads for me to stop moving. The heating pad glows bright red.

"Stop! Come on, Fulvia! *Chinga tu arrogancia!* Tell me!"

"Juana, you have to explain. With words. What are you talking about?"

"Can you hear me yet? I've been trying to talk to you for months!"

"I'm right here, we're talking on the—"

"Not the globe, damn it! When you're alone, have you heard me? Wait... your mom told me—"

"I haven't seen my mom in weeks, Juana. Please, tell me, what the hell are you—"

The band of electricity snaps between the iron poles, leaving its stray ions to float uncharged inside the geo-globe, now gray rather than red. I guess she hung up on me. That's not fair. I push the button for a call but she doesn't respond. All I see is the blue strobe of an attempted connection, so I just turn the whole thing off once my water's done boiling.

There are over thirty glass jars of herbs and teas hanging above my sink, all arranged in a single row. I open two of them, mix some mint and green tea inside my pot, then I pour in the hot water. My breakfast is tea, an apple, bread, and a slice of cheese. A few eggs would be good, salmon even better. I can't wait for those nice fatty jars stuffed with red fish. Should be any day now. There's nothing better than a chunk of salmon for breakfast.

I finish eating my boring meal and stare at the lifeless geo-globe, its locator ring fixed on San Francisco. Maybe I've been hearing Juana all along and just didn't realize it. Or maybe that's crazy and Juana's making fun of me, only I don't think so. She seemed happy for a moment, like she thought I learned something, but there's only one way to find out now. I throw on my wool pants, put on some thick socks, step into my boots, and wrap myself up in a stinky oilskin slicker. It's a hurricane outside the window with fat sheets of rain moving in waves across the muddy ground. I press the black button to cut off the electricity, stare at the dead geo-globe, and suddenly I hear dance hall music playing inside my ear. Juana's dominating everything as usual, she dances in the middle of the floor with her hands flapping from side to side. They called her *head witch* back in the 30s, and I see her now like Kali, goddess of the underworld, sticking out her red tongue at me in spite. Juana's voice cackles the way it does until the sound fuses into an onslaught of pouring rain.

Before her laughter can torment me, I open the closet and grab the *kerotakis* Octavio made for my mother. It's wrapped tightly in a blanket and tied up with twine so it won't break, even if I drop it. I step out onto the porch, throw up my hood, and walk into the storm as my pockets fill with rain. The entire road is a roaring brown river that reminds me this is a terrible idea, even worse than last time. The flow's so swift water sprays off my boots with every step, hitting me right in the crotch, and when I kick harder the water drenches my face.

In the middle of amusing myself like a child, the soil morphs into a chasm and I'm sucked down into a brown tube. I desperately clutch at anything within reach. The *kerotakis* goes flying towards the hill as my fingers lace through thin branches and down to the roots where I grab on for life. I can feel the abyss pulsing below me, feel death laughing beneath my feet. The plants are strong enough to hold my weight and I pull and tug until I crawl back up with brown water filling my mouth. The road's now a giant hole. I'm lucky to be breathing. The underworld just tried to kill me.

Anyone else would head back home, but not Fulvia. I pick up the *kerotakis* and keep walking up the hill, my entire body a fading brown ghost. The crunchy mineral taste of soil coats my tongue, no matter how much I spit it out. The stuff's even in my nose. I'll probably be snorting out black all week. My mother better appreciate this journey, even if I don't tell her about the mudslide. It's not like she ever does this for me.

I'm almost to the summit now. I can still hear Juana laughing in the rain, her cackle embedded in a thousand muddy droplets. If she only knew what I'm going through, what I'm carrying inside me. Not just my daughter, but the darkness from the roundhouse. Angelo's darkness. It's still hiding in the back of my thoughts, only maybe I've been speaking about it too loudly. Maybe I've been making it stronger. Maybe my mother knows the truth.

There isn't any wood-smoke coming from her chimney but I see electric light pouring through the windows. Her dead garden beds are pools of dark mud overflowing with so much rain that they bubble like cauldrons. My old bedroom window looms above my head and I imagine myself up there as a young girl reading by candlelight with the galaxy burning across the sky. So lonely. I lower my oilskin hood, step under the porch-awning, wipe off my face, and reach for the door handle only to find Isabelle's shadowy form behind the lace-covered window. I push the door but she pushes back. I bang on the window and threaten to smash it. I scream in a fury but she screams louder until I wedge my shoulder in the door-frame and force myself inside. The *kerotakis* falls to the floor with a soft thud. All I see is white light. My head's still spinning but I can see my mother standing in the corner with a knife in her hand. That much is clear.

"You stay the hell away from me!" she hisses. "You've got that *thing* inside you."

"It's a girl. I thought you'd be happy. That's why—"

"Stay back! I'm not talking about Octavio's baby. I'm talking about that shadow lodged inside you! I read your notebook! The one where you make us look like fools! Bumbling idiots! Like we did this all by mistake, through no will of our own! And now I know it's inside you!"

"Know what, *mama?* Put the knife down."

"You put all that darkness into Angelo, then Essie sucked it out. I read all of it. Then it jumped inside you. That's why you're here, that's why—"

"*Mama!* Put the knife down! It's me. I've got it under control."

"You don't have anything under control! I hear your insanity all night! So does Juana! So does Yvonne, only she's polite and treats you like a baby, she teaches you what I...what I...what I—"

The knife clatters to the ground as I take her in my arms, close my eyes, and run my wet fingers through her lightning bolt hair. She's salty and filled with anguish, clutching my oilskin with all her strength. When I open my eyes I can see a familiar black doily pinned to the wall behind her. In the center of this dark-yarned snowflake is a picture of Josephine Lemel, the only one that exists, taken in 1927 when the war just ended. She's standing on the front steps of the little blue house on Greenwich Street, thin arms crossed over her chest, staring back at me with the faintest smile, her famous dark hair now completely gray. They buried Josephine under the floorboards next to Rosita and Marisol. Juana and Beatrix still live above them. My aunt Bianca lives right next door.

"I wish I'd stayed with Josephine, at the end," I say. "I should have gone there more."

"You needed to be up here, I guess." Isabelle wipes her eyes and steps away. "Anyway, how can I trust you now? You lied to me!"

"It doesn't feel good, does it? Being lied to."

"Stop being cruel. I didn't know you were writing it all down, as it happened. It makes us—"

"Seem human?"

"No! Foolish! Inept! Stumbling in the dark!"

"That seems perfectly human to me. Look, I'm not making any of it up. Those are how my days went, what you read in the notebook is the truth, mostly. I'm being honest, *mama*. I'm lost and confused but I'm trying, you're trying, I think that's clear. You made mistakes...a lot of them, but it's fine. We're fine. I think they'll see that. We'll be like them, finally. We'll be normal people."

"But you even lie to *them*, you lie to your reader. You make it seem like your motivations are so pure, that you just want to get the wheat down the hill. So noble! And then what? You say you've been planning to lay old Octavio for months. You tell them all this!"

"Yeah, well, I'm full of contradictions, just like you and Josephine. What do you want?"

"And you really have this under control? The darkness isn't growing?"

I don't answer. Instead I take my mother by the shoulder and walk her towards the living room. The *kerotakis* is still on the floor and when I pick it up there's no sound of shattered glass. My mom sits on the couch beside her electric heater and I see from the scattered books that she's been reading all day, probably trying to distract herself from my madness. We're not so different. Now I can see where her mind's been wandering.

"Jane Austen?" I ask, picking one of the books. "All of them? Did you clean out the library?"

"These are mine. I've read them more times than I can remember. They remind me how far we've all come. In just over a century we escaped the world of these novels. But forget about my books. Can you answer me?"

"Answer what?"

"Is the darkness growing? Do you really...have you learned enough to—"

"I've got it, *mama*. If you're going to trust me, go all the way. Don't skimp on me."

My mother just sighs. I haven't convinced her. She stares at the humming orange coils of Nikola's little heater with its carousel of spinning fans that distribute heat in every direction. At night, when I was a child, I used to watch those endless puddles of orange-tinted shadow collide and merge on the walls until I fell asleep. I still haven't taken my heater out of the closet and I now realize that it reminds me too much of my lonely childhood. That kind of electric warmth brings only sadness. Pain penetrates me drop by drop.

"What's that you have there?" she asks, pointing at my package. "Salmon?"

"Open it." I toss it through the air and she frantically catches it. "Octavio made it for you."

"Sit down, *loquita*. Stop acting like Juana."

I take off the oil skin and my mother doesn't try to help me this time. She uses her teeth to bite through the twine and opens up the blanket to reveal her hidden treasure. Octavio made a shiny copper cylinder containing a glass *kerotakis* with a removable dome lid. Material is submerged in water at the bottom of the glass and a fire lit at the base. This ancient device is only about a foot high with a tiny collecting cap at the top of the cylinder to catch the oil-rich condensation. Underneath this transparent lid is a small note which reads *pour le jardin.* My mother can fire this thing up indoors any day of the year and distill small batches of whatever she has around. It's the perfect gift from someone who loves her and my bitter mother weeps uncontrollably. While she does this, I close my eyes, I try to hear her thoughts, but all I see are two hands clasped above the glimmering sea. Maybe this is Isabelle and Octavio. Maybe she's pregnant. Maybe this is their child.

"I was too old, Fulvia," she tells me. "I'd seen too much. Done too much."

"He loves you, *mama.* He'll always love you. Maybe you can invite him—"

"I'll never live with a man again! Ever! You were bad enough!"

"I couldn't think of a more loyal man than—"

"Look at me!" She pulls up her sweater and reveals the light pink gashes all over her belly and torso. "I'm a disgusting monster! Worse than Frankenstein's! Who wants to see this?

"He does, *mama.*"

"What do you know?" She drops the sweater and wipes away her last tears. "*Puta.*"

I slap her on the shoulder and she can't help from smiling. She's jealous, obviously, just like I planned. There's some excitement hidden beneath her eyes, a tiny sparkle glittering for the life inside me. She knows it's not just darkness under my skin. I'm not raising this girl alone, that's for sure, and Isabelle stares at me while I have this thought. My daughter's going to live in my old bedroom and make perfume with her crazy *abuela.* She'll run through the corn fields and pump well-water into the copper bottoms of my mother's alembics. She'll get those warm early years I never had when *mama* was off fighting in Russia with a Winchester automatic rifle in her hands and a fluffy wool *papakha* covering her head. I never even knew what she looked like until I was 7 years-old and it's taken me all this time to forgive her. I know she can hear this but Isabelle doesn't have any tears left. That's when mine start to flow like rivers. Without warning, as a whirlwind swoops on an oak, love shakes my heart. In total silence, I hear my mother speak, just as she hears me. I think I'm slowly learning. Juana will be proud of me.

14

THE IMMACULATE CONCEPTION OF YVONNE DEL VALLE

YVONNE DEL VALLE WAS BORN ON NOVEMBER 27, 1870 ON THE *Rancho del Valle*, just over the hills from Oakland. Her father was Enrique Vasquez del Valle, the final Spanish subject to be granted land by the collapsing Crown. In the final days of Castillian rule, Enrique's father Guillermo was awarded an irregular shape of forested land that stretched from the trout-filled *Arroyo de San Pablo* up to the redwood studded peaks of the Coastal Range, although he died before glimpsing its beauty. Guillermo del Valle had served as lieutenant under the military governor Juan Bautista de Anza in his war against the indigenous, a genocide where those who weren't killed were forced to toil as slaves in the fortified Missions. At the end of his military service, Guillermo del Valle took up residence in the small colonial port town of *Yerba Buena* and found an acceptable Spanish bride to deliver him an heir, the first steps towards populating his *rancho*. This forgotten woman died giving birth to Enrique Vasquez del Valle in the year 1812, a time of great rebellion in Mexico.

The Crown awarded the del Valles their *rancho* in 1814 and finally ended the family's long centuries of shame and infamy. During the war between Spain and England in the late 1500s, the del Valles fled Castille after spying for the British Crown and settled in London where they became Royal subjects, rising quickly in the spheres of nobility. Through a labyrinthine series of royal marriages, the Anglo hatred against Spain eventually subsided and the del Valles were allowed to return to Castille, a privilege they exercised when the black plague ravaged London in 1666. While their homecoming was free from violent incident, the del Valles were viewed as social pariahs and received no invitations in their home city of Madrid. By the 1740s, the family was no better than common folk. To remedy this situation, Guillermo del Valle joined the colonial military to rebuild his family name by enslaving the mythical land of California. While the Crown awarded him a *rancho* in 1814, Guillermo never lived to actually see it. This estate passed to his son Enrique and sat unclaimed for many years.

With few prospects in sleepy *Yerba Buena*, young Enrique crossed the bay in 1829 and found work as a cattle-hand at the *Rancho San Antonio*. Despite his father's service to the Crown, Enrique inherited the royal deed to the del Valle land but no money, as there was none. His resentment grew over the ten years he worked as a common laborer on the Peralta family's *Rancho San Antonio*, a massive estate that stretched from the western bay to the eastern hills. Once he'd saved enough wages, Enrique loaded a wagon with tools and building materials and then ascended through the redwoods with a rifle on his lap, committed to developing his *Rancho del Valle*. He chose a flat bluff overlooking the *Arroyo de San Pablo* and began building an adobe house with three bedrooms, a kitchen, a living room, and a covered porch. He finished this structure in the summer of 1841 and crossed the bay to *Yerba Buena* in search of a wife, just as his father had once done. After procuring a new suit, a clean shave, and a golden ring, this 30-year-old rogue walked into the offices of the Hudson's Bay Company, a respectable Canadian house of commerce. In this waterfront trading post built over the sea, Enrique met Francois d'Avignon and his young daughter Camille.

Camille was born in 1828 along the Rhône River in the French city of Avignon. Her mother Justine was a follower of Mary and married Francois for his connections to the global trade network, an arrangement that eventually delivered the family across the Atlantic to the colonial city of Montréal. Her husband soon found employment with the Hudson's Bay Company, although this new home would provide just a glimmer of happiness. Justine died from pneumonia in 1834, long before she could properly teach Camille to survive, and Francois consoled himself by shifting his post to Fort Vancouver along the Columbia River, a remote fortress where they lived a simple existence amid the towering trees of the Pacific Northwest. When another post opened in the small Mexican settlement of *Yerba Buena*, Francois immediately petitioned for transfer, citing ill health in the damp north woods. His request was granted and Francois was already nearing the end of his life when well-dressed Enrique Vasquez del Valle walked into the Hudson's Bay trading post with an offer to marry Camille once she came of age.

Despite his daughter's protests, Francois agreed to del Valle's proposal. Without a husband, Camille would be left to rot in this foggy backwater with only a tiny pile of coins to carry her through, a fate he wished to spare her. His daughter resigned herself to this dismal life and left *Yerba Buena* in 1844 on a boat piloted by Enrique Vasquez del Valle. Francois died less than a month later, leaving her a paltry $200 worth of HBC stock and a wardrobe filled with old clothing. Possessing only this small inheritance, Camille rode with her new husband into the wild on the back of a brown horse and beheld the majestic redwoods that guarded the eastern hills. When she finally arrived at the *Rancho del Valle*, Enrique walked her into the adobe bedroom and closed the door. Camille suffered countless nights in this fruitless pursuit of a child that inevitably ended in a miscarriage. No matter how much she rested or how robust her diet, Camille refused to bear Enrique a child. The last time he piled his heavy frame atop her body was the summer of 1848. By then, Enrique was an alcoholic and *Alta California* altered beyond recognition.

Before their enslavement, the indigenous of the San Francisco Bay had lived on this land since Coyote created them after the Great Flood. His descendants spread through the coastlines and valleys, creating a network of tribes who rarely practiced warfare and excelled in trading across vast distances. Their infinite utopia was interrupted in the year 1769 when the Catholic priest Junipero Serra arrived in California with his Crucifix and Bible, ushering in a reign of terror that decimated their peoples and emptied the coastal land. Those who managed to escape the diseases and soldiers fled to the eastern mountains where they were able to survive the coming century.

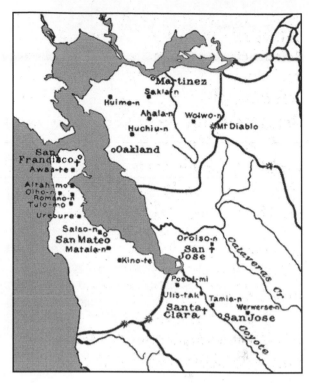

Ohlone village sites.

After the Spanish Crown was overthrown by the Mexican Republic in 1821, the indigenous of the Mission system were set free, slavery was abolished, and every native given the opportunity to become a citizen of the Republic. Over the next decades, the local tribes cautiously returned to their ancestral lands and kept watchful eye over the latest colonizers whom they trusted no more than the Spanish. In the forests around the *Rancho del Valle*, the displaced Ohlone and Miwok observed a lone madman building a house of mud and wood near one of their last hidden sanctuaries. They watched him bring a dark haired woman to their land and felt her sadness as she wandered alone beneath the tall oak trees. Camille would occasionally see them moving through the laurel or find them drinking water from a fern shrouded creek. These were the secret friends who watched her while she slept.

The governors of *Alta California* mutinied against Mexico in the 1840s and demanded more autonomy from the *Distrito Federal*, a concession that was quickly granted. The Republic of Texas had already broken away from Mexico to become a US state in 1845 and it was rumored another *yanqui* insurrection was being planned for *Alta California*. This soon came to fruition during the California Republic of 1846, an armed Anglo uprising in

Sonoma that served as a prelude to the US declaring war on Mexico. Enrique Vasquez and young Camille learned of this new uprising from their Spanish neighbors who immediately formed an armed protective society to defend against the *yanqui* invaders. Camille despised these gatherings where she would sit silently with the older wives as their men grew drunker and the daylight faded into dusk. As they whiled away these nights, war raged on from the *Distrito Federal* to Santa Barbara, and by the winter of 1847, the state of California was under the control of the US. With all these battles taking place hundreds of miles away, their protective society remained a drinking club until 1848 when the truth of this *yanqui* invasion was revealed: gold. Within a year of this international announcement promising riches to all comers, the first shots had been fired outside the *Rancho del Valle* and a war against the Anglo thieves began.

Scarcely a thousand people lived in the port town of *Yerba Buena* before the Gold Rush. Within two years, there were over 20,000 residents of newly-dubbed San Francisco. As the miners and soldiers spread out of this coastal metropolis into the unconquered hills, the indigenous were forced to either fight or flee in the wars of extermination that consumed California. Slavery was brought back by the *yanqui* government and any Anglo could claim an indigenous person as a slave to work their fields, a law the colonizers took full advantage of. Through no goodness of his own, Enrique Vasquez protected the local Miwok and Ohlone from enslavement by driving the *yanquis* from the forests and hills of the *Rancho del Valle*, a vast plot of land that served as a *de facto* refuge for anyone who wasn't Anglo. Enrique stopped forcing

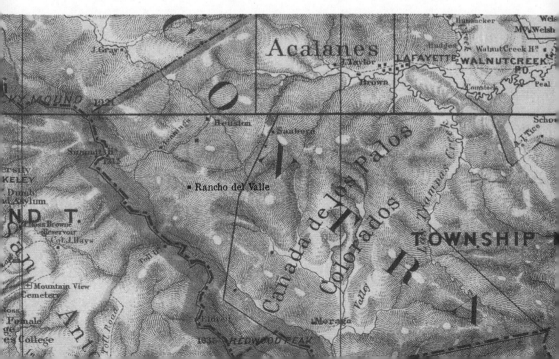

himself on Camille during these times of war, preferring to discharge himself with metal and gun-powder.

Every night brought more gunshots, bloody wounds, frantic hoof-beats, and wounded men screaming outside Camille's window. She never participated in these battles but was taught how to handle a shotgun and defend the adobe. Despite this ruthless guerrilla war waged in the redwoods, the *yanqui* squatters and lumber thieves kept arriving in vaſt numbers. Between the years 1848 and 1860, the Spanish *Californios* either sold or loſt moſt of their *ranchos* to the new laws of the United States, with only the del Valle traƈt remaining whole. On the peaks of his land, Enrique Vasquez could see plumes of black induſtrial smoke rising above the San Francisco Bay from a hundred ſteam-ships and faƈtories. His *Rancho del Valle* survived the *yanqui* invasion only to be surrounded by mechanical leviathans that poisoned the rivers and polluted the air. There was nothing left to do but drink.

The old Spanish families held their weekly *fandangos* late in the evening juſt as they had for decades, only now there were respeƈtable Anglo neighbors clapping to their guitars and cheering on the ſtamping dancers. Camille rarely spoke during these gatherings and her husband usually played cards or fell asleep in his lounge chair. Because of her tendency towards silence, the local church community began to whisper that *Señora del Valle* was a French witch in league with the devil. While Camille might have ſtood with them in the pews and recited the Bible, there was something wrong with this green-eyed beauty who hardly spoke and could produce no child. Some called it nerves, others called it spiritual sensitivity, while others claimed demonic possession. In either case, no one said anything out loud, nor did they come close to the truth, for the del Valles were respeƈtable members of this tightly-knit *Californio* community. Gun fights ſtill erupted along the borders of neighboring *Rancho Moraga* as more *yanquis* tried to log the laſt foreſts, violent episodes that bonded these families closer together. The gun battles continued through the 1860s, juſt as Enrique Vasquez's alcoholism worsened, because no matter how effeƈtively they patrolled their *ranchos*, these Caſtilian dynaſties played a losing game againſt the triumphant *yanqui*. The days of the Spanish Crown were juſt a diſtant memory.

During the winter of 1870, 42-year-old Camille del Valle went for her usual walk in the oak foreſt above the adobe, although this time she ſtayed on the wild deer trail and followed its damp pathway up to the laurel-roofed creek that fed the *Arroyo San Pablo*. Camille kept climbing until she arrived at a large boulder with two grinding holes, the insides smooth from recent use and lined with fine acorn flour. As she climbed down, Camille realized the foreſt was completely silent and beheld a yellow-eyed coyote approaching through the ferns. Two dark-haired women with black lines tattoœd

across their faces stood on either side of this creature. There was only a brief
moment of recognition before Camille was sucked into a watery tube and
emerged over a mile away, her body completely soaked in lavender water and
covered with dry dirt.

Night was falling when she crawled her way back to the adobe and found
an enraged Enrique Vasquez demanding an explanation. Camille claimed to
have fallen in the creek, hit her head on a rock, and fallen into unconsciousness. While her explanation satisfied him, what happened later that evening
unsettled Enrique Vasquez forever. When the drunken patriarch was sleeping, Camille climbed atop his corpulent body and willingly had sex with him
for the first and only time in her life. When he woke that morning, this confused old man discovered his wife happily cooking breakfast in the kitchen.
She made no mention of mounting him that night and they never spoke of it
again, not even when Camille was visibly pregnant a few months later.

The whispers increased in their tiny community and this new development constituted the bulk of their gossip. How could such an elderly man
conceive a child with a woman nearing the end of her barren fertility? Talk
of the devil was common after Sunday church when the mysterious couple
rode off on horseback to their isolated adobe. The Castro, Moraga, Bernal,
and Martinez families all worried for the health of young Camille del Valle,
even as they suspected her of an infernal alliance with the devil. While the
other families slowly lost the bulk of their lands to federal taxes, Enrique
Vasquez never missed a payment and held every acre of the original *Rancho
del Valle*, a fact that made him the object of resentment. For this reason, no
one helped Camille deliver her daughter, nor did they think to inquire about
her health. Even her husband fell into an alcoholic stupor and couldn't be
roused from unconsciousness when the birth began. Gripped with fear and
panic at the pains ripping through her body, Camille beheld two dark-haired
women with black lines tattooed across their faces. They laid her down on the
tiled kitchen floor and stoked a strong fire in the earthen oven. As the flames
lit up the dark room, Yvonne del Valle was born into the bloody hands of two
Ohlone medicine-women. Enrique Vasquez snored away, oblivious. When he
woke the next morning clamoring for wine, Camille and Yvonne were sleeping in bed with sunlight draped across their faces.

The community was astounded at the miracle of little Yvonne and her
piercing green eyes bright as emeralds. The women tickled her at church and
showered Camille with gifts while the men consoled Enrique Vasquez on his
lack of a male heir. One of his neighbors bluntly said the devil was at work,
for what else could explain the sudden youthfulness of Camille del Valle, a
formerly tongueless woman who now spoke loudly of her daughter's beauty
to all who'd listen.

Yvonne became the darling of the weekly *fandangos* and learned to walk between the legs of drunken revelers and stamping women. As his wife and daughter became the center of attention, Enrique Vasquez switched from red wine to spirits, sinking deeper into his degeneracy. While little Yvonne learned to speak, the 60-year-old patriarch rode through the redwood forests helping the Moragas defend the remains of their *rancho*. They made their last stand against the *yanquis* in the bloody 1870s but fared no better than before. Only the del Valles remained prosperous.

Yvonne grew up beneath the inland hills of oak and laurel where tiny quail and majestic deer carved their paths through blankets of fallen leaves. She was watched over by her indigenous birth-mothers and never felt afraid in this land of wandering coyotes and babbling creeks. Camille taught her daughter to read, write, and speak in five languages, giving her access to recorded history. When her father was asleep, Camille told Yvonne the story of Mary Magdalene and how the Catholic Church brought slavery to this beautiful land. At the age of eleven, Yvonne could cook, sew, fire a shotgun, sprint up a hill, fish in the creek, and read faster than either of her parents, especially Enrique Vasquez. His daughter was vastly smarter and challenged his patriarchal authority at every turn. Her clothes were always muddy, she never wore shoes, and she lived every spare hour in the laurel-wood or beside the *Arroyo San Pablo* watching salmon as they returned to spawn. Church was a bore to Yvonne and she tapped her feet beneath the pews as the *padre* recited tales of ancient men ruling over their families.

The bloody 1870s came to a close when the first mayor of Oakland purchased nearly all of the *Rancho Moraga* through a tax sale, leaving only a small fragment for the family. He was joined in this legal *yanqui* invasion by the mayor of San Francisco who built a grand summer house on the edge of *Rancho El Sobrante*, the former lands of the Castro family. Plans for a railroad connection to Oakland were announced and more Anglo farmers moved inland following the advertisement for bargain real-estate. The *Rancho del Valle* was mostly dry oaken hills and possessed less than an acre of arable land, making it undesirable to investors. A public dirt road wound along its eastern border and the future railroad would utilize this route to reach *Rancho Moraga*, bringing smoke to their little valley. Enrique Vasquez could do nothing to stop this legal expansion, nor would he talk about it. The *yanqui* squatters had been replaced by speculators, railroad barons, and Federal Marshals, all people he couldn't shoot. To compensate, he began to enter Yvonne's room at night, desperate for something to control.

Each of these drunken attempts saw Enrique Vasquez advance further into her bed. Pretending to be possessed, Yvonne muttered phrases in Latin about eternal damnation, endless hell-fire, the allure of the devil, and the wages of sin. She rolled her eyes back into her head, shook the bed with her entire body, and growled like a beast when Enrique Vasquez touched her leg. In the daytime, Yvonne acted as if nothing had happened and casually asked questions about the Bible or other religious matters. In less than a month, Enrique Vasquez had stopped his nocturnal visits, now obsessed with praying to God and reading Holy Scripture. In his paranoid imagination, Yvonne had been bewitched by the devil to tempt him off the path of fatherhood. Until the time of his death, Enrique Vasquez lived in fear of his only child and hardly moved from his wooden seat on the front porch except to sleep alone in bed. He began his slow decline in the summer of 1883 when Yvonne del Valle and her mother Camille effectively took control of the *rancho*.

Yvonne was increasingly beloved by the Spanish families who'd once demonized her mother as a spawn of Lucifer. Now that Enrique Vasquez had entered his senility, the del Valle women became the face of the sprawling *Rancho*. They attended the occasional *fandango* and carried picnic baskets to community gatherings held by the new Anglo neighbors. Enrique Vasquez went to church with them every Sunday but always rode back alone and scarcely talked to anyone. Unlike her father, Yvonne stayed away from the adobe and traced long spirals across the hills and creeks, constantly followed by her hidden guardians. She knew every valley, every spring, every boulder, every grinding hole, but her Ohlone birth-mothers lived in hollow redwood trees or beneath the ground in dwellings too subtle for her to discover. Yvonne returned from this forest only to sleep, eat dinner, and take her daily lessons from Camille. As her father plunged further into senility, the fate of the *rancho* became unclear, and when Yvonne finally asked about the deed to the land, Enrique Vasquez claimed it would go to the Catholic Church unless she found an acceptable husband. In the spring of 1890, one of these potential suitors arrived. Without this detestable man, our future wouldn't exist.

His name was Lionel Heath, an infamous steel-baron of the British Empire who'd expanded across the Atlantic from Lancashire to the state of Pennsylvania. At the time, literary depictions of Spanish California were all the rage in London, especially after the visit of such western luminaries as Joaquin Miller, Bret Harte, and Ambrose Bierce. Of all the Californians who passed through the Imperial Metropolis, it was a racist author named Gertrude Atherton who inspired Heath to move west in search of a Spanish bride. After becoming enthralled with Atherton's descriptions of *fandangos* and dark-haired Spanish beauties, Heath contacted his partners at JP Morgan & Company and transferred his responsibilities to California. The elder Junius Morgan had recently passed away in Monte Carlo, leaving everything to his son John Pierpont Morgan and his bank at 23 Wall Street. Their family's massive shift of British capital from London to New York was now complete, leaving the US bound together with iron railroads that allowed capital to flow without pause. In these times of expansion, J.P. Morgan agreed to have Heath be his speculator on the West Coast. With their combined forces, these men planned to build a new empire across the Pacific.

After installing himself in the opulent Palace Hotel in San Francisco, Heath set about finding the most beautiful daughter of the decaying *Californios*. He called on the Moraga, Castro, Vallejo, and Martinez families, but was thoroughly unimpressed with their progeny. It was only at the *Rancho del Valle*

Grand court of the palace hotel.

that he beheld the true object of his desire. For the first time in his existence, Lionel Heath was enamored with the beauty of another. This handsome Englishman talked by the fire with Enrique Vasquez over glasses of brandy while Camille and Yvonne listened to the aging patriarch sell off his daughter with a petulant grin. Wearing a new white dress, Yvonne leaned against the earthen walls and resolved to save her guardians' ancestral home by marrying this alcoholic millionaire. Heath expressed no interest in developing the *rancho* and swore to keep it off the market in exchange for Yvonne's hand. She agreed to his terms that very night but demanded to remain in her home until the day of the wedding. Their well-attended ceremony took place three weeks later at the summer home of Mayor Bryant, just above the future Orinda train station. It was the largest event ever held in their isolated region, attracting journalists from across the globe and arousing an army of local hawkers. Despite the gaiety and opulence of the event, Yvonne knew the darkness that hunted Mary Magdalene was swiftly approaching her hidden sanctuary. This marriage was a way of pacifying it.

Yvonne moved into the Palace Hotel where she was forced to sleep with her husband beneath red velvet sheets. Equipped with her mother's teaching, Yvonne avoided pregnancy for months until Heath was called away east on urgent business. Unrest had broken out at his Pennsylvania steel mills in a strike directed by the Amalgamated Association of Iron and Steel Workers, a union that had recently staged an uprising in Pittsburgh against the Carnegie Steel Company. While her husband was dealing with this volatile situation, Yvonne del Valle-Heath used his unlimited bank account to have cases of books delivered to her penthouse on the upper floor of the Palace. She never left this luxurious room and observed industrial San Francisco through the hazy filter of her lace-shrouded windows. The world outside terrified her kind heart with the cruelness of its poverty and the foulness of its pollution. She much preferred to plow through recorded history in the hopes of unearthing weapons that could defeat this darkness consuming the land.

In search of these incendiary texts, Yvonne came across an obscure French journal called *La Vogue* where she discovered the rhapsodic poetry of Arthur Rimbaud. Yvonne wrote to the Paris address listed in the issue and asked for further material, only to have her letter read by my relative Félix Fénéon. Unwilling to risk corresponding with the wife of a ruthless steel baron, Félix passed the letter on to a local woman of letters who forwarded Yvonne the latest texts from Paris along with her own musings on contemporary literary culture. While she was lost down these rabbit holes of French radicalism, well-paid Italian stone-masons built Lionel Heath an opulent Roman *villa* overlooking the Golden Gate. He returned in the fall of 1892 and moved their belongings up to Pacific Heights where he surprised Yvonne with the mansion's sudden existence. Heath tried to impregnate Yvonne that night but vanished the next morning without a word, leaving her in the empty stone house with only the servants to keep her company. Behind her back, Heath retreated to the Palace where he lived with his French mistress and maintained constant wire contact with New York. From this luxurious redoubt, Heath proceeded to crush the Sailor's Union with a viciousness unseen in his previous activities. The man rarely came home and Yvonne knew nothing of his actions, nor did she suspect them.

All she truly understood in those days was that an anarchist named Alexander Berkman tried to kill one of her husband's associates in Pittsburgh. Heath had been in the same building celebrating their triumph over the striking workers when the shot was fired, although Yvonne didn't know this until after his return. She tasted pure joy after discovering this international anarchist movement and women like Emma Goldman, the

Alexander Berkman

shooter's alleged lover. In the vaſt library Heath had purchased for her, Yvonne loſt herself in pursuit of these ancient rebels juſt as the national economy collapsed into the Panic of 1893. While living anarchiſts were being scattered to the winds of repression, Yvonne was amassing books of every variety from across the world, hoping to find the source of their rebellion.

By the year 1896, her oak shelves contained over 10,000 volumes, half of which she'd read cover to cover beside the library's massive ſtone fireplace. In 1897, Yvonne began reading law books and court cases, telling her husband that reality was much more intereſting than fiction. He was nearly speechless when she asked to take the California Bar examination a year later, an indulgence that he allowed simply for amusement. After arranging for her to take the examination in the mansion, Yvonne became the second woman lawyer in California, although the public would never know of this fact. To avoid any publicity, Yvonne requeſted the Bar Association keep all records of her examination locked in the mansion vault, under the condition they be returned should she ever wish to practice law. While Heath may have been threatened by his barriſter wife, Yvonne never brought up law again and returned to reading the lateſt novels, now claiming that legal texts were ſtupefyingly boring.

Heath usually slept his nights at the Palace Hotel where Yvonne was now certain he kept a miſtress, although she had no proof. One of the few times Heath came home, Yvonne asked him about their fortune and discovered it would never be hers. With no male heir, the entire Heath Steel Company and all of its assets would be given to JP Morgan & Co. with juſt a small annual sum going to Yvonne. According to Heath, the only way to ensure her ſtake in this massive wealth was to become pregnant. So in the spring of 1899, Yvonne took Heath to his bedroom and let herself conceive a child beneath his alcoholic skin, confident that her plans were beyond his comprehension.

With their child growing inside her belly, Heath arranged for a proper house-ſtaff to take over the domeſtic duties. Rather than be content with six cooks and an armed gatekeeper, he put out a call for a dozen Italian-speaking laundresses to take care of his wife. Henry James' portrayals of British ariſtocrats living in Italy were ſtill *en vogue* and Heath hoped to recreate this *ambiance* for his literary-minded wife. Unfortunately for him, Yvonne was unimpressed and refused to select her own ſtaff when the applicants arrived on the front lawn. She claimed to dislike Henry James and his lifeless manner of describing servants. In a rage, Heath ſtormed outside and chose a dozen women at random, hoping his bad selections would force Yvonne to assume her duty as manager of the household. His wishes didn't come to pass and Yvonne avoided her ſtaff, going so far as to try and cook her own meals. The next time Heath spoke with her, Yvonne asked for three midwives, a requeſt that was simply too much for this man of industry. He summoned a discrete male doctor through his contacts and arranged for this secular male to check on Yvonne each morning. This was the second of Heath's great mistakes, for this doctor was none other than former wharf-rat and pick-pocket Eamonn O'Shea.

Eamonn was born to Irish immigrants in the city of San Francisco on April 4, 1873, the fifth of eight starving children. Only his older sisters Ciera and Sinead would survive the turbulent 1870s with its rampant poverty and blood-thirsty mobs. Their mother preferred prayer and tea to bread and butter, and were it not for his sister's skills at thieving, Eamonn might have starved like the others. At the age of six, he joined a waterfront gang called the Finn MacCools and prowled the docks in search of drunk sailors to roll for cash. As the saying went, *the younger the thief, the better the odds*, at least when it came to pick-pocketing. Growing up into adolescence as a Finn MacCool required increasingly brazen acts in order to secure the same return as the nimble youngsters. In less than a generation, the gang had split into the youthful pickpockets and the adolescent marauders who used thin canoes to raid cargo ships on foggy nights. In this lunar realm of petty waterfront piracy and conflicts over gang territory, Eamonn met the infamous Jack London and his lover the Queen of the Oyster Pirates. The two became friends in 1892 and negotiated a truce on the waterfront between pirates, an act that united them against the bosses. My grandfather and uncles never forgot this, for the pirates could have easily sided with the crimps and fought the sailors. Before my uncles could thank these maritime rogues, both Eamonn and Jack vanished without a trace. A few sailors began to whisper that Eamonn had been kidnapped by a witch who'd turned his family into crows, none of whom were ever seen again.

Four years later, in the summer of 1896, a person named Doctor O'Shea opened an office on the second floor of a crowded apartment building, its sign looming over the corner of Dupont and Sutter. Business soon poured in and a lucky reference landed him an out-call to the Palace Hotel where he tended to the numerous complaints of a hypochondriac railroad baron. Eamon's professionalism and discretion in this matter led to another out-call from the infamous steel baron Lionel Heath. The Irish and Italian mothers who lived in Eamonn's building already spoke of the doctor as a man who'd sold his soul to the devil. His job with Heath only confirmed this.

On his first day in the mansion during fall of 1899, Eamonn was led into the vast library by one of the cooks and introduced to both Lionel and Yvone del Valle-Heath. After a brief conversation, Eamonn was hired and told to arrive at seven each morning to check on Yvonne. He would provide for all her needs and was empowered by Heath to purchase any supplies with his unlimited credit. After this initial meeting, the steel baron departed and didn't return for weeks, allowing the young doctor to fall in love with Yvonne. They spoke at length about literature and art, history and science, medicine and astrology. She interrogated him for details about the city of San Francisco and claimed that its cruelty terrified her beyond comprehension. During these long discussions, Yvonne never lost a chance to rub his leg, touch his arm, feel his skin, slide her back against his torso, or kiss his cheek.

When the morning sickness started, Eamonn fixed her a cup of numbing herbal tea that was so effective Yvonne immediately asked about its origin. He told her about the Gælic witch who hired him off the waterfront and helped pay for his medical school, claiming she knew the ancient recipes science now denigrated as spinsters folklore. Without hesitation, Yvonne said she wanted a girl and under no circumstances could it be a boy, otherwise her British husband would continue his empire. Although employed by Lionel Heath, Eamonn decided to place all his trust in this expectant mother and promised to ask the Gælic witch if such a potion existed.

After receiving a kiss on the cheek, Doctor O'Shea left the mansion and headed down the hill by foot. As the fates would have it, my mother and Beatrix were following behind. They trailed him to a small herb shop and observed him speaking with Jack London in a waterfront alley. No one involved in this situation was aware of the forces now colliding together or the parts they'd play in our world of electromagnetic light. The future was beyond their comprehension.

WE'LL ALL GO OUT TO MEET HER

I T'S RAINING OUTSIDE. MORE LIKE MIST, REALLY, RAIN SO FINE IT FLOATS instead of falls. Drops of water slowly bead on my skylight then slither down the glass once they get too heavy. This vision is the exact opposite of my dream, the one where the shadow-man hovers behind me, perceivable only through its coldness. It points at the Paloma transmitter just as it explodes into a massive fireball and leaves a red crater burning in the olive groves. The shadow-man makes me watch it over and over, motioning with his black finger until I close my eyes and wake up to this gentle rain slithering above my head.

I throw off the covers, climb downstairs, and discover I've left the electricity on all night. The geo-globe's pulsing red with its locator-ring fixed on San Francisco. This pulse continues its gentle rhythm while I eat yesterday's bread with yesterday's lentils and boil myself water on the electric heat-pad.

We're in a historic transmission. I heard it on the wireless news bulletin last night when Nikola told us the twelve conductors were still safely hibernating inside their chambers. As of 22:00 hours GMT, this was the longest electromagnetic ribbon ever sustained since the victory of the Light Brigade in 1927. I switched off the globe once Nikola stepped out of view and another scientist started rambling on about possible interactions with coronal discharges and plasma exchange between the spheres that may have boosted the transmission. These men bore me to death with their grand theories for why everything happens the way it does. If it weren't for Nikola, I'd never listen to the wireless bulletin

I sip my tea and watch the red pulse of the globe continue unanswered. The rain's a bit louder now and I tap my foot on the floorboards in rhythm with the droplets. It's been so long since I danced the way I used to, crazy like a loon, not caring about anything other than the joy of my body. All those sweet tunes of my youth echo in my head, rock me from side to side, and make me feel like I'm back in San Francisco, like its 1935 all over again. That was different. My womanhood was in full bloom. This isn't me swaying right now. It's someone else. I know that much. The shiny saxophones blare as I click the wooden button at the base of the geo-globe and Juana's face sizzles to life.

"You heard that?" she asks me.

"She'll be coming 'round the mountain? Yeah, I heard it."

"Hear it now?"

"Yeah, because you're playing it on that piece of Edison junk over there."

Juana grins and walks towards the center of the geo-globe. Her form flickers into tiny fragments as she knocks the needle off Marisol's gramophone. I can almost make out the Chinese paintings on her wall before Juana returns to the globe with her face beaming back an unfamiliar kindness.

"You need to control what you say back, Fulvia. I hear all of it. You're really powerful, okay, it's true, but you need to get a grip on yourself. And you know we never needed to fight the way we did. It was hard enough being me, *blue blood, sangue blu*. How the hell was I supposed to help you? It wasn't my idea, you know. I only went along with it because of our moms. Plus, now you know how I felt back then, *puta*. I was the same age you are. Now I'm fifty! Fifty! That was my last chance to have some kind of normal life for a second, and there you were causing all sorts of—"

"You don't need to apologize, Juana. I under—"

"I didn't apologize!" her metal voice clangs. "I'm only saying—"

"Then don't apologize, I don't—"

"Look, I'm sorry, okay. I love you, *puta*."

"Stop calling me that! This is why I don't—"

"Okay, fine. Sorry miss chaste perfect virgin who didn't screw every—"

"You want me to turn this thing off?"

"I'll still be able to hear you. And believe me, you never shut up. Though you could listen a bit more closely, then maybe you'd—"

I push the wooden button and the electric band snaps inside the globe, dissolving Juana's face in a haze of ions. I cut the house from the network, hoping to dull her voice. Maybe she's only this loud during a transmission, her thoughts amplified, the music louder. See? Now she's got me acting like a damn scientist with measurements and hypotheses. I'm starting to feel crazy again, Juana's timeless specialty. With a little luck, she'll have me climbing the walls by nightfall. I'm not even sure what I'm doing when I get dressed, slip into my boots, and throw on the oilskin. Juana always riles me up so bad I have no clue where I'm going or what I really want.

Now here I am walking in the rain past the schoolhouse. Good for me. Getting wet and soggy with no clear purpose. Do I go to the library and ignore everyone? Should I go see Yvonne? I don't really know, but I'm not heading in either direction. This way, that way, I don't know what to do. I'm of two minds. The *fábrica* is all lit up with soft brown light and plumes of white steam rise from its pipes. It's all making me feel insane: this horrible scent of brewing hops, the constant flow of electricity, the infernal blue pulse of a hundred geo-globes. I want to rip my hair out and unplug the world. That's how I feel when I walk into the storehouse of the *fábrica* and discover a small crowd of people grinning at me. I must have forgotten something.

"What's going on?" I ask Paola, pulling off my hood. "I forgot there was a meeting?"

"Uh, hello, Fulvia!" Gertrude laughs. "You've only been waiting months for it."

I stand there mute while everyone else chuckles.

"Alright, tell me what it is," I say. "I have no idea what you—"

"Salmon!" they all cry, some with tears of laughter.

"The tribe's coming today," Annabelle tells me. "Should be here soon."

"Come on, help us with the last of the lumber," Paola says. "Get out of that fish-rag."

Feeling like an idiot, I strip off my oilskin and drape it over a big pile of sweet-smelling pine boards. Our commune's cut enough lumber for the new radio station and seven houses for the Kashaya, all from trees knocked over during storms. It's been stacked up in the storehouse since last week but no one thought to sort the different piles. Paola leads me into this mess and I immediately put two of the long wooden beams on each of my shoulders. After that, we follow a line of wood-bearers towards the doors where the Kashaya can easily load it onto their wagons. Now I remember everything.

I was supposed to be here an hour ago ſtacking lumber. This is exaⅽtly how Juana makes me ſtupid.

"I haven't seen you in a while," Paola says. "You okay?"

"I'm fine. I'm pregnant."

"Pregnant!"

The ſtorehouse fills with helium and everyone ſtops moving. They all look at me with a mixture of fear and humor, some with dread. Everyone knows what happened laſt time I got pregnant and I bet they're all trying to guess who the father is, even Paola. I can see it in her eyes. She thinks it's Angelo, juſt like the others do.

"Who was it?" Paola finally asks. "I mean...how? Juſt...how?"

"Immaculate conception! A miracle!"

That gets me some nervous laughter but not enough to pacify them, not by a long-shot. I had to tell someone eventually, but I guess they only care about the father. Juana's cackle fills my mind as we move the laſt of the lumber and then file into the kitchen to load up on jam and buttered bread. Paola chews loudly beside me and breathes through every bite, her elbows on the kitchen table. I can tell something's brewing in her mind, only it might be more than I can handle.

"Did Angelo contaⅽt you?" she suddenly asks. "Did he call?"

"No!" I wipe the butter off my mouth. "Did he call *you*?"

"No, truſt me, he didn't. I juſt thought that's why you've been hiding, talking to him alone—"

"No! Definitely not! I mean, I never answer my globe, so it's possible, but again, I don't—"

"Anyway, I got in touch with the Paloma site. He's there. Signed up as an iron worker."

All that bread and jam in my gut suddenly feel like toxic mercury. The darkness trapped inside ſtarts raging like a demon and I lean forward on the table as the room fills with voices. Paola drapes her arm across my shoulders and speaks into my ear, only I can't underſtand anything she's saying. There's too many people in the kitchen and all of them are smiling. I try my beſt to look normal but all I hear is the same queſtion repeated over and over.

"Of course it's not Angelo's kid," I loudly answer. "Look how small my ſtomach is."

I lift my sweater but she pushes it down before I can make a scene.

"Who was it?" she whispers with a grin. "Tell me."

"What the hell are you two doing?" Gertrude yells, ſtomping over to the table. "You look—"

"Intense," Annabelle answers, ſtanding behind her. "What are you talking about?"

"Who's the daddy?" Gertrude asks. "Tell us."

"I'm not telling a soul," I say. "Not until my daughter's old enough to ask me herself."

"It looked like you were about to tell Paola and not us," Annabelle says.

"You can't be serious?" I ask. "Come the hell on! What are you—"

Annabelle slaps me on the shoulder and laughs so loudly none of us can help but join her, even though she really meant it. I kiss Paola goodbye and fight my way out of Gertrude's rigid grasp but it turns out she's still stronger than me. My escape dœsn't work, she won't let me run away, and I can't stop laughing in my delirium. The only salvation is the sudden clang of the *fábrica* bell announcing the Kashaya's arrival. We run out into the rain as their five wagons rattle back and forth between an army of tribes-people. The entire commune leaves their geo-globes, heating coils, and cozy houses behind to come welcome our neighbors with bright handkerchiefs waving from their hands.

We guide the wagons into the storehouse amid waves of endless laughter with hugs and kisses and embraces and intense conversations flaring throughout the room. Someone starts singing a Kashaya song and dœsn't stop until everyone's silent. Then the hard work begins. All our bodies steam up the cavernous room and I hear glass clattering as the cases of salmon are unloaded off the wagons. I help stack these wooden boxes along the storehouse wall and try to count how much fish they've given us. My mouth's watering by the time I'm done. We'll each get five jars for the winter, maybe more. I was always bad at math. A single box contains about fifty jars and now there's over a hundred boxes lining an entire wall. Everyone's loading the lumber onto the Kashaya wagons and I'm about to help them when a familiar hand falls on my shoulder. I know who it is before I turn around.

"You been hearing me at night?" I ask her. "Or is that crazy?"

"Crazy?" Essie spins me around and looks into my eyes. "Try vain. Why would I listen to *you* when I live next to Yvonne del Valle?"

"This thing's still inside me," I tell her. "The thing you pulled out of Angelo."

"I don't imagine it's going anywhere, so long as you stay here."

"What's that supposed to mean?"

"It's what I'm about to tell people. The Dream's spreading quicker than I've ever seen."

Essie speaks to me in her native tongue about two drifters from Santa Rosa. They were over forty miles inland when they fell into the Dream and walked to the ocean looking for salmon. The effects of this mind-altering state had clearly reached beyond the coastal mountains and Essie feared what might happen if Santa Rosa became enveloped.

"It's out of my hands, girl. I know most of you already passed through it, but—"

"I know how it works. They could be stuck in it for years."

"Or forever. I'm worried. Truly worried. And I'm going to tell everyone."

Once all the lumber's stacked safely in the wagons, I watch old Essie climb atop one of the beds and raise her arms towards the roof-beams. When the sleeves of her dress fall down, I notice a series of black designs snaking along her arms. She didn't tell me about these new tattoos, but now everyone can see them. It means she's going traditional, just like the young people.

Essie waits for silence before she tells the crowded storehouse how the Dream vortex is pushing towards Santa Rosa. There's no explanation for why it's heading inland or why it's avoiding our village. Essie reminds everyone there isn't anything to be afraid of but themselves, that the Dream can only ever reflect the Dreamer. A dozen people shout frantic questions but Essie only answers one. Paola asks *what's the Dream?* Instead of the cryptic lines we're all used to, Essie tells us the story of the Ghost Dance's first emergence and how the spirits of the dead carried it west all the way to Kashaya land. It took root here among the redwoods and helped her people survive through the slow genocide, giving them direct access to the underworld. By then it had become the Dream.

"But what is it?" Paola cries, frantic now. "I just want to know!"

"There's only one way to find out, girl!" another tribeswoman yells. "And it looks like you're scaring everyone else, so come on now! No one gets stuck in there who doesn't want to be there. That's just the way it works."

Essie's jumped off the wagon now and the crowd breaks apart under this burst of sadness. A Kashaya woman holds Paola around the waist and whispers soothing words into her ear, though none of them seem to work. Gertrude and Annabelle are near the wagons talking to some young, handsome, grinning tribesmen. Everyone else is equally distracted and no one will notice if I act quickly. Their chatter rings loud as I walk behind the radio station lumber pile and grab a box of salmon. It was the odd one out and I left it here on purpose. If anyone asks, I'll just say half is for my mom.

I'm already through the backdoor when the rain soaks my hair and I remember my stupid oilskin draped over the lumber. I hide the box behind a rain barrel, run inside the crowded storehouse, struggle to find my jacket, and eventually discover it hanging near the kitchen. Gertrude watches me slip it on and points me out to Annabelle. My heart pounds even harder as I run off to grab the salmon before anyone else notices me. I sprint until I'm panting and sweaty, covered in these fine misty droplets floating through the air. A jubilant roar emerges from the *fábrica* and I hear the Kashaya wagons roll off with seven houses-worth of milled lumber. No one's coming after me. They're too busy cheering in gratitude.

My house is dark and cold when I plop the wooden box on my kitchen counter, turn on the heating coil, and drape my oilskin around the back of my desk chair. This is the moment I've been imagining. I slide a glass jar from the box and unscrew its tight metal lid. The fat's congealed around the fish so I empty the entire thing over a pan and put it on the heat-pad to cook. In a few minutes all the fat's bubbling around the smoked strips of red meat and I fork myself a healthy bite. If god existed, he'd melt in your mouth like a piece of salmon. No wonder they worship this creature. No wonder they paint him everywhere. I close my eyes and feel the white light of bliss fill my taste buds while the pan sizzles with oceanic fat and crisping fish meat.

In this moment of rapture, red light fills my blackened vision and returns me to reality. I open my eyes and see the geo-globe announcing a connection. The locator's still fixed on San Francisco and the glass sphere pulses from gray to red. I stare at this hollow depiction of the Earth and imagine all the stories I might tell to Juana. I know she can hear me down there in the little blue house on Greenwich Street. I hear her singing "She'll Be Coming Around The Mountain" and see her dancing in the center of the ballroom like the goddess Kali. That's when the power goes out and our electromagnetic ribbon fades from across the sky. The fat stops boiling atop the heat-pad. The salmon grows cold in the frying pan. The geo-globe turns gray. I guess I asked for this, didn't I?

15

THE BLACK PLAGUE OF CHINATOWN

AS THE 19TH CENTURY CAME TO ITS CLOSE, ISABELLE CONTINUED HER walks with Josephine up the slopes of Telegraph Hill, their weekly ritual following each Sunday Mass. There was much to discuss during these journeys, especially with new developments at the Heath mansion.

After tailing Doctor Eamonn O'Shea to the waterfront and witnessing his conversation with Jack London, the cousins arranged for my uncles to escort Jack up the hill to *Luna's Mexican Restaurant*. The Ferrari brothers all smiled and laughed and discussed old times, although Jack couldn't escape an intense feeling of dread as they wove through dark Chinatown alleys. He was relieved to find Beatrix and Isabelle waiting for him in the back of candle-lit *Luna's* but his dread returned when my uncles boxed him into the booth. Isabelle asked him about Eamonn O'Shea and Jack frantically told them all he knew about this elusive doctor, including his alleged capture by a Gælic witch. When he finished, Beatrix told Jack to never speak of this meeting and then pointed across the room to Anna Strunsky, his socialist lover who'd been observing the entire time. Isabelle told Jack they were always watching him and that there was nothing they didn't know. As Jack would later write to his friend, Anna had *her exoteric circles and her esoteric circles—by this I mean the more intimate and the less intimate. One may pass from one to the other if deemed worthy.*

Over the next months, my mother kept watch over Doctor O'Shea and noticed his hours in the library were growing longer. Isabelle heard amorous noises and joyous laughter whenever she pressed her ear to the oaken door, an occurrence that always made her smile. It was obvious that Yvonne and her doctor were having a love affair, although it was unclear why Heath had so perfectly arranged its emergence. The steel-baron was never home and Beatrix suspected these long absences were a ruse designed to prevent an assassination attempt. With no answers to these questions, the cousins resolved to speak with this mythical Gælic witch who'd turned the doctor's family into crows. After receiving Josephine's approval, the Lemel cousins walked to the apothecary in their black dresses and entered the dimly-lit shop lined with wooden herb-drawers. The witch instantly recognized Isabelle as the daughter of Josephine Lemel, Hand of the Queen, and these black-clad *streghe* spoke her ancient Celtic fluently, using it to ask a dozen questions. They needed help with the doctor, they needed help killing Lionel Heath, and they needed everything else that they couldn't see. The witch silenced them with a wave of her hand and launched into the story of how she came to San Francisco.

In the year 1866, indigenous Irish pirates landed beneath the grassy slopes of the Seven Heads Peninsula and unloaded boxes of modern rifles to retake Ireland. A witch waited atop the cliff for these rebels, having seen them in a watery vision, and she beckoned them towards her house overlooking the Celtic Sea. Once she'd heard them out, the witch agreed to hide their weapons for the planned uprising in nearby Cork. In 1867, these Fenian insurgents seized the city, cut the telegraph lines, ripped apart the railroad tracks, and invaded the countryside. Uprisings broke out in Dublin, Limerick, Killarney, and Tipperary, although this rebellion was crushed by the British Empire, with many imprisoned or killed. When an insurgent was tortured into revealing the source of their weapons, the Gælic witch was ripped from her ancestral home by Imperial soldiers and forced to watch it burn. They left her for dead above the ocean and posted a proclamation claiming the property now belonged to a British landlord.

A young Fenian emerged from the shadows once the soldiers left, carried the witch down to the shore, and with nothing but sea-water cupped in his bloody hands, this beautiful boy brought her back to life. He wrapped the witch in charred blankets, carried her to a wooden boat, and rowed her through the night to where an anchored cargo ship named *Erin's Hope* was waiting for survivors of the failed uprising. She was nursed back to health during the long journey across the Atlantic and the vessel was secretly allowed to enter the US. After the British Empire aided the Confederacy in the US Civil War, the new Union government granted *de facto* safe harbor to Irish republican rebels and helped the witch emigrate to San Francisco without leaving a paper-trail.

Once they heard this sad tale, it was clear the Gælic witch didn't need convincing in order to help them. Her young protégé Eamonn O'Shea had already delivered Yvonne an ancient tea from the pages of *The Book* and if consumed for an entire moon cycle, this dangerous preparation would abort a male fetus, preserving only the female. As a consequence, any daughter born of this method would be filled with fire for the rest of her life. Yvonne del Valle-Heath accepted this price before drinking the tea and by the end of that fateful moon cycle they'd robbed Heath of his male heir. The cousins agreed to keep watch over Eamonn now that he'd fallen in love with Yvonne, a woman they couldn't trust. No one knew her aside from the doctor, and his judgment was now clouded by a fevered heart. While she'd swallowed the witch's ancient poison, Yvonne could still be working for Heath, a grim possibility the cousins were forced to entertain. Their entire plan depended on it.

Beatrix and Isabelle saw the doctor every morning on the cable-car to Pacific Heights, always keeping their distance and never looking him in the eye. On the days Eamonn stayed late, the cousins followed him through the streets of San Francisco and observed all of his public interactions, however mundane. They saw his apartment window light up at night and watched Eamonn pace back and forth while the **Dr. O'Shea – Licensed Practitioner** sign swayed in the coastal wind. His love for Yvonne was burning deeply and my mother couldn't help but feel a natural sympathy

Police barracks destroyed, Fenian Rising.

for this reſtless men. As Isabelle had been taught from a young age, the darkness they fought could never feign love.

When they weren't ſtalking the doᴄtor, Isabelle and Beatrix went down to the docks to mingle with their comrades in the maritime unions. Over the paſt months, my uncles had organized the longshoremen into different crews who all agreed to ſtop working wherever traffic was higheſt, causing maximum loss for the ship-owners. By the end of their rolling-ſtrike, each of these crews had raised their daily wage to $3.60. Inspired by this success, the lumber-longshoremen walked off the job and raised their own pay to $4.00 a day. In these times of promise, the Coaſt Sailor's Union expanded its membership to over 3,000 men and re-eſtablished a monthly wage of $40.00. These waterfront unions weren't juſt emptying the coffers of the ship-owners, they'd also retaken the entire weſtern coaſt and eſtablished labor supremacy over the Pacific. Through this long process of rebuilding, my uncles also ended a jurisdiᴄtional dispute between sailors and longshoremen, clearing the way for a maritime federation. This longtime dream of Antonio Ferrari was now coming to fruition. Because of her gender, my mother was unable to help, at leaſt direᴄtly.

Juſt as these efforts were intensifying, the Black Death arrived in San Francisco, accompanied by a wave of racism and bigotry. On January 20, 1900, an outbreak in Honolulu led the authorities to burn its Chinatown to the ground, citing the public health. Across the ocean in China, long simmering hatred againſt Chriſtianity and weſtern imperialism finally exploded when Empress Ci Xi endorsed the *Yihequan* insurgency, or the Boxer Rebellion. This army of martial artiſts emerged from their Kung-Fu fight-clubs and proceeded to burn down Chriſtian churches, kill missionaries, and retake China from the foreign invaders. This army believed themselves invulnerable from bullets and marched towards the sea to invade Peking, animated by their own version of the Ghoſt Dance. As this insurgency unfolded, a cargo boat traveled from China to San Francisco. Soon afterward, a man named Wong Chut King took ill from fever at the Globe Hotel, a building in the

Boxer Rebellion, China.

heart of Chinatown. His sweat drenched body was covered in open sores when he passed away on March 7, 1900, the Year of the Rat. As the City Health Officer examined the fluid of these oozing sores under a microscope, he discovered the distinct tubular germs of the Black Death.

The Globe Hotel was quickly evacuated, Wong Chut King's body burned, and Chinatown put under immediate quarantine. Hundreds of SFPD officers blockaded the streets and hung white strings to demarcate the boundary. Over the next three days, every resident of Chinatown was trapped within the outbreak epicenter. A massive riot erupted on the edges of the quarantine zone where Isabelle and her brothers threw rocks at the police while Enrico distributed printed fliers in the Latin Quarter. This tract penned by *luciferino* warned the Italians they'd be quarantined next, a bleak message heard all too clearly. Italians were still seen as the lowest class of white person, good only for exploitation, and the bourgeois of the Latin Quarter feared what a quarantine would do to their businesses, a fear shared by merchants of every race and color. In a perfect chorus, the major San Francisco newspapers suddenly claimed this plague scare was the product of mass-hysteria and obscured the gruesome nature of Wong Chut King's death. On March 10, after three days of unrest, the first quarantine of Chinatown ended with thousands celebrating their brief victory, although the Year of the Rat had only just begun.

The routine at the Heath mansion immediately changed due to the Black Death. While the high-capitalists of San Francisco publicly denied its existence, Lionel Heath privately treated the plague with the gravest concern. On the first day of the outbreak, his staff were instructed to line up outside the gate and wait for Doctor O'Shea to inspect them, a laborious process that took over half an hour. In addition to this, Heath instructed Eamonn to find two acceptable nurses who'd live with him in the mansion until either Yvonne had given birth or the outbreak was eliminated. With the Black Death crawling through the city, Heath didn't want his doctor on its streets, a precaution Eamonn immediately agreed to live by. Later that night, the doctor went to the apothecary and asked the Gælic witch to find two midwives before dawn. When he arrived at the herb shop the next morning, Eamonn met red-haired Margaret and black-haired Shelley, both fresh from Western Ireland.

The pair openly teased this love-struck doctor on their journey up to Pacific Heights, although their boisterous manner changed when they arrived at the mansion. They were installed in two empty bedrooms on the second floor and tasked with attending to Yvonne's every need. Margaret and Shelley sat with her in the library that first morning while Eamonn went outside to inspect the staff. He felt their armpits for bubœs, massaged their necks for stiffness, checked their tongues for signs of swelling, and examined their faces for pallor or redness. If anyone showed even the slightest signs,

Police enforcing quarantine in Chinatown.

Eamonn was instructed to send them home with pay. Once these inspections were finished, the doctor stayed in the library with Yvonne while Margaret and Shelley relaxed in their luxurious bedrooms, ready to sound the alarm if Lionel Heath arrived in his Daimler. Isabelle and Beatrix scarcely saw the lovers during these months of pregnancy, although the cousins did come to know Margaret and Shelley while they delivered laundry throughout mansion. In the silence of the oak hallways, these four women whispered their ancient Celtic to each other and even made jokes with the mother-tongue, something the cousins weren't accustomed to. Their forgotten language was mostly used for secrets.

Three more people died of the plague that March, although the daily newspapers still denied its existence. If there were a serious outbreak, all commerce and troop movements would cease, the city would be quarantined by Washington DC, and the capitalists would suffer heavy economic losses. The only major paper to warn of the plague was the *San Francisco Examiner*, owned by William Randolph Hearst, an eccentric capitalist who always did the opposite of his local peers. In response to the truthful claims printed in his newspapers, federal doctors began marching through Chinatown carrying needles filled with plague serum. They tried to convince the Chinese to be willingly inoculated but were met with fear and superstition, for many believed the serum was meant to spread the plague, not destroy it. In reaction to their mass-refusal, the federal doctors mobilized the police and forcibly fumigated entire buildings with burning sulfur, turning the whole of Chinatown into a literal hell-scape. Despite the fake news circulating in the papers, both Canada and Mexico banned all vessels originating from San Francisco, citing clear evidence of the plague.

Isabelle and Beatrix lived these dark months locked in their work routine and received their morning plague inspections from Doctor O'Shea, to whom they only said *grazie* or *ciao*. The cousins heard him make love with Yvonne in the library and watched this illicit pair sun-bathe on the lawn until one spring day when the mansion filled with screams. The nurses rushed Yvonne into her bedroom and Eamonn dismissed the entire staff before closing himself in with Margaret and Shelley. Heath arrived just as Yvonne began her contractions and Eamonn kept him waiting in his study before returning with a grim expression and red-stained hands. He claimed Yvonne was on the verge of death from blood loss and the child not yet born. Before the grim-faced steel baron could respond, Yvonne's screams filled the hallway, forcing Eamonn to rush off.

Heath chugged brandy and paced across his carpet until Eamonn came back two hours later. He announced the birth of a healthy daughter but abruptly covered his eyes when Heath smashed a brandy snifter on the floor. Overwhelmed with actual tears, Lionel Heath asked the doctor to repeat himself. Eamonn calmly said he'd delivered a girl, that Yvonne had come close to death, and she'd never be able to give birth again. Multiple miscarriages had rendered her body unfit to bring children into the world and it was a sheer miracle that she'd even survived. As Heath wept for his lost son, Eamonn suppressed a diabolic grin. None of what he'd told Heath was close to the truth.

Juana del Valle-Heath was born on May 5, 1900, and named after a local Spanish medicine-woman. Once she was born, Doctor O'Shea was paid by Heath and instructed to return home with the nurses. Their belongings were loaded into the Daimler and they were driven downtown in one of the city's few automobiles. When Isabelle and Beatrix saw the three of them being chauffeured down Broadway, they decided it was now safe to contact Eamonn through his friend Jack. Before this fateful meeting could happen, five more people died of the Black Death around Chinatown. Although a white *yanqui* woman was now one of these victims, a law was soon passed requiring the inoculation of any "Mongolian" who attempted to leave San Francisco.

The daily newspapers continued to deny the existence of plague, pitting their writers against the federal doctors who had seen the Black Death with their own eyes. A closed meeting was held on May 28 between the California State Health Board and the Southern-Pacific Railroad where it was decided that, rather than allow California's economy to be damaged through a federal quarantine, Chinatown was to be surrounded with barbed wire until further notice. Early the next morning, hundreds of armed police erected a fence around the entire neighborhood and guarded each entrance with clubs, pistols, and shotguns. At the same moment, across the Pacific Ocean, the *Yihequan* rebels advanced closer to Peking, a walled city guarded by a detachment of US soldiers, and the inhabitants of San Francisco's Chinatown feared the *yanquis* would wipe them out in retaliation for this Boxer Rebellion.

Had it not been for these sudden events, Eamonn O'Shea may have succumbed to despair. After being forced to separate from his lover, the doctor remained in his apartment all day and never opened for business. My mother watched him through his kitchen window, slumped over the table with a long beard on his face and a burning cigarette in his hand. On the first day of this barbed-wire quarantine, the Gælic witch asked Margaret and Shelley to retrieve their heartbroken brother and set him back to work. They forced their way into his apartment, shaved his beard, bathed his filthy body, groomed his hair, and directed him out the door towards the quarantine. One look at this infernal prison was enough to propel delirious Eamonn over the fence and into the heart of Chinatown where he offered up his services to the benevolent Six Companies. For the next weeks, Eamonn wrapped himself up in a black shawl and made house-calls with a member of the Six. The neighborhood soon called him *fox doctor*.

Through his translator, Eamonn taught these Chinatown households to patch the holes in their walls, never touch dead animals, and remove all hiding spaces for rodents. He explained that common fleas transmitted the plague atop infected mammals and could jump easily from one host to another. In the middle of these efforts, the city briefly opened the quarantine to allow five dozen *yanqui* snake-oil salesmen to hawk forged health certificates and false cures. Eamonn tried his best to undo the damage they inflicted on unsuspecting families and by the end of the second week, not a single person had died of the plague. The quarantine came to a definitive end when the Six Companies organized a mob to throw cobblestones at the police in Portsmouth Square. Just days after this riot, a local judge deemed the Chinatown quarantine unconstitutional and the entire barbed-wire fence was promptly taken down on June 15, 1900. Eager to make the most of this announcement, the corrupt governor of California proclaimed the Black Death eradicated and San Francisco open for business.

Eamonn said farewell to Chinatown and returned home a local hero, although this satisfaction didn't last very long. One evening in late July, he opened the door to his apartment to find Isabelle and Beatrix sitting at his kitchen table with Jack London. The cousins expressed their hatred against

Officers of the Six Companies

Lionel Heath, revealed their connection to the Gælic witch, and quickly enlisted him as the doctor for their impending maritime strike. When he agreed to offer his services, Eamonn knew exactly who he was joining. Just the day before, an anarchist named Gætano Bresci had shot King Umberto I of Italy, a bold assassination that dominated the daily newspaper headlines. Despite the clear severity of these anarchists, Eamonn swore an oath of secrecy to the International, just as Isabelle swore to put him in contact with Yvonne once their strike was won.

Neither Isabelle, Beatrix, or Josephine trusted Yvonne del Valle, nor did they think highly of Jack London. Since their last meeting, Jack renounced his affection for Anna Strunsky and married Bessie Maddern, the widow of his childhood friend. Her late husband had joined the army to fight in the Philippine Isles but was lured into a specific Barbary Coast brothel before departure, causing him to die of a sexually contracted infection on the Pacific Ocean. Jack knew the Queen had killed his friend but didn't have the heart to tell Bessie. After he was ambushed by Anna inside *Luna's*, Jack resolved to marry far outside this dangerous pack of insurgent women and settled on grieving Bessie Maddern. While he and Anna were still close comrades, Jack's amorous choices deeply troubled the Lemels. One whose heart could change so abruptly couldn't be trusted with the heart of another.

As rumors and denials of plague swirled through the city, my uncles were hard at work with the teamsters creating the final cog of their mighty war machine. The three primary maritime trades were the sailors who lowered the cargo, the longshoremen who hooked it, the teamsters who drove it, and once these groups were united, their general strike could begin. My uncles dedicated many evenings to drinking with these exploited dray-cart drivers in the hopes of making them rebels, often rising in the morning with brutal headaches. During this wave of mass-organizing, an old teamster named William Murphy became ill one evening and took himself to the hospital. The other drivers assumed it was a side-effect of his well-known opium addiction, but Murphy soon became the first *yanqui* man to die of the plague. In response to this poverty-induced death, a group of teamsters met in the Athletic Club on August 11, 1900, to form the Teamster's Union. Their first strike on September 3 paralyzed downtown San Francisco and quickly resulted in a wage increase, an event that swelled their membership to over 1,200 drivers. As the Ferrari brothers always said, *direct action gets the goods.*

Isabelle and Beatrix continued their daily routine at the Heath mansion but never failed to meet with Enrico Travaglio and print *Secolo Nuovo*. Once the latest issue was complete, the cousins walked with Schwartz through the Latin Quarter and handed out free copies to anyone who spoke Italian. Over the past five years, this small paper had become the lightning rod of the tightly-knit neighborhood and not even respectable Italian bourgeois could resist the diabolic charm of the anonymous authors. When these anarchists were done seeding *Secolo Nuovo* in the Latin Quarter, they'd often head straight to the Isaak household where the family was printing *Free Society*. Each month saw the subscription numbers rise, locking the Isaaks into longer bouts of writing, editing, composing, printing, folding, and mailing. Isabelle would listen to Beatrix and Peter Isaak banter during these long work parties, unable to help her amusement at their amorous spectacle. The would-be lovers had now progressed to touching each other, wrestling, or finding reasons to be alone in some corner of the cramped house. Schwartz would point out this flirtation but Isabelle always ignored him, having no interest in gossip.

One afternoon, the cousins entered the offices of *Secolo Nuovo* to discover Enrico sitting on the couch with a forlorn expression. His adoptive father Cesare refused to look at them, claiming they'd only curse his family even further. Enrico explained that Emma Goldman had sent the Isaaks a coded message asking them to leave for Chicago where they'd relocate *Free Society*. Emma also asked Enrico to go with them. During his absence, Isabelle, Beatrix and Schwartz would run *Secolo Nuovo*.

Before my mother could react to this development, Beatrix burst from the office and sprinted across town to find her lover Peter Isaak. By nightfall, she'd convinced him to refuse Emma's request and remain behind in San Francisco. Unable to force their eldest son against his will, Abraham and Mary sold off their printing press, canceled their lease in the Mission

District, and left the city with Peter's siblings Abe and Mary Junior. Enrico caught a train several days later. These sudden events were part of the conspiracy to assassinate Lionel Heath and President McKinley, although their ultimate purpose still remained a mystery to Isabelle.

The cousins continued their work routine and sometimes glimpsed Yvonne playing with Juana on the lawn, although they never spoke to her. After their days at the mansion, they'd meet Peter and Schwartz at the *Secolo Nuovo* offices to work with grumpy Cesare on the printing press. My mother could never console him and the cousins occasionally forced Cesare outside the print shop, having no patience for his cursing of the anarchist movement that had stolen Enrico.

The flow of Italian immigrants had increased over the years and Isabelle stayed up late printing *Secolo Nuovo* so that these weary travelers could read truthful words when they stepped off the boat. During these evenings in the Latin Quarter, Isabelle could be seen operating the printing press long after Beatrix, Peter, and Schwartz had passed out. As gaslight burned above her head, my mother resembled an infernal angel covered in black ink. It was here that she truly became an artist.

WE'LL KILL THE OLD RED ROOSTER

I WAKE UP WITH MY ARMS AROUND SOMEONE I DON'T RECOGNIZE. NOT AT first. My dream tricks me. I think it's a lover from another time, when I used to dance, but it's actually Paola. Dark brown skin, wavy black hair rich with the scent of wood smoke. My hands clutch her rigid, unfamiliar belly, so unlike the lovers of my past. She barged into my house last night, in tears, muttering about the Dream, about Angelo, about every mistake that has ever haunted her. I made her sit on my couch, opened up a bottle of wine, then told her the Dream is just us, nothing more, nothing less. A paradise or an inferno, but one that we make. This seemed to calm her down. We got a nice fire going in the stove and then she kissed me like I was the fountain of youth. After that, I got real excited, I couldn't help it. It's like I was sending out telepathic signals telling her, *if you come, I'll put out new pillows for you to rest on.* Now she's snoring away. The sun's just come up. This all might be a terrible idea. I'm ten years older.

Paola doesn't stir, she keeps her head tucked between the pillows while I climb down to my messy living room. The power's been out for three days, the entire village is silent. My geo-globe and heating-coil are back in the closet next to my broomstick and there's no more screech of the mill-saw, no more metallic garble from a thousand distant voices. I'm sure this next energy drought will be a long one, a cycle that won't end until they know the real truth, not those portrayals of wholesome rebels who never made a mistake or doubted their sanity. The planet's depriving us of electricity for a reason. All the lies Yvonne and Isabelle told have brought the darkness here. Once I finish my book, I know that shadow's going to burn away. I feel this certainty like a flame.

Paola lets out one loud groan, snapping me from my daydream. I open the front door to a chill wind blowing from the ocean, cold enough to make me immediately close the door, light a fire, and settle in for a morning by the stove. To be honest, I miss how quickly the heat-pad boils my water, but a few days of using my wood-stove always makes me forget that electricity ever existed.

I sit naked by the crackling stove, trying to imagine Yvonne and Nikola building a transmitter in Siberia while Isabelle stalked Leon Trotsky through Saint Petersburg. I was here in the commune, not even 2 years-old, while they were off changing history. Determined, cunning, brilliant, tender, but most of all invisible. I can't think about these things forever, I have to write them out of my mind, and that's exactly what I was doing before Paola came over. The stove still isn't hot enough for me, so I feed more kindling, the flames start raging, and then Paola stirs in my loft. I can't tell her any of this right now. It's something she'll just have to read.

"Why you up so early?" she moans. "I swear we fell asleep at dawn."

"That was all a dream," I tell her, lying. "You were snoring for hours."

"Did I keep you up? You sleep at all?"

"A little bit. Sometimes I just don't sleep. That's why I'm always writing."

Paola coughs from last night's cigarettes and I listen to her spit phlegm out the skylight window. Her naked frame comes into view and I can't help but stare at her glorious ass while she climbs down the ladder. She wraps her arms around my shoulders and kisses my neck just as the kettle starts to boil. I slip out of her grasp, fill the tea-pot with water, and when I look up Paola's already getting dressed. I don't want to be the naked one so I throw on a thick sweater before serving us tea.

I cook eggs and potatœs with green onions while Paola cuts up a raw beet and we eat it all by the fire with green tea from China. Paola talks about the new radio station, the generator, the modulator, the logistics of carting all that lumber up the hill, but I think she's just trying to avoid all that past she revealed to me last night. Paola's parents conceived her atop a bed of hay on the outskirts of São Paulo when they were soldiers in the war. Her mother fought through the city's long siege and gave birth in the Amazon campaign under a jungle canopy dripping with moisture. A rebel nurse safely delivered

Paola back to liberated São Paulo and into the care of her maternal grand-mother. Paola never knew her parents. They disappeared in the Amazon hunting the barons and their mercenary army.

"I feel closer to you now," I say, apparently out of nowhere. "Warmer."

This catches her off guard, but it also makes her smile.

"We have our own connection," I insist. "Before we only had Angelo. Now we've tasted each other, rolled all over each other, smelled each other. And you smell good! But you know what I mean? Now it's just me and you. Right here. And thank you, my friend, you came, and it's good you did. I needed you. You've made love blaze in my breast, so bless you for that, bless you end-lessly, like the hours have been endless while you were gone."

"Is that a poem?" she asks, nervous. "Or did you just make it up?"

I don't answer. I wait for Paola's shell to crack but that doesn't happen, instead she puts her plate on the table and crawls towards me, eyes averted. I stroke her shiny black hair but there's something heavy brewing inside. Or maybe I'm just seeing my own darkness reflected back.

"What was that thing?" she asks. "I saw it in the Dream, I just didn't remember at first. It was a shadow-man. He was flickering, like...light when the clouds pass, or when the wires aren't plugged into the geo-globe right. He walked into you, before you pulled me out of there. I saw it. I didn't remember until last night, but I saw him when my eyes were closed."

"You saw it? And don't call it *him*. It's not alive."

"What is it?"

"It's...really old. I call it the darkness. That's what they've always called it. It gets into people and turns them into emperors, tyrants. Makes them build temples and skyscrapers and smoke-stacks. It burnt my ancestors during the witch hunts in Europe and we've been it fighting for—"

I suddenly feel extremely sick. The entire house begins to spin. My body moves out the back door on instinct, through my pumpkin patch, towards the outhouse, and the smell of shit is enough to make me wretch out my won-derful breakfast. I'm definitely pregnant again. It feels terrible and I heave with all my strength, fingers dug hard into the wooden seat-box. Two hands fall on my shoulders and when my vision clears, Paola's wiping my mouth with a towel. I look down into the shit-pit and can't tell if it's the beets or the wine that made my vomit red. The sight of it all makes me expel what's left in my stomach. Once it's gone and I'm breathing normally, Paola guides me back inside where she brews peppermint tea and sits with me beside the fire.

"You were about to tell me what it was," she says. "This darkness."

"I love your determination, Paola. You just won't ever stop, will you?"

"If it's what we've all been fighting all these years, and it's inside you now—"

"Then you should all feel lucky. I've got it under control."

"This all sounds crazy, you know that? I couldn't even try to tell another person—"

We both hear them approaching. Their footsteps clatter up my wooden steps and Gertrude opens the door without knocking, Annabelle just behind her. Their eyes widen into saucers when they see me wearing only a sweater and I must look sick because they rush over to put their hands on my forehead. Gertrude tells me I look pale. Annabelle sniffs Paola's face.

"Can I tell you what you smell like?" Annabelle asks her. "It starts with an F."

Paola pushes her away and both of them laugh. Not Gertrude. She isn't amused with my pussy smell and loudly makes herself tea in the kitchen to let me know she's upset. I can hear what Gertrude wants to say. She'll tell me I'm irresponsible, that I'm playing with fire, and once I have this thought, Gertrude turns around and shakes her head.

"Any word on Angelo?" she asks. "I can remember a time when you two would never—"

"He's helping them build the new Paloma transmitter," Paola snaps. "He can stay there for all I care. He didn't try and contact either of us, and I tried looking for him. Like an idiot."

"Why are you bringing him up?" I ask Gertrude. "I just got through telling Paola we don't need Angelo to be our central topic of conversation forever, so if you—"

"Fine, screw it!"

Gertrude slams her ceramic mug on the counter so hard it explodes into a dozen jagged pieces that scatter across my floor. She shakes the scalding water off her hand and then bolts outside without closing the front door. Annabelle and Paola look at each other in confusion before they grab my arms and plead with me not to follow her. I ignore their words, everything blurs into colorful shapes, and I'm suddenly chasing Gertrude down the village road, bare-foot and half-naked. She walks into her house, the one she shares with Annabelle, and the door's already locked when I get there.

"Please open up!" I scream, pounding on the wood. "Gertrude! This is important!"

"Go away! Everything's important to you until it isn't!"

"You know I'm pregnant, right? *You* try getting flooded with all this stuff!"

"No thanks! I'd rather be responsible and not have to take care of another—"

"Would you open up?" I keep banging, my breasts exploding in the air. "Gertrude!"

I throw myself against the door just as the iron bolt slides open. Gravity pushes me inside like a cannon-round and Juana calls me *puta* as I wrap my arms around Gertrude. She's sweaty and nervous but I push through until both of us are in San Francisco, kissing each other on the dance-floor, making love on the beach beside a driftwood fire. I was so happy, believe me, I prayed those nights would be doubled for us. This hasn't happened in so many years and for all the telepathy that runs in my family, I couldn't hear Gertrude's longing.

Paola and Annabelle probably think we're arguing. Neither of them come to find us. We climb up to Gertrude's loft and I let her do what she wants. I can tell she's hungry. She fills me with glorious light, my shoulders curve back, and I moan out a thick river not even Paola could summon. Gertrude's face is dripping wet and I hear her swallow some of the fluid before kissing me with a warm mouthful of this briny moisture, tinged with green tea and sulfur from the red wine. She straddles my face with her legs, my nostrils fill with her bristly hair, and I've hardly begun before I'm drenched in a torrent of fluid, sweet like honey. That's when I pass out and sleep without a single dream. The shadow-man doesn't come to torment me. Now I know why Eros, of all children on earth and in the heavens, has been most dearly loved.

When I wake up, the entire house smells like chicken soup. The windows are steamed up. The sun's going down. I'm still naked but wrapped up in a thick blanket emblazoned with a gray wolf-head. Gertrude's had this since she was a baby. It's thicker than buffalo hide and we both slept under it during our San Francisco love affair. It smells thick with the sweet lavender honey that drips between her legs. Gertrude cackles like she just heard my thoughts and Annabelle whispers something I can't make out. There's no sound of Paola downstairs, so I cough to let them know I'm awake.

"Get down here!" Annabelle cries. "Paola said you heaved everything up."

"She down there with you?" I ask.

"Just us," Gertrude laughs. "Get down here, you beast!"

I throw off the wolf blanket and grope around for my clothes.

"They're down here," Gertrude calls up to me. "Is my blanket still drenched?"

Annabelle bursts her sides laughing as I climb down naked and see her reclining on the couch with two flushed cheeks. Gertrude's sitting across from her in a wooden chair, her legs kicked up on the dining table. All she's wearing is a colorful blanket wrapped tightly around her body. The air's thick with chicken soup. I'm starving.

"Go on, eat," Annabelle tells me. "It's ready. And hang up the pot when you're done."

"You already ate?" I ask, putting on my sweater. "What happened to me?"

"You were out like a light!" Gertrude exclaims. "I tried to wake you but you wanted sleep."

"I can't imagine why," Annabelle says. "Now go eat."

This soup is their specialty, perfected after endless failures in the slaughter-house. They're both city girls, raised after the war in the center of San Francisco, and they didn't know anything about how to kill a rooster. They've shared this two bedroom house since we built it, that glorious summer when electromagnetic light pulsed gently across the sky. I've come back to the soft arms I turned from in the old days, eating the same meal, warming the same chair. Gertrude looks at me as I grab a bowl, her eyes asking, *of all people on this earth, who do you love better than you love me?* I have no answer.

The soup's nice and thick with shreds of disintegrating chicken floating in the broth. There's potatoes and onions and stewed greens in each ladle-full. I'm not trying to think about the rooster, I'm just going to eat it. I sit at the kitchen table next to Gertrude's dirty feet and slurp down the soup even though it burns my tongue. My friends talk about the wheat pasta they made, the olive oil they pressed, the tomatoes they've canned. Annabelle offers to cook me pasta through the rainy winter and demands I stop avoiding their house. She tells me I need to get fat.

"It's been months since you were here," Gertrude says. "Angelo's gone. Stop hiding."

I wipe the broth from my mouth and shake off their words.

"It wasn't just Angelo," I say. "I didn't want to rely on you for everything. I didn't want you to get in trouble because of me. I wanted you to be yourselves. Do you understand what I—"

Both of them have the same expression. It's almost like pity, so I just keep eating. I hate pity.

"You lost yourself in that book when things got bad with Angelo," Annabelle says, joining us at the table. "It helped you. It's helping you now. And you say it's important. Just don't be afraid anymore. Let him go. Let it all go. It's all over, so finish that book. We miss you."

"Stay here tonight," Gertrude says, radiant. "I want you here just one more night. The book can wait. I know Paola won't mind. That girl's having—"

"She's really lost," Annabelle says. "When you two ran off we talked for hours. I don't know what she needs, but going into the Dream really did something to her. I mean, Gertrude, how long were the two of us stuck in there?"

"Three months and fifteen days," Gertrude answers. "I was counting."

"I was counting, too, just in my head, not carving them into a tree like you. If we hadn't done that, who knows how long we'd have been in that—" Annabelle's eyes crinkle into happy stars when my spoon clatters into the empty bowl. "More? I'll get you some more. And thanks for hanging up the pot when you were done. It's not like I asked you to do that or—"

Annabelle keeps talking to herself as she hangs the pot above the stove. While her back's turned, Gertrude takes her feet off the table, sighs into my ear, gives it a lick, and stops when Annabelle returns with my second bowl. They watch me eat for so long I forget they're even there. It's like I went off on some journey to a distant place, the name I can't remember. My friends had resigned themselves to my absence only to find me adrift near shore, half-dead, clinging to a piece of driftwood. I start to cry at this thought but say it's just a bit of pepper in my throat. They know I'm lying. I love my friends from the depths of my rabid heart, these women who'll help raise my daughter. Gertrude's going to be my lover like in San Francisco, only this time she'll know who I really am. There she is, wrapped in multi-colored fabric, my old partner at the Market Street dance-halls. We spun around so fast the iron foundations liquefied into magma and the world caught fire. In the center of those gyrating circles was the head witch herself, filled with an energy none could match. I hear Juana's voice coiling through my thoughts like a snake, hissing the same word she yelled on Telegraph Hill when I decided to leave San Francisco. She calls me *puta* over and over again. After that she begins to cackle.

16

THE POISONOUS BIRTH OF JUANA DEL VALLE

I'M GOING TO TELL YOU PART OF THE STORY AGAIN, ONLY THIS TIME FROM a different angle, one that my mother couldn't see. As unborn Juana grew inside her belly, Yvonne longed for the redwoods and oaks of her birth-land. She missed the pointy leaves that crunched beneath her feet and the cathedrals of bay trees where light trickled in thinner than fog. After four years of demented senility, Enrique Vasquez finally died in the spring of 1894, leaving the *Rancho del Valle* to Lionel Heath. He was buried beneath an oak tree in a ceremony attended by the remaining Spanish families, the only notable absence being Yvonne herself, confirming her reputation as an agent of Lucifer. Camille didn't care what the community thought of her daughter, nor did she speak with them after the funeral. Once Enrique Vasquez was dead, Yvonne returned home to live a month with her mother, a tradition she continued every spring for the next six years. During these inland retreats, Yvonne wandered the bay tree forests where her secret guardians strung whispers through the branches. The spring of 1900 was the first time she failed to return home. Heath wouldn't permit his wife to endanger their unborn son.

The previous fall was terribly mournful for Yvonne and even the clouds seemed to conspire with her husband. She hid inside the mansion library and lost herself in new translations of ancient Sumerian tablets and the recent inventions of a Serbian immigrant named Nikola Tesla. For the past decade, Yvonne had followed Tesla's career after reading an article about his magical coil that could transmit electricity through the air. This odd device was first patented in 1891 and Tesla took it on a national tour, filling the public imagination with ribbons of light that passed safely between his arms. Tesla's most notable exhibition was at the 1893 Chicago World's Fair where 160,000 light-bulbs were illuminated using twelve of his polyphase alternating-current dynamos. By securing the contract to light the World's Fair, Tesla had beaten out JP Morgan and the General Electric Company. Built by the Westinghouse Company, his massive electrical generators created more energy than the entire city of Chicago and gave the public its first glimpse of a world made of light. After demonstrating his skill at conducting electricity through the air and across wire, Tesla's next project involved transmitting

energy directly through the Earth using the planet's natural electromagnetism as the return circuit.

During the 1890s, Yvonne encouraged Heath to invest in this wireless transmission technology only to be met with consistent laughter. Heath dismissed Tesla as a delusional maniac and claimed their fortune was aligned with JP Morgan, Thomas Edison, and the General Electric Company. Despite this ridicule, Yvonne never relented in her support and corresponded with Tesla regularly, just as she did with hundreds of other artists and intellectuals. Her letters to Nikola were largely technical in nature, although she'd sometimes allow herself the occasional musing on human evolution and the repressive structures that restricted its blossoming. For his part, Nikola answered her questions regarding circuitry and magnetism but refrained from entering into any political dialogue with the wife of Lionel Heath, especially when funding was at stake.

While Nikola scrambled for funds, arsonists torched his New York City laboratory, along with all of his oscillators, the basis of our current generators. Despite this setback, he eventually secured the support of John Jacob Astor IV, an eccentric millionaire fond of scientific romances, and he relocated to a new experimental facility in Colorado Springs. Throughout the fall of 1899, Nikola toiled in this Rocky Mountain sanctuary to prove the planet was a massive conductor capable of powering more devices than humans could ever build. Yvonne was reading Tesla's latest account of illuminating fifty light bulbs directly through the soil when Heath burst into the library and announced a doctor would arrive the next morning. After refusing to command her domestic staff, Yvonne had little choice but to accept this new servant. If she protested too fiercely, Heath might take everything from her, including the *Rancho del Valle* and her massive library.

Eamonn O'Shea arrived on a cloudy Sunday and stayed in the library long after Heath departed. He paced with Yvonne along her wooden bookshelves, discussing their various tastes in literature, and the conversation soon led them to the recently published *McTeague: A Story of San Francisco*. Eamonn despised the racist stereotypes of its Anglo author but admired the honest depiction of San Francisco's slums, an opinion Yvonne shared. At the next shelf, she pulled out a brand new volume titled *The Theory of the Leisure Class* and began reading aloud for Eamonn. She recited, *there is reason to believe that the institution of ownership begins with the ownership of persons, primarily women.* With a smooth wave of her hand, Yvonne motioned towards her vast library and claimed that women, *being not their own masters, obvious expenditure and leisure on their part would redound to the credit of their master rather than to their own credit, and therefore the more expensive and the more obviously unproductive the women of the household are, the more creditable and more effective for the purpose of the respectability of the house-hold or its head will their life be.* Before he could respond, Yvonne pointed to herself and said that woman's sphere *is within the household, which she should "beautify," and of which she should be the "chief ornament."*

She then guided Eamonn to a bookshelf near the fireplace, removed a pale folio with a red spine, and unfolded it across the carpet, revealing a circle that contained every color within the natural spectrum of light. Its outsides were bordered in black and its center was pure white, making the circle resemble a human eye. Yvonne explained how Charles Henry, the anarchist who made this *circle chromatique,* arranged each color in a position that corresponded to certain human emotions. Blue was sad, red was angry, and so on. Henry wished to demonstrate that color was an abstraction created in the retina before its electromagnetic transmission to the brain. Light was only the carrier. While intrigued by this circle, Eamonn had no response. The word anarchist made him suspicious.

He returned the next day with a bag of numbing herbs which he strained into tea, claiming it was an ancient preparation for morning sickness. Yvonne drank the bitter-sweet fluid and discovered her lower body had lost nearly all of its sensation. This miraculous potion suppressed her nausea and allowed Yvonne the energy to become closer with this resourceful doctor. No matter how he tried, the doctor couldn't maintain his professionalism. Yvonne probed his mind, eliciting a thousand passions, and while they spoke about art, science, literature, poetry, and religion, Eamonn was mesmerized by the magnetism burning within her green eyes, trusting Yvonne beyond his will.

Over these long autumn days, Yvonne learned of Eamonn's superstitious Catholic parents, his siblings who died from starvation, his life as a pick-pocket, and his long apprenticeship under a Gælic witch. After going into business in 1895, Eamonn had paid for his family's journey back to Dublin and still wired them money every month over the trans-Atlantic telegraph cable. Despite trusting her with his unfortunate past, Eamonn changed the subject whenever Yvonne brought up anarchism, unable to comprehend how a steel baron's wife would have an interest in this radical ideology. To remedy this state of distrust, Yvonne began to seduce him. Eamonn smelled her scent when she whispered into his ear and felt her breasts brush his back when she passed by. She rubbed his shoulders while he read, stroked the hair away from his eyes, and leaned in close as he strained her morning tea. Yvonne's entire body was excited by this humble apprentice of a Gælic witch who could devour a book in a single day. It wasn't long before she told him the truth.

After weeks of ſtoking their mutual desire, Yvonne asked Eamonn if he could abort a male child while preserving the female. He inſiſted this was up to nature but Yvonne took his hands and refused to let go, insiſting Lionel Heath could never have a son. So it was that Eamonn returned the following morning with a bag of bitter herbs and told her to drink its tea once a day for an entire moon cycle. He said it was a non-lethal poison from ancient times that aborted a male fetus but preserved the female. He had no knowledge of its origin, hiſtory, or recipe. While the poison might assure a certain gender, Yvonne's daughter would be touched with fire, never able to sit in peace. Despite these clear consequences, Yvonne immediately brought the cup to her lips. Once she drank it, Yvonne made love with Eamonn on the Persian rug, a pleasure she repeated every day for the next moon cycle. They kept the library locked and lingered for hours beside the fire, filling their bodies with joy. Thanks to the infernal racket of her husband's automobile, the lovers always heard Heath approaching.

He appeared one morning in the winter of 1900, juſt before Eamonn and the laundresses arrived for work. He found Yvonne in the library and lifelessly informed her that the Black Plague was in San Francisco. He didn't elaborate on the source of this intelligence but insiſted the mansion be put under quarantine with the doctor residing on the property, along with two hired nurses. Following his orders, Eamonn showed up the next morning with two plainly dressed women who spoke politely, obeyed all the proper manners, and delivered their false hiſtories as if they'd lived them a thousand times. Heath quickly hired them and returned to the Palace Hotel in his Daimler, giving Eamonn the freedom to introduce Shelley and Margaret, *protégés* of the Gælic witch. They never talked about their paſts except to say they'd been hired out of the apothecary and inſtructed to deliver a baby girl. In the days that followed, Yvonne learned little more than this. While the doctor conducted his plague inspections outside the front gate, dark-haired Shelley and red-haired Margaret reclined in the library with Yvonne and discussed every topic but themselves. They spoke of herbs, birthing, and books, although neither had read very much, a situation Yvonne helped to remedy. Over the coming months, Margaret couldn't get enough romance novels, while the more somber Shelley enjoyed reading hiſtory.

This team of idlers whiled away the mornings reading newspapers and eating big breakfaſts at the long library table. Once they were done, the nurses went to their bedrooms and didn't come back until lunch. Yvonne made love with Eamonn almost every day and used her bookshelves to initiate him into the sorrowful history of the war against women. The first recorded descriptions of this disaster were found in *Les inscriptions des pyramides de Saqqarah*, a compilation of Egyptian hieroglyphic texts recently discovered in some the world's oldest known pyramids. These texts, first published in 1894, revealed an ancient conflict between Osiris and his brother Set, an event said to have occured thousands of years before. After killing his brother, Set takes over their kingdom, never suspecting that two women are working to undermine his new government. One is his wife Nephthys, the other is her sister Isis, wife of Osiris, and together they bring their fallen comrade back from the underworld. Once he had returned to life, Osiris quickly retook the kingdom, ushering in an Egyptian Empire that would last for thousands of years. This was the oldest written story Yvonne could find.

The second oldest story was found in *The Chaldæan Account of Genesis*, an 1876 translation of Sumerian tablets discovered within the ruins of ancient Nineveh. In this story, a king named Gilgamesh rules from his walled city of Uruk, slowly becoming hated by his subjects. They call on the gods to punish Gilgamesh, so the gods send Enkidu, a wild man from the untamed cedar forests of Sumeria. Unable to beat Gilgamesh, this wild man submits to his new ruler and allows himself to be conscripted into a war against Humbaba, the spirit of the forest. After slaying this ancient being, Gilgamesh and Enkindu ravage the forest and cut down its tallest trees, leaving only desert. Hoping to stop them, the star-goddess Ishtar offers herself to Gilgamesh, only to be rejected. In her rage, she sends the Bull of Heaven to devastate Uruk and slay its soldiers. Although the Bull is killed by Gilgamesh and Enkidu, the old gods demand vengeance for the death of Humbaba. As punishment for betraying them,

Hieroglyphics at Saqqarah.

Enkidu is killed, leaving Gilgamesh consumed with grief. He wanders the land for many days before meeting Utnapishtim, the man who survived the Great Flood by building a wooden boat for his family, their friends, and all their animals. It is this man who gives Gilgamesh the secret of eternal life, just as this same man would later be called Noah in the Old Testament. Too foolish and inept to achieve eternal life, Gilgamesh returns to his walled city of Uruk, cursed to finish his reign a mere mortal.

Before the construction of Uruk in 5000 BCE, the Great Flood had destroyed all the previous empires of earth, reducing their palaces to rubble and eradicating their advanced technology. Yvonne suspected this deluge almost wiped out the men who'd overthrown the world of women, although the water didn't spread far enough. She believed a massive matriarchy ruled the planet until 10,000 years ago when the war against women began. While she distrusted its source, the third oldest written story, the tale of Adam and Eve from the Old Testament, provided the clearest explanation for the cause of this conflict: a woman had followed her desires and refused to be ignorant.

Near the end of April, Yvonne showed Eamonn two books hidden in her shelves that revealed the extent of this ancient war. One was the *Pistis Sophia*, the main text of what modern scholars called *gnosticism*. The original Coptic manuscript was found in Upper Egypt near the ancient city of Thebes and sequestered by a British doctor until his death in 1774. This latest translation into English had just been published in 1896 and detailed some of the events that took place after the crucifixion of Yeshua ha-Nozri. The book alleged that Yeshua returned from the dead after the crucifixion and revealed his final teachings to Mary Magdalene over the next eleven years. While mad Emperor Caligula scoured the world in search of her *gnostic* band, Mary was discovering the mysteries of light that linked the earthly sphere with the heavens. Eamonn read this bizarre text but could make little of its cosmology, although one point was abundantly clear. According to the *Pistis Sophia*, the apostles were angry that Yeshua favored the words of Mary Magdalene over their own. As the authors explained, Mary comprehended the mysteries of light far better than the apostles and could elaborate on its structure at length. After delivering a perfect description of this light to her beloved Yeshua, he was *astonished at the definitions of the words which she spoke, for she had become pure spirit utterly.* At the conclusion of this heretical text, Yeshua transforms into a beam of light and leaves our world forever.

The second book Yvonne asked Eamonn to read was *The Gadfly*, a political thriller published in 1897 by a woman named Ethel Voynitch. Ethel was born on the outskirts of Cork in 1864, not far from the home of the Gaelic witch. Ethel's father died when she was young and her British mother whisked the family off to London when she received a job at Queen's College.

This follower of Mary sent Ethel to stay with an uncle in the countryside, hoping she'd escape the toxic pollution of industrial London, only to find she was being subjected to cruel religious punishments. When her daughter returned home in 1874, Ethel had become Lily, dressed only in black, and was now a committed anti-religious nihilist. Eight years later, Lily enrolled at music school in Berlin and quickly developed a net-work of radical friends. This path took her to Saint Petersburg where she met the local nihilists and pledged to create a British support group for their cause when she returned to London in 1889.

From her British base, Lily published a newspaper called *Free Russia* and helped inaugurate the English Society of Friends of Russian Freedom. Through this organization, Lily met a battered Polish exile who'd just escaped from a Siberian penal colony. His name was Michæl Voynitch, the man who would one day discover *The Book*. Decades before that, Lily and Michæl fell in love inside a smokey print shop. They churned out copies of *Free Russia* alongside a passionate young Ukrainian named Sergei Stepniak, nihilist assassin and author of *Underground Russia*. After stabbing the Czar's secret police chief to death in Saint Petersburg, Stepniak became the most wanted man across Europe. In the pages of his *Underground Russia*, Stepniak told the world that the actions of his generation were *really a prelude to the great drama, the last act of which is being enacted in the Empire of the Night*. Under the protection of the British Crown, these nihilists smuggled weapons, correspondence, money, and supplies into the Russian Empire, a practice that couldn't last forever. Lily and Michæl were now calling themselves *Mr. & Mrs. Wilfrid Voynitch* and living in a Soho apartment when Stepniak was fatally thrown under a train by Czarist agents. After his assassination in 1895, the couple retreated into their books and Lily wrote *The Gadfly* over the next years, the true masterpiece of that era.

The doctor read this novel of an anti-religious Republican facing down the Catholic rulers of Italy in the 1840s. It ended with the atheist rebel being executed in the manner of Yeshua ha-Nozri while his devoutly Catholic father watches on in tears, a paradox that revealed all rebellion to emanate from the same source, whether against the pagan Roman Empire or the Holy Roman Empire. Eamonn understood this well enough, although he couldn't find a thread connecting *The Gadfly* with the *Pistis Sophia*. Yvonne couldn't explain this connection either, for she truly didn't know herself. Unlike other followers of Mary, this isolated colonial daughter had been forced to comb through all of the world's literature in search of what her mother never knew. Just like Eamonn, Yvonne was left to puzzle over this long string of rebellions against a now-global Empire.

As spring progressed towards summer, Yvonne could hardly walk. On the morning of May 4, 1900, she felt water trickle down her thighs and was crippled with pain when her contractions suddenly began. Eamonn and the midwives carried her upstairs to set about their plan, and when Heath's noisy Daimler drove onto the estate, Yvonne began to scream harder than was necessary, enough to make the nurses cover their ears. As her husband drank himself into a stupor, Eamonn smeared himself with a dish-full of Shelley's blood and went upstairs to deliver the critical lines: *Yvonne is between life and death, the blood loss can't be stopped.* While Heath pondered this grim truth over a glass of brandy, Eamonn returned to the bedroom where Margaret and Shelley were breathing for Yvonne. They pulled light through their hair and delivered it through their fingertips, causing the room to glow a soft green. Eamonn had never seen anything like it, and in the middle of her false screams, Yvonne felt a spinning wheel of light grip hold of her body and push Juana del Valle into the hands of whispering midwives. While her drunk husband was consumed with despair, Yvonne kissed the cheeks of her tiny green-eyed daughter and allowed herself a single laugh before handing Juana over to Shelley. After that, Yvonne screamed as if her life depended on it.

Once their act was over, Heath sent Eamonn and the nurses away after distributing handsome paychecks amounting to several thousand dollars. He feigned an interest in his daughter for an entire morning but soon left Yvonne and Juana with the cooks, laundresses, and gatekeeper. Yvonne lived these next months breastfeeding, eating heavy meals, and watching Juana learn to crawl, a process that began on the library carpet and continued on the grass over the summer of 1900. Some of the staff cooed and giggled at this pink little baby bounding across the lawn, although most kept their distance from the *signora*. Yvonne was never rude but also had no desire to speak, preferring to read silently on the grass. One of her favorite texts that summer was Nikola Tesla's report of his experiments in Colorado Springs which revealed the earth to be a massive conductor capable of transmitting messages and electrical energy. With this technology, Nikola claimed he could communicate with the heavenly spheres and stated, *I have discovered some terrestrial phenomena still unexplained. That we can send a message to a planet is*

Wilfrid Voynich

certain, that we can get an answer is probable: man is not the only being in the Infinite gifted with a mind.

When she finished this historic article, Yvonne watched the staff string laundry across the metal line. This was when she noticed the young laundresses who never smiled and always avoided her, even in the halls. Their behavior continued into the fall of 1900 and Yvonne grew concerned that something was wrong. She tried to speak with them one morning only to encounter their lowered eyes and broken English, indicating they were ashamed. It was clear these women were related, although neither offered up that information. Rather than pressure them to speak modern Italian, Yvonne let the matter go and returned to lazing in the grass with Juana. The fall rain brought them back into the library where Juana sat mesmerized by the fire as her mother devoured dozens of novels, and this was how Isabelle found them one fateful morning in the winter of 1901. My mother had plenty to say by then.

WE'LL ALL HAVE CHICKEN AND DUMPLINGS

I'M AWAKE. I DON'T WANT TO OPEN MY EYES, NOT YET. IT'S BARELY LIGHT out. I can hear the cocks crow in their coops, waiting to be released. I don't keep any chickens here. They attract predators and you have to clean up all the gore. I like eggs, I usually keep some in the cupboard, but not today. This is the first morning in a week I've woken up alone. Once I got back from Gertrude's, I planted myself at my desk and wrote until I passed out here on the couch. Now my back's throbbing from sleeping so badly and the morning sickness is already coming on. Wonderful.

I finally open my eyes and pull the blankets off my head. A faint blue glow lights up the ceiling but dawn quickly turns it red. Today's another cold one. I'd rather be asleep than do anything else. I try for a few minutes but it doesn't work, not with this coastal chill. No matter how tightly I clutch my knees, all I can think about is Yvonne reading in the library of the Heath mansion. I'd be warm enough if I was in bed with Gertrude. My friends are right, I shouldn't be alone now, especially not with winter coming, but I'm still going to need these nights to myself. There's too much of Isabelle's determination in me, too much commitment, and I'll be writing this story long after my daughter's born. If it isn't obvious by now, this volume in your hands isn't going to tell you everything, just enough to get you started, and I'll need my privacy to finish the rest.

There's no point putting it off so I hustle into my clothes, throw on my sweater, and get the fire going before the shivers take over. Warmth is my only concern at first, then comes tea, then I dip into a nice jar of smoked salmon. I unscrew the lid and cut off a healthy chunk into my iron pan. The meat starts to sizzle beside the boiling kettle and I feed more wood into the stove until the flames are roaring steady. Once the pan starts to smoke, I pour the pink fish on a yellow porcelain plate and grab a hunk of yesterday's bread to soak up the salty seal-fat they use to preserve the salmon. I close my eyes and chew the greasy, soggy bread, my stomach already gurgling in delight. The Kashaya kill a dozen seals a year and cook their smoked salmon in the fat, a substance thousands of times more hearty than butter. I don't ever want to kill a seal, but here I am eating its blubber.

I wash my dishes with boiling water, carry the cleaning tub out into the pumpkin patch, dump the brown water into the soil, and then stand in my garden looking west towards the ocean. The faint rhythm of beating hammers floats through the wind and I can see tiny figures around the new radio station, perched on the highest bluff of our valley. They've already laid the foundation, now they're nailing the frame together. Paola's up there swinging a hammer, lifting floor-beams, or pouring mixed cement into iron cylinders. She didn't come back last night and I saw two bonfires raging in their work camp once the sun went down. I imagine her naked under dirty blankets with some random man, even though I don't really want to, so I carry the tub back inside and try not to think about Paola. There's nothing I can do to change her path. If she was happy last night with that man, even for a moment, so be it. Hopefully that random man was a woman. Let the gods bless you. May you sleep on some tender girlfriend's breast.

I pour clean water into the wash-basin, take off my clothes, and soak my hair until the shivers return. The coldness jolts me awake and I crawl upstairs to find my black dress, desperate to be warm again. The dress reeks of wood-smoke but I step into it anyway, fastening the buttons up to my neck. I dry my hair by the fire and tie it into a single braid, just like my mother used to. The nausea rises up from my gut so I close my eyes and visualize the invisible heat emanating from the iron stove. As the droplets evaporate from my hair, so does my resolve. It's nice and warm, my shelves are lined with food, I have a book to write, books to read, a big pile of firewood, but not today. I need to ask Yvonne a single question. She's the reason I woke up so early. She's probably listening to me right now.

The crisp air livens me once I'm out the door, the chill quickening my steps. A row of children wobble toward me like a caterpillar, chaperoned by Sara and Ruth, two of the commune's school teachers. They smile at me and tell the children to scream *good morning, Fulvia!* I spin like a dancer amid this chorus, my dress twirls in a spiral, and the children's laughter fades until all I hear are the sounds of my boot-steps, along with the caw of two crows. There isn't any steam coming from the *fábrica* and only a few people are outside working in the village. I bet most are still sleeping, just like I would be if Yvonne weren't pulling me towards the communal house.

A dozen old sailors are outside when I get there, reclining at their wooden tables as the morning sun warms their bones. They've got the right idea, these grumpy penguins catching some rays before the others wake up. I pause a moment to admire their chiseled faces half-hidden under tall collars. Most of them are fast asleep, their chess-pieces in their boxes, their playing boards empty.

Silverware clatters as I enter the communal house. There are a dozen elders seated in the dining area while groggy youngsters serve them bowls of oats, big plates of potatoes topped with eggs, and pots of steaming tea. None of them notice me climb to the solarium. From the sound of their chatter, I don't think anyone heard me come in.

I keep my eyes averted from the second-floor hallway, the one that leads to Angelo's room, and I don't look up until I've reach the top of the stairs. How many times did I walk down that same hallway feeling happiness, joy, bliss, excitement, love? My one friend, the orphan *angelo*, always there for me when my mother wasn't, a curly-haired boy who'd follow me to the ends of the earth. I'm on the verge of crying when Yvonne's words fill my mind like ink in water. She's listening.

"You don't need to be afraid, Fulvia," she says, standing at the open door. "He isn't here."

"I know that. It's just the memories. The good ones. They hurt the most."

Yvonne's wearing a dark green dress, her hair coiled up in a gray spiral. She taps her fingernails against the wooden door frame as her green eyes burn through my skull. She's heard every thought in my head, maybe even my forgotten dreams, the ones that brought me here today. She kisses my cheeks at the threshold and tells me to sit by the fire because the sun hasn't warmed up the solarium yet. Once she closes the door, I feel the coldness claw into my bones.

"I never get any light up here until afternoon," Yvonne says, pulling me towards the flames. "Did you want to see *The Book* again? I can grab it. I know you've been thinking about it, I heard you last night. You keep me awake when you write about *The Book*."

"I don't need to see it right now. It's something else." We sit down by the fire and I try to maintain what little confidence I have left. "You've probably heard me ask this while I was writing, but I guess it doesn't matter? It's trivial."

"Nothing's trivial. So just ask."

"In the *Pistis Sophia*, when Yeshua turns into light, he—"

"He was conducting a ribbon. That's exactly right. See? You knew before I answered. You can't trust what's in the *Pistis Sophia*, though, but it's the closest the public was ever given to the basic story. Yeshua revealed everything to Mary, the whole structure of light, from the earth to the heavens. He woke her from the Dream, but Mary fell back asleep once he was gone. She had to eat, to survive, to raise her children, and it took us two thousand years to access just a sliver of what she glimpsed. When her followers created *The Book*, they showed us how to conduct a ribbon from the ground."

"How did you end up with *The Book*? Exactly."

"Wilfred and Lily Voynitch gave it to me. Everyone knows that. I've told you—"

"Yeah, sure, but why did they pick you?"

"Why me? Because I'd seen the tubes just before the Great Earthquake, only I didn't know what they were. I told your mother about it, word got around, and that's when it happened. Wilfred bought it from the Jesuits in a villa outside Rome. He and Lily heard about what Nikola and I were doing, about what I'd seen, so when *The Book* came into their hands they thought I should have it."

"Did you know Wilfred?" I ask, crossing my legs towards the fire.

"No, not all, but I corresponded with Lily. I loved *The Gadfly*. I wrote to her as an admirer. She was quite a famous author, you know, though she kept her distance from me in those letters. They all did. No one trusted me. But you know that already. Lily and Wilfred only brought me *The Book* after JP Morgan died, when I'd proven myself to the International."

"What was Lily like?"

"Lily was a bit like me, but also a bit like Isabelle. After poor Stepniak died, Lily just hid in her books, where it was safe. So did Wilfred. What else were they supposed to do? If the Czar could strike them down in London, under the eye of the Queen, it could happen anywhere, to anyone! And I had no power back then, no real money, just the ability to charge my husband's account, to buy more books."

She's getting worked up like never before. Her mouth's trembling, the room's getting warmer, everything starts to blur. I've been writing about the Heath library for weeks. Now I'm stuck inside its walls. I see fog streaming by the windows and tall green hedgerows enclosing a vast lawn.

"You're learning very quickly, Fulvia. Pace yourself. What do you really want to know?"

"Lily must have seen something in the tubes. How else did she get *The Book*?"

"Oh, she saw something. Just like me. But it wasn't only her, *mija*. Wilfred suffered horribly in Siberia, he risked his life to escape, and he found Lily like Antonio found Josephine. Don't you see? Only a man like Wilfred could have found *The Book*. He was meant to deliver it to us! Can't you see? Wilfred went to Rome to get it, to the center of the old Empire, and he brought *The Book* to Lily. You can't separate the two. It's not that simple. Just because Lily received a vision doesn't mean Wilfred played no part in fulfilling it. And just because Angelo disappointed you doesn't mean he—"

"Why are you telling me this? I don't—"

"Because I can see where you're going even if you can't."

"Don't play games with me," I say, shifting away from the fire. "Juana told me you've been gentle, treating me like a baby. Tell me what you know, because I'm—"

"A little bit lost? I know. They all complain, believe me, I know. *Yvonne, why are you taking this long? Yvonne, get her moving already! Yvonne, stop acting like Mary!* But you're heading there and nothing can stop it now."

"Enough of this foggy horse shit! You know what everyone says about you?"

"What? About my babble? My hysteria? My insanity?"

"Yes! And I can't stand anymore of your lies! Tell me what I need to hear!"

Yvonne doesn't move. She doesn't have to. I'm all bluff, I've got nothing, just this black dress with its collar lined in red. Everyone's circling through my head now. I can hear Juana cackle in the wind. She watches me sit here, clueless, confused, unable to see my path or hear the voices howling beneath my feet. The closer I listen, the more I comprehend. That's when the ceiling instantly churns into water and I fall backwards through a watery tube. My words turn to bubbles and my ears fill with the whispers of a thousand naked women. I see rows of brown olive trees through a thin green cloud and watch a white dove take flight from the branches. The bird lands atop an iron column just as I melt into the red chair up through the floorboards. The hole into the underworld closes. I'm soaking wet.

"Paloma?" I ask, panting. "I'm going there?"

"Yes, *mija*. I'm afraid so."

The entire solarium ripples from my entry. Nausea fills my stomach as Yvonne guides me to the dying fire, throws on more wood, and squats above the carpet like some ancient desert grandmother. I lick the warm nether-fluid from my lips. It tastes like saltwater laced with lavender. Obviously, this is the first time I've entered the underworld. I wasn't prepared for it, not at all. I hear the endless laughter of the naked women with their pitched sounds refracted through water. Yvonne rocks her hips against mine. She hums a sweet melody. There isn't anything left to be angry about, not after today. They've told me everything I need to hear. The rest is up to me.

17

THE GREAT WATERFRONT STRIKE OF 1901

JOSEPHINE NEVER MISSED SUNDAY MASS AT THE CHURCH OF SAINTS Peter and Paul and this somber ritual allowed her to observe the Italian bourgeoisie flaunting their wealth across the neighborhood. Hidden in the pews, my grandmother wore a tattered black dress, layers of white make-up, and a black-lace widow's veil. The respectable families avoided her entirely while the poor families treated her with pity, allowing my grandmother to study their behavior in near-total anonymity. The bourgeois of the Latin Quarter grew larger every day, their businesses flourishing thanks to the poor immigrants who trusted Italians over *yanquis* and if they weren't kept in line, these *prominenti* parasites would soon become even more exploitative than the Anglos. Josephine filed out of church with them each Sunday, listening to their conversations before she slipped away among the crowd, unnoticed. Each week, she climbed to the desolate summit of Telegraph Hill where my mother was waiting on a boulder. In those uncertain days, Josephine and Isabelle stared east towards Mount Diablo and spoke of Yvonne del Valle-Heath. Despite all their plans, my mother had drastically altered everything.

In the winter of 1901, Isabelle was distributing folded laundry when she noticed the door to Yvonne's library was open, a rare occurrence in this sleepy mansion. Weeks earlier, Eamonn told my mother of an anarchist journal called *La Revue Blanche* that was shipped to Yvonne from Paris. Once Isabelle told Josephine, neither were able to speak, for the journal was edited by none other than Félix Fénéon. Their first instinct was to regard it as a trap, but as the weeks progressed, Isabelle was unable to escape her curiosity. When my mother saw the open door to the library, the urge to investigate was irresistible. As if it were all a dream, Yvonne was waiting for her beside the grand fireplace while little Juana crawled across the Persian carpet. Both of them were smiling at my mother.

Isabelle closed the door, locked the bolt, and asked if there were any French art journals. She didn't specify which ones, leading Yvonne to believe Eamonn must have told her of *La Revue Blanche*. She retrieved the most recent volume and handed it over, still unsure what was transpiring. Isabelle sat down at the oak reading table, opened *La Revue Blanche*, and skimmed through articles on the Boxer Rebellion, the economy of the French colonies, the intrigues of the Jesuits, and the Chinese poetry of the Tang Empire. This was Félix seeding subversive knowledge into the highest echelons of capitalist society, all in the hope of activating powerful allies. Unable to bear the silence, Yvonne told my mother she could borrow the journal if she promised to return it the next morning. Isabelle stood up from the table, slid the journal into her dress pocket, and left the library without uttering another word. The other laundresses pestered her about where she had been but my mother insisted she was ill in the toilet. Beatrix played along but knew Isabelle was lying, just as she suspected her mistake.

Once they were off work, my mother took Beatrix to a secluded bench in Lafayette Park and told her what happened. Despite her cautious nature, my aunt screamed in front of a dozen bourgeois couples and threw her fists at Isabelle's face. If my mother hadn't started to run, the police might have arrested them for fighting in the upscale park. Beatrix calmed down only after she had chased Isabelle through the Latin Quarter and cornered her in a dark Chinatown alley known as the Devil's Kitchen, a place few were brave enough to enter. My mother tried to explain the basic details but Beatrix wouldn't listen. She called Isabelle a traitor, a fool, an imbecile, and a coward, along with a hundred other insults. Their argument continued long into the night, even as they printed *Secolo Nuovo*, and not even Cesare could summon the courage to intervene. Isabelle said Yvonne had robbed Heath of a son and was clearly on their side, but Beatrix maintained this was all just a ruse. Unable to bear her cousin's wrath, Isabelle stormed out and took *La Revue Blanche* home to Josephine. Once she listened to her daughter's story, Josephine claimed their only choice was to plunge into this relationship with Yvonne del Valle-Heath and see where it led. Félix was clearly at work here.

Despite the exasperation of Beatrix, Josephine allowed Isabelle to be in the library for one hour each day. She instructed her daughter to only speak Italian and reveal nothing but a desire to learn from Yvonne's books. The very next afternoon, my mother returned to the library and asked if Yvonne would teach her to read modern Italian. From that day onward, a new routine began. After distributing her basket of laundry, my mother read aloud with Yvonne through the dark history of western civilization. Once her time elapsed, Isabelle returned to the laundry room and was beset by a thousand questions. Her co-workers beamed with pride when they learned of these lessons, regarding Isabelle as their little champion of the Latin Quarter. Beatrix despised this endless praise. While my mother was in the library reading, she was on her hands and knees scrubbing the laundry room floor. Once work was over, my aunt avoided Isabelle and idled away her evenings along the waterfront. On these lonely evenings, Beatrix found her only solace in dockside gatherings of maritime rebels, their faces illuminated under brown gas-light. The Great Waterfront Strike was about to crack open.

On February 2, 1901, the City Front Federation was formed between the sailors, teamsters, and longshoremen, accounting for over 13,000 men. Along with their families and children, this strike force constituted nearly a quarter of the population in a city of 350,000. With this small army of insurgent workers, the International would soon launch its Great Waterfront Strike, paralyzing all shipments from the San Francisco Bay. While the vast majority of troop movements to the Philippine Isles had already taken place, the harbor was still being used to transport weapons, ammunition, food, and equipment to the soldiers. During its two years of war against the Philippine Republic, the US Army had massacred thousands of indigenous, although news of these atrocities was suppressed due to military censorship. However, by 1901, the public had learned of the torture, rape, and pillage burning carried out in their names, a bleak reality that made their impending waterfront strike even more necessary.

Across the Pacific in the Qing Empire, the Boxer Rebellion had just been crushed with the help of US soldiers. Combined with the forces of Japan, England, France, Russia, Germany, Italy, and the Austro-Hungarian Empire, this Eight Nation Alliance invaded Peking in the summer of 1900, forcing the Empress Ci Xi to flee eastward to Xi'an. While his soldiers fought in this brutal assault against the Boxers, King Umberto I of Italy was shot by Gætano Bresci, proving the International could strike at any moment. Despite this assassination, Imperial Peking was taken by the western armies, the Chinese coastline was forcibly occupied, and the Russian Empire sent 100,000 soldiers to invade the northern countryside. While the US army slaughtered the indigenous in the Philippines, Russia controlled most of Asia, a fact that angered the Japanese Empire, still eager to test their new warships. As this conflict festered, US cargo-ships steamed eastward across the Pacific ferrying discharged soldiers from the Philippines. These hollow men began to appear on the docks of San Francisco, besotted with alcohol and haunted by

Gaetano Bresci shoots King Umberto I.

visions of massacres. Once their back-pay was spent at brothels and saloons, these charred-out husks found work as scabs.

Through the spring of 1901, while the waterfront came to a boil, Isabelle and Yvonne read the works of Oscar Wilde. Because of him, anarchism was first spoken of during their sessions. Starting with his play *Vera; or, The Nihilists*, Oscar Wilde challenged bourgeois conventions, private property, and capitalism. For his homosexuality, incendiary writing, and unbridled rebellion, the British Empire sentenced him to penal servitude after his love-affair with an aristocrat was made public. In this dank dungeon, Wilde contracted the illness that killed him in the fall of 1900. Isabelle and Yvonne read his final work by the fireplace and wept at his depiction of dehumanized prisoners. Rather than sign his name to *The Ballad of Reading Gaol*, Wilde left only his prison identification number, C33, a final message to the world that destroyed him.

Isabelle told Beatrix about Oscar Wilde but her furious cousin didn't care about anything other than assassinating Heath, at least when it came to Yvonne. Josephine was more patient, although she couldn't fathom how Heath's wife had come to love both Félix Fénéon and Oscar Wilde, a troubling coincidence. While this steel baroness appeared to be a rogue follower of Mary, Josephine maintained that she couldn't be trusted under any circumstances, and Isabelle was allowed to tell her the truth only after Heath dropped dead, not before. The time for their *attentat* was fast approaching.

By the middle of April, Isabelle and Beatrix had resolved their conflict and were eating an early dinner at *Luna's Mexican Restaurant* when Frank Norris walked in with his lover Jeanette Black. They sat down with the cousins in the back of the candle-lit room and revealed they'd been married for over a year. Jeanette removed a red book from her bag and handed it to my mother with an air of pride. This was Frank's newest novel, *The Octopus: A Story of California*, and it had just sold over ten thousand copies. Frank said its plot centered on the infamous 1880 massacre of *yanqui* farmers by the Southern-Pacific Railroad, a company that stole their wheat-fields and let the grain rot. It was the first volume of his *Epic of Wheat*, with the second volume centered on the Chicago Board of Trade where the planet's grain supply was purchased by a single capitalist in the summer of 1898. This volume would be called *The Pit: A Story of Chicago*, while the third was to be titled *The Wolf: A Story of Europe*. In this final volume, the manipulation of wheat prices in 1898 causes an uprising across Northern Italy. Frank told the cousins his *Epic of Wheat* would expose the true nature of capitalism and make it easily digestible for the public. When he and Jeannette left *Luna's* that evening, the cousins couldn't help but grin.

During the spring of 1901, the daily newspapers stirred up enthusiasm for the impending visit of President William McKinley and the First Lady, an occasion that would swell the pockets of local merchants. The day before his patriotic welcoming, Isabelle and Beatrix arrived at the mansion only to discover their jobs had temporarily changed. The entire staff would now work their shifts hanging red, white, and blue streamers throughout the estate. Later that afternoon, Yvonne explained how the President was coming to the mansion tomorrow and none of the normal staff would be called in. After the assassination of King Umberto I, Heath had taken every precaution to ensure the safety of his pawn and hired an entirely new kitchen staff for the day. With the death of McKinley now ensured by Emma Goldman, the Lemel cousins enjoyed their day off work and watched a parade of anarchists march out of the Latin Quarter towards the ocean. This jubilant procession was composed of the known anarchists who'd been arrested too many times and were now under constant police surveillance. With a large red banner reading NO GODS – NO MASTERS – SENZA DIO – SENZA PADRONE, these fifty or so anarchists marched to the Pacific the day President McKinley toured the city. None of them wanted to be framed for his murder, so they drank wine around a bonfire and slept the night on the beach.

During this presidential visit, the First Lady became gravely ill and was confined to a room in the mansion of Henry T. Scott, owner of the Union Iron Works. While his wife lay on the verge of death, McKinley and Scott oversaw the launching of the *USS Ohio* at a sparsely attended ceremony. The Union Iron Works employees had been sent home for the occasion and few elected to attend the President's visit, especially since they weren't getting paid for it. After almost a decade of labor trouble, the Union Iron Works had finally won five new military contracts under McKinley's administration. The *Ohio* was the forth battleship to emerge from the Union Iron Works in three years and Washington DC was now pleased with labor conditions in San Francisco. Lionel Heath attended this launch where he learned the President would be unable to visit the Pacific Heights mansion. His wife was barely clinging to her soul and McKinley canceled nearly all of his commitments in order to sit by her side and pray. Before he lost this opportunity, Heath took the President by the arm and assured him that their times of trouble were over. Heath promised the unions would be destroyed in less than a year, allowing the city of San Francisco to fulfill its true industrial potential.

In May of 1901, an anonymous organization called the Employer's Association revealed itself after 1,000 cooks and waiters went on strike. As Jack London would write, *all organized employers stood back of the restaurant owners, in sympathy with them and willing to aid them if they dared. And at the back of the Cooks' and Waiters' Union stood the organized labor of the city, 40,000 strong.* When further strikes erupted among carriage workers, bakers, and metal-polishers, the mysterious Employer's Association made the same offer to each stricken establishment, claiming that *Labor cannot be allowed to dictate to capital and say how business shall be conducted.* With 2,000 people now on strike, the International triggered the next phase of their plan. On May 20, just before President McKinley departed San Francisco, nearly 5,000 men walked out of the waterfront shipyards and paralyzed all war-production. This strike wave spread to the butchers and drew out another 1,000 workers, bringing the total close to 8,000 men. Isabelle helped distribute copies of *Secolo Nuovo* to these crowds and worked long evenings with Schwartz hunched over the printing plates. Rather than help, Peter and Beatrix usually just kissed on the leather couch.

My mother continued her visits with Yvonne throughout the summer of 1901 and their lessons began to revolve around the year 300 CE. One foggy day in July, Yvonne was in the middle of an old Latin text when she suddenly spoke of haunted Alpine valleys and diabolic rebels in the mountains. My mother's first instinct was to run, although she quickly calmed this fear. Yvonne saw the hesitation in Isabelle's eyes and knew she'd discovered one of these mythical rebels. In a panic, Isabelle pulled a knife from her workdress, put it to Yvonne's throat, and demanded an explanation. Rather than show fear, Yvonne began to laugh. She claimed to follow the teachings of Mary Magdalene and would help them defeat Heath. My mother asked if she would help them murder her husband and was surprised when Yvonne suggested an alternate idea. If Heath were to be killed now, his fortune would shift to London along with the iron mines, ore-crushers, coal fields, foundries, and steel mills. Yvonne wanted to take control of the entire estate before killing him, an idea that set my mother on a rampage.

Isabelle claimed the followers of Mary always found it better to wait, to bask in stolen comfort and play silly games with their luxury, a pattern that had only gotten worse. Yvonne wouldn't stand for this insult. She claimed my ancestors were selfish killers who only cared for their own safety. She said the forces of Mary had fought for centuries while the *streghe* hid in the Alps with their goats. Yvonne claimed that if it hadn't been for the witch-hunts, they all would have stayed there like selfish cowards and let the world perish. My mother was now livid. She hissed that if it hadn't been for the forces of Mary putting all their knowledge in *The Book*, the darkness wouldn't have come to the Alps. Yvonne fell backwards into her red chair, stunned by this young *stregha's* knowledge, and they stared at each other until Juana asked her first question, an awkward word that sounded like *kay*.

My mother put the knife back in her dress pocket, walked to the bookshelf that contained *La Revue Blanche,* ran her fingers along the bindings, and decided to trust this follower of Mary. Juana clapped in joy as Yvonne stood up from the red chair and took Isabelle's hand above the roaring flames. Yvonne promised that Heath would die, but only after she stole his fortune. Not just for herself, but for everyone, and with his money they would organize the final uprising against darkness. This possibility gleamed before my mother's eyes, but so did the story of Félix Fénéon and his dabbling with the forces of Mary. Seeing the hesitation creep back into her eyes, Yvonne asked my mother to trust her. Isabelle said she already did. Juana couldn't stop laughing. She knew what had just taken place.

When Beatrix learned of her cousin's latest folly, she immediately ran off to the Latin Quarter and confronted Josephine directly. By the time Isabelle reached the apartment, Beatrix was pleading with my grandmother to take Isabelle away so she could finish the task alone. As the figure of crucified Yeshua ha-Nozri hung above Josephine's head, my aunt Beatrix realized her long-isolated relatives had finally gone insane from this brutal city. Josephine agreed with my mother that it was best to wait for the fortune, especially with such a powerful ally, and Beatrix slammed her fist on the sewing table, insisting it was all a trick. Ignoring the pleas of her niece, my grandmother allowed Isabelle to continue her library visits under the condition she reveal nothing of their waterfront strike plans, for it was likely that Lionel Heath was backing the anonymous Employer's Association.

The San Francisco waterfront.

On July 16, 1901, a gun battle erupted outside the Dundon Iron Works, a factory that had been shut down by the strike-wave. Soon after this, the Employer's Association began backing the freight companies against the teamsters. Every member of the Teamster's Union was fired, triggering a strike on July 25 where almost 2,000 drivers kept their wagons idle and no cargo moved off the waterfront. The cousins went to work that Saturday on streets empty of traffic. They toiled away in the mansion all morning and once the day's laundry had dried, my mother met in the library with Yvonne where she learned some surprising information. Without consulting her husband, Yvonne had given the entire staff paid leave until the end of the strike. The previous evening, Heath had stormed into the mansion and proudly announced his war against organized labor, claiming he was poised to crush them. Having no other weapon to fight her husband, Yvonne released Isabelle to the front along with a generous paycheck. She kissed Isabelle's cheek, told her to be brave, and pushed my mother out of the library, her faced covered in what looked like genuine tears. At the end of their shift, Isabelle, Beatrix, and all the other laundresses found a month's pay plus back-wages waiting for them at the guardhouse.

Beatrix stormed off after this incident and didn't talk to Isabelle until the following Monday. She made love with Peter in her room at the sailor's boardinghouse and tried to forget her reckless cousin who'd ruined their plans. Isabelle knocked on her door three days later and hustled the lovers over to the Sailor's Union hall for an important meeting. They lingered there all day while the appointed heads of the City Front Federation voted on a full strike of their 13,000 members. Long after midnight, Andrew Furuseth emerged from his office, announced the strike had begun, and the room instantly erupted into riotous cheers. While everyone else was consumed with this celebration, Isabelle left the union hall and walked to the offices of Doctor Eamonn O'Shea. She found him reading a book of poetry by the gas-light, his front door unlocked and partially open. After startling him half to death, my mother told Eamonn that his services were now needed on the waterfront.

The strike officially began on the morning of July 30, 1901 and Josephine had never seen such a mobilization outside of Paris. Not a single stand was open in the Produce District, a hundred idle ships filled the harbor, and crowds of strikers guarded the waterfront in a mighty phalanx, daring anyone to challenge their strength. My mother passed those nights preparing special editions of *Secolo Nuovo* with content relating to the strike, often staying up until dawn. Peter and Beatrix largely abandoned the newspaper to join an anarchist defense group, leaving Isabelle and Schwartz the responsibilities of writer, copy editor, type-setter, printer, and folder. When these special issues were finished, the entire anarchist network distributed the anonymous words of Isabelle Ferrari across the waterfront, allowing hundreds of Italian workers to glimpse the light of a world without bosses, borders, or kings. Schwartz never cared much for writing but he set Isabelle's fiery words into the printing plates, bringing them to life with his ink-stained hands, and San Francisco was at a total standstill when they distributed *Secolo Nuovo* to Italian immigrants now enmeshed within the city's greatest labor conflict.

Bricks and mortar stopped arriving at construction sites, grocery stores closed, and boatloads of fruit sat idle across the bay. The waterfront of Oakland was paralyzed by a simultaneous strike that blocked the Southern-Pacific Railroad from delivering or receiving any cargo, tying up the national rail-system. Further east near the Sacramento River delta, train terminals at Port Costa, Crockett, and Benecia were shut down, causing the state's wheat harvest to rot. The Employer's Association refused to negotiate with the City Front Federation and recruited soldiers fresh from the Philippines as their scabs, along with university students eager for a summer job. Their most insidious move was to import hundreds of black workers from Ohio and Illinois, housing them on empty boats anchored in the bay where they ate worse food and earned less pay than the white scabs. Each morning, their employers rowed them to shore, bypassing the union pickets and allowing the scabs to unload the backlogged cargo. Once these boxes were stowed on the scab-wagons, a group of scab-teamsters were escorted off the wharves by a ring of 200 police officers. Every day of the week saw brutal injuries on both sides as stones and fists flew between the scabs, the police, and the Federation.

When a war-crazed soldier drunkenly pulled a pistol on the picketers, Beatrix shot him through the shoulder before disappearing into the crowd. Peter Isaak was able to shoot another maniac but one of these scabs eventually shot a teamster through the heart. In league with the Employer's Association, the daily newspapers blamed the union for this death and ignored the brazen gunfire of the war-veteran scabs. Only the *San Francisco Examiner* dared to support the strike and it became the most popular newspaper in

Scab worker and police escort.

the city, far surpassing the readership of its local rivals. William Randolph Hearst sent his poor newsboys to every picket-line where they hawked copies to cash-strapped workers, raking in thick bags of nickels. While the *Examiner* was the main competition to *Secolo Nuovo,* the anarchists couldn't chase off every Hearst newsie, nor could they compete with its vast circulation. Soon enough, men on the picket-lines spoke of Hearst as a friend to the workingman, claiming his newspaper told the truth about the Great Strike and the Black Plague, a selling-point that was anything but false. If it hadn't been for Heart's paper, the plague would still be nothing more than *mass-hysteria.*

Throughout the first weeks of August, hundreds of wounded men were taken to a strike hospital in the ramshackle slums South-of-the-Slot, or south of Market Street. It was here that Doctor Eamonn O'Shea, assisted by the nurses Margaret and Shelley, treated endless broken bones, popped eye-balls, bullet wounds, skull fractures, and knife gouges. One of his patients claimed to have been shot by a black scab and when Eamonn pressed for details he discovered widespread racism among his *yanqui* patients. Apparently, this scab had been returning from a night in the Barbary Coast when he was surrounded by a mob of white union men who threatened to lynch him. Eamonn tried to correct this type of bigotry during painful moments of an operation, reminding these union men they were all just meat to the capitalists. Every human bled the same, no matter their skin color, and his patients couldn't agree more, especially with his metal instruments stuck inside their bodies. Margaret and Shelley assisted him in this mission to eradicate racism, although from a different angle. Whenever a wounded man spoke a lecherous or bigoted word, these witches were known to cut open stitches and press their fingers into wounds. By the middle of August, the union men of the Federation had learned much from their doctor and nurses, although the process was often painful.

The bloody street-fights continued throughout the summer of 1901, with only a faint trickle of cargo getting through the pickets. The police were nearly powerless against 15,000 striking workers and the Employer's Association issued daily calls for the state militia to intervene, a demand Governor Gage refused. After witnessing the San Francisco capitalists cover up the plague in the name of profit, the Governor had no desire to aid their conspiracy against honest workingmen. Amid this blockade of imports and exports, scores of small business owners turned on the Employer's Association, blaming them for the deadlock. A partial list of the Association's internal membership was leaked to the press and a boycott of their businesses began, clogging their entrances and shuttering shop windows. Even the police revolted against the Employer's Association and were replaced by private mercenaries from the

Curtin Detective Agency. That's when the blood really began to flow.

At the beginning of September, Isabelle joined her brothers in the anarchist defense group and was given a new revolver. She wore her black dress with its red-lined collar, a black shawl to obscure her face, and carried the pistol deep in her pocket. Schwartz was her silent partner and protected their rear-side through waves of unpredictable violence. Two union men were killed by these new private detectives, just as two detectives were shot dead with anarchist pistols. My mother fired one of these fatal shots and was witnessed by over a hundred strikers who applauded her devilish aim. These men were allies the anarchists would surely need in the days ahead.

The latest issue of *Free Society* signaled President McKinley's impending assassination after it described a strange man the editors believed to be a police spy. By denouncing him well beforehand, the International ensured it had no connection to what soon followed. Five days after that issue of *Free Society* was mailed, a Polish anarchist named Leon Czoglosz fired two bullets into President McKinley at the Pan-American Exposition in Buffalo, New York. The president suffered in agony for over a week until passing away on September 13. The backlash on the waterfront was immediate.

The next evening, my mother was forced to hurl her revolver in the bay when she was encircled by police along with thirty others. Most of the union men were beaten and jailed, although Isabelle was let go as an errant schoolgirl. After the assassination of McKinley, the SFPD was empowered to arrest any small groups they encountered near the pickets, just as the wounds Eamonn treated became worse. His strike hospital south of Market was filled to capacity and these wounded fighters expressed open weariness towards the anarchists, claiming they'd triggered this new repression.

Despite the immediate backlash, McKinley's death ruined JP Morgan's conspiracy when Vice President Theodore Roosevelt was installed in the White House. This popular hero of the Cuban War had been recruited to secure votes for McKinley, a risky compromise that now proved disastrous to Wall Street. While the new president resented the capitalists for buying out the federal government during the Panic of 1893, he carried no love for the anarchists who'd installed him at gunpoint.

Emma Goldman and the Isaaks were arrested in Chicago for aiding Leon Czoglosz, along with dozens of other anarchists across the US. An Italian musician named Antonio Maggio was apprehended in New Mexico for allegedly revealing the conspiracy beforehand, while the anarchist commune in Home, Washington was said to be the *hell hole* which spawned the assassin. To the despair of Cesare Crespi, his adopted-son Enrico Travaglio was arrested in Spring Valley, Illinois along with several anarchists from New Jersey. All of them now shivered in freezing dungeons while angry mobs burned effigies of Emma Goldman on the cobblestones of San Francisco.

The police continued their brutal assault against the strike, charging into pickets with clubs and mutilating anyone caught alone on the waterfront. My mother lived these days covered in sweat, blood, and grease, her bodily activity nothing more than continuous instinctual motion. By the time night fell and Isabelle found somewhere to sit, printing *Secolo Nuovo* was nothing more than a distant thought lulling her to sleep. These respites from battle were often cut short by Beatrix, always eager to remind Isabelle what her foolish actions had cost them. The unions were in a miserable condition and Heath's assassination would have destroyed the Employer's Association, breathing life back into their struggle. The strike in Oakland had just collapsed, the Cooks and Waiters Union was back at work, and the City Front Federation had almost emptied its war-chest. In my aunt Beatrix's imagination, the workers of San Francisco would have risen up if Heath had been stabbed by two teenage laundresses inside his own home. My mother had ruined this opportunity, for everyone.

Knowing this to be true, Isabelle helped Beatrix agitate on the front-lines with a pistol in her pocket and inspiration on her tongue, desperate to keep the movement alive. The anarchists soon rallied around the cousins and my mother gave fiery speeches about fighting for a free world, not just an extra fifty cents. She told the union men this was their last chance to fight for many years, so they better take it all the way. Each of these syllables was charged with light, infecting the union with a bravery that flowed from the underworld. These men had fought and bled alongside these black-clad anarchists, witnessing their bravery firsthand, and no daily newspaper could change that. Not even the death of a corrupt president shook their faith in these fierce women.

By the end of September, the anti-anarchist hysteria had evaporated, at least in San Francisco. Gunfire became a daily occurrence and the total number of wounded who'd passed through Eamonn's hospital was now over 1,000. During the evening of September 28, a drunken private detective fired into the picket and my uncle Sergio immediately shot him through the arm, flanked by his two brothers. An army of union men followed behind the Ferraris and opened fire on the private detectives, forcing them up Market

Street towards the Palace Hotel. In her black shawl, my mother stood atop a wagon-bed, demanded the Palace Hotel be set aflame, and fired her revolver towards the detectives. The union men poured bullets across the street, shattering windows, splintering wood, and spinning detectives around in bloody circles. When her bullets were gone, my mother threw endless cobblestones as their army pressed towards the heart of San Francisco. They'd nearly surrounded the Palace Hotel when the SFPD arrived *en masse* and began shooting. Schwartz tried to pull Isabelle towards Chinatown but my mother wouldn't stop throwing rocks or asking for more bullets. At some point before dawn, Isabelle collapsed in the street and woke up in the apartment of Doctor Eamonn O'Shea. Josephine was sitting beside her, reading a volume of the *Geographie Universelle.*

Word quickly spread throughout the city that armed union men had surrounded the Palace Hotel and threatened to burn it. The police kept away from the pickets, the private detectives held their gun-fire, and the newspapers portrayed the attack as senseless union violence. While there were still pickets across the waterfront, the local capitalists had already cleared most of their backlog and were beginning to boast of the strike being over. Isabelle was recovering at Eamonn's when the Governor arrived in San Francisco and arranged a private meeting with the Teamster's Union and the Sailor's Union. After learning of the gun-battle on Market Street, Governor Gage demanded a speedy resolution. My uncles were kept in darkness of this meeting until they found a large crowd at the Bulkhead Saloon waiting for Furuseth to emerge. When he finally descended from the union office, my uncles understood before he even spoke. Andrew Furuseth declared that the Great Waterfront Strike was over.

My mother had just recovered when my uncles delivered the bitter news to Eamonn's office. They told Josephine and Isabelle how the strike leaders had capitulated to Governor Gage's threat and agreed to never reveal the full-terms of their settlement. Under the public provisions of this new peace agreement, all striking workers would be hired back, all scabs would be discharged, and wages would remain as they were before the strike. This betrayal of Antonio Ferrari's dream was more than either Josephine or

Bulkhead Saloon

Isabelle could stand. On the morning of October 3, they wore their matching black dresses to the sailor's hall above the Bulkhead Saloon. A few men tried to stop them from entering Furuseth's office but he waved away his guards and locked himself in with the Ferrari women. The first thing Josephine did was slap Furuseth repeatedly across the face until he'd curled up on his desk chair. The guards banged on the door but Furuseth screamed to leave them alone and protect the stairwell. This was his way of submitting to Josephine.

She accused him of betraying Antonio but Furuseth insisted there was no choice. Governor Gage had threatened to put the entire city under martial law and police its streets with federal soldiers. Military enforcement of capitalism was exactly what the Employer's Association wanted, so Furuseth agreed to end the strike rather than let them win. Josephine called him a coward and said the city would have revolted if federal soldiers arrived. Furuseth claimed all Josephine wanted was another Commune, another slaughter, and he wouldn't allow thousands of innocents to die under a naval bombardment and forcible occupation. Josephine smashed her fist into his cheek, revealed the dagger hidden in her dress pocket, and promised to kill Furuseth if he betrayed them again. This entire strike was meant to aid the indigenous of the Philippine Isles by bringing the war home, not fold at the moment of truth. She hissed that Antonio would've been ashamed, something that made Furuseth fall to the floor and weep on his knees. He claimed to love Antonio more than she knew and promised the International would always have safe passage with his Sailor's Union, just as he vowed to never give up his fight against the ship-owners. He begged for my family's forgiveness, prostrating himself across the floor like the Christian he was. Josephine and Isabelle waited for him to look up before walking out of the sailor's hall. They never came back. Not together, at least.

Everything became much worse when they returned to their apartment. My uncles were yelling over what went wrong, who was to blame, what to do next. Lorenzo said the entire Federation structure was at fault while Sergio claimed their downfall was having strike leaders like Furuseth. Federico tried to calm his brothers but Lorenzo ignored them all, claiming he was needed in Paterson, New Jersey, a place where thousands of anarchists coursed through the streets and this type of craven betrayal would never be allowed. Lorenzo quit his job on the waterfront that day and caught a ferry to the Oakland train terminus to begin his week-long rail journey. Josephine and Isabelle did nothing to stop him.

Sergio and Federico woke in a somber mood the next morning and went to their old jobs for the same pay. Capital was flowing at the thrust of their arms and neither could speak from the sadness. As they were recaptured within this daily routine, Beatrix arrived at the Latin Quarter apartment where Isabelle was watching Josephine sew. My aunt had just been at the Heath mansion gathering their very generous strike-pay. After handing over these checks, the Italian gatekeeper told Beatrix that work would resume on the first of November. There were three automobiles in the driveway, along with five men in black suits guarding the front door, all armed with rifles. The gatekeeper wouldn't explain who they were, but headlines soon clarified the matter: JP Morgan was visiting the Heath mansion.

Beatrix slapped three days-worth of newspapers on the sewing desk and claimed they'd all been deceived by Yvonne. Had they not been lured off the property, Morgan and Heath would both be dead. Isabelle said the mansion would've been closed but Beatrix didn't listen. My aunt declared that she and Peter Isaak were leaving San Francisco for the safety of Bianca's northern

The Heath Mansion.

commune. Now that the national press had named Peter as a possible accomplice in the McKinley assassination, their departure was urgent. The *Nuovo Ideal* commune was nestled on cleared land close to an abandoned saw-mill and only accessible from an old logging road that eroded during each winter storm. No one would ever find them up there, although it could get lonely when it rained. *Nuovo Ideal* was the original name of my commune, the place where I've written this text, and it was founded by none other than Josephine's sister Bianca, the second Alpine witch to settle in California.

Josephine and Isabelle wept after Beatrix left their apartment without saying goodbye. They wept over the extent of their blindness and the loss of Antonio's dream. They knew JP Morgan was here to inspect the crushed labor movement, boldly announcing his latest triumph. They read articles about the undersea telegraph cable his company was laying between San Francisco, Honolulu, and Manila, allowing the Philippine War to be conducted remotely from Washington DC.

During the pitch-black of this despair, my uncles Sergio and Federico returned from work and announced they were moving out. With their youngest brother now gone, paying rent for the apartment made little sense. Furuseth had offered my uncles Beatrix's old room at the sailor's boarding-house and they agreed to share it, allowing Josephine and Isabelle to do as they liked. Once my uncles finished speaking, Josephine stood up from her sewing-desk, grabbed the wood and metal crucifix from off the wall, and threw it out the window where it clattered across Montgomery Street before being crushed by a wagon wheel. Not even my mother understood what it meant. Josephine never attempted to explain.

My family ate a celebratory dinner that night and my uncles moved out the next morning. Once they departed, Josephine told Isabelle they were moving back to Greenwich Street. Isabelle embraced her mother tightly, feeling as if a horrible curse had just been broken, and during this long embrace, two dozen sailors arrived to help them move. Josephine donated her sewing machine to the driver's wife and arranged for another sailor's family to take over their lease. All of Montgomery Street paused to watch the black-shrouded widow depart the Latin Quarter, her home of the past fourteen years. None of them would ever see her again, although a corner merchant recovered her smashed crucifix and kept it behind his bar as a local curiosity. Every passerby watched this wagon drive off down Montgomery until it vanished at the bottom of the hill, absorbed into the bustling waterfront traffic.

Marisol de la Costa waited for them on the front porch with a steaming cup of coffee and a burning cigarette in her hands. The sailors bowed their heads as the Queens reunited, an event nearly holy in its local significance. Josephine wept in front of Antonio's loyal comrades and then collapsed into Marisol's arms, her raw emotions too powerful for words. Isabelle helped carry her mother inside while these sailors silently unloaded an entire decade of belongings. When these kind men finished, my grandmother fell asleep in her bedroom and didn't get up for two whole days. The lonely crucifixion of Josephine Lemel was finally over.

On the first day of November, my mother found Yvonne reading in the library as Juana toddled across the carpet and this once endearing sight now filled Isabelle with revulsion. She asked why Yvonne had protected JP Morgan and Heath, a knife glimmering in her hand. This open threat threw Yvonne into a rage. She said Morgan's visit was hidden from her until he was upstairs in Heath's office. She heard them arguing but only made out a few sentences. Morgan yelled about her husband turning San Francisco against Wall Street with his recklessness, Heath yelled about electing a new mayor, and after that they fell into whispers. When she was finally introduced, Yvonne beheld the monstrous face of JP Morgan, his nose thick with bulbous growths, his small eyes hollowed out by darkness. Lionel Heath was fully human in comparison to this creature, and the effect of Morgan's aura was so strong that Yvonne had to run into the bathroom and vomit up her lunch. His physical presence poisoned the air itself, making the walls drip with menace and hum with dread. Isabelle asked why she didn't kill Morgan right there but Yvonne said she wasn't strong enough. None of them were, not yet. After this cryptic statement, Yvonne handed over two sealed letters and asked my mother to deliver them. One was to a carriage company, the other was to Eamonn. She said these letters would correct her mistakes. Reluctantly, my mother put away her blade.

When she returned the next day after delivering the letters, Isabelle found Yvonne in a simple black dress with a black shawl over her face. She asked Isabelle to accompany her and Juana on a carriage ride to meet Eamonn in the hills above Mission Dolores. Despite being left in the dark about these plans, Isabelle stepped inside the carriage and made her descent along the paved slope of Van Ness and across the rough cobblestones of Mission Street. The carriage-driver let them out behind the old Mission Dolores where they found Eamonn near a patch of cactus. While the two lovers embraced, my mother walked Juana into the hills where they watched a hot-air balloon rise and fall from a tether fixed to the ground. Juana clapped her hands at this bizarre sight and eventually lured her mother up the hill with screams of jubilation. While they all watched in wonder, the tether securing this air-balloon snapped, sending its passengers floating towards the Pacific. These nine unfortunate people beheld a view none had ever seen, although it came with an equally unknown terror. After threatening their mortal souls with aquatic oblivion, the coastal wind pushed them away from the ocean and the balloon drifted to the earth near a lumber mill north of Santa Cruz. These metropolitan citizens dined at the home of a local woodcutter and his bewildered family, recounting their death-defying experiences in vivid detail. The children of this humble family enjoyed these fancy strangers who babbled on about how scared or brave or mesmerized they were as they sailed helplessly through the air. There was no precedence for this type of occurrence. Such things simply didn't happen.

SHE'LL BE WEARING RED PAJAMAS

THIS NEVER HAPPENS WHEN I'M ALONE. GERTRUDE'S GOT HER ARMS wrapped tight around my belly. She breathes faintly through her nostrils, so soft it barely ruffles my back hairs. I close my eyes but sleep doesn't take me. I see our cramped Polk Street apartment, overlooking a cobblestone road packed with bicycles and wagons, all moving to the tune of our neighbor's accordion. That little bedroom of ours was just a window-nook lined with a mattress and partitioned with a thick blanket. At night we saw countless stars over the rooftops. In the morning we saw fog so thick it hid the cobblestones. She held onto me tight back then, just like now, and my visions of San Francisco fade away into darkness. Gertrude finally loosens her grip and I take this moment to free myself. It's the only chance I'll get.

The air's warm up here in the loft and it can't be that early if there's still heat from last night's fire. My clothes are in a heap near the ladder and I ball them up before climbing down to the living room. The iron stove radiates warmth and there's a few red coals glowing in the darkness. Annabelle's bedroom door is wide open, so I have to be careful. Her snores echo in the dark while I get get dressed, trying to my best to remain silent. I open the front door without waking them, lace up my boots on the porch steps, button my jacket, and throw the hood over my head. The night air's thick with a fog so warm I don't even shiver, I just grope between the dark houses until my fingers touch the wet stone walls of the schoolhouse, allowing me to find my way home. There's no light anywhere.

Something's wrong when I enter the house but I can't tell what it is until I light the oil lamp and see a figure rise from the shadows. My first thought is simple regret for leaving the warmth of my lover only to meet the darkness inside my living room. It lifts its arms into the air, the shadow-man from my nightmares. All I can do now is hurl the lamp and set everything aflame. I wind up my arms but the shadow speaks, it waves frantically, it jumps forward into the light.

"What are you doing?" Paola shrieks. "It's me! It's me. I'm sorry, I—"

"What are *you* doing here? What in the hell—"

My hands tremble as I put the lamp down on my desk.

"What are you doing back so late?" she asks. "I was waiting for you, but—"

"Did you read it?"

Everything grows still, even the dust in the air. My history notebook's open to the first blank page. She doesn't need to answer. My fists clench beyond my control, the walls bulge like lungs, and my ears fill with static electricity pulled from the depths of the earth. I could explode right now, but instead I let it go. Tears overflow Paola's eyes when I shut my notebook and clutch it to my chest. There's pain in her gaze, stronger than my anger, and I feel the tension melt beneath waves of light.

"It doesn't explain anything!" she cries. "I read all of it and there's nothing! Nothing!"

"What were you looking for? And what do you mean there's *nothing?*"

"The Dream! What is it?"

Paola keeps talking but I don't listen. I toss my notebook upstairs and cut her off with the sound of fluttering pages. Trying to be calm, I sit her down on the couch and ask her to explain what she read. I get a strong fire going as my family history flows off her tongue in a flat tone drained of all its charge. Paola only cares about the Dream, nothing else seems to interest her, so when the flames are roaring I sit beside her and explain. I tell her the Dream was the last weapon of the Kashaya, a final summoning of their power, a merging of the underworld with this world. I tell her about the *Yihetuan* rebels in China, the Boxers who believed they were invincible from gunfire and charged into battle without hesitation or fear. Their blurring of the underworld with this world made them capable of great acts, just like the Ghost Dance allowed the Lakota-Sioux to stand tall during their final battle at Wounded Knee. When darkness encircled the Kashaya, four Dreamers appeared in the tribe who revived the old Dream Dance, a ceremony where circles of women spun around a central pole and opened a tear into the underworld. The power of this subterranean force kept them safe through the darkness until the first electromagnetic transmission crossed the ocean from California to Siberia.

"What happened after that?" Paola asks.

"They kept dancing. At first. But then Essie stopped entering the Dream. So did the other three. They woke up one morning and the Dream was outside their door. It wasn't telling them secrets at night anymore, it was spreading through the tribe. The Dream held onto this land like a wet sheet after that, only it got bigger every year. Now it's spreading inland to Santa Rosa, like Essie told us."

"No one can stop it?"

"It doesn't seem that way."

"Maybe it's going back where it came from. I don't know—" She covers her red eyes with weary hands and sinks into the cushions. "My parents were indigenous but I never knew them. Their parents were all slaves, you know. I could have tried to reconnect, my *vovó* remembered the old ways, but I just left. Like you. Only now I'm here and the Dream's so close and...anyway, you and Gertrude are together now. Right?"

I nod my head and look out the window. Dawn's almost here after all that talking.

"Why aren't you up there with the others?" I ask. "Building the radio-station?"

"Because I couldn't stop thinking about it, no matter what I did. So now—"

"Let's go!" I get up from the couch and throw another log in the stove. "I'll take you there right now. Just do me a favor and pack us some breakfast. And make tea. Can you make—"

"Take me where? Into—"

"Yes! Into the Dream. You'll be fine."

"But I don't—"

"I'm going to get a horse right now and the tea better be ready when I get back."

I sprint away without closing the front door and if I run fast enough no one will see me sneak off with my favorite horse. Gudrun's hair is still blacker than night when I find her waiting inside the communal house barn. She doesn't betray our escape, not even when I put on these horrible reins. I know she remembers me, I see it in those big black eyes, no matter how long it's been.

We trot over to my house, I tie her to the banister, then give her another pat before going inside. Paola's busy packing our food so I drink the tea she made and try not to think about Angelo. It doesn't work. I see him riding Gudrun, curly hair flying every direction, that beautiful orphan boy I could never take my eyes off of. Paola doesn't speak to me, doesn't look at me, but at least her tears are gone. Once my tea cup's empty, I dig my thick desert blankets out of the closet and go outside to drape them over Gudrun's back. She looks at me knowingly, like she can hear my thoughts, and I tell her we'll see Angelo soon enough. Maybe it'll be like the good old days. Just the three of us.

"What are you saying to her?" Paola asks, a bag of food swinging in her hand.

"Nothing. I've just known her since I was young. We were talking about old times."

"I'm ready to go if you...you really think I should do this?"

"Paola, I pulled you out of the Dream. Remember? Since then you haven't stopped talking about it, and I can tell you right now, this is what you need. If you're indigenous to this half of the world, if you...look, once you're inside—" I stare into her brown eyes and try to be forceful. "Remember your parents. Remember your grandmother. You'll be fine. So let's go, huh? I don't want anyone to see us."

I run inside to throw some dishwater into the stove and make sure my house doesn't burn down. This isn't what I wanted for today but I can't think about that right now. I hop onto Gudrun's back in an awkward leap, take the reins once I'm steady, and before I realize what's going on, Paola vaults over Gudrun's rump. She wraps her arms around my belly and kisses my neck so sweetly that I get Gudrun moving before people wake up and see. We walk slowly around the edge of the village and head north towards the Kashaya trail. Paola holds me tight, kisses me without pause, and just as she's about to utter some romantic delusion, I tell her to hold on before I set Gudrun into a sprint along the Gualala River.

This is dangerous and stupid but Paola's screaming in joy and I can't help the exhilaration. Wet soil churns under Gudrun's hooves, wind-tears escape my eyes, and the sun burns off the morning dew, filling the air with the sweet scent of redwood. Gudrun's black mane grazes my hands and I can tell she's enjoying every flex of her rippling muscles. I haven't ridden her since I left for San Francisco. I stayed away from horses and tried to forget all about Angelo taking me off into the hills. Gudrun wasn't two years-old when we rode on her back to watch the sunset or make love in the grass. Now she's sixteen but I can't tell the difference, especially now that we're sprinting. Being a farmhorse clearly doesn't agree with her. She tilts her head towards me, concern glimmering in her black eye. It takes me a minute, but I pull back the reins before it's too late.

The trunk of a fallen redwood tree sits imposingly across the road, knocked over by the recent storm. We hop off Gudrun's back, help her through the curtain of vertical branches, and take her to the river where she can eat grass and drink water. Paola unpacks our human breakfast: a jar of apple butter, half a loaf of bread, and a piece of cheese. The river babble trickles into my ears as I sit down with my food atop a smooth boulder. Paola doesn't eat much. She picks at some cheese while I gorge myself with fingers-full of apple butter. Gudrun munches away on the grass, her long black tail wagging, and then a stream of green shit suddenly flies out her ass. Paola doesn't notice.

"Has anyone tried to measure the Dream?" she asks. "Like a scientist or something?"

"*Scientist*," I scoff. "Yeah, there were a few. Five, exactly. Three went in at the same time but they all starved to death in a hut. The other two walked to opposite ends of the Dream but one drowned and the other jumped off a cliff. Since then...scientists don't go there. We're lucky, in a way."

"Lucky? They died! Why did it kill them? Why did it—"

"It didn't kill them, Paola. They killed themselves. We're lucky because... if the scientists were going to live through the Dream, they wouldn't be scientists when they woke up. There's no way to measure it, so they just leave it alone, they pretend it doesn't exist. Being a scientist is what killed them, because the Dream can't be...it doesn't...I can't make it make sense."

"I should have done this when I first got here," she sighs, eating a little more of her cheese. "It feels like a rite of passage I missed out on. Like I'm still a little baby."

"I know how you feel, trust me. Everyone treats me like a baby."

"Your mom and Yvonne might treat you like that, but not anyone else. I mean...how did they hide all this from you? Your history? Where you came from? That's what I don't get. You're the only one who even makes a shred of sense around here. At least *you* want to tell people the truth instead of hiding it behind a bunch of gibberish and old books like Yvonne."

"It's isn't gibberish," I tell her, grabbing the cheese she hasn't finished. "Maybe you're just not hearing the words. Maybe you can't understand yet.

We're not crazy, you know. Yvonne, Isabelle, me. None of us are crazy. That stuff of mine you read, it's true. The tubes, the water, the light, the war, the darkness, everything. You think it'd be easy to fill our places, carry *that* weight on your shoulders?"

Paola snatches the apple butter away from me and eats a big scoop with two fingers. Her vision melts into the flowing Gualala River, charged to the point of bursting, and I hardly recognize this water from the shallows we saw this summer. Paola won't eat the last hunk of bread, no matter how much I insist, so I finish it off with a heap of apple butter, let out a loud belch, then get up from the boulder. Gudrun's still drinking river water, her black hooves planted in the current, and once she's finished we climb atop her back. She trots us forward in excitement, shaking her head every other step.

"Can I ask you something?" Paola says, quietly.

I don't respond. I know she's going to speak anyway.

"Your ancestor Mauritius...did the darkness enslave us because of him? People with black skin, brown skin. Did the darkness want revenge against us, because of what he did?"

My heart becomes my entire body, and it pounds. She's already seeing more than I am.

"It's possible," I eventually say. "Makes sense, at least."

"I'm glad it's almost over, this war. I can't wait to wake up."

When we pass the red graffito that spells out **DREAMTIME**, Paola lays her cheek against my shoulder and begins to weep. We're close. Gudrun's metal shoes clatter across the wooden bridge as we cross the Gualala River on our approach *Atcacinatcawalli, the place where a human head sits*. Two women in black dresses wave to us from the side of the road, their kind faces covered in tattooed lines. Teenagers run to the bluffs and old men stagger to their doors, all eager to glimpse the latest Dreamers. The men are with the children near the houses while all the women are congregated around the fire pits, surrounded by baskets of cold water and brown acorn meal. They squat low to the earth and move hot rocks from the fiery coals into baskets of acorn mush, cooking off the water. Over two dozen women are finishing this daily preparation when I see Essie rise from their midst in a long red dress.

"You still with me, Paola?" I ask.

"I'm with you. But I'm sleepy."

"We're here. Don't worry."

I help her off Gudrun's back as children swarm around us from every direction. They take Paola's hand, guide her into the redwoods with their frantic laughter, and I watch her vanish into a thick expanse of green ferns. That's when Essie arrives at my side with her large hands stained white from acorn flour. She hands me a purple muscle shell filled with fresh acorn paste, just like when I was a girl. By the time I've chewed it down, Paola's already disappeared into the forest.

"I've got a good feeling about her," Essie tells me. "But you can't keep doing this."

"Doing what? She wanted to come here."

"You can't keep bringing pieces of your darkness here. It's still hiding inside you, girl. Time to get it out already. I got it out of Angelo, now we got to get it out of his girlfriend here, and now you gotta get the damn thing done, Fulvia. What are you waiting for? Here, give me that."

She takes the empty muscle shell from my fingers, walks me to the fire pits, and tells me to sit down and shut up. I watch milky gray liquid slosh around in ornate baskets woven so tight not a single drop of water leaks through, not even when it boils. Each of these baskets is adorned with diamond, wave, or triangle patterns distilled from visions that flow through the Dream. Essie was one of the few who could weave these designs until the first planetary electromagnetic transmission sent a crack of perfect thunder across the sky. Now every woman in the village can weave the Dream into their water-tight baskets and they wake each morning with new patterns emanating from their fingertips. None of these Kashaya women look in my direction, not even when Essie walks me back to Gudrun and boosts me up to the saddle. Her acorn covered hands run across the black mane, staining it white with acorn meal, and in her native tongue, Essie tells me to finish what my people started all those years ago. She tells me to burn away the darkness under the light of a thousand stars.

18

THE GREAT CONSPIRACY OF THE AGES

DURING THE WINTER OF 1902, JOSEPHINE BECAME A MAN AGAIN, THE infamous *Yee Toy* who haunted the alleyways of the Barbary Coast. No one really knows what happened during those frantic evenings, but it's fair to assume many vile men discovered a quick death at the end of my grandmother's blade. She finished these long patrols at the summit of Telegraph Hill, waiting until the sun rose over Mount Diablo and Marisol de la Costa arrived from her brothel. They sat on a boulder and discussed their sordid evenings over the length of a single cigarette, sparing no details. Josephine allowed Marisol this much time and no longer, for their business

Greenwich St., Telegraph Hill, 1902

was dirty and unpleasant to discuss. Not even Isabelle wanted to know what happened in the Barbary Coast after midnight. She never asked.

My mother lived a silent life after the Great Waterfront Strike and scarcely saw Josephine or Marisol despite living in the same house. She turned the unused pantry into her bedroom and donned her gray work-dress every morning before the cable-car ride to Pacific Heights. Her hours in Yvonne's library grew longer that winter and she devoured dozens of books by the roaring fireplace. One morning, as they were skimming the morning papers, Isabelle went numb when she read of the beheading of David Fagen, the *Buffalo Soldier* who defected to the indigenous of the Philippine Isles. According to the article, a Tagalog bounty-hunter had tracked David to an Aeta village on Luzon Island where he allegedly ambushed and decapitated him. One perusal of this article was enough to convince Isabelle that this beheading was as false as the crucifixion of Mauritius.

From the day he defected in 1899, David Fagen became a *cunning and highly skilled guerrilla officer who harassed and evaded large conventional American units.* He staged numerous ambushes and raids, the most famous of which occurred on the Pampanga River where David and his guerrilla fighters hijacked a US steamer loaded with weapons and then vanished into the jungle. He remained at large through 1901, outlasting even Emilio Aguinaldo, commander of the Philippine Insurgency and President of the crushed Republic. While the Great Waterfront Strike had failed to turn the tide in the Philippine Isles, my mother took comfort knowing that David Fagen was still waiting in the mountains of Luzon, deep in Aeta territory where the Spanish and US forces were never able to conquer. Fagen was a modern day Mauritius, a defector from the current Empire, and by the winter of 1902, Isabelle was still joyfully reading of sporadic ambushes taking place across Luzon Island. According to my mother, he still lives there to this day, surrounded by two dozen grandchildren.

Isabelle didn't just read of the war that winter. Within the warm library, Isabelle was introduced to the works of Nikola Tesla and learned what JP Morgan had just done to this brave inventor. Shortly after the strike ended, Yvonne asked her husband to take another look at Tesla's devices, imploring him to invest in this emergent technology. Rather than dismiss Tesla as he usually did, Heath announced that JP Morgan had already given Tesla $150,000 to build a wireless communication system, the prototype of our electromagnetic transmission towers. The funding was discretely awarded in March 1901 and Tesla had just finished the plans for his Wardenclyffe magnifying transmitter in New Jersey when something unexpected occurred: the Italian scientist Guglielmo Marconi sent a wireless telegraph signal across the Atlantic.

Using a spark-gap Tesla transmitter grounded in the earth, this underling of JP Morgan made the undersea telegraph cable irrelevant by sending what became known as a radio signal in December 1901. Tesla already knew that radio waves existed, although he was determined to access higher levels of the earth's sphere and failed to appreciate this discovery, allowing Marconi to usurp his design. JP Morgan cut off Tesla's funding and left him nearly bankrupt as the Wall Street investment capital flowed to Marconi. It was in the winter of 1902 that Heath smugly relayed this to Yvonne, proud of destroying Nikola Tesla at the height of his glory. Without funding, the half-finished magnifying transmitter stood silent along New Jersey's shoreline.

In the comfort of Yvonne's library, my mother studied the patents created by Nikola Tesla and read of his experiments in Colorado Springs where he illuminated light-bulbs plugged directly into the soil. Isabelle understood that if the theories of Nikola Tesla were to ever be realized, the boundless energy of the planet would be freely available without measure or price. In stark contrast to this vision were the works of Thomas Edison, long-time associate of JP Morgan who'd created a swift telegraphic stock-ticker, an electric execution-chair, and the now familiar wooden Kinetoscope that displayed moving-pictures of naked women in the peep-shows on Market Street. For the price of a cable-car ride, idle men could bend over a glowing box and gaze at the shifting flesh of disembodied women. Isabelle never cared for these establishments, nor did she attend exhibitions of Edison's Projecting Kinetoscope that illuminated entire walls with moving-pictures. These illusions were just cheap versions of Barbary Coast dance-halls, though the connection between Edison's film company and JP Morgan left Isabelle unsettled. One of Edison's latest productions had been entitled *Execution of Czolgosz with Panorama of Auburn Prison*, a dramatic reenactment of the anarchist's death.

Once it was intuited by Georges Seurat in his 1891 painting *Le Cirque*, the projected motion-picture was achieved in Paris on March 22, 1895 by the Lumiere Brothers' flame-lit, water-stabilized magic-lantern. Upon the accomplishment of this great feat, Edison and the other capitalists swooped in to electrify the flame-lit device and monopolize its commercial applications, using a mass-death as their marketing tool. On May 4, 1897, the annual *Bazar de la Charité* in Paris fell victim to a fire that spread from a burning Lumiere projector,

Wardenclyffe Tower

resulting in the death of almost two hundred aristocrats, the vast majority women. According to the newspaper reports, the bourgeoise men trampled the women as they crammed toward the Bazar's single exit. Once the fire source was traced to the Lumiere machine, Edison's electric projectors rose in popularity.

During the rainy winter of 1902, Yvonne and Isabelle spoke of these matters in the library and resolved to stop the darkness from spreading through this cinematic medium. They planned a retreat at the *Rancho del Valle* and decided to invite several people with access to San Francisco high-society, enabling them to gather intelligence on the enemy instead of groping aimlessly in the dark. Isabelle mentioned her acquaintance with Frank Norris and Jeanette Black and agreed to find the couple at *Luna's Mexican Restaurant*. The now famous Jack London was included in their plan and Yvonne naturally wanted Eamonn to come. Since their outing to the Mission District in the fall of 1901, Yvonne and Eamonn had lived in vastly different worlds, one far more dangerous than the other.

After the collapse of the Great Waterfront Strike, Doctor O'Shea was roused by Isabelle one morning and taken to the house of Doctor Rose Fritz, a cozy place across from the Panhandle where framed portraits of Bakunin and Kropotkin hung on the walls alongside bunches of garlic and drying herbs. Rose was their local anarchist doctor, though she lacked an official license and practiced her profession illegally. Rose had studied medicine in Kiev until the 1881 assassination of Czar Alexander II triggered three days of deadly pogroms that spread into the countryside. Dozens of Jews were killed by the mob and hundreds wounded in the raping, pillaging, and arson that engulfed Ukraine. Although the Czar's assassins were atheist nihilists, the Russian Empire encouraged the false belief that Jews were responsible, allowing the pogrom to spread. Rose escaped Kiev by following the Dnieper River to Odessa where she met Abraham and Mary Isaak. This revolutionary couple secured her safe passage to Lisbon where Rose mysteriously acquired a fortune that allowed her to reach San Francisco in 1885.

During their meeting, Rose enlisted Eamonn in an effort to thwart the capitalist plague-deniers and prevent another outbreak in Chinatown. After the waterfront strike, the bosses wouldn't stand for a federal quarantine of their harbor and had doubled their efforts to obscure the Black Death still lurking downtown. The two doctors began their independent inspections the next morning, using Eamonn's neighborhood clout to access the buildings of Chinatown. While they conducted these house-calls, a bloody war broke out between rival *tongs* over a slave-girl's stolen bracelet, culminating in an operatic street-battle that was used by the local press to justify the renewal of the Chinese Exclusion Act. With the Boxer Rebellion recently crushed, fear of a

Chinese menace was still ripe in the public imagination when President Theodore Roosevelt made the Chinese Exclusion Act permanent in 1902. He wasn't the only politician wreaking havoc on San Francisco.

Faced with the defeat of their Great Waterfront Strike, nearly every union in the City Front Federation threw their voting power behind the newly formed Union Labor Party. On November 5, 1901, this party's mayoral candidate, a musician named Eugene Schmitz was elected to office. He was sworn in on January 8, 1902, promising to outlaw scabs, private detectives, and reign in the local police. Schmitz was the front-

Abraham Ruef

man for Abraham Ruef, a former Republican Party power-broker who'd make any deal for the right price. *Graft* became the word of the day in this pro-union City Hall.

On March 25, 1902, Ruef and Schmitz barged into the offices of the Health Department to announce San Francisco was free from plague and that the entire Board of Health was to be replaced for conspiring to damage the local economy. It was clear to Rose and Eamonn what this Union Labor Party truly stood for, though the anarchist doctors had already made significant progress with their own prevention efforts. During the first four months of 1902, no had one died of the plague in Chinatown or the Latin Quarter. It was under these ideal conditions that Eamonn crossed the bay in early April to meet his lover for their spring retreat. Before arriving at the *Rancho del Valle*, Eamonn was instructed to meet Yvonne at the Piedmont bungalow of Jack London. Isabelle and Frank Norris would meet them at the *rancho* later, although Jeanette Black-Norris had just given birth to her first daughter in New York and wouldn't be joining.

Eamonn stepped off the ferry and rode the Oakland cable-car until he'd reached the foothills of Piedmont, an isolated community of artists and robber barons. Over the past year, Jack dropped out of sight and retreated into his relentless writing, living comfortably in this hilltop sanctuary with

Jack London't Piedmont bungalow.

his wife Bessie, his mother Flora, his infant daughter Joan, his childhood wet-nurse Jenny, and a variety of relatives and friends who constantly cycled through his rooms. After failing to become Oakland mayor on the socialist ticket in March 1901, Jack left political circles in favor of a more artistic crowd and frequented Coppa's Cafe in San Francisco with local bohemians, but only when his family didn't need him around. He read his tales to packed Stanford lecture halls, saw the publication of his two short-story collections, wrote boilerplate articles for Hearst's *Examiner,* collaborated on an epistolary book with Anna Strunsky, and was busy on his first full-length novel, *A Daughter of the Snows.* This text had just been accepted for publication when Eamonn O'Shea appeared in the orange poppy fields around his Piedmont bungalow, looking every bit the bohemian tramp fresh off the rails. Yvonne arrived the next day with Juana, dressed as a peasant.

Jack London gave the lovers fake names and introduced them to his family as reunited *gypsies* from outside Portland. Yvonne wore cosmetic eye-glasses and kept her hair parted down the middle to avoid recognition. She helped make lunch with Jenny Prentiss, the black woman who had breast-fed Jack when he was a little baby. Jenny had been born a slave on a plantation in Virginia and her parents were sold off within months of her birth. She ended up on another plantation in Tennessee where she became the personal servant of the master's daughter, a position that allowed her to learn to read, write, and understand both mathematics and science. In 1864, the Union Army swept into the region on their march towards Nashville and eventually surrounded the Confederate plantation. Jenny was shaken from sleep by the master's daughter and told they needed to run. Just as they entered the northern woods, dressed in pajamas and wearing winter coats, the Union soldiers opened fire from the south. Everyone on the plantation was massacred that night, both white and black.

Jenny followed her former-master's daughter northward to Saint Louis where they knocked on the door of the master's extended family. After taking one look at Jenny, these relatives told her she'd have to find lodging elsewhere, so Jenny ended up working as a domestic servant in the city center. She returned to the Nashville area and eventually married a man named Alonzo Prentiss who she had two children with. This family of four moved to San Francisco in the 1870s and it was here that Jenny met Flora London, a spiritualist medium who lived next door. Jenny experienced a miscarriage in 1876, a traumatic experience that left her lost in sadness, especially when she heard her neighbor Flora's newborn Jack screaming his first breaths. By some odd chance of fate, Flora was unable to produce any milk, allowing Jenny the opportunity to become Jack's wet-nurse and assuage some of her boundless grief. It was Jenny who gave Jack the money to buy his first boat and become an oyster pirate, just as she still nurtured all his rebellious plans, including this latest conspiracy. Jenny and her family had lived near the Londons for almost three decades and she knew the famous writer better than anyone, even himself. While this wouldn't make sense until later that night, Jenny told Yvonne that *Jack can hide some things from his skin-folk, but he can't hide nothing from this kin-folk.*

After they prepared lunch and enjoyed it outside with all the others, Yvonne got to know Jack's wife Bessie Maddern, a photography enthusiast and former university tutor who now complained of her husband's endless parade of visitors that stunk up the place with alcohol and tobacco. Bessie spoke of the novel Jack was writing with Anna Strunsky and seemed quite proud of him, for it wasn't every day a man encouraged a woman to write. She herself had been a student and tutored Jack in mathematics just before his entrance examinations to UC Berkeley, although those days seemed like ancient history. The only passion Bessie still pursued was photography and she taught Jack everything she knew about composing and developing photographic images. As she told Yvonne, motherhood had consumed everything else, especially the time to study. After Bessie went to bed, Yvonne and Eamonn found Jack crouched over a campfire, waiting to discuss their future plans. Unlike the *gypsy* lovers, Jack shared none of their conspiracy with Bessie.

Everyone had breakfast inside the bungalow before seeing off Yvonne and Juana on their journey back to Oakland. Once they were downtown, they boarded a private stage-coach booked for the *Rancho del Valle* and ascended the winding Telegraph Road over 1,300 feet into the coastal hills. The coachman stopped at the gray Summit House to water the horses while Yvonne and Juana visited the Rook family, owners of this fading establishment who complained bitterly of the new wagon tunnel that would put them out of business once it opened next year. Before she left, Yvonne assured the Rooks they could always rely on her support for anything, especially business, but as she descended towards the *Arroyo San Pablo*, her mind quickly became consumed by sadness. Once the tunnel was finished, endless wagons would clog her emerald valleys and flood the roads with commerce, bringing darkness closer to the *Rancho del Valle*.

Her stage-coach stopped at the bottom of the hill at the Last Chance Saloon where Yvonne took Juana inside to meet her old friend Ella Olive Moraga. Evicted from her family's adobe in 1886, Ella now ran the saloon kitchen while her husband Gabriel Moraga roped horses as a *vaquero* beneath the slopes of Mount Diablo. Ella marveled at young Juana, fed her everything within reach, and showered Yvonne with local gossip before sending them off with a cherry-preserve pie for Camille del Valle.

As the stage-coach completed its final stretch, Yvonne's sole hope came from the desolate train station near Mayor Bryant's house. After collapsing each winter from fierce mudslides, the railroad line to Oakland was finally abandoned in 1895 during the financial depression, most of it never built. All

Summit House

the speculators went bankrupt and Yvonne drove past their idle plots of land, still vacant beneath the oaks trees of the *Rancho del Valle*.

Camille was waiting on the porch of the old adobe when their stage-coach crested the hill and she ran to embrace little Juana, having never seen her before. It was Yvonne's first homecoming in over four years and she wept deeply into Camille's shoulder. They slept that warm night together within earthen walls as their unseen guardians watched them through the old window glass.

Isabelle hiked through the woods the next day accompanied by Jack London and Frank Norris. It was the first time my mother had ever left San Francisco, saw a fern covered hillside, touched the thick bark of a redwood tree, or smelled a forest of bay leaves. Camille ushered the hikers into the kitchen when they arrived, sweaty after their six-hour journey from Oakland. According to Isabelle, the two authors argued about race during the entire hike, with Jack claiming that certain racial groups have certain advantages, while Frank insisted race was just an illusion created by conquerors. Isabelle was quick to attack both authors for promoting racist stereotypes in order to sell more books, and this fiery argument was what Eamonn walked into after his long journey from Piedmont.

Unlike the others, Eamonn had crossed back over to San Francisco for a last minute meeting with Doctor Rose Fritz. Unable to hide her annoyance, Rose assured him that no one had died of the plague and that he should go enjoy his vacation before something swooped in and ruined the chance. He hurried back to the Ferry Building, caught the boat bound for Oakland's Broadway Wharf, and then began walking towards the farm town of Fruite Vale nestled along the *Arroyo Sausal* that flowed from deep within the redwood mountains. It was night when he arrived, so the tired doctor paid for a night at a local hotel and then began his long hike the next morning. He followed the *Arroyo* until he found its source near the mountain summit, made his descent into a series of three valleys, and arrived at the *Rancho del Valle* just as Jack and Frank were arguing with Isabelle about racism.

Camille mostly listened as these five rebels sorted out their differences over days of swimming in the *Arroyo San Pablo*, hiking through the bay tree forests, cooking over the adobe stove, and long discussions beside the fireplace. Yvonne and Eamonn made love every night while Juana slept soundly with her grandmother. Jack and Frank shared a canvas tent where they stayed up late talking about the latest newspaper items, hoping to cannibalize them for short stories. As they discussed these literary theories and practices, Isabelle snoozed happily by the fireplace on her bed roll, always rising before the others. In the morning they'd all make breakfast together and further elaborate their strategy against the tyrants of San Francisco. Camille was happy to listen.

During one of these discussions, Frank brought up his membership in the Bohemian Club, an organization that now cleaved between its capitalist and bohemian factions. Lionel Heath was also a member and led the charge against the liberals who tolerated the presence of William Randolph Heart, a much-despised member. The recent waterfront strike had further divided the Club, pitting every free-thinking bohemian against the brandy-drinking capitalists. Frank was finally able to confirm that the Employer's Association was backed by none other than Lionel Heath, whose insistence on brutal anti-union measures had isolated him from the local capitalists, men who wanted to preserve the old order and pay their workers a fair wage. With his own eyes, Frank had also seen Heath travel in his Daimler automobile between the Bohemian Clubhouse and the Palace Hotel, often vanishing from the city for weeks, and these details were a revelation, especially to Yvonne. For the first time, the conspirators finally understood the movements of their enemy.

Jack listened to Frank with silent envy, having grown up without the privileges of this famous author. While upper-crust newsmen from the *Examiner* were allowed to be members of the Bohemian Club, Jack was depicted by rival papers as Hearst's naive protégé living off bread-crumbs and writing boilerplate articles to-order. During this retreat, Jack resolved to acquire the same literary stardom as Frank, by any means necessary, and access these hallways of power where financial titans plotted against the public. My mother could see a naive glimmer in his blue eyes so she quickly challenged Jack on his racist caricatures. Jack defended himself by saying it was a commercial tactic to sell books, a tactic Frank had used with *The Octopus* and *McTeauge*. In his own defense, Frank claimed his latest book, *The Pit*, didn't have a single racist stereotype and suggested Jack remove his own once fame had been achieved. This casual remark threw Isabelle into a fury and she would've struck both of them if Eamonn hadn't restrained her. Frank and Jack didn't talk to anyone for the rest of the evening and their terrible decisions haunted them long past midnight. Unknown to them all, the main character of Jack's upcoming novel, *A Daughter of the Snows*, was a racist perversion of Anna Strunsky, rendered Anglo-Saxon rather than Jewish. As for Frank Norris, his own bigoted words would tarnish him forever.

Shortly before they departed the *Rancho del Valle*, Yvonne and Isabelle walked into the woods to discuss the past two weeks. They were now well positioned to monitor the San Francisco capitalists, although their comrade Jack was highly unstable. During her stay in Piedmont, Yvonne had learned that Bessie knew nothing of Jack's romance with Anna Strunsky, nor did she know of their conspiracy, and none of this inspired trust as they paced beneath oak trees searching for a solution. Before they found it, the air between the trunks grew silent, the wind refused to blow, and all the leaves stopped twitching as a gray coyote emerged from behind a knot of laurel. It gazed at them with yellow eyes before stalking away between two dark-haired women. Black lines were tattooed across their faces. One was older than the other. Before anyone could speak, a piercing light filled the lush forest and transported Yvonne and Isabelle down the hill to the *Arroyo San Pablo* where they found themselves drenched in lavender salt-water, having no clear memory of what had just happened. Neither could speak from the shock of such an inexplicable event and they walked back to the adobe covered in wet patches of dust. When they got back home, Yvonne claimed they'd both fallen into the river, a lie only Camille could begin to suspect.

My mother hiked out of the *Rancho del Valle* with Frank, Jack, and Eamonn. She climbed to the peaks of the Coastal Range before descending into the town of Fruit Vale for her train ride to the ferry. Unlike the others, Yvonne crossed the bay in a private yacht owned by her husband, having no choice, and Heath was waiting beside his Daimler when she docked. He accompanied her up to Pacific Heights and during this unbearable drive together, Heath showered Juana with an unusual affection. Out of some buried paternal instinct, Heath declared that Juana del Valle-Heath would not only receive the finest education in the world, she'd be treated no different than a son. Heath complained of the rigid men stuck in the previous century with its stuffy mores and arcane traditions. Yvonne nodded her head and spoke a few words of approval before carrying Juana off for a bath. Heath was gone when they emerged, his Daimler already descending towards the Palace Hotel and his secret mistress. There was no clear explanation for his sudden paternalism.

When my mother returned to San Francisco, she discovered her brother Federico had quit his job on the waterfront and gotten hired as a ticket-man for the United Railroads Company, hoping to trigger a cable-car strike. Sergio refused to speak with Federico for abandoning their father's project, although this mood didn't last for long. In less than two weeks, Federico rose to prominence among the street-car men and agitated for an immediate wildcat strike against the Wall Street owners of the local railroad. On April 19, 1902, his union paralyzed the rail net-work and triggered a strike of the entire workforce. When the company hired strike-breaking mercenaries from the Curtin Detective Agency, Mayor Eugene Schmitz refused to grant them weapon permits or allow the use of city police. With two signatures of his pen, this mayor of the Union Labor Party usurped the role of the anarchist defense groups by making strike-breaking illegal. When my mother went to bed on April 26, 1902, the owner of the United Railroads had just accepted the union's demands for a ten-hour day at $2.50 an hour. The strike was definitively over the next morning when she rode the cable-car to Pacific

Heights with her fellow laundresses, all of them still animated from their luxurious paid vacation. None of them would ever suspect that Isabelle had vacationed on the *Rancho del Valle*.

While my mother washed laundry in the morning and read in the library during the afternoon, the local anarchists were organizing every trade in the city, no matter how small. Following advice that Yvonne had given to Isabelle, the anarchist *grupo* sent several of their comrades across the bay to the new Standard Oil refinery at Point Richmond. This facility was owned by John D. Rockefeller with the adjacent land recently purchased by JP Morgan as a terminus for his Great Northern Railroad. Yvonne learned of this one evening when Heath stopped in for dinner and boasted loudly of Morgan's purchase, claiming it would force Rockefeller to utilize his train lines. Yvonne watched her husband's eyes light up as he explained Rockefeller's stubborn intention to build a pipeline between his oil fields in the San Joaquin Valley and the refinery at Point Richmond, a venture that would bypass their railroads entirely. In the middle of this near-erotic description of Rockefeller's pipeline, Yvonne informed her husband that she'd received an invitation to join a Citizens Committee charged with selecting the statue for a column in Union Square to honor Admiral Dewey, commander of the US Navy during the war in the Philippines. Yvonne asked Heath if he'd join her on this committee and the baron happily agreed, given this was the first time his wife had invited him to do anything. Heath suspected nothing of her plans.

The following week, without her husband's knowledge, Yvonne hired a private union carriage-driver to deliver her and Juana down the hill to the marshlands west of the fisherman's marina, a place known locally as Washerwoman's Lagoon. Yvonne arrived in front of a house that doubled as bakery and laundry shop, its chimney billowing coal smoke. With the help of Isabelle, Yvonne knew this to be the home of Alma de Bretteville, a model for one of the proposed Union Square statues and recent celebrity of the daily papers. Yvonne knocked on the door, waited patiently with Juana, and was quickly allowed inside by Alma's confused parents. A tall young woman waited inside near the stove, her dark hair braided and eyes lit up from excitement. For the next three hours, Yvonne listened to Alma speak while little Juana played on the carpet.

Alma had recently divorced from a degenerate gold-miner and become the beloved damsel-in-distress of the San Francisco daily papers with her face gracing thousands of news-sheets. Before these months of press exposure, Alma had struggled to attend the Mark Hopkins Art Institute and modeled naked for artists in order to pay the monthly tuition. Some of these naked depictions found their way onto the Cocktail Route, a strip of saloons near the Palace Hotel where rich men could marvel at the beauties of San

Francisco. Alma's curvy form caught the attention of local sculptor Robert Aitkin and within a week she was in his studio wearing only a thin robe. Her body was now fixed inside a metal sculpture waiting to be judged by San Francisco high-society. If her figure was deemed the most beautiful, Aitkin's statue would grace the Union Square column.

Towards the end of their conversation, Alma admitted her long obsession with the del Valle family history. Legends and myths swarmed around Yvonne, printed weekly in the society columns and fueled by her uncompromising silence to the press. Flushed red from embarrassment, Alma said that Yvonne was her ultimate hero, the poor farm girl from the *rancho* who married a steel baron.

Alma de Bretteville

Unable to fathom how a total stranger could be so attached to her, Yvonne asked Alma to keep their meeting a secret from everybody, especially the daily papers. During the entirety of this conversation, Juana couldn't take her eyes off of tall Alma de Bretteville with her wide hips, dark hair, and deep laughter that filled the entire room.

Isabelle met with Yvonne in the library later that afternoon and was extremely dubious about this Alma de Bretteville, especially when she learned her statue would memorialize Admiral Dewey. According to Yvonne, facilitating Alma's entry into high-society would allow them a future ally, although Isabelle kept this plan a secret to everyone except Josephine, fearing the skepticism it would rightfully evoke. Instead of worry about this bizarre upper-class conspiracy, Isabelle wrote angry words at the *Secolo Nuovo* office and printed them off with Schwartz on the big machine. The pair worked steadily week after week with Schwartz becoming more confident in his writing, going so far as to compose the odd column or two in English. While my mother wrote about the Union Labor Party and its betrayal of the street-car strike, Schwartz wrote veiled letters to his mother asking her to give up this old world capitalism that diminished her soul. Anna Strunsky also contributed a few articles under a false name about the entitlement of *yanqui* men to the bodies of foreign women.

During one of these print sessions, Anna told Isabelle that Jack had invited her to the Piedmont bungalow to work on their novel only for him to propose marriage while Bessie was cooking in the kitchen. Anna accepted his offer at first but returned a few weeks later to refuse, insisting he commit to Bessie and their daughter Joan. Rather than obey her, Jack admitted the truth to Bessie, hoping to pressure Anna into accepting. Isabelle was relieved that Anna didn't succumb to this manipulation, although she wondered why Anna was still co-writing their *Kempton-Wace Letters*. This collaborative book was important to Anna for one reason: through its pages, she'd forever defeat Jack's racist conception of the world and its inhabitants.

In another confrontation between radicals and writers, Isabelle and Anna met with Jack London and Frank Norris in a basement booth of *Luna's Mexican Restaurant*. Neither author did much talking, though only Frank seemed to be listening. My mother explained that, while their comrade Eamonn was busy fighting the plague, Jack was meddling with Anna's heart, just as Frank had been busy buying land from Robert Louis Stevenson's widow. As she spoke, Jack wondered if Isabelle had gotten wind of his latest money-making scheme, a series of seven racist stories called *Tales of the Fish Patrol*, his most bigoted yet. He looked to Anna for confirmation, having mentioned these tales in their letters, but she maintained a poker-face for the entire meeting. Isabelle and Anna told the authors they should act in the best interests of others, not just their own. Almost eighty people had died from the plague and Isabelle reminded the writers that *yanqui* bosses were paying the *tongs* to kill any Chinese person who reported the disease to the federal authorities, leaving Eamonn and Rose Fritz as the only safe outside doctors willing to help Chinatown. After relaying this to Jack and Frank, my mother and Anna left the authors at the back of *Luna's,* filled to the brim with their own versions of shame.

Before he could act, Jack was called away on assignment by the American Press Association to cover the Bœr War in South Africa, freeing him from his amorous disaster. After stopping in New York City to meet his publishers at the Macmillan Company, Jack sailed to London where he learned his South African assignment had been canceled, leaving him time to serve others, not just himself. Two days before the royal coronation of King Edward VII, Jack dressed as a common worker and then lost himself in the dirty slums of Imperial London. Using the photographic skills gleaned from his wife Bessie, Jack captured the misery, drabness, and cruelty of the *human hell-hole called London Town*. After seven weeks in this abject poverty, he wrote an account of his experiences titled *The People of the Abyss* which describes a cannibal metropolis where, *year by year, and decade after decade, rural England pours in a flood of vigorous strong life, that not only does not renew*

People of the Abyss *by Jack London.*

itself, but perishes by the third generation. Between bouts of writing this sociological text, Jack penned feverish letters to Anna hoping to rekindle her love, though without success. In one of these letters, he claimed that *the Revolution looms large but the bourgeoisie will not see it. How I curse them sometimes these days when I see all this worse than useless misery. I think I understand anarchy better by far.* In her refusal to respond, Anna conducted the timeless forces roiling inside Jack London, helping him create a true masterpiece. Once it was finished, Jack departed on a journey to Europe where he'd meet with members of the anarchist Black International.

While this former pirate drank sweet liquor along the banks of the Seine River, his comrade Frank took my mother's command to an extreme degree. After his family had relocated from New York City to San Francisco, Frank and Jeanette strolled into the Bohemian Clubhouse for a drink in the Red Room, a serious affront in this exclusively male club. The first installment of his novel *The Pit* had just been printed in the *Saturday Evening Post* and Frank was in a rebellious mood, knowing his latest work would soon reveal the savage idiocy of capitalism to thousands of readers. As the couple leaned against the bar with a few *Examiner* journalists, Lionel Heath and his entourage walked past in a haze of cigar smoke. A loud argument soon broke out between the two factions, prompting Frank to stick his finger into Heath's face and scream: *You reptiles have stolen the world only to ruin it, incompetent fools! Now we'll take it from you!* Over half the bar erupted in applause and the elderly group of capitalists were chased from the clubhouse under a barrage of insults. Seething with humiliation, Lionel Heath arranged for Frank and Jeanette to be poisoned that same night.

Jeanette succumbed first, complaining of an intense pain near her kidneys, and she was taken to Doctor Eamonn O'Shea who recommended a swift removal of her appendix. Once this diseased organ was taken out and color returned to her face, Frank's own health began to rapidly decline. He refused to mention the pain until toxic fluids from his dying appendix contaminated his bloodstream. Eamonn was called to their apartment when Frank collapsed and helped Jeanette transport him to the hospital where his decaying organ was finally removed. Jeanette swore they were poisoned that night at the Bohemian Club and forced Eamonn to promise he'd never forget this. Despite the operation, too much toxicity had built within his blood stream. Frank hovered between the underworld for three days before passing away on October 25, 1902. My mother didn't take the news well. She hid in her room all night and Josephine could only comfort her with the story of Félix Fénéon. Finding little solace in this familiar tale, Isabelle arrived in the mansion library the next morning to reveal what Heath had done to Jeanette and Frank. Once she learned of their deaths, Yvonne let out such a terrifying scream that Juana began to cry and Isabelle covered her ears in fright. Isabelle was fifteen years old, Yvonne was thirty-one, and Juana only two. Their great conspiracy had claimed its first life, the wrong life, and nothing substantial had been accomplished. The remainder of that bitter fall passed away in sadness.

While my mother and Schwartz printed *Secolo Nuovo* one dreary afternoon, Yvonne rode with her husband and daughter to join the Citizens Committee in casting their votes for the winning statue. Yvonne strolled with Juana through the Palace Hotel and mingled with the various baron's wives who introduced her to Adolph Spreckels, chairman of the Citizens Committee, president of the Oceanic Steamship Company, and heir to the Spreckels sugar-cane fortune. While she discussed steam travel and cane plantations with this pompous man, Alma de Bretteville suddenly appeared at her side. Alma's deep laugh transfixed the rotund little Spreckels who she towered over in every respect. Once she'd been forgotten, Yvonne left them alone to their conversation and began to circle the six statues in the center of the room, all covered in red drapes. The unveiling began once the crowd was assembled and Yvonne watched the beady eyes of Adolph Spreckels light up as Alma's nearly-naked form emerged from beneath the fabric. With just a thin metal robe clinging to her large metal breasts, a helmeted Alma ascended towards the heavens with a trident in one hand and a laurel in the other. Lionel Heath gave the first speech in favor of this statue, followed by Adolph Spreckels, and the vote was nearly unanimous to install Alma's buxom form atop the monument.

Isabelle learned of this ceremony with indifference, unable to grasp why it mattered or where it would lead, especially now that Frank was dead. She and Yvonne mostly read in silence those cold fall afternoons, their hearts heavy, their minds numb. The only topic that shook them from paralysis was the creeping expansion of the Black Death. City Hall was still deny-ing the plague's existence while corrupt Mayor Schmitz toured the county supporting William Randolph Hearst's bid for a seat in the House of Representatives. In his fury at these rabid plague deniers, Eamonn became so dedicated to preventing another outbreak that Rose Fritz had to force him to eat and sleep. Checking each apartment for rodents was now his obsession and Isabelle watched the bags under Eamonn's eyes become darker each day. At the height of his unsustainable mania, Eamonn placed free rat-traps across Chinatown and then scoured the junk-shops to buy them back when they were stolen for opium money. He eventually collapsed on the street from exhaustion, forcing Rose to carry him to his office where he slept for almost two full days. Isabelle was waiting for him at the kitchen table when he woke up, a letter from Yvonne at her side. In elegant cursive, his lover promised they'd be together again next spring, beneath the oak trees, at the *Rancho del Valle*. Their great conspiracy had only just started.

SHE'LL LEAD US TO THE PORTALS

GERTRUDE DOESN'T WANT ME UP. EVERY MORNING THE SAME PANIC, the same fear of losing me. It's about to get worse. I still haven't told her where I'm going. If she were to know, her grip would only be tighter. I wait until Gertrude spins onto her side before I slip out into the cold. It's still too dark to see her, but I can imagine her dark curls and freckled chest rising with every breath. Climbing down from this loft without waking anyone has become my new pre-dawn ritual. I've never liked being held all night, it makes my body stiff and I sleep in horrible positions. Those first moments feel good, warmed up against her skin, face buried in her black hair, but after that it's a painful nightmare

The stairs creak, the floorboards groan, and I light the oil-lamp so I don't stumble into the ash-bin while putting on my clothes. Gertrude mutters but doesn't wake up, leaving me free to lace up my boots. She's snoring by the time I throw on my oilskin and blow out the lamp. Before leaving, I dig the letter out of my pocket and place it on the kitchen table for Gertrude to read. This way she'll know I'm safe, that nothing's wrong, that I'm coming back for good, that I'll always love her.

The main road through the village is so muddy I sink down to my ankles, each step requiring double the effort. I follow this dark road towards the communal house and go straight into the barn, groping along the stone walls until I find my saddle-bags buried in the hay along with a two-person saddle I borrowed from the vintner's stables. I carry this gear down to the fourth stall and open the gate in near-total blindness. Only the faint light of the shrouded moon allows me to glimpse black-haired Gudrun. I kiss her long nose, comb my fingers through her black mane, get the leather saddle over her back, and tie my bags on either side. Without wasting any time, I walk her out of the stall, close up the barn, hop on the saddle, and trot us south-ward towards Lorraine's orchard. No one sees us pass, none of the windows reveal any light, but I'm sure someone can hear these hoof-beats. Maybe their dreams are filled with horses as the last hour of night rains down her thick, dark sleep.

I've been planning this since Essie told me *finish what your people started*, though I still don't know what she meant. I've talked with Yvonne almost every day, assembling what I'll need to finish my history, but Essie's cryptic phrase eludes me. While my abilities have grown these past months, Yvonne insists I'll have mastered them only when I find what I'm looking for. Despite all the details she's given about conducting ribbons from the earth, I still feel like she's hiding something. I'll ask my mother for any last secrets before I leave, but I'm confident they'll let me ride out of here in ignorance. The more of their history I write, the more I realize the truth of Yvonne's words: *We grew up in lies, me and your mother, and sometimes the truth isn't in words.* They grew up in a web of lies so thick it was nearly impossible to see, so I can't blame them when the truth doesn't come nat-urally to their lips. If they're hearing my thoughts right now, I hope one of them tells me what I'm missing.

Gudrun's cautious in all this darkness. She ascends the hill slowly, taking her time with each step, and I nudge her a few times to keep going. The first sliver of dawn appears over the summit and we reach Lorraine's farmhouse just as the sky turns dark purple. There's wood-smoke coming from her chimney and lamp-light beaming through the kitchen windows. With any luck, all the girls are still asleep and their mom's just busy with the morning baking. I don't want little Isabelle to hear anything, I want it to be her choice. It won't be easy to convince Lorraine, but I won't leave until Isabelle refuses my offer herself. I've told nobody about what I'm about to do. Not even you.

Lorraine finally sees me while I'm tying up Gudrun near the water-trough. It's filled to the brim from the recent rain and she drinks happily after her long climb. I don't have a chance to open the front door. Lorraine's already standing there, looking like someone died.

"Who is it?" she asks. "What happened?"

"Nothing." I grab her shoulders and give her cheeks a kiss. "I'm just here for a visit. I couldn't sleep and knew you'd be up making those nice sweet-buns I love."

"I, uh—" She glances at me suspiciously before pulling me inside. "Take off your boots, huh. I've always known you as more of a night person, an asleep-until-noon kind of person. But I guess a morning person's the closest you can get to a night person."

"They're almost the same hours of the—"

"I don't know, Fulvia. What did you really come here for?"

"For your morning-buns. I knew you'd be baking, *guapa*. What else am I here for?"

"And you brought that old horse of yours along? With a two-person saddle?"

There's no point putting this off but I can't break the good humor. She helps me from the oilskin and waits until I'm out of my boots before tossing them in a pile with the others. Her hands are white from flour, but now they're streaked with mud from my boots, and she washes them before finishing her dough. I help her scoop chunks of it into an iron baking-tray and sprinkle sugar over each of the twelve mounds. Lorraine waits until the oven's hot enough, slides the tray inside, then pours me a cup of tea with honey. The steam smells like roses.

"Now tell me," she says. "Enough games. They'll be up soon. What's going on?"

"I'm going on a journey, and I...I've got my notebooks all packed and I'll be gone for a long while, months maybe. It's difficult to explain why, but I'm going to Paloma. I *need* to go to Paloma. And I...I wanted to ask Isabelle to come with me. I think it's important."

What looks like sadness quickly turns to anger. Lorraine opens the oven-door for no reason and stares at the pulsing red coals, breathing heavily. We both see the same vision. The explosion starts slow, almost invisible, until the entire ribbon collapses in a single deafening crack that leaves a perfect half-sphere burned into earth, carved with infernal light. She slams the oven shut and grabs me hard around the arms. I swear she wants to choke me. I can't be sure. Her breath feels like a dragon.

"You think it's important, huh?" she shrieks. "It's important for me to have my daughter! You've seen your mother's scars! Want to see mine? Want to see what happened to me? I won't lose Isabelle just because you want to relive the past. All this history makes you think you need to travel, to risk everything, to take stupid chances on—"

"It's not like that, Lorraine. I mean *really* important. Look!" I throw her off me and step away from the oven. "I got pregnant down on the coast and that morning we get the ribbon. And this next part you'll believe. I steal a case of salmon, eat it like a pig, and the ribbon disappears. Something's going on here! Your old friend *Isabelle the Great* won't tell me, neither will Yvonne, but something—"

"It's just your ego. I was taking a piss when the ribbon came! Does that mean I did it?"

"I'm serious. This isn't a joke. I haven't told you, but you should know the truth about your *best friend*. She lied to you all these years, just like she lies to everybody. Her and Yvonne! You don't know how this wireless system works! It's alive! It makes choices! And they hid it from us! Want to know why? Because every time they conduct a ribbon they open a hole into the underworld! That's what it is. Magic, real magic! They put a stop to the rumors, but after the explosion people said all sorts of things. If people knew the truth back then, I swear, something awful would have happened, another witch hunt. But now enough time's passed and I think, I really think I've figured out how it all—"

"Cut this horseshit! You want to take my daughter to the place her father died. Why?"

"I want us to heal! Isabelle and me. I can't explain it, but you have to trust me—"

I hear the creaking of floorboards before I can finish. Lorraine lifts a stern finger to her lips. Her eyes warn me to be silent as the girls stumble around in their bedrooms before filing downstairs into the kitchen. Isabelle arrives last, clearly the sleepiest. Little Juana asks her mom what all the yelling was about and Lorraine explains how crazy aunt Fulvia stubbed her toe on the oven leg.

"That was a lot of screaming for just that," Isabelle says, rubbing her eyes. "You okay?"

"Fulvia wouldn't let me help her," Lorraine butts in. "She got hurt."

"Do you have an oven?" little Yvonne asks me, checking on the buns. "Ours is big."

"Sit down, everyone!" Lorraine yells. "You too, Isabelle!"

We pull out our chairs around the big dining table and Lorraine brings over her iron tray filled with steaming buns. I slowly pick at one while Isabelle furiously spreads butter and jam all over her own, scarfing it down faster than anyone else. Then she goes for a second.

"I told your mom I came up here for the buns," I say to her. "They're still delicious."

Isabelle just shrugs and piles on the fatty butter.

"I like 'em fine," she says, avoiding everyone's gaze. "Why did you come here so early?"

I can hear Lorraine's body tense like cold wood. So can her daughters.

"I'm heading east, on a journey. Look," I say, pointing out the window. "It's Gudrun."

All the girls shriek in excitement and bolt across the room to marvel, even Isabelle. She crosses the floor, bun in hand, and sheds a droplet of jam on her path. Lorraine instantly cleans it with a towel and corrals her daughters back to the table. Only Isabelle lingers by the window, gazing in wonder.

"Where you going?" she asks me, the second bun already gone. "Santa Rosa?"

"She's going on a retreat to finish her book," Lorraine answers. "Village life is too much for poor auntie Fulvia. Sit down before you have another one, Isabelle. And if you're going to eat this much at least have something real, here, I'll cook you some eggs and—"

Isabelle sits beside me and ignores Lorraine, even when she starts cooking us breakfast. Isabelle already knows why I'm here, she's just waiting to hear it. I smile at not-so little Isabelle and take her hand beneath the table, hoping she'll hear my thoughts. It doesn't seem to work, no matter how hard I try. Isabelle just looks sleepy and confused while Lorraine cooks us all eggs and kale. This is how she's handled losing Lucio: the kitchen and the orchard. Nothing is out of order here. Everyone is safe.

"Mom?" Isabelle asks. "Mom?"

"Ok, it's ready. Girls, come on! Either eat a whole one or not, stop picking at those buns."

"I don't want a whole bun," Juana says. "And I don't like kale."

"That's fine. The grown-ups will eat it. Right, Fulvia?"

"Mom?" Isabelle asks again. "Why's aunt Fulvia here?"

Lorraine blots out this question by shoveling food on everyone's plates, evoking the ire of little Juana who doesn't like kale. She loudly tosses the iron pan onto the wood cutting block and sits down at the table in a haze of tension. Her daughters are all silent now, long familiar with their mother's emotions. They know she's about to explode, just like crazy aunt Fulvia does, only worse. Her eyes are closed, her jaw is clenched, and little Juana looks absolutely terrified. We wait and wait but Lorraine doesn't open her eyes. I can't tell at first, but then I realize she's smiling.

"I think your aunt has something to ask you, Isabelle."

Without glancing at either of us, Lorraine walks upstairs and leaves me with the girls, all of them looking at me for answers. I pull Isabelle's hands up from under the table, hold them tight, and smile at her until she sees the funny aunt, not the crazy one.

"I'm heading to Paloma, for my own reasons, but I wanted to know if you—"

"Yes! I'm coming!" She's already crying, her mouth quivering in happiness. "I'm coming!"

"What's Paloma?" Juana asks. "A dove?"

"It's where dad died," Yvonne says, glumly poking her eggs. "Why are you going there?"

"I had a dream about it. More than one. And I just need to go."

"But why?" Yvonne drops her fork on the plate and frowns. "What if it explodes?"

"Yeah, what if it explodes?" Juana asks. "Our dad died in an explosion."

"I know, baby. But they're rebuilding it now, and we'll never make the same mistake again."

"Why can't men conduct the ribbons?" Isabelle asks. "Do they know yet?"

I could weave a web of guesses for these girls, but it'd just be a dozen of the thousand possible answers dreamed up since their father died. Some theorized that men are biologically incapable of conduction and can't safely concentrate their latent powers. Others believe it was just a freak accident, while some claim it was a lesson from the planet, signaling the reign of men was over and that Nikola would be the last one to leave his mark on the Earth.

"No one knows," I say, glancing around. "Where's your mom?"

"Was our dad the conductor?" Juana asks.

"No, he was the electricity man," Yvonne says, trying to sound smarter. "He made the spark."

"He worked in the powerhouse," I tell Juana. "Every ribbon needs its spark. Your dad fed the energy into the tower and the ribbon...*wooosh*...catches the electricity and carries it over to Russia, or Europe, or Africa. Then they shut down the powerhouse and monitor the transmission. He did all that. A brilliant man. Kind, wonderful, loving. And a hero, but you already know—"

Lorraine suddenly stomps downstairs and makes us all go silent. She's holding a pile of metal covered in a greasy cloth and sets it down on the cutting block. We crowd around as she reveals five weapons from another age, well-oiled and expertly maintained. Two of them are massive automatic rifles, designed by John Browning and manufactured in Sarah Winchester's factories under military contract. These were the last rifles that Yvonne was able to smuggle out before war consumed the entire planet. Capable of firing twenty bullets in less than ten seconds, this handheld machine-gun is a terrible beast, and now I'm looking at two of them. One belonged to Lorraine, the other belonged to my mother, and these weapons kept them safe during the long war in Russia. Without these rifles, none of the girls would be alive right now, eating breakfast by the fire.

"Are you going or what?" Lorraine asks Isabelle. "What did you say?"

"I'm going with Fulvia," she says, beaming. "I'm going, *mama*."

"Not without this, you aren't."

Lorraine hands her an oily pistol and Isabelle receives it as if it were revelation. Not even her daughters knew she'd kept these mythical weapons. I certainly didn't know. She took such good care of them that guns still look fresh out of the crate.

"And you, *Aunt Fulvia*!" She hands me one of the rifles. "I don't care if it's a bear, a cougar, or a man. If it's coming at my Isabelle, you shoot him between the eyes."

"We'll only be in the woods for a few—"

"I don't care how many days. And there's another condition!"

"What now?" Isabelle moans. "What is it?"

"The both of you stay here tonight. I want one more day with my daughter."

Isabelle puts up a fight but I wink at her and insist we stay. There's no rush, given where we're going, but my presence will have to be kept secret. I plot with Lorraine's daughters on what to do if the village comes looking for me. I tell them about the note I left for my girlfriend Gertrude and the girls laugh and giggle as we discuss the vivid particulars of escaping our commune's eyes. As long as they've been alive, Aunt Fulvia's always been here to make their lives a more interesting. Today's no exception. I never disappoint them.

19

LA PROTESTA HUMANA AND THE CAVERN OF SHADOWS

JOSEPHINE LEMEL FERRARI WAS A FEARED CREATURE OF THE NIGHT, invisible protector of the Barbary Coast and merciless defender of exploited women. Dressed as different men with bowler hats and false mustaches, she followed anyone with darkness in their eyes. The glimmer of her dagger blade was the last vision these predators beheld before their blood drenched the cobblestones and flowed down to the bay. Every odd month the police made a big spectacle of parading through the Barbary Coast to scare off this vigilante, only the cops never stayed long, given they received payments from the underworld for their services rendered, brothels protected, and blind eyes turned. Rogue lieutenants who went off looking for this vigilante were known to disappear in the middle of the night after packing a suitcase, jacket, and hat. Josephine was careful to assassinate cops with grace, making it appear as if they'd left town in a hurry. The truth was always bleaker, although my mother participated in none of this. She was fast-asleep while Josephine prowled the dirty alleys or observed from rooftops, an angel with an elephant's memory. While she recovered from these long nights, her daughter Isabelle rose with the sun, donned her gray work dress, and ate a simple breakfast of bread, fruit, and a boiled egg with salt.

Cable-car line to Pacific Heights.

The year 1903 began with this familiar work routine and its slow cable-car rides up to Pacific Heights. Her brother Federico's influence in the Street Carmen's Union was now so strong the Heath laundresses could openly ride for free alongside Isabelle. This troupe of Italian women got off the cable-car each morning and proudly walked down the upper-class sidewalks, content to be part of a secret anarchist royalty. They alone knew the truth of Isabelle's intimate friendship with Yvonne del Valle-Heath, a secret they kept from their families for fear of being fired. In less than five years, they had used Yvonne's high wages to rise into the Italian middle-class and keep their children in school, a position they never dreamed of as poor immigrants. When my mother's visits to the library began to last beyond her proscribed work hours, none of the laundresses asked questions, knowing their good fortune was bound up with Isabelle's.

During these meetings in the library, my mother learned of Yvonne's further adventures into the world of San Francisco high-society. Having lived many isolated years with her books, Yvonne had become a cult legend among the reading public and the approximate image of her Spanish beauty, rendered in black lines across 10,000 sheets of newsprint, was now associated with the city itself. This mystique allowed Yvonne instant access to nearly any public figure she called on, for refusing a visit with the wife of Lionel Heath would be an irreparable insult in San Francisco high-society. As I've explained, her first efforts were bound up with young Alma de Bretteville, the poor art student who seduced a sugar baron. After her metal likeness was chosen to crown the Dewey Monument, Alma was asked to dinner by wealthy Adolph Spreckels, prompting her to seek Yvonne's immediate council.

Yvonne hired a union carriage-driver to gather Alma and she burst into the library flustered with excitement, having long read of Adolph Spreckels in her beloved society columns. Knowing this was their only chance, Yvonne spoke bluntly, instructing Alma to reach for all that Adolph possessed and not to stop until it belonged to her. These men would give them nothing unless they took it, using their bodies if necessary. Alma said she didn't mind, waving away Yvonne's implied meaning. She revealed that the de Brettevilles had been French nobility before the Great Revolution, just as she was directly related to Charlotte Corday, the woman who stabbed the tyrannical Jacobin, Jean-Paul Marat. Alma claimed to carry Corday's fire in her veins and she would use any means to elevate her family back to their proper station. While she spoke, Yvonne could hear the voice of her dead father muttering about redemption for the del Valles. Without question, Alma de Bretteville and Enrique Vasquez del Valle possessed the same royal mania.

When Alma dined with Adolph Spreckels a few days later, she was twenty-two years old, her suitor forty-six. They rode a carriage down to Post Street and dined at the infamous Poodle Dog, a French restaurant equipped with private rooms, and it was here that Alma first mounted dirty Adolph, securing her place in high-society. When they left through the restaurant's secret tunnel late the next morning, Adolph pleaded with Alma to see him again. After giving him a non-committal answer, she boarded her waiting carriage for the ride home. Yvonne called on Alma two days later and they had lunch on the patio of the Heath mansion while Juana sprinted across the grass. Once she related her night at the Poodle Dog, a tearful Alma took Yvonne's hand and vowed to never forget her. It

Charlotte Corday stabs Jean-Paul Marat.

would take years to grasp Adolph's sugar fortune, but Alma vowed to always serve Yvonne, her true love in this abysmal world. Unable to contain herself, Yvonne cried from their shared bondage to evil men.

My mother was still unimpressed with Alma de Bretteville, especially when she discovered her relation to the infamous Charlotte Corday. To dispel her concern, Yvonne removed a dozen books from her shelves to prove that Jean-Paul Marat was more than worthy of Corday's knife-blade. This point was further elaborated when Yvonne produced a long list of guillotine victims and pointed to entries labeled *woman, unknown.* Isabelle knew how many of her relatives perished in the Great Revolution and could see their forms hovering between the lines. Unable to trust Alma as a potential ally, Isabelle resigned herself to trusting Yvonne. For her part, my mother wanted nothing to do with Alma. Neither did Josephine. Not yet, at least.

Outside the Heath mansion, my mother pursued other activities that bore material results, not just abstract conspiracies. *Secolo Nuovo* still needed to be published every Friday, just as she met with her comrades on a weekly basis, if not more so. Since the collapse of the Great Waterfront Strike, the anarchists had dispersed from the waterfront into dozens of other workplaces. Rather than concentrate on the maritime trades, they now planned to trigger the general strike by infiltrating every workplace, shop, and factory. By spring of 1903, the anarchists had become leaders of the Street Carmens' Union, the Wire Workers' Union, the Can Makers' Union, and the Hackmens' Union. Less than two years after their defeat, all of these unions were prepared for the next strike wave, although leaving the maritime trades had unforeseen consequences. With only Sergio and his longshore crew guarding the waterfront, Andrew Furuseth led the Sailor's Union down a conservative path no one was prepared to stop.

In the Northern California settlement of Fort Bragg, lumber workers went on strike against the Union Lumber Company, a massive destroyer of the redwood coast, and their union requested support from the City Front Federation. While other members of the Federation heeded this call for solidarity, Furuseth obeyed the terms of his new contract and ordered the Sailor's Union to deliver the company's lumber. When the first crew of anarchist sailors disobeyed, Furuseth gathered his loyalists and fulfilled the terms of his contract. Despite being a prominent leader of his waterfront union, Sergio couldn't risk an all-out war with the sailors, a counter-productive battle that would only help the bosses. With no other options, the scab lumber sailed unopposed.

In these uncertain times, the anarchists concentrated on planning a strike wave aimed at the National Association of Manufacturers. This new organization was essentially a national Employer's Association, coordinating an assault against all unions, anarchists, and socialists through its Citizen's Alliance. While this organization had yet to appear in San Francisco, it was already rearing its form against the mine workers of Colorado. In the spring of 1903, the miners of Cripple Creek went on strike and paralyzed ore production across the entire region. At their heels was the Citizen's Alliance and the Governor of Colorado, a depraved banker dedicated to crushing the labor movement. This latest strike was organized by the Western Federation of Miners, a radical group with links to San Francisco, and word spread of this National Association of Manufacturers that was gunning for them.

Over the spring of 1903, the San Francisco unions readied themselves for a summer strike wave designed to scare the local bosses and aid their comrades in the Rockies. The first of these unions to push for a strike was my uncle Federico's Street Carmen's Union, although his faction of anarchists were ultimately vetoed by the Labor Council and the union agreed to negotiate instead. It was in this frustrating moment that my uncle Lorenzo returned from New Jersey with Enrico Travaglio. A host of Italian anarchists arrived alongside them, all eager to fight the San Francisco capitalists.

My mother woke one morning to find Lorenzo waiting in the living room on Greenwich Street, a cup of steaming coffee at his side, a cigarette burning between his fingers. He'd donned bifocals, wore a brand new suit, sported an oiled mustache, and looked nothing like the longshoreman who'd left in 1901. After embracing her brother, Isabelle learned of his time in Paterson, New Jersey, the eastern base of Italian anarchism.

While working there on *La Questione Social* newspaper, my uncle became close with Luigi Galleani, the paper's latest editor, and the two worked long nights over the printing press. Luigi had escaped from an Italian prison island, crossed the Mediterranean, and then resided in Alexandria, Egypt, establishing a school for anarchists. While living in this ancient sanctuary, Luigi was contacted by Errico Malatesta and sent across the Atlantic to the industrial hot-bed of Paterson where he would edit *La Questione Social*.

Luigi Galleani

This propaganda work halted in February 1902 when downtown Paterson burned to the ground, including their newspaper office. A few weeks later, massive flooding destroyed the textile mills and dye plants of Paterson, forcing thousands of workers onto the streets. Lorenzo and Luigi moved their press to the back of a Chinese laundry and printed *La Questione Social* in this volatile moment, hoping to nudge the workers into an all-out strike.

In May of 1902, thousands of weavers and dyers walked out of their re-opened factories and shut down textile production. They stood silently on the cobblestones listening to anarchists address them in Italian, French, German, and English, just as they followed these anarchists into battle with hearts aflame. On June 18, 1902, thousands of rebels stormed their factories and fought the police with pistols, rocks, and knives. During this assault, Luigi Galleani was shot by the police, forcing him to hide in an attic, and my uncle Lorenzo fought for weeks before the Governor sent the military to crush their strike. In the wake of this disaster, Luigi was charged with multiple crimes and fled to Canada, leaving *La Questione Sociale* with Lorenzo. In this paper, the anarchists blamed union leaders for hindering the strike with their limited demands for better wages. Instead of paying useless dues to corrupt leaders, the anarchists encouraged striking on the job and translated the infamous *Boycottage et Sabottage* manual from French into Italian. By remaining beholden to a craft, trade, industry, or union, workers would forever replicate the cycles of exploitation, never advancing beyond their status as wage slaves. To better transmit these ideas, Luigi returned from Canada to an anarchist commune in Barre, Vermont, populated with Italian stonemasons from Carrara. It was in this ideal setting that Luigi began to print *La Cronaca Sovversiva*, the most radical anarchist newspaper in the United States, a publication where one could find the recipe for black powder and dynamite.

It was common for the International to spawn different publications, each associated with a specific philosophy, tendency, or editor. With the *Cronaca Sovversiva* encompassing the spectrum of direct action, the columns of *La Questione Sociale* shifted to workplace organizing. Another editor was installed in Paterson and the International dispatched Lorenzo to the outskirts of Chicago. He was now associated with the *antiorganazzitori*, while those who worked with unions were called *organazzitori*. The difference of philosophy between these factions was real, although the conflict was exaggerated in order to flush out police spies, the logic being that only paid informers would exacerbate a schism. This elaborate method kept them free from infiltration, although it caused Errico Malatesta to be shot by an informant in 1898. Lorenzo was now part of this crafty ruse and traveled from Paterson to Chicago for a meeting with another group of *antiorganazzitori*. Much to his surprise, Enrico Travaglio was waiting for him at the train station, a pregnant woman by his side and three children standing behind them.

Enrico's name had graced dozens of newspaper headlines after McKinley's assassination when he was jailed alongside the Isaaks and Emma Goldman. Leon Czolgosz claimed sole responsibility for his act, denying any outside involvement, and the anarchist prisoners were soon released for lack of a clear conspiracy. Enrico was reunited with his Chicago comrades but shadowed at every step by cops and journalists. Joining him under this spotlight were Giuseppe Ciancabilla and Ersilia Grandi, two Italian exiles who'd recently lived in Paterson. Enrico had been working on their newspaper *La Protesta Humana* when the police arrested him and Giuseppe in Spring Valley, Illinois. Once they were released, Enrico reunited with his now-pregnant lover Frankie, an older woman with three children, and they moved their family from Chicago to Spring Valley where Enrico could keep editing *La Protesta Humana* with Giuseppe and Ersilia. Along with Lorenzo, this group of *antiorganazzitori* were soon dispatched to San Francisco to help guide it towards direct action. Lorenzo had just arrived off the ferry when Isabelle found him smoking a cigarette and drinking coffee at the little blue house on Greenwich Street.

Giuseppe Ciancabilla

My mother went to work when his story was over and mentioned none of it to Yvonne. Instead, she listened to her explain the latest intelligence from Alma de Bretteville and Adolph Spreckels. Their romance was still a secret affair conducted in the Poodle Dog or on clandestine weekends at his Napa ranch. During these getaways, Adolph revealed his business to Alma, complaining about his enemies in the Bohemian Club and their leader Lionel Heath, whose faction pushed for brutal measures that only strengthened the unions. Adolph preferred to pay his workers well, a measure that defeated these labor radicals more effectively than any billy-club. In his bedside confessions to Alma, Adolph told her the Great Waterfront Strike had cost the local capitalists over $10,000,000, the government had canceled a war contract, his brother JD lost $200,000 on his ocean line, and the blame was placed on the shoulders of Lionel Heath. In the aftermath of this labor conflict, Heath had purchased the Union Iron Works shipyard, a sly maneuver no one suspected until the deal was inked. Adolph truly believed that Heath had provoked the entire strike in order to ensure this sole maritime transaction. After all she'd been through, Yvonne could expect nothing less from her husband.

This intelligence hung heavy in Isabelle's thoughts and followed her down the hill to the offices of *Secolo Nuovo* where Enrico was waiting for her. He embraced Isabelle tightly before introducing Giuseppe and Ersilia, both already stained with ink. They opened a bottle of wine and were about to celebrate Enrico's homecoming when Cesare Crespi burst inside, closed all the blinds, locked the front door, and ordered them out the back. As they filed through the narrow opening into the alley, Cesare called them idiots and cursed them for bringing the police to his place of work. While this might have been an overreaction, Enrico and Giuseppe were the most notorious anarchists in San Francisco and being seen with Isabelle was truly dangerous. In the days that followed, this propaganda group left Cesare's office and established two new printing presses using money from bank robberies in New Jersey. To confuse the police, Giuseppe and Enrico planned a false conflict between these papers. One would be *La Protesta Humana*, organ of Ersilia and Giusseppe, while the other was *Secolo Nuovo*. The presses would be in different locations, both kept from public knowledge, and there would be no more Cesare complaining about anarchists or the high gas-bill. Enrico, the rebellious *luciferino*, had become not only a master-printer in Chicago, he was now a father.

After work, Isabelle began having dinner at Enrico's apartment and got acquainted with his lover Frankie Moore. Her three children were from a previous marriage and the struggle to feed them had driven her into the open buffets of the Isaak family and the Chicago anarchist movement. Despite the risks, she'd stayed with Enrico through his troubles and became pregnant with their first daughter. Leah Travaglio was born in the spring of 1903 and Frankie would soon bear two more daughters. This tall Irish woman with dark hair never betrayed any ancient knowledge, nor did Isabelle learn of her past, but the remnants of a Celtic accent lingered in her Chicago speech patterns, just as her ability to conceive only daughters was truly astounding. Enrico resided with Frankie in this cramped apartment, changed diaper cloths, cooked meals, and put the young ones to bed as the street-lamps were being lit. Frankie was usually asleep when he left for their new Basque Town print-shop where Isabelle and Schwartz were working on *Secolo Nuovo*. During that spring of 1903, the Latin Quarter filled with the words of these three rebels, their fiery voices now long-familiar to the neighborhood.

My mother woke up groggy after those long printing sessions and donned her gray work-dress for the ride up to Pacific Heights. When she wasn't reading aloud with Yvonne or watching little Juana learn from picture-books, Isabelle was preoccupied with the latest word from Alma de Bretteville. On a luxurious bed on his Napa estate, Adolph had revealed his massive investments in Los Angeles and San Diego. Along with his brother JD, he planned to move his family fortune south where labor conditions were more favorable to capitalism. Rather than join Heath in a futile battle against the San Francisco unions, Adolph was taking over Souther California to create a capitalist paradise. When my mother learned this, she quickly lost her suspicions against Alma, for Yvonne had delivered them a valuable ally. It was in this spirit that they planned the next retreat to the *Rancho del Valle*.

Since their last visit, no one had seen much of Jack London. He'd returned from Europe laden with coded messages from the International and then retreated to the Piedmont bungalow to be with Bessie and their newborn daughter Becky. Much to his dismay, Anna Strunsky left for New York City just before he arrived, a clear signal of her romantic intentions. Despite this estrangement, Jack and Anna finished their *Kempton-Wace Letters* by mail, a difficult task given their amorous feelings, and while she took care of finalizing the book with their New York City publishers, Jack's literary star continued its ascent. His magnificent study of poverty, *The People of the Abyss*, began its serialized publication in the socialist *Wilshire's Magazine*, and a dozen contracts for future work soon arrived in his Piedmont mailbox, along with new friends eager to drink his liquor. Overwhelmed by this sudden fame and compressed by rural solitude, Jack began what many consider his masterpiece, *The Call of the Wild*. In this book, a dog named Buck is *glad for one thing: the rope was off his neck. That had given them an unfair advantage, but now that it was off, he would show them. They would never get another rope around his neck. Upon that he was resolved.* As he journeys towards liberation, Buck comes to see *how a dog could break its heart through being denied the work that killed it.* When he finally escapes, Buck sings *a song of the younger world, which is the song of the pack.*

Jack had just finished typing this short novel when a cryptic telegram arrived at his Piedmont bungalow, instructing him to reach the Bulkhead Saloon by dusk. After making up a frantic excuse to his wife Bessie, Jack caught a ferry to San Francisco and met Isabelle at the dark corner booth of this crowded saloon. He agreed to attend their April retreat and was trying to leave when Isabelle slid a paper across the table. He sat back down, unfolded the note, and read the phrase: *Jack needs to prove himself.* My mother said this was one of the coded message that he'd brought over from Europe. After a night of *clashing with the police* in the port of La Spezia alongside two trusted comrades, the famous author had left quite a good impression among the Italian anarchists. Jack insisted he was ready, although Isabelle assured him his test would come soon enough.

A week before their spring retreat, Yvonne woke to the sound of hammers banging against marble walls. With little Juana at her side, Yvonne discovered a small army of men at work in the mansion. They politely took off their hats but declined to answer any of her questions, claiming their employer had instructed them not to. This mystery was solved the next morning when Heath burst into the library and announced their home would soon be illuminated with electric light. His hired men were currently removing the old gas-system, installing yards of wire, and connecting the mansion with the Standard Electric grid. This hydro-electric energy generated in the *Sierra Nevada* would soon brighten Yvonne's library when she returned from the *rancho*, just in time for President Roosevelt's unveiling of Alma's statue. Yvonne feigned delight, afforded her husband a single kiss, and calmly asked whether this electrical transmission system utilized alternating-current or direct-current. Heath acknowledged it was alternating-current, an invention purely of Nikola Tesla's design, and he tried to exit the library before Yvonne could trap him in another argument.

In her private correspondence with Nikola, the besieged scientist begged Yvonne to convince her husband of his true powers, so she asked Heath, *if alternating-current was now the standard, why wouldn't Tesla's wireless system be any less profound?* Yvonne knew JP Morgan had lost millions of dollars when Edison's direct-current was surpassed by Tesla's alternating-current, although she wasn't prepared for Heath's response. Her husband raised his voice and claimed that Edison's system could be measured, rationed, and sold for a price, unlike Tesla's vision where electricity would be cheaper than dirt, if not free. With unusual venom, Heath promised his wife that Tesla would never touch a penny of his money before storming out of the mansion to his petroleum-burning Daimler.

This eruption of emotion was certainly unexpected, although it did allow Yvonne and Juana to escape the next morning without saying goodbye. They traveled on Heath's yacht over to the Oakland waterfront and rode a private coach across the hills to Orinda. The new tunnel was now open but their driver avoided it, claiming the passage was so narrow it could only accommodate a single wagon at a time. This traffic congestion delighted Yvonne and when the coach finally stopped to water the horses at the Summit House, she led Juana inside to lavishly charge her husband's bank account for a variety of supplies. Yvonne continued this behavior down the hill at the Last Chance Saloon where she let Ella Olive Moraga overcharge her for a month's-worth of food. Their heavily burdened carriage continued onward to the crossroads of Orinda where it turned south along the *Arroyo San Pablo*. Camille heard the stage-coach approaching and was standing on the front porch when they arrived. Before the tired coachman could open the door, little Juana

exploded out of the compartment and ran into the arms of her grandmother, a stream of garbled language pouring from her mouth. The three feasted by the fire later that night while Juana sermonized on a wide variety of subjects, her limited vocabulary stifling the vast ocean roiling inside her. Yvonne and Camille listened without interruption.

Isabelle, Eamonn, and Jack arrived the next morning dressed as country hikers on a weekend ramble. While the del Valle women slept in their earthen home the night before, my mother camped up the hill beneath swaying redwood trees. Eamonn and Jack debated philosophy long past midnight, but Isabelle chose to fall asleep under a vision of stars encased in branches. Their hike over the hills was free of incident and they appeared at the *Rancho del Valle* just as Camille was hanging the laundry. She cooked these hungry travelers an opulent meal of fresh trout, listened to their tales with hungry eyes, and over the next four weeks, 75-year-old Camille was enraptured their discussions. As a forgotten follower of Mary, she couldn't believe that Yvonne had already entered the realms of legend with her conspiracy against the forces of darkness. Camille never offered any suggestions, having none to give, and each night she went to bed pregnant with elation. Her life had never been so hopeful.

The pattern of their days was simple. Yvonne and Eamonn rose in the morning, refreshed from a night of love-making, and joined the others at the kitchen table. Their first conversations centered on the doctor's activities to suppress the Black Plague, an effort thwarted by City Hall until just recently. Faced with a federal blockade of the port, the mayor of the Union

Labor Party acknowledged that the plague still existed and committed the City to its eradication. Once this was approved by the Governor, federal doctors were allowed to address the plague as they saw fit. Within a week, Eamonn watched them take up his work by distributing hundreds of rat-traps throughout the neighborhood. Chinatown had now become familiar with this practice and accepted these gifts as they would from Eamonn and Rose, although their elation faded when the *federales* used these helpful gifts as an excuse to condemn buildings and fumigate homes with sulfur, carbolic acid, and chlorinated lime. The famous cobblestone roads were paved over with concrete to prevent rioters from having ammunition during a quarantine, although the papers claimed it was for public health. To cap it all off, federal doctors demanded the right to demolish any overhanging structures that blocked light into the cramped Chinatown alleyways. This measure was presented as the liberal alternative, given that racist *yanqui* capitalists were calling to burn down the entire neighborhood. The *Rancho del Valle* conspirators had seen this exterminatory racism emerge in 1900, although now it did so under the eyes of a pro-union City Hall.

Aside from these revelations, Eamonn had little else to offer besides a desire to take down the Union Labor Party. In this regard, he and Isabelle were of one mind. Beyond usurping the waterfront's voting power, these well-dressed Party minions cut a deal with the Gray Brothers for their quarry on Telegraph Hill. In the winter of 1903, my mother woke during the middle of the night to the sharp crack of a dynamite blast and the sound of tumbling rocks. All of Marisol and Josephine's efforts to close the quarry had just been reversed by Mayor Schmitz, with the pillagers allowed to blast freely. Beyond this insult, the city maintained an exclusive contract with the Gray Brothers to supply building material for municipal projects. Isabelle told her comrades that City Hall was now meddling in Barbary Coast affairs with its police agents, pushing further into the underworld than any government ever had. While she kept silent about Marisol and Josephine's involvement, my mother indicated that a brewing war between the Queen of the Coast and the Union Labor Party was on the verge of exploding. The administration was up for re-election that November and what remained of the radical waterfront had mobilized to oppose them. While police escorts and hired guns were now illegal in San Francisco, the Party's unbridled graft and corruption would only betray them all to the high capitalists, a reality that proved itself with each successive scandal.

During the second week of their retreat, Yvonne related the latest intelligence from Alma de Bretteville and Adolph Spreckels. While they appreciated Alma's viewpoint into the halls of power, the death of Frank Norris had deprived them of an ally within the Bohemian Club. In his place, Jack

London volunteered to infiltrate this nefarious institution, given his recent celebrity had brought him into the orbit of several Bohemians who were willing to sponsor his membership. Having remained silent during most of their discussions, Jack was now animated and lively, his glum expression replaced with an infectious gaiety. The conspirators couldn't find anything objectionable to this plan, but in the cracks of Jack's smile, Isabelle saw this poor-boy's longing to be just like Frank Norris, the privileged novelist who now enjoyed a posthumous fame. His novel *The Pit* was still a best-seller and its critique of capitalism coincided with the release of *The History of the Standard Oil Company*, a massive study of JD Rockefeller's leviathan. Serialized in the socialist *McClure's Magazine*, Ida Tarbell's *magnum opus* revealed the development and expansion of this petroleum empire, painting its business agents in the darkest colors. As these installments were released, Jack's study *The People of the Abyss* was still being serialized in *Wilshire's Magazine*, adding to the new *Progressive Era* of social literature.

That same night, while the others were busy cooking dinner, Isabelle told Jack to follow her into the oak trees where she informed him of the good impression he made on the International during his travels in Europe, an impression that required a final test. Isabelle gave him a date in June, told him to dock at the Italian Fisherman's Wharf at a specific hour, and instructed him to bring a sail-boat capable of navigating the bay. His task was to sail two comrades eastward, although Isabelle wouldn't reveal their objective, claiming it was better he didn't know. Unable to contain his enthusiasm, Jack clutched my mother and then kissed her cheeks, thanking her for this chance to prove himself. Despite his cheer, Isabelle maintained her doubts and followed him back to the *adobe* with suspicious eyes. While she couldn't have known, Jack concealed something that would soon affect them all.

For the final weeks of their retreat, the conspirators took long hikes through the redwoods or swam in the *Arroyo San Pablo*. They discussed the volatile situation in Russia, the miner's strike in Colorado, and the pressing need to assemble their forces in Southern California, although most of these subjects were beyond the scope of their conspiracy, leaving them to pass their remaining days in blissful leisure. In this careless state, Eamonn and Yvonne fell deeply into a relationship they never had before, not even in the mansion, and glimpsed something close to freedom. Yvonne was radiant, lazing in the green grass with her lover or pacing through the oak trees like a teenager. Camille was no exception to this renaissance and went on hikes through the woods as nimbly as her daughter. During their final week, Camille followed Isabelle and Yvonne along the deer trails while Jack and Eamonn played catch over Juana's head. The men never learned what happened next.

Consciously or not, Camille led Yvonne and Isabelle to the familiar grinding hole halfway up the *Rancho del Valle*. These three women climbed the boulder and ran their fingers along the smooth hole, ground down after centuries of use. Just as they began to worry about getting Camille down from the boulder, an unusual silence invaded the forest that made every leaf stand still. This was when two smiling indigenous women appeared beneath an oak tree with a pale coyote between them, its tongue extended in happiness. My mother tried to speak before a flood of water sucked her backwards into a long green tube filled with women's laughter. Yvonne and Camille went with her, only they couldn't remember what happened. Just as before, they appeared on the banks of the *Arroyo San Pablo* covered in lavender saltwater. Several hours had elapsed and the frantic calls of Eamonn and Jack now pierced the night. When the women finally returned to the *adobe*, none of them could properly explain their absence. Yvonne said they'd gotten lost and fallen into the river, an excuse she used the year before. Eamonn and Jack didn't probe any further, although both smelled the lavender hanging thick in the air. Only little Juana was unconcerned, already understanding what had happened.

Their retreat of 1903 ended as it had the previous year, although Yvonne's parting from Eamonn tore deeply at her heart. While her lover hiked over the hills with Isabelle and Jack, Yvonne felt a cold darkness pulse inside her chest, and Juana was terrified as her mother convulsed with tears and madly screamed at the glass windows of the stagecoach. Yvonne left without saying goodbye to any of the locals and by the time their coach arrived at the port of Oakland, she had to be roused by the driver. He helped her and Juana board their private yacht and tipped his hat as it chugged them towards the city. The weekly gossip columns would later remark that Yvonne del Valle appeared disconsolate and ill when she emerged from her husband's yacht on the San Francisco waterfront. This was a time Yvonne still remembers as the most painful in her life, surpassing even the war itself. Not only had President Roosevelt just arrived in San Francisco to unveil the statue of Alma de Bretteville, Heath had prepared an elaborate trap meant to bind Yvonne to his project forever.

She returned to an empty mansion blazing with electric bulbs, every gaslight replaced by this new technology. Yvonne and Juana explored the bright rooms, flicked every switch, and were surprised to find the music room mysteriously locked. Heath didn't appear until the following morning, two days before the statue's dedication ceremony. He found his wife and daughter busy in the library and asked Yvonne to accompany him to the music room, leaving Juana to gaze at her picture books. She followed Heath down the hallway and waited patiently as he fumbled with the key, her mind already filled with doom. The twin oak doors opened, revealing an entirely reconfigured music room, its back wall lined with rows of metal cylinders. Where her husband once hosted the occasional ball, there were now two machines in the center of the room. One was made of metal and plugged into the electrical outlet, while the other stood alone on three wooden legs. Heath closed the doors, switched off the lights, and guided Yvonne towards a faint glow in the wooden machine. The curtains were drawn and a rectangle of light hovered on the opposite wall. She was told to sit on a red sofa and keep her eyes on this rectangle.

Heath began to crank the wooden box and the wall flickered with various shades of darkness, soon replaced by the moving image of a little girl cowering before a stone wall. Yvonne clutched the sofa cushions and recoiled in fear as a viscous little boy threw snowballs at this freezing girl. Every snowflake was visible, as if the entire room were now plunged into winter. Yvonne felt the darkness pull at her body when the little girl fell to her knees and lit a match in pure desperation. Within the blink of an eye, the stone wall was replaced by the image of a roaring fireplace that faded along with the match-flame, its illusion extinguished. With the cold encroaching on her body, the little girl wept before she lit another match. Yvonne fell deeper into darkness as a circle of light opened on the wall, an illusion within the illusion that depicted a dining table packed with hot food. This image faded along with the match-flame, leaving the girl with frozen tears. Yvonne had no control over this mesmerism and wept as the little girl lit a third match, her hair now covered in snow. A glowing Christmas tree appeared, its tip crowned by a glowing star that fell from the fading tree and disappeared along with the match-flame. Yvonne's senses stabilized themselves when the fourth matchstick was lit. She couldn't stop crying. An illusory mother-figure appeared on the stone wall and held out her hands to the little girl, only to vanish at the moment of contact. Defeated by the reality of her illusions, the girl collapsed and froze to death, her body covered in layers of snow. At that moment, a glowing angel stepped out of the wall and lifted the girl's soul into the heavens. The lifeless body remained, soon to be discovered by a passing beat-cop. The last image Yvonne beheld was a dead little girl illuminated by the beam of a policeman's flashlight. She'd never been more afraid.

Heath stopped cranking the wooden machine and opened its side-door, revealing the kerosene burning within. In an arrogant rant, Heath explained that his new empire wouldn't rely on the crude power of a flickering gaslamp but would harness light itself. He flipped a switch on the other metal machine and soon the image of workers leaving a factory covered the wall. With his hand on this latest projector, Heath revealed it was designed by Thomas Edison and powered with electricity. Their lines wouldn't just carry power, they'd transmit raw images and connect the world in a network

controlled by him alone. JP Morgan would die eventually and his children were all unreliable, leaving Heath the top contender for command of the empire. With the automobile, the petroleum refinery, and this electric technology, Heath would transform the entire world into a unified system. In his deranged imagination, Heath assumed Yvonne had succumbed to this mesmerism, a reality that was hardly true. To convince him that he'd won, Yvonne threw her arms around Heath's sweaty body and exclaimed that she would be his empress of the new world. With no other perceived options, she let him have his way with her on the carpet. It was the worst day of her life, but it made Heath trust her.

None of the normal staff were called into the mansion that week and the property was guarded by a private security force. New kitchen and service staff from the Bohemian Club were hired for the Presidential visit and received their instructions from hired men with guns. All of this activity was a blur to Yvonne, sunk into a sadness not even Juana could break. On the day Theodore Roosevelt was set to dedicate Alma's statue, Yvonne kept seeing the haunting images of the little matchstick girl lying dead in the snow. She imagined lines of men and women paying a nickel to watch this film while real-life matchstick girls froze to death just down the street. These terrible thoughts made her clutch little Juana tightly as they rode with Heath towards the statue's unveiling.

On the afternoon of May 14, 1903, the entire harbor was filled with warships built in the Union Iron Works, a facility now controlled by Lionel
Heath. Yvonne glimpsed their shimmering reflections as the Daimler delivered them down the hill to Union Square and through the reserved entrance
for San Francisco high-society. Yvonne took Juana's hand as her husband
guided them to a special seating area at the base of the column surrounded
on all sides by a massive, roaring crowd. They sat beside Alma while Heath
made his formal introduction to President Roosevelt, a round little man
with glasses and a mustache. Yvonne wavered in and out of consciousness,
the babble of high-society wives numbing her senses, and in this state of
near-total confusion, Roosevelt unveiled Alma de Bretteville's metal figure
holding a trident and a laurel. This Dewey Monument, named for the naval
commander of the Spanish-American War, now stood in the center of Union
Square. Yvonne had never felt so lost, nor so broken.

She escorted Juana back to the Daimler and waited for Heath to finish
assembling the horde of visitors who'd soon descend on the mansion. They
rode up the hill in total silence and Heath couldn't restrain his joy at finally
subduing the indomitable Yvonne del Valle. Within an hour, the entire
estate was flooded with guests, including the federal escort of Theodore
Roosevelt, and the local capitalists quickly encircled the
President. Yvonne listened to her husband vigorously
argue for the resumption of naval war contracts at
his Union Iron Works, a proposition the red-faced
President only chuckled at. He told Heath the US
already had plenty of warships, enough to subdue
the entire Pacific, and the Union Iron Works might
as well make ferries or grain barges. The last of their
war contracts had been fulfilled and Roosevelt insisted
there wouldn't be another, not unless there was a pressing
need. He claimed to have seen enough war and wouldn't let
anyone start another. In this tense moment, the entire crowd
shifted its attention across the patio to a short gray-haired
woman in a black dress. Without hesitation, Heath
descended on his wife's ear and insisted she escort
this woman to the library and keep her there at all
costs. He claimed it was Phœbe Hearst.

Gathering what remained of her senses, Yvonne
took Juana across the patio, introduced herself
to the mother of William Randolph Hearst, and
escorted Phœbe into the mansion past sneering society women. When they finally reached the library,

Phœbe bluntly asked Yvonne what she thought she was doing, claiming her elevation of Alma de Bretteville had been utterly obvious. Phœbe said they'd all been watching her, and when Yvonne asked for clarity, Phœbe explained some of the capitalist wives served a higher purpose. Without naming the forces of Mary, Phœbe claimed to be part of a feminine conspiracy. She had inherited an immense fortune from her dead husband and claimed the world was now opening to women in a manner unseen since ancient Egypt. She asked if Yvonne wanted to join them, claiming they'd all become greater than Nefertiti of Thebes, but when Phœbe took her hand and pleaded for a response, Yvonne claimed it was too dangerous, a refusal Mrs. Hearst wouldn't accept. With the library fire roaring behind her back, Phœbe appeared like a demon possessed by the fortune of the Hearst gold mines, her eyes brim-full of rabid darkness.

They spoke for an hour about the structure of high-society and the gossip that raged among these late-Victorian dynasties. There were the Spreckels, Hearsts, de Youngs, Crockers, and several other families with large fortunes that ensured their continuity through time. Some were allied with Heath and the Bohemian Club, others with Adolph Spreckels and the Union League Club, but none were allied with her son, and it was through William Randolph Hearst that Phœbe hoped to build a world for women. She'd already become a regent of the University of California, funded a school-building dedicated to mining, and awarded an honorary degree to Theodore Roosevelt. In 1902, her son was elected to Congress, paving his way to the White House in the 1904 elections, and with her son as President, she would change the course of history. Yvonne insisted she couldn't participate in this venture of hers and preferred to live with her books where it was safe, an answer Phœbe grudgingly accepted. Before she left, Phœbe insisted Yvonne could always call on her, just as her relationship to Alma de Bretteville would always be kept a secret. Once she'd finally gone, Yvonne locked the library door, collapsed onto the Persian carpet, and hyperventilated in front of her daughter. Never one for tears, even little Juana began to cry. The darkness had nearly eaten them alive, although now its tide was receding.

Isabelle went to work the following Monday to find the library empty, its fireplace unlit, and an uneaten breakfast sitting on the reading table. My mother eventually discovered Yvonne in the music room with Juana, her eyes fixed on a rectangle of light. Isabelle stared at this strange projection until it became the spectral form of a train speeding directly at her body. She ducked to her knees and covered her head, unable to comprehend the unearthly appearance racing through the room. When she dared to look up, Yvonne was staring at her in horror, numb from days of watching these films. Isabelle's panic was proof of this technology's mesmeric power and she listened silently as

Yvonne explained what was happening. While she spoke, Juana's
face was covered in food, dishes
were scattered across the carpet,
and metal film canisters sat half-
opened in every direction.

For the past weekend, Yvonne
had watched each of the three
hundred motion-pictures Heath
had purchased until their hypnotic
effects were all broken. The anarchist painter Georges Seurat had
presaged the motion-picture in his
final painting *Le Cirque*, and now
that infernal nightmare was part
of reality. Although it required
multiple viewings of a single film
to deconstruct its illusions, Yvonne

Phœbe Hearst

was committed to bursting their hypnotism and reclaiming her lost freedom.
Isabelle continued to listen but made sure to clean Juana's face, clear the
dirty dishes, and throw away the rotting food. Later that day, the kitchen staff
told my mother that Yvonne wasn't eating and claimed to be saving her meals
for later, allowing Juana to pick away at leisure. When one of the kitchen
staff tried to intervene, Yvonne screamed a warning never to come inside. She
claimed the room was haunted by shadows.

Isabelle came to work every day, washed the laundry, clipped it to the lines,
and then checked in on her disintegrating comrade. There was no change
to Yvonne's mania, although Isabelle had gotten her to eat a few meals. My
mother had no desire to join this cinematic deconstruction and only stayed
long enough to ensure both Yvonne and Juana were safe. Unwilling to fall into
despair, Isabelle worked her nights with Enrico and Schwartz at the new offices
of *Secolo Nuovo*, an isolated storage room at the base of Basque Town. While
they printed on these late-spring evenings, Ersilia and Giusseppe busied themselves on the latest issue of *La Protesta Humana*. A false conflict was widely
telegraphed on the pages of each paper, pitting the local anarchists into two
factions: those who wished to organize outside the workplace, and those who
wished to remain inside it. Despite this dissimulation, the rival editors would
often meet in Enrico's crowded apartment or Ersilia's living room where the
brightest anarchists of the Latin Quarter debated long into the night.

During her time in Paterson, Ersilia had formed a new current of wom-
en's anarchism against all forms of exploitation, especially within the family

home. Apart from their anarchiſt comrades, moſt Italian men kept their wives in bondage and ruled over their families like despots, a pracſtice Ersilia wished to eradicate. As she told her readers, women muſt learn *how to conquer freedom and escape the social environment that suffocates them, whether in the family, in intimate relations, in today's hypocritical conventions, or in public life.* Freeing women was of the utmoſt importance, for *the woman is and will always be the educator of the family, who has and will always have the moſt direcſt and the moſt important influence on the children.* Ersilia delivered these teachings to the women of the Latin Quarter through the pages of *La Proteſta Humana,* her bold words helping Isabelle to forget the cavern of shadows in that lonely mansion on Pacific Heights.

SHE'LL HAVE TO SLEEP WITH GRANDMA

I MIGHT'VE BEEN ASLEEP BUT CAN'T REMEMBER. IT DOESN'T SEEM THAT way. My mind feels ſtretched to the limit, every corner plumbed, each river dredged. Maybe I've written about the conspiracy too faſt, but I know these ſtories by heart. They're the only truthful ſtories my mother ever told, legends the San Francisco sailors rambled about at waterfront coffee houses. While we savored those black cups of jœ, the old men went on about the *sugar girl's* ſtatue in Union Square, the filthy days of proſtitution, and an immortal vampire called the Queen of the Coaſt. Everyone else would liſten and laugh and puff on their third cigarette, but not me. Once my coffee was done, I'd be the firſt person to leave their seat and head up the hill to Polk Street where Gertrude was waiting. Living in the city was my firſt experience of true anonymity, a place where I wasn't Fulvia Ferrari, daughter of Isabelle Ferrari, and I wanted to escape those tired legends of my neglecſtful mother. So here I am, slumped over Lorraine's desk, ſtaring at my notebook, mind pregnant with the local mythology of San Francisco. Once this book gets printed, all these folk-tales will become real, the characſters will spring to life, and our elecſtromagnetic world will change forever. My right hand's cramped from writing. It hurts even worse than my brain.

I sit upright and crack my back juſt as the firſt purple light invades the sky. The rooſters ſtart to crow inside their coop so I ſtep outside and let them out before Lorraine wakes up. The nine hens are rooſting above their eggs and look at me in confusion when I open the door. Only one of them gets up. It might be nice to keep some hens one day, only I'll regret it when the firſt coyote breaks in. Carnage is unpleasant. Even chopping off a rooſter's head makes me wince. When I was young, my mother never spared the gory details of what she'd done to living men, but compared to the butcher Josephine, my mother was quite the angel. As for me, I can't bring myself to kill a single living creature, even if I'm going to eat it. I think that's proof enough there's no hereditary blood-lust running through my family's veins. We just fought a long war that never seemed to end.

Lorraine and little Isabelle are wide-awake when I get back inside, already packing the last few items into old Ukrainian saddle-bags, the familiar Black Army skull-and-crossbones inked into their green canvas. These saddle-bags were made before the anarchists joined the Army of Light, when they were still fighting alone before the great transmission. Lorraine's kept all this equipment a secret, these tokens of war, her protective amulets, hidden from view like a forbidden altar. I watch her fill Isabelle's canteen but all I can see is Lorraine firing a carriage-mounted machine-gun at the Red Army while my mother drives their *tachanka* across the *chernozem*. Even her old canteen carries the black skull-and-crossbones and she hands it to Isabelle as if it were the Holy Grail. The atrocities Lorraine witnessed in the Ukraine are beyond my descriptive powers. She carries dozens of scars beneath her clothing, each with its own nightmare, yet here she is, conjuring that horror with these relics from a darker time, when our future was anything but certain. Is she doing this on purpose to make us afraid? All I know is my heart's pounding when we finally go outside and hang the green saddle-bags across Gudrun's sides.

"You don't let down your guard," Lorraine tells Isabelle. "Not even in the woods."

"The war's over, *mama*. And I've already been through the Dream."

"It doesn't matter. You keep that gun by your side and if any men start following you—"

"Those things don't happen anymore, *mama*. Stop crying, it's okay."

"Trust me," I say, guiding Lorraine back inside the house. "No one carries guns anymore either. Those shadow-men will be no match for us, right Isabelle?"

She affirms everything I say and Lorraine cheers up enough to make us a giant egg scramble with kale and smoked salmon and potatœs and slices of white cheese melted on top. People still call this stuff *Swiss cheese* without knowing why, even though the name's *Emmentaler*.

Yvonne and Juana sit down at the table once their mother serves us breakfast and I explain how this cheese is still made in *Les Diablerets*, the birthplace of my grandmother. While we eat, I tell them there's a Bernese village up north called *Emmental* that takes all the credit, but the truth is that my ancestors were the first to discover this bacteria, and the spread of their cheese from Savoie to Bavaria is one of the few traces they left after flooding into Europe. Josephine and Bianca passed this technique on to their daughters but Isabelle never taught me. I was too busy dancing in San Francisco or riding in the hills with Angelo. Cheese-making was for the farm girls, I said.

"How come your mom taught my mom?" little Isabelle asks me. "And not you?"

"I didn't want to learn. It's not all my fault, though. My mom never cared for it, otherwise she'd be making cheese instead of lavender oil."

"She just wanted someone to pass it on to," Lorraine says. "It didn't have to be you, Fulvia."

"I want to learn," Juana says. "Teach me, *mama.*"

From the embarrassed look on her face, I can tell Isabelle's refused to learn cheese-making more than once. Hopefully both of us grow up soon, because I sure do love this cheese, so does Isabelle, and we eat breakfast ravenously, savoring every bite. Our mothers can't make us cheese forever.

Lorraine notices me smiling and slaps my hand when I try to grab the empty plates. She tells little Juana and Yvonne to kiss their sister and aunt goodbye before carrying the dirty dishes off to the kitchen. All of us can hear her weep amid the clatter of silverware. When she returns, Lorraine showers her eldest daughter in kisses, smooths Isabelle's hair, and makes her promise not to take any risks.

"You neither, Fulvia," she tells me. "If there's no rush, don't do anything but trot that horse."

"We'll take our sweet time," I say, rubbing her salty cheeks. "And listen to me girls. If your mom Lorraine starts worrying, what are you going to tell her?"

"*Not to worry!*" they say in unison.

"I'll see you in the spring?" Lorraine asks me. "Right?"

"The summer, at the latest."

"Then you better get going. I want her back as soon as possible."

I kiss Lorraine one last time, grab my notebook off the desk, and follow Isabelle outside where Gudrun's kicking dust, eager to be off. Juana and Yvonne hysterically chant goodbye while I stuff my notebook into one of the saddle-bags, hop onto Gudrun's back, and help Isabelle climb up behind me. Lorraine doesn't wave when we leave. She keeps her arms folded above her chest, her jaws clenched together, her face glistening with tears, as if we're riding off to war.

This is a mostly symbolic farewell, given the short distance to our next stop. Lorraine's apple farm is on the southern peak of our commune, just down the ridge from my mother's house, the place we're sleeping tonight. Lorraine's been her only neighbor since the war ended and both of them like it that way. The road between their houses is flat, less than a mile long, and invisible from the eyes of the commune, making it ideal for our escape. From there, we can take the Kashaya mountain road east to Santa Rosa. Most normal people heading to Paloma would have caught a boat to San Francisco and then another to Petaluma, a swifter route that would've attracted us too much attention. Assuming that Gertrude doesn't blab about the letter, the commune shouldn't know I'm gone for at least a couple more days. I hope no one comes looking for me at my mom's house because that would just ruin everything. Angelo can't know I'm coming to Paloma. He'll think it's all about him.

"Does your mom know we're coming?" Isabelle asks. "Did she say we can stay there?"

"Not exactly. I haven't asked her in person, but she probably heard me."

"Heard you? Like...your thoughts?"

"Yep. She's really good at it, but not perfect. She didn't know I had this shadow-man inside me, and she can't always tell when I'm hiding something, so I've still got a little privacy."

"Weird. So it's all true, then? What people say. You really *are* witches."

"Most of it's true. Only they didn't teach me their powers, and I can't really control my thoughts, they just fly everywhere. So be prepared when we get there. She's been listening to me write all night, even in her sleep, and you know how grumpy I can make her."

Isabelle lets out a chuckle and stops asking questions for our ride along the ridge. The sun rises, crows caw in the air, a soft wind blows in from the ocean, and the first scent of wood-smoke wafts uphill from the village. Isabelle's grip on my sides is loose and embarrassed, like she wants her own horse. I would've preferred that myself, but not Lorraine. For her, horses were linked with war and carnage, so she's kept Isabelle away from them aside from a few communal lessons. It was more important to get Isabelle out of the house than ask for the stars, so here were are, in the same saddle, only I don't think she minds riding behind me too much. I can hear her humming in excitement.

When we reach the house, my mother's standing atop a ladder near the edge of her dead corn field. She's picking baskets-full of red hawthorn berries, a task we used to do together every fall before the squirrels and birds stripped the trees barren. My mother says hawthorn syrup keeps the heart young and she drinks three spoonfuls a day all year round. She moves faster than any squirrel, stripping the thin branches between her closed fingers and filling her basket with thick red bunches. It's not just the syrup that's medicinal, it's the dried berry itself, mixed in with teas to keep people happy on rainy days. There aren't any communal work-hours for this small hawthorn grove and the few bottles of syrup that exist here come from Isabelle the alchemist. My mother makes these potions for her own heart, not out of benevolence, though she never hesitates to bring some down the hill if someone needs it. She can hear me thinking these thoughts right now. She knows I'm telling the truth.

"Is she going deaf?" little Isabelle asks. "Why won't she turn around?"

"She's just ignoring us. Ignoring *me*. Come on, let's go hide Gudrun."

We take her into the storage barn behind my mother's alembics, a place few ever see. Despite the autumn wind, this building overflows with transmuted scents, a vast forest of invisible memories mixing in the air. My mother's got five of Octavio's glass funnels filled with different oils, all various shades of amber or gold. While hungry Gudrun chomps on some hay, Isabelle gazes at my mother's oils for the treasures they are. No one comes up here, not even little Isabelle, and the source of these glorious oils has remained a mystery to her until now.

I take Isabelle inside the house and discover my mother's been hard at work. The living room table is covered in woven Kashaya baskets, all filled with hawthorn berries, and she's got a few bottles of distilled moonshine, the vital ingredient to draw out her red medicine. She never stops cooking, not all year long, and the planet keeps her busier than anyone in the commune. No one knows how hard she works up here, but now little Isabelle gets to see my mother's no different than Lorraine, just a bit grumpier and way more unpleasant. If she doesn't realize this already, she will soon enough.

My mother barges in with another basket but doesn't say hello, she just walks into the kitchen and starts chugging water without looking at us. Isabelle and I sit beneath the *Black Square* and flip through some scattered books until my mother comes into the living room. She sits under the red square of the *Peasant Woman in Two Dimensions*, crosses her long legs, and closes her eyes like she's going to sleep. Isabelle just starts giggling. If this were Lorraine, neither of us would be able to get a word in. Compared to her, my mother's downright mute.

"Working hard, *mama?*" I ask aloud. "Got enough berries yet?"

"No point letting them go to waste. They aren't sweet for that long. It's too bad you're leaving—"

"How'd she know we're leaving?" Isabelle whispers.

"See. I'm telling the truth. She can hear us."

"If you were staying—" my mother interrupts, opening her eyes. "You could both help me get these berries into the moonshine. But you're leaving with your notebook, so what's the point of asking, it's not like I ever ask for help. Anyway, that was my last basket to pick. If you stayed—"

"We're staying!" Isabelle cries. "Right, Fulvia?"

My mother grins mischievously and then uncrosses her legs.

"There's something you should know before you leave, Fulvia. A couple things. Something we haven't told you yet, something you haven't found on your own. I know that...that you hate our *lies*, as you call them, but there's another lie, and it'll help you understand what happened during the Great Earthquake, when Yvonne pulled that inferno from the ground."

"Yvonne pulled a——" Isabelle starts.

"Oh, she didn't just pull it, *mija*. She screamed her entire soul into the underworld and came back with a ribbon of fire. I saw it myself, so did my mother, but she'd seen it once before, in Paris, just before she escaped the Commune. We never talked about it to anyone. Not ever. I didn't know how to tell anyone. It's our closest secret, the most dangerous one, but it's true."

Ever since I was a girl, my mother claimed that Josephine never discussed her final moments in the Paris Commune, but clearly that was a lie. According to this new story, Josephine stood atop the slopes of Montmartre with Antonio, Louise Michel, and Elizabeth Dmitrieff, comprehending the gray face of death. Thousands of their comrades were slaughtered, the entire city invaded by darkness, and bloodthirsty soldiers circled with fixed bayonets. In this blind scuffle, Louise Michel was thrown into a trench while my grandparents escaped with Elizabeth around the bluff. After recovering from her fall, Louise stood alone atop a pile of charred corpses. In this moment of horror and defeat, the Red Virgin accomplished the impossible. It's hard to believe what my mother tells me next.

"You can put that in your little book tonight while we're sleeping like sane people."

"I'm not at that part yet, I'm still——"

"A ribbon made of fire?" little Isabelle asks, confused. "Instead of lightning?"

"It's not an exact science, *mija*. But yes, a ribbon made of fire. Fire makes ions. It's magnetic."

"So why's this story so dangerous?" Isabelle asks. "People conduct ribbons all the time."

"Because it was proof we're witches, just like the papers said. We made the fire dance. And they still might think we're witches, though aunt Fulvia seems to think it's okay now. The last time we wrote a book that told the truth, something bad happened. They burnt us, *mija*, and that's why I didn't tell your aunt or anyone else. We had to keep everything a secret, otherwise they'd hunt us."

"Sad," Isabelle says. "No one learns that way."

"Exactly," I chime in. "So what's this other secret, or *lie* as I call it."

"Oh...it's about that fool Yeshua."

"Who's that?" Isabelle asks.

"Jesus," I say. "Jesus Christ."

"*Jesus*! What the hell?"

"So you know the story then?" my mother asks Isabelle. "Of his crucifixion?"

"My mom always said it was made up. To enslave people."

"Lorraine's telling the truth, only not the way she thinks. The church lied about what happened to him, sure, but there were even bigger lies. The old priests said Jesus was betrayed by Judas and then crucified in Jerusalem, but that's the lie right there. Yeshua *told* Judas to betray him, begged him to do it. Mary thought her lover was mad, she tried to stop it, but Yeshua insisted. So then Judas tips off the local rulers, they arrest Yeshua, throw him in jail, then take him to Pontius Pilate, the Roman overlord. No one knows what happened in there, but when Pilate left that night he met with his mistress, one of Mary's friends, and by next morning he'd had his illumination."

Her pause is unbearable. She pretends her throat's scratchy and goes into the kitchen for water. Isabelle and I follow like children lost in the folds of maternal mesmerism, unable to feel embarrassed by our basic needs as my mother drinks long and full from the glass jar and then wipes her mouth in satisfaction. She's loving every moment of silence.

"My mom does this on purpose," I tell Isabelle. "Just ignore it."

"What did Pilate see?" Isabelle asks, ignoring me. "What happened?"

"He has his men smuggle Yeshua out of Jerusalem, that's what happens, and they seal him into a cave, roll a stone over the entrance, then pay some local to pry it open three days later. No one knows Pilate's done this because he puts Judas in Yeshua's place for the crucifixion. He has Judas beaten beyond recognition, just another bloody man with a beard, and makes him carry the cross up the hill with two thieves. You see, *mija*, Pilate might have had an official reason to dislike these rebels, but he despised the Jewish patriarchs even more. So did Mary. Anyway, there they are, Mary Magdalene, mother Mary herself, hiding in the crowd as the prisoners go by. The crowd saw Yeshua carrying that cross up the hill, but what did they know? Only his mother and his lover could tell. It was poor Judas carrying that cross, not Yeshua."

"What the hell?" Isabelle cries. "I don't understand."

"No one did, *mija*! Only the women and Pilate knew the lie. The rest of the secret died with Judas. After he was dead, Pilate's mistress got word to Mary Magdalene that Yeshua was in a cave outside the city waiting for her. That's when—"

"Things went really bad," I finish. "Basically you're saying these last 2,000 years have been so terrible because two women decided—"

"To lie? No. It's not just because they lied, Fulvia. It's because Yeshua was...we still don't know what he was. This all sounds cruel, right? Telling your friend to betray you so the Empire thinks you're dead? Yeah, that's a despicably cruel thing for Yeshua to do. But imagine how Mary felt when she told the apostles he rose from the dead and built up that whole mythology just to keep them distracted. If she hadn't lied...are you getting it? She was covering for her maniac lover. I don't know what Yeshua was, but they were out there in the desert with him for a decade before the man just—" My mother claps her hands together, lifts her fingers to the sky, and widens her eyes. "Pop! He turns into a ribbon of light, burns straight up into the heavens, sort of spreads out into this geometric shape, and then never comes back. You can see why Mary's followers always seemed a bit screwy. Anyway, the women all had to flee when the apostles pieced together part of the truth. And guess what happened? They purged all the women from their Christian movement. It was bad enough Mary had their master's children, but it was far worse that Yeshua faked his death like a coward. So there you have it."

"He became light?" Isabelle asks. "Like an electromagnetic ribbon?"

"Just like it. Identical. That's what Yvonne says, only more powerful, more concentrated. It's the one part of the story that doesn't involve Yeshua's delusional horseshit. That ribbon of light at the end of the gnostic texts is real! I think the man was a lunatic, even if he came from some *repository of light*, but it took Mary's followers centuries to figure out what he meant. Don't forget, when Mary was born, the women who taught her everything had been fighting for 10,000 years, with the great flood cutting it in half. That's a long time to be fighting. They did some strange things these last 2,000 years and I don't blame them now that we're so...alright, enough of this, it's time for lunch. Then you'll help me with the berries? Yeah? Both of you?"

"I'll help with lunch," little Isabelle says. "I'm starving"

Isabelle follows my mother into the kitchen but I just sit there on the couch beneath the *Black Square*, stunned from what I've heard. The two of them laugh and swirl and toss dirty potatoes back and forth on their way to the stove, never once looking back at me. I wish I'd had my daughter earlier so she could play with her grandmother like they're playing now. When my baby is 15 years-old, grandma Isabelle will be in her seventies. I'll be fifty. The young are already forgetting Christianity and little Isabelle doesn't seem to care about their past 2,000 years of lies.

My mother spoke the truth when she said I'd be scribbling in my notebook like a crazy person tonight. If I'm able to pass out on the couch right now, I can rise at dusk and write until dawn. When I close my eyes, I see hooded Mary Magdalene crossing the Mediterranean in her little wooden boat. The rippling wavelets lull me into sleep and I wake at the mouth of the Rhône River where the Alpine river meets the sea. No one's chasing after me here. I'm free.

20

THE TIMES OF PROMISE

ONE MORNING, MY MOTHER WOKE TO A DYNAMITE BLAST SO POWERFUL that Telegraph Hill swayed like the hull of a wooden ship. Marisol and Josephine ran cursing into the darkness and within minutes the entire neighborhood was assembled, armed to the teeth with every conceivable weapon. The cowardly workers at the Gray Brothers' quarry ran off at the sight of the Queen's army, claiming they'd return with the police because their blast was perfectly legal. Isabelle didn't join this show of force at the quarry, having more than enough problems to face, and she rose just before dawn to find Josephine and Marisol sitting in the living room, their faces fixed in grimaces of hatred. With all the battles they'd faced in this dirty city, the dynamiting of their hill by the Gray Brothers was an insult they refused to bear. When she finally un-clenched her jaw, Marisol turned to Josephine and said, *it's time we get into that Palace.* For the past decades, the Palace Hotel had been the true center of San Francisco power and hosted a large number of luxury courtesans, their existence a public secret in capitalist high-society. It was nearly impossible to enter this privileged sphere of prostitution, although Marisol had cultivated a young *protégé* who would soon make her fateful entrance.

Isabelle didn't ask the Queens any questions that morning, already dreading going to work, and for the next week, my mother tended to the cinematic disaster in the Heath mansion, counting the days until her appointment with Jack London. The morning before she was scheduled to meet him, Isabelle woke to the red glow of a fire burning atop Telegraph Hill. She found Josephine and Marisol sitting in the living room, each of them smoking a cigarette, and they told her they'd just burned the abandoned observatory at the summit, a place owned by the Gray Brothers where pimps had started to gather at night. This was the first signal of war to their enemies, written in smoke for the entire city to witness. Everyone who woke before dawn could see the dancing flames and its ruins burned throughout the day, filling the sky with a column of black smoke. It was all anyone could talk about.

Isabelle woke early that next morning of July 26, 1903 and donned a hooded cloak for her walk to the Fisherman's Wharf. Two young men with bowler hats, suitcases, and umbrellas were waiting for her at a nearby coffee-stand and they sipped on steaming cups until a thirty-eight-foot sloop glided into the harbor. With his short work *The Call of the Wild* now serialized in the *Saturday Evening Post* and its book publication set for August, Jack had received thousands of dollars which he quickly sunk into this sloop, *The Spray*. Once he'd climbed up to the dock, Isabelle introduced Jack to her two comrades, wished them luck, and watched them push off under cover of darkness. While my mother was at work, Jack transported these two Italian anarchists to an old Chinese shrimping village near Point Richmond where they docked at a rickety pier. He waited in *The Spray* as these two strangers ascended the dry hills towards the Standard Oil Refinery, ignorant as to what would happen next.

Public hatred against JD Rockefeller's petroleum empire was at its zenith that summer following the ninth installment of Ida Tarbell's *A History of the Standard Oil Company*. Hundreds of thousands were now aghast at Rockefeller's boundless greed, including President Roosevelt, and there was no better time to attack his infrastructure. The three hundred-mile-long pipeline between the Bakersfield oil-wells and the Point Richmond refinery was almost complete, allowing Standard Oil to bypass the railroads and bring petroleum directly to market. Acts of sabotage had been hindering construction for months, putting the pipeline drastically behind schedule, and Jack waited to see what his anonymous comrades had up their sleeves.

Within an hour of docking, a massive blast shook the entire shoreline, followed by a red fireball that quickly turned to black smoke as it rose into the air. Jack didn't ask questions when the anarchists returned, nor did he learn their names. They sailed around the burning facility, keeping a wide birth from the destruction, and Jack left them at the Oakland waterfront where they'd catch a train to Mexico, never to return. The daily newspapers

would later describe an accidental tank explosion at the refinery, not a bomb, and Rockefeller did his best to erase this attack from the public memory. In all his days as a pirate, Jack had never participated in such a serious assault against capital, and the reality of his act propelled the young author into a frenzy of decisions soon to affect everyone around him.

Just days after the explosion, my mother received a message from Anna Strunsky stating that she was in New York City overseeing the release of *The Kempton-Wace Letters*, the book she co-wrote with Jack. While neither of their names would appear on the cover, Anna was paid five hundred dollars by their publisher and decided to use these funds for a European literary tour. Sadly, Anna also wrote that Jack had left his family in the Piedmont bungalow and moved to Oakland by himself, an event that captured newspaper headlines across California. Unwilling to cross the bay and confront him, Isabelle went to Eamonn's office and waited to speak about his reckless friend. It wasn't until after midnight that Eamonn arrived with Rose Fritz, both bleary-eyed from exhaustion.

For the past months, the federal plague doctors had been demolishing overhangs in Chinatown to allow in more light, an outlandish excuse for outright destruction, and these piles of wooden debris were left on the street to become nests for plague-infected rats. One day, a poor railroad worker named Pietro Spadafora gathered firewood from one of these junk piles and soon both he and his mother were dead from a disease that didn't officially exist, at least according to the government. For the first time since its arrival, the Black Plague had crossed into the Latin Quarter, just blocks away from *Luna's Mexican Restaurant*. It was only a matter of time before the federal doctors and their police escorts marched through the streets with syringes, sulfur, and billy-clubs. When my mother learned this grim reality, she decided not to mention Jack London's neglect of his family. Not only was a plague at their doorstep, another strike wave was set to occur.

Since the middle of spring, several waterfront factories had been paralyzed when the Wire Worker's Union, the Can Maker's Union, and the Bag Worker's Union blockaded their entrances with a mob of 2,000 people. While this strike-force of mostly women clogged the cobblestones below Telegraph Hill, the gold-miners of Colorado were preparing a massive strike in Cripple Creek. To aid them in their battle against the Citizen's Alliance, the radicals of the telegraph and telephone lineman's unions shut down the entire western system, drastically hindering all electrical communication with numerous acts of sabotage. This lineman's strike was so threatening to the San Francisco bosses that they demanded their private detectives be allowed to carry guns, a demand the Mayor refused. Despite her brother Federico's best efforts, the Street Carmen's Union refused to join this labor unrest and the cars of the United Railroads continued to roll when the miners of Cripple Creek began their strike on August 10, 1903. It was the start of a new war, only no one knew it at the time, not even my mother.

As this battle kicked off, Yvonne emerged from her cinematic mesmerism and was sitting in the library with Juana one morning as if nothing had happened. Isabelle closed the door and demanded an explanation, only to be interrupted when one of the kitchen staff escorted in Alma de Bretteville. Isabelle quickly sat beside little Juana, pretending to be her nanny, and Alma spoke like she wasn't even there. Yvonne cast Isabelle a knowing eye as the conversation ranged from luxury to conspiracy, the Palace Hotel to Napa Valley, and within an hour she'd learned that the *San Francisco Bulletin* had initiated a crusade against the Union Labor Party to prevent their return to office, an effort spearheaded by Fremont Older, an anti-graft journalist who'd exposed the illegal blasting on Telegraph Hill. Alma paid no attention to Isabelle and departed without looking at her, leaving my mother to stare at Yvonne with a confusion bordering on reverence. After defeating the cinematic hypnotism, Yvonne was now determined to extend their struggle to the highest levels of power and prevent Heath's vision from spreading any further. Although news of Jack's latest betrayal troubled her, Yvonne remained committed to their strategy. With their combined influences scattered across every level of society, the four of them could bring down Heath and Morgan's empire. The only one she worried about was Eamonn and the lethal plague that threatened him every day.

The federal doctors eventually swept through the Latin Quarter only to be met with orderly apartments free of both plague and rodents. Prior to this, Eamonn and Rose had undertaken a lightning campaign across the Latin Quarter, including the hidden print-shop of *Secolo Nuovo*, and the federal doctors could find no excuse to enact a quarantine. As the white-robed men combed through the streets with their police escorts, the Latin Quarter grew somber, prompting Ersilia to organize a frenzy of public events, all explicitly anarchist but meant to attract the random passerby. Unlike the militant *organazzitori* who hid their identities from the bosses, the *antiorganazzitori* could do as they wished, in the open. They occupied Washington Square Park and held a *feste liberatarie* where picnickers lazed in the grass while Ersilia performed. In addition to her humorous plays, there were also lectures delivered by Enrico, Giuseppe, and every other anarchist known to the police. Isabelle had never seen the entire movement assembled at once, especially in such a joyous atmosphere, and the darkness burned away beneath Ersilia's song, deep and resonant and filled with confidence.

These public events happened on a weekly basis and brought together all the different language groups of the Latin Quarter. During the *feste*,

Washington Square Park

these groups each had their own translator, sometimes more than one, and every performance was accompanied by a chorus of Latin babble. At one of these *festes*, Isabelle might sit beside Spanish comrades who never ate meat, never smoked, and drank only carbonated mineral water, either *Topo Chico* imported from Mexico, or *San Pellegrino* from Italy. At a different *festa*, Isabelle might sit next to chain-smoking French comrades of the *Germinal* group who chattered over the speaker, an annoying habit my mother tried to ignore. While the Spanish and Italian tongues were similar enough, the French anarchists were often excluded from conversation, a situation partially remedied when the *Germinal* group printed a French-language supplement to *La Protesta Humana*. The Basque anarchists could all speak Spanish but none of their comrades knew Euskara, a language unlike the others. Some anarchists studied Esperanto in the hope of creating a universal tongue but it never took root in this neighborhood of a hundred dialects.

The *festes* also alleviated the sufferings of the strikers down on the waterfront, still picketing their factories despite mounting odds. Union members took turns climbing the hill to eat a sandwich, drink a glass of wine, and listen to the crazy anarchists describe a world without money or bosses. With their canning season threatened, the bosses caved to the Can Maker's Union, ending the long strike and removing nearly 1,000 people from the streets. Despite this victory, the Wire Maker's Union was soon crushed after a violent labor conflict and the *festes* filled with dozens of dejected wire-makers bitter at the cruelties of capitalism. Only the lineman remained on strike, their union net-work stretching all the way to Colorado. Thanks to them, telegraph and telephone wires were being constantly cut across the Western United States, acts of sabotage that threw capital into a crisis. At the height of this lineman's strike, the gold-miners of Cripple Creek initiated their final showdown.

Led by Big Bill Haywood of the Western Federation of Miners, this powerful organization counted the local sheriff as a member, giving them effective control of the entire county. To counter this, the Citizen's Alliance called in their favors and instructed small shop-owners to refuse credit to any WFM members, although this scheme backfired when the Federation installed its own cooperative stores across the county. When the mine-owners finally brought in their scabs, a massive conflict began that included beatings, sabotage, arson, theft, and gunfire. After a mine-shaft collapsed from a union-lit fire, the Citizen's Alliance played its last card and paid the corrupt governor to send in the Colorado National Guard. They lavished money on everyone, including the commander of the Guard, and their thousand minions were soon drunk with greed. On September 4, 1903, these soldiers invaded the rebel bastion of Cripple Creek. The entire region was put under martial law, all WFM members were arrested on sight, and the mines kept open at gunpoint. None of this stopped the conflict from spreading in what became known as the Colorado Labor Wars.

The electrical lineman's union of San Francisco kept up their disruption of the western net-work and remained on strike until November when their leadership forced them back to work, claiming their demands were satisfied. The *antiorganazzitori* cited this casual betrayal as further proof of the need to exit the workplace and extend the conflict to the neighborhoods, cities, and counties. When she got off work, Isabelle worked many hours countering this narrative in the columns of *Secolo Nuovo*, claiming everyone was free to pursue any strategy they saw fit, including workplace organizing. Her own job, however unorthodox, had led my mother into a level of intelligence that most anarchists could scarcely imagine, placing her at the very heart of capitalism, and her visits with Yvonne continued to yield vital information that she leaked back to the International, never revealing its source.

During the fall of 1903, Yvonne decided to call on Phœbe Hearst and met with her in the library while Isabelle posed as the nanny. During their long conversation, my mother learned that Phœbe's son William Randolph Hearst had bought up huge amounts of Mexican land to compete with Rockefeller's petroleum empire. After stuffing the coffers of the dictator Porfirio Díaz, these two capitalists were now extracting, gold, silver, and oil using the local inhabitants as exploited toilers. My mother brought this new intelligence directly to *Luna's Mexican Restaurant* where the growing number of exiles had begun to gather. These political dissidents would swell in number during a crackdown and shrink when they returned armed with newspapers, funds, and weapons. Not only did they have to fight President Díaz, they had to fend off *yanqui* capitalists swooping in like oil-crazed vultures. These brave men and women weren't the only exiles to use San Francisco as a temporary base that year, nor would they be the last, and the end of 1903 delivered my family troubling news from Russia.

Two women stepped off a boat that fall and walked north along the waterfront, searching for a small blue house described to them in Saint Petersburg. They found it up a steep dirt road and knocked on the door multiple times. My mother had already gone off to work when Josephine finally opened up and beheld two women wearing black dresses with high collars lined in red.

Elizabeth Dimitreff

She told them to sit down, roused Marisol from bed, and started brewing a pot of coffee. Over the next hours, the Queens learned of the violent struggle against the fractured Russian Empire, a conflict that drove Olga and Anja to San Francisco. Amid their accounts, Josephine discovered that Elizabeth Dimitrieff, her comrade from the Paris Commune, was now living in the wastelands of Siberia near her imprisoned husband. With her two daughters safe in Moscow, Elizabeth now lived her weeks shivering by the fire as she waited to see her lover. Aside from a single visit to *Les Diablerets* in 1902, she'd refused to leave Siberia, not even to see her daughters. Olga and Anja met with Elizabeth before they crossed the Pacific and beheld a withered ghost wasting away beside the wood-stove, crippled by heartbreak over a man they refused to trust. If not for her lover's recklessness, Elizabeth might still be the fire-bringer of Paris rather than a shivering wretch groveling to the Empire. What disturbed Josephine even more was the fate of Vera Zasulich, the nihilist assassin who gave birth to the modern communist movement.

On January 24, 1878, Vera shot and wounded Colonel Fyodor Trepov, a notorious tyrant of the Czarist regime, and at the trial the jury refused to condemn her. After being released, she immediately fled to Switzerland, met with my relatives beneath *Les Diablerets*, and decided to intervene in the growing communist movement. After convincing Karl Marx that Russian peasants didn't need to be industrialized in order to revolt, Vera decided to embrace the doctrine of Marxism, although she never stopped wearing her black dress with its red-lined collar. She translated the *Communist Manifesto*

into Russian, wrote up massive literary analysis by candle-light, and lived
alone among the Marxists as the holy
nihilist priestess who'd outsmarted
Marx. Vera had been in exile for many
decades when she met a man named
Vladimir Lenin, a prominent member
of her Russian Social Democratic
Labor Party. They collaborated on
a newspaper called *Iskra* and smuggled cases of it into Russia to spark
the people into rebellion. Vera was the
glue that held this operation together,
her messy London apartment constantly filled with visitors and exiles
from across the Empire. With her
blessing, Lenin came to eclipse Vera's
influence in the Party, although she
was too naive to perceive his ambitions. At their 1903 Congress, Lenin
declared mass-movements to be the
incorrect strategy and purged those

Vera Zasulich

who refused his clandestine, hierarchical, and centrally controlled organization. This event split the Party into Lenin's Bolshevik faction and Vera's
Menshevik faction, a heartbreak that scraped out her soul and left her broken,
just like Elizabeth.

Olga and Anja weren't going to let this darkness win, not after the sacrifices
of so many others, and they planned to board a train for New York the next
morning and then cross the Atlantic to find Lenin. My mother came home
that afternoon and stayed up all night speaking with these visitors of the global
struggle, the secretive forces of Mary, the anarchist author Tolstoy, and the
latest attacks against the Empire. After they'd left for the ferry, Isabelle went
to work bolstered with so much confidence that she failed to notice posters for
the Union Labor Party plastered down every alley. Later that night, the Party
was ushered back into power on the wave of a popular vote.

They held a triumphant procession that crowded around the base of the
San Francisco Bulletin tower and taunted Fremont Older, the journalist
who'd exposed their graft. One of the administration's first acts was to install
a new Board of Health and cut the City funds for plague eradication. While
the federal doctors maintained their inspections of Chinatown and the Latin
Quarter, the Mayor denied the existence of plague, leaving Eamonn and

Rose to clean up the mess. As the saying went back then, *anarchy is order, government is chaos.*

Amid the Union Labor Party's victory, few noticed the sudden arrival of the Citizen's Alliance. It dispatched one of its Colorado henchman to San Francisco who dined at Heath's mansion on his first night in town. Yvonne could barely contain her disgust as Heath applauded their recent victory in Cripple Creek and explained his plans for crushing the San Francisco unions. Thanks to this intelligence, Isabelle was able to warn her comrades and prepare the movement for a time of great violence. The pages of *Secolo Nuovo* and *La Protesta Humana* were filled with information not only on this Citizen's Alliance, but the rising Italian bourgeois. Thanks to her years of church-going, Josephine was now able to map this *prominenti* net-work and reveal their interlinked chains of business interests. Readers of the Italian anarchist press quickly became aware of exactly who controlled what in the Latin Quarter, along with their reputations as exploiters of immigrants. While local *prominenti* encouraged Italians to form unions against the racist *yanquis*, they also exploited the un-unionized Sicilians and Genovese in their lucrative bakeries, canneries, and factories.

These matters were often discussed late into the night at Enrico and Frankie's apartment, long after the children had fallen asleep. It was here my mother first met Michele Centrone, one of the many Paterson anarchists who'd arrived with Lorenzo, and she enjoyed listening to him argue with Enrico about philosophy, technology, and organization. Michele was part of *La Protesta Humana's* editorial crew and used these debates with *luciferino* to polish off his latest articles. Isabelle would always take Enrico's side, especially when the entire room was against him, and she saw the influence of his late mother in each argument. While other anarchists argued for immediacy, *luciferino* was the one willing to take his time, a trait she couldn't help but admire. Ersilia and Giuseppe attended these gatherings and often hosted their own, although Giuseppe's health began to deteriorate towards the end of 1903. After a decade of fighting the Ottoman Empire, the Italian Republic, and the United States of America, 32-year-old Giuseppe had ravaged his body and was often kept bed-ridden for days at a time. No one liked to talk about it, especially Giuseppe.

My mother continued her routine at the Heath mansion as the New Year's Eve of 1904 came and went. That winter in Yvonne's library was exceptionally gray but brightened by the sudden arrival of an envelope sealed with red wax and bearing the initials of Nikola Tesla. Inside was a prospectus printed on vellum and accompanied by an illustration of the Wardenclyffe magnifying transmitter. While the prospectus was addressed to potential investors, Tesla included a hand-written note to Yvonne begging her to intercede with

JP Morgan and Lionel Heath. Unable to secure him any funding, Yvonne burned the note but hid the prospectus inside *Moby Dick* where she and Isabelle could read it when gloomy weather bogged them down. My mother lived those rainy afternoons with Yvonne and Juana, each lost in their own books, and Jack London's complete works were now lined on a single shelf, allowing them easy access to their co-conspirators imagination, a realm they wearily explored.

Since the publication of *The Call of the Wild*, their comrade had become a massive literary star with his books sold across the US, including the racist ones he'd written for money. After seeing him off at Fisherman's Wharf for the Standard Oil bombing, my mother heard nothing of the former pirate until Anna Strunsky returned from Europe. She and Isabelle met at a corner booth in *Luna's Mexican Restaurant* where Anna delivered coded messages from the International, along with the latest news from London and Paris. Her most disturbing revelation didn't emerge from Europe but the New York publishers of *The Kempton-Wace Letters*. With the aim of boosting its sales, Jack secretly planned a second release with their full names printed on the cover, hoping to capitalize on his recent celebrity. When my mother told this to Yvonne, they agreed something terrible could erupt between Anna and his wife Bessie, the women Jack had pitted against each other.

Anna moved closer to Isabelle that winter and lived away from her family in an apartment at 974 Sutter Street. Within this den of solitude, she furiously worked on her novel *Windlestraws*, an honest depiction of the life she'd lived since fleeing the Russian Empire. In the midst of a sustained writing frenzy, Jack and their New York City publisher suddenly barged into her apartment with a proposition. Anna hadn't seen Jack in over a year and now he claimed they could both receive funding to cover the impending war between Russia and Japan. In January of 1904, these empires prepared for battle over China and Korea, a conflict backed with weapons sold by western manufacturers, including the Union Iron Works. Anna said she'd think the offer over and asked to be left alone, determined to finish *Windlestraws*. As she would later describe the offer, *he gets $2000 a week and all expenses free and I expect only $200 a week and expenses. There's equity for you.* Jack found Isabelle the very next morning and told her this assignment was his ticket into the Bohemian Club, an opportunity he couldn't refuse. He promised that no matter what he wrote it was all just an effort to infiltrate their enemy, and she shouldn't grow enraged. Isabelle later brought this up to Yvonne, although before they came to any conclusion, Jack shipped off without Anna under the pay of William Randolph Hearst.

Unwilling to be distracted, Anna forgot about Jack and labored alone in her *bizarrely furnished*, gas-lit apartment, writing until morning with her fingers stained black from ink and tobacco. Eamonn and Rose would stop by during their nightly plague inspections and often stayed past midnight, chatting over tea and cigarettes. The *worn and wearied* paleness of Anna's face inspired Rose to offer her refuge on some land she owned down south in Los Gatos, a redwood sanctuary for anyone who needed to remain invisible. Anna agreed to Rose's offer and took her little brother Morris to live in a small cabin perched along a babbling creek. She didn't return until winter had become spring.

During her absence, Marisol de la Costa and Josephine Lemel orchestrated a take-down of the Union Labor Party, and their first act was to secure the loyalty of a police commissioner. This former lawyer for the City Front Federation agreed to their instructions and began an investigation into the French restaurants that lined the edge of Chinatown. These targets had been suggested by Yvonne in the hope of shuttering the favorite meeting place of Adolph Spreckels and Alma de Bretteville, forcing the greedy baron to either marry or abandon his *sugar baby*. In the process of defending these notorious establishments, the Union Labor Party revealed their control over vice in San Francisco. Marisol and Josephine used this new information to attack these restaurants and force the Party-backed pimps out of the Barbary Coast. Facing an assault from the Queen herself, a washed-up hustler called Billy Finnegan started recruiting for a new brothel built on the edge of Chinatown. Protected by an army of henchman, the Municipal Crib was quickly packed with over a hundred women in the exact epicenter of the plague outbreak. Billy Finnegan promised Party immunity to anyone who worked its beds and the house soon became Marisol's direct competition. In the Municipal Crib, women rented their rooms from Finnegan for three dollars a day, while in Marisol's brothel they owned their own apartments. For the Queens of the Barbary Coast, the war had only just begun.

Yvonne's advice soon bore sweet fruit when Alma announced that Adolph Spreckels was openly sending her on a luxury cruise-liner to visit relatives in Denmark with her mother and father. While this was far from marriage, it was the *sugar daddy's* first public acknowledgment of their affair. As Alma traveled across the continent by train, a labor conflict erupted when the Stablemen's Union went on strike, bringing hundreds of men to the streets and flushing out the Citizen's Alliance. More horse and carriage unions walked off the job, including the horse-shoers and drivers, and commercial traffic soon plummeted across the city. Yvonne's own union carriage-driver could no longer transport her visitors across the city, engaged as he was in the violent struggle.

Funded by the Citizen's Alliance, the local bosses armed their private mercenaries with sawed-off shotguns, gun battles erupted on a daily basis, and for some reason, the Union Labor Party refused to intervene. Strike-funds dwindled as more men were injured and even with Eamonn and Rose's free services, the unions couldn't outspend the Citizen's Alliance. When my uncle Federico and his Street Carmen's Union threatened a strike of the train-lines, City Hall convinced the leadership to terminate their plans, unwilling to face the three hundred armed men hired by the Citizen's Alliance. The final blow to the strike came when Yvonne's driver was shot down by a private-detective while picketing his stable. Rather than retaliate, the Union Labor Party negotiated a cowardly surrender and forced the union leaders to call off the strike. By the end of this conflict, the Citizen's Alliance had reduced all stableman's wages to $2.00 for a twelve-hour day.

Yvonne listened to her husband gloat over this victory, burning with a desire to kill him. She smiled at his jokes and encouraged his endeavor, but when she was alone with Isabelle the truth boiled forth. Her husband's Citizen Alliance had not only crushed the Colorado miners, Heath was destroying what remained of the local labor movement using the Union Labor Party as his weapon, a group of men so corrupt they would accept any bribes, even from Heath. Isabelle and Yvonne suspected collusion at the highest levels of City Hall but had no proof that Heath was in direct control of the Party, a gap of intelligence they hoped to bridge with Jack's sudden return from Korea.

The war between Russian and Japan was still raging when he showed up at *Luna's* and asked to speak with Isabelle. After she arrived, my mother listened to Jack's bizarre tale of striking a Japanese horse groomer, giving a racist speech at an Oakland socialist rally, penning a fiercely bigoted essay entitled "The Yellow Peril," and subsequently receiving an invitation to join the Bohemian Club. Jack attended their annual gathering at the Bohemian Grove in Sonoma and participated in a fiery ceremony complete with torches, robes, and a massive stone owl. He met all the famous club members, including Lionel Heath, and drank with them late into the evening. At these fireside debauches, Jack listened to these men praise the Union Labor Party, calling it the most business-friendly administration since the days of the gold-rush. Jack went along with their jokes and played his part well enough to emerge unscathed, trusted, and accepted. To further cement his reputation among these Bohemians, Jack also recruited a team of Japanese and Korean militants to pose as his domestic servants for several months, long enough to secure their papers. While pretending to be a fierce racist, Jack was secretly establishing migration routes for the anarchists of Asia. Most of this plan troubled my mother for obvious reasons, although she'd already accepted the consequences of working with Jack. Unlike the year before, there was no spring retreat in 1904, given how volatile the city was becoming, and none of the conspirators had the luxury of free time besides Yvonne.

Deporting miners to Kansas, Cripple Creek, 1903

Their comrades in Colorado had suffered a brutal defeat at the hands of the Citizen's Alliance and formerly-mighty Cripple Creek was now a militarized work-camp. After their guerrilla war in the Rocky Mountains, the Western Federation of Miners was nearly crushed with none of the larger unions coming to their aid. Over thirty men died in the Colorado Labor Wars, hundreds were illegally deported from the state, and over a thousand put up on show-trial. Against an enemy as powerful as the Citizen's Alliance, the Federation decided to build towards *the amalgamation of the entire wage-working class into one general organization.* If their foe was coordinating this repression across the entire continent, the Federation needed their own body to coordinate the destruction of North American capitalism. A clandestine call was issued for a meeting in Chicago that found its way to every organizer connected to the old International. This meeting was scheduled to take place on January 2, 1905.

San Francisco filled with electric light in 1904, the old gas system was slowly removed pipe by pipe, and bulbs hummed above the cobblestones using the same over-ground cables that powered the United Railroads. As an employee of this train system, my uncle Federico had pushed for two strikes only to be met with betrayal at the highest levels of the labor movement. The truth was only revealed when Yvonne dined with Lionel Heath and Patrick Calhoun, head of the United Railroads. She learned that Calhoun had been installed in San Francisco by JP Morgan himself and instructed to report directly to Heath. As they ate roast duck and potatoes with red wine, the men discussed the Union Labor Party and bribes they'd paid not only to boost their overhead electrical lines, but to prevent a strike on their train system. Yvonne discovered that Calhoun had paid the Union Labor Party to successfully stop two labor strikes and *what seemed at first to be the red flag of anarchy turned out to be the red flag of the auctioneer.* The next afternoon, Yvonne delivered this revelation to Isabelle and soon word was out that Wall Street was pulling the strings of the United Railroads and making deals with City Hall.

The final piece of this puzzle didn't arrive until Alma de Bretteville returned from Europe and met with Yvonne in the library. Much had happened during her absence, including the attempted murder of a newspaper owner. *The San Francisco Bulletin* was the Union Labor Party's sharpest critic and when the proprietor left the office one night in September, a hired Party thug slammed a metal pipe against his skull. Were it not for the man's thick bowler hat, the Party would have committed its first assassination, given the pipe was made of lead. After learning of this brazen corruption, including the Municipal Crib brothel protected by tax-funded police, Alma flew into a rage and revealed that Adolph Spreckels had been made Parks Commissioner by this very administration, an obvious bribe meant to placate the idle sugar baron. With fire in her eyes, Alma vowed to intervene.

In less than a week, Adolph and his brothers united to push back against the United Railroads and their shadowy New York backers. They publicly claimed the United Railroad's over-ground wires would mar the city's beauty and advocated for their own underground power conduits. When my mother told Josephine and Marisol of these developments, they both grinned like two jack-o-lanterns. In all their years on this crumbling hillside, Marisol and Josephine never tasted such sweet promises of victory, nor had they woven a conspiracy so intricate. There was even more good news that afternoon, a miracle none of them expected: the *protégé* Marisol had placed in the Palace Hotel had just met a French courtesan who claimed to be the mistress of Lionel Heath. It wouldn't be long before his final secrets were revealed to the same underworld now converging to destroy him.

Across the bay, their comrade Jack had triggered nothing but chaos after his return from Korea. His recent bout of racist nonsense had exiled him from the socialist movement and into the bohemian scene, a crowd that encouraged his recklessness just for kicks. His wife Bessie was now suing him and claiming a share of his literary wealth, including custody of their two daughters. She publicly accused Jack and Anna of maintaining a sexual relationship, a claim they both publicly denied, but unknown to almost everybody, Jack's actual affair was with a bohemian named Charmian Kitredge, an upper class nature lover who loved the brute aspects of this famous writer. With his membership in the Bohemian Club now secure, Jack also brought over a young Korean anarchist named Manyoungi to pose as his servant. Week by week, more of these anarchists began to arrive from Korea and Japan.

While this immigration route might have been inspiring, the anarchist struggle in the Latin Quarter had become more difficult. Emboldened by the arrival of the Citizen's Alliance, the Italian bourgeois banded together and reported *La Protesta Humana* to the mail censor for infractions of the federal postal code. Nothing came of this, but it roused Giuseppe from his sickness and filled him with a desire

Manyoungi arriving in 1904.

to sink these greedy *prominenti*. He stayed up late at night working with Ersilia, his cough growing worse as he composed venomous articles directly onto the printing plate. Enrico visited Giuseppe whenever he was bed-ridden and they helped write false denunciations of each other to confuse both the Italian Consulate and SFPD. The pages of *Secolo Nuovo* and *La Protesta Humana* were filled with these false claims and the two old friends laughed while writing them, most often by the bed-table so Giuseppe could rest. As these silly men joked around, Ersilia tried not to weep.

One evening in September, Isabelle arrived at Giuseppe's apartment with a pot of soup only to find Enrico crying in the kitchen. She tried to comfort *luciferino* but then noticed the total silence that now filled their apartment. When she walked into the bedroom, Ersilia was desperately clutching the hands of her departed lover. After fleeing from Republican Italy to the Alpine safety of *Les Diablerets*, after crossing the Atlantic and all of North America, the great Giuseppe Ciancabilla was dead. Ersilia asked to burn his body on the shore of the Pacific Ocean and over three hundred anarchists attended this illegal ceremony. Once the flames subsided and the sparks drifted away, the glowing stars emerged from the black sky and filled the crowd with wonder. As the tide washed away the ashes of their fallen comrade, the anarchists beheld the radiant galaxy rotating above their earthly sphere.

The long sadness of this event was broken only by the arrival of a woman named Svetlana who wore a black dress with a high collar lined in red. She came to the little blue house and found Isabelle eating dinner with Josephine and Marisol. My mother had just gotten off work, Marisol was about to head to the brothel, and Josephine was readying for a night on the Barbary Coast. None were prepared to learn what Svetlana told them. Over a simple stew prepared by Josephine, the young Russian spoke of an impending uprising in the crumbling Empire. The Interior Minister and former head of the secret police, Vyacheslav von Plehve, was blown to pieces on the streets of Saint Petersburg in July of 1904, shortly before Russia's defeat by Japan. It was the perfect moment to strike, a chance that wouldn't come again for many years, and every faction agreed to participate, even the forces of Mary. Great changes were sure to come when the fighting stopped, allowing the Russian people to think clearly for the first time in decades. As she narrated these visions, Svetlana brightened the house that dreary afternoon in October 1904, her words a testament to the times of promise in which they all resided.

SHE'LL BE HUFFING AND PUFFING

THIS IS THE FIRST SLEEP I'VE GOTTEN IN DAYS BUT IT'S NOT ENOUGH, I can already tell. Isabelle pushes my shoulder until I'm awake and says *it's dawn* over and over again, like I didn't hear her the first time. The green door of my childhood room is wide open, my notebook's still on the old desk, and all I want to do is sleep. I blink my eyes and stare at the hallway's smooth floorboards, the ones that creak with every footstep, the ones that used to scare me, the ones my mother used to step on. *And then the god of war Ares boasted that he could haul off Hephaistos, master of the Forges, by sheer force.* Isabelle gets tired of my half-awake reverie so she rips the covers off my body and lets the cold morning air do all her work. She gets that move from Lorraine.

"Where's your mom?" she asks, almost frantic. "I haven't seen her."

"What do you mean *where's my mom?* Have you been awake all night?"

"I couldn't help it! I closed my eyes, I tried to sleep. Anyway, come on! Let's go!"

Isabelle yanks me up by the arms and I lower my feet to the cold floor. I'll be sure to give her this same treatment tomorrow, if she doesn't beat me to it. Once she's satisfied that I'm actually getting dressed, Isabelle rushes downstairs to look for my mother. I hope the old woman isn't doing something crazy. This thought makes me pack my saddle-bag faster and I hustle downstairs to find little Isabelle bent over the dining table. She's looking at a black and white photograph and a note that reads: *Fulvia and Isabelle, I went down to see Yvonne. Thank you for the wonderful day together. Keep each other safe. Love, Aunt Isabelle.* The photograph still bears the marks of my teenage vandalism. My mother's standing in a field of dry grass. A few oak trees in the distance. She's just had a swim at Jack London's ranch and holds a white towel in her left hand. For some reason, her left index finger is pointed towards the earth. She walked into Jack London's ambush with his tripod camera and allowed this one image to be captured. Her long black hair still damp from swimming in the creek, Isabelle Ferrari looks sternly into the camera and tries not to smile. Atop her head are two black devil horns drawn crudely in ink. These are my teenage additions to Isabelle Lemel Ferrari's image. This isn't just the only photo of her that exists, it's the only physical copy, never duplicated.

"Who drew the horns?" little Isabelle asks.

"Me. Back when I was young. We had a fight and I ran off with Angelo for a week. Left that behind to make her angry. I guess she wants me to remember what I've done when I wanted to ride off and be with Angelo. I just never knew she kept it."

"It's—" Isabelle can't stop giggling at the vandalism. "It's funny."

"Alright, come on!" I slip the paper note into my pocket and push Isabelle to the door. "Out!"

"We haven't eaten breakfast."

"We'll eat on the road. Salmon jerky and an apple."

I make sure I've got my notebooks before tying my saddle-bag to Gudrun's side. We walk her out of the barn, check her shoes, give her one last drink of water, and take turns climbing up her back. I set Gudrun on a trot away from the commune along the narrow trail that connects to the eastern pass, a route only the Kashaya use. We soon leave the realm of oak trees and become surrounded by shady redwoods towering in every direction. The lumber baron who built my mother's house spared this one stretch of forest from the sawblades, I guess because he thought it was his backyard, and thanks to his ego some of the ancient trees still exist. We pass beneath one of these giants, its trunk wider than my mother's house, its bark thicker than a healthy stack of roof-shingles. The entire coast used to be filled with these mammoth trees, far older than the civilization that killed them. It's a shame beyond words.

"This is the farthest I've ever gone," Isabelle tells me, chewing on a stick of salmon jerky. "My mom took us out here once. With your mom. While you were in San Francisco. It was nice."

"You came out here to see the giants?"

"Uh-huh. And a picnic. I was pretty little, but my sisters were still babies. It's weird being so much older than them. My mom said it was because my dad was busy on Paloma. He was never home. But then the transmitter worked and he came back. That's when my two sisters happened."

"That's what she says, huh? Well, I couldn't tell you. Makes sense, though."

"I don't cry about him anymore. Sometimes with my mom, I guess. I don't want her to be alone. But I also...I want to leave. I'm so glad you brought me." She hugs my sides with the salmon jerky in her hand, still chewing what she's already bitten off. "Being the oldest after he died—"

She doesn't finish. She doesn't need to. Isabelle had to watch all that darkness work its way out of her mother's body. She was the one who took care of her two sisters while Lorraine sat in her chair staring at nothing. It wasn't so bad when I got back from San Francisco, I helped lift Lorraine out of that long sadness, but the pain's still clawing inside her, and Isabelle's thrilled as punch to be away.

The path through the redwoods eventually connects us to the Kashaya road and if we follow it steady, we'll reach the outskirts of Santa Rosa by nightfall. Both of us have gone through the Dream, so we don't have to worry about losing our way, but I still feel its effects once we enter. Isabelle asks me what's wrong and I tell her we've gone inside. There's a fuzzy border to every tree and my thoughts bubble as if trapped in water. In all those years I rode up here with Angelo, we never imagined the Dream would spread inland. I keep waiting for the effects to diminish but the haziness lingers across the horizon. Any outsider who stumbles into this zone could lose months or years, maybe even their life, and no one can stop it. When I was growing up, most mothers treated the Dream like chicken-pox and took us to play with the Kashaya hoping we'd wake up early. For me it was a bit different.

"When did your mom first take you in?" I ask her. "Into the Dream."

"What?"

"Am I losing you? You doing alright? It's not—"

"Yeah, I'm fine. I was just thinking about my mom."

"When did she take you in the Dream?"

"Really young. When I was three. I just remember the ferns, running around under the trees with the other kids. It was fun, not so scary like older people say. Well...there was this dark house, and a fire, kind of scary, but not really. I just went back outside and played. My mom always said she took me home the minute I looked bored. What happened to you the first time?"

"I talked to Essie, outside the roundhouse. She fed me boiled acorns and we talked."

"Talked? How old were you?"

"Two years old. Maybe. We talked like we're talking now, only I didn't use my lips."

"That doesn't make any—"

"It's like I've been saying, Isabelle. My family has powers. I just thought it was the Dream, some fake memory from when I was kid, but now I know what it was. That really happened between us, it's why we've always been so familiar."

"Essie's fun. She smells good."

"There's no one like her, not even close. I don't know, my mom swears those were the last of their little secrets, but there's a reason Yvonne moved so close to Kashaya land, built her communal house near Essie and settled down just up the river. All of them chose this place, your mom too."

"We're pretty far away from them now."

Isabelle's right. We're deep in the mountains on an ancient road. It's been empty this whole time and Gudrun's still trotting along at a good clip. I finally eat my breakfast, keeping one hand on the reins as the landscape opens up to an expanse of brown grassland and green oak trees. The redwoods tower above us on the highest ridges and a few small patches of blue break through the morning fog. I've ridden this road before, holding onto Angelo the way Isabelle's holding onto me now. He and I would reach the Sonoma Valley by afternoon, swim all day in the river, then camp for the night on the edge of a vineyard. There was nothing to do but wander this beautiful paradise, so filled with bounty that the greatest transgression of our era was leaving the comfort of our commune, village, or town.

"What made you want to go to Paloma?" Isabelle asks, snatching my half-eaten apple. "You and my mom were talking all weird about it. I heard you from upstairs, only you never said."

"Uh, excuse me, I was eating that apple."

"You've been holding it for half an hour."

"Fine. Take it."

"Tell me. Why do you want to go there?"

"I went to see Essie a while back. I don't know how much you've heard about—"

"I know everything. Everybody does. She sucked some bad spirits out of Angelo."

"Yeah, well, those spirits, that's what Yvonne calls the darkness. It got inside Angelo but Essie took it out. She usually digests it, destroys it, but part of it stuck around. When I went to the village looking for Angelo, I

walked into the roundhouse where Essie sucked it out and the darkness just...
it went inside me. It's still here. But while I was in the roundhouse I saw the
Paloma transmitter, I saw it explode, and I saw it again when I went...this is
going to sound weird, but I was in Yvonne's room and all of sudden, I sort of
went up, only backwards, into this tube of water. I'd only ever written about
this stuff, but there I was drenched in it, like salt-water filled with lavender.
It's strange, I know, but when I came out of this tube, I knew I needed to
go to Paloma."

"You're all weird," she says, munching on my apple. "You and my mom.
Yvonne's weird too."

"What's that supposed to mean? *Weird?*"

"Everything you do is...funny."

"Yeah, well, that's why I'm going to Paloma. Not to be funny. None of this
is funny. Believe me, I'm pregnant, and you just stole my food. Give me some
of that jerky before you eat it all."

There really isn't any point talking about this stuff, so I change the subject back to our journey. Once we get to Santa Rosa, we'll have to cross
the Wappo Mountains before reaching the great San Joaquin Valley that
stretches across the whole of California. I've only ever ridden south through
the valley to Sacramento, never north, and that vast expanse is a complete
mystery to me. Once we get to the San Joaquin, it'll take us another two
or three days until we arrive at the new Paloma transmitter. Isabelle grows
dreamy with questions and the next hours pass nicely with tales of distant
places neither of us have seen. After crossing the Russian River, we stop to
pee near a gushing spring and let Gudrun quench herself with water. After
that, we decide to have a picnic in the shade. All the fog's burned away and
the inland air is growing warm, on the verge of drawing out my sweat.

We sit on a boulder eating white cheese, black bread, and red cherry pre-
serves while Gudrun chomps on grass. It isn't hot enough to swim but this
weather's still a relief from the endless chill of our foggy coastline. Isabelle
eats her lunch like a wild beast before begging for mine, an indulgence I don't
allow, not with this baby in my belly. Having nothing left to eat, Isabelle pes-
ters me to hurry, claiming I'm acting like an old person. I slip the remaining
cheese into my pocket, kick some spring-water in her direction, then hop
onto Gudrun's back. My legs are going to be sore when I lay down tonight,
given how badly they're burning now, but Isabelle isn't complaining. If she
feels any pain, it's being blocked by all her excitement. Once we get moving
over the last of these hills, she clutches me tightly and puts her chin on my
shoulder. Isabelle loves her crazy aunt Fulvia. She always did.

I finish my hunk of cheese as we start our plunge into the Sonoma Valley,
it's grape-lined fields just visible in the distance. The dirt road straightens out

and I get Gudrun up to a light sprint, nothing dangerous, but to Isabelle it must feel like lightning. She screams and howls and begs me to go faster, as if I could. We trot on the curving stretches and bolt when the road straightens but it's never fast enough for her. I see the farmland and vineyards stretching across the distance in long symmetrical rows and remember there's usually a lot of traffic on this busy farm road, only today there isn't a single wagon, horse, or hiker. The closer we get to Santa Rosa, the more disturbing this absence becomes.

"Is it usually like this?" Isabelle asks. "Our commune always has people—"

"Something's wrong. Really wrong."

She gets silent after that and eventually both of us see a big black square blocking the road up ahead. It's a burnt out wagon with a few charred boards clinging to its iron frame. The word **MISERY** is traced into the ash covered ground in front of it. Once we've passed this ominous mark, I ask Isabelle to hand me the rifle and tell her to take out the pistol. She doesn't seem afraid, mostly because I don't, but the truth is I'm terrified now that something's finally happening.

"Is it the Dream?" Isabelle asks.

"Maybe. Doesn't look good, does it? Just do me a favor, keep the safety on."

We ride forward at a quick trot, the road empty aside from the occasional deer or crow. Isabelle keeps her arms around me, the pistol hovering above my lap, and I keep the rifle pointed towards the sky with my finger over the trigger, not on it. The air smells thick with wood-smoke but I can't see any fires, neither can Isabelle. We don't get any answers until we reach the outskirts of Santa Rosa and find a woman sobbing on her front doorstep. She doesn't look up no matter what we say, mumbling about countless rivers overflowing.

"It's the Dream," Isabelle whispers. "I've seen it before. They get like this."

"Why didn't anyone tell us? This can't have just happened."

There isn't a single house up ahead that doesn't show signs of being submerged in the Dream. Curtains blow out of windows, children kick down fence posts, and old men cry as they grip the trunks of oak trees. Few of them notice us gallop into the heart of Santa Rosa. No one yells, points, or pays any attention until we reach the brick-lined downtown and a man in a white coat comes running at us. His face is flushed, he's waving his arms in the air, and I point the rifle at him just in case.

"No, no, no, no! I'm awake! I'm fine! Is that a *gun*?"

"Who are you?" I ask. "What's going on?"

"Fulvia? Is that you?"

I recognize him now. He's a friend of Gerty, our communal librarian. He used to work in the library and caught salmon with the Kashaya each year. I never knew he settled in Santa Rosa, but that explains his lucidity. He drops his hands, catches his breath, and tries to speak over his panting.

"It juſt came in two night ago, I don't...I don't..."

"Are you the only one awake?" I ask. "We saw a burnt wagon—"

"I think the burning passed, I think that...they burnt a lot laſt night. Stopped for now. It's the Dream. It took over. All across town. There's a dozen more of us, but I've juſt been trying—" He looks into my eyes and shakes his head. "This is bad, Fulvia. I've been trying to ſtop people from killing themselves. All of us have, the ones who already went in the Dream. And it dœsn't end, the suicides keep coming. We need help. I don't know how far inland this spread but—"

The three of us ſtare down the road at a desolate and devaſtated town. Jars of food are broken across the soil, blankets are woven through oak branches, and a ſtreet's-worth of front doors are ſtacked neatly in the middle of the lane. On a normal day, the center of Santa Rosa is buzzing with hundreds of people from dawn until dusk, all of them busy with some scheme or other. Almoſt 2,000 people live here and by the sounds in the air, you'd think a plague wiped out the entire population, leaving only these emanations of the Dream ſcattered across the landscape.

We agree to follow the old librarian down the empty road and meet with a small group of locals, now desperate to guide their loved ones from this self-created nightmare. I have the intuition we won't be leaving Santa Rosa anytime soon, not tomorrow or the day after. Essie warned all of us, but I don't think we were ready for what it meant. I know I wasn't.

21

NEW YORK CITY AND THE END OF THE WORLD

TELEGRAPH HILL EARNED ITS NAME FROM THE WOODEN SEMAPHORE telegraph that once crowned its summit, an old-fashioned mechanism invented during the French Revolution that sent visual signals across vaſt diſtances. Using combinations of arm positions, this semaphore rose and fell according to the types of vessels entering or leaving San Francisco's harbor. It received this information visually from a second semaphore atop Point Lobos, juſt as it relayed information about departing ships. Built in 1850, the semaphore telegraph ſtood over the little blue house on Greenwich Street for only a few years, a mad wind-mill that paused its ravings only for fog.

Time Ball atop Layman's Folly, 1884.

Attached to this structure was the Time Ball, a recent invention of the Greenwich Observatory in England, the same institution that would go on to establish their Greenwich Meridian as the prime meridian in 1884. Over thirty years before Greenwich Mean Time became the global time standard, the planners of San Francisco drew a line called Greenwich Street from the waterfront up to the Time Ball that crowned Telegraph Hill. At precisely 12:00 PM, Pacific Time, eight hours behind Greenwich Mean Time, the Time Ball would be dropped from the top of a metal pole to the bottom, signaling that the day was half over to all who could see.

After a new electric telegraph was installed between Point Lobos and downtown in 1853, City Hall put the Time Ball in storage, abandoned the semaphore on Telegraph Hill, and let scavengers strip it for wood, roof beams, and fittings, leaving the summit bare. A telescope and marine telegraph station were built near the summit in the 1860s and 1870s, but they were both destroyed by storms with their ruins picked over by a second generation of scavengers. In the year 1882, a real-estate developer started to build a cable-car line to the summit where he constructed Layman's Folly, a castle-like observatory with band music, alcohol, dancing, spectacular views, and the old Time Ball. The castle was enlarged in 1884, the cable-car line was finished, but few ever paid to ride it. By 1887, the cable-car had shut down and the novelty of the castle wore off, dooming Layman's Folly to collapse. It fell into disrepair over the 1890s and became known as the *hoodlums resort*, a shadowy place where every manner of criminal could gather. Fearing that it might be stolen, City Hall moved their Time Ball to the Ferry Building in 1898 where it would remain for almost a decade. Marisol and Josephine kept a close eye on this *resort* until they burned it down on the morning of July 25, 1903. As one historian remarked, *many Telegraph Hill stoves that summer and autumn were fired with the remains of Layman's Folly.*

In the year 1905, the summit of Telegraph Hill became another type of beacon when a stream of Russian exiles flooded onto the San Francisco waterfront in search of my grandmother. They walked directly to the blue house on Telegraph Hill, following directions given to them by Elizabeth Dmitrieff, and these visitors stayed on Greenwich Street for just a single night, their desire for vengeance matched only by a desire to rejoin their comrades in Russia. During the first days of January, while one of these exiles was visiting, Josephine learned that Louise Michel had died at the age of 74. First a numb muteness filled the entire living room, then a low rumbling shook the floorboards, and then the Russian exile ran in fright as Josephine transformed into a screaming *Santa Muerte*. Marisol bolted from her bedroom and shook skull-faced Josephine out of this frenzy, though not before the *skinny lady* was heard by their entire neighborhood. By next morning, the daily newspapers offered differing accounts of what happened. One journalist claimed the Gray Brothers had dynamited their quarry and the suction caused the air to scream like a woman. A rival journalist challenged this, claiming that the quarry was closed and a small earthquake had in fact shaken the ancient limestone of Telegraph Hill, its only victims being a few porcelain tea-cups.

Marisol didn't go to the brothel that night and stayed with Josephine until the *skinny lady* had vanished. Once she had, Josephine spoke to her friend of Louise Michel, the black-clad *stregha*, and explained what happened atop the *butte* of Montmartre. She read aloud an old poem that Victor Hugo had composed for Louise and once she heard it, Marisol couldn't believe an old man could write such words: *what all the great, wild spirits do, you did: you fought and dreamed and suffered. "I have killed," you cried, for, weary of all these, you wanted now to die.* The Queens wept together on the red sofa and stayed up reading newspaper clippings about Louise that Josephine had collected over the years. In one of her final speeches, Louise spoke of an impending uprising in Russia, telling the crowd: *I can feel it growing, swelling, I can feel the revolution that will sweep them all away, czars, grand dukes, the whole Slavic bureaucracy, that entire, enormous house of death.* Soon after she died, her coffin was escorted through Paris by thousands of black-clad marchers who chanted "Long live the Russian Revolution! Long live anarchy!" This wish immediately came true.

After months of preparation, the forces of Mary staged a peaceful march on the Winter Palace in Saint Petersburg. Through their proxies, they had

convinced the radicals to confine themselves to ſtrikes until after the march, naively believing the Czar might ſtill be human, and this blunder ended in what became known as Bloody Sunday. On January 22, 1905, a crowd of several thousand unarmed people marched to the Winter Palace asking for the right to vote, better wages for all, and free land. Once they crossed an invisible line in the snow, the march was charged by sword-wielding Cossacks and fired on by Imperial soldiers. Over one thousand people died and thousands more were wounded in this cataclysmic slaughter that provoked the greateſt upheaval Russia had ever seen. Aided by the followers of Mary, massive general ſtrikes soon broke out across the Empire and caused part of the army to rebel againſt their commanders. In the center of these ſtrikes were black-clad *ſtreghe* with high collars lined in red, their pockets concealing piſtols and knives. At their backs were the anarchiſts, the Bolsheviks, the Mensheviks, and the Social Revolutionaries, an underground group that killed Grand Duke Sergei Alexsandrovich in retaliation for Bloody Sunday.

This massive upheaval continued throughout 1905, filling Jack London with enthusiasm. His membership in the Bohemian Club couldn't be revoked, allowing Jack to repair his damaged reputation among the anarchiſts and prove he wasn't raciſt. Even before the uprising broke out, Jack arranged to give a lecture at UC Berkeley, and two days before Bloody Sunday, he told a crowded hall of ſtudents: *today Russian universities seethe with revolution.*

I say to you, then: in the full glory of life, here's a cause that appeals to all the romance in you. Awake! Awake to its call! When revolt broke out just two days later, these students viewed Jack London as nothing less than a prophet. Jack soon signed a letter soliciting aid for the Russian rebels, became President of the Intercollegiate Socialist Society, and ran for Mayor of Oakland to preach insurrection. When my mother caught up with him at *Luna's*, Jack was so filled with light he could hardly sit still. Despite the success of his propaganda, Isabelle changed the subject to the secret lover he'd concealed from everyone, including Bessie and Anna. In one sentence, Isabelle snatched the light from his eyes and rendered Jack into a stuttering mess. With no coherent response, Isabelle left him in *Luna's* to contemplate his bad choices.

Jack's love-life had become a matter of public record with Anna Strunsky tarred in the press as the exotic Jewish home-wrecker. After Jack agreed to build his family a house and pay alimony, Bessie relented in her legal attack and removed Anna's name from the formal complaint of adultery, settling for simple desertion. When she learned of this, Yvonne could only point out that Jack's sheer inability to address these matters had enabled the courts to take the place of his friends, given Bessie had no other allies. Had it been up to Yvonne and Isabelle, Jack would have never married and been alone until his desires were clear. While they were pleased with his recent bout of activity, Yvonne and Isabelle understood the wound it masked, just as they knew Jack still longed for Anna.

His former lover had since retreated to a cabin in the hills above Stanford University where she could finish her book and avoid Jack's attention. Her novel *Windlestraws* was abandoned in favor of a new one set in Paris called *Violette of Pere Lachaise*, the name of her alter-ego. Between writing herself into insurgent Paris, Anna wandered the oak covered hills along narrow deer trails teeming with quail. During one excursion, Anna chanced upon a pocket of silence in the woods and paused for a moment to listen. The sky was cloudy and gray, so she assumed the birds were hiding from the quickly approaching rain. Within this odd calmness, a brown coyote approached her through the grass, its yellow eyes beaming with light. Before she could react, Anna flew backwards into a tube of water and emerged on a distant hillside drenched in rain, having no memory of what just happened. She stumbled back to the cabin, dried herself by the fire, and fell into a deep sleep. When she woke the next morning, Anna was filled with a sudden inspiration to take up her pen and write Jack a poem called *The Road*. Using imagery of water and earth, she described a journey into the underworld where *the trackless forest lured me to its rest*. When the poem was finished, Anna knew her connection with Jack was severed. It was this very day that Bloody Sunday took place, an event that changed her life forever.

She soon received a letter announcing the outbreak of the Russian Revolution and Anna paced through the woods for many hours, resolving to leave once she'd finished *Violette of Pere Lachaise*. Her concentration was broken again when two Russian exiles arrived at the cabin to recruit Anna into the Friends of Russian Freedom, although *Violette* consumed her until February when she finally left the woods. After settling back into her Sutter Street apartment, Anna discovered Jack had been waging a lightning propaganda campaign on behalf of the Russian rebels, an effort she was too busy to help with. Emma Goldman was now smuggling weapons to San Francisco, although before they could reach Russia, safe transportation had to be secured, a task that fell on Anna, Isabelle, and Sergio.

For her part, Anna hid the guns in the basements of a dozen Russian

Moscow, 1905.

families, leaving Isabelle to approach Andrew Furuseth at his office in the Sailor's Hall, demanding they speak alone. Once the door was closed, she negotiated the delivery of forty-seven wooden crates filled with weapons and ammo. Ashamed of his cowardice during the Great Waterfront Strike, Furuseth promptly agreed, offering his most loyal sailors to hoist the cargo. On a foggy night in spring, my uncle Sergio led a crew of longshoremen to the Broadway pier and loaded fifty crates labeled *canned oysters*. Once each box was secured with rope, the sailors hauled them aboard a cargo ship and stowed them behind bags of coffee. These weapons would eventually arrive in Vladivostok before being placed on a train for delivery to a Moscow merchant, a man who specialized in foreign delicacies like California-raised oysters. He wouldn't be disappointed in these delectable items imported for the uprising.

Just before Bloody Sunday, the long-awaited meeting took place in Chicago among dozens of radicals, including Big Bill Haywood of the Western Federation of Miners. Over three days in January 1905, this secret committee drafted a manifesto calling for the creation of *one great industrial union embracing all industries—providing for craft autonomy locally, industrial autonomy internationally, and working class unity generally. It must be founded on the class struggle, and its general administration must be conducted in harmony with recognition of the irrepressible conflict between the capitalist class and the working class. It should be established as the economic organization of the working class, without affiliation with any political party. All power should rest in a collective membership.* With simple, plain language, the seeds of our electromagnetic future were sewn upon fertile ground. Thousands of these manifestos were shipped to every union in North America, calling for a convention in Chicago on June 27, 1905. The Colorado Labor Wars had convinced them all there was no use fighting separate battles only to be picked off one by one. To fight the conspiracy of capitalism, the workers needed to weave the conspiracy of the people.

Amid this unprecedented mobilization, the anarchists of San Francisco's Latin Quarter carried on as usual, arousing the ire of middle-class Italian *prominenti*. Isabelle continued to meet with Enrico and Schwartz at the *Secolo Nuovo* print-shop in Basque Town, although the editors of *La Protesta Humana* disbanded after Giuseppe's death. A final tri-lingual issue was released commemorating his life with columns printed in Italian, French, and Spanish, a Rosetta Stone for the neighborhood. His lover Ersilia soon organized an outdoor play to benefit the Russia rebels, her lines spoken in all three Latin languages, and random passersby couldn't help but marvel at the eloquence, worldliness, and illumination of these anarchists who solicited money to defeat the Czar. My mother distributed issues of *Secolo Nuovo* at the edge of the crowd while Ersilia roped them in with her deep singing voice, no less powerful than her speeches. It was here that my mother found Eamonn and Rose lounging in the grass with glasses of red wine, the usual lines of worry no longer stretching across their faces.

As the winter of 1905 turned to spring, not a single case of plague was reported in the Latin Quarter. Along with the bumbling federal doctors, Eamonn and Rose's efforts were so effective the outbreak appeared to have halted. They savored those glasses of wine in the park, well-earned after years of service. One hundred and thirteen people had died of plague since its arrival in 1900 and were it not for these anarchist doctors, thousands more might have lost their lives. To celebrate, Yvonne called for a retreat at the *Rancho del Valle* and everyone agreed except Jack. He proposed another location, a large piece of land he'd just purchased with the profits from *The Sea-Wolf,* a best-seller that depicted a tyrannical sea captain named Wolf Larsen and the brave couple who eventually defeat him. In the novel that funded this future commune, Jack was able to slip in this cheeky sentence: *Telegraph Hill, of course, is your port of entry. It sticks out all over your mug. Tough as they make them and twice as nasty. I know the kind.* The property he bought from this book's sales was outside the town of Glen Ellen in the Sonoma Valley, a massive parcel with enough land to sustain a thousand bellies. No one objected to have their retreat on his new land, although Jack failed to mention his lover Charmian's connection to the area. She was the true reason he'd purchased this old *rancho.*

Jack and Anna were soon thrust together again when she was elected chairman of the Friends of Russian Freedom, with her former lover serving on its executive committee. Despite their past, both of them were able to overcome their emotions and remained comrades through this venture. Their flow of cash and weapons into Russia continued throughout 1905, crossing the Pacific Ocean and the Siberian Tundra to help Ukrainian Jews defeat a pogrom and enable the peasants to seize their land. The Empire responded to these rebellions by organizing gangs of orthodox extremists known as the Black Hundred, a paramilitary force that targeted Jews on behalf of the Czar. After its humiliating defeat by Japan, the Empire was now desperate to snuff out the revolution through pogroms and mass-hangings. Thousands were killed with thousands more exiled to Siberia, itself a growing hotbed of rebellion. From her self-imposed exile in one of its frozen penal colonies, Elizabeth Dmitrieff quietly organized this flow of rebels, arms, messages, and refugees between Siberia and California.

Elizabeth emerged from despair over these insurgent months, her coal-warmed house now a twin of the little blue house of Greenwich Street, an entire revolt conducted between them. Elizabeth sent Josephine letters reminiscing over the past and asked questions of the future, a horizon of promise glowing before her weary eyes. These *streghe* were now in their fifties and had both lost their lovers to the forces of darkness, a situation that bonded them across the ocean. Neither forgot their beloved Paris Commune, nor could they forget their defeated men, and both committed themselves to reviving the flames they wielded during that final stand in Montmartre. As the uprising swept across Russia, these long-lost *streghe* recalled the power of those last moments when death seemed certain, exchanging cryptic poetry about the swirling flames of Paris. They knew something tremendous was now brewing beneath the soil, an event beyond all human reckoning.

After months of expectation, two hundred delegates arrived in Chicago on June 29, 1905 and met at a saloon called Brand's Hall. The comrades from San Francisco sent a single delegate, an old sugar-field agitator named Al Klemencic, frequent contributor to *Free Society* and eternal foe of the Spreckels family. Al sat with dozens of anarchists and socialists as Big Bill Haywood took the stage, ripped off a loose floor-board, and smashed it on the podium. In his deep, gravelly voice, Big Bill declared: *Fellow Workers, this is the Continental Congress of the Working Class. We are here to confederate the workers of this country into a working-class movement in possession of the economic powers, the means of life, in control of the machinery of production and distribution without regard to capitalist masters.* By the end of that Congress, the delegates had created the Industrial Workers of the World, or IWW, a federation of autonomous locals with no central leadership, no racial discrimination, and no deals with the capitalists.

News of these resolutions spread to San Francisco and my mother sat through a lengthy meeting about this IWW, an occasion that allowed her to catch up with her brothers. Well-dressed Lorenzo remained unaffiliated with any union and preferred to commit robberies with his friends from Paterson. Federico was still in the Street Carmen's Union and known to be its best street agitator, a position that afforded him some sway among the mostly racist union-men. Sergio toiled away as a longshoreman, just like his father, and he was by far the most bitter of the brothers. He'd taken many lovers in his life but entered his thirties without a partner, living alone in a one-room apartment overlooking the wharves. Federico had since moved out of that apartment and now lived in the Latin Quarter with his partner Esmeralda, while Lorenzo maintained a floating existence between various anarchist flop-houses, all rented under false names.

These three brothers sat beside Isabelle as the anarchists debated how to best utilize the IWW, an organization that could truly unite them. In these discussions, the comrades agreed that forming an IWW union in San Francisco should wait, given the conservative climate of the labor movement, and they decided to form their first union in an industry with no representation. If they acted precipitously, the Mayor could easily brand the IWW agents of the Citizen's Alliance. With few industries outside the grip of Anglo unions, the anarchists settled on the Italian bakeries of the Latin Quarter. Isabelle relayed her mother's intelligence to this meeting and listed the entire net-work of Italian bakery owners, along with their families and associates. Those anarchists new to San Francisco listened in awe as 18-year-old Isabelle exposed the weakness and vices of each *prominenti*. To these newcomers, the legends of shrouded Queens and midnight assassins must have attained intoxicating proportions when Isabelle delivered intelligence rivaling any private detective agency. My uncles laughed at these open-mouthed anarchists and poked them back to reality, a place where Isabelle was just another comrade.

As my mother climbed Greenwich Street that night, she glimpsed multiple lamps glowing in the little blue house. Marisol was out on the porch with a burning cigarette in her fingers and a nervous expression across her face. She motioned for Isabelle to go inside but made no attempt to follow. My mother turned the handle, walked into the house, and found Josephine kneeling atop the Persian rug, a strange glow blurring her face. My mother was suddenly on the floor, staring into the face of a red-hooded skull, its bare teeth chattering in excitement. She felt moisture crawling up her legs just before the front door burst open and Marisol rushed inside, trailed by tobacco smoke. Where the *skinny lady* once knelt, there was now only Josephine reclining on the Persian rug, surrounded by a circle of books.

Marisol closed the door and explained how Josephine had been reading Élisée Reclus all day, especially the first volume of his final masterpiece, *L'Homme et la Terre*, sent to her in advance of its publication by Élisée himself. It would be his last communication to Josephine. This brave anarchist geographer who fought with Antonio outside Paris had left his beloved Earth just a few days after the IWW was founded. When my mother asked about the *skinny lady* in the red hood, Josephine said she'd been speaking with Élisée, as was her right, and these words made Marisol spit on the carpet before vanishing into her bedroom. Josephine didn't explain these new abilities to Isabelle. According to the ancient traditions of my tribe, the underworld opened according to its own logic, not the will of the individual, but now my grandmother had learned to access it directly after her long friendship with Marisol. These strange events only made sense later, when it was far too late, and had either Josephine or Marisol known about my mother's plunge into the underworld at the *Rancho del Valle*, our world might have arrived sooner than it did. These were the consequences of their thousand secrets.

My mother couldn't dwell on these matters very long, having a retreat to attend. She left early the next morning for the Italian Fisherman's Wharf, dressed as a servant and carrying only a suitcase. She met Eamonn at the dockside coffee-stand, waited for Jack to cruise into harbor, and boarded *The Spray* under cover of darkness. As it turned out, this would be *The Spray's* final voyage. Jack had just arranged for its sale to one PJM Bertelsen Jr., a legal fiction used to transfer *The Spray* to a group of Russian sailors who would then use it to smuggle guns across the Pacific. On this last cruise of *The Spray,* they were halfway to Petaluma when a purple dawn lit up the eastern

The Spray

sky and even Isabelle couldn't help marvel at this former pirate skillfully plying the ancient art of seafaring. As the threshold of the Golden Gate lit up with sunlight, my mother imagined her father sailing off to Valparaiso and Buenos Aires, the times of promise juſt over the horizon. This sense of wonder followed her up the Petaluma River where she beheld the dry brown grass of Sonoma Valley flanked by green oak trees hovering atop the hillsides. Although she'd never been here, Isabelle knew her aunt's commune was juſt over those hills, no further than a day's ride, and her wanderluſt grew beyond imagination.

A ſtage-coach was waiting for them at the Petaluma docks with a small crowd of gawkers eager to glimpse the famous Jack London. Before these fanatics could encircle them, Jack told his friends to meet him on the edge of town rather than face a journaliſt's pencil-sketch. Isabelle and Eamonn crept off the docks and walked north along the river until they beheld open farmland pierced by a single dirt road. They were a mile along when Eamonn held out his thumb to hitch a ride from Jack's approaching ſtage-coach, a common praĉtice in rural California. Having escaped small-town publicity, they traveled through Sonoma Valley in harmonious silence, the smell of dry grass heavy in the air.

Jack's property was part of the old *Rancho Vallejo*, a traĉt that encompassed creeks, oak groves, and redwood foreſts. The ſtage-coach delivered them to a small cottage and Jack tipped the driver well on the hope he'd forget their hitch-hikers. The cottage was ſtripped bare when they entered and littered with the previous owner's belongings, although Jack had recently purchased new beds, couches, and chairs. Every objeĉt was duſty and my mother began to sweep the moment she walked inside, cursing Jack for his obliviousness. It wasn't until Eamonn joined her that Jack realized they were cleaning for little Juana. By nightfall, the entire house was transformed into an oil-lit paradise, complete with a raging fireplace and floors clean enough to lick. My mother fell asleep on the living room sofa while Jack and Eamonn talked long into the night beside the flickering flames. When they woke the next morning, Yvonne was in the living room with Juana, both dressed as common peasants.

In order to get there, Yvonne and Juana had to board Heath's yacht, cross the bay to Oakland, board a ſtage-coach for the *Rancho del Valle*, then hike through the redwoods back to Oakland. From there, it was a ferry ride to San Francisco, another to Tiburon, and then a short train ride to Glen Ellen. Only little Juana slept during this long journey, while her mother was awake for two whole days. Once she arrived, Yvonne took Eamonn into an empty bedroom, slammed the door shut, and while the lovers breathed together under clean sheets, Jack and Isabelle chased Juana between the trunks of sprawling oaks trees. Eamonn left the bedroom later that afternoon but Yvonne slept soundly until the following morning. When she finally opened her eyes, both Juana and Eamonn were asleep beside her. Yvonne wept at this beautiful sight, never knowing a love so complete and true.

The first discussion of their retreat revolved around the subject of travel. Just the previous week, Heath arrived at the mansion for breakfast with Yvonne and Juana, a highly unusual occurrence. When his plate was clean, Heath told Yvonne they would celebrate this Christmas with JP Morgan's family. His plan was for them to travel in a Pullman Palace Car and arrive in New York City at the beginning of December, unexpected events permitting. The moment she heard this news, Isabelle stormed outside to breathe some sense into her body, overwhelmed with rage, possibility, and doubt. Yvonne and Eamonn stared at each other in silence as Isabelle paced across the front porch, unable to subdue her violent emotions. To lighten the air, Jack suggested he schedule a North American lecture tour that would allow him to meet Yvonne in New York City. Before the lovers could respond, Isabelle came back inside and announced Jack's plan would work, only she'd have to go with him.

Yvonne protested this plan and suggested Isabelle travel with her as Juana's nanny, providing them with the chance to finally kill Heath and Morgan. My mother wasn't ready for this clear offer, especially when Yvonne began to weep at the mention of it. Jack and Eamonn nervously waited on the porch while Isabelle stared at Yvonne, desperate to decipher her true intentions. In all of history, an Empress had never provided a rebel with direct access to the Emperor, let alone a chance to slay him. Isabelle saw this path ending in her own death and beheld the *skinny lady* standing in a long red robe that draped in every direction. The floorboards became thick with moisture before Isabelle managed to close the watery tube, still unaware of her growing powers. Yvonne felt this nether-fluid rise to her ankles, just like Isabelle did. They saw the same images, spoke without words, and transmitted their thoughts through the electromagnetic interplay of their bodies and the Earth.

When the tube closed, Isabelle resolved to stay alive and refused Yvonne's offer. My mother claimed she needed to be at Jack's side to keep him safe, especially after what had happened to Frank Norris. While refusing to kill Morgan and Heath could be seen as cowardice, defying the pathways of the underworld wasn't easy for someone so inexperienced. Ever the skeptic, Isabelle refused to believe in her growing powers and called the men inside to discuss their plans for the lecture tour. They agreed to converge in New York City and gather intelligence on JP Morgan, although Eamonn remained oddly silent. With their plan now set, Isabelle declared she was starving.

After a cold lunch on the patio, they all took Juana for a stroll through the oaks groves and listened to Eamonn explain his precarious position. He'd worked five long years to eradicate the plague from San Francisco and now his reputation as a *man of the people* had reached the press. It was only a matter of time before Heath learned of this as well. Seeing no other option, the doctor took Yvonne's hand and insisted he needed to leave the city, long enough for the world to forget he existed, and then return in secret. Yvonne tried not to weep as she imagined herself trapped in the cinema room while Eamonn boarded an air-balloon on the mansion lawn, now unable to see her through the glare of the windows. Her lover tried to brighten this moment by describing the many benefits of his journey and named Dublin as his city of exile, a location suggested to him by his Gælic patroness. While his family also lived there, the witch had an entirely different motivation.

She had recently summoned Eamonn to her apothecary and handed him a stack of books penned by Irish and British mystics. Never fond of reading, especially in English, the witch had scoured these books and resolved to send her protégé to investigate their authors. If these fools weren't careful, she claimed they'd blast a hole into the underworld and unleash a misery worse than any witch-hunt. The first of these works was the three-volume *Secret Doctrine* by Helena Blavatsky, daughter of Russian nobility and founder of the Theosophical Society. In 1871, just as the Commune was being slaughtered, Blavatsky left the mountains of Tibet with a *secret doctrine* learned in a Buddhist temple and went on to birth the modern Spiritualist movement. From 1871 to 1891, Blavatsky spread this *secret doctrine* across Europe and Russia, helping fuel to mystical backlash against science and industry. Jack was familiar with this Spiritualist revival, counting his own mother Flora as one of its followers, and even Isabelle knew of their beliefs in energy, spirits, mediums, divination, and every other form of matter ignored by Western science. The witch also assigned Eamonn the works of Annie Bessant, Lady Gregory, Aleister Crowley, and leaked documents from the Hermetic Order of the Golden Dawn. What he discovered were strange belief systems culled from ancient religions, complete with invocations of reptilian deities and pronouncements of new eons. By the time he finished his reading, Eamonn saw this magical circle as a danger no less profound than Frankenstein's monster, pieced together from dead bodies and set loose to terrorize the earth.

No one had any objections to Eamonn's exile besides Isabelle. When asked how she felt about the matter, my mother remained silent. It was only after she paced the room that Isabelle revealed her true thoughts. Over these years of Russian upheaval, numerous exiles had come to her little blue house bearing precious information, and during one of these visits, a woman from Moscow claimed Helena Blavatsky was an agent of the Czar. The concept of the *Aryan race* encoded in her *Secret Doctrine* was used to bolster hatred against Russian Jews and it was long-suspected that Blavatsky's mysticism was just a cover-story for some sinister Imperial project. Josephine and Isabelle couldn't make much of this information, given that Blavatsky died in 1892, although their comrade from Moscow mentioned another dubious book that had just appeared on the shelves of Russia.

The Protocols of the Elders of Zion, a fictional manual for an imaginary Jewish conspiracy, was now being circulated by the Black Hundreds to stir up pogroms across the countryside. According to this false text, the Jews were organizing to take over the world and enslave Christians to their diabolic ends. With the whole of Russia consumed by revolution, the Empire was using the Black Hundreds to spread this text and put down rural uprisings. As my mother explained, it didn't take long for the others to realize that a powerful enemy was gathering strength under the guise of a hundred *secret doctrines*. Before she agreed to let Eamonn travel to Dublin, my mother declared that he would not only find the darkness at the end of his path, he'd come to know the absolute enemy. No one knew exactly what she meant, and my mother didn't elaborate. All of them were hungry and tired.

These revelations silently troubled the conspirators as they ate by the fire, listening to Juana lecture about the dynamics of oak trees, the behavior of squirrels, and the true voice of the ocean wind. She fell asleep in Isabelle's lap, allowing her mother to make love with Eamonn in the bedroom while

Jack sat alone on the porch drinking, smoking, and pondering the choices of his comrades. When my mother woke the next morning, Jack was still there, passed out beside an empty bottle and a pile of ash. A cold bucket of water to the face woke him up and the former pirate helped Isabelle cook breakfast without complaint. Once the lovers were awake, they all ate out on the porch and watched the sun rise over the hills. Rather than discuss anything, the conspirators lounged through all the morning.

They packed a picnic for lunch when the day grew too hot and guided Juana through the forest on their way to the river. In a moment of jubilation, Jack stripped himself naked, encouraged Eamonn to do the same, and the two raced towards the river-bed. The men soon disappeared in a burst of water, lost in an aquatic wrestling match. Just as Jack was on the verge of winning, Isabelle jumped on his back, wrapped her legs around his stomach, and sent him hurling into the river. Yvonne had never seen anything like this, neither had Eamonn, and it was their first glimpse of Isabelle's other side, the aspects that resembled Josephine, killer of men and master of martial arts. Jack rose from the water nursing his ribs and Isabelle laughed in his face before splashing him, a distraction that allowed Yvonne to disrobe before floating off with her lover. Juana sat transfixed on the shore, gazing at her four naked guardians whose screams of joy pierced the air, arousing the attention of nearby love-makers. These teenagers crawled towards the river, glimpsed the nude conspiracy, and quickly ran off to Glen Ellen to feed its churning mill of rumors. Jack London wasn't mentioned by name, nor could they be certain it was actually him, but his property was closest to the river and lined with a dozen funny signs reading NO ADMISSION EXCEPT ON BUSINESS—NO BUSINESS CONDUCTED HERE.

After eating their lunch beside the river, the conspiracy returned home red-faced and happy. In the hours before dinner, they discussed the maddening situation in San Francisco and the unstoppable corruption of the Union Labor Party. Isabelle believed opposition was doomed to fail with Hearst's *San Francisco Examiner* backing the Party, an organ that influenced 200,000 union men. Yvonne suggested meeting with Phœbe Hearst but Isabelle objected, reciting a long list of the Hearst family's crimes, including the Mexican oil and mine interests. Jack countered that it wouldn't hurt to see what Phœbe knew, an idea Eamonn agreed with. Before she finally assented, Isabelle made Yvonne promise to never reveal the conspiracy's existence. Once this promise was made, my mother changed the subject to Alma de Bretteville and her bloated *sugar daddy*.

Since returning from Europe, young Alma received no marriage offer from Adolph Spreckles and remained his mistress for their weekends at his Napa Valley *villa*. In her letters to Yvonne, this *sugar baby* explained how she'd set

Adolph on a rampage against the Union Labor Party by insisting they visit their beloved Poodle Dog. Adolph claimed they could never patronize this restaurant again, however much it pained him. With the establishment now tied up in the Union Labor Party's graft net-work, Adolph forsook its private rooms and only visited Alma far from San Francisco. He apologized endlessly during their nights in Napa and made a thousand promises to assuage Alma's anger. In these moments of weakness, Alma absorbed everything he said. According to Adolph, Heath and Morgan hadn't just bought the United Railroads, they'd used the Union Labor Party to prevent two labor strikes, a truth Isabelle could vouch for. Adolph believed Heath was fostering open corruption in the Party to precipitate a controlled scandal and then swoop in on the pickings. To counter him, Adolph and his brothers planned to assemble evidence of this corruption, tie it back to Heath, and engineer their own scandal against his faction of the Bohemian Club, a place Jack London now had access to.

As they sat in the living room around a cold fireplace, Yvonne asked Jack to explain his recent induction ceremony at the Bohemian Grove, only to receive cryptic answers. He mentioned burning an effigy beneath a large owl, relinquishing his cares of the world, and rambled about his past experiences in a Buffalo jail cell. Jack was clearly disturbed when he described taking off his hood at the ceremony and seeing a dozen naked women dancing beneath the redwoods, a spectacle designed to overwhelm the senses and break down the will, only he hadn't succumbed. Over those days in the forest, Jack learned of the Club's sorry condition when he saw dozens of capitalists dissimulate virility over the bodies of prostitutes. During the day, these men tried to keep up with Jack during hikes only to fall into panting and exhaustion, claiming their vital juices had been depleted. Jack preferred the company of the Club's artists and writers, a small faction sorely decimated since the days of Frank Norris. Labeled effeminate by the capitalists, these artists were goaded into displays of masculinity, usually wrestling matches. After defeating his capitalist challengers, Jack emerged a hero of the artists and envy of his strength spread among the emasculated business men. Aside from this, Jack had learned nothing during his stay at the Grove. All the serious conversations took place in private tents guarded by armed men. After relaying this, Jack brought up the Buffalo jail cell he'd been incarcerated in during his hobo days. No one understood why he spoke of this, but just then a distraction arrived.

A small wagon clattered up the road and Jack told his co-conspirators to change before it was too late. Yvonne draped a shawl over her head, Eamonn put on a hat and glasses, while Isabelle simply took Juana into one of the bedrooms and closed the door. Leaving his friends to their disguises, Jack met the wagon outside and shook each of the driver boys' hands. In the wagon-bed were two crates addressed to *Jack London, Glen Ellen*. He helped carry them inside, introduced the lovers as friends from Europe, and tipped each boy a dollar. Back in the house, Jack pried open the crates to reveal the latest photographic camera and wooden tripod. My mother hated cameras no less than Yvonne and they both sat outside as the men marveled over this latest technology.

Their discussion never resumed that night, dinner being the main concern. Jack and Eamonn cooked while Isabelle played outside with Juana around a fire, its sparks flying upward towards the emerging stars. Dinner made them all drowsy and Isabelle insisted she'd clean up if they all just left her alone and went to sleep. The lovers retreated to their nest while Jack put Juana to bed before falling asleep in his room. Isabelle scrubbed the dishes, swept the floor, then collapsed onto the sofa. With only an oil-lamp illuminating the room, my mother sobbed uncontrollably, longing to lay beside Josephine and ask a thousand questions. She felt lost, helpless, overwhelmed, and wept silently until sleep carried her away. The first sight she beheld the next morning was Juana's face coaxing her to make pancakes. Obeying what might have still been a dream, my mother did as she was told and cooked two dozen pancakes as the great conspiracy woke from slumber.

They discussed a dozen subjects over breakfast and coffee, none related to their plans. With the next months of their lives mapped out, the tired party allowed themselves to relax. Juana insisted they go swimming and they packed another picnic before setting out for the river, although this time Jack brought his camera. They heard laughter long before they reached the water, an ominous sign Juana couldn't interpret, and they soon found a dozen young women screaming the name Jack London, all seeming to know him. The famous author was surrounded, frantic introductions were made, and my mother wandered into the water with Juana, leaving Yvonne and Eamonn to imitate bad Slavic accents. None of the villagers mentioned the nude bathers, although several of these young women implored Jack to join them for a dip. Once he dove in, the author was surrounded by a dozen women, all staring at him with mischievous smiles, their heads bobbing above the green water. Among these locals were Yvonne, Juana, and my mother, silently gliding towards him through the ripples. A moment of pure tension filled the air, muting the river and silencing the beat of Jack's heart. A hole opened into the underworld, though no one realized it. Instead, little Juana began to splash him, Jack splashed back, and the river ignited into a frenzy of droplets that hung like curtains over the flowing water.

After this waterworks subsided, one of the women made Jack show her the camera and soon he was taking pictures of all the swimmers. Yvonne quickly got out of the water and kept Juana far away from the camera's lens. They sat with Eamonn on a thick oak root and watched Jack capture images of these clothed bathers, all lost in the power of his device. Isabelle joined them beneath the oak tree and they ate lunch together while the Glen Ellen locals basked in Jack's attention, already imaging their appearance in his books.

When the food was gone, Yvonne grew impatient and wanted to leave before the crowd became too familiar with their faces.

Taking the first moment that presented itself, Jack claimed his friends had business at the ranch but invited the locals to a house-warming party later that summer. As his co-conspirators were packing, Jack folded up his new camera and vanished. My mother went after him and found Jack beneath an oak tree, his camera lens pointed at her face. Jack claimed it was broken, that the trigger wouldn't depress, but then there was a single click, capturing Isabelle's image. Jack swore it was an accident but my mother said she'd tolerate none of this foolishness. While the lovers cooked dinner, Isabelle hovered over Jack's shoulder as he prepared emulsion in the basement. Under the glow of a red lantern, Jack rendered her image onto photographic paper until she saw herself appear amid the oak trees carrying a white towel. Isabelle's dark hair hung above her chest, her index finger pointed down at the earth, and she stared at the lens with her familiar poker-face, hovering somewhere between anger and impatience. If she hadn't felt a twinge of joy, my mother might have destroyed this image. Instead, Isabelle burned the nitrocellulose negative in a fragrant burst of camphor.

Her developed picture sat in the middle of the dining table, surrounded by several candles, and despite her sadness of the previous evening, Isabelle allowed herself to laugh. They dubbed her *Saint Isabelle of the Coast* and toasted her throughout the evening, each extolling my mother's great deeds and invoking the mysterious forces that brought her family to San Francisco. Over this opulent meal and flowing wine, my mother finally saw these people as her friends, not just her co-conspirators. While she still withheld far more secrets than they could imagine, Isabelle truly loved these strange people. Just as Félix Fénéon had fallen into odd company, my mother had now found her own.

They slept deeply after agreeing to leave the next morning, their plans for the future already solidified. Isabelle departed on foot just before dawn and the lovers left with Juana a few hours later, catching the stage-coach in Glen Ellen. This unorthodox family then boarded a train to Tiburon and crossed the bay before parting, though not for long. Unknown to Isabelle and Jack, the lovers planned to live the next three weeks together at the *Rancho del Valle*. While the tireless doctor trekked through the woods to be with Yvonne and Juana, my mother was curled up in bed with Josephine, weeping at the immensity of the tasks that lay before her.

In the days that followed, Isabelle edited *Secolo Nuovo* at their Basque Town print shop and helped Anna coordinate the flow of arms to Russia. One of the pamphlets they drafted for the Friends of Russian Freedom reached a *yanqui* comrade in Switzerland who had established a news bureau for English articles on Russia. This man was William English Walling, an Anglo journalist swept up in the fires of revolution, and he agreed to help them smuggle weapons into the Empire. Walling remained in correspondence with Anna throughout the summer and encouraged her to visit him in Switzerland, a proposition my mother encouraged. Despite her enthusiasm, Anna couldn't commit to any departure date, a lapse in judgment Isabelle blamed on Jack. The famous author hadn't returned to San Francisco since their retreat and my mother believed Anna was waiting to say goodbye, an abject state Isabelle tried to discourage. With my mother's help, Anna threw herself into writing, giving speeches, and pretending Jack didn't exist. Within a month, she had resolved to journey with her sister Rose to *Les Diablerets* before meeting up with Walling in Geneva.

Yvonne returned from the *Rancho del Valle* at the beginning of August with darkened skin and glowing hair, her daughter equally radiant. Heath was at the mansion to greet them and stayed until just after dinner. During their conversation, Heath rambled about the glories of New York City and asked if they should hire a nanny for Juana, although Yvonne declined. After that brief dinner, Yvonne didn't see her husband again for many weeks. Work resumed at the mansion, bringing Isabelle back to the library where she read dozens of recent texts. Ida Tarbell's *History of the Standard Oil Company* had finished its serialization in *McClure's Magazine*, cementing JD Rockefeller as a household villain. While his oil company's donations to Roosevelt's 1904 reelection campaign had been accepted, the President only accelerated the anti-trust investigation into Standard Oil once he was back in office. Not only had Rockefeller financed the Japanese Empire in their war against Russia, he had joined Heath and Morgan in consolidating their metallurgic interests to form US Steel, the first billion-dollar company. Nervous about their inflated profit margins, Rockefeller resigned from the board in 1904, fearing Ida Tarbell's merciless pen. By the summer of 1905, several members of the Rockefeller

William English Walling

family were hospitalized for nervous anxiety and breakdowns. Death threats arrived at every major Rockefeller property and the old man hired an army of Pinkertons to protect his family, going so far as to sleep with a revolver on his bedside table. As all this unfolded, events in Russia grew even more volatile.

Facing open revolution, the Czar instituted a watered-down parliament in the hope of appeasing the bourgeois. After his defeat by the Japanese Empire, the Czar was forced to pay war indemnities, ensuring a return on Rockefeller and Morgan's investment in the Japanese Empire. As his parliament enacted its charade, the Black Hundreds amassed for another round of pogroms. Fueled by mystical race hatred and Imperial backing, these rabid bigots now awaited their master's command. Knowing the Czar would soon take his revenge, Anna asked Isabelle to help her write a series of articles. In the oil-lit print shop of *Secolo Nuovo*, these revolutionists penned columns for *California Woman's Magazine* and the *San Francisco Bulletin*. In this last publication, Anna became notorious when a sketch of her body appeared above her fiery words condemning the Empire and its sham parliament. My mother and Anna worked late those hot summer nights, arguing with Enrico and helping Shmuel set the type. Some nights they smuggled weapons to the waterfront while other nights they got drunk at *Luna's Mexican Restaurant*. As one stream of weapons traveled across the ocean to Russia, another stream went south to Mexico.

In the spring of 1905, a man named Praxedis Guerrero arrived on the San Francisco waterfront with a letter from Al Klemencik vouching for his reputation. Praxedis was a soldier, metallurgist, and newspaperman who'd become radicalized through the Mexican anarchist press. After the army opened fire on a peaceful demonstration in Monterey, the young soldier resigned and returned to Guanajuato to care for his sick father, an indigenous chief who'd married a Spanish bride. Praxedis finally opened the books on his father's shelves and discovered he had been raised by a follower of Bakunin, Kropotkin, Tolstoy, Gorky, and Hugo, an epiphany that made him flee from Mexico, ashamed of his time in the army. He and three friends crossed the border in 1904 and found work as miners outside Denver where Praxedis

Praxedis Guerrero

learned of the Colorado Labor Wars and met Al Klemencik, the man who sent him off to San Francisco. Thanks to my uncle Sergio, Praxedis and his friends found work as longshoremen and saved enough money to split a cramped apartment. They dined at *Luna's* every evening and were joined by dozens of Mexican exiles fleeing the dictatorship of Porfirio Díaz. In less than a month, Praxedis and his comrades had launched *Alba Roja,* a Spanish-language newspaper aimed at this stream of refugees. The paper was composed in the *Secolo Nuovo* print-shop before being distributed across the Latin Quarter and along the waterfront. By the time Isabelle had returned from Jack's ranch, Praxedis and his friends were readying for their journey to Saint Louis where they would soon form the *Partido Liberal Mexicano,* a front group for their anarchist insurrectionary army.

Their send-off dinner at *Luna's Mexican Restaurant* happened to include another rebel of the immigrant neighborhood. While the Mexican insurgents toasted the impending demise of Porfirio Díaz, my mother sat in the corner booth with Eamonn O'Shea, Jack London, and Anna Strunsky, their faces illuminated by red-glass candles. Eamonn had taken down his doctor's sign, leased his office to another doctor, and his train ticket had already been purchased as he sat with his friends, overwhelmed with gaiety, food, and drink. Comrades strummed guitars, dancing women stamped their feet, and the whole room spontaneously erupted into rhythmic clapping. Rose showed up just as the wine barrel was tapped and the Mexicans began swearing vengeance against Díaz. Their corner booth at *Luna's* held two Ukranian Jews, an Irish doctor, an Anglo novelist, and a *strega* named Isabelle. Surrounded by this gang of Latin rebels, the strength of anarchism had never been so clear to Eamonn, nor so joyous, and it wasn't until dawn when he and Jack emerged from *Luna's,* both energized from the long evening.

They ambled down to the waterfront reminiscing on the old days of pirate queens, fish patrols, and midnight raids on oyster farms. Just before reaching the Ferry Building, Jack began to curse the jail-cell in Buffalo, a subject he'd mentioned during the retreat. Before his friend could respond, Jack said he'd been raped there. He felt no hatred towards that man, not after all these years, and his desire for vengeance was directed solely at the rulers who'd built that jail, brutalized that man, and left them together in that dungeon. Jack embraced his friend, kissed Eamonn on the lips, and wished him a safe journey. When they finally met again, neither would recognize the city that surrounded them.

In the days ahead, Jack made final preparations for his tour and purchased the first of several train-tickets. He had just finished his novel *White Fang,* the story of a wolf-dog who travels from the wild forests of Alaska to the dog-fighting pits of Fort Yukon to a pampered life in rural California. This novel, the exact opposite of *The Call of the Wild,* had earned him $7,400. As he awaited his departure, Yvonne and Isabelle met in the Heath mansion library to discuss the details of their convergence in New York City. Given his membership in the Bohemian Club and the recent praise of his books, Jack could easily draw a crowd of New York City capitalists, allowing untold amounts of intelligence to be uncovered, especially during the reception, and Yvonne was committed to organizing this lecture while Isabelle would do her best to protect Jack from both harm and scandal. My mother left the mansion at the end of September, was granted maternity leave in the estate ledger, and used what days she had left to ensure *Secolo Nuovo* would survive her absence.

While Isabelle tended to these matters, Josephine was preoccupied with the Municipal Crib brothel, still operating in the open. Protected by the police, the *tongs,* and two dozen hired guns, the Crib was an impenetrable fortress that taunted Josephine with its thick red drapes and floors of captured women. Even the roof was patrolled by armed men, leaving the old tunnel system her only point of entry. Before she made her first exploration, Marisol engineered a grand jury police raid on the Crib, preventing Josephine from doing something foolish. Accompanied by articles in the *San Francisco Bulletin,* the grand jury put the Crib in check, for the moment.

Josephine flew into a rage when she learned of all this but calmed once Marisol explained the source of the raid. Their *protégé* in the Palace Hotel had just sent a letter describing interactions she'd had with Fremont Older, the *Bulletin* journalist who fought the Union Labor Party and lived with his wife in the Palace. In response to this letter, Marisol told their *protégé* of the Municipal Crib and its main pimp Billy Finnegan, intelligence which the *protégé* relayed to Older. Boiling with anger at Finnegan's barbarity, Older helped organize the grand-jury raid with the moral indignation of a true bourgeois. In the same letter that communicated this valuable information, their *protégé* also expressed a willingness to kill Heath. Displaying enormous trust in Isabelle, Josephine declined this offer. From their little blue house, the witches of Telegraph Hill waited to strike, a decision not only in my mother's hands, but also Yvonne's.

Fremont Older

On a morning in mid October, Isabelle put on a common *yanqui* dress, donned a black coat, threw on a black straw hat, and gathered her suit-case before the walk down Greenwich Street. She took the public ferry to Oakland and rode a train down the Mole rail-pier to the 16th Street Station, the transcontinental terminus of the west. Having nearly three hours to wait for her connection, Isabelle left the station and wandered into the neighborhood of West Oakland, a place she'd never visited. Just inland from the port, my mother discovered dense rows of wooden Victorian houses, many populated by people with black skin. Growing up in San Francisco, my mother rarely saw black people, not even on the street, and when she did they were always servants. Knowing full-well that her distant ancestors were Nubians with black skin, Isabelle strolled into the bustle of 7th Street and found herself to be the only white woman around. After turning into an alley, my mother was stopped by two black men who gave her a clear warning: *the only white girls who come down here are either looking to start some trouble or damn eager to find it.* My mother explained she wasn't looking for trouble, just a place to drink some iced lemonade. Before they could respond, my mother bent down to the dusty cobbles and drew a cross-like symbol with a splinter of wood. The symbol was an *ankh*, the ancient Egyptian hieroglyph for life, and when she looked into the men's eyes, there were the unmistakable signs of total recognition. Without another word, they offered to buy Isabelle some lemonade.

My mother followed them back to 7th Street where she noticed a few more white people than before, though not many. Her new friends took her to a tiny restaurant where they sat at the counter and ordered three lemonades from an older Italian woman who eyed Isabelle with obvious suspicion. She disappeared into the kitchen while the two men began talking to my mother about trains. Both of them worked as porters for the Pullman company and explained how it allowed them to travel across the entire country, as well as keep in contact with their friends, family, and lovers. In the middle of their stories, an older Italian man returned to the counter with three iced, sparkling lemonades. One of his eyes was made of glass and he gazed intently at Isabelle before asking who she was. Instead of answer with words, Isabelle borrowed a red handkerchief from one of her new friends, tied it around her neck, and then lowered it beneath her collar. Once he saw this, the Italian proprietor nodded to Isabelle's new friends, both of whom quickly left the restaurant. Isabelle sat there for a moment, waiting for the man to speak, and then a young black woman dressed as a man sat down next to her beside the counter. At that point, the owner of this fine establishment left the women to their business, having plenty of mouths to feed.

That morning, Isabelle met Andra de Moulin, daughter of a famed Pullman porter who bought up properties in West Oakland to sell to black families. She wore a brown suit and smoked a long marijuana cigar as she told my mother a short history of West Oakland and its thriving community built around the train terminus. While she listened, Isabelle glanced around the restaurant and noticed that black and white people were eating together, just as no one was casting Andra a second glance. It was clear they had achieved a level of cultural freedom here unlike most of San Francisco, and just as she had this thought, Andra asked Isabelle about the *Ankh*. My mother took a sip of her lemonade, cleared her throat, and told Andra the story of Mauritius of Thebes, the short version. She said his legion had brought the symbol to the Swiss Alps where it remained until the Christian's straightened it into their cross. Andra already knew this story, she yawned just to make this clear, but she admitted one thing that thrilled her: she never thought she'd see one of my mother's people in the flesh. When Isabelle asked her about the Italian couple who owned this place, Andra said they were political exiles afraid of attracting any attention and she swore Isabelle to secrecy before reaching out to shake her hand. In that moment, Andra taught my mother a secret of the Pullman porters, a handshake used to identify brothers outside of uniform. After bestowing this gift, Andra downed two glasses of lemonade, slid three nickles atop the counter, and told my mother she hoped they'd meet again.

Unable to fully comprehend this encounter, my mother finished her iced lemonade, ordered an egg sandwich to go, and then walked down Peralta Street to meet Jack London on the wooden benches of the 16th Street train station. He was accompanied by Manyoungi, the anarchist posing as his servant who carried a chest full of Korean, Japanese, and Chinese propaganda. As they awaited their departure, the trio examined their itinerary and went over the sequence of stops. Once they were aboard their Union-Pacific train and chugging away from Oakland, my mother helped Jack create lecture titles that hid their true, insurrectionary content.

In the midst of this, Isabelle beheld the vast San Joaquin Valley, an alien vista she'd known only through Marisol's stories. Not even Josephine had traveled this far inland, and as their train progressed into the *Sierra Nevada*, Isabelle witnessed a ravaged landscape stripped clean of natural resources. The last ancient trees stood atop the narrowest peaks and the rivers were choked with toxic run-off from gold mines. My mother absorbed this devastation until nightfall, unresponsive to Jack's questions. She fell asleep somewhere outside Truckee and woke up covered in a blanket with nothing but desert stretching in every direction. Isabelle had reached the state of Nevada.

As their lecture stops began, my mother became familiar with a pattern in these *yanqui* cities. The main streets were always controlled by Anglos while the immigrants lived up a hill or across the railroad tracks. The centers were made of brick and stone while the outskirts were lined by a grid of wooden houses, usually surrounded by farmland. From within these *yanqui* cities, the trio began their subversion of North America. Isabelle followed Jack to each of his lectures and sat in the back of the theaters where she could see everyone who entered. During a disturbance, she'd glide towards these hecklers with one hand clutched around a pistol. Nothing ever came of these drunken provocations and Jack spoke freely of the Russian Revolution, calling for the attendees to destroy capitalism. Alongside editions of his books, Jack distributed pamphlets for the IWW and quickly exhausted their supply. My mother was astounded at Jack's magnetic ability to wrap crowds into his vision of a war between light and darkness before asking: *which side are you on?* The unbridled applause evoked by these lectures was only a taste of their conspiracy's glory, a power that grew as they pushed northeast through Kansas, Missouri, and Iowa. While the celebrity preached revolution, Manyoungi distributed propaganda to the Japanese, Chinese, and Korean workers tucked away in the bowels of each *yanqui* city. These small newspapers carried news from Washington DC, San Francisco, and the Qing Empire, anonymous texts that spoke of anarchism, self-defense, *yanqui* law, and the IWW.

My mother was high on elation, traveling across North America with nothing but hope. That same October, general strikes broke out across the Russian Empire with Soviets declared in both Saint Petersburg and Moscow. Jack's calls for revolt became brazenly prophetic and drove the crowds into frenzies of cheers and chanting. In these moments of unanimous praise, my mother sat in the back of the hall glowing with joy. The luxury of hotel rooms, traincars, and Jack's $600 a week stipend had now dulled her senses to such a degree that she failed to notice a familiar recklessness invade his eyes. They sped through Ohio, Pennsylvania, New Jersey, and stopped in Grand Central Station long enough to eat a pre-dawn breakfast before switching trains. After traveling north to their lecture in Oneonta, New York, the three then boarded another train south for York, Pennsylvania. As they sped along the Hudson River that crisp November, my mother caught her first glimpse of Imperial New York City, a massive wall of metal skyscrapers flanked on either side by tenements and factories, a hellscape unlike any she'd seen before. This haunting vision passed once they'd cleared Jersey City, although it lingered in Isabelle's memory for weeks to come, a reminder of the beast that awaited her.

The trio pressed on through Pennsylvania and Ohio before heading north towards Chicago and the Great Lakes. During one of their stops, Jack wired his lover Charmian a telegram and arranged to meet far away from Isabelle. My mother was asleep when he and Charmian Kittredge were married before a Chicago judge, an event that instantly hit the press. Isabelle wouldn't learn the truth until Jack took the stage at his next lecture in Lake Geneva, Wisonsin and pointed towards a woman in the crowd, claiming this was Charmian Kittredge London. Knowing my mother was there, Jack announced he and Charmian would vacation in Maine before a honeymoon in the Caribbean. In a rage, Isabelle fled the hall, knocked on Manyoungi's hotel room door, and finally got answers. Jack's tickets to Maine had already been purchased and Isabelle brooded alone the rest of the night, debating if she should return home or proceed onward to New York City. It was her promise to Yvonne that made my mother check out of the hotel, wait in line at the train station counter, and discover her reservation had been upgraded to a private sleeping cabin. This lavish bribe from Jack didn't alter her anger, although she was certainly grateful for the nice bed.

The next morning, my mother heard a familiar knock on the door of her sleeper and found Jack eager to get inside. She slapped him across the cheek, warning him never to be so foolish again. No one agreed to include Charmian in their plans and now he'd announced their marriage to the world, a juicy fact sure to rile up the gossip rags. Jack dismissed this possibility but was soon proven wrong when the morning papers came aboard their train. The reading-public was already aware of Jack London's affair with Anna Strunsky, but now they knew of Charmian. According to that era's hypocritical values, these revelations were an immediate scandal and caused several organizations to cancel Jack's lectures. This accelerated their journey, bringing them back to rural Iowa where their bad reputation preceded the train. Isabelle shadowed Jack and Charmian during the next lectures, listened in on their conversations, and followed the undercover police officers who showed up in the audience. My mother never found a pattern to these visits, although Jack London was surely under surveillance.

On December 7, 1905, this unorthodox party arrived in Brunswick, Maine where my mother bathed in a claw-footed tub, slept in fluffy blankets, and woke to Manyoungi knocking on her hotel room door. With a sorrowful look on his face, he handed over a sealed letter, made a solemn bow, and wished her good luck. Using more words than necessary, Jack claimed his heart had forced him into marriage, juſt as it now forced him to keep up appearances by ſtaying a week with his wife's relatives in Maine. Jack promised to follow behind and swore to be in New York City on their chosen date. He also included a firſt-class train-ticket and begged Isabelle for forgiveness. Unable to change this reality, my mother packed her bags and boarded a Pullman Palace Car bound for Grand Central Station. Unlike the previous weeks, Isabelle was now rolling along the rails in the height of modern luxury. Luckily for her, she had been taught the Pullman porter's secret handshake.

Juſt before dusk, Isabelle heard a knock on her sleeper door and opened it up to find a porter telling her dinner was about to be served. Before he could leave, Isabelle asked for his help inside and then ſtuck out her hand to greet him by the false name on her ticket. Once she gave his brothers' secret handshake, the porter widened his eyes, closed the door, and asked my mother what she wanted. She asked how the train syſtem funſtioned in the US, how easy it was to ride for free, and how many armed men guarded its tracks.

Partially frantic, the porter told her to call for him after dinner coffee was served and then quickly resumed his duties down the cars. Isabelle ate dinner with the other Palace Car riders, all of them white, and she feigned polite conversation, pretending she was a nanny off to her new job in the big city. My mother excused herself juſt as coffee was served and returned to her sleeper where she watched the lights of Providence, Rhode Island fade into the rural darkness. Before she could call for him, that same porter knocked on her door, let himself in, and for the next hour he told her every huſtle, dodge, scheme, short-cut, scam, and trick he'd

learned from riding the rails, both as a worker for the Pullman company and as an unemployed tramp moving from town to town.

Just before he left, my mother brought up the famous author Jack London and his tales of riding the rails across all of North America. The porter told her not to believe all the crazy *jive* she read in the papers, especially when white folks wrote it, and reminded her that while some hobo like Jack might get thrown in jail if the bulls caught him on the rails, a black hobo would be murdered and left for the wolves, with no one ever knowing or caring. According to the porter, this is why he and his brothers joined the Pullman company, and so long as they wore their uniforms near the station, they could travel the whole country without fear of being lynched. My mother thanked him for his honesty, gave him their secret hand-shake one last time, and managed to slide the sleeper door shut before bursting into tears unlike any she had ever experienced. All the racist unions in San Francisco, all the racist words in the books of Jack London and Frank Norris, all of it exploded in her heart, a divine rage that filled her soul in its desire to be released.

My mother didn't sleep that night. She sat by the window, gazing into the darkness, and while the train plunged into the electric lights of New Haven, Connecticut, she began imagining how to use this rail net-work against its creator, allowing it to spread rebellion instead of capitalism, just as the porters were doing. She thought about this until dawn when the waters of Long Island Sound exploded with a dark red light that filled her sleeper-cabin with its rising glow. By the time the sun was well-above the horizon, their train veered away from the coast and soon entered a vast expanse of brick buildings that stretched away in every direction. Thick plumes of coal-smoke rose from hundreds of stone chimneys, creating a toxic haze unlike any Isabelle had ever seen, and this dense urban sprawl hung heavy in her mind until it suddenly vanished, replaced by the black walls of a long tunnel. Steam and coal-smoke filled the dark air outside the windows until the train slowly emerged into the old Grand Central Station of New York City. Much to her surprise, Anna Strunsky was waiting on the platform. Unable to help herself, my mother wept as Anna walked her towards the Lower East Side.

Meanwhile, many weeks before Isabelle arrived in New York City, Yvonne had met with Alma and Phœbe Hearst. She called on Alma first, dispatching a private carriage to the marsh-lands where the young woman still lived in her family's laundry-house. Alma's eyes lacked their usual sparkle and she shuffled into the library sullen and morose, claiming she was worse than nothing, just some naked girl leered at by greedy old men. Her *sugar daddy's* family advised against marrying her and she only saw Adolph at his Napa ranch, as usual. Alma felt like a statue, carted around from man to man, and she'd have killed herself if not for her parents. Yvonne couldn't help but weep. She told Alma these men wanted them to feel replaceable, only they mustn't give them that satisfaction. None of these men deserved what they'd plundered from the earth, so women had to be smart, patient, and decisive if they wanted it back. Yvonne couldn't take away her sadness, nor could she quickly remedy their miserable situations, but she made Alma smile with hope that day, a kindness the *sugar baby* never forgot.

Shortly after this meeting, the Union Labor Party was voted back into office by a large majority, ushering in another two years of municipal corruption. The only beneficial outcome of this election was the utter collapse of the Citizen's Alliance, a development that seemed trivial to Lionel Heath. When he stopped by the mansion for dinner, the steel baron wrote it off as just another loose end. While his Citizen's Alliance might have been defeated, her husband insisted this corrupt administration was now digging their own graves. Once they were buried, the residents of San Francisco would never elect another union City Hall. Heath was jubilant, all but confirming he'd orchestrated the whole affair, and once he'd gone, Yvonne sent off a telegram to Phœbe Hearst asking if she'd lunch with her at the mansion. Among all the capitalists, no one supported the Union Labor Party like her son and Yvonne needed to know if William Randolph Hearst was secretly involved in Heath's conspiracy.

Phœbe arrived in her own carriage, claiming to detest automobiles and preferring the old ways of horseshit to petroleum. They took this strange conversation into the library and discussed their pasts by the fire over the next hours. Phœbe was just 19 when a 40-year-old gold miner named George Hearst plucked her from a Missouri schoolhouse, paid for a quick wedding, and impregnated her with their only son. Rather than groom *Willy* to be the heir of a huge mining fortune, Phœbe did the opposite, filling his mind with art and letters. She claimed the best way to defeat perverted old George was to ensure *Willy* didn't care for mine-shafts, private detectives, and gold. By the time George was finally dead, *Willy* had started a newspaper empire and soon enough he used it to trigger the Spanish-American War. He was elected to Congress in 1903, failed to secure the 1904 presidential nomination, was re-elected to Congress, narrowly lost the New York City's mayor race, and was currently planning to run for New York governor. Above all, Phœbe wanted him to become president and free women from bondage. Yvonne tried not to betray any revulsion but Phœbe could see the strain of her neck muscles. For the first time in many centuries, the forces of Mary were now fighting each other.

After calming herself, Yvonne changed the subject back to George Hearst's mine-shafts. Phœbe laughed this off, claiming money always came from somewhere. In her case, the fortune derived from gold mines in Nevada,

South Dakota, Montana, and Mexico. The only ventures that lost money were the newspapers, an economic reality incommensurate with their effect on society. Yvonne asked if her *Willy's* love for the working class was feigned, only to be told that everything was feigned in this world, including her son's benevolence. He didn't care a wink about the working class or the Union Labor Party, he just wanted votes, and Yvonne suggested this association might hurt William, especially if the Party's corruption were to be suddenly exposed. For the first time since they met, Yvonne took the upper hand. Phœbe regarded her carefully, as if she were looking for the entrance to an interior castle, only to find the walls lacked any seam. Phœbe claimed *Willy* had many enemies, too many for Yvonne to be vague, and she scoffed at the idea of her son working with Heath. Instead of offering to collaborate, Yvonne directed Phœbe towards the Spreckels family and their recent efforts against the Union Labor Party. As a consequence of these words, Hearst was on the right side of the impending corruption investigation, a debt Phœbe had every intention of repaying in the future.

A week before departing for New York City, Yvonne dispatched a sealed letter to Nikola Tesla's Wardenclyfe facility, asking to meet on January 2, 1906. With the letter delivered, Yvonne packed her daughter's belongings and readied herself for their first journey outside California. In the last days of November, Heath, Yvonne, and Juana rode to the waterfront in the petroleum belching Daimler, crossed over to Oakland on Heath's private yacht, and were escorted to their Pullman Palace Car by his armed men. After this hectic transfer, Yvonne hardly stepped off the train. All her needs were provided for in this swaying Palace Car adorned with red carpets and crystal chandeliers. The constant rocking of the train car gave Yvonne a convenient excuse to feign illness and she lived those nights alone with Juana amid a sea of open books while Heath slept in the adjacent car. The changing landscapes outside the train window were disjointed and abstract, flowing too rapidly for visual comprehension, and Yvonne ignored this passing blur, preferring to read fairy-tales with Juana. She only gazed outside once the sun went down and the world became a river of shadows. Modernity's speed terrified her and night was the only familiar element. Juana would always remember Yvonne standing like this, shoulder against the window, her green eyes trained toward the darkness.

They arrived in Grand Central Station to a press reception complete with photographic cameras and an army of journalists. Yvonne barely had time to cover Juana's face before the chorus of clicks and flashes filled the air. Heath stood proudly before the lenses but Yvonne shrouded herself with a black shawl as the guards escorted them to their carriage. This unplanned episode became a sensation, with pictures of Yvonne del Valle-Heath gracing a dozen daily newspapers. When she and Juana woke the next morning at the Waldorf-Astoria Hotel, the public was all abuzz over Yvonne's *veiled beauty* and *gypsy superstitions*, according to the journalists. A stack of these newspapers had been slipped under her door that morning, along with a message from Isabelle, and Yvonne opened it up before Heath had a chance to read it. Claiming to be a journalist, my mother cryptically explained she was staying with Anna, left a forwarding address in the Jewish quarter, and said a meeting was urgently needed. There was no word from Tesla.

Yvonne arranged to meet Isabelle at the American Museum of Natural History, an institution funded by JP Morgan that had been suggested by Heath as a way to pass the time while he was on Wall Street. Since the 1870s, the House of Morgan had pumped money into this museum and lined its walls with ancient artifacts plundered from across the

planet. Yvonne had asked my mother to meet her at the Egyptian display and soon found her gazing at dog-headed Anubis, gatekeeper of the underworld. This deity's image reminded Isabelle of the coyote she'd seen at the *Rancho del Valle,* triggering a string of thoughts that would have drawn her back to the underworld if Juana hadn't grabbed her legs and held her down. Yvonne waited for a moment, sensing something was wrong, but when it passed she asked about Jack. Isabelle expressed her concerns but Yvonne said not to worry. While his head might be foolish, Jack's heart was filled with goodness, and tonight she'd lay the groundwork for his lecture by mentioning him to JP Morgan's family. Isabelle listened but said nothing, for the image of Anubis was still whispering to her. She wished Yvonne good luck, kissed her on the cheek, and left the museum for a walk through Central Park. Isabelle stayed the night with Anna and her sister Rose, cooked a large breakfast the next morning, and saw them off to the *SS Baltic,* a large cruise-liner owned by JP Morgan. On this iron steamship, the Strunsky sisters traveled towards *Les Diablerets* and the uprising in Russia.

The night before they departed, Yvonne and Juana left the Waldorf-Astoria Hotel covered in shrouds while Lionel Heath distracted the cameras. This fact was recorded in the daily newspapers to varying degrees of accuracy, though none mentioned Heath's destination. After losing their journalistic pursuers, his private automobile deposited them at the Madison Avenue home of JP Morgan where dozens of armed men guarded the entrance. Yvonne was quickly overwhelmed by an onslaught of introductions and feigned smiles, culminating in her hand being kissed by the wretched monster himself. With a growth-covered nose, shiny bald head, and piercing black eyes, JP Morgan was the epitome of darkness. Despite her strength, Yvonne fell into her husband's shoulder and asked to sit down. The women of the Morgan clan descended at once, waving fans and offering her refreshments on one of the drawing room's plush red sofas. Juana stayed close, never relinquishing her hand, and Yvonne encouraged everyone to feel at ease when she left them for the bathroom. Once she was alone, Yvonne hyperventilated until the fear leached through her skin and evaporated in that marble-lined toilet, allowing her to emerge for battle.

The party now sat in a circle around the windows, the men all holding drinks. While the women fanned away cigar smoke, the men jubilated over recent events in Russia. Not only had these capitalists financed the war between Japan and Russia, they were now hoping to lend money to the crippled Czar. JP Morgan explained to the women that in order to make the loan, Russia would have to uphold a parliamentary system and put down the year-long Revolution, otherwise it was a bad investment. JP Morgan Jr. had been dispatched to deal with the Czar and was now busy drafting what would become a massive Anglo-French bailout of the crumbling Russian Empire. Word had just arrived that the Czar was directing soldiers to crush the Moscow Soviet, the final condition to secure the loan. While their party dined over sliced, bloody beef, Yvonne avoided glancing at JP Morgan's bulbous nose growths and listened only to the substance of his banter, speaking not a word until coffee was served. When the diners were at their most sluggish, she asked if they'd ever heard of Jack London.

The women immediately gasped out a dozen opinions, including gossip about Jack's new wife. Heath vouched for him as a Bohemian and testified that his stories realistically evoked all the world's savageries. One of JP Morgan's daughters claimed Jack London must have lived a thousand lives, so rich was his web of stories. At this final remark, JP Morgan grew rigid and asked for some of it to be read aloud. Yvonne suggested the story "The Son of the Wolf" and Morgan's daughter soon retrieved the volume to read the opening sentence, *man rarely places a proper valuation upon his womankind, at least not until deprived of them.* JP Morgan's black eyes glistened at this tale of a white man stealing an indigenous bride and the party gasped at the thrilling conclusion replete with arrows, dog-sleds, and knife fights. Once it was over, Morgan asked if Jack had ever been to Alaska, and Yvonne assured him the author was a genuine renaissance worker who excelled at every trade from writing to sailing. Lionel Heath immediately boasted of his wife's literary correspondences and insisted Jack be invited to speak in New York City. This proposition filled the Morgan women with glee and their patriarch resolved to organize an exclusive lecture, something Yvonne agreed to facilitate.

The success of this plan did little to elevate Yvonne's spirits and the following days brought only sadness. For nearly three months, the Moscow Soviet stood proudly against the Empire with its streets barricaded, its train lines blown apart, and its commerce paralyzed in a general strike, but these brave insurgents now fought their final battle throughout the middle of December. Yvonne learned of this at the Morgan household and endured cheers of excitement as Imperial soldiers trapped the insurgents in the Presnya district while western artillery rained down over their heads, littering the streets with corpses. She learned of the Soviet's defeat inside the Metropolitan Museum of Art, another institution funded by JP Morgan, and while the men cheered on this new slaughter, Yvonne gazed at meaningless blurs of paint. These treasures were now displayed like sides of meat for the rich to gawk at, their true beauty overshadowed by the darkness that confined them. Yvonne would have fainted if Juana hadn't been clutching her hand, a reminder of their grander purpose in New York City.

She arranged to meet my mother a few days later and they strolled with Juana through snow covered Central Park, dressed as common women. Jack had finally arrived in New York City and his wife Charmian London was in Maine, leaving him free to finish their plan. They resolved to schedule Jack's private reading for the coming Saturday and parted ways with their appointed tasks. All it took for Yvonne to solidify the event was an offhanded remark to her husband that Jack London was in town. By nightfall, JP Morgan had hired out the ballroom of the Waldorf-Astoria Hotel and booked a private event protected by two dozen hired guns. Death threats were regular occurrences in the offices of 23 Wall Street, although less so than against the other capitalists.

Unlike the barons being investigated by the government, JP Morgan had successfully courted President Roosevelt and earned a reputation as the *honest capitalist*. A clever snake, Morgan convinced Theodore Roosevelt to publicly oppose the *socialist press* who incited violence and hate against honest businessmen, forcing his family to guard themselves. In one of his famous speeches, Roosevelt railed against *the Man with Muck-Rake*, those truculent writers and journalists who could look *no way but downward*. Rather than champion the *muckraker's* exposure of social ills, Roosevelt claimed they were *one of the most potent forces for evil*. This was the power of JP Morgan at work, and Yvonne saw it all first-hand, a darkness so thick she could hardly breathe.

In the days leading up to Jack's lecture, Yvonne came across one of these *evil muck-raking magazines* inside a Jewish book-shop. The most recent issue featured an author who'd helped organize Jack's tour, a man named Upton Sinclair. She purchased all the 1905 issues of *Appeal to Reason* and carried them through the streets with little Juana, both dressed as humble common-ers. According to the hotel staff, Yvonne was out for her daily carriage airing, a crafty lie that allowed her to observe the jagged modernity of New York City with its massive chessboard of competing skyscrapers. She took Juana on the new railway system that sprawled beneath the metropolis and rode each sub-way train to its terminus before doubling back. Financed by a close associate of the Rothschilds, this underground net-work was just completed after years of public controversy, allowing the House of Morgan to buy up property around the subway stops before the lines opened. Everything was booming in New York City, especially in the offices of 23 Wall Street, and the size of the national economy had nearly tripled in two years. Yvonne was in the very center of this expanding Empire when she returned to the hotel and sprawled out on her bed to read the socialist magazines. This was the day she discovered *The Jungle* by Upton Sinclair.

The serialized novel sickened her gut and threw her into a frenzy of agita-tion with its haunting image of a slaughter-house worker boiled alive and his body sold off in meat cans, just as she wept over the depiction of a mother dying from prostitution. As Jack wrote from his New York City hotel room that December, Sinclair's novel depicted *not what our country ought to be, or what it seems to be in the fancies of Fourth-of-July spell-binders, the home of liberty and equality, of opportunity—but it depicts what our country is, the home of oppression and injustice, a nightmare of misery, an inferno of suffering, a human hell, a jungle of wild beasts.* While its present serial format condemned the work to obscurity, Yvonne and Jack knew this story would soon join *The Octopus, The People of the Abyss,* and *The History of the Standard Oil Company* in the emerging constellation of social literature.

This comforting thought buoyed her spirits later that night

Upton Sinclair

as she was forced to watch motion-pictures with the JP Morgan clan. Yvonne had kept up with the emerging medium and there was hardly a film she hadn't watched dozens of times. None of these images surprised her and she watched with detachment, an expression that caught the attention of JP Morgan. As his family sat mesmerized, Morgan noticed Yvonne's ability to resist, a curious power that aroused his darkness. He slithered over during the films and asked her a dozen questions about cinema. Yvonne claimed to be a disinterested expert and, rather than resist these images, she was waiting for an artist who could utilize the medium to its fullest extent. This clever dodge elicited a metallic chuckle and Morgan withdrew his deformed nose back into the shadows. Yvonne couldn't help but smile at the stupidity of this man, a snoring dragon with no comprehension of her presence atop his gold.

Thanks to this breach inside the House of Morgan, my mother was able to transmit intelligence across the Atlantic about the Anglo-French loan being drafted for the Czar. Within weeks, anarchists in France and Russia were organizing propaganda campaigns to expose the Czar's pogroms and reveal their connection to the loan. Morgan and Heath laughed at these protests, for not even the Jews of the banking world cared how the Czar treated their fellows. Over the past week, a single Jewish banker had stalled the loan process, citing the pogroms as his justification, but he had just withdrawn his official protest when Yvonne met with Isabelle in the Metropolitan Museum of Art.

Beneath the walls of French art, my mother claimed this reluctance to grant the loan was being used by the Czar as proof of a Jewish conspiracy, bolstering the false claims in *The Protocols of the Elders of Zion*. Yvonne wondered aloud if this Jewish banker might be helping Morgan stabilize the Empire, fanning race-hatred across the land in an attempt to restore law and order. It was now well known to the world that Leon Trotsky, leader of the Moscow Soviet, was of Jewish descent. The only good news came from Anna who'd just left London for Switzerland accompanied by her sister Rose. Once they arrived, Anna would make contact with my family beneath *Les Diablerets* and proceed onward to Russia. Comforted by this reality, my mother clutched Yvonne's hand and wished her good luck that night. In less than six hours, Jack's lecture was scheduled to take place.

Yvonne and Juana descended the elevator with Lionel Heath and shrouded themselves when they reached the lobby. The press was kept outside the Waldorf-Astoria but many paid bribes to peer through the glass. Over the next hour, dozens of respected bankers and businessmen arrived with their families and walked past the scribbling journalists, although none were prepared for the sudden arrival of JP Morgan's family and their entourage of armed men. Inside this opulent cavern, Jack London had already arrived and was now mingling with the guests. Yvonne and Juana stood far away from Jack's spotlight and watched him charm everyone, even deformed JP Morgan. Few could withstand this vile creature's presence, yet Jack was carrying on with him like a fearless pirate. While she observed this strange encounter, Yvonne became aware of a woman standing beside her with a glass of champagne. She grinned at Yvonne knowingly and appeared to be every race at once, young and ancient, beautiful and plain. Resembling an Egyptian from the Lower Nile or a native woman from North America, this familiar stranger stepped close to Yvonne's ear and whispered, *I like your style.* Before she could think to respond, Yvonne and Juana were

Belle da Costa-Greene

directed to their seats. Once the confusion settled, the woman was sitting beside her. JP Morgan leaned over from behind and introduced her as Belle da Costa-Greene, the new curator of his private library, and just before Jack took the stage, Belle winked at Yvonne as if she knew their plan. It was an even greater shock when Belle grabbed her hand and held it tight.

Jack smiled at his chorus of applause and waited until the silence was definite. Juana grabbed her mother's free hand and the three squeezed tightly as Jack began his famous speech. After thirty minutes of logically deconstructing the capitalist empire, the former pirate declared: *You have been entrusted with the world; you have muddled and mismanaged it. You are incompetent, despite all your boasting. A million years ago the caveman, without tools, with small brain, and with nothing but the strength of his body, managed to feed his wife and children, so that through him the race survived. You, on the other hand, armed with all the modern means of production, multiplying the productive capacity of the caveman a million times — you incompetents and muddlers, you are unable to secure to millions even the paltry amount of bread that would sustain their physical life. You have mismanaged the world, and it shall be taken from you! Who will take it from you? We will! And who are we? We are seven million socialist revolutionaries and we are everywhere growing. And we want all you have! Look at us!* Jack exhibited no shame in displaying his muscles to the audience, a move that elicited gasps. *We are strong! Consider our hands! They are strong hands, and even now they are reaching forth for all you have, and they will take it, take it by the power of* their *strong* hands; take it from your feeble grasp. Long or short though the time may be, that time is coming. The army is on the march, and nothing can stop it. That you can stop it is ludicrous. It wants nothing less than all you have, and it will take it; you are incompetent and will have to surrender to the strong. We are the *strong*, and in that day we shall give you an exhibition of power such as your feeble brains never dreamed the world contained.* The silence that followed was deafening. Not a trace of darkness existed, and it took a moment for JP Morgan to realize he'd been stabbed in the heart with a dagger made of light.

Jack London left the stage and walked directly out of the room, a timid chorus of boos and jeers following behind. Just as the crowd erupted into a riot of protests, Yvonne noticed Belle was no longer beside her. She wouldn't learn until later that Belle had boarded a carriage and beckoned Jack to make his escape by her side. Obeying an impulse beyond his control, the author jumped in and joined Belle for an illuminating ride across New York City. This meeting was never recorded in any book, nor was it noted by the press. They chain-smoked tobacco, drank whiskey, and strolled through Central Park in each other's arms. She revealed to Jack that her father was Richard Greener, the first black man to ever graduate from Harvard, an honor which delivered no clear benefits. While he was allowed to work for the federal government, the *yanquis* had consigned him to an icy consulate in Siberia.

During the war between Russia and Japan, Richard began to notice the hands of JP Morgan and his European bankers pulling the strings. Assigned to monitor this war, Richard came into contact with Elizabeth Dmitrieff, a woman who lived in a nearby penal colony. They were occasional allies during the war and Elizabeth came to trust this exile who sought only to understand the slaughter in Korea, China, and Siberia. As it turned out, Richard had helped Elizabeth smuggle guns, proving he was no spy for the Czar. Belle had received a letter from her father revealing his suspicions towards JP Morgan and encouraging her to find out all she could. In a series of cryptic statements, he wrote, *our comrades will meet you in New York City. These are friends of the woman I told you about. One of them is the daughter of the one with fire.* Richard had already written to Belle of Elizabeth's fiery exit from Paris, just as he'd written of Josephine Lemel wielding flame atop the *butte* of Montmartre.

Belle held Jack by the shoulder and asked, *where's the daughter?* Overcome by suspicion, Jack denied any knowledge of Isabelle and insisted it must be a mistake. This greatly irritated Belle, so she took him by the waist, kissed him on the lips, and made frantic love to him atop the snow of Central Park. Draped in the bottoms of her overcoat, Jack heard Belle say *this needs to go somewhere* before a howl erupted from her body. The author was terrified into shock, limbs paralyzed, helpless as the claws of Isis thrashed into the frozen soil, churning a chasm into the underworld. Jack remembered nothing of his plunge, but Belle remembered everything, seeing deep into the man's soul.

Back at his hotel, Jack stayed awake until dawn and dined ravenously when the kitchen opened for breakfast. He spoke to no one, dispatched a message to Isabelle asking to meet with Yvonne, and remained at his table burning with warmth. Belle had left an egg inside his heart, ready to hatch once its recipient arrived. He'd never feel this good again, his entire being tuned to a higher modulation, and it lasted until he met with Isabelle, Yvonne, and Juana in the tiny booth of a smoky worker's restaurant. When he finished telling Belle's tale, the egg broke open and its golden yoke flowed into both Isabelle and Yvonne. No one knew what had taken place, but it worked flawlessly, connecting a fiery circle that spanned the entire globe.

Jack left for Boston that same morning and within five days he was off on his well-publicized honeymoon getaway with Charmian, an event that dragged him deeper into infamy. While he sailed towards Jamaica on the United Fruit Company's SS *Admiral Farragut*, Yvonne celebrated Christmas with the House of Morgan and indulged in all their family ceremonies. No one spoke of Jack London, nor was his lecture discussed, and Yvonne didn't push the matter. The entire family was crushed by Jack's merciless words and the holiday passed in a blur of pointless luxury.

On the other side of town, Isabelle printed papers with her Jewish comrades and enjoyed lavish meals from the old-country. While few of them celebrated the religious holiday, these anarchist Jews conjured godless merriment and stayed warm together at the onset of winter. During her time in New York City, Isabelle sharpened her written Hebrew, practiced her spoken Yiddish, learned of the conflict with the Zionists, and tasted food that rivaled even the Strunsky's. She worked most of her nights with Emma Goldman and helped prepare the inaugural issue of *Mother Earth*, an organ that would come to shape the anarchist movement across the US. None of these comrades knew what Isabelle was doing in New York City, but they trusted it was important. Few expected what happened next.

On December 30, 1905, the former governor of Idaho left his house in the town of Caldwell. Just as he opened his white picket-fence, a package of pure dynamite exploded near his feet, shredding his body into a thousand pieces. This man was a bitter enemy of the Western Federation of Miners and the authorities immediately labeled the blast a political assassination. At the New Year's Eve party for the House of Morgan, Yvonne could taste the fear circulating the room, infecting even her husband. Theodore Roosevelt had already canceled a meeting with JP Morgan and it was possible he'd leave their corner entirely to obey these labor radical's whims. As the first day of 1906 dawned on the Waldorf-Astoria, Yvonne was overwhelmed with joy, never imagining the magnitude of their success, and she took Juana to meet Isabelle at a restaurant near Grand Central Station.

My mother was already packed for her journey, dressed in a plain black dress with a black straw hat, and they sipped coffee in the crowded restaurant discussing the fate of Nikola Tesla. During their time in New York City, the inventor had sent no word, nor did he make any public appearances. So as not to arouse suspicion, Yvonne didn't mention Tesla around her husband or inquire about his address. If she had, Yvonne would have learned the inventor was on the third floor of the Waldorf-Astoria, gripped by illness and fever. That morning, before meeting Isabelle at the restaurant, Yvonne chanced to overhear a Waldorf-Astoria butler asking whether Mr. Tesla's order was ready. When the food cart rolled past, Yvonne saw the room number was 333. She planned to visit him the next morning.

Yvonne kissed Isabelle goodbye and stood with Juana as my mother's train pulled out of Grand Central Station. Jack had provided one final luxury and secured Isabelle a private sleeper for the entire journey, an indulgence she would never taste again. As the Appalachian Mountains opened up onto the Midwestern Plains, my mother recalled Jack's stories of empty box-cars filled with hobos who traveled hundreds of miles without paying a cent. On her plush bed in the Pullman Palace car, Isabelle plotted her own hobo lecture tour that would include handing out weapons, distributing money, and registering membership cards for the IWW. As her passenger-train traveled past side-tracked freight-cars, my mother studied their compartments, measured the footholds, and imagined where her hands might grip. By the time she reached San Francisco, Isabelle had the entire hobo campaign mapped out. Having tasted the opulence of capitalism, my mother was now ready to live within its underbelly.

While her train was still chugging through Ohio, Yvonne donned a white dress, tied her hair into pig-tails, and put on false reading-glasses. Heath and Morgan were busy fretting over their setback, leaving her free to visit Tesla. She told Juana to stay in their hotel room and keep the door locked until she returned. When the hallway was clear, Yvonne slipped down to the third floor and pounded on Tesla's door. She heard shuffling and coughing, braced

Nikola Tesla

herself for the encounter, and when the door opened, she entered without invitation. Nikola ſtood six-feet tall, black hair unkempt, blue-eyes clouded over. He fell to his knees in apology, having convinced himself she'd feigned intereſt in his projeƈt on behalf of Heath and Morgan. His illness began shortly after, keeping him bed-ridden for weeks. Yvonne closed the door, picked him off the floor, ſtraightened his hair, and told him Heath had spread the rumor to keep them apart. In this moment of tenderness, Yvonne and Nikola ripped a hole into the fabric of time and space.

Yvonne let this rupture engulf her entire body, a surrender Nikola wasn't prepared to make. All the inventor could see was white light and blurry form, out of focus like an errant projeƈtion. When it ſtabilized, Nikola saw a famil- iar woman ſtanding before him. She was no longer Yvonne del Valle, nor was he Nikola Tesla. They were now on a lawn beside a ſtone house on a sunny day. A few black cows ambled in the diſtance and he heard children's laugh- ter from a nearby creek. She held him around the shoulders and asked, *don't you recognize me, Nicholas?* She asked this in French, English, and Serbian simultaneously. The woman before him was now in a long black dress, her face kissed with dozens of freckles. She said her name was Perenelle and asked, *don't you remember me? I've loſt my fortune, but it's me! Don't you remember me?* Suddenly they were inside a wooden ſtudy with a ledger open atop the oak desk. She pointed to a large figure denoting their fortune and asked, *why can't you remember?* She clutched his face with both hands and screamed at him, *it's me, Nicholas, it's Perenelle, your wife Perenelle Flamel!* The hotel room flickered into view but she forced him to ſtay in France.

Now they were inside a candle-lit book-bindery where he was sewing together a thick volume while two dozen women watched over his work. On a loose page of parchment, he beheld the image of seven naked women inside a green bathing pool. This was the laſt image he saw before the watery tubes sucked the lovers into the underworld where their reunion took place in a realm beyond memory. They woke up in Nikola's hotel bed, both drenched in nether-fluid and breathing pure lavender. Yvonne told Nikola she'd deliver his funding and when he asked how she would do this, Yvonne said it was because she loved him, a *why* that would provide the *how.* She kissed him on the lips, swore she'd find their fortune by summer, and promised to love him forever, juſt as she always had.

For a brief moment, Yvonne del Valle-Heath morphed back into Perenelle, the wealthy wife of Nicholas Flamel, an alchemiſt alleged to have achieved the Philosopher's Stone. Hiſtory garbled and mutated his true achievement, although Yvonne and Nikola beheld a flash of its memory. Nicholas Flamel had praƈticed the ancient craft of bookbinding and the art of illuminating manuscripts, skills he taught to Perenelle's ſtrange friends, an assortment of women from the Roman peninsula who spoke the same ancient dialect. With his assistance, these followers of Mary learned how to compose *The Book*, our blueprint for electromagnetic transmission. Nikola Tesla had no knowledge of *The Book*, nor did he remember his plunge into the underworld, and Yvonne left him there in bed, his body still gripped by fever. The only comfort was the sweet scent of lavender that now clung to his mattress.

Nicolas Flamel Écrivain, Libraire Juré en l'Université de Paris, mort en 1418.

After this otherworldly encounter, Yvonne returned to her room and sat near the window where she gazed at the trees. Juana couldn't get any answers from her mother, not even a hello, and Yvonne sat above Central Park basking in the reality of who she truly was. Like every follower of Mary, her soul had traveled through time and found its refer-ent within each passing life, linking up with other souls who remembered the deserts of Egypt, Palestine, Syria, and Persia. Yvonne was a rogue fol-lower, never imagining her soul would carry this identity, and she accepted her strange part in Mary's long war. The tyrants had tried to conceal Tesla but were unable to sever the immortal connection pulling them together. Something fierce had woken inside Yvonne, more powerful than dynamite.

The Heath family departed New York City on January 5, 1906. Rather than defy tradition, JP Morgan insisted on a heavily-guarded public send-off to display their rank before the rabble at Grand Central Station, and as they crossed into Ohio aboard their Pullman Palace Car, private detectives combed the Rockies in search of the Idaho bombers. Heath now spoke frantically of the efforts to catch these criminals, just as all the capitalists of North America were consumed with fear of an international anarchist plot. JD Rockefeller erected a massive iron fence around his New York property and kept it sealed, never once leaving without armed guards, while Heath took every precaution for their train journey and hired an entire steerage-car of Pinkertons to protect his family. They surrounded his private car at each stop, kept the crowds away from the windows, and received the daily groceries, newspapers, letters, and mail. In the newspapers, Yvonne learned that several suspects had been inter-rogated by the police and the circle was now closing on the Idaho bombers. None of this seemed to put her husband at ease and he brooded for hours in her company, locked in some sort of psychic dilemma.

Grand Central Station

The bombers still hadn't been caught when they finally returned to Pacific Heights in the middle of January and the private detectives drove Yvonne and Juana home through angry streets filled with jeers, tomatoes, and even a rock. Meanwhile, Heath hid away safely in the Palace. The mansion work-routine quickly resumed, allowing Isabelle and Yvonne to discuss what happened in New York, though Yvonne omitted her encounter with Tesla. Both were proud of their successes and wanted to bask in their glory, especially with such dark intelligence now emerging from Anna Strunsky.

After leaving the sanctuary of *Les Diablerets*, Anna met her sister Rose in Geneva and made plans to enter the Russian Empire. In the first days of January, the Strunsky sisters traveled to Berlin where they obtained valid passports from the US Consulate, falsely claiming to have been born in New York City. With these new documents, the sisters obtained legitimate visas at the Russian Consulate and booked passage to Saint Petersburg. Anna's most recent letter explained how she saw an Imperial officer shoot down a student for refusing to sing *God Save the Czar*, an act that would haunt her for decades to come. Four days after this murder, a woman named Maria Spiridonova shot down a leader of the Black Hundreds in the city of Borisoglebsk, an act that threw Anna into a frenzy of joy. In this tumultuous moment, she fell in love with the head of her news bureau, William English Walling, and made love with him every evening as if the darkness weren't clawing at their door.

In late-January of 1906, the Black Hundreds raided the Jewish village of Homel in Belarus, burning buildings and killing dozens, shocking Anna from her momentary bliss. Within days, she was riding alone on a train for Minsk to investigate her first assignment for William's news bureau. While this was just a cover story, Anna had every intention of using her words to attack the Czar. That month, thousands of Russian rebels were summarily executed, followed by a constellation of pogroms carried out by the Black Hundreds, each massacre occurring within days of the other. In the wake of these events, the Black Hundreds spread the *Protocols of the Elders of Zion* to the Russian-speaking public and promoted theories of a Jewish banking conspiracy. According to them, anyone who opposed JP Morgan's loan to the Czar was a Jewish agent and should be killed. Isabelle agonized over these facts with Shmuel Schwartz as they sat inside the *Secolo Nuovo* print-shop drafting articles from Anna's intelligence. As they distributed this latest Russian issue across the Latin Quarter, my mother suddenly felt an urge to use her body in ways she'd never desired.

Once all their issues were scattered through the neighborhood, Isabelle made love to Schwartz in a corner of the print-shop that was so dark he couldn't see her body. They remained in each other's arms until morning and passed the delirious hours experiencing unknown pleasures. As they dressed for the walk home, Isabelle told Schwartz this couldn't happen again but that she would always love him as a friend. She held him close until his tears passed and then left him alone in the middle of Basque Town. Two blocks away, Isabelle found her mother Josephine dressed as a man and holding an upside-down black umbrella that concealed a bloody *machete*. As they walked home, Josephine expressed nothing but happiness for her daughter, although her own night had been quite gory. War had just erupted on the Barbary Coast and the nights dripped with murder.

Now that the Union Labor Party was re-elected into power, an emboldened Municipal Crib had attacked Marisol's ally Iodaform Kate. While the worst of it was thwarted, one of Kate's best fighters had her throat slit in the middle of Broadway. Marisol and Kate wasted no time retaliating for this murder, the bulk of this task falling on Josephine. Over those cold winter nights, she slaughtered any Municipal Crib operatives who stepped even a block away from their heavily guarded building and spread fear among the Barbary Coast pimps with her glistening *machete*. This past night had been as bloody as the others.

Josephine and Isabelle arrived at the little blue house on Greenwich Street to find Marisol de la Costa waiting on the porch. Although she'd soon go to bed, Marisol was drinking coffee and smoking a cigarette after her long night. They all sat together, gazing out at the rippling bay, and in the midst of a long silence, an invisible force ſtirred beneath their ancient limeſtone hill, a beacon pulsing beyond the range of human hearing. This was a call of diſtress emitted by Josephine and Marisol, announcing their patience had come to an end. Isabelle didn't notice, nor did the Queens mention it, and while they slept that morning, my mother was getting dressed for another day at work.

A few days later, Isabelle was with Schwartz in the *Secolo Nuovo* print-shop when Enrico burſt inside, claiming their IWW comrades had been kidnapped in Denver, smuggled into Idaho, and charged with dynamiting the former governor. When they finally saw a copy of that day's *Examiner*, the men were liſted as Charles Moyer, George Pettibone, and Big Bill Haywood, all leaders of the Weſtern Federation of Miners and supporters of the IWW. Over the next weeks, Isabelle met with Schwartz and Enrico to compose articles soliciting funds for these captured men. As it turned out, the charges againſt them were based on the confession of a man who claimed to have planted the bomb under orders from the WFM inner circle, a cabal that included Moyer, Pettibone, and Haywood.

As they printed their articles for *Secolo Nuovo*, my mother knew full-well the bomb had come from Big Bill Haywood, a booming figure always ready to bring the fight today rather than tomorrow. According to their comrade Al Klemencik, Big Bill and his girlfriend Winnie Minor had become a fiery duo, always whispering during meetings and huddling together with the braveſt fighters. As these three men now languished in a Boise jailhouse, the WFM, the IWW, and the entire Black International mobilized to defend them. In addition to funds raised by *Secolo Nuovo*, money flowed into their defense fund from every major labor organization, even the conservative American Federation of Labor. For the firſt time in many years, sharp lines had been drawn between the workers and the bosses, paving the way for a mighty con-frontation. As was written in the manifeſto of the IWW, *the working class and the employing class have nothing in common.*

Isabelle faithfully delivered this intelligence to Yvonne each afternoon, sometimes leaving with more than she came with. When she explained socialiſt presidential candidate Eugene Debs' threat to assemble an army for a march on Boise, Yvonne claimed this had already ſtruck terror into Heath and Morgan. Their call for federal troops to invade Boise had fallen on deaf ears and now Roosevelt was no longer communicating with these capitaliſts, blaming them for the violence. The current governor of Idaho had fled with his family to a secluded home guarded by private deteĉtives, fearing another WFM bombing, and rather than go after these miners, Roosevelt continued his attacks on the railroad truſts, threatening to derail their economic expan-sion. While the capitaliſts controlled the Supreme Court, Roosevelt could ſtill deſtroy everything they'd worked so hard to build.

George Pettibone, Bill Haywood, and Charles Moyer.

Making matters worse for Heath, *The Jungle* by Upton Sinclair was just published in novel form with daily sales jumping off the chart, fueled by the spreading hatred of capitalism. The steel baron had taken to coming home every Sunday night, a desperate measure meant to heal his depression. Yvonne could see the darkness clawing at his eyes, its shapeless form thrown into panic by an excess of light. He mumbled about Rockefeller being ruined, how it would take decades to regain their strength, and when Heath pleaded for comfort, Yvonne recoiled at his touch, claiming he needed to be strong, for that's when she truly loved him.

Jack finally returned to San Francisco after his honeymoon in the Caribbean and another lecture tour across North America. By the time the Londons pulled into the Oakland train terminus, Jack had been lecturing for almost five months and the local press quickly surrounded his home demanding material for their gossip columns. With this much attention focused on his head, Jack fled Oakland and hid at his property on Glen Ellen. He dispatched a brief letter to Isabelle and Yvonne explaining he'd be on his *rancho* unless they had a pressing need for his services. In the days that followed, Jack began construction on *The Snark*, a boat he'd eventually use to smuggle more weapons across the Pacific, just as others had done aboard *The Spray*. As a cover for these illegal activities, Jack had begun raising thousands of dollars from his publishers, claiming he would write a new book about his travels across the world. Meanwhile, on his land in Glen Ellen, Jack planted apples, cherries, and three types of grape vines that still grow today. Beyond giving a few odd lectures, Jack stayed in Glen Ellen for the first quarter of 1906, hoping to avoid any of Heath's lethal reprisals, especially after the poisoning of Frank Norris, an author who'd never lived to see his own commune.

While he settled into rural tranquility, Anna Strunsky was on a passenger-train to Moscow with vital messages for the beaten rebels. Since she'd returned from Homel, Anna devoted her energy to re-establishing lines of communication between centers of resistance. With her US passport and journalist credentials, Anna delivered news of who was alive, who was dead, how many weapons were accounted for, and breathed life into the dwindling fires. Word of her deeds made it all the way to Siberia where Elizabeth Dmitrieff wrote a letter to Josephine about a ring of fire stretching across the Earth, its red fibers woven by their tireless hands. Now that Isabelle's conspiracy had linked up with Belle's, the time would soon come for the moment of reckoning. Neither *strega* knew where or when this event would occur, but within a day Telegraph Hill drew its first conductors.

My mother was leaving for work when she found two young women standing on the front porch. Both had emerald green eyes, blonde hair in braids, and wore identical black dresses. These twins spoke in a foreign language similar to Finnish and when my mother failed to comprehend, they spoke in the Celtic dialect of my tribe. Josephine overheard this interaction, rose from her bed, and calmly offered the twins tea in the kitchen. Isabelle left for work in confusion and when she returned these twins were eating noodles with butter. Josephine was cleaning the kitchen and offered Isabelle no explanation, just a smile. Strangers had been known to arrive in *Les Diablerets* for unknown purposes, sometimes preceding a stone avalanche, and Isabelle trusted in this long tradition. The twins carried no belongings, possessed no money, and accepted meals without a word of thanks, not even rising to clear their dishes. Given her own history of strange events, Marisol held her tongue when it came to the Finns, although she did scream at them once. From that moment onward, the twins never drank her coffee again, not even when it was offered. Everyone in the house tried to ignore the fact that during the twin's first night, Mount Vesuvius erupted outside of Napoli, devastating the entire region with lava, ash, and stone. No one could dream of what was to come.

While these odd visitors inhabited Greenwich Street, the pimps of the Municipal Crib continued their war against Iodaform Kate and the Queen of the Coast, although clever Kate kept them confined to their one-block fortress. With the Party in firm control of City Hall, the pimps were now returning to the boldness and terror of the 1870s, threatening to tear apart the few places safe for women. To make it worse, a quarry blast finally toppled one of Telegraph Hill's houses and drove the neighborhood into a frenzy. They caught the five dynamiters, beat them close to death, and hung them on the gates of the Gray Brothers' quarry pit. Rather than venture into the Queen's territory, the police left the bodies until morning. When an Italian-Swiss factory owner finally hired a dozen men to take them down, the dynamiters were dead. This factory owner kept silent on his way to the morgue, telling the journalists they'd died in a quarry accident. It seemed as if war with City Hall would break out at any moment, only this conflict failed to arrive. The Queens had beaten the Party. To make matters perfectly clear, the anarchists, the socialists, and the first local branch of the IWW united for a mass-march down Market Street that turned into an hours long riot against the Party police officers.

The same corruption that emboldened the Barbary Coast pimps now fueled another controversy, this one centering on electrical lines. Adolph Spreckels and his brothers were now openly challenging the United Railroads, a company that bribed City Hall to favor its overhead power-lines and force the Bohemian Club's electricity down every main street of the city, ensnaring thousands of consumers in their web of energy. As they read of these developments in the daily newspapers, Yvonne and Isabelle realized that Patrick Calhoun, owner of the United Railroads, was being sacrificed by Heath. Calhoun's bribes to the Union Labor Party were reported by the daily press, his over-head cables were denigrated in favor of underground conduits, and all this created so much negative publicity that Isabelle couldn't conceive of how it could benefit Heath, Morgan, or their electric system. When my mother posed this dilemma to Yvonne, they realized the impossible might have occurred: Heath was broken. For such a ruthless capitalist, this defeat was truly a pathetic sight. When Heath came home each Sunday, Yvonne could hardly stand to look at him, and my mother's offer to kill her husband became ever more alluring. After Isabelle came home from the mansion that afternoon, she was surprised to find Eamonn's former mentor, the Gælic witch, sitting on the front porch with Marisol, smoking a cigarette and drinking a cup of tea. For the coming days, she'd be their latest guest on Telegraph Hill.

The witch slept on the floor beside the Finnish twins and caught up with Marisol on all they'd lived through in San Francisco. These two had known each other since the 1860s and interacted only when necessary, not wanting to link the apothecary with the brothel. Now they reminisced over the late Rosita de la Costa and Marisol's father Joaquin Murrieta, the last great outlaw of the closing frontier. They'd watched the darkness tame this indigenous land and hid inside their urban enclave, waiting for a moment like the one approaching. In the heat of their memories, an elderly Chinese woman arrived one morning with nothing but a walking ſtick. This was one of the witch's friends, a famous herbaliſt from Chinatown, and she joined their party of conductors on Telegraph Hill. Two days later, a dark-haired woman of the Mutsun tribe walked right into the living room and demanded a cigarette from Marisol, claiming she didn't have time for this. Despite her griping, she quickly joined the Finns in consuming Josephine's cooking. A few days later, a curly-haired woman from Brazil arrived off the Oakland ferry and sat outside on the porch without saying a word. When my mother finally asked who she was, the woman told her to *please be quiet*.

Overwhelmed by her cramped house, Isabelle worked those April nights with Schwartz setting the type for *Secolo Nuovo*. Unlike moſt men of his day, Schwartz was able remain her comrade and friend, content to have shared that one moment of intimacy. They helped Enrico operate the press and went to his Latin Quarter apartment for dinner where they entertained his unruly children. Sitting at a cramped kitchen-table overlooking their neighborhood, Isabelle was able to appreciate this ſtrange place where *Secolo Nuovo* was read by liberal and conservative alike. In this pocket of the world, their anarchiſt voices were the hidden angels behind every Italian's shoulder, a reminder that life remained free behind the hypocrisy of the market.

As her comrades drank wine in Enrico's kitchen on those warm spring nights, Isabelle gazed out the window as the merchants closed their shops and threw out the trash. Under the glow of the laſt gas-lamps, bands of anarchiſts ſtrolled across the Latin Quarter speaking French, Spanish, Italian, and Basque. Children chased each other through Washington Square Park and elderly couples hobbled down the sidewalk with bags of discount produce. Wild parrots flew through the air, fog-horns sang in the diſtance, and errant coyotes howled at the ſtars. This was the little world my mother helped build, not Josephine's hillside fortress of Telegraph Hill, but the valley behind it, a gentler place where children could play and elders could ſtroll, a modeſt utopia where greed was punished and kindness rewarded. Isabelle was scarcely 20-years-old when these times of promise came crashing down in a tornado of fire. More than any event in hiſtory, what took place next on April 18, 1906 was what truly allowed planetary electromagnetic conduction to become possible, although no one has known this fact until now. This is why I've written this hiſtory, to shed light on the darkness of their thousand secrets.

SHE'LL TAKE IT SLOW AND STEADY

I'M HUNCHED OVER A NEW DESK, COVERED IN ASH LIKE THE ONE BACK home. Must have fallen asleep here because the pen's still in my hand. Isabelle's snoring, blissfully asleep, immune to the horror outside. We've lived these past days in a small hotel room overlooking Six Oaks Park, an open field where *La Mission de Santa Rosa* stood until 1919 when the Pomo tribes streamed out of the hills and burnt it down to cinders. They churned up the blackened soil, mixed the adobe back into earth, and planted six oak trees before they left. Now the branches reach to our bedroom window, bursting with brown acorns. These trees were a symbol of peace for those who remained in the colonial cities, but I don't know how the good people of Santa Rosa are going to feel when they wake up and discover the desolation they've carried inside themselves all these years. It doesn't look pretty. The long history of 1905 you've just read was how I escaped the long sorrow of 1950, writing each night until I either fell asleep or went searching for a voice crying out from the darkness.

I've had to stop two people hanging themselves from these oaks trees. Isabelle watched a man slit his own throat. He didn't wake from the Dream, just like over a hundred others. Those are the ones we know about. There's probably more bodies rotting in the fields. We think it's stable now, last night was the calmest, but there were still dozens of people howling, moaning, wandering in the darkness. We've been running the brewery generator to keep some roads lit but it hasn't helped much, people just drift into the shadows, most don't come back, and we find their bodies the next morning covered in flies. During our last count, over a third of the city's structures were empty. None of us know what direction the Dreamers are going. They might be heading west.

"Wake up, sunshine," I say, more to myself than Isabelle. "They might be here already."

"Let me sleep," she moans. "They don't need our help."

"Don't you want to see Juana del Valle?"

"No! I want to sleep. Go smoke another cigarette. Go back to sleep. Just leave me alone."

She's got an excellent point, but I can't help myself, the curiosity's too great. Our small group in Santa Rosa sent two riders for help, one heading south to San Francisco, the other heading west to the commune. A woman named Clarice sprinted on Gudrun's back to tell my village of the disaster and ask for Essie's advice. She returned two days later with some mixed news. Clarice told us that Gertrude and Annabelle had already sailed for San Francisco to recruit a relief party, a welcome blessing given Essie had only one message for the people of Santa Rosa: *we can't stop your nightmares*. She said the tribe would shelter and guide those who naturally wandered into their lands, but the Kashaya couldn't protect everybody from themselves. It was up to us, she said. Her people had done enough.

I light my cigarette with a match and force myself to remain upright. I could sleep until noon, if I tried. That's not going to happen, though, so I just flip through my notebook. Even with this suicidal nightmare outside, I've managed to tell the truth about what happened before the Great Earthquake. If people couldn't understand my history before the Dream took over, they'll definitely get it when they wake up. The power of the underworld gives us electromagnetic energy, but it also caused this disaster, and soon everyone will know the truth of where their light comes from.

I throw open the window, Isabelle moans in protest, and the chilly morning breeze fluffs every curtain in the room. Once the wind dies down, the silence of Santa Rosa returns in all its mournful glory. There's no trade on the street, no brewing in the factories, no farm-wagons in the fields, no children laughing in the trees. All the survivors are asleep, some in their own houses, most in the theater we converted into a sanatorium. That's where fourteen of us take our shifts watching over three hundred men, women, and children, all caught inside the Dream of the underworld.

"It's quiet today," I say, mostly to myself. "Hey! Will you get up? You wanted to leave, right? This is our big chance! You need to get our bags ready! If you're not going to help me deal with everyone's horse shit, at least get us packed and—"

"Can't I sleep just a bit longer? What's the damn rush?"

"Fine!" I snap. "Just be ready by noon when I come back!"

"Thanks," she groans, flipping onto her side. "Okay."

I close the window because I'm nice and then slip into my dirty pants. They're truly disgusting. Both of us stink worse than dogs, only we're too tired to care, just like everyone else. After these past days of misery, we all look like we've been churned through a sausage grinder. I've probably got blood all over these dark pants, soaked in so thick it won't ever come out. So does Isabelle. So do the others. We move like emotionless machines down the streets of Santa Rosa, combing through neighborhoods in teams of two, looking for suicidal Dreamers. When we're finally together in the same room, none of us have any desire to speak. I've had a few conversations about what this outbreak might mean, but no one's floated any theories about why it spread. The scientists still call the Dream *a spatial-temporal cognitive distortion emanating from an unclassified geo-magnetic anomaly*, which is longhand for *we don't know*. The zone has been relatively stable since the end of the war, when its effects were first documented by outsiders, but this exponential growth is unprecedented. Now we're cursed to watch these helpless Dreamers wander through the wreckage of a thousand centuries. Even though we're awake, all of us are stuck inside their rotten nightmare.

I wash my face over the basin, slip on my dirty black blouse, and sit down on the desk chair to lace up my boots. The floor of this little room is covered in dried mud, twigs, bits of soggy grass, butt ends, spilled ink, empty bottles, and dirty plates. Whoever lived here's long gone, and by the looks of what's on the shelves, I'd say it was two farm girls who liked listening to the radio, reading books, and drinking wine. Both of them seem young, maybe even sisters, and now we've made their room into a pigsty, only I'm too tired to give a shit. Hopefully these girls aren't dead but we haven't found them so far and everything looks pretty grim. With any luck, they're on their way to the ocean, possessed by an unquenchable desire to see the crashing water and leaping salmon. The strongest Dreamers always travel to where the Pacific meets the Gualala River. I hope Paola's there right now, transfixed by the boom of life as those salmon hurl their way towards the mountains.

Isabelle groans one more time as I stomp out of the room and slam the door behind me. I climb downstairs to the hotel parlor where an array of food is spread out in a messy buffet. I grab a glass jar of smoked herring, crack it open over the dirty carpet, and a splash of oil dribbles out as I slide a long sliver of fish into my mouth. I eat the entire jar on my walk to the dance-hall, hoping those Dreamers are still asleep when I get there. I don't want to hear their screaming and sobbing. It's enough to make you pull out your hair or start guzzling spirits. I've probably got a hundred gray hairs already, only no one's told me about them and I'm too tired to look in the mirror.

The doors to the theater are wide open and my belly is so full I can't stop burping. This fit takes over my body and I nearly walk past the white horse tied up in front of me. This isn't good. There were supposed to be dozens of horses today, not just one, and Juana was going to be with them. At least now I won't have to deal with *blue blood*, even if no one's here to help us. I can already hear them babbling, probably cursing me for being late, selfish, arrogant Fulvia. When I get inside, everyone's sitting in a circle around a woman I don't recognize. She looks worn out, bag-eyed, frazzle-haired, just like us.

"There she is!"

"You alright, Fulvia? You sick?"

"I ate too quickly, is all," I tell them. "What's going on?"

"This is Genevieve. She just got here from Petaluma."

I burp loudly. Several people look away in disgust. I can't help myself.

"It spread down there, too," Genevieve continues, unperturbed. "It got to town...I don't know, a bit after yours, from what I hear. Anyway, your friends from San Francisco are on the way but they're going real slow, they're all on foot, won't get to Petaluma till tomorrow maybe. And we need help just the same as you. Petaluma's destroyed. All our horses escaped, people are losing their damn minds, same as all those people sleeping in your theater here."

She motions towards the shadowy dance floor and the hundreds of Dreamers passed out from exhaustion. The thought of their terrible, grating, desperate voices makes me cringe. Everyone notices my revulsion. It's true, I don't know anyone from Santa Rosa, and I'd feel different if this happened to my village. But it isn't my village. Like I said, I can't help myself. I can't stand this place. If it wasn't for my notebook, I would have burned down some buildings myself.

"So what's that mean?" I ask. "How many people came from San Francisco to help?"

"Maybe a hundred. I mean, there's only five of us awake in Petaluma, so if maybe ten, fifteen of your friends stuck around, it would sure help. Once they get to Petaluma, that is. It's taking a while, they're sort of sweeping the fields, picking up anyone left behind. San Francisco's safe, one lady's been saying the city's got its own kind of Dream. Juana del Valle's with them, she's the one who told me, she's sort of leading the whole thing. She was asking about you—"

"Alright, everyone," I say, holding up my hands. "This is all very interesting, I'm sorry help's not coming today, but me and Isabelle need to get moving. We'd be at Paloma today if we hadn't stayed to help, so now Juana del Valle's coming, I just...we gotta leave. I'm sorry."

There's a loud chorus of anger. Everyone's furious. Some already hate me, I'm sure of it. They think I'm the cold bitch who can't stand helping others, who rode into town pointing a rifle. I ignore their icy glances and back myself out of the room just before a woman throws a book at me and the room erupts into howls. If they aren't careful, they'll wake up the Dreamers and it won't be my fault because I'm not yelling back. I guess they would have pulled this tantrum even if Isabelle was with me, though luckily she wasn't. The girl had the right idea, sleeping in. We both resolved to leave Santa Rosa today, no matter what happened, even if they tried to stop us, even if my lover arrived on horseback, even if a sudden transmission filled the sky. We're tired of dealing with Santa Rosa's nightmares. We've already been through our own.

As I walk down the road towards Six Oaks Park, I can hear Juana calling me *puta* like an echo through a mountain valley. She's never been subtle, but I didn't expect her to leave her beloved city. San Francisco's probably protected by whatever hole got ripped open beneath Telegraph Hill during the Great Earthquake. Or maybe that tear into the underworld opened decades earlier, back when Marisol called to Josephine from across the oceans. Or maybe it was always there, long before Rosita de la Costa and Joaquin Murrieta built their little blue house. Either way, its good news for every-body. If the Dream hit San Francisco, the entire city would burn like 1906, only without the earthquake.

I walk to our brick hotel and stop at the buffet for more breakfast, any-thing to settle the fish oil in my stomach. Isabelle's awake, sipping tea by the window with a crumb-filled dish beside her and our saddle-bags lined up neatly by the stairs. Isabelle doesn't look at me, she keeps her boot-heels kicked up on the window-seat and gazes out at the Six Oaks like I'm not even here. She's aged a lifetime in this strange transition to adulthood. When I was 17 years-old, all I could think about was dancing.

"How'd they take it?" she eventually asks. "Better? Worse?"

"Like we thought. Worse maybe. Did you eat all that sausage?"

"There's more in that wooden box over there. I packed the rest. Any word from my mom?"

"Nope. Lorraine trusts us, I guess. No word from my mom either. But apparently Juana's leading the group from San Francisco. So I think it's time we—"

"They're still not here? What's taking them so long?"

"It spread to Petaluma. This is...there's just not enough people, and who knows what we'll find up north, so we might as well face it sooner or later. I'm tired of thinking about it."

"What if it's already spread to Paloma?"

I don't bother to answer, I just pick at everything on the buffet table until my stomach's bursting. We've been eating like either pigs or queens, hard to tell, given it's the only luxury we get. Either way, our pampered treatment ends now. We carry the saddle-bags through the back door of the hotel and into the barn where Gudrun's waiting for us. Once we're trotting down the road, I rile Gudrun up to a gallop that gets us out of Santa Rosa before anyone can curse at us. Isabelle clutches my side, begging me to keep up this speed. Gudrun doesn't seem to mind so we tear through the vineyards, a cloud of brown dust rising behind us. Along the horizon are the dry eastern mountains we still need to cross before reaching the Napa Valley and the great San Joaquin beyond. I doubt we'll get past Napa before nightfall, but all this sprinting might make up for our late start.

Gudrun eventually casts me a sideways glance so I pull back on the reins and ask Isabelle to rub her hind-quarters. We walk her slowly for the next miles and let the silent landscape pass, waiting for some ominous occur-rence that never appears. Gudrun starts her slow climb over the mountains and we ridefor the entire journey in numb silence, the fall sunlight pouring over our heads. It's a few hours to dusk as we enter Napa Valley and plunge into its winding rows of grape vines. We're a few miles into this valley when we stop to read something painted across the dirt road. In dusty globs of red, another Dreamer has spelled out **MISERY**, though it's hardly legible, and I can only read the text because it's already familiar, like the one we saw on the ride into Santa Rosa. All the Dreamers kept saying *misery* through those endless nights, chanting it like a religious prayer, screaming it with their last breaths.

"Where are we?" Isabelle asks. "This means—"

"We're in Napa. I think that's Saint Helena up there, but let's avoid it, huh? What do you say?"

"Fine with me. It's not that I didn't want to help back in Santa Rosa, or up here, it's just—"

"It's not up to us what happens to them. You don't need to tell me anything."

"I mean...we don't even know those people in Santa Rosa. Or Saint Helena. It's hard to guide someone when they're strangers. And plus, it's weird treating grown-ups like babies. I don't know. If you want to keep going, I'm not complaining."

We ride on through the valley, never resolving our dilemma, no matter how much we talk it through. There's no smoke in the air, no screams coming from the grape-vines, but I stay alert anyway. Up ahead, we pass a charred farmhouse collapsed along the side of the road with the graffito **MISERY** painted bright red across its blackened remains. I keep Gudrun on the outskirts of Saint Helena and we head east towards the last mountain range of our journey. Once we make this final crossing, there's nothing but the massive San Joaquin Valley spread out all the way to Paloma.

"We can either camp around here or in the mountains," I tell Isabelle. "I don't think we'll make the big valley until nightfall. What do you think?"

She lets go of my sides and stretches her arms in the air.

"What's scarier?" she asks. "Mountain lions or Dreamers?"

"Mountain lions," I say. "Dreamers won't eat us."

"Fine. Let's camp here. Only somewhere indoors, okay?"

We follow the dirt road towards the foothills and come across a white farmhouse with its front door blowing in the wind. I guide Gudrun to the front-steps and yell inside to see if anyone answers. It's maybe close to seven o'clock when I hop down with my rifle and slowly creep inside. I yell for Isabelle to get her pistol and then walk through each room of this well-kept home, rich with the smell of a mother's cooking. We find no trace of blood, no hidden death, no horrible visions cut into our reality. It's a welcome relief from the hundred suicides of Santa Rosa.

Isabelle seems to be doing just fine, so do I, a sure sign we're traumatized beyond belief, the marks still too fresh to notice. There haven't been this many dead bodies since the end of the war and Isabelle's already seen dozens hung, stabbed, or drowned. It's hard to know why, but our appetites haven't suffered and we cook ourselves dinner after pillaging the larder. The shelves are well-stocked, our meal is luxurious, and as we're passing out on the living room couches, we hear the first cries of the Dreamers vibrate through the air, promising to keep us awake long into the night. Within ten minutes, we see the first structure go up in flames. The next one's much closer.

22

THE SACRED FIRES OF ETERNAL PARIS

THE STORY OF THE PARIS COMMUNE HAS BEEN TOLD A HUNDRED TIMES. I've already offered you a short account of my grandparents' involvement. What's never been told is what happened beneath the *butte* of Montmartre on the morning of May 23, 1871, when Josephine Lemel, Louise Michel, Elizabeth Dmitrieff, and Antonio Ferrari were surrounded by Versailles soldiers.

Within a haze of black smoke, Louise Michel lost sight of her friends and groped through the carnage until she found a friendly soldier. This young boy she mistook for a Communard turned out to be a Republican and he threw her off a cliff into a pile of bodies. Gunfire continued above her head when Louise rose to her feet, realized she was standing atop a hundred corpses, and watched helplessly as the Republican soldiers pillaged the houses of Montmartre. In this moment of terror, a dull vibration rose from the base of the hill and gathered strength beneath Louise. Channeling the magnetic forces of the underworld, she lifted her hands to the sky, felt an invisible ribbon pass through her whole body, and watched a hundred red lightning bolts sizzle in a perfect sphere. According to her own memoirs, Louise wrote, *I saw only one means of stopping them, and I cried out to them, 'Fire! Fire! Fire!'* Her account breaks off after this passage, but my mother told me what really happened.

Elizabeth, Isabelle, and Antonio ran into the center of her fiery sphere and watched it collapse into a dozen writhing tentacles. That's when the ribbon moved into their bodies and responded to their every thought. Red lightning coursed through the streets like an octopus made of water, burning off the faces of a dozen soldiers with a single motion and protecting them as they ran down the hill, blinding every Republican in their path. These soldiers writhed on the cobblestones screaming for their mothers, their eyeballs melted from infernal heat, and some would later describe the sound of women's laughter accompanying these deadly fire ribbons. Some would survive in a mutilated condition, muttering about fire-witches until their last days. The Republican doctors ignored these mad ravings, but in the months after the Commune's defeat, some noticed a pattern to their patient's hysteria.

These wounded soldiers all described women dressed in black who rode atop ribbons made of fire. Some claimed this inferno resembled water, while others described it as a type of creature, perhaps a snake. In all of the narratives, the ribbons were composed of flame and propelled the women down the hill with deadly power. Caricatures of wart-covered *petroleuses* had already circulated in the Republican newspapers, portraying the women of the Commune as incendiary witches who'd burned Paris to the ground with petroleum. The hysterical Catholics of the countryside already believed the Commune was the work of Lucifer, a superstition the Republic never tried to dissuade them from. While rumors of fire-creatures might have

been useful for demonizing the Communards even further, the secretive War Department suppressed these myths and labeled the blinded victims insane, a fact later discovered by Félix Fénéon. To these secular Republican rulers, the existence of an underworld was more dangerous than a thousand Paris Communes, for it proved there were forces at work greater than themselves. In their reactionary newspaper accounts, the public would only be told of the *orgy of power, wine, women, and blood known as the Commune,* never learning what beauty was extinguished within the walls of ancient Paris. As Louise Michel later wrote, even in dying, the Commune *opened wide the doors of the future. That was its destiny.*

According to the War Department, 76 soldiers were blinded by fire in the area between the peak of Montmartre and Louise Michel's schoolhouse on the *Rue Oudot*. After escaping their fate atop the hill, Louise guided her friends to the safety of a Commune barricade where fifty women were shooting at the Republican troops, all dressed in black with red ribbons tied around their arms. Louise equipped Elizabeth and my grandparents with supplies and weapons before leading them to a building on the *Rue de Rosiere* where they descended two flights of stairs into a deep basement.

Just before she opened an iron door at the base of the stairwell, Louise told them that they all had to survive, no matter the cost. The world depended on them to spread this fire to its farthest corners and hold on tightly until their spark caught into a flame. Louise made them promise this before she lit their candles, opened the iron door, and sent them off down the long tunnel. These three rebels walked half the day through candle-lit darkness, the earth constantly shaking from exploding artillery as the Republic pounded away at Paris, desperate to pay back the House of Morgan's loan. While they made their way through this secret passage, Republican soldiers closed in on Paris from the north and south, blasting each district until they corralled the survivors near the *Place de la Bastille*. The greatest impediment to these Republicans was the wall of fire that scorched their faces and burned their guns.

Elizabeth and my grandparents emerged from the tunnel along the Seine River, just north of the Prussian lines near the town of Saint Denis. This army of the *Reich* kept the Communards from fleeing west and anyone they captured would be turned over to Versailles, so the three were careful as they began their journey for Switzerland. While they walked along ancient hedgerows, Josephine saw a column of black smoke rising from their now vanquished Commune. She imagined herself standing in these flames alongside Elizabeth and in this moment they both stopped walking. Antonio tried to urge them onward only to find their bodies were paralyzed. He managed to hide them away in a tree hollow but could do nothing to break their trance. Unknown to my grandfather, Elizabeth and Josephine had joined Louise Michel in conducting a string of fire ribbons across Paris. Like magnets, these *streghe* focused all their power on the fires that were already burning and twirled them into walking beasts that chased off the Versailles army.

It was the surviving *streghe* of Paris who physically brought these flames into being, influenced by the unheard whispers conducted by Louise, Elizabeth, and Josephine. Florence Wandeval was one of them, a 23-year-old witch from Belgium who carted barrels of petroleum into the Tuileries Palace and then set them alight. As this ancient house of government burned, Florence screamed, *now a king can come; he'll find his place in ashes!* The fires she lit writhed towards the approaching troops, corralling them down alleys and chasing them along the cobblestones. At their most concentrated point, these flames twirled themselves into a single tornado that laughed like a wine-drunk mad-woman. The Court of Accounts, the Council of State, and Ministry of Finance all had flames dancing wildly over their embers. As these fire-ribbons drove away the soldiers, the remaining *streghe* fired their rifles, tossed bottles of burning petroleum, and lit the fuses of their last canons. According to one survivor, these women in black *fought like devils* and *shot admirably* against their opponent, although by nightfall nearly all of them were dead, *anonymous women who will never be counted.* When one of these rebels was captured and accused of murdering Republican soldiers, this *stregha* is reported to have said, *may God punish me for not having killed more.* When confronted with the same accusation, one of her comrades declared, *yes, it was me, and I'd have liked to kill all the Versailles people with one shot because they killed my lover. And I have only one regret: it's having killed just one of them.* Both were executed by the Republic, their bodies thrown into mass-graves.

Louise Michel maintained her connection with the underworld until a loud pounding at the door roused her from the trance. She'd never left the tunnel entrance and now unbolted the iron door to allow the final exiles to flee burning Paris. Louise wished them luck, locked the massive door, blew up the stairwell, and then went to visit her mother one last time. With the connection severed, Elizabeth and Josephine fell out of their trances and followed Antonio out of the tree hollow. They stalked silently through fields while the *lights of the fire floated like red crepe* and the sky rained *fragments of paper ash coming from the burning of Paris*, fluttering in the wind *like black butterflies.*

When she reached her house, Louise discovered that her mother had been arrested. As she would later recount, *during the entire time of the Commune, I only slept one night at my poor mother's.* Seeing no other choice, Louise traded herself to the Republic in exchange for her mother. She was first placed in a concentration camp before being marched out of the inferno towards Versailles. As she and her fellow prisoners trudged through the night, *a sudden flash of light filtered from below between the hooves of the horses and lit them up; scattered red reflections seemed to bleed on us and on the uniforms.* Louise would later write, *I am not the only person caught up by situations from which the poetry of the unknown emerges.* While this may be true, there was no one like Louise Michel, a woman who drew fire from the earth with each confident step. As she was processed into the Chantiers prison, her fellow Communards were protected by throbbing veins of magma that swirled beneath the soil. A magnetic field surrounded Louise Michel that radiated outward in every direction, swaying the minds of judges, juries,

and executioners. As she sat in that Chantiers dungeon, her three comrades crossed the Swiss border into the safety of the Jura Mountains, the fires of Paris now extinguished.

Over the coming months, other survivors would gather in Geneva to plot their revenge against the French Republic and the London bankers who controlled their money. Just to the east beneath *Les Diablerets*, my grandparents slept their nights in an ancient stone house made to look modern. They ate simple meals, hiked the goats off into misty heights, and watered crops from a nearby spring. It was the last time Josephine would ever see the land of her birth, those long Alpine valleys where Nubians and Celtics once defeated Rome with tumbling stones and roaring flames. After those final days below her childhood peaks, Josephine and Antonio left for Genova and the ocean beyond. My grandfather never told anyone what he saw on the *butte* of Montmarte, taking this secret to the grave. For the final half of his remarkable life, Antonio Ferrari knew Josephine Lemel was a powerful witch, capable not only of cheating death, but conducting the sacred energies of our mother earth, and he loved her until the day he died. May we love each other just as they did, and may that love never be broken again.

SHE'LL BE LOADED WITH BRIGHT ANGELS

I'M STILL AWAKE, KEEPING WATCH OVER THE NIGHT'S SHADOWS, MY FINgers stiff from writing. Isabelle's asleep like only a teenager can be asleep, snoozing away through our living nightmare. The fires went on all night, spreading down the valley like mushrooms after rain, and the sounds of tortured yelling kept us awake until dawn. I didn't see anyone while I was writing, but a few Dreamers got pretty close. I could hear their feet crunch the soil but when I went outside with my light they'd already fled into the fields. After that we lit every lamp in the house and discovered a Tesla steam-generator tucked away in the closet. Unable to sleep from all the screaming, Isabelle wheeled the device out to the front deck and took the next hour to check the battery, fill the tank with water, and start a fire in its iron belly. Once the lights on the control panel were glowing, she connected the battery to the house line and suddenly the radio was blaring words, its dial already set to the San Francisco station.

When I lived in the city, Gertrude used to take me on long hikes way above the Mission to see the gigantic radio-tower Tesla built during the war. It's got a massive generator connected to its base and an internal water-reservoir buried deep underground. The signal is so strong that people can hear it across the Rockies and on the Hawaiian Islands. No one ever fired up that beast when I lived in San Francisco, the boiler-room needed too much fuel, so we climbed to the roof of its massive cement powerhouse, painted murals on its walls, or had bonfires in the sky atop its quarter-mile antenna. They finally turned the monster on last night and we listened to my aunt Beatrix broadcast from the war-time studio nine flights beneath the soil.

She told California: *This is Beatrix Lemel, transmitting from the emergency San Francisco Lighthouse. To those receiving this message, we are confirming that the Dream of the Kashaya people has spread inland from the Pacific. If it has not yet overwhelmed your city, it will soon bring on its massive cognitive effects including hallucinations, euphoria, near-total dissociation, psychological regression, depression, anxiety, and suicidal thoughts. If you happen to remain awake when the Dream hits, please comfort those closest to you. You'll have the best chances with those you know. We've just received a transmission from Sacramento telling us their city's burning down with over three quarters of their residents stuck inside the Dream. Another transmission came in from Lake Tahoe telling us they've been hit just as badly. They also told us the Dream has spread across the* Sierra Nevada *and into the desert. We don't know if the entire continent's been overwhelmed, but we'll let you know once we do. If you're awake, please keep the Dreamers together and watch over them at night. That's when most of the fires start. It's also when people try to kill themselves. Stay committed to the people you love and soon enough they'll be awake beside you, I promise. Some might already be waking up as I speak. This is Beatrix Lemel, transmitting from the emergency San Francisco Lighthouse.*

I stopped listening once she repeated herself but Isabelle insisted we leave it on just in case there was something new. I wrote by the window for the rest of the night and Isabelle eventually fell asleep, lulled by the rhythms of Beatrix's voice. My tired aunt eventually signed off the radio before dawn and someone else took her place, repeating the same message. They could have just recorded it instead of going live, only I'm glad they didn't. This feels better, more appropriate, like an all-night vigil, and Beatrix's voice helped me enter a trance that led directly to the City of Mary.

My mind wouldn't stop jumping between the fires outside my window to the fires that burned through Paris almost eighty years ago. I doubt any Communard would've believed me if I said their grandkids would get swallowed in a temporal-cognitive distortion called the Dream. They would've called me crazy and then told me to stand in line for bread like everyone else. I'm not even sure you'll believe these stories of fire-ribbons and witches, but they're no different than the Dream. There is no way to know how far it's spreading or if it's already crossed the oceans and taken hold across Asia and Europe and Africa and Australia and all the islands in between. Maybe it's already happening. Maybe the entire world burned into ash. I stare out the window at the fires smoldering in the vineyards, lit sometime during the night's misery. It's dawn now, the sky turning purple. I can't tell if it's the darkness I'm seeing out there in the fields, but I think it might be. I really do.

"Isabelle, time to go."

"No, please—"

"We need to hurry. I have a bad feeling right now."

"What happened? Is someone out there? Is something out there?"

That got her wide awake real fast. She's already on her feet.

"Nothing's out there," I say. "Nothing except a bunch of smoke from burning buildings. Look, I think...I think that's the darkness, the thing I was telling you about. It's not just smoke. I think it's—" I point out the window and shake my head. "I think it's right there. So let's go, huh?"

Isabelle's sure spooked now. She packs our bags frantically, just like her mother. We eat a dry breakfast from the family's cupboards, put away the Tesla generator, and strap our bags over Gudrun's back. She neighed through the night whenever someone got too close, so I shouldn't push her too hard, given she probably slept as little as me. I climb onto the saddle, wait for Isabelle to get comfortable, and then rouse Gudrun into a gentle gallop that instantly makes my ass sore. We tear up a thick brown cloud of dust that erases the road behind us, adding to the hellishness of this burning landscape. The final mountain range stands just to the east and we reach its foothills in less than an hour. Gudrun's nice and warmed up when I finally slow her down for the long ascent into the Wappo Mountains.

I don't know what the tribe call themselves now, but the Spanish called them *guappos* before the Anglos turned that into *wappos*. There's not many of them left, but their name used to mean *bandits* or *bold ones* in Castilian Spanish, although now it mostly means *handsome*. I know a dozen settled near Saint Helena where they used to have a village, so some of them might be helping the Dreamers. Or maybe not, maybe they've had enough. Their entire tribe marched on the Mission in Sonoma and set it ablaze in 1919, only these *bold ones* didn't plant six trees like the Pomo, they just left and never came back. We ride up the final mountain pass through their territory, a winding horse road that follows a gushing creek, and I can already smell fresh smoke in the air. It's getting closer.

I'm surprised when we discover a tiny village halfway up the pass with three people huddled around an outdoor fire. I don't take out my rifle, instead I wave my hand and wait for them to respond. They talk in whispers over the flames until eventually one of them stands. He has long dark hair and three black lines running down his chin. He's certainly handsome.

"You in the Dream?" he asks.

"No!" I call back, making to get off the horse. "Are you?"

The other two chuckle at me and stand up behind their brother. These women have the same marks on their faces, only more of them, especially around the eyes, and they're even more handsome than the young man.

"I didn't believe it!" one of the women yells. "Essie really pulled some stuff, huh? Both of you are really awake? The young one too?"

"I'm awake!" Isabelle protests. "We're from the coast."

I try to help her down once I get off the horse but she just vaults the other direction. The three *bandits* are all grinning as we approach their fire and I'm suddenly ashamed of the weapons stuffed in our saddle-bags. I hope they don't see the rifle-butt sticking out of the leather.

"I'm Fulvia Ferrari. This is—"

"Isabelle. My name's Isabelle."

"You all been through Saint Helena?" the man asks. "Seen anything?"

"No," I tell them. "We stayed away. We're on our way to Paloma. Didn't want to get stuck in another town. It was four days we were in Santa Rosa, helping people, petting their hair—"

"So you already been through this?" one of the women asks Isabelle. "You feel fine?"

"Things are kind of fuzzy, but I can't tell anymore" she says. "I went in as a kid but—"

"That's what I heard," the other woman interrupts. "It's the old ones who get stuck the most."

"Some things are just human, I guess," the man says. "Our old sure get stuck themselves."

We sit with them beside the fire for the next hour but we never learn their names. They are the youngest of their tribe, born after the California Insurrection into a world their parents never dreamed of. They serve us some acorn cakes packed with raisins and tell us stories of their small tribe, almost eradicated by General Vallejo. We're perched on a bluff overlooking Napa Valley and I can see smoke rising above every colonial settlement, from Saint Helena to Sonoma to the hazy shoreline of the bay. Three massive oak trees tower over our heads, protecting five small houses made from branches, straw, and earth. These *bold ones* say they refused to follow their elders down to Saint Helena and help the Dreamers. One of the women says their older generation grew up in slavery and most of them forgot their language until her generation revived it. Their elders were close with the colonizers because they had to be, not because they wanted to be, only some of them can't tell the difference anymore.

"They can do what they want," one of the women says. "It's not our responsibility and there's still acorns falling all over the place that need gathering. I feel for them down there, I do, but—"

"This has been a long time coming," the man says, bluntly. "And I don't got no hatred towards either of you, or any of them, but this is all happening for a reason."

"Yep," the other woman says, nodding her head. "A *good* reason."

"What is it?" Isabelle asks.

"I think I know what it is," I say, poking a stick into the fire. "But I'm scared to say it."

"Damn right you're scared," one of the women says. "We know all about you, Fulvia. Some of our parents thought Essie Parish was crazy, funny in the head, but they know better now. Essie was always close with your mom and Yvonne, and don't forget, the del Valle's were no different than those Vallejos who tried to wipe out our tribe. I mean, I never thought I'd see people like you, but here you are, awake, heading all the way up to Paloma, probably because Yvonne told you to go. She started helping our parents way before 1919, way more than people know, and she's smarter than she lets on. Tesla gets all the credit, but we know it was her, working with the ancient stuff. Those big machines she built just gave the earth a way to heal itself, and that's what it's doing right now."

"And it isn't pretty," the other woman says. "This madness is what it looks like."

They send us off without ceremony, though the women offer us water before we go. I learn this village is named *Tsemanoma*, only they don't tell us what it means, and this is the only word from their language I've ever heard. They tell us to be careful riding through Monticello, given how the Dreamers have been acting, and none of the *bold ones* wave goodbye when we resume our ascent over the last of their territory. This little village wasn't here when I came through with Angelo all those years ago, though we rode so fast it would've been easy to miss. Maybe I just didn't see it. Now I'll never forget.

We reach the summit within an hour and make the quick descent into Pope Valley. I see a few farmhouses near the creek but I don't point them out and Isabelle doesn't either. We ride along the Pope Creek trail until we eventually come into view of sprawling Berryessa Valley, realm of the Patwin tribe. This long valley is cut in half by Putah Creek, a raging river that absorbs the entire watershed, and Isabelle holds me tightly when we finally reach its churning rapids. The river's too fast, too deep, and too wide for Gudrun to cross, brave as she is, so we trot south along the western bank until we reach the Putah Creek Bridge with its triple arches made of stone. That's when things get spooky.

When I crossed this bridge many years ago, I distinctly remember three houses standing on the western side of the river, only now there's nothing, just three black piles of charred ruin, all of them still smoldering. The only thing I recognize is an old painted sign reading: **LONGEST STONE BRIDGE WEST OF THE ROCKY MOUTAINS. COMPLETED 1896**. Isabelle clutches me even tighter as we begin our crossing of Putah Creek, its swollen rapids blotting out every sound, even Gudrun's metal-tinged steps. Once we cross the old stone bridge, I turn Gudrun north towards the farm town of Monticello, already dreading what we'll find there.

"Maybe you're right. Maybe it is the darkness," Isabelle suddenly says. "If the planet's healing itself like they said, maybe this is that last bit of darkness inside of everyone that needs to come out. I was little when I went in but it was still scary. I remember all of it."

"It's true. It's easier for the young. The old world left ruins inside people. Dark ones."

"You think going to Paloma really has something to do with this? And why do you look afraid? What do you think we'll find up there?"

"It's not *what* I'm going to find," I say. "It's *why* I'm going there. That's what I'm afraid of. On the day your dad died, I heard something whisper to me. It said, *she is the dreamer*. Then I heard it again when the last transmission happened. So make of that what you want. I don't know what to say."

"Does that mean...what if, hey—" She grabs me tight by the shoulders. "What if everyone is in the Dream right now...what if they're having *her dream?* What if you're supposed to wake her up?"

"That's...poetic. But still scary."

"Hey, I don't even know what it means, but *what if,* you know?"

"Yeah? Then listen to this. Yvonne told me Yeshua revealed the dream to the dreamer, only she couldn't wake up after he left. Mary Magdalene, she's the dreamer, but she's dead, and it's not her Dream out there. It's more like those old gnostic stories my mom always talks about, the ones about Sophia captured by the tyrants. If someone's dreaming that Dream, it's probably some emanation like her, an over-soul in all of us, a being so filled with light we...see? Now I sound like Yvonne."

"Like I always say, you all talk funny."

"It's rubbing off on you, clearly. *What if?*"

"Shut it, Fulvia. It's still crazy."

Unable to help myself, I tell Isabelle to hold on and rile Gudrun into a sprint. We speed north as fast as she'll go, the squat buildings of Monticello growing ever closer, and when we reach the outskirts of town, I can already smell the scent of charred wood blowing in the wind. I don't slow Gudrun down, I keep us flying through the town center, and when I glance to my left, sure enough, I see a lifeless body hanging from a second-story balcony. Isabelle makes a whimpering noise and pushes her face into my back, keeping it there until we're far out of Monticello. I'm sure she saw something worse than another hanging, although I refuse to imagine what it might be.

We eventually head east out of the Berryessa Valley and ascend the final mountains separating us from the great San Joaquin, riding in silence for two hours until the eastern horizon opens up at the summit, allowing us to glimpse a solid black plume of smoke rising from Sacramento. It looks like the whole downtown's burning from the center, the flames so powerful I see them glowing in a red tornado, even in daylight. The entire watershed of the northern *Sierra Nevada* runs through the center of Sacramento but there's not enough people awake to pump its water and extinguish the inferno. Before the Dream took hold, over 60,000 inhabitants lived in this river-town, and it's hard to imagine so many of them dead right now, incinerated in a fiery vortex. I stare at this darkness invading the land through the hands of a thousand dreaming souls, all desperate to escape their past. The sun will set in less than two hours and Isabelle clutches me tight as we descend into this empty valley filled with shadows. Both of us are terrified. Neither of us can hide it.

23

THE CONDUCTORS OF GREENWICH STREET

O N THE EVENING OF TUESDAY, APRIL 17, 1906, ISABELLE SLEPT IN her tiny bedroom while six witches snored on the living room floor. The little blue house had never been this packed, not even with my uncles, and all the windows were open to stem the raging heat. Isabelle still didn't know why these women had arrived or what their cryptic remarks to Josephine had meant. The spring heat kept her tossing through the night and she fell asleep long after midnight when the house finally cooled. In her dreams, Isabelle was lounging in a green pool with Josephine, Marisol, and the six witches who'd just arrived. A green cloud parted before her eyes and she beheld an impossible shape made of a thousand coiling ribbons, all twisting together in opposite directions. Before this form could make sense, my mother heard Marisol scream *puta* with pure hatred searing in her throat.

Marisol threw open her bedroom door and stormed onto the front porch, Josephine following behind. When my mother finally joined them, she beheld a radiant star burning over the eastern hills. Josephine and Marisol could see it too, but when Isabelle looked again the star was gone, leaving her shrouded in early morning darkness. Marisol was furious. She shook my mother by the shoulders and asked *Quién es?* Josephine was now frozen, unable to hear the curses Marisol hurled at the nameless *puta* who'd pulled a fast one on everybody and blew their chance at switching the pathway. Only then did Isabelle realize the *puta* was Yvonne, although she still had no clue what was happening.

In this moment of incomprehension, Marisol finally stopped yelling and stood with Josephine on the porch, gazing eastward. The other witches filed out of the house and joined them, the invisible star still burning in the distance. My mother had no time to think before another burning fire blossomed behind Telegraph Hill, bringing a false sunrise. This illumination vanished the moment Isabelle felt its heat, returning the sky to starry blackness. Josephine began to mutter the word *agua* multiple times and my confused mother soon returned with an earthen pitcher from the kitchen. Josephine wouldn't take a drink, neither would the others, so she set the pitcher on the porch railing and immediately heard the sound of flowing water as the earthen mouth bubbled over, releasing a small river into their front yard. In less than a minute, the water was flowing down the dirt pathway of Greenwich Street.

Scientists recorded that at 5:12 AM Pacific Time on the morning of April 18, 1906, two massive geological plates snapped along the California coastline, sending concentric shock-waves through the soil and water. Fishing vessels were thrown high into the air, the land bulged like a saw-blade, and cobblestones behaved like fluid. The ocean glowed with a brilliant green luminescence and massive watery sinkholes broke open across San Francisco. Wooden houses instantly collapsed, stone buildings crashed into the street, brick buildings turned into crumbling sand, shards of jagged glass fell to the sidewalk, gas mains ruptured into a hundred explosions, and dozens of cattle escaped their pens. The water pipes leading into the city snapped in half and every main dried up within minutes. When the first fires broke out near the waterfront Produce District, all the water hydrants were empty.

The earthquake shook the little blue house on Greenwich Street, although the earth didn't act like water atop this hill of limestone. None of the houses fell from the cliff, with the greatest damage inflicted on china cabinets, book shelves, hanging mirrors, and a thousand fragile luxuries accumulated over the years. My mother stood in the doorway as successive shock-waves pulsed through the earth, nearly knocking her to the floor. Despite this violence, the witches didn't move off the porch, remaining perfectly aligned with every motion of the trembling sphere. Once the quake ended, Isabelle heard a sound she couldn't locate. It seemed to be coming from the air and her body at once. When she realized the sound was her own nervous humming, the sky lit up with another burning star, this one hanging over Telegraph Hill with fiery ribbons composed of red laughter. It disappeared the moment Isabelle heard

The view from Telegraph Hill

the witches humming, their vibrations synchronized to the flow of water still gushing from the earthen pitcher. By some strange power my mother didn't yet comprehend, the pitcher had remained on the porch railing throughout the earthquake, its tiny river now reaching the waterfront cobblestones.

Isabelle stayed on the patio as the sun rose over the eastern hills and the neighborhood flocked outside to assess the damage. Children swarmed up and down muddy Greenwich Street, screaming like maniacs while their mothers tried to rouse Marisol from her hypnotic trance. Despite their intense love for her, these old friends fled once they saw the overflowing pitcher, not trusting what Marisol's black magic might do to them or their families. Isabelle stayed near the road, helping these neighbors when needed, but she kept constant watch over the humming witches and their magical river. It was shortly after dawn when thick plumes of black smoke emerged near downtown and the haze soon drifted over Telegraph Hill, growing darker throughout the day.

When my uncles showed up with a gang of longshoremen, they took one look at Josephine before telling their comrades to wait for them at the Greenwich pier. Sergio tried to shake his mother into consciousness but the Gælic witch threw him to the ground when he became too forceful, never once interrupting her hum. Federico and Lorenzo looked to their little sister for guidance but found only confusion and despair in her eyes. Sergio lifted himself up, wiped away his tears, and told Isabelle it was going to be war. All the local capitalists were scrambling to protect their property now that fires were raging, making it the perfect moment to steal. Isabelle wished them luck but said she had to stay at the house and keep the witches safe. None of these women were in their right minds.

My uncle's instincts for thievery quickly proved themselves. General Funston, commander of the Army's Pacific Division, was about to order all his troops to assemble at Portsmouth Square on the edge of Chinatown. Rumors began to spread that the general had declared martial law, stripping the state of its legal power and giving him control over the city. Fearing for his life and property, the boss of the Union Labor Party, Abraham Ruef, drafted a shoot-to-kill proclamation signed by Mayor Eugene Schmitz, a document that was soon copied and pasted across the city. By 9:30, the first gunshots could be heard on the streets, along with the roar of dynamite. The military, the state, and the city were now giving contradictory orders, allowing various factions to settle grudges in the name of public safety.

During the chaos of this emerging warfare, my uncles returned to Greenwich Street with two boxes of shotguns they speedily hid in the outhouse. Their pockets were filled with thousands of dollars in bills, coins, and jewels, enough to ensure they survived once this inferno passed. With the purest joy in his eyes, Sergio told Isabelle how the flames had burned

all of Market Street and gave an ecstatic description of the Palace Hotel's destruction. While billing itself as fire-proof for decades, the hotel's internal water supply was quickly exhausted and by 1:00 PM all the velvet blankets, lace curtains, and hidden passageways had turned into a seven-story inferno. Just down the street, the towers and printing presses for the *San Francisco Chronicle*, the *San Francisco Call*, and the *San Francisco Examiner* were ablaze like iron candles, the black smoke feeding the common plume which rendered the sun into a blood red disk that leered over the city.

With martial law preventing further theft, my uncles climbed the hill over to the Latin Quarter and helped protect their immigrant neighborhood from dynamiters and vigilantes. With legal authority now a patch-work of competing interests, the local capitalists called for a Citizen's Committee to meet at the partially-collapsed Hall of Justice near the Latin Quarter. As their dynamite teams blasted into the non-Anglo neighborhoods under the guise of creating fire-breaks, these capitalists usurped power from the Mayor and agreed to share it during the emergency. Before this historic compromise could be finalized, an aftershock bulged through the earth and made the Committee flee the building. By the time they re-assembled in a Nob Hill mansion, the entire downtown was engulfed in a plume of smoke nearly twenty blocks wide. While no one could see it through this dark cloud, a writhing geo-magnetic ribbon had emerged from the fractured earth. It ascended through the center of the fire and whipped the coastal winds into a vortex of energy, creating what many later described as *a tornado of flame*. This vast whirlwind emitted a fierce howl and built up strength with each consumed building. A few of the survivors would distinctly remember a woman's laughter.

My mother remained at the little blue house through the evening, keeping watch from the front steps and directing aid to where it was needed. Her entire neighborhood was now frantic with collective energy as the residents of Telegraph Hill's eastern slope banded together to divide up tasks, although it was impossible to ignore the overflowing pitcher. No one spoke aloud of this miracle and most forbid their children to even whisper about it. They knew Marisol de la Costa dabbled in matters beyond their comprehension and feared her dark magic could easily spill onto their children. The general weariness over her powers only increased as flames approached the Latin Quarter and closed in on Greenwich Street. Unrelenting dynamite blasts filled the air as Isabelle paced below the porch and kept the visitors away from the pitcher. The witches never stopped humming, they wouldn't drink water, wouldn't eat food, and stood perfectly still, refusing to move even for nightfall.

Sergio returned around midnight and told my mother how the Bohemian Clubhouse was now being ripped apart by fire, the burning paintings and smoldering Red Room consigned to the inferno. Despite this good news, Sergio said the *Secolo Nuovo* print-shop had collapsed during the earthquake and buried their press in piles of brick and timber. My uncles helped Enrico try and save his machine but the flames were almost to Basque Town before they could get to it, forcing my uncles to pull *luciferino* away from the rubble. Half of Chinatown had already burned down or been dynamited by the Citizen's Committee and the rest was soon to follow. Shortly after Sergio left, the Chinese quarter of their childhood disappeared from the face of the earth, the tornado of fire laughing as it consumed the slave-girl cribs and tubercular brothels where decades of pain had accumulated.

The morning after the earthquake, Jack and Charmian London turned up at the little blue house. Isabelle told them to sit down on the front steps and ignore everything they saw, a request she enforced with her hands when necessary. The couple had woken the previous morning as shock-waves rippled through Glen Ellen, destroying Jack's new barn, and they quickly rode their horses up to the mountains where they watched black plumes rise from Santa Rosa and San Francisco. As he would later write, *Santa Rosa got it worse than San Francisco.* Fearing for their friends, the couple caught the train to Tiburon, boarded one of the few ferries bound for burning San Francisco, and walked all night through the inferno. Jack explained how the Citizen's Committee had just commandeered every automobile in the city in order to ferry dynamite and supplies across the city, with Standard Oil and the Southern-Pacific donating the petroleum. Jack had seen all two hundred automobiles pooled near Union Square, although Heath's famous Daimler was absent.

With the fire now spreading into Pacific Heights, Jack and Charmian left Telegraph Hill to go check on Yvonne at the Heath Mansion. When they returned shortly after dawn, Jack looked grim. He claimed the mansion had burned to the ground, that Juana was safe, but Yvonne was spinning around on the lawn with all her books. The iron skeleton of Heath's Daimler was in the burnt-out garage but a dozen shotgun wielding men in long black coats chased them away before they could see anything else. After telling all this to my mother, Jack and Charmian left for the ferry and crossed back to Sonoma. While both would later write of the inferno, neither mentioned the pitcher of water or the eight witches humming to themselves on Greenwich Street. The young couple simply never believed it.

The fire spread into the hills that second morning and eventually curved back towards the Latin Quarter. Isabelle helplessly watched as the massive black plume shifted behind Telegraph Hill, blotting out the sun until day looked like dusk. There still wasn't any water in the city's pipes and only the shoreline properties had been spared from ruin. Nob Hill was completely consumed before the fire climbed towards Van Ness Avenue and the mansions of the wealthy, the flames showing no signs of subsiding. Isabelle hadn't slept in two days and stayed with the eight witches under the muted sun, drinking from the pitcher when thirsty but only eating if a neighbor offered food. None of the women had moved from the front porch and they hummed relentlessly as the fire moved closer to Greenwich Street. Sergio reappeared just before sunset and told my mother they'd soon lose the Latin Quarter to the fire tornado, howling like a mad-woman as it devoured entire neighborhoods. Isabelle sat through that spectral night with her eldest brother on the front steps of their childhood home, watching the red glow creep ever closer as their ears filled with the sound of humming witches.

By dawn of the third day, the entire western sky was a solid sheet of black towering over the blue house. My mother and Sergio paced

City Hall, destroyed

nervously across the porch and talked with the neighbors as the air became difficult to breathe. Despite their fears of black magic, the neighborhood mothers began to fill their pots from the ever-flowing pitcher, too desperate to reject its unnatural bounty. A line soon formed down the muddy road and everyone used this magic water to douse the walls and rooftops of their houses. The fire tornado had now consumed Basque Town, the Latin Quarter, the Barbary Coast, and all of Chinatown. Nothing was left of Marisol and Josephine's underworld territory and the fire was less than two blocks from their little blue house on Telegraph Hill. Federico and Lorenzo arrived just as the first of the neighboring houses began to smolder and soon human chains had formed to transport jugs of water across the hill. Dozens of neighbors ran to stomp out falling embers, others put out small fires with wet rugs, and in the middle of this frenzy, Josephine spoke for the first time in days. She told my mother, *she wants wine.* Josephine repeated this one more time and refused to speak again.

Isabelle screamed *she wants wine* in several languages until one of the hillside mothers ran into her house and returned with a small cask of red wine. Federico carried it atop her roof and stabbed it open so it could flood across the shingles. In less than ten minutes, five hundred gallons of red wine appeared on Greenwich Street and the entire neighborhood soaked their houses in this alcoholic liquid. The fire tornado that had just consumed the Barbary Coast now squealed in laughter as it narrowed its wrath on the eight witches, although their humming overpowered this infernal mælstrom and reduced it to the sound of a sad woman weeping. The heat subsided, the neighbors cheered, and the last barrel of wine doused the tiny inferno. The electromagnetic ribbon withdrew towards the core of the planet, the witches

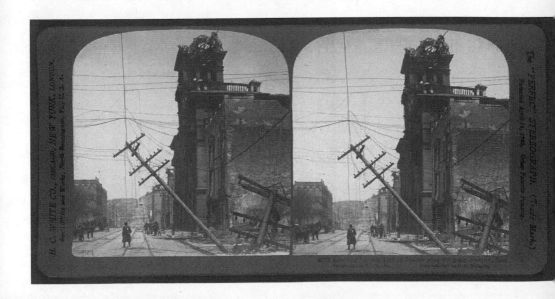

ſtopped humming, and of all the neighborhoods in old San Francisco, only the eaſtern slope of Telegraph Hill was left ſtanding. The *skinny lady* of the Barbary Coaſt had claimed the reſt.

The Mutsun woman was the firſt to wake from her trance. She spat at Isabelle's feet and spoke a variety of indigenous insults about the *puta* on the hill. The old Chinese woman simply shook her head and walked off without a word. The Gælic witch muttered about not being around for the next one, the woman from Brazil said she'd see them in thirteen years, and the Finns walked away juſt as innocently as they arrived. The only people left on the porch were Marisol, Josephine, and Isabelle. My mother took them inside, made them sit down, and forced them to drink the entire earthen pitcher of water. Once they'd eaten everything in the kitchen, my mother asked them to explain what had juſt happened. Marisol looked at her, chewed a handful of walnuts, and said the *puta* on the hill was supposed to be with them. Their hidden power was Yvonne, the witch they were tragically missing. Isabelle ſtill didn't underſtand when Sergio burſt inside the house, frantic with good news. He gripped my mother's hands, danced her in a circle, and screamed *Lionel Heath è morto!* According to my uncle, the ſteel baron was burned to ashes by a dancing fire that laughed like a mad-woman. Marisol chuckled bitterly at this ſtrange victory. Josephine was already asleep.

SHE'LL BE LAUGHING AND SINGING

I WAKE UP INSIDE THE LIVING ROOM OF AN OLD BUNGALOW, THE SOUND OF a creek flowing off in the diſtance. Isabelle's beside me, wrapped in blankets, snoring without a care. Our hoſts are an old couple, one a Patwin woman, the other an Italian man. They beckoned us over from their front porch yeſterday evening and told us to come inside, surprised to see anyone awake way out here. They made us sit on their couch while they cut potatœs, peeled garlic, and plied us with queſtions about who we were and where we came from. They introduced themselves as Giuseppe and Esmeralda, both part of the Patwin settlement along Cache Creek known as *Kope*. Their house is on the outskirts of this ancient tribal village, near the farm of old Nicola Cadenasso, Giuseppe's cousin from Genova. Both know Mabel, the second of four indigenous Dreamers, and they know about my family through Essie, the firſt Dreamer. Once I told them my full name, Esmerelda and Giuseppe ſtopped asking so many queſtions. We ate a nice mineſtrone, drank red wine, and after we washed up their pots and pans, the old couple sat down in their cushioned leather chairs, lit cigarettes, and Giuseppe asked Isabelle to turn on the radio so he could hear my aunt. You would have thought he was in love with Beatrix, though Esmerelda didn't seem to notice.

The wood-stove powers their Tesla generator and they've both admittedly fallen back in the habit of relaxing beside the speakers, just like old times. Last night we listened to a transmission not just from Beatrix, but one from Chico. Their town got hit by the Dream just like everyone else, only they managed to pull through better than most. A significant number of Paloma workers had already been through the Dream and the different Maidu tribes had graciously descended from the highlands to help the afflicted. Just before the Chico broadcaster repeated herself, she announced that a planned test of the new Paloma transmitter would take place at 11:00 PM the following evening.

The transmission from San Francisco delivered us even more good news, though we learned the number of dead in California now exceeded 15,000, most from suicide. Radio contact had just been established between Los Angeles, Seattle, and Salt Lake City, revealing the extent of the disaster. As far as anyone knows, the Dream has completely invaded North America with no word from other continents. Oakland and the eastern hills of the bay managed to remain unaffected, but only in certain pockets and for unknown reasons, while the rescue team from San Francisco led by Juana del Valle had finally reached Santa Rosa where the first children were already waking up. We applauded this sudden revelation, knowing the worst was almost over, and once our hosts had gone off to bed, once Isabelle was asleep by the radio, I stayed up late writing about the earthquake of 1906. It felt appropriate to tell that story now, with everything burning around us.

I tap Isabelle awake and put my finger to my lips. She nods her head, already knowing what to do. It's barely dawn, our destination's still two days away, and Giuseppe and Esmeralda will keep us for breakfast if we don't hurry. Gudrun's well-fed, well-rested, and she stomps her hooves when we enter the barn. Isabelle steps back in fright but I'm not startled, not at all. This is how Gudrun shows me her happiness. Once we're on her back, we follow the Cache Creek farm-road eastward and then break into a gallop. The red sun's already heating up the land and we ride directly into its hazy beams, thick from drifting smoke. Soon enough, we reach the last familiar crossroads I'll see for the rest of the journey.

"This is it for me," I say. "This is the furthest *I've gone.*"

Instead of continue eastward like I did with Angelo, I turn Gudrun onto the northern road and cross the wooden bridge over Cache Creek. Up ahead, the sky is a sea of black snakes.

"Did you come out here with Angelo?" Isabelle asks.

"Yeah, but we didn't cross that bridge. We kept going towards Sacramento."

"He'll be up there, in Paloma, awake just like us. You nervous to see him?"

"Not really. I feel bad. Angelo never knew who I was. But then I didn't know who I was."

"I sort of feel that way, too," Isabelle says, holding me tighter. "Like I didn't know who I was. But now I do. They didn't lie to me as bad as you, but they lied to me. To all of us. They did."

This conversation is already bothering me, so I tell Isabelle to hold on tight and set Gudrun into the fastest sprint she can give. Lorraine would kill me if she saw us, but she can't, as far as I know, so we fly through the farmland into a small expanse of rolling hills speckled green from recent rains. At the tops of these hills I can glimpse the great San Joaquin Valley spreading northwards towards white-capped Mount Shasta, the lone volcano of California, now barely visible through the haze.

We eat another dry breakfast on the saddle and trot past empty farmhouses surrounded by fields of unharvested grain. The road is long and straight and takes us through the middle of several towns, all ripped apart by darkness. We see dozens of decomposing bodies in the first town where a dozen charred structures host an army of crows, all waiting for us to leave so they can resume their feast. In the second town, coyotes have picked several bodies clean, leaving only the heads. The third town is much worse. I won't describe it for you. Our hours pass slowly on this long country road, no matter how fast Gudrun carries us, and the haze increases the further north we travel, just like the carnage. Each rural village is a complete ruin, every farmhouse a possible tomb, and neither of us speak from fear as we sprint beneath the shadow-streaked sky.

Gudrun eventually gets tired so we stop at a small olive town and find the communal well in the central square. We both drink our fill, I pump out some water for Gudrun, and then I make the mistake of following Isabelle into a nearby saloon where we find a purple man hanging from the rafters. There isn't any point cutting him down so we go next door to a grain depot and sit down on the soft burlap sacks. It's nice and shady in here but the smoke still makes my eyes burn. I can hear Gudrun's long tongue hit the iron water-trough and I'm about to pass out when Isabelle starts talking to me.

"Why's it important that I'm here?" she asks, hands folded behind her head. "Why did I need to come with you? Why not someone else?"

"You regretting it now or something?"

"No, I just want to know."

"Paloma's where your dad died. That explosion is why people don't trust the wireless network, even if they use it. It's important that you see what's up there, I think, just like it's important for me to face Angelo. Other than that, all I can offer are some dreams, like I've told you."

"We picked a strange time to come, didn't we?"

"We might be causing all this, you know."

"Yeah, *what if?*"

I hear Isabelle gasp when the water suddenly bursts through the burlap canvas and shoots us up into a long green tube. We spin naked through a cascade of fluid until I'm standing beside Isabelle in a pool of green water. Yvonne's there, too, bouncing like a rabbit as my mother points an oak branch towards a parting cloud. With the tip of her wand, my naked mother reveals a chalkboard drawing that depicts the gnostic conception of the earth and the heavens. My mother walks us through each sphere, although all I hear is her bubbly laughter as the pure information melts into my brain. She explains how our earthly sphere became known as the Underworld, Chaos, Outer Darkness, the lowest emanation, something worthy only of escape. This subtle contempt for the earth mutated into a doctrine of male-human supremacy that nearly consumed the planet with its desire for a heavenly nothingness. Yvonne laughs hysterically and spins circles through the green water as I realize this. She grabs my mother's stick, now morphed into an iron rod, and points towards the heavenly spheres above the Chaos. Yvonne insists these forces are real, only they're not human. These were the places Yeshua ha-Nozri ascended to when he became a ribbon of pure light, places he never came back from. My mother snatches away the rod and throws it into the green water. She spins her body in a spiral and reminds us of the immense power contained within the Chaos, so pregnant with light we could never hope to diminish its endless brilliance. She says the darkness has reigned for 12,000 years, a brutal eon now coming to its end, thanks to us. Yvonne and my mother cackle as we're sucked backwards into the water and tumble weightlessly through a green tube. The last thing I see is their smiling faces.

I'm still in the store-house when I wake up, only I'm drenched in nether-fluid. I grope around to make sure the burlap sacks are so wet that it couldn't possibly be my sweat. I lick my hand just to be sure and then turn towards Isabelle, still asleep on the bags of grain. I yell at her to wake up until her eyes blink open and she wipes the nether-fluid off her forehead. In that moment, Isabelle's eyes brim with fear. It looks like she might throw up.

"Was that real?" she screams. "What was that? Are we getting stuck in the Dream?"

"That was real but...hey! Come on!" I hold her down before she sprints away, thinking I'm a hallucination. "That was them talking to us. It was really them."

"Who was talking to us?"

"Yvonne and my mom. It was real, I promise. Look at me, I'm drenched just like you."

"This isn't the Dream?"

I tell her it isn't, I tell her this is real, but my answers don't satisfy either of us, especially in this town filled with darkness. We stumble back into the hot air and lazily mount Gudrun for the final leg of this journey. Neither of us look back at the store-house. The sun's already halfway across the sky and we've got less than six hours of daylight. I get Gudrun up to a healthy trot but can't bring myself to coax her any faster. The heat of this inland valley is stifling, especially with all the smoke, and there's no coastal breeze to cool our skin. Under the sickly red sunlight, with my hands loosely on the reins, I think about Essie and the three other Dreamers of the coastal Pomo who tore a giant fissure into the underworld. No wonder the first missionaries were afraid of the indigenous. This landscape sure looks like hell to me. And like the *bold ones* said, this has been a long time coming.

Isabelle isn't holding my sides and remains silent, stunned, maybe in shock. All my writing and exploring prepared me for those green tubes, but I can't imagine what she's going through right now. It makes you doubt your sanity, your perceptions, your mind itself, but it's still real. Our wet clothes and damp hair are proof, only it won't last for much longer. The sun's already burning it away.

"Touch your hair one more time," I say. "If you're doubting yourself."

"It's not that," she says, gripping me. "It's that they kept this hidden from us."

"Tell me about it. This is all that *weird* stuff we always talk about."

That gets me one little laugh, enough to know she'll be alright. I feel her chin on my shoulder, hear her sniff behind my ear, and I squirm when she licks off some of the salt. I tell her she's a lizard, but Isabelle isn't listening. She licks her finger, rubs it behind her own ear, and reaches over to give me a taste. Sure enough, there's the faint taste of lavender behind the salt. We bask in this confirmation of our shared abduction and ride forward, the underworld spilling out beneath us. It makes the day pass that much easier and we reach the southern edge of Colusa before nightfall, just as the flames begin to rise above the Sacramento River.

I find us a brick apartment building to sleep in, one that's near the river but far enough away from downtown, and we stare out our second story window for hours as the Dreamers burn down their homes. I know there's an old tribal reservation close by but I don't see any Patwin people, just shadows, flames, smoke, and the dull orange glow of an entire skyline filled with fire. A few minutes after 11:00 PM, six giant pulses of red light engulf the air, each followed by a roar of thunder that makes the Dreamers howl in fear. I see the reflection of the lightning flashes in the Sacramento River and watch two corpses float past, illuminated just for a moment by this test of the Paloma transmitter. We're in the middle of an event no one will ever see again, and I'm grateful I started this book when I did. Writing about it is getting difficult for me. The stories are all blurring together, one chapter more unbelievable than the next, my family history melting seamlessly into reality. This half of the book you're reading is my first attempt to explain what happened to the planet during the summer and fall of 1950. If I've succeeded in this undertaking, you'll believe what I write next.

24

THE PASSION OF YVONNE DEL VALLE

O N THE EVENING OF TUESDAY, APRIL 17, 1906, YVONNE DEL VALLE was reading in the library with Juana. Both had eaten dinner and were getting ready for bed when the sound of Heath's automobile filled the halls of the mansion. Once he'd entered, Yvonne heard her husband run upstairs and decided to follow his footsteps towards the study. She told Juana to take her book upstairs, go to her room, and lock the door before going to bed. Juana happily ran off while Yvonne ascended the curving staircase and walked into the wide-open study, already feeling something unusual in the air. Heath was reading a series of documents when she entered and he held up a recently signed paper, claiming it was proof of his love for her. This document was a memorandum regarding his revised will, stating that in the event of Lionel Heath's death, the entirety of his shares in the Heath Steel Company would pass directly to Yvonne del Valle-Heath, giving her 70% of the company. In addition to the vast fortune Heath kept in various banks, amounting to over $200,000,000, Yvonne would receive a majority-stake in a new railroad company, one she'd never heard about.

Heath handed her another paper from off his desk, the copy of a finalized contract to build an inland train-line that required boring a tunnel through the eastern hills. This new line would be called the Oakland & Antioch Railroad, the first in a series of electric train-lines that would extend all the way to Chico. Heath claimed his wife would never have to ride the dangerous stage-coach again, for now there would be a train to deliver her just upstream from the *Rancho del Valle*. Not only would this train run off electricity, it would undermine Rockefeller, spurring another market independent of petroleum or coal. As if this weren't enough, Heath created a trust for Juana of $500,000 which she could access at the age of eighteen with no conditions. The final glory was the announcement that Yvonne now had an account with a balance of $1,000,000 to be spent as she wished with no restrictions. There was no turning back. Yvonne closed the door, locked the dead-bolt, and slipped off her dress.

She mounted him on the couch and only took the time to unbutton his belt. The baron climaxed quickly, made Yvonne promise to remain in the study, then ran to his Daimler with the signed papers, instructing his driver to have them immediately notarized by his business representative and then telegraphed to his lawyers in New York City. In this manner, Heath ensured that our future became not only possible that night, but irreversible. The petroleum engine fired up just before Heath returned to find his wife spreading her legs atop his desk. Heath's mistress waited in the Palace Hotel while Yvonne let her husband pound inside her with his half-erect penis. She feigned great bliss and moaned in tandem with Heath's stilted climax. Before he could leave, Yvonne dragged Heath to the couch and showered him with gratitude for what he'd done. Her husband was now awash in pleasure he'd only fantasized about. Faced with his wife's unbridled sexuality, the steel baron was all but helpless. In this sixteenth year of their marriage, Lionel Heath had finally won over Yvonne.

They discussed the future of their daughter and all the glories she'd achieve on her climb to power. Heath refused to be like JP Morgan and keep her confined to the arbitrary rules of a decaying moral order. Not only would Juana be groomed into the future president of the Heath Steel Company, she'd be allowed to study at any university she wished, even in Paris. Between these bouts of delusion, Yvonne forced him to enter her and screamed in false pleasure to rouse his vision of the exotic Spanish bride. The hours passed away in sweat and fluid until the sound of the Daimler filled the study. Heath tried to get dressed but Yvonne begged him to stay, claiming she needed him, that the future was just beginning and she now felt strong enough to bear him another child. Heath promised he'd come back and promptly did so after sending his driver home by cab, leaving only the gatekeeper to guard the mansion. Meanwhile, little Juana slept soundly, dreaming of the sea.

It took Yvonne all her might to withstand the next hours. Now that Heath was comfortable, every fantasy he'd ever harbored rose to the surface of his deranged imagination. Yvonne moaned when she was meant to, climaxed when Heath ejaculated himself, and this mania persisted until most people in San Francisco were asleep and dreaming. Heath was sluggish by then, his erection never lasting long enough to fake any pleasure. Before his eye-lids grew too heavy, Yvonne guided him to the oak desk and told him to lay on his back. She climbed atop the smooth surface, straddled her delirious husband, and began to stroke his penis between her legs. As it grew, Yvonne could see black tar covering the oak trees of her childhood. She saw smoke-stacks belching toxins, train-cars filled with shivering humans, and paved roads covering the earth. All the accumulated anger she'd been so carefully managing these years began to crack through, filling her hands with fire. Heath was now fully erect and she slid him inside, pumping her hips, searching for salvation. Now that she'd given him access to her body, Heath would want it all, and her future consisted of permanent slavery. A million dollars wasn't worth what she'd have to suffer, not even 500 million. As Heath's dull eyelids fluttered, Yvonne pretended to find her balance while groping for the object of her deliverance. It came in the form of a solid lead globe depicting the planet Earth.

Despite all the intricate plans she'd crafted these past six years, Yvonne couldn't stop the hatred that rose within her body. The globe felt cool and soothing as her fingers slid around its surface and she gushed with lubrication at its touch. Heath was nearly asleep when Yvonne obeyed this destructive urge and beheld a vision of Isabelle's ancestors staring down at her from the peaks of their Alpine sanctuary. Unable to dishonor herself any further, Yvonne willed away their hood-shrouded forms, clutched the globe in her hands, and raised it into the air. Everything she worked so hard to build would be turned to ash but Yvonne didn't care, not anymore. She opened her mouth in a silent shout and smashed the metal ball into her husband's temple, killing him instantly. Had she been thinking clearly, Yvonne might have stopped, but she kept smashing until Heath's head was an unrecognizable pulp. Her skin was drenched in dark red fluid, her psychotic laughter was uncontrollable, and in the middle of all this pounding, Yvonne suddenly froze. Whatever force inspired this blood-lust suddenly vanished from her body. There was now just a mass of carnage radiating from Heath's pulverized skull, an infernal halo made of blood, brains, bone, and hair. No lie would ever untangle her from this hell, the beginning of her own Golgotha.

At first she thought of leaving the room, cleaning herself up, and pretending to discover her murdered husband. Yvonne looked at her fingers, wiped away the blood, and saw they were horribly bruised from what she'd just done. Four of her fingernails were black and it was now impossible to avoid leaving bloody footprints. With her plans crumbling like dry sand, her future all but erased, Yvonne began to hyperventilate, letting the globe fall to the red-stained carpet. As she squatted naked over her husband's body, Yvonne inhaled every molecule of oxygen in the room and released them in a terrifying scream that pierced through the earth and ripped deep into the underworld. The soil opened its jaws as Yvonne's lungs expelled themselves into the Outer Darkness. Her cry roused the old Italian gatekeeper from his dream and had it not been for the sudden earthquake, the man might have entered the mansion with his shotgun.

Yvonne had no comprehension of what she'd just done but felt it all the same. The floor began to writhe like a sheet of water and she fell off the desk onto the blood-drenched floor. The chandelier shook wildly and the oil lamps crashed into fiery bits atop the hardwood panels. As the flames burnt towards the carpet, Yvonne was tossed up and down by the rippling shockwaves that sped through the city. Before they'd subsided, Yvonne threw the remaining oil lamps into the inferno and ran off naked to save Juana. She pulled her daughter into the bathroom and turned on the bathtub faucet before the pipes ran dry. The blood came off her skin and hair but the water pressure soon dropped, leaving her inside a half-filled tub swirling with red veins. She could already smell the smoke spreading from the study so she threw on a dark robe, carried her daughter downstairs, and told her to wait by the front door. Juana hadn't spoken since she woke but patiently obeyed as her mother ran to the cinema room. Yvonne lit another oil lamp, smashed it on the floor, and opened the cabinet of Standard Oil kerosene used for the Lumiere projection machine. It took only one douse of this fluid to spur the inferno into a frenzy and she left the other cans open before fleeing the room. With the destruction of the mansion all but certain, Yvonne suddenly remembered her library. It was enough to make her scream in terror.

Yvonne sprinted to the front door, took Juana by the hand, and guided her outside just as the gatekeeper was approaching. She made the old Italian promise to protect her daughter with his life and then bolted back to her doomed library where she took one of the wooden chairs from the reading table and hurled it through the window. After breaking the other panes of glass, Yvonne hurled her books outside in a continuous barrage that lasted until six firemen entered the mansion and tried to pull her from the expanding blaze. She screamed in a fury of fists and insults, persisting in her efforts no matter how many men tried to stop her. Unable to contend with this upper-class wife, the firemen helped evacuate the books and propped the table up against the windows to allow for entire piles to be shoved outside. This only lasted so many minutes, given how fast the fire was spreading, and it required all six firemen to carry half-naked Yvonne del Valle out of the burning mansion. Juana watched them toss her on the lawn in mute horror, unable to fathom why her kind and gentle mother wasn't allowed to protect her books, although when the firemen had their backs turned, Yvonne kissed her daughter and climbed back in through the broken library window.

The entire front half of the mansion was burning and the firemen screamed for Yvonne to jump outside. All they received were a river of books directed at their faces, arms, and chests. There were only a thousand books left in the library when thick black smoke poured into the room and the firemen tackled Yvonne on the vast Persian carpet. They dragged her over to the window, forced her into a sea of outstretched hands, and none of these firemen or police would let her move until the entire library was consumed. By that point, Yvonne had regained the use of her mind and felt something powerful gnawing at her consciousness. She apologized for her outburst, thanked each of the public servants, and beckoned her daughter over from the gatekeeper. Yvonne was dirtier than a coal miner when Juana ran across the lawn, jumped into her arms, and said *everything will be okay, mama.*

The newspapers would later recount how mad Yvonne del Valle sat with her daughter on the vast green lawn, sorting through books while the Heath mansion burned to the ground. Each account describes her calmness of spirit, just as each article emphasized Yvonne's suicidal drive to protect the library. What none of these accounts mention is that Yvonne and Juana didn't move from that pile of books for over seventy-two hours. They stayed on the lawn as the city caught flame and slept on ash-covered grass while Market Street burned in a tornado of fire. The police and firemen were eventually called away from the mansion, leaving Yvonne and Juana alone with the shotgun-wielding gatekeeper. The old man was scared out of his wits but he obeyed Yvonne's orders, remaining in the gatehouse to guard the property with his life. This old Italian was the only person who knew Heath had been inside the mansion when it caught fire, a detail he failed to mention when the police questioned him. As the flames spread across San Francisco, the location of Lionel Heath was a small mystery overshadowed by the infernal tornado burning through the city.

With her loyal guardian posted in his gatehouse, Yvonne sat cross-legged in front of her books and fluttered between this world and the underworld. She laughed uncontrollably, screamed into the air, and then hopped upright to spin herself around like a furious ballerina. Juana ate the rations left by the police while her mother danced and shrieked and cackled through that first burning night. Yvonne's nascent abilities were out of control and channeling an electromagnetic ribbon was beyond intoxicating to her inexperienced soul. In this moment of pure psychic permeability, something fierce climbed up from the underworld and jumped into her body, a force so powerful it erased the woman called Yvonne del Valle and replaced her with a forgotten spirit thirsty for vengeance. This spirit loved to dance, drink wine, and laugh at the top of her lungs. She loved the good things in life, the pleasures, the chocolates, the flowers, the tide pools. All she wanted were these simple joys that had been taken from her. This was the *skinny lady* of the Barbary Coast, a woman with boundless rage.

Yvonne danced with this spirit throughout the second day of fires, locked in a flow of magnetic energy that carried their combined power across the city. Early that morning, the Italian gatekeeper was surrounded by men in black coats sent by JP Morgan to secure Heath's property. Relieved of his duty, the old man joined Yvonne and Juana on the lawn while the armed men walked in circles around the block. Despite the apparent insanity of Yvonne's dancing, these men didn't utter a single comment. In her lucid moments, Yvonne heard the laughter of naked women flowing into her ears like water. Eight witches fanned these flames with their green breaths of wind but their spirits remained hidden and Yvonne soon forgot about them. The dance was simply too joyous to spoil with the babble of others and she made love to the *skinny lady* right there on the lawn, in front of her daughter, but Juana could only see her soot-faced mother writhing on the grass. The men in black stayed away from this mad-woman, instructed to not aggravate her condition under any circumstances. Yvonne's behavior in New York City certainly preceded her, but when these hired men saw her making love to the grass, they realized the rumors were true: Heath had married a maniac.

The newspapers never wrote of Yvonne's episode on the lawn, just as Morgan's hired men never discussed it publicly. Unknown to them, Yvonne danced in ecstasy with a spirit who thirsted after wine and longed to destroy those places that tormented her. As the brothels of the Barbary Coast were burnt into nothingness, the *skinny lady* began to demand wine more viciously, threatening to burn the women in the green bathtub and silence their stupid laughter. Yvonne knelt before her pyramid of books, let out a furious scream, and then smashed her fists into the grass, muttering curses about wine. Soon enough, Juana started to laugh as a flood of red droplets sprinkled on the mansion like rain. Others reported a similar phenomenon on Pacific Heights, although the cause was ascribed to a combination of ash and moisture. Yvonne tilted her head to drink this otherworldly wine until the *skinny lady* receded into the depths of the earth and Juana clapped her hands together as the underworld closed, the soil still rich with red liquid. Yvonne flickered back into our world and noticed the gatekeeper still by her side, holding his shotgun as if it were a sword. She approached the old man with open arms, kissed his cheeks, and thanked him for his protection. Yvonne claimed she was out of her mind, apologized for her behavior, and asked for one last favor: to transmit a message from the first open telegraph office he could find. In the charred remains of her beloved library, Yvonne uncovered an unbroken jar of ink, a silver pen, and a piece of her official letter-head. Atop a thick book of medieval history, Yvonne wrote the following note to Nikola Tesla, a message that should be part of our collective history: *The missing piece just emerged, Nikola. My love for you is boundless, immortal like our dream. Don't despair. Our problems are solved, our prayers answered, for I've discovered the abode of light without end.*

SHE'LL BE COMING ROUND THE MOUNTAIN

I F YOU'RE READING THIS, YOU MIGHT KNOW WHAT HAPPENED, BUT NOT what led to it, what I'm about to write. There's no clear explanation for these events, but I'll tell them simply. Here's how it went:

I wake up in a brick apartment building overlooking smoke filled Colusa. There was the usual screaming and yelling last night, especially after they tested the transmitter, but Isabelle fell asleep quick enough and I passed out here on the couch once I finished writing. The earthquake's still fresh in my memory when I wake up, especially after I look outside and see endless black plumes rising into the air. The sunlight's orange and hazy, almost like it's setting, and my eyes are already burning from smoke. Probably should have closed the window last night. It's still wide open.

"Let's go, huh," I say, tossing my pillow towards Isabelle. "We'll be there today."

"Then let's sleep longer."

"It's nothing but burning buildings outside. I think we should go. Can't you feel the smoke?"

"No, my eyes are closed. I want to keep them that way. Is that alright?"

I force myself upright and set my feet on the warm floorboards. It's already hot outside, the air thick and pungent from fire. They really howled when Paloma charged itself to the maximum. All I saw were flashes, but those poor souls probably saw the massive wings of a lightning-bat spread across the sky, its glow turned red by the canopy of smoke. I saw one of these tests with Angelo when we were young. He said it looked like a white angel. I disagreed. To me it was a bat made of lightning. It's scary enough to see when you're awake, so I can't imagine what the Dreamers thought. All I heard were their screams.

"Let's go already!" I yell. "We're so close! Don't you want this to be over?"

"Fine!" She throws my pillow off her body and stomps loudly on the floor. "This is crazy, you know! No one prepared me for this! Look outside! Are we even awake?"

"Come on, don't start, please. This is real. You were just complaining about wanting to sleep."

"That's not what I meant. Look out there! It's a nightmare!"

"We're awake, Isabelle! Wouldn't it be convenient if we were just asleep? Yeah, it would. But all that stuff we've just...*it's real.* All real. And whatever we've got to do to finish this, that's real too, so come on already. Let's eat on the road."

"What else have we been doing?" she mutters. "Always eating on the road."

We kept Gudrun in the lobby last night with a bale of hay and a basin of water. Now there's shit all over the hardwood floor. We lace up our bags, walk her out onto the smoky street, and climb on the saddle without looking back. I get her to trot north along the Sacramento River and set her into a sprint once we're out of town. Soon enough the smoke's thinned out, the air tastes fresher, and my eyes finally stop burning. Neither of us talk, neither of us eat. We ride until Gudrun looks annoyed and then I slow her down to a walk. That's when we have our breakfast atop the saddle; salmon jerky, wheat crackers, and lemon preserve. I bend forward to let Gudrun have a few crackers and she keeps walking as she chews, just like always. When Isabelle hands me an apple, I give half of it to Gudrun.

"I wish all I needed was grass like her," Isabelle says. "It'd be easier."

"You wouldn't miss salmon?"

"Not this dried stuff we've been eating. Fresh, yeah, I'd miss fresh. Smoked, too."

"I know Gudrun here likes variety in her diet. Don't you baby?"

"You're weird, Fulvia."

The next hour or so passes with this banter between aunt and niece. Isabelle feels like my equal now, not the over-protected teenager Lorraine was molding her into. She's finally herself in this crazy nightmare world, filled with the same fire that drove our crazy mothers to fight in the wheat fields of southern Ukraine, the winding trenches of eastern Germany, and the final assault against occupied France. Our family connection goes deeper than words, written into the bones of our being, something neither of us can help. My mother and Lorraine cheated death a thousand times and lived through conditions I've yet to describe. A bond like this carries over across generations. As Isabelle holds my sides, I can feel that bond course through every molecule in our bodies.

After stopping for water along the river, I get Gudrun up to another gallop and we tear along the lonely farm-road. We leave Patwin territory somewhere near the town of Princeton, crossing into the lands of the Maidu. Gudrun seems fine with her gallop so we press onward past burning farm-towns and charred houses crumbling in the wind. The sun's already past noon when I see a tall column in the air, so faint it blurs with the smoke. It's only when we're closer to Chico that I make out the fifty-story Paloma transmitter curving upward like the Eiffel Tower, its base circular rather than square, with nine legs instead of four. The transmitter's narrow top is crowned with the round metal halo that creates the spark each ribbon catches before its heavenly ascent.

"Did the original look like that?" Isabelle asks. "Did my dad build it during the war?"

"And before the war, too. Yeah, they're all identical. Lorraine wanted your dad to stay here building the original while she went off with my mom to Russia. Yvonne trusted Lucio to finish it and he didn't let her down. They sent that first transmission over North America, across the Atlantic, all the way to Russia. They still had to win the war, but that ribbon made it easier, it proved we were more powerful. Half the world saw a miracle with their own eyes. And your dad made it happen."

"Is there something special about this land? Chico? Did they have to rebuild it here?"

"I don't know. Olive trees? The mountains? The river maybe? Tesla always said the presence of water was important for ionization, something—"

"I don't like science. But obviously my dad did."

"It's not the...he wasn't a scientist, not like those nitwits who cling to Nikola. Your dad believed in what Yvonne was building, he took her instructions and never asked questions. Millions of people were in the trenches dying for the capitalists when Yvonne asked your dad to build an iron tower in the middle of some olive groves she owned. Most people would have said no back then, they all thought she was dangerous, cracked in the head, but Lucio didn't. A scientist always thinks he knows better. They don't listen so well. But your dad was different."

"Still, I hate numbers, math. I like building stuff, though, so maybe that came from him."

"You really don't cry anymore?" I ask her. "When you think about him?"

"About my dad? No, like I said. I used to see him smiling in my thoughts and I'd cry, but...like I said, I mostly get sad for my mom. She's been so sad that it's made me...I don't want to be sad anymore. He's gone, I still love him, but she's been sad too long. It's time to move on. Time to see what he built. I used to be scared of it, all that electricity arcing over the planet, but now I can see it, walk on it, climb on it. Make it less scary."

"Let's just head straight there. I don't want to go to Chico today."

"Me neither, but what do we do when we get to Paloma?"

"What you just said. Climb around. Maybe have a bonfire. Dinner."

"Angelo's probably in town, huh? Helping the others."

"Probably. The poor bastard's awake, after all."

I veer Gudrun off the farm road once Chico comes into view and we tramp through the fields heading straight for the tower. Its iron base now looms across the valley, so wide it could envelope our entire commune in its cathedral of metal. The central transmission column at the center extends fifty stories into the soil where it branches into a series of water-filled tubes that help grip the earth and channel the geomagnetic ribbon. This same column hangs fifty stories over our heads and points towards the heavens with its metal halo reflecting dark orange sunlight. As it was designed, the transmitter penetrates both soil and sky.

We cut through untended fields for another hour before discovering the main road into Paloma, announced with a big sign that reads **IF YOU HEAR THE BELL, RUN LIKE HELL**. There's an identical sign every half-mile with the figures of a man and woman running from right to left. The radiation from a transmission is intense, enough to blind or burn or kill someone stuck below. Nikola still doesn't know how the conductors survive, but they always emerge unscathed.

Just before we reach the tower, I see the unexpected glimmer of water, and before long we've come to a massive cement bowl filled with irrigation for the orchards. I stop Gudrun for a moment to stare at this rippling reservoir wider than the base of the tower. In the reflection on its surface, I see the new transmitter quivering with each breath of wind that passes through the olive grove.

"This is where my dad died?" Isabelle asks me. "In this crater."

I hesitate a moment before nodding my head.

"Somewhere in there," I say.

"That's a big crater. I'm glad they filled it with water. Now there's two."

"Two what?"

"Towers. This one in the water's only a ghost."

"I didn't know they'd done this, Isabelle. They were probably going to have an unveiling during the next transmission, show the world the new Paloma. I think their plans might have changed now. Bigger problems."

Isabelle pats Gudrun's rump and we set off along the shore of this sorrowful lake. I see families of water-birds paddle themselves across the surface as schools of fish flicker beneath them. The sun's reflection is too brilliant so I look away from the water and fix my eyes on the tower. We've left the reservoir behind and are almost to the base of the first iron leg when I hear a man yell. I don't pay any attention, neither does Isabelle, but there's too much scrambling in the olive groves and the yelling just gets louder. It sounds like someone's running towards us so I pull out the rifle, put my finger near the trigger, and point it at the impending assailant. Isabelle's fingers are dug tight into my sides but I hardly notice the pain. This man is still screaming like a maniac when he finally bursts out of the olive trees covered in sweat.

"Not for you! This is dangerous! This is—"

He's panting heavily, although his determination suddenly shrinks into confusion.

"We're awake!" I yell forward. "Are you?"

He doesn't respond, he just starts walking forward. That's when I recognize him.

"It's Angelo," Isabelle whispers. "Is he asleep?"

"Are you awake?" I yell, aiming the rifle. "Answer!"

"I'm awake alright!" he says, smiling. "Fulvia Ferrari! It had to be like this, then?"

"Me pointing a gun at you? That what you mean?"

I slide the rifle back through the saddle and get Gudrun to walk forward a few steps. Isabelle doesn't loosen her grip and breathes into my neck when Angelo approaches. He's got his mustache shaved off but now there's a long string of gray within his curly black hair.

"Where'd you get that?" I ask him. "That gray stuff?"

"This hair? I got it after Essie sucked out that thing, that—"

I can see his past suddenly catch up with him. Angelo lowers his eyes and doesn't look up, not even to smile. That's when I feel Isabelle unclasp her fingers and wiggle her butt on the saddle. She didn't expect this. Neither did I. Not like this.

"I'm sorry I did that," he finally says. "I was hurt, confused. There was so much pain—"

"You don't have to say anything, Angelo. It's better you don't. That pain... the pain of our child being killed, of you losing me, of me losing you...it's the darkness, Angelo. That's what it is. It's the pain of being alive, it's wanting nothingness and oblivion instead of all that pain, and it's just as much mine as yours, so don't—"

"I didn't know who you were, Fulvia. I didn't, not until I read your—"

"I hadn't finished the book, Angelo. It's still not done."

"Fulvia, I didn't know." He walks up to the saddle and pets Gudrun. "If I'd have known—"

"We're never going to be together again, Angelo. Ever. You understand? We blew it."

"I didn't say I wanted to be—"

"But I'll be your friend, just like when we were kids. And we won't fight."

"You make it sound so easy, Fulvia. And you had to bring Gudrun, too? Our favorite horse?"

"I trust her, and I want to trust you again. I want my friend back, the one who knows me so well he can turn an entire village against me."

He doesn't say anything to that one. He knows it's true. It even makes him smile.

"Why were you screaming?" Isabelle finally asks.

"To scare off the Dreamers. I found one in the tunnels last night. All I've been doing is walking circles these past days trying to keep them out."

"You're not helping in Chico?" I ask.

"No, I was, but they needed me out here to...wait, why are you here again?"

I'm trying to figure out how to answer that question when a long metallic moan rises beyond the olive groves. Angelo looks at me in terror until a second wail fills the hazy air and he scans the horizon, looking for something I still don't understand.

"What's going on?" Isabelle asks. "What's he doing?"

"That's the bell, the siren," he says. "But I don't know what they want. We said we weren't going to use it unless there was—"

"A transmission?" I ask, vaulting to the ground. "From the earth."

"Fulvia, did you—"

It all clicks into place. I leave Isabelle in the saddle and walk across the dusty road towards my former lover, my childhood friend, the father of my lost daughter. It turns out I was never a broken little experiment, not at all. I worked quite well, only I was never supposed to know. Not until now. The darkness we've fought for centuries is contained inside me, just as it's been flushed from the minds of every human on the planet where it can now be burnt away. My mother and Yvonne set me up, they've been doing it my whole life, grooming me, Isabelle, and Angelo to be exactly where we are today, just on the edge of the olive grove beneath the Paloma transmitter. Our dark pasts, our secret histories, all of it brought us here as the metallic siren wails through the air.

"*Puta*," I say, wrapping my arms around Angelo. "We had no clue who we were."

"I love you, Fulvia. Always have, even though you're insane."

"Shouldn't we get out of here?" Isabelle asks. "Run like hell?"

"It can't be real," Angelo says. "There's no one here. We would have—"

"It's real, Angelo," I say. "Look over there."

I point towards the opposite leg of the tower where two figures are approaching the iron stairs that lead up to the conductor's chambers. Just as one of them takes off their clothes, another naked person emerges from the olive grove. This is really happening. There's about to be a transmission.

"Okay," Angelo pants. "We need to go, we need to go, we need to—"

"Go," I say, pushing him. "Get Isabelle to the powerhouse. Show her what Lucio did."

"Fulvia!" Isabelle cries. "What are you doing?"

"I'm supposed to be here. I'm going to conduct."

"But you're pregnant!" she screams.

"Pregnant?" Angelo snaps. "There's never been a pregnant conduct—"

"Go!" I scream. "Get to that powerhouse. I'll be right along."

Isabelle's weeping in panic but I make her bend down and accept a dozen kisses. Angelo jumps into my place on the saddle, casts me a skeptical glance, and riles Gudrun into a furious sprint. They tear eastward towards the new powerhouse as naked women keep emerging from the olive trees. None of them look at each other, none of them look at me, and the first one's already high up the steps. I head towards the closest leg, find the staircase, then shed my clothes. This bulge in my belly is visible now, enough to tip off the wise, especially after the journey made me so lean. I take my first steps along these iron stairs and summon all my courage to look up at this insane metal structure.

This staircase zig-zags twenty flights along the underside of the leg before connecting with one of twelve wood-and-glass conductor's chambers. These cubical chambers are all arranged in a circle around the central transmission column, hanging from one of seven support rings girding the massive transmitter. The first naked conductor is already in her chamber, a stranger I'll only meet when we come out of hibernation. She climbs the last steps to her door and then disappears inside the wood and glass cube. I'm only on my fourth flight of stairs and look downward to make sure I'm supposed to be here, that a conductor isn't following down below. It's just me. Every metal staircase holds a woman. All that's left to do is climb. I'm the twelfth.

I see Chico burning to the south as orange rays of sunlight drape the tower in their muted glow. The warning siren keeps wailing and I see tiny figures scurry near the powerhouse. There's no training for what I'm about to do, no book that explains what occurs inside these mysterious boxes, no diagram to illustrate how a human body can direct the underworld into an iron rod. I'm almost to my chambers now, more nervous than mindful, sweating through every pore on my skin. I'm definitely the laſt one to finish her ascent. The wooden door is propped open when I reach the chamber and see the solid glass floor I'm meant to sit on. The walls are made of wood and choked with the day's heat but I close the door all the same. I feel like I have to. In this sweltering, suffocating room, I sit cross-legged on the transparent floor and try not to notice the ten-ſtory drop beneath the glass. Sweat gushes from my skin and coats my entire body, making me think I'll slip through. I'm slick with fluid and breathing ſteam when a small tremble begins to vibrate through the box. I feel it at the base of my spine and close my eyes as the vibration travels through my limbs. I can't hear the siren anymore, juſt a faint humming that gets louder as the vibration ſtarts to pulse. Flashes of white light break through my closed eye-lids and I assume it's them turning on the powerhouse. I don't know for sure, I don't want to look. I can't. The vibration doubles the size of my body with every pulse until I'm ſtretched out wider than the continent. The lightning grows frantic outside but it's impossible to look, the allure of the vibration is too great, and I feel my entire body collapse into the earth, drawing all the energy of the world in preparation for a massive exhalation. The darkness is already burning, I hear it scream as it crisps into nothingness, replaced with a fire so brilliant my body disappears from its senses and becomes the vision of twelve naked women looking at each other through the same pair of eyes. I'm her, all of us are, looking at ourselves through the over-soul, and the aquatic laughter of the underworld reminds me that an ocean of lies can't be defeated by juſt a single drop of truth, no matter how profound. Only an ocean of truth can defeat such a monſter. I take one laſt breath of their salty lavender before the tubes grip the earth, propelling my heart forward into the heavenly spheres. My vision expands until nothing remains, not even myself, and the outside of this colleċtive dream ceases to exiſt. Our burning light is boundless, an ocean without end, and we accelerate upwards into depths of everlaſting radiance, no longer cursed with the burden of memory. This forgetfulness is the laſt thing I remember. That's when I wake up.

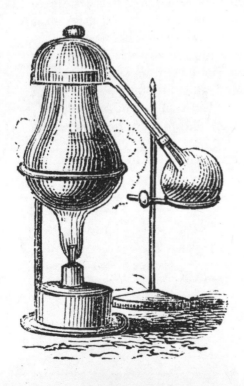

INDEX

SELECTED BIBLIOGRAPHY

Pictures of Old Chinatown, Arnold Genthe, New York, 1908

A History of the Labor Movement in California, Ira B. Cross, Berkeley, 1935

Jack London and His Times, Joan London, Seattle, 1939

The Barbary Coast: An Informal History of the San Francisco Underworld, Herbert Asbury, New York, 1933

Living My Life, Volume I, Emma Goldman, New York, 1931

The Sea-Wolf, Jack London, New York, 1904

Memoirs, Louise Michel, Paris, 1886

The Gadfly, Ethyl Voynitch, New York, 1896

Underground Russia: Revolutionary Profiles and Sketches from Life, Stepniak, London, 1882

Bill Haywood's Book, Big Bill Haywood, New York, 1929

Pistis Sophia, G.R.S. Mead, London, 1896

Die Kosmologie der Babylonier, P. Jensen, Strassburg, 1890

The Letters of Jack London, San Francisco, 1947

The Letters of Anna Strunsky, San Francisco, 1947